Charles de Rochefort, John Davies, Louis de Poincy, Raymond Breton, John N. Brown

The History of the Caribby-Islands

viz. Barbados, St Christophers, St Vincents, Martinico, Dominico, Barbouthos,

Monserrat, Mevis [sic], Antego, &c. in all XXVIII.

Charles de Rochefort, John Davies, Louis de Poincy, Raymond Breton, John N. Brown

The History of the Caribby-Islands
viz. Barbados, St Christophers, St Vincents, Martinico, Dominico, Barbouthos, Monserrat, Mevis [sic], Antego, &c. in all XXVIII.

ISBN/EAN: 9783337198282

Printed in Europe, USA, Canada, Australia, Japan

Cover: Foto ©Andreas Hilbeck / pixelio.de

More available books at **www.hansebooks.com**

THE HISTORY OF THE Caribby-Islands,

VIZ.

BARBADOS, St. CHRISTOPHERS, St. VINCENTS, MARTINICO, DOMINICO, BARBOUTHOS, MONSERRAT, MEVIS, ANTEGO, &c. in all XXVIII.

IN TWO BOOKS.

The First containing the NATURAL; The Second, the MORAL HISTORY of those Islands.

Illustrated with several Pieces of Sculpture, representing the most considerable Rarities therein Described.

WITH A CARIBBIAN-VOCABULARY.

Rendred into English
By *JOHN DAVIES* of *Kidwelly.*

LONDON,

Printed by *J. M.* for *Thomas Dring* and *John Starkey,* and are to be sold at their Shops, at the *George* in *Fleet-street* neer *Clifford's-Inn,* and at the *Mitre* between Middle *Temple-Gate* and *Temple-Bar.* 1666.

Whitehall, June 2. 1665.

By Permiſſion and Licence from the Right
Honourable Mr. Secretary *Morice* this
Book may be Printed.

Jo. Cook.

Sir EDWARD BYSCHE.

Moſt honoured Sir,

YOu have ſufficiently ſatisfied the World of the Curioſity you have for whatever, in any meaſure, deſerves it: You were pleas'd to give me a hint of the Piece I here preſent you withal; and your recommendation of the Original might well raiſe in me a hope of your readier acceptance of the Tranſlation. It is the nobleſt of humane Actions to vouchſafe a kind Entertainment to the Diſtreſs'd, whether Nature or Fortune hath made them Calamitous. The equality of Miſery makes the Endurers of it moſt commonly the more compaſsionate; ſo far as that thoſe who have been firſt reliev'd charitably direct others to the ſame Almoners.

Thus do I bring to your doors a company of poor *Caribbians*, to offer you their Reſpects and Submiſsions, in the name of all thoſe Iſlands, whereof their Anceſtors have been heretofore poſſeſs'd in the Ocean of *America*: They are in hopes, that neither the obſcurity of their Origine, nor the harſhneſs of their Language, nor the barbariſme of their Manners, nor their ſtrange courſe of Life, nor the cruelty of their Wars, nor their ancient Poverty, nor

 laſtly

lastly the unconstancy of their Fortune, will hinder your favourable Reception of them. And what heightens this hope of theirs, is, an imagination, that you, who find leisure to bestow your Eye and Thoughts on so infinite a Multitude of Volumes as press from all parts of the World into your Library, may be pleas'd with something that is done among them; and that the History of the *Caribbies* may entertain you, not only with a delightful Variety, as to the divertisement of the Sight, but also with many occurrences capable of exciting your Admiration.

What may be further said on their behalf, I leave to be express'd in their own natural Rhetorick, and bethink me of making some Apology for my self; which is only this, That the presumption of the present Address is in some measure the effect of your Goodness and Candor, and that it had been but a necessary expression of my Gratitude, had I many years since profess'd how much I am,

Most honoured Sir,

Your most humble and much

obliged Servant,

J. DAVIES.

THE
PREFACE,

Giving an account of both the *Original* and *English* Edition of this Work.

THE *Relations we have from remote Countries, for the most part, come attended with this misfortune; that many times they are written by Persons, who, being concerned therein, for some Reasons and Considerations only known to themselves, make it their business to disguise the Truth, and represent things otherwise than they are. Sometimes also we have to do with certain Writers, who, in cold blood, and to gratifie their own humour, would impose upon our credulity, as it were out of a defiance of being disproved. And lastly, it is our fate to receive Pieces of this nature from men little vers'd in study, and so such as are not able to lay down things with the requisite exactness, inasmuch as, upon many occasions, they take one thing for another, and relate not things truly and naturally, though they have not any intention to deceive us. On the contrary, it is a great advantage, when such Works are composed by Authors, in whom these three conditions are found combining together; to wit, That they are unconcerned; That they dally not with Truth; and, That they have all the Requisites for the right framing of their Relations.*

Those who shall cast their Eyes on the present History, are to expect therein these advantages: For as to the two first of the forementioned Conditions, that is, to comprehend them under one word, Sincerity, the Authors of this Work presume to attribute it to themselves, since it is an Elogy any one may innocently assume to himself, if his own Conscience give him not a check for so doing: But for the third, which relates to the ability of the mind, though

an

an over-earneſt pretention thereto may ſeem to proceed from a certain vanity and ſelf-confidence; yet when all circumſtances ſhall be conſidered, the ingenuous will eaſily be induced to allow them even that alſo.

For 1. *The Relations they had to work upon came from Perſons who had been Eye-witneſſes of what they delivered, diſ-intereſſed, and of known integrity, and endued with the abilities requiſite to manage ſuch a Work.* 2 *There was a deſign of this Hiſtory drawn at* Paris, *ſome years before it came abroad, and then thought worthy publiſhing, by divers intelligent men, to whom it was communicated, who carefully read it over, and honoured it with their Remarks. Yet that it might come forth with greater exactneſs, it was laid aſide, till the obſervations of after-Voyages had added much to its perfection. So that if the Publick receive any ſatisfaction from this Hiſtory, it will have reaſon rather to congratulate, than quarrel at its delay; ſince it comes out now more enriched and exact, than it would have been, at the firſt proffer of it to the Preſs. For beſides that many Obſervations and Relations came ſince to hand, the Authors made alſo great advantages of the private Diſcourſes they had with one Father Raymond, eſpecially as to the Moral part of the Caribbian Hiſtory. For this man having lived many years in thoſe Iſlands, and had much converſation with the* Caribbians *of* Dominico, *came by that means to be acquainted with their Language, their Manners, and the moſt particular Cuſtoms of that Nation. From the ſame F.* Raymond *they had alſo the Caribbian Vocabulary, which may be ſeen at the end of the Book.*

They thought fit to divide the Hiſtory into two Parts, the Natural and the Moral, in imitation of that of the excellent Joſephus Acoſta, *and they hope the Piece will be found ſuch as to anſwer the Title; comprehending in the former whatever is of the natural growth of the Country, as* Plants, Fruits, Flowers, Birds, Beaſts, &c. *and under the latter, whatſoever relates to their* Manners, Cuſtoms, Religion, Vertues, Vices, &c. *Not that they would have it inferr'd thence, that this Treatiſe ſhould contain whatever might be written on the ſubject of the* Caribbies;

nay

nay they acknowledge, that both the Natural and Moral part of this History might be much enlarged; but with this advertisement, that if every part of the New-world were so diligently examined by Historians as this hath been, the Old-world would have a much more particular account thereof, than it hath at the present.

They have also thought it not beside their purpose, especially in the Moral part of the History, to cite the Writings of divers other well-known Authours, not out of any design to enlarge the Volume, as some might haply imagine; but to make a certain parallel between the Morality of our Caribbians, and that of divers other yet Barbarous Nations; which they conceiv'd would not be undelightful to some, even though they looked on them as so many digressions from, or interruptions of the Carribbian History. But what censure soever may be passed on them, they hope that if any shall think them not necessarily relating to the main design of the Draught, they may nevertheless view them with a certain pleasure, as the Drapery, consisting of Flowers and Fruits, &c. for the greater ornament of the Piece.

Discourse is the image of the thought; but the Draught of a thing by way of Painting or Graving represents the thing it self. From this consideration it came, that this Piece is further adorn'd with several pieces of Sculpture, to the end that the Ideas of the things particularly treated of might be the more throughly imprinted in the Readers mind, by a sensible demonstration thereof.

Thus much as to the Authours and Directors of the Original Edition. The Publisher of the English hath only these few Remarks to trouble the Reader withal.

1. That possibly those of the English Nation, who are inhabitants in the Caribbies, may have peculiar names for divers of the Plants, Beasts, Birds, Fishes, &c. mentioned in this Treatise, much different from those which the Publisher hath used. Some of them, upon consultation with such as had lived in those parts he made a shift to get, and in all likelihood might have gotten most of the rest, had not the breaking forth of the last years Contagion caus'd most of the Inhabitants of London, to retire to their Country Habitations and Friends.

2. The

2. *The Reader is to note, that where some accident is said to have happened four or five, or some other number of years since (as for instance, pag. 14. where it is said in these words, that, two years since they were forced to quit their Villages, &c.) it is to be referred to the coming forth of the Original Edition, which was in the year* M. DC. LVIII.

3. *That whereas there might well be expected before this Work a Map of the* Caribby-Islands *in general, as also particular ones of the most eminent Islands, the Reader is to content himself with this satisfaction from the Stationers, that if an accurate one of the whole, that is such a one as might have been suitable to the other Embelishments of the present Work, could have been procured, it should not have been wanting: With this further assurance, that if what is done at the present meet with the reception expected, the next Impression shall be furnished not only with the forementioned Map, but also some other Pieces of Ornament, whereof the last years distraction, and want of time now have obstructed the insertion.*

Lastly, whereas many persons of worth (though more in the Original then in the Translation) are mentioned in several places as Inhabitants of the foresaid Colonies, there is only this to be said; that as the instancing of them adds somewhat to the certainty of the Relations; so it may likewise serve to undeceive many Europæans, *who are either so ill-informed of those Islands, or so prejudic'd against them, as to be perswaded, that, for the most part, they are only the refuges and receptacles of Bankrupts and debauched persons; the contrary being most certain; to wit, that they are inhabited by an infinite number of Families of good repute, which live civilly and in the fear of God.*

J. D.

THE
HISTORY
OF THE
Caribby Iſlands.

THE FIRST BOOK.

Containing the NATURAL Hiſtory of thoſe ISLANDS.

CHAPTER I.

Of the Scituation of the Caribbies in general ; the Temperature of the Air, the Nature of the Country, and its Inhabitants.

Etween the Continent of that part of *America* which lies Southward, and the Eaſtern Quarter of the Iſland of Sᵗ *John Porto-Rico*, there are certain Iſlands making up together the Figure of a Bow, and ſo diſpos'd that they croſs the Ocean, as it were by an oblique line.

They are by ſome called the *Antilles* of *America*, probably upon this account, that they make a kind of bar before the greater Iſlands, which are called the Iſlands of *America* : If ſo,

B   the

the word should be *Ant-Isles*, as being compos'd of the Greek word 'Αντι, which signifies *opposite*, and *Isles* or *Iles* : But the English commonly call them the *Caribby*-Islands, and the *Caribbies*. There are also who call them the *Cannibal*-Islands, from the names of the ancient Inhabitants; and they are read in some under the name of the *Camercane* Islands.

These Islands were first discovered by *Christopher Columbus*, under the Reign of *Ferdinand* and *Isabella*, King and Queen of *Castile* and *Leon*, in the year of our Lord, One thousand four hundred ninety and two.

There are numbred of them in all twenty eight, lying under the Torrid Zone, acounting from the eleventh degree of the Æquator, to the nineteenth Northward. Some Authors, as *Linscot* in his History of *America*, taking the name of the *Antilles* in a more general signification, attribute it to the four greater Islands, to wit, *Hispaniola*, *Cuba*, *Jamaica*, and *Porto-Rico*, as well as to these twenty eight.

The Air of all these Islands is temperate, and healthy enough, especially to such as have lived any time in them. The Plague heretofore was not known in these Parts, no more than it was in *China*, and some other places of the East : But some years since most of these Islands were much troubled with malignant Fevers, which the Physitians held to be contagious. That corruption of the Air was occasion'd by some Ships which came from the Coast of *Africk*; but now there is no talk of any such Diseases.

The heats are not greater in these parts than they are in *France* during the Months of *July* and *August*; and through a particular care of Divine Providence, between eight and nine in the morning there rises a gentle East-wind, which many times continues till four in the afternoon, refreshing the Air, and allaying the soultriness of the heat. *Josephus Acosta* affirms, That in the greater Islands of *America* this cooling wind blows about Noon. Thus through all the compass of the Torrid Zone, the wise Disposer of humane concernments hath ordered cool and regular Winds, to alleviate the scorching heats of the Sun.

It is never cold in the *Caribbies*, and Ice is a thing was never seen in those parts; nay, it would be accounted a kind of prodigy to find that where,

> *All things are clad in a perpetual green,*
> *And Winter only in the Snow of Lillies seen.*

But the Nights there are extreamly cool; and if a Man be uncovered during that time, he is apt to catch Colds, and great and dangerous pains in the Chest and Stomach : Nay, it hath been observ'd, That those who have expos'd themselves uncover'd to that pleasing coolness, if they have escaped pains and

gripings

gripings in the Stomack, have turn'd pale, yellowiſh, and ſwell'd-up, and in a ſhort time loſt the lively vermilion Complexions they had before.   There are indeed others attribute theſe effects to their feeding on *Caſſava*, which is commonly eaten in theſe Iſlands inſtead of bread, and may poſſibly have ſome quality not conſiſtent with the natural conſtitution of the Inhabitans of our Climates.   There is the ſame temperature in the night time at *Peru*, and in the *Maldivas*.   And thoſe who have travell'd to *Jeruſalem*, and through all the hot Countries, do affirm, That the greater the heats are in the day time, ſo much the colder are the nights; the reaſon whereof is, that the great Vapours rais'd by the Sun in the day time, being condens'd at night, and falling down in Dew, do extreamly cool and refreſh the Air.

The Æquinox laſts in theſe Iſlands neer one half of the year, and all the reſt of it the longeſt days are fourteen hours, and the ſhorteſt nights ten.   And thus hath the Divine Wiſdom beſtow'd of thoſe Parts of the World which lye moſt expos'd to the ſcorching beams of the Sun, long and cool nights, to recover and reſtore to vigour what the too neer approaches of that Planet had dry'd up and almoſt blaſted in the day.

Nor can the Year be here divided into four equal and diſtinct parts, as we do in *Europe*: But the Rains, which are very frequent there from *April* to *November*, and the great Droughts which reign all the reſt of the Year, make the only difference which may be obſerv'd between the Seaſons.

Now how theſe different Conſtitutions and Temperatures of the Air ſhould be called, there is a great diverſity of Opinions. Some conſidering, that as in theſe Parts there is in a manner no *Crepuſculum* or Twilight (which is a certain competion of, or ſomthing between night and day) ſo neither is there any Spring or Autumn to make a certain connexion between Summer and a kind of Winter, which they admit there.   Others maintain on the contrary, That there is no juſt reaſon that that part of the Year which goes under the name of Winter, ſhould be ſo called, in regard the Earth there is never cover'd with Froſt or Snow, which are the unwelcom attendants of Winter, but at all times cloath'd with a delightful Verdure, and almoſt in all ſeaſons crown'd with Flowers and Fruits, though in a different meaſure; whence they conclude, That the Year may be diſtinguiſh'd into three different and equal parts, and thoſe be called Spring, Summer, Autumn; though not ſo eaſily diſtinguiſhable as haply they may be in ſeveral parts of the World.

But the common expreſſion of thoſe people, who make up the Colonies now planted in theſe Iſlands, is not conſiſtent with this diſtinction; for they take the ſeaſon of the rains to be Winter, and that of the droughts, which is fair, clear, and pleaſant, to be Summer.   'Tis true, * *Acoſta* quarrels at the * *Lib. 2*

B 2

Spaniards,

Spaniards, for expressing themselves in that manner, and taking those rainy moneths for Winter. He affirms, that the time of the drought and fair weather is the true Winter in all the Torrid Zone, because then the Sun is at the greatest distance from that Region; and on the contrary, that the season of Rains and Mists ought there to be called Summer, by reason of the nearness of that Planet. To speak properly and rigorously, there is some reason we should comply with the sentiment of *Acosta*; yet inasmuch as not only the *Spaniards*, but also many other Nations, express themselves otherwise, we shall keep to their terms rather, especially in a thing of so little consequence.

But how rainy soever this Season may be in the *Carribies*, those who have liv'd there several years affirm, that there hardly passes a day, but the Sun is seen. The same thing is said of the Island of *Rhodes*; whence Antiquity dedicated it to the Sun, out of an imagination, that that Star had a particular care of it.

The Ebbing and Flowing of the Sea is regulated in these Countries, as in our parts; but it rises not above three or four foot at most.

The greatest part of these Islands are cover'd with several sorts of excellent Woods, which being green at all times, afford a very delightful prospect, and represent a perpetual Summer.

The Soil, in most places, is as rich and as pregnant as in any part of *France*; Insomuch that all those Islands that are inhabited, give not the Inhabitants any occasion to repent them of the pains they take. In which particular, they differ much from those Countries of *New-France*, where the poor Savages are so put to it to get their subsistance, that their Children, going out of their Hutts in the morning, and finding their Parents a hunting, are wont to cry out as loud as they can, *Come Tatous*; *come Castors*; *come Orignacs*; calling thus to the relief of their necessities those creatures, which yet come not in their sight as often as they stand in need thereof.

The same inhabited Islands are also furnished with good sources of fresh Water, Springs, Lakes, Brooks, Wells and Cisterns, and some of them have fair Rivers. There are further in several places Mineral-waters, which are successfully used, in order to the curing of divers Diseases. Brimstone is got out of the bowels of the Mountains in divers places; and the bright silver spangles which the Torrents and Rivers bring down along with them, and are found in the sand, and the froath of their waters, after they have been over-flown, are certain *indicia* and discoveries, that there is Crystal to be had in them, and that there are also Mines of those precious Metals, which are so much sought after by most men.

Those

Those running waters, which deserve the name of Rivers, are never dry'd up, even in the greatest droughts, and extreamly well stor'd with Fish, for the most part different from those seen in *Europe*. But there is such abundance on the Sea-coasts, that the Inhabitants will hardly take the pains to fish in the Rivers.

The Vine thrives very well in these Islands, and, besides a wild kind of Vine they have, which grows naturally in the Woods, and bears a very fair and large Grape, there are in all the Inhabited ones great Gardens, with the Walks set about with Vines; nay in some places perfect Vine-yards, as those in *France*, which bear twice a year, and sometimes oftener, according to the cultivation bestow'd on them, with respect had to the Moon and conveniency of the Seasons. The Grape is excellent good, but the Wine made of it will not keep many days; and therefore there is but little of it made.

As for Wheat, which grows in *New-Spain* as well as in any place of the World, it grows no further then the blade in the *Carribbies*, and is only for the making of Green-sauce, in regard that Grain requires winter, and the soil there being too rank, it shoots forth too much at first, and there is not strength enough left in the root to force it to staulk and knit in the ear. But if tryal were made of the sowing of Barley and Rye, and other Grains which require heat, its probable they would thrive well. And yet, should they come to maturity, and with great increase, the Inhabitants, being at little trouble to get *Manyoc*, *Potatoes*, *Turkey-wheat*, and several kinds of Pulse, would not take the pains to put them into the ground.

All the natural Provisions of these Islands are light, and of easie digestion; in regard the Country being hot, the stomack ought not to be burthened, as may be presumed in colder Climates. Upon this account it is, that such as are newly come into these parts are advis'd to eat little, and often. Nor doth what is eaten breed much blood, and therefore Phlebotomy is not much used.

These Islands are inhabited by four different Nations; whereof the first are the *Indigenæ*, or *Originary Inhabitants*, who have lived there time out of mind; and these are the *Carribbians* or *Canniballs*, of whom wee shall give a perfect accompt in the Second Book of this History. The other three are the *English*, the *French*, and the *Dutch*. The establishment of these foreign Nations in those parts happen'd about the year of our Lord one thousand six hundred twenty five, since which time they have so encreas'd, that the *English* and *French* are now become a very numerous people; as will be seen more at large in the sequel of this History.

CHAP.

CHAP. II.

Of each of the Caribby I-flands *in particular.*

THat we may obferve fome order in the Defcription we intend of each of thefe Iflands in particular, we fhall divide them into three Claffes; whereof the firft fhall comprehend thofe which lye towards the South, and are neereft the Line; the fecond thofe which lye Northward; and the laft, thofe which are commonly called the Lee-ward Iflands, which reach Weftward from St *Chriftophers*, the beft known of them all.

T A B A G O.

THe firft, and moft Southerly of all the *Caribbies* is *Tabago*, or *Tabac*, diftant from the Equinoctial, Northward, eleven degrees and fixteen minutes. It is about eight leagues in length, and four in breadth. There are in it feveral pleafant Mountains, out of which arife eighteen Springs or fmall Rivers, which, having drench'd the Plains, fall into the Sea. It is conceiv'd the air of it would be healthy enough, if the Trees were cut down, and the ground opened.

The extraordinary height of the Trees growing in this Ifland argue the fruitfulnefs of its foil. There are in this the five kinds of four-footed creatures, whereof there are but one or two in any of the other Iflands. As 1. a kind of *Swine*, not much furnifh'd with briftles, which have a certain hole on their backs. 2 *Tatous*. 3 *Agoutis*. 4 *Opaffums*, and 5 *Musk-Rats*, all which we fhall defcribe in their proper place. Not to mention the Wood-Quifts, Turtles, Partridges, and Parrats, which are commonly feen there, it affords abundance of other Birds, not known in *Europe*.

The Sea which encompaffes this Ifland is abundantly furnifh'd with all forts of excellent Fifh. Sea-Tortoifes come in multitudes to hide their Egges in the fand, which lyes on the fhoars. On the Weft and North fide of it, there are Bayes, where Ships may fafely Anchor.

About fixteen years fince, a Company of Burghers of *Walcre* in *Zealand* fent thither 2co men, to plant a Colony there, under the States-General of the United Provinces, and call'd the Ifland, the *New-Walcre*. But the natural Inhabitants of the Country, fearing the Neighbourhood of thofe Foreigners, maffacred fome of them, which forc'd the reft, who were troubled with ficknefs and feared the treatment their companions had receiv'd, to retire elfewhere. Whereupon the Ifland

was

was a long time deſtitute of Inhabitants, and frequented only by ſome *Caribbians*, who, coming and going to their Wars, ſtruck in there to get neceſſary refreſhments; as alſo by ſome French of the Iſlands of *Martinico* and *Gardeloupe*, who came thither to fiſh for *Lamantine* and *Tortoiſes*, at certain ſeaſons of the year.

But now the *Zealanders* are re-eſtabliſh'd there, and about three years ſince *Lampſen*, an ancient Burgo-maſter of *Fluſhing*, and one of the States-General, ventur'd to people the Iſland anew. He brought thither, in his own Ships, ſeveral gallant perſons, who are likely reſtore the Colony which his Country-men had planted there before.

This Iſland lying next to the Continent of that part of *America* which lyes Southward, lyes very convenient for a Commerce with the *Arovagues*, the *Calibis*, the *Caribbians*, and ſeveral other *Indian* Nations; and the keeping together of a conſiderable force of men, which might be eaſily ſent over into the Continent, and lay the foundations of a powerful Colony.

GRANADA.

THe Iſland of *Granada*, lying at twelve degrees and ſixteen ſcruples on this ſide of the Line, does properly begin the Semicircle of the *Antilles*. It is in length about ſeven leagues, the breadth not the ſame in all places, reaching North and South like a Creſcent. The French became maſters of it about ſix years ſince. They had at the beginning great conteſtations with the *Caribbians*, who, for ſome moneths, diſputed the poſſeſſion of it with them by force of arms. But at laſt Monſieur *Parquet*, Governour of *Martinico*, who had reſolv'd, at his own charge, to make an eſtabliſhment there, oblig'd them, out of a conſideration of their own concernments, grounded principally on the great advantages they received from the Neighbourhood of the French, to leave him quietly poſſeſs'd of it.

The ground produces all manner of the Country proviſions, as Sugar-Canes, Ginger, and excellent Tobacco. The air is very healthy. It is well furniſh'd with Springs of freſh water, and places of good Anchorage for Ships. It hath alſo abundance of fair Trees, ſome excellent for their fruit, others for their fitneſs for building. There is good Fiſhing all about it, and the Inhabitants have alſo good Fiſhing and Hunting in and about three little Iſlands, called the *Granadines*, lying North-Eaſt from it. The firſt Governour of this place was, Monſieur *Le Comte* Governour of *Martinico*, who was ſucceeded by Mon. *dela Vaumeniere*. It hath ſince been bought by the Count of *Serillas*, of Monſ. *Parquet*.

B E K I A.

BEKIA.

THe Iſland of *Bekia* is diſtant from the Line twelve degrees and 25 ſcruples. It is ten or twelve leagues about, and would be fruitful enough, if it were cultivated. There is in it a good Haven for Ships; but inaſmuch as it is not furniſh'd with freſh water, it is not much frequented, unleſs it be by ſome *Caribbians* of St. *Vincent's*, who ſometimes go thither a fiſhing, or to dreſs ſome ſmall Gardens they have up and down there for their diverſion.

St *VINCENT.*

THe Iſland of St. *Vincent* is the moſt populous of any poſſeſs'd by the *Caribbians.* Its Altitude is ſixteen degres North from the Line. Thoſe who have ſeen the Iſland *Ferro*, or *Fietro*, one of the *Canaries*, affirm, that this is much of the ſame figure. It may be about eight leagues in length, and ſix in breadth. There are in it ſeveral high Mountains, between which are very fruitful Plains, if they were cultivated. The *Caribbians* have many fair Villages, where they live pleaſantly, and without any diſturbance. And though they have a jealouſly of the ſtrangers that live about them, and ſtand on their Guard when they come to their Roads, yet do they not deny them the Bread of the Country, which is *Caſſava* , Water, Fruits, and other Proviſions, growing in their Country, if they want them, taking in exchange, Wedges, Hooks, and other implements of Iron, which they much eſteem

BARBADOS.

THe *Barbados*, which is the ſame that is called by the French *Barboude*, lyes between the 13 and 14 degree, North from the Equator, and Eaſtward from St. *Alouſie*, and St. *Vincent.* The Engliſh, who planted a Colony there in the year *M.DC.XXVII.* allow it to be about 25 leagues in compaſs, but greater in length then breadth. There is in the whole Iſland but one River, which truely deſerves that name : but the Countrey lying low and even, there are, in ſeveral places, Pools and Reſervatories of freſh water, which ſupply the ſcarcity of Springs and Rivers. Moſt houſes have alſo Ciſterns, and Wells which are never dry.

At the firſt Cultivation the Earth promiſed not much; but experience hath evinc'd the contrary, it plentifully producing Tobacco, Ginger, Cotten, and eſpecially Sugar-Canes, inſomuch that, next to St. *Chriſtophers*, it is the moſt frequented by Merchants, and the moſt populous of all the *Antilles.*

About

About the year 1646. they accounted in it about twenty thouſand Inhabitants, not comprehending in that number the Negro-Slaves, who were thought to amount to a far greater.

There are many places in this Iſland, which may juſtly be called Towns, as containing many fair, long, and ſpacious Streets, furniſh'd with a great number of noble Structures, built by the principal Officers and Inhabitants of this flouriſhing Colony. Nay indeed, taking a full proſpect of the whole Iſland, a man might take it for one great City, inaſmuch as the houſes are at no great diſtance one from another; that many of thoſe are very well built, according to the rate of Building in *England*; that the Shops and Store-houſes are well furniſh'd with all ſorts of Commodities; that there are many Fairs and Markets; and laſtly, that the whole Iſland, as great Cities are, is divided into ſeveral Pariſhes, which have very fair Churches. The moſt conſiderable of the Inhabitants think themſelves ſo well, that it is ſeldom ſeen they ever remove thence.

This Iſland is very famous in all parts, by reaſon of the great abundance of excellent Sugar it hath afforded theſe many years. 'Tis true, it is not ſo white as that which comes from other parts, but it is better eſteemed by Refiners, becauſe it hath fairer grain and yields more, when it is purifi'd.

Sᵗ L U C Y's.

Sᴛ *Lucy's* Iſland lyes at 13 deg. 40 ſcr. on this ſide the Line. It was heretofore frequented only by a ſmall number of *Indians*, who came to fiſh thereabouts. But ſome time ſince, the French of *Martinico* came and kept them company. There are two high Mountains in the Iſland, which are very cold. They are ſeen at a great diſtance, and are called by the French, *Les Pitons de St. Alouſie.* At the deſcent of theſe Mountains, there are pleaſant Valleys cover'd with great Trees, and water'd with Springs. The air is conceiv'd **to** be healthy, and that the ſoil will be fruitful, when it ſhall **be** a little better diſcover'd then it is yet.

MARTINICO.

Tʜᴇ Iſland of *Martinico*, which the Indians call'd *Madanina*, lyes **at** the altitude of fourteen degrees and thirty ſcruples on this ſide the Line. It is about ſixteen leagues in length, of an unequal breadth, and about forty five in compaſs. The Soil of it is pleaſant, which makes **it** at this day one of the moſt populous of all the *Caribbies*.

The *French* and *Indians* are joyntly poſſeſſ'd of it, and have
C   liv'd

liv'd a long time in very good correspondence. Monf. *Parquet* is the prefent French Governour of it.

Of all the *Caribbies* this is the moft uneven Ifland, that is, the moft full of Mountains, which are very high, and intermixt with inacceffible Rocks. The fruitful parts of it confift in certain round Hills or eminences; as alfo in very delightful fkirts of Mountains, and fome Plains or Valleys, which are extreamly pleafant.

The Mountains of it are not to be inhabited, and ferve for the feeding and retreat of wild Beafts, Serpents and Snakes, whereof there is great abundance. Yet are thefe Mountains well furnifh'd with wood, which, in bignefs and length, exceed any in *Europe*, and bears fruit and food for the wild Boars and Birds.

As for the Hills and fkirts of Mountains, they are for the moft part, inhabitable; and of a good foil, but very troublefome to manure. For fome of them are fo high and fteepy, that people can hardly work on them without danger, or at leaft without holding by a Tobacco-ftalk, or fome Tree with one hand, that they may work with the other.

The Tobacco which grows on thefe eminent places is ever the beft, and efteem'd above that which grows in the Valleys, and bottoms, which have not fo much prefence of the Sun. For the Tobacco, which grows in bottoms, and places encompafs'd with Woods, is ever full of yellow-fpots, as if it were burnt, and neither takes well, nor keeps well. Thefe enclofed places are alfo unhealthy, and thofe who work in them contract an ill colour, and the new-comers, who are not accuftomed to that air, do fooner, in thefe, then in any other places, catch that griping of the Belly, which is fo common in thefe Iflands.

There being two different Nations in this Ifland, it is accordingly divided between them, to wit, the *Indians*, the natural Inhabitants of the Country; and the *French*, who laid the foundations of this Colony in *July*, in the year 1635. under the Conduct of Monf. *Defnambuc*, who brought them from St. *Chriftophers*, and left them in quiet poffeffion of this place.

That part of the Ifland which is inhabited by the Indians is comprehended in one quarter, which is called the *Cabes-terre*, without any other diftinction.

The part occupied by the *French*, and called *Baffe-terre*, is divided into five quarters, which are by them called, *La Cafe du Pilote*, *La Cafe Capot*, *Le Carbet*, *Le Fort St. Pierre*, and *Le Prefcheur*. In each of thefe Quarters there is a Church, or at leaft a Chappel, a Court of Guard, and a Magazine for Arms, about which are built feveral large and fair Store-houfes, both for the Commodities that are imported, and thofe of the growth of the Ifland.

The

The Quarter of the *Case du Pilote* is so called from a Savage Captain, who had sometimes lived there, and glory'd much in the name *Pilot*, which the *French* had given him. He discover'd to Monf. *Parquet*, the engagements which those of his Nation entred into against him.

In the Quarter of *Case Capot*, there is a very noble *Savanna*, (thus they call in the Islands pleasant Meadows and Pastures) which hath, on the one side the River called *Capot*, and on the other, many fair Edifices.

The *Carbet* Quarter hath its name from the ancient Inhabitants, who sometime had there one of their greatest Villages, and a publick House which they called *Carbet*, a name yet common to those places, where they have their meetings. The *French* Governour liv'd in this Quarter a long time, having built a noble Brick-house, neer the Haven, in a pleasant bottom, refresh'd by a considerable River, which falls down out of the Mountains. The Indians, who never had seen Structure of any such material, look'd on it at first with a great astonishment, and having attempted to shake it, by the strength of their shoulders, but not stirring it, they were forc'd acknowledg, that if all Houses were so built, the Tempest which they call the *Hurricane* would not prejudice them. But since, the Governour not having his health perfectly there, he made a present of it to the *Jesuits*, together with the Gardens about it, as also the rarities and curiosities of the Country, and several other habitations dependent on it, and a great number of Negro-slaves, who cultivate them.

Fort St. Pierre, or St. *Peter's* Fort, is the place where the Governour now lives. There are in it several great pieces of Cannon, some of Brass, some of Iron. This Fort commands all the Haven. About a stones cast from the Governours, stands the fair Colledge of the *Jesuits*, situate on a pleasant River, which is thence called, *The Jesuits River*. This Structure is of Free-stone and Brick, very delightful to the eye. The Avenues also want not their temptation, and, all about it, are Gardens and Orchards, producing whatever is most delicious of the growth of the Islands; as also several Plants, Herbs, Flowers and Fruits brought thither from *France*. There is also a Vine-yard, which yields yearly good store of Wine.

The *Le Prescheur*, or the Preachers Quarter, contains an even low part of the Country, very considerable for its extent, and several high Mountains, upon the skirts whereof, there are a good number of fair Habitations.

Between the *Cabes-terre*, and the *Basse-terre*, there is a kind of bottom, where is abundance of that Wood by which the Tobacco climes up. There they have also the Reeds, wherewith the Hutts are Palisado'd; as also the wild *Mahot*, the bark whereof serves for several things about the house.

C 2

Most

Moſt of the Houſes in this Iſland are of wood, very convenient, and delightful to the eye. The moſt conſiderable are built on certain eminences. That advantageous ſituation contributes much to their health who live in them, for the air is clearer then that of the Valleys. It alſo adds much to the beauty of thoſe pleaſant Structures ; and cauſes a very divertive proſpect.

The beſt Haven of this Iſland lyes between *Carbet* and St. *Peters* Fort. It is more ſafe then any of the neighbouring Iſlands, as being encompaſs'd with high Mountains, which ſecure the Ships lying in it from the violence of all winds.

Between *Caſe du Pilote*, and a bottom called *Culde Sac des Salines*, there is a Rock, running about half a league into the Sea, which is called the *Diamond*, from its figure, and is a retreat for an infinite number of Birds, and among others Wood-quiſts, which breed in it. It is hard getting up to it, yet ſome viſit it, as they paſs by, when the young ones are fit to eat.

There is another place on the ſame ſide as the *Diamond*, into which Ships are brought, to be refreſh'd, and mended. The Sea there is always calm, but the air not healthy, in regard the Sea-men commonly catch Fevers, which yet are not very dangerous, inaſmuch as they ſhake them off, as ſoon as they depart thence.

Beſides the Torrents, which in times of rains fall down with great violence, and the inundations of this Iſland, there are nine or ten conſiderable Rivers which are never dry. Their ſources are at the aſcent or foot of the higheſt Mountains, and having watered the Valleys they fall into the Sea. They are prejudicial to the places neer them, in regard that when they overflow, they root up Trees, undermine rocks, and make a deſolation over the Fields and Gardens, carrying along with them, the houſes which lye in the plain Country, and whatever oppoſes the impetuoſity of their courſe. This inconvenience hath oblig'd the Inhabitants of this Colony to take up their habitations on the tops of thoſe little Mountains, wherewith their Iſland is richly furniſh'd ; for they ſecure them from theſe inundations.

But what is moſt conſiderable in this Iſland, is the multitude of the Inhabitants poſſeſſing it, who are thought to amount to nine or ten thouſand perſons, not comprehending in that number the Indians and Negroes, who are neer as many. The mildneſs of the Government and the advantageous ſituation of the Iſland contribute much to the advancement of it and the multiplication of its Inhabitants. For moſt of the *French* and *Dutch* Ships, bound for *America*, ſo order their courſe, that they may touch here, rather then at any other of the Iſlands : and as ſoon as they have caſt Anchor in any of the Havens, to

take

take in the refrefhments neceffary for them, they fet a fhoar
their Paffengers, if they be not exprefly oblig'd to bring them
to fome other place.   Nay it hath often hapned that whole Families, which had left *France*, with a defigne to pafs over into
fome of the other Iflands which lye beyond this, and are not inferior to it, either as to Air or Soil, being wearied out with
the inconveniences of a long Voyage, have fetled here to avoid
expofing themfelves to the fame again.

Among the great multitude of people which make up this
Colony, there are many perfons of worth and quality, who
after their honorable imployments in other parts of the world,
have at laft made choice of this place, for their repofe and retirement.   Among thefe are particularly to be mentioned
Monf. *Courcelas*, Lieutenant-General under the Governor, a
perfon who by his excellent conduct hath gain'd the affections
of both Inhabitants and Strangers; Monf. *Le Comte*, and Monf.
de L'Oubiere, as being the principal Officers.

At the beginning of our Defcription of this Ifland, we faid,
that the *French* and *Indians* lived there a long time together in good correfpondence.   But the Letters that came
thence lately, giving an account of the ftate of it, affirm, that
about four years fince, the *Caribbians* made an infurrection,
and have continued a War with the French ever fince; that
fince that time, thofe Barbarians had done great mifchiefs in
the French Quarters; and that neither the height of the Mountains, nor depth of the precipices, nor yet the horror of vaft
and dreadful folitudes, which till then had been accounted an
impenetrable wall, lying between the feveral divifions of both
the Nations, hindred not their falling upon them, and filling
their habitations with fire, maffacres, defolation, and whatever the implacable fpirit of revenge could fuggeft to them of
greateft cruelty, to feed their rage, and fatisfie their brutality.

Of the occafions of this Rupture there are feveral accounts
given.   Some attribute it to Monf. *Parquet's* eftablifhing of
French Colonies in the Iflands of *Granada* and St. *Lucy*, without the confent of the *Caribbians*, who thereupon took occafion of difcontent.   Others affirm that they took up Arms, to
revenge the deaths of fome of their Nation, Inhabitants of the
Ifland of S. *Vincent*, whom they believe to have come to their
end by drinking fome poifon'd Strong-water which had been
brought them from *Martinico*.

Immediately upon the breaking forth of this War, and the
firft devaftations made by the *Caribbians* in one of the *French*
Quarters (which, according to their cuftom, was by a bafe fur-
prife) thofe who envy'd the glory of thofe Colonies, and their
progrefs and eftablifhment in thofe Iflands, fcattered their ma-
licious reports, That the *French* would never be able to keep
under

under thofe Barbarians; That thofe of the fame Nation, who live in *Dominico* and S. *Vincent's*, had fecretly apply'd themfelves to all their Allies of the Continent, to incite them to engage in an unanimous War againft the *French*; That the more eafily to effectuate that defign, and make their Party ftronger, they had gone fo far as to treat of a Peace with the *Arovagues*, their ancient Enemies: And, That they had fo far engag'd all thefe Salvages in their Quarrel, that they were refolv'd with a joynt-force to fall upon the *French*, and over-run them with their multitude.

It is not certainly known whether there were really any fuch Affociation againft them or not; but certain it is, that the effects 'of it appear'd not; and that after the firft Irruptions of the *Caribbians* of *Martinico* into the *French* Quarters, which were indeed with fome advantage of the Barbarians, they have been fo unfuccefsful in their Enterprifes fince, and worfted fo with the lofs of the chief amongft them, that about two years fince they were forc'd to quit their Villages, and leave their Gardens to the difpofal of the Victorious, and retire for fafety into Woods, and inacceffible Rocks and Mountains. So that the World is now perfwaded of the contrary, *viz.* That if thofe Barbarians fhall make any further attempt to recover themfelves out of that wretched Confternation in which they live, by the force of Arms, they will in all likelyhood be forc'd either to quit the abfolute poffeffion of the Ifland to the *French*, or accept of fuch Conditions of Peace as they can obtain, to renew the ancient Alliance, which they have been but too forward to break.

CHAP. III.

Of the Iflands which lye towards the North.

THe Iflands we intend to defcribe in this Chapter, lying more towards the North, are confequently more temperate. They are alfo more frequented than thofe of *Tabago*, *Granada*, and S. *Aloufia*, in regard the Ships which have refrefh'd themfelves at *Martinico*, and fall down thence to S. *Chriftophers*, may vifit them one after another, without any diverfion out of their Courfe.

DOMINICO.

THe Ifland of *Dominico* lies at the altitude of 15 degrees and 30 minutes. It is conceiv'd to be in length about 13.

League

Leagues, and not much lefs in breadth, where it is at the great-eft. There are in the midft of it feveral high Mountains, which encompafs an inacceffible bottom, where may be feen from the tops of certain rocks an infinite number of *Reptiles*, of a dreadful bulk and length.

This Ifland is inhabited by the *Caribbians*, who are very nu-merous in it. They have a long time entertain'd thofe who came to vifit them with a ftory of a vaft and monftrous Serpent, which had its aboad in that bottom. They affirmed that there was on the head of it a very fparkling ftone, like a Carbuncle, of ineftimable price; That it commonly veil'd that rich Je-wel with a thin moving fkin, like that of a mans eye-lid; but that when it went to drink, or fported himfelf in the midft of that deep bottom, he fully difcover'd it, and that the rocks and all about receiv'd a wonderful luftre from the fire iffuing out of that precious Crown.

The fupream Perfon of this Ifland was heretofore one of the moft confiderable among thofe of the fame Nation. For when all their Forces marched out to Battel againft the *Arovaguer*, their common Enemies of the Continent; he had the conduct of the Van-guard and was known by a particular mark which he had about him.

When any *French* Ships come neer this Ifland, there are im-mediately feen feveral Canows, in each whereof there are three, or but four *Indians* at the moft, who come to direct them to the Havens, where they may fafely Anchor. They commonly bring along with them fome of the Country Fruits, whereof having prefented the Captains and other Officers with the choiceft, they proffer the reft in exchange for Fifhing-hooks, grains of Cryftal, and fuch trifles, as they account precious.

MARIGALANTA.

THe Ifland of *Marigalanta* lyes at the altitude of 15 deg. and 40 minutes. It is a flat Country, and well furnifh'd with wood, which argues it would be fertile enough, if it were once reduced to culture. It hath always been frequented by the *Indians*, as well in order to Fifhing, as for fome fmall Gar-dens which they have in it.

The laft Letters from the *Carribies* brought news that Monf. *d'Howel*, Governour of *Gardeloupe* had lately peopled this Ifland, and built a Fort in it to keep under certain *Indians*, who would have oppofed his defign, and had kill'd twenty of thofe whom he had fent thither at firft to difcover the Coun-try; and that upon that accident he had fent over thither three hundred men, who retreated in the night time to a great Vef-fel they had in the road, till fuch time as the Fort was made tenable.

tenable. The *Caribbians* of *Dominico*, the better to continue the good correspondence there is between them and the Inhabitants of *Gardeloupe*, who are their next Neighbours, affirm they had no hand in that Maſſacre, and excuſed themſelves to Monſ. *d' Howel*, imputing it to thoſe of their Nation, who live in the other Iſlands.

SAINTS.

BEtween *Dominico* and *Gardeloupe* there are three or four ſmall Iſlands very neer one another, commonly called the *Saints* : They are at the ſame Altitude as *Marigalanta*, Weſt from which they lye, and are as yet deſert and unhabited.

The Iſland of *Birds* lyes more Weſt then the forementioned, at fifteen degrees, and forty five minutes. It hath that name from the infinite number of Birds, which breed in it, making their Neſts even on the Sea-ſhoar : They are for the moſt part eaſily taken with the hand, not fearing men in regard they ſeldom ſee any. This Iſland lyes very low, and is hardly perceiv'd till one be very neer it.

DESIRADO.

THe Iſland *Deſirado* was ſo called by *Chriſtopher Columbus*, as being the firſt diſcover'd by him of all the *Caribbies*, in his ſecond Voyage into *America*. And as he called the firſt place he diſcover'd of this new World *San Salvador*, whereas before it was called *Guanabani*, which is one of the *Lucajos*, at the altitude of 25 degrees and ſome minutes ; ſo he called this *Deſirado*, from the obtaining of his *Deſire*. It lies ten Leagues from *Gardeloupe*, North-eaſt, and from the Line 16 degrees and 10 minutes. The ſoil of this Iſland is good ; and conſequently it will not be long ere it be Inhabited.

GARDELOUPE.

GArdeloupe is one of the greateſt and nobleſt Iſlands of any poſſeſs'd by the *French* in the *Caribbies*. It was heretofore called by the Indians *Carucueira* ; but the *Spaniards* gave it the name by which it is now known. Some would have it preciſely at 16 Degrees ; others add therto 16 minutes. The Circumference of it is about 60 Leagues, and, where broadeſt, about nine or ten in breadth. It is divided into two parts by a little Arm of the Sea, which ſeparates the *Grand'-Terre* from that which is properly called *Gardeloupe*. The more Eaſterly part of this latter is called by the French *Cabes-Terre*, and that towards the Weſt *Baſſe-Terre*.

That part of it which is called the *Grand'-Terre* hath two
Salt-

Salt-pits, where the Sea-water is converted into Salt, as in ſeveral other Iſlands, by the force of the Sun, without aſſiſtance of Art.

That part which is inhabited hath in ſeveral places, eſpecially towards the middle of it, divers high Mountains, whereof ſome are full of bare and dreadful Rocks, riſing out of a Bottom, encompaſſed with many inacceſſible Precipices; others are cover'd with delightful Trees, which are to them at all times a kind of pleaſant Garland. At the foot of theſe Mountains there are ſeveral Plains of a vaſt extent, which are refreſh'd by a great number of pleaſant Rivers, which occaſioned heretofore the *Spaniſh* Ships to touch there, to take in freſh water for the continuance of their Voyage. Some of theſe Rivers when they are overflown bring down pieces of Wood that have paſs'd through the Sulphur-mines, that are in one of the moſt remarkable Mountains in the Iſland, which continually caſts up ſmoak, whence it is called the *Sulphur-Mountain*. There are alſo in it Springs of hot water, which have been found by experience good for the Dropſie, and all Indiſpoſitions proceeding from a cold cauſe. There are between theſe two parts of the Land two great Gulphs, whence thoſe Inhabitants who delight in Fiſhing may at any time take Tortoiſes, and ſeveral other excellent Fiſh.

The *French* firſt planted themſelves in this Iſland in the year *M. DC. XXXV.* M. M. *du Pleſſis* and *l' Olive* were the firſt Governours of it, with equal authority; but the former dying ſeven moneths after his arrival, and the other becoming unfit for Government by the loſs of his ſight, there was ſent over Monſ. *Auber*, one of the Captains of St. *Chriſtophers*, who chanc'd to be then at *Paris*. This Colony owes its conſervation and welfare ſince to the prudence and conduct of this worthy Governor, who ſignaliz'd his entrance into that Charge by the Peace he made with the *Carribians*, and ſeveral good Conſtitutions in order to the welfare of the Inhabitants, whereof we ſhall give a more particular account in the ſecond Book of this Hiſtory.

Monſieur *d' Howel* is now Lord and Governor of this Iſland, which is yet better ſince his eſtabliſhment, for the number of the Inhabitants is much encreas'd, and they have built very fair Houſes, and brought ſuch Trading thither, that now it is one of the moſt flouriſhing and moſt conſiderable Iſlands of the *Caribbies*.

There are in it very fair Plains, wherein the ground is ordered by the Plough, a thing not to be ſeen in any of the other Iſlands. And after the Plough, it bears Rice, Turky-wheat, the *Manioc*, whereof *Caſſava* is made, *Potatoes*, nay, in ſome places Ginger and Sugar-canes, with great increaſe.

The reformed *Jacobins*, or *White-Friers*, are poſſeſs'd of some part of the best Land in this Island, on which they have many delightful Plantations. The good condition wherein they are is to be acknowledg'd an effect of the care of the R. Father *Raymond Breton*, who, amidst many great difficulties, preserv'd them to his Order.

In that part of the Island, which is called *Basse-terre*, there is a little Town which grows daily bigger : It hath already several Streets adorned with many handsome houses of Timber, most of two Stories, of a convenient structure and delightful to the eye. Besides a fair Parish-Church, there are in it a Colledg of *Jesuits*, and a Monastery of *Carmelites*, brought thither lately by the Governors means; as also several Storehouses, well furnish'd with Provisions and Commodities, requisite for the subsistance of the Colony.

The Governor lives in a Castle, not far from the Town. It is built four-square, having at each corner Spurs and Redoubts of Masons work, of such thickness as to bear the weight of several great Pieces of Brass, which are mounted there. A little beyond the Castle there is a very high Mountain which might somewhat incommodate it; but the Governor not omitting any thing that might contribute to the ornament or security of the Island, hath planted some great Pieces there, and to prevent surprise of an Enemy, he hath made a kind of Cittadel there, which is at all times furnish'd with Provisions and Ammunition. The *Cabes-terre* hath also a considerable Fort, which secures the whole Quarter; it is called St. *Mary's* Fort.

Many persons of quality have made their retirement into this Island, and have set up a great number of Sugar-Mills.

ANTEGO.

THe Island of *Antego* lyes at the Altitude of 16 degrees, and 11 minutes, between the *Barbados*, and the *Desirada*. It is in length about six or seven leagues, the breadth not the same in all places; The access of it is dangerous for Shipping, by reason of the rocks which encompass it. It was conceiv'd heretofore, that it was not to be inhabited, upon this presumption, that there was no fresh water in it : but the English, who have planted themselves in it, have met with some, and have made Ponds and Cisterns, which might supply that defect. This Island is abundant in Fish, most sorts of wild Fowl, and in all of tame Cattel. It is inhabited by seven or eight hundred men.

MONT-SERRAT.

THe Iſland of *Mont-Serrat* receiv'd that name from the *Spaniards*, upon the account of a certain reſemblance there is between a Mountain in this, and that of *Mont-Serrat*, which is not far from *Barcelona*; and it hath kept the name ever ſince. It lyes at the Altitude of 27 degrees. It is about three Leagues in length, and almoſt as much in breadth, ſo that it ſeems to be almoſt of a round figure. 'Tis conceiv'd there are in it between ſix and ſeven hundred men.

What is moſt conſiderable in this Iſland is a very fair Church, of a delightful Structure, built by the contributions of the Governor and Inhabitants. The Pulpit, the Seats, and all the Joyners and Carpenters work within it, are of the moſt precious and ſweet-ſcented-wood growing in the Country.

BARBOVTHOS.

THe Iſland which the Engliſh call the *Barbouthos*, lyes at the Altitude of 17 degrees, and 30 minutes. It lyes very low, and is in length about five leagues, lying North-Eaſt from *Mont-Serrat*. The Engliſh are the Inhabitants of it, and the Colony may amount to between four and five hundred men, who find whereupon to ſubſiſt conveniently.

It is ſubject to this annoyance, which is alſo common to the Iſlands of *Antego* and *Mont-Serrat*, that the *Caribbians* of *Dominico*, and other places, do many times commit great ſpoils in it. The enmity and averſion which thoſe *Barbarians* have conceiv'd againſt the *Engliſh* Nation in general, is come to that height, that there hardly paſſes a year but they make one or two irruptions, in the night time, into ſame one of the Iſlands it is poſſeſ'd of; and then, if they be not timely diſcover'd, and valiantly oppos'd, they kill all the men they meet, ranſack the Houſes and burn them, and if they can get any of the Women or Children, they carry them away Priſoners into their own Territories, with all the Booty they have a mind to.

ROTONDA.

THe Iſland called *Redonda*, or *Rotonda*, from its round figure, lyes at the altitude of 17 degrees, and 10 minutes. It is a very little one, and at a diſtance ſeems to be only a great Tower, and taking a proſpect of it one way, a man might ſay it were a great Ship under ſail. It is of eaſie acceſs on all ſides, by reaſon the Sea about it is deep, and without rocks or ſhelves, which might be dangerous to ſhipping.

D 2   *NIEVES.*

NIEVES.

THe Island called *Nieves*, otherwise *Mevis*, lyes at the altitude of 27 degrees, and 19 minutes, Northward. It is not above six leagues about, and in the midst of it there is but one only Mountain, which is very high, and cover'd with great Trees up to the very top. The Plantations are all about the Mountain, beginning from the Sea-side, till you come to the highest part of it, the ascent being commodious enough. This Island may easily be compass'd either by land or water. There are in it divers springs of fresh water, whereof some are strong enough to make their way to the Sea: Nay there is one spring, whereof the waters are hot and mineral. Not far from the source there are Bathes made, which are frequented with good success, in order to the curing of those diseases for which the waters of *Bourbon* are recommended.

The *English*, who planted themselves there in the year *M.DC.XXVIII.* are still the Inhabitants of this Island, and they are now thought to be between three and four thousand men, who subsist and live handsomly, by the trade they drive in Sugar, Ginger and Tobacco.

This Island is the best governed of any in the *Caribbies.* Justice is there administred with great prudence by a Council, consisting of the most eminent and most ancient Inhabitants of the Colony: Swearing, Thieving, Drunkenness, Fornication, and all dissolutions and disorders are severely punish'd. In the Year *M.DC.XLIX.* Mr. *Lake*, a knowing person and fearing God, had the Government of it. He is since departed this life.

There are in this Island three Churches, which have nothing extraordinary, as to Structure, but are very convenient as to the performing of Divine Service. For the security of the Vessels that are in the Road, and to prevent the invasion of an Enemy, there is a Fort built, wherein are several great Pieces which command as far as the Sea. It secures also the publick Storehouses, into which all the Commodities that are imported, and necessary for the subsistance of the Inhabitants, are disposed. And thence it is, that they are afterwards distributed to those private persons who stand in need thereof, provided those who have the over-sight of them think them solvent persons, according to the time and price agreed upon, and ordered by the Governor and Council.

A further recommendation of this Island, is, that it is divided only by a small arm of the Sea from that of St. *Christophers*, the noblest and most famous of all the *Caribbies.* Having given but a short Description of the other Islands, what we

shall

shall give of this, as being the chiefest, will be somewhat larger.
but with it reason, we shall assign it a Chapter by it self.

CHAP. IV.

Of the Island of St. Christopher.

St *Christophers* was so called by *Christopher Columbus*, who finding it very pleasant, would needs give it his own name.   He was engag'd to give it this name from a consideration of the figure of its Mountains, the Island having on its upper part, as it were upon one of its shoulders, another lesser Mountain, as St *Christopher* is painted like a Gyant, carrying our Saviour upon his, as it were a little Child.   Its altitude is at 17 degrees, 25 minutes.

It is about 25 leagues in compass.   The Soil being light and sandy, is apt to produce all sorts of the Country Fruits, as also many of the choicest growing in *Europe*.   It lyes high in the midst, by reason of some very high Mountains, out of which arise several Rivers, which sometimes are so suddenly overflown through the rains falling on the Mountains, so as that there is none seen at the extremities of them, or in the Plains, that the Inhabitants are many times surpriz'd by those Torrents.

The whole Island is divided into four Cantons, or Quarters, two whereof are possess'd by the *English*; the other two by the *French*; but in such sort, as that people cannot cross from one quarter to the other, without passing over Lands of one of the two Nations.   The *English* have in their part a greater number of little Rivers then the *French*; but in requital, the latter have more of the plain Country, and Lands fitter for cultivation.   The *English* also exceed the *French* in number; but the latter have more fortified places, and are better armed.   The *French* have four Forts, well furnish'd with great Pieces, which carry a great way into the Sea; and one of them hath regular works, like a Citadel.   The most considerable next that lyes at the Haven, or Anchoring-place, called *Basse-terre*.   There is in both a constant Guard kept : And to prevent the differences which might happen between two different Nations, each of them upon the Avenues of their Quarters hath a Guard which is renew'd every day.   The *English* have two fortifi'd places, whereof one commands the great Haven, and the other a Descent, not far from *Pointe de Sable*.

This Island is furnish'd with a fair Salt-pit, lying on the Sea-side, which the Inhabitants commonly call *Cul-de-Sac*.   Not
far

far thence, there is a small Point of Land, which reaches out
so far towards the Island of *Nieves*, that it is not above half a
league of Sea between the two, insomuch that there have been
those who have swam from one to the other.

It is conceiv'd there is a Silver-mine in St. *Christophers*; but
in regard the Salt-pits, Woods, Havens, and Mines are common to both Nations, no body looks after it: Besides, such
an enterprise would require a great stock, and an infinite number of Slaves.   The true Silver-mine of this Island is Sugar.

A man may easily compass the whole Island by Land,
but cannot pass through the midst of it, by reason of several
great and steepy Mountains, between which there are dreadful precipices, and springs of hot water: Nay there are some
springs of Sulphur, which hath occasion'd one of them to be
called, the *Sulphur-Mountain*.   Taking the Circumference
from without, the body of the Island seems to extend it self,
by a gentle descent, down to the Sea-side, and is of an unequal breadth, according as the Mountains dilate their skirts
more or less towards the Sea, or the more the Sea advances,
and forces the land against the Mountains.   The Soil, as far as
it is cultivated, that is, to the steepy ascent of the Mountains,
is divided in a manner about into several stages or stories,
through which there are drawn fair and spacious ways, in a
strait-line, as much as the places would permit.   The first of
these lines of communication begins at about a hundred paces
from the Sea-side; another three or four hundred paces higher, and so ascending to the third or fourth, whence a man may
take a very pleasant prospect of all the Plantations from thence
downwards.

Every Stage, which makes a kind of girdle, or enclosure, greater or lesser about the Mountains, according to the greater or lesser distance of it from the Mountains, hath also its ways, which
like so many crossing streets afford an easie access to those
who live higher or lower; and this with such a noble symmetry, that when a man compasses the Island by Sea, he cannot
imagine any thing more delightful, then to see that pleasing
verdure of so many Trees, which are planted along the high-
ways, and are the divisions between the several Plantations.
The prospect is such, that the eye can hardly be wearied with
it: If it be directed upwards, it is terminated by those high
Mountains, which are crown'd with a perpetual verdure, and
cloath'd with precious Woods: If downwards, it is entertain'd by the delightful prospect of Gardens, which taken in
from those places where the Mountains are inaccessible, are
thence by a gentle and easie descent continu'd to the Sea-
side.   The delightful bright-green of the Tobacco, planted
exactly by the line, the pale-yellow of the Sugar-Canes,
when come to maturity, and the dark-green of Ginger and
                                                 Potatoes,

Potatoes, make ſo delightful a Landſkip, as muſt cauſe an extraordinary recreation to the unwearied eye. What very
much adds to this delight, is, that in the midſt of every Plantation, or Garden, there may be ſeen ſeveral fair houſes of different ſtructures, particularly thoſe which are cover'd with red
or glaz'd ſlate, contribute a greater luſtre to that pleaſant per-
ſpective. And in regard there is a perpetual aſcent in the Iſland,
the lower ſtage or ſtory deprives not the ſight of the pleaſure
ariſing from the proſpect of that which lyes at a greater diſtance ; but a man may at one graſp of the eye, as it were in an
inſtant, behold all thoſe delightful diviſions, all thoſe ways
which look like ſo many walks of an Orchard, planted with
ſeveral ſorts of Trees ; all thoſe Gardens regularly beſet with
divers Fruits ; and all thoſe Edifices, which for the moſt part
are not diſtant one from another above a hundred paces. In a
word, ſo many agreeable objects offer themſelves to the eye,
at the ſame intuition, that it is at a kind of loſs on which moſt
to faſten it ſelf.

There is indeed a certain neceſſity, for the greater convenience of the Inhabitants, and eaſier managing of their employments, that their houſes ſhould be diſtinct one from another,
and plac'd in the midſt of that piece of ground which they
have to manure. The French, beſides the houſes they have
thus diſpos'd at certain diſtances, have, in their Quarter of
Baſſe-terre, a Town which grows bigger daily, and whereof
the Houſes are of Brick and Timber. It lyes neer the Haven,
where commonly Ships lye at Anchor. The moſt conſiderable
of the Inhabitants, and Foreign-Merchants have Store-houſes
there.

The French and Dutch Merchants, who reſide there con-
ſtantly, are well furniſh'd with excellent Wines, *Aqua-vitæ*,
and Beer, all ſorts of Stuffes, of Silk, or Wooll, fit for the
Country, and generally all the refreſhments, which being not
of the growth of the Iſland, are yet neceſſary for the better
accommodation of the Inhabitants. All is ſold at a reaſonable
rate, and in exchange for the Commodities growing in the
Country. In the ſame place live ſeveral ſorts of Trades-men,
whoſe employments are neceſſary to Commerce and civil Society. There is alſo a Hall for the adminiſtration of Juſtice,
and a fair Church able to contain a very great Congregation :
The Structure is of wood, rais'd on a foundation of Free-ſtone :
Inſtead of Glaſs-windows there are only turned Pillars, after
the faſhion of a Balcony. It is cover'd with red Slate.

The *Capuchins* for ſome years had the overſight of the ſaid
Church, and the charge of the Souls, as to the French, over
the whole Iſland : but in the year one thouſand ſix hundred
forty and ſix, they were diſengag'd from that employment by
the unanimous conſent of the Inhabitants, who civilly diſmiſs'd
them,

them, and receiv'd in their ftead *Jefuits* and *Carmelites*, who have very fair Houfes and Plantations, which are manured by a great number of Slaves belonging to them, through whofe means they are very handfomly maintained. The R. F. *Henry du Vivier* was the firft Superior of the Jefuitical Miffion.

His Excellency the General hath alfo built a very fair Hofpital, in a very healthy place, where fuch fick perfons as are unable to effect their recovery at their own houfes, are attended, and maintained, and vifited by Phyfitians and Surgeons, till they are reftored to their former health. Strangers alfo who fall fick in the Ifland are receiv'd in there. Order is alfo taken that Orphans be difpos'd into convenient houfes, where they are brought up and inftructed.

There are many noble Structures built both by the the Englifh and French; but the moft magnificent of any is the Caftle of the French General, the particular Defcription whereof we fhall neverthelefs forbear, in regard it makes not much to the Natural Hiftory of the *Caribbies*.

Of the Englifh building the moft confiderable are thofe of the late Mr. *Warner*, firft Governour General of this Nation; Mr. *Rich's*, his fucceffor; Mr. *Everard's*, and Col. *Geffreyfon's*, which may well be ranked among the moft noble, and beft accomplifh'd of any in the *Caribbies*.

The Englifh have alfo built in this Ifland five very fair Churches, well furnifh'd within with Pulpits, and Seats, of excellent Joyners work, of precious wood. Till the late Times, the Minifters were fent thither by the Archbifhop of *Canterbury*, to whofe Diocefs it belongs.

CHAP. V.

Of the Lee-ward Iflands.

ALL the Iflands lying Weft from St. *Chriftophers* are commonly called the Lee-ward Iflands, inafmuch as the conftant wind of the *Caribbies* is an Eaft-wind, with fome point of the North, and that there is feldom any Weft or South-wind. Of thefe there are nine principal ones, whereof we fhall give an account in this Chapter, according to the order they are placed in the Map.

St EVSTACE.

THe Ifland of St. *Euftace* lyes North-Weft from St. *Chriftophers*, at the altitude of feventeen degrees, and forty minutes. It is about five leagues in compafs. To fpeak properly,

perly, it is but a Mountain rising up in the midst of the Ocean, much like a Sugar-loaf, which is thought to be the figure of Mount *Tabor*, and the *Pic* of *Teneriffe*, save that the last named is incomparably higher. The Colony inhabiting it, consist-ing of about sixteen hundred men, acknowledg the Sovereign-ty of the States-General, who have granted the Government of it to Monf. *Van Ree*, and his Associates, Merchants of *Flush-ing* in *Zealand*.

This Island is the strongest, as to situation, of all the *Carib-bies*, for there is but one good descent, which may be easily de-fended; so that a few men might keep off a great Army: But besides this natural Fortification, there is in it a strong Fort which commands the best Haven, the Guns of it carrying a good distance into the Sea.

The Inhabitants have neat houses, and those well furnish'd, as their Country-men have in *Holland*. Only the very top of the Mountain is cover'd with Wood; all the compass is manur'd. It can hardly be credited what quantities of Tobacco it hath heretofore and still doth yield.

Though the top of this Mountain seems to be very picked, yet is there a kind of bottom of a large extent, affording a re-treat to a great number of wild Beasts. The Inhabitants are very industrious in keeping on their Lands all sorts of Poultry, as also Swine and Conies, which breed exceamly.

There are no Springs in this Island; but there are now few Houses but have a good Cistern to supply that defect: There are also Store-houses so well furnish'd with all things requisite to life, and the accommodation of the Inhabitants, that many times they have wherewith to pleasure their Neighbours. The Inhabitants live decently and Christianly, and cannot justly be reproach'd with those crimes which some have impos'd upon them. There is in the Island one Church, which hath from time to time been supply'd with very able Pastors; of whom one was Mr *May*, who, among other Writings, put out a Learned Commentary on the most difficult places of the five Books of *Moses*, wherein there are many curious Observations of Na-ture.

St *BARTHOLOMEW*.

THe Island of S. *Bartholomew* lies North-east from S. *Chri-stophers*, at the 16. degree of Altitude: It hath but lit-tle ground fit for manuring, though it be it be a considerable compass: The Governour-General of the French, *de Poincy*, peopled it at his own Charge about fifteen years since: It af-fords several sorts of excellent Trees, which are much esteem'd; an infinite number of Birds of several kinds; and a kind of Lime-stone, which is fetch'd thence by the Inhabitants of the
E	other

other Iſlands.   There is no ſafe coming in for Ships of great
burthen, by reaſon of the many Rocks which encompaſs it.
Such perſons as are enclin'd to ſolitude cannot diſpoſe themſelves to a fitter place for it than this is.

SABA.

THe Iſland of *Saba* lies North-weſt from S. *Euſtace's*, at the
altitude of 17 degrees and 35 minutes: A man would think
it at a diſtance to be only a Rock; but the Colony of S. *Euſtace*,
which ſent over men to manure It, hath found in it a pleaſant
Valley, able to employ many Families, who live contentedly in
that delightful retirement.   Only Shallops can come neer it.
The Fiſhing about it is very plentiful : Nor is there any want
of other Refreſhments that are neceſſary.

St MARTIN.

THe Iſland of S. *Martin* lies at the Altitude of 18. degrees
and 16 minutes : It is about ſeven Leagues in length,
and four in bredth : There are in it excellent Salt-ponds, which
had oblig'd the *Spaniard* to build a Fort in it, the better to ſecure the poſſeſſion of it; but about nine years ſince he demoliſh'd the Fort and quitted the Iſland: Which being obſerv'd
by Monſieur *de Ruyter*, who commanded one of the Ships which
Monſieur *Lampſen* commonly ſends into *America*, and who then
ſailed by this Iſland, he went to S.*Euſtace's* to raiſe men, whom
he brought thither, and took poſſeſſion of it in the name of the
States-General.

The news of the *Spaniards* departure thence coming at the
ſame time to the *French* General, he preſently diſpatch'd thither
a Ship very well mann'd, to recover the right and pretenſions
of the *French*, who had been poſſeſs'd of the ſaid Iſland before
the uſurpation of the *Spaniard* : Since the *French* and *Dutch*
have divided it, and live very friendly together.   The *French*
have there about 300 men.   The Salt-ponds are in the *Dutch*-
Quarter.   The *Dutch* are more in number than the *French* :
Lampſen and *Van Ree* are the Directors of the Colony.   They
have very fair Houſes, large Store-houſes, and a conſiderable
number of Negroes, who are their perpetual Slaves.

There is no freſh water in this Iſland, but what when it rains
is receiv'd into Ciſterns, which are common enough.   There
are ſeveral little Iſlands about this, very convenient for the di-
vertiſements of the Inhabitants.   There are alſo Ponds of ſalt
water, which run up far into the Land, in which are taken
abundance of good Fiſh, eſpecially Sea-Tortoiſes.   There are
in the Woods Wild-Swine, Quiſts, Turtles, and an infinite
number of Parrots.   There are alſo ſeveral Trees, out of which
                                                        diſtil

diſtill ſeveral ſorts of Gums: but the Tobacco which grows here being eſteem'd beyond that of any of the other Iſlands, the Commerce of it is ſo much the more conſiderable.   The French and Dutch have their diſtinct Churches in their ſeveral Juriſdictions.   Monſieur *des Camps*, the preſent Paſtor of the Dutch Church was ſent thither in *September*, 1655. by the Synod of the *Walloon* Churches of the United Provinces, under whoſe ſpiritual inſpection this Colony is.

SNAKE.

THe Iſland named the *Snake*, is ſo called from its figure; for it is a long tract of earth, but very narrow, winding almoſt about neer S. *Martins* Iſland, whence it is very plainly perceiv'd.   There is not any Mountain in it, the ground lying low and even.   Where it is broadeſt there is a Pond, about which ſome Engliſh families planted themſelves about ſeven or eight years ſince, and where they plant Tobacco, which is highly eſteem'd of thoſe who are good judges in that Commodity.   The Iſland lyes at 18 degrees and 20 minutes on this ſide the Line.

SOMBRERO.

THe Iſland *Sombrero* lyes in the midſt of thoſe Banks which lye about the Channel, through which the Ships bound for *Europe* do paſs.   It lyes at 18 degrees and 30 minutes. The Spaniards called it *Sombrero*, from its having the figure of a Hat.   It is not inhabited.

ANEGADO.

ANegado, which lyes under the ſame degree as *Sombrero*, is alſo deſert, and of dangerous acceſs.

VIRGINS.

THe *Virgins*, greater and leſſer, comprehend ſeveral Iſlands marked in the Map by that name.   There are numbred in all twelve or thirteen of them: They reach Eaſtward from St. *John de Porto-Rico*, at the altitude of 18 degrees, North of the Line.   Between theſe Iſlands there are very good Anchoring places for ſeveral Fleets.   The Spaniards viſit them often, in order to Fiſhing, which is there plentiful   There are alſo in them an infinite number of rare both Land and Seafowl.   They afford ſo little good ground, that after a tryal made thereof in ſeveral places, it was concluded, that they deſerved not Inhabitants.

    Ste CROIX.

S^{te} *C R O I X.*

THe laft of all the *Caribbies* of the Lee-ward Iflands is the
Ifland of *Sante Croix,* or the Holy Crofs.   It lyes at 18
degrees and fome minutes.   The *Caribbians* who were forc'd
thence by the Spaniards, call it *Ayay* : It was much efteem'd
among them, becaufe it was the firft Ifland that Nation poffefs'd
themfelves of when they came from the North to feek a convenient habitation to lay the foundations of their Colonies, as
fhall be reprefented particularly in the Second Book of this
Hiftory.

The Soil of this Ifland returns with good intereft whatever
is fown in it : there are in it fair and fpacious Plains, of a black
earth, and eafie to be manured : there are alfo feveral fair and
precious kinds of Trees good for Dying and Joyners work.
The Air is good, but the Waters not fo wholfom, if drunk immediately after they are drawn : To take away the ill quality
they have, they are put to reft a certain time in earthen veffels,
which makes them good ; and thence it is conceiv'd that the
bad quality proceeds from their mud, as is obferved in thofe of
the *Nile.*

This Ifland is now poffefs'd by the French, who have rais'd
it to a great height after its feveral changes of former Mafters.
The French General fupplies it with Inhabitants at his own
charge.

It may be nine or ten Leagues in length, and neer as much
in breadth, where it is broadeft.   The Mountains are neither
fo high nor fhuffled fo neer together, but that people may get
up to the tops of them, and that there is good ground enough
befides to find work for many thoufands of men.

CHAP. VI.

*Of Trees growing in thefe Iflands, whofe Fruit
may be eaten.*

OF the Trees growing in thefe Iflands fome bear good
Fruits, which contribute to the nourifhment of the
Inhabitants ; others are fit for Building, Joyners work,
or Dying : There are fome alfo very fuccefsfully ufed in Medicine , and fome which only delight the Smelling by their
fweet fcent, and the Sight by their ever verdant Boughs and
Leaves.

Of thofe which bear Fruits fit for Food, and may be feen in
Europe,

Europe, there are only here *Orange-trees*, *Pomegranate-trees*, *Citron-trees*, and *Lemon-trees*, the bulk and goodneſs whereof far exceeds thoſe of the ſame kinds growing elſewhere.

ORANGE.

OF *Oranges* there are two kinds, yet of the ſame figure, and diſtinguiſhable only by the taſte: ſome are ſweet, others ſharp, both extreamly delicate. The ſharp are a great convenience to houſe-keeping, for they are uſed inſtead of Verjuyce and Vinegar; but the ſweet excell in goodneſs: Some indeed call the *China-Orange*, the Queen of *Oranges*, and real Muſk-balls under the colour and figure of *Oranges*: But however ſome may celebrate the delightful ſweetneſs of the *China-Oranges*, there are others prefer the excellent taſte and picquancy of our *American-Oranges*.

POMEGRANATE.

THe *Pomegranate-trees* grow alſo excellently well in all theſe Iſlands, and bear Fruits fair to the Eye and pleaſant to the Taſte. In many places theſe Trees ſerve for Paliſadoes about Courts, borders of Gardens, and the Avenues of Houſes.

CITRONS.

OF *Citrons* there are three kinds, different as to bigneſs, and which conſequently are not all called *Citrons*. The firſt kind, which is the faireſt and largeſt, is called *Lime*: it is only good to be preſerv'd, having very little juyce; but preſerv'd, it is excellent. The ſecond kind is the *Lemon*, about the bigneſs of the *Citron* brought from *Spain*: but its juyce is little, in compariſon of its bulk. The little *Citron*, which makes the third kind, is the beſt and moſt eſteem'd: it hath a very thin ſkin or pellicle, and is full of a very ſharp juyce, which gives an excellent taſte to Meats, and a picquancy to ſeveral Sawces: it is a particular Fruit of *America*. Some curious perſons have in their Gardens a kind of very ſweet *Citrons*, both as to their peel and juyce, which as to bigneſs and taſte come not behind thoſe which grow in *Portugal*.

All other Trees growing in the *Caribbies* have their Leaves, Flowers, Fruit, and Bark, of a Figure, Taſte and Colour different from thoſe of our Countries.

GOYAVIER.

GOYAVIER.

TO begin with the Fruit-Trees; there is some account made of the *Goyavier*, which comes neer the figure of the *Laurel*, save that the Leaves are softer, of a brighter green, and more cottened on the lower-side. The Bark of this Tree is very thin and smooth: It shoots forth at the roots several suckers, which if not taken away, will in time make a thick wood about it, as far as there is any good ground. Its branches, which are thick and well furnish'd with leaves, are loaden twice a year with little white Flowers, which are follow'd by several green Apples, which become yellow, and of a good smell when they are ripe. This Fruit hath on the top a little posie like a Crown, and the meat within is either white or red, full of little kernels, like those of a *Pomegranate*; whence the Dutch call it the sweet *Pomegranate*: It is about the bigness of a *Pearmain*, and ripens in one night.

Being eaten green, it is astringent: whence it is used by many against Bloody-Fluxes: but being ripe it hath a quite contrary effect.

PAPAYER.

THe *Papayer* is a Tree which grows without boughs, about 15 or 20 foot high, big proportionably to its height, hollow and spongious within, whence it is used to convey Springs and Rivulets to diverse places. There are two kinds of it; one commonly found in all the Islands. The leaves of it are divided into three points, much like the leaf of the *Fig-tree:* They are fastened to long tails, as big as a mans thumbs, and hollow within. They shoot out of the top of the Tree, and bending downwards, they cover several round fruits, about the bigness of the great *Quince-pear*, which grow round the boal to which they are fastened.

The other kind is particular to the Island of *Sante Croix*. It is fairer, and hath more leaves then the former: but what causes it to be more esteem'd is its Fruit, which is about the bigness of a *Melon*, and of the figure of a womans breast, whence the *Portughese* call it *Mamao*.

There is this particularly remarkable in these Trees, that they bring forth new fruits every moneth in the year. The flower of both kind is of good scent, and comes neer that of *Jessemine*. The Fruit of the latter is accounted among the choicest entertainments of the Islands, in as much as being come to perfection it hath a firm substance, and may be cut in pieces like a *Melon*, and is of a very pleasant taste. The rind is yellow, intermix'd with certain green lines, and within it is full

of

of little ſeeds, round, viſcous, and ſoft, of a picquant taſte, and approaching that of Spice. This fruit fortifies the ſtomack, and helps digeſtion.

MOMIN.

THe *Momin* is a Tree grows up to the bigneſs of an *Apple-tree*, and bears a large fruit of the ſame name. 'Tis true, the Iſlanders commonly call it *Coraſol*, becauſe the ſeeds of thoſe they have was brought from *Coraſol*, an Iſland poſſeſs'd long ſince by the Dutch, who have there a good Fort, and a numerous Colony, which hath ſpred it ſelf into ſeveral other Iſlands neer it. This Fruit is like a little Cucumber not fully ripe; the rind of it is always green, and enamell'd with ſeveral ſmall partitions like ſcales: if it be gathered in its maturity it is within as white as cream, and of a mixture of ſweetneſs and ſharpneſs, which much heightens the taſte of it. This Fruit is extreamly cooling, and pleaſant to the palate: In the midſt of it lyes the ſeed, which is of the bigneſs and figure of a Bean, very ſmooth, and of the colour of a Touch-ſtone on which a piece of gold had been newly try'd; for it ſeems to ſparkle with little golden veins.

JUNIPA.

JUnipa, or *Jenipa*, being the ſame Tree which the *Braſilians* call *Janipaba*, and the *Portuguez*, *Jenipapo*, grows up to the bigneſs of a *Cheſnut-tree*, the boughes of it bowing down towards the ground, and making a pleaſant ſhade: The leaves of it are long, like thoſe of a *Wallnut-tree*: It bears a kind of flower like thoſe of *Narciſſus*, and they are of a good ſcent. The wood of it is ſolid, and in colour of a pearly grey. The Inhabitants cut down theſe Trees while they are yet young, to make ſtocks for Muskets and Fire-locks, in regard the wood being eaſie to be wrought, may be excellently poliſh'd. Every moneth it is cloath'd with ſome new leaves: It bears a kind of Apples, which being ripe ſeem to have been baked in an Oven, about the bigneſs of an ordinary Apple: Falling from the Tree they make a noiſe like that of a gun diſcharg'd: which proceeds hence, that certain winds or ſpirits pent up in the thin pellicles which encloſe the ſeed, being ſtirr'd by the fall, force their way out with a certain violence. Whence it may be concluded, that it is the ſame Fruit which the Indians in *New-Spain*, by a barbarous name call *Quant la Lazin*.

Theſe *Junipa-apples* eaten without taking away the little skin within them, are extreamly binding. This Fruit is much ſought after by Hunts-men, in regard that being ſouriſh it quenches thirſt, and comforts ſuch as are wearied by travelling.
The

The juice of it dyes a very dark Violet, though it self be as
clear as rock-water:nay when it is applied twice to the same part
of the body which a man would dye, it makes the place appear
black.   The Indians use it to fortifie the body, and to make it
more supple before they go to the wars.   They are also of a
perswasion that this colour renders them more terrible to their
enemies.   The tincture this Fruit gives cannot be taken away
with Soap; but after nine or ten days it disappears of it self.
The Swine which eat of this fruit when it falls off the Tree,
have the flesh and fat of a violet colour, as hath been found by
experience.   The same thing hath been observ'd in the flesh of
Parrots, and other Birds, when they have eaten of it.   There
may be made of these Apples a drink pleasant enough, yet such
as is only us'd among the Indians and Hunts-men, who have no
setled habitation.

R A I S I N.

THe *Raisin-tree*, or *Vine*, which the *Caribbians* call *Ouliem*,
      grows up to a midling height, and creeps in a manner
along the ground on the Sea-side : but in good ground, it
grows up high, as one of the most delightful Trees of the Fo-
rest.   The leaves of it are round, and thick, intermixt with
red and green.   Under the bark of the trunk, having rais'd a
white soft substance about two inches thick, a man finds a
wood of a violet colour, solid, and fit for excellent pieces of
Joyners work. It bears in its branches such fruits, as when they
are ripe might be taken for great violet Grapes; but instead of
kernels, every Grape hath under a tender pellicle, and under a
very small substance, which is a little sowrish, cooling, and of a
good taste, a hard stone like that of a Plumb.

A C A J O V.

THere are three kinds of Trees known by the name of
      Acajou; but of those, only that we shall here describe
bears any fruit : 'Tis a Tree of no great height, spreading its
branches down towards the ground : The leaves of it are fair
and large, closing to a roundness before, and divided by certain
veins.   The flowers of it at the first shooting forth are white,
but afterwards they become incarnate, and of a purple colour :
They grow in tuffes and bushes, and they send forth so sweet a
scent, that it is easie to distinguish the Tree which bears them :
These flowers fall not till they are thrust off by a kind of *Chestnut*, much after the form of an Ear, or a Hares kidney.   When
this *Chestnut* is come to its growth, there is fram'd under it a
very fair Apple, somewhat long, which is crown'd with that
as a crest, which as it ripens becomes of an Olive-colour, while
                                                        the

the Apple puts on a thin delicate skin of a lively Vermilion. Within it is full of certain ſpungious filaments, which yield a kind of ſweet and ſharp juice extreamly good to quench thirſt, and accounted very good for the ſtomach, as alſo in ſwoonings and fainting, being qualifi'd with a little Sugar: But if it chance to fall on any Linen, it makes a red ſtain therein, which continues till ſuch time as the Tree brings forth new flowers.

The Indians make an excellent drink of this fruit, which being kept ſome days inebriates as ſoon as the beſt French-wine would. The Nut which is above, burnt, yields a cau-ſtick oyl, which is ſucceſsfully uſed to mollifie, nay to take away Corns, and the callouſneſs of the feet. If it be crack'd there is within a kernel, cover'd with a thin pellicle, which being taken away it is of an excellent taſte, and its vertue is to warm and extreamly to fortifie the Stomach.

This Tree bears but once a year; whence the Braſilians number their age by the Nuts growing on this Apple, laying up one for every year, which they keep very carefully in a little basket for that purpoſe. If an inciſion be made at the foot of this Tree there will come forth a clear and tranſparent Gum, which many have taken for that which is brought out of *Arabia.* The ſeed of the Tree is in the Nut, which put into the ground grows without any trouble.

I C A C O.

THe *Icaco* is a kind of ſmall Plumb-tree which grows after the form of a Briar; the branches of it are at all times loaden with ſmall long leaves: Twice a year they are dreſs'd with abundance of pretty white or violet flowers, which are fol-low'd by a little round fruit, about the bigneſs of a Damſin, and that being ripe, grows either white or violet, as the flower had been before: This fruit is very ſweet, and ſo lov'd by ſome Savages living neer the Gulf of *Hondures,* that they are called *Icacos* from their much feeding on theſe Plumbs. Thoſe who have travell'd among them have obſerved, that when theſe fruits are ripe they carefully ſecure the propriety thereof to themſelves, and to prevent their Neighbours, who have none in their Quarters, from ſpoiling the Trees, have Guards ſet on the Avenues of their Country, who with Club and Dart op-poſe ſuch as ſhould attempt their diſturbance.

MONBAIN.

THe *Monbain* is a Tree grows very high, and bears long and yellowiſh Plumbs, which are of a ſcent good enough: But the ſtone being bigger then all the meat about it, they are not much eſteem'd, unleſs it be of ſome who mix them in the drinks of *Ouicou* and *Maby,* to give them a better taſte. The

Swine feeding in the Woods are always fat when thefe fruits are ripe; for there falls abundance of them under the Trees as they ripen, which are greedily devoured by thofe creatures. This Tree yields a yellow Gum, which cafts a ftronger fcent then the fruit. The branches thruft into the ground eafily take root; whence it comes that they commonly fet thofe Clofes with them where they keep Cattle.

The *Courbary* for the moft part grows higher, more leavie and bigger then the *Monbain*. It bears a fruit the fhell whereof can hardly be broken, and it is about four fingers long, two broad, and one thick: Within the fhell there is two or three ftones cover'd with a foft meat, as yellow as *Saffron*. It is of a good tafte; but if much of it be taken it extreamly clogs the ftomack, and hinders refpiration. The Savages in cafe of neceffity make a drink of it, which well ordered is not unpleafant, that is, when it is well boild with water. The wood of this Tree is folid, of a colour inclining to red. The Tree being old yields a Gum which is hardened by the Sun, and will continue clear, tranfparent as yellow *Amber*, and of a good fcent. Some Indians make Buttons of it, of feveral fafhions, of which they make Bracelets, Neck-laces, and Pendants, which are handfom, glittering, and of a good fcent.

INDIAN FIG-TREE.

THere is in moft of thefe Iflands a great Tree, which the Europeans have called the *Indian Fig-tree*, becaufe it bears a fmall fruit without any ftone, which in figure and tafte comes neer the French Fig: Otherwife it hath no refemblance to our Fig-trees; for befides that the leaf is of a different figure, and much narrower, it grows in fome places to fuch an exceffive bulk, that there are of them fuch as many men put together cannot encompafs, in regard the Trunk, which commonly is not even in its circumference, fhoots forth on the fides from the very root to the place where the boughs begin, certain excrefcencies which reach four or five foot about, and which by that means make deep cavities, ftanding like fo many Neeches. Thefe Excrefcencies which are of the fame fubftance with the body of the Tree, are alfo enclos'd with the fame bark as covers it, and they are feven or eight inches thick, proportionably to the Trunk they encompafs. The wood of this Tree within is white and foft, and there are commonly cut out of thofe long pieces which fhoot forth out of the Trunk, Planks for Flooring, Doors and Tables, without any fear that the Tree fhould dye: For, in a fhort time it fo eafily recovers the prejudice it had receiv'd, that it can hardly be perceiv'd there was any thing taken from it. All thofe who have liv'd in the Ifland of *Tortoifes*, which lyes North from

Hifpaniola,

Hispaniola, have seen in the way which leads from the Plains
of the Mountain to the Village, which the French call *Mil-
plantage* , one of these Trees which may well afford shelter
to two hundred men under the shade of its branches, which
are always loaden with leaves very thick and bushy.

SERVICE-TREE.

THere is in these Islands a kind of *Service-tree* much different from that in *France* ; for it is of an excessive height,
pleasant to the eye, and adorn'd with fair leaves and branches.
It bears a pleasant fruit, round as a *Cherry*, of a yellowish colour, spotted with little round spots ; when it is ripe it falls off
of it self : It tastes like a *Sorb-apple*, and thence it came to be
so cal ed : It is much sought after by the Birds.

The PRICKLY-PALM.

ALL these Islands have *Palms*, nay some have four several
sorts of them.   One is called the *Prickly* or *Thorny-Palm*,
having that name from the prickliness of it, the boal, branches,
and leaves being furnished with prickles very sharp, and so
dangerous, that whoever is prick'd thereby will be troubled a
long time, if a present remedy be not applyed : Those which encompass the trunk are flat, about the length of a mans finger,
of the figure of a Tooth-pick, smooth, and of a tawny colour
inclining to black.   The Negroes before they come neer it
make a fire about the foot of the Tree to burn up the prickles,
which are as so much armour to it.   Its fruit consists in a great
tuft, which contains several greyish, hard and round Nuts, within which are kernels good to eat.   Of this kind of *Palms* some
Negroes get a sort of Wine by making incisions in the branches.
It is probably the same Tree which the *Brasilians* call *Ayri*.

FRANC-PALM.

THe second kind is the *Franc-Palm* : It is a strait Tree of
extraordinary height.   The roots of this Tree are above
ground, round about the stock two or three foot high, and
about the bigness of a Hogshead : These roots are small proportionably to the height of the Tree they sustain ; but they
are so confusedly shufled one within another, that they afford
it a substantial support.   One thing particular to this Tree is,
that it is bigger above then below : While it is young the bark
is tender, of a dark-grey colour, and mark'd at every foots
distance with a circle, which discovers very neer how many
years it hath been in the ground : But when it is come to its
full growth, it is all over so solid and smooth, that there is
F 2   nothing

nothing to be seen. The top of it is adorned with several fair branches chanell'd, and smooth, which have on each side an infinite number of leaves, green, long, narrow and very thin, which add much to its beauty. The tenderest of these branches, which are not yet fully blown, start up directly from the middle of the Tree, while the others which bend downwards all about make it as 'twere a rich and beautiful crown.

This Tree disburthens it self every month of some one of its branches, as also of a bark which is loosned from below, which is four or five foot long, about two broad, and of the thickness of tann'd leather. The Inhabitants of the Islands call this bark *Tache*, and they use it for the covering of their Kitchins, and other places belonging to their habitations, as they make use of the leaves neatly ty'd together in little sheaves to cover their houses.

We have purposely ranked the *Palms* among the Fruit-trees of these Islands, in regard all of them, the *Latanier* only excepted, contribute somewhat to the nourishment of men. For if the *Prickly-Palm* before described, afford Wine, this bears on the top of its trunk, and as it were in its heart, a whitish marrow or pith, very tender and savory, tasting like a small Nut, if eaten raw, and being boiled, and seasoned with the thin and white leaves which encompass it, and are as it were so much linen about it, it may be numbred among the most delicious dishes of the *Caribbies*. The French call that marrowy substance, and the leaves enclosing it, *Chou de Palmiste*, Palm-Cabbage, for they put it into the Pot instead of Cabbage, and other Herbs.

Cleave the trunk of this Tree in two, and take away, as may easily be done, a certain filiamental and soft matter, which lyes within, the remaining wood, which is by that means made hollow, and a good inch thick, makes excellent long gutters, which will last a great while. They are used also to cover with one piece only the roof of the *Cazes*, and to convey water to any place. Turners and Joyners make of this wood, which is almost black and easily polish'd, several excellent pieces which are naturally marbled.

Pliny writes of Trees so prodigiously high, that an arrow could not be shot over them: and the Author of the *General History of the Indies* speaks of a Tree so high that a man could not cast a stone over it. But though the *Palm* we now describe much exceeds all the other Trees of the *Caribbies*, yet dare we not affirm it to be of such an extraordinary height, since that from the foot of the Tree there may be easily observ'd a fair branch, which rising out of the top of the trunk, is always turn'd towards the Sun-rising. It is renew'd every year, and when it is come out of its case, it is enamell'd with an infinite number of little yellow flowers, like golden buttons,

tons,

tons, which afterwards falling, their places are ſupply'd by certain round fruits, about the bigneſs of a ſmall Hens egge. They are faſten'd together as it were in one cluſter, and that theſe flowers and fruits might be ſecured againſt the injuries of the weather, they are cover'd above by a thick bark, which on the outſide is hard and of a greyiſh colour, but within of a kind of Vermilion-guilt, cloſing upwards like a Pyramid. This precious fan is nothing elſe but the caſe which kept in the flowers before they were fully blown, and being opened below ſpreads it ſelf into a hollow figure in the midſt, and pointed at the extremities, the better to cover both the flowers and the fruit.

LATANIER.

THe third kind of *Palm* is called the *Latanier* : This grows up to a conſiderable height, but not very big. In ſtead of branches, it hath only long leaves, round above, and ſpread at the extremity like a fan. They are faſtened to certain great ſtalks which come out of certain filaments, that encompaſs the top of the trunk, like a thick piece of Canvaſs, red and very clear. Theſe leaves ty'd up in little bundles, ſerve to cover the *Cazes*, and of the rind which is raiſed from above the tails or ſtalks, may be made Sives, Baſkets, and ſeveral other little curioſities, which the Indians account the beſt of their Houſhold-ſtuff. Of the wood of this Tree, as alſo of that of the *Franc-Palm*, they make Bows, the Clubs they uſe in fighting, in ſtead of Swords, *Azagayes*, a kind of little ſharp Launces, which they dart at their enemies with the hand, and they ſharpen therewith the points of their Arrows, which by that means are as piercing as if they were of Steel.

COCOS.

THe fourth kind of *Palm*, and the moſt excellent of all is that which is called *Cocos*, that famous fruit of which Hiſtorians tell ſuch miracles. But it is to be obſerv'd that the *Cocos* of the *Weſt-Indies* grow not neer to the height of thoſe in the *Eaſt-Indies*, the trunk commonly not exceeding twenty or twenty five foot in height, of a bigneſs proportionable thereto. It is better furniſh'd with branches and leaves then the *Franc-Palm*. The Iſlands of *Monaca* and *Routan*, at the Gulf of *Hondures*, are famous for their abounding with theſe Trees. The Iſland of S. *Bartholomew* of the *Caribbies* have alſo of them, and thence they were brought to S. *Chriſtophers*.

The fruit grows upon the very trunk, at the ſhooting forth of the branches. It hath the form of a Nut, but is without compariſon much bigger ; for one of them ſometimes weighs
about

about ten pound. From the firſt bearing the Tree is never found without fruit, for it bears new every moneth. The ſhell is ſo hard and thick that it may be poliſh'd, and figures engrav'd upon it, and made into Cups, Bottles, and other Veſſels. It is encompaſs'd with a thick covering which is all of filaments.

When the *Coco-nut* is opened, there is firſt met with a meat, white as ſnow, which is extreamly nouriſhing, and taſtes like an *Almond*: There is ſo much of this marrowy ſubſtance in every fruit as may well fill an ordinary diſh. It is very firmly faſtened within the ſhell, and in the midſt of it there is a large glaſs full of liquor, clear and pleaſant as perfum'd Wine: ſo that a man may be well ſatisfi'd with one of theſe fruits at a meal. It is only this water which is turned into ſeed, and among other vertues hath that of clearing the face of all wrinkles, and giving it a bright and Vermilion colour, ſo it be waſhed therewith as ſoon as the fruit is fallen from the Tree.

Who deſires a particular account of the *Cocos* and its uſes, as well in Phyſick as Houſe-keeping, may read the large deſcription of it made by *Francis Pyrard*, in his Treatiſe of the Animals, Trees, and Fruits of the *Eaſt-Indies*.

Some from the neerneſs of the names do ſometimes confound the *Cocos* with the *Cacao*, which grows in the Province of *Guatimala*, neer *New-Spain*, which is alſo a famous fruit all over *America*, for its being the principal ingredient in the compoſition called *Chocolate*. This drink taken moderately cauſeth Venery, Procreation and Conception, and facilitates Delivery, preſerves Health, and impinguates: It helpeth Digeſtion, Conſumption and Cough of the Lungs, Plague of the Guts, and other Fluxes, the Green-Sickneſs, Jaundiſe, and all manner of Imflammations and Oppilations: It cleanſeth the Teeth, and ſweetneth Breath, provokes Urine, cures Stone and Strangury, expells Poyſon, and preſerves from all infectious Diſeaſes; all which vertues are attributed to it by ſeveral creditable Authors.

The *Cacao* which was to be ſeen in the *Caribbies*, in the year one thouſand ſix hundred forty nine, in a Garden of an Inhabitant of the Iſland of *Sante Croix*, which was then in the hands of the *Engliſh*, is a Tree much like an *Orange-tree*, ſave that it grows not up ſo high, and that it hath larger leaves. It is commonly planted in ſhady places, even under other Trees, that they may keep off the heat of the Sun from it, which might otherwiſe occaſion the withering of its leaves. Its fruit is about the bigneſs and neer the figure of an *Acorn*, or a middle ſiz'd *Olive*, and grows in great long cods, or huſks, which are ſtreaked in ſeveral places with little partitions along the ſides.

CHAP.

CHAP. VII.

Of Trees fit for Building, Joyners-Work, and Dying.

WE have hitherto given an account of thoſe Trees, whoſe Fruits contribute to the ſubſiſtance, and refreſhment of the Inhabitants : we ſhall now treat of the moſt conſiderable in order to the Building of Houſes, and Furniſhing of them by the help of the Joyner. Which done, we ſhall ſpeak of all thoſe other Trees of ſeveral colours, whereof the Dyer may make uſe in his Profeſſion.

A C A J O V.

THere are few of the Iſlands but afford good Trees for the Carpenters and Joyners-Work. Of theſe one of the moſt conſiderable is the *Acajou*, which grows to that exceſſive height, that the *Caribbians* will of one trunk make thoſe long Shallops called *Pyrages*, which are able to carry fifty men. It ſhoots forth many branches which grow very cloſe together, by reaſon of the abundance of leaves they are loaden with. The ſhade of this Tree is very delightful ; nay ſome affirm that it contributes to their Health who repoſe themſelves under it.

There are two ſorts of *Acajou*, which differ only in the height of the trunk, and colour of the wood. The wood of the moſt eſteem'd is red, light, of a good ſcent, and eaſily wrought. It hath been found by experience that it receives no prejudice from the Worm ; that it rots not in the water when it hath been cut in ſeaſon ; and that the Cheſts and Cabinets made of it communicate a good ſcent too, and ſecure the Cloaths kept in them from Vermine, which either breed in, or get into thoſe made of other wood. Hence ſome have imagin'd it to be a kind of *Cedar :* There are alſo made of it Shingles for the covering of Houſes. Some Maſters of Ships who Trade to the *Caribbies* many times bring thence Planks of this wood, which are of ſuch length and breadth that there needs but one to make a fair and large Table.

The other kind of *Acajou* is of the ſame figure, as to the outſide, as that before deſcribed ; but it grows not up ſo high, and the bark and pith taken away, the wood is white : Newly fell'd it is very eaſily wrought ; but left abroad in the air, it grows ſo hard that there can hardly be any uſe made of it. The Inhabitants uſe it only for want of other, becauſe it is ſubject to worms, and putrifies in a ſhort time. If an inciſion be

made

made in the trunks of thefe Trees, they will yield abundance of Gum, whereof there might be a good ufe made, if any tryal had been made of it.

ACOMAS.

THe *Acomas* is a Tree grows up to the height and bulk of the *Acajou*, and is no lefs efteem'd by Carpenters and Joyners. Its leaves are fmooth and long enough: It bears a fruit of the bignefs of a Plumb, which come to maturity, is of a yellow colour, pleafant to the eye, but too bitter to be mans-meat. The Wood-Quifts grow fat on it at a certain time of the year, and during that time, their flefh is of the fame tafte as the fruit they have eaten. The bark is of an Afh-colour, and very rough, the wood heavy and eafily polifh'd, and according to the places where it grows, the heart of it is red, or yellowifh, or inclining to violet. If the bark be opened, there will come forth a milky liquor, which grows hard like Gum.

ROSE-WOOD.

THe wood called *Rofe-wood* is fit not only for the Carpenter, but alfo for the Joyner; and therefore is numbred among the moft confiderable. And here we cannot but acknowledg, that if the ancient Inhabitants of the *Caribbies* had any defign to make a firm fetlement of themfelves there, they might find not only things requifite for their fubfiftance, but alfo delicacies and curiofities, as well in order to their nourifhment and cloathing, as to the building of their Houfes, and the furnifhing of them when they are built. But the flattering imaginations of a return into the place of their birth, whereof moft have their hearts full, induce them to a neglect of all thofe confiderable advantages which thefe Iflands prefent them withall, and an indifferency, if not a contempt, for that abundance of precious things which they fo liberally produce. For not to fay any thing at prefent how eafily they might makes Stuffes of the Cotton growing here; how they might keep all forts of Fowl, and tame Cattel, which breed there as abundantly as in any place in the World, they might, no doubt, enrich themfelves very much by feveral forts of precious wood, through the Trade they might drive into feveral parts of *Europe*, fince they think not fit to make ufe of them in order to the better accommodation of their habitations. The defcription we fhall make of fome of thefe rare Trees in this and the next Chapter will make good this Propofition.

Of thefe, as we faid before, the *Rofe-wood* is to be ranked among the chiefeft. This Tree grows to a height proportionable

onable to its bignefs.   The trunk of it is commonly fo ftrait,
that it is one of the greateft ornaments of the *Caribbian* Forefts.
It is cover'd with many fair boughs, and thofe loaden with foft
leaves, downy on one fide, and neer as long as thofe of a Wallnut-tree.   During the feafon of the Rains it bears white flowers, of a good fcent, which growing in bufhes, or as it were
Pofies, add very much to the natural beauty of the Tree.
Thefe flowers are follow'd by a fmall blackifh and fmooth feed.
The bark of the boal is of a whitifh-grey : The wood within is
of the colour of a dead leaf, and when the Smoothing-plane
and Polifher hath pafs'd upon it, there may be feen feveral
veins of different colours, waving up and down, which gives
it a luftre, as if it were marbled · But the fweet fcent it cafts
forth while it is handled and wrought caufes it to be the more
efteem'd, and procur'd it the name it is now known by.   Some
have imagin'd, that that fweet fcent, which indeed is more pleafant then that of a Rofe, fhould have given it the name of *Cy-
prian-wood*, and indeed in fome parts of the *Caribbies* it paffes
under that denomination.   This Tree grows in all the Iflands
after the fame fafhion, as to the external figure ; but the wood
of it is marbled with divers colours, according to the difference
of the foil where it had its production and growth.

INDIAN-WOOD.

THE *Indian-wood* is alfo a precious Tree, and of good
fcent : Of this there is fuch abundance in the Ifland of
S. Croix, and feveral others, that there are in them whole Forefts of it.   It is not inferior to the *Rofe-wood*, but grows bigger and higher when it meets with good ground.   The roots of
it fpread themfelves very deep into the ground, and the trunk
is very ftrait : The bark is fmooth, thin, and even all over, of
a bright filver-grey colour, and in fome places inclining to yellow, which is a diftinction between this Tree and all others : It
flourifhes once a year, in the feafon of the Rains, and then it
renews fome part of its leaves.   The wood of it is very folid
and weighty, whence it comes that it may be polifh'd, and
fome Savages make their Clubs of it.   Having taken off a Ver-
milion-pith which is under the bark, there appears the heart of
the tree, which is extream hard, and of a Violet colour, for
which it is much efteemed by the curious.

The good fcent of this tree confifts particularly in its leaves :
they are of the fame figure with thofe of the *Guava-tree*, and when
they are handled, they perfume the hands with a fweeter fcent
then that of the *Laurel :* they derive to Meat and Sauces fo delicate a *gufto*, as might be attributed rather to a compofition of
feveral Spices, then to a fimple leaf : It is ufed alfo in the Baths
prefcrib'd by Phyficians to fortifie bruifed Nerves, and dry up
G   the

the fwelling which remains in their Legs who have been in malignant Fevers.

Befides the *Acajou*, before fpoken of, there are in thefe
Iflands feveral forts of trees whereof the wood is red, folid,
weighty, and not fubject to worms and putrefaction. They
are excellent for both Carpenter and Joyner.

IRON-WOOD.

BUt above all there is a particular account made of the *Iron-
wood*, fo called, becaufe in folidity, weight, and hard-
nefs, it exceeds all thofe we have yet defcribed. This tree,
which may be ranked among the higheft and beft proportioned
of any in thefe Iflands, is well furnifh'd with branches, and
thofe with little leaves with fharp points, and divided neer the
ftalk. It flourifhes twice a year, to wit, in *March* and *September*. The flowers of it, which are of a Violet colour, are fucceeded by a fmall fruit about the bignefs of a Cherry, which
as it ripens grows black, and is much fought after by the Birds.
The bark of the trunk is of a brownifh colour : The wood is
of a very bright red being newly fell'd, but lying abroad in the
air it lofes much of its livelinefs and luftre. The heart of the
Tree is of a very dark red, like that of *Brafil*, and of fuch hard-
nefs that the wedges muft be very fharp and well try'd before,
to bring it to the ground. But the wood of it being fair to the
eye, folid, eafie to be polifh'd, and more incorruptible then either *Cedar* or *Cyprefs*, it abundantly requites by all thefe excellent qualities the pains is taken about it before there can be
any ufe made thereof.

There is alfo another Tree known by the fame name, but it
is not comparable to the former : It bears only fmall leaves,
and when it flourifheth, it is loaden with abundance of Pofies,
as it were, rifing up above the branches like fo many Plumes of
Feathers, which give it an extraordinary ornament. It is of a
great height, and the inner-bark is yellowifh or white, according to the places where it grows. All the wood of this Tree,
the heart only excepted, which is very fmall, very hard, and
inclining to black, is fubject to worms; whence it comes that
it is not commonly ufed, but for want of other.

There are in the *Caribbies* many Trees fit for Dying : The
moft efteemed and beft known are the *Brafil-wood*, the *Yellow-
wood*, the *Green-Ebony*, and the *Roucou*.

BRASIL-WOOD.

THe *Brafil-wood* is fo called, becaufe the firft brought into
Europe came from the Province of *Brafil*, where it grows
more abundantly then in any other part of *America*. Of this
                                                                    kind

kind of Tree there are not many in the *Caribbies*, and what there is, is only in thoſe Iſlands which are moſt furniſhed with dry rocks.   The trunk of it is not ſtrait as that of other Trees, but crooked, uneven, and full of knots like the *White-Thorn*. When it is loaden with flowers there comes from it a ſweet ſcent, which fortifies the Brain.   The wood of it is much ſought after by Turners; but the principal uſe of it is for Dying.

YELLOW-WOOD.

THe Iſland of *S. Croix* is the moſt famous of all the Iſlands for its abundance in rare and precious Trees.   There is one very much eſteem'd for its uſefulneſs in Dying : It grows up to a great height, and the wood is perfectly yellow.   When the Engliſh had the Iſland they ſent much of it to their own Country.   It is called the *Yellow-wood*, from its colour.

GREEN-EBONY.

THe *Green-Ebony* is commonly uſed in ſome excellent pieces of Joyners-work, becauſe it eaſily takes the colour and luſtre of the true *Ebony*.   But the beſt uſe of it is for Dying, for it colours a fair Graſs-green.   The Tree is very buſhy by reaſon its root ſhoots forth a great number of Suckers, which hinder it from growing ſo high and big as it might, if the ſap were directed only to the trunk.   The leaves are ſmooth, and of a bright-green colour.   Within the outer-bark there is about two inches of white inner-bark, and the reſt of the wood to the heart is of ſo dark a green that it inclines to black : but when it is poliſh'd, there appear certain yellow veins which make it look as if it were marbled.

ROUCOU.

THe *Roucou* is the ſame Tree which the *Braſilians* call *Uru-cu*.   It grows no higher then a ſmall *Orange-tree* : Its leaves, which are pointed at one end, have the figure of a heart : It bears flowers in colour white, mixt with Carnation; they conſiſt of five leaves, in form like a Star, and about the big-neſs of a Roſe : They grow in little buſhes at the extremities of the branches.   Theſe flowers are ſucceeded by little huskes, in which are encloſed ſeveral ſeeds about the bigneſs of a ſmall Pea, which being come to ripeneſs are of the moſt bright and lively Vermilion colour that can be imagined.   This rich Dy-ing-Commodity which is enclos'd in the ſaid husk is ſo ſoft and viſcous that it ſticks to ones fingers as ſoon as it is touch'd.

   To get this precious liquor they ſhake in an earthen veſſel

the ſeeds unto which it is faſtened ; then there is poured thereto warm water, in which they are waſh'd till ſuch time as they have loſt their Vermilion colour ; and then when this water hath reſted a while, they dry in the ſhade the dregs or thick Lye which is at the bottom of the veſſel, and then it is made up into Lozenges or little Balls, which are very much eſteem'd by Painters and Dyers when they are pure and without mixture, as thoſe are whereof we have now given the deſcription.

The wood of this Tree is eaſily broken: It is very good for firing, and if the fire ſhould be quite out, it is only rubbing for a certain time two pieces one againſt another, and they will caſt forth ſparks like a Fire-lock, which will ſet fire on the Cotton, or any other matter ſuſceptible thereof, that is laid neer to receive it. Of the Bark of it are made Lines which laſt a long time. The Root of it gives a delicate *guſto* to Meats, and when there is any of it put into Sauces, it communicates to them the colour and ſcent of *Saffron*.

The *Caribbians* have of theſe Trees in all their Gardens, are very careful in the ordering and keeping of them, and eſteem them very highly, becauſe from them they have the bright Vermilion with which they make their Bodies red : they uſe it alſo in Painting, and to give a luſtre and handſomneſs to thoſe veſſels which they make uſe of in their houſes.

There might well be numbred among the Trees fit for Dying moſt of thoſe which yield any Gums : For thoſe who have had the curioſity to make a tryal thereof, have found by experience, that being mixt in Dying they heighten the darkeſt and dulleſt colours, by a certain livelineſs and luſtre which they communicate thereto.

CHAP. VIII.

Of Trees uſeful in Medicine, and ſome others, whereof the Inhabitants of the Caribbies *may make great advantages.*

THe great diſpoſer of all things, having aſſign'd all Nations the limits of their ſeveral habitations, hath left no Country deſtitute of means requiſite for the convenient ſubſiſtance of the men placed therein ; and that they might be eye-witneſſes of the in-exhauſtible treaſure of his ever to be adored Providence, he hath impregnated the Earth with the vertue of producing not only the Proviſions neceſſary for their nouriſhment, but alſo ſeveral Antidotes to ſecure them againſt

the

the infirmities whereby they might be aſſaulted, and divers
ſovereign Remedies for their recovery when they are fallen into them.   Not to make mention of any other part of the
World, we may affirm it of the *Caribbies*, that they have all
theſe rare advantages in a very great meaſure : For they do not
only entertain their Inhabitants with a delightful variety of
Fruits, Roots, Herbs, Pulſe, Wild-Fowl, Fiſh, and other
delicacies for the Table, but they alſo ſupply them with a
great number of excellent Remedies to cure them of their indiſpoſitions.   And this the judicious Reader may eaſily obſerve all through this Natural Hiſtory, and particularly in this
Chapter, where we ſhall deſcribe the Trees which are very uſeful in Medicine.

CASSIA-TREE.

THE *Caſſia-tree* grows up to the bigneſs, and comes neer the
figure of a *Peach-tree*, the leaves of it being ſomewhat
long and narrow : They fall off once a year, in the time of the
great Droughts, and when the ſeaſon of the Rain comes in, it
puts forth new ones: They are preceded by ſeveral Poſies of
of yellow flowers, which are ſucceeded by long Pipes or Cods
about the bigneſs of a mans thumb, and ſometimes a foot and
a half, or two foot in length: They contain within them, as in
ſo many little Cells, that Medicinal Drug ſo well known to the
Apothecaries, called *Caſſia*, which the *Caribbians* call *Mali Mali*.   Before the fruit is grown to its full bigneſs and length it is
always green, but as it advances to perfection and ripeneſs it
becomes of a browniſh or Violet colour, and ſo continues, hanging at the branches.

When the Fruit is ripe and dry, and the Trees which bear it
are ſhaken by great winds, the noiſe cauſed by the colliſion of
thoſe hard and long Cods ſtriking one againſt another is heard
at a great diſtance : This frightens the Birds, and keeps them
from coming neer it; nay ſuch men as are ignorant of the cauſe
of that confuſed ſound, if they ſee not the Trees ſhaking, and
ſtirring their branches and fruits, imagine themſelves neer the
Sea-ſide, and think they hear the agitation of it, or take it for
the claſhing of Arms in an Engagement of Souldiers.   'Tis the
obſervation of all thoſe who have viſited that part of St. *Domingo* where there are whole Plains, and thoſe of a large extent, full only of theſe Trees.   It is thence, in all probability,
that the ſeed of thoſe growing in the *Caribbies* was brought.
Thoſe ſticks of *Caſſia* which are brought from *America* are fuller
and more weighty then thoſe which come out of the *Levant*,
and the Drug within them hath the ſame effects and vertues.

The Flowers of the *Caſſia-tree* preſerv'd with Sugar gently
purge not only the Belly, but alſo the Bladder.   The ſticks of
Caſſia

Caſſia conferv'd while they are green have alſo the ſame vertue. But the pulp taken out of the ripe fruit operates ſooner and more effectually. Many of the Inhabitants uſe it with good ſucceſs once a moneth, a little before meals; and they have found by experience that this gentle Medicine contributes much to the continuance of their good conſtitution.

MEDICINAL NUTS.

THe *Medicinal Nuts*, which are ſo common in all the Iſlands, grow on a ſmall Tree, which is for the moſt part uſed to partitions between the Gardens and Plantations. If it were not hindred from growing, it would come up to the height of an ordinary Fig-tree, which it ſomwhat reſembles in figure. The wood of it is very tender and pithy, and it ſhoots forth ſeveral bracnhes which ſcamble confuſedly about the trunk: They are loaden with pretty long leaves, green and ſoft, round below, and ending in three points.

Out of the wood and leaves of this Tree there comes a milky juice, which ſtains Linen: nay there is no pleaſure in being neer it when it rains, for the drops which fall from the leaves have the ſame effect as the juice: It bears ſeveral yellow flowers conſiſting of five leaves, which when they are fully blown look like ſo many ſtars. The flowers falling, there come in the places of ſome of them little Nuts, which at firſt are green, then turn yellow, and at laſt black, and a little open, when they are ripe. Within every Nut there are three or four ſtones, in ſo many little cells, the rind whereof is blackiſh, in bigneſs and figure ſomwhat like a bean. The rind being taken away, there is in every one of them a white kernel of an oily ſubſtance, which is incloſed and divided in the midſt by a thin film or pellicle: Theſe kernels are of a taſte pleaſant enough, not much different from that of Small-Nuts: but if they be not moderately eaten they will violently purge both upwards and downwards, eſpecially if the ſkin which encloſes them, and the pellicle dividing them in the midſt be ſwallow'd: To moderate their quality, and that they may be taken with leſs danger, the way is to cleanſe them of thoſe ſkins and pellicles, and put them for a little while upon the coals; then being beaten, or bruis'd, four or five of them may be taken in a little Wine, as a vehicle or corrective.

The boughs of this Tree being cut off and thruſt into the ground do eaſily take root. The *Portuguez* extract an oyl out of the kernels, which is good enough for the uſes of the Kitchin, and may alſo be uſeful in Medicine.

CINAMON.

CINAMON.

THe Tree which bears that kind of *Cinamon* which is so common in all the Islands, may be ranked among those which are useful in Medicine, since its Aromatick Bark is sought after by all those who are troubled with cold distempers, and successfully used to disburthen the chest of the viscous and phlegmatick humors which oppress it. The sweet scent and perpetual verdure of this delightful Tree have perswaded some that it was a kind of Laurel: but it grows much higher, its trunk is also bigger, its branches larger, and its leaves, which are not altogether so long, are much softer, and of a more lively green. The bark of it, which is cover'd by an Ash-colour'd skin, is thicker, and of a whiter colour then the *Cinamon* which comes from the *Levant :* It is also of a sharper and more biting taste : but being dried in the shade, it gives a pleasant taste to Meats.

The Islands *Tabago*, *Barbados*, and *Sante Croix* are accounted to be better furnish'd then any of the rest with several sorts of wood, which experience hath found very useful in Medicine : For they afford *Sandal-wood*, *Guaiacum*, and *Safafras*, all which are so well known, that we need not in this place make any particular descriptions thereof.

COTTON-TREE.

THere are several other Trees very common in all these Islands, whereof the Inhabitants may make very considerable advantages. The *Cotton-tree*, called by the Savages *Manoulou-Akecha*, may be ranked among the chiefest, as being the most profitable. It grows up to the height of a *Peach-tree*, the bark is of a brownish colour, the leaves small, divided into three parts : It bears a flower about the bigness of a Rose, under which there are three little green and sharp-pointed leaves, by which it is encompassed. This flower consists of five leaves which are of a bright yellow colour, having towards the stem small lines of a purple colour, and a yellow button or crown encompassed with little filaments of the same colour : The flowers are succeeded by a fruit of an oval figure, about the bigness of a small Nut with its shell : when it is come to maturity it is all black on the out-side, and opens in three several places, at which appears the whiteness of the *Cotton* lying within that rough covering : there are in every of the fruit seven little beans, which are the seed of the Tree.

There is another kind of *Cotton-tree* which creeps along the ground like an unsupported Vine : this bears the best and most esteemed *Cotton* : Of both there are made Cloths, and several cheap Stuffs, very useful in House-keeping.   SOAP-

SOAP-TREE.

THere are two forts of Trees which the Iflanders ufe inftead of *Soap*: one of them hath this quality in its fruit,
which grows in clufters, round, yellowifh, and about the bignefs of a fmall Plumb, which hath alfo a hard black ftone within it that may be polifh'd : It is commonly called the *Soap-
fruit* : the other hath the fame vertue in its root, which is
white and foft : both of them lather as well as any Soap ; but
the former ufed too frequently burns the Linen.   Thefe Trees
are called the *Soap-trees* from the vertue they have to whiten
Cloaths.

The ARCHED-INDIAN-FIG-TREE.

THe *Arched-Indian-Fig-Tree* is a Tree thrives beft in fenny
places, and on the Sea-fide : Its leaf is green, thick, and
of a good length : the branches which bend down to the
ground, no fooner touch it but they take root and grow up into other Trees, which afterwards produce others, fo that in
time they fpread over all the good ground they meet with,
which is by that means fo hardly reducible to bear other
things, that it will yield no profit : under thefe Trees the wild
Boars, and other beafts are fecurely lodg'd. They are alfo in many places the lurking-holes of the Inhabitants of the Iflands,
who having garrifon'd themfelves within thefe Trees, defie all
enemies : There is further this great advantage made of them,
that there being no Oaks in thefe Iflands, their bark is good for
Tanners.

GOURD-TREE.

NOr may we forget the *Gourd-tree*, of which are made the
greateft part of the Houfhold-veffels, ufed not only by
the Indians, but the Foreigners who are Inhabitants of thefe
Iflands : 'tis a Tree grows up to the height and bignefs of a
great Apple-tree ; its branches are commonly well-loaden
with leaves, which are long, narrow, and round at the extremity, faften'd by bufhes to the branches, and fometimes fhooting
out of the trunk it felf: It bears flowers and fruits moft moneths
of the year ; the flowers are of a greyifh colour mixt with
green, and full of fmall black fpots, and fometimes violet :
they are fucceeded by certain Apples, whereof there can hardly be found two on the fame Tree of equal bignefs, and the
fame figure ; and as a Potter fhews the excellency of his Art by
making on the fame wheel, and of the fame mafs of clay, Veffels of different forms and capacity ; fo Nature fhews here a
miraculous

miraculous induſtry, by loading the ſame Tree with fruits different in their form and bigneſs, though the productions of the
ſame ſubſtance.

Theſe fruits have this common, that they have all a hard
woody bark of ſuch a thickneſs and ſolidity, that Bottles, Ba-
ſons, Cups, Diſhes, Platters, and ſeveral other Veſſels neceſſary to Houſe-keeping may be made thereof: they are full of
a certain pulp, which being ripe becomes of a Violet-colour,
though before it had been white: amidſt this ſubſtance there
are certain ſmall flat and hard grains, which are the ſeeds of
the Tree. Thoſe of the Inhabitants who are moſt addicted to
Hunting, in caſe of neceſſity, quench their thirſt with this fruit,
and they ſay it hath the taſte of burnt-wine, but is too aſtrin-
gent. The Indians poliſh the bark, and give it ſo delightful
an enamel with *Roucou*, *Indico*, and ſeveral other pleaſant colours, that the moſt nice may eat and drink out of the veſſels
they make thereof: Nay ſome are ſo curious, as to think them
worthy a place among the Rarities of their Cloſets.

MAHOT.

OF the Tree called *Mahot* there are two kinds, *Mahot-
franc*, and *Mahot-d'herbe* : the former is the more ſought
after, as being the ſtronger : it grows not very big, in regard
the branches creep along the ground : the bark is very thick,
and eaſily taken from the Tree : there are made of it long
Laces or Points, which are ſtronger then the Lines of *Teil*,
which are uſed in many places : they are commonly uſed to
make up Rolls of *Tobacco*, and to faſten things about the
Houſe: as for the latter *Mahot*, it is uſed where the former is
wanting; but it eaſily rots, and is not comparable to the other
as to ſtrength.

In a word, there are in theſe Iſlands ſeveral other Trees not
known in *Europe*, whereof ſome only delight the eye, ſuch as
are that which is called *Mappou*, and divers kinds of thorny
wood : others only ſatisfie the ſmelling by their ſweet ſcents ;
others have venemous qualities, as the *Milkie-tree*, as alſo that
whoſe root reduced to powder and caſt into rivers inebriates
the Fiſh; the *Mancenilier*, which we ſhall deſcribe in its proper
place, and an infinite number of others, the wood whereof is
white, ſoft, and of no uſe, and have yet got no names among
the foreign Inhabitants of thoſe parts.

H

CHAP.

CHAP. IX.

Of other Trees growing in thefe Iflands whofe Fruits or
Roots contribute to the fubfiftance of the Inhabitants,
or ferve for fome other ufes.

IT hath pleafed the great Contriver of all things to divide
that Element, which we call Earth, into feveral Countries,
each whereof he hath endued with certain advantages and
conveniences not to be found in other places, that by fuch a
delightful variety of things he might make a more diftinct
and remarkable demonftration of his own all-cherifhing Providence. But it muft be acknowledg'd, that in the diftributi-
on which the Divine Wifedome hath made of its bounties,
the *Caribby Iflands* have had a very large portion : For, to confine our felves to the defign we intend to profecute, not only
the greater forts of Trees, which we have defcribed in the former Chapters, contribute to the Shelter, Nourifhment, Cloathing, Health, and feveral other accommodations of the Inhabitants ; but there are alfo divers fhrubs, or leffer Trees,
which either fhoot forth Roots, or bear Fruits conducing to
the fame purpofe, as fhall be feen in the perufal of this
Chapter.

MANYOC.

INftead of Wheat the Inhabitants make ufe of the root of a
fmall Tree called *Manyoc*, by fome *Manyot*, and by others
Mandioque, of which is made a kinde of Bread delicate
enough, called *Caffava :* whence it is alfo fometimes called the
Caffava-tree. This root is fo fruitful, that a fmall parcel of
ground planted therewith will feed more perfons then fix
times as much fown with the beft Wheat could do : It fhoots
forth crooked branches about the height of five or fix foot,
eafie to be broken, and full of fmall knots : the leaf is narrow
and fomewhat long : at nine moneths end the root comes to its
maturity : **Nay** it is reported, that in *Brafil* it grows to the
bignefs of a mans thigh in three or four moneths. If the ground
be not too moift the root may continue in it three years without corrupting, fo that there needs no Store-houfe, 'or Garret
to put it up in ; for it is taken out of the ground as it is fpent.

To propagate this Root, you muft take of the branches, and
cut them in pieces about a foot in length : then make trenches
in your Garden with a Hoe, and thruft in three of thofe fticks
triangle-wife into the earth which had been taken out of the
trenches,

trenches, and wherewith a little hill or tump had been rais'd :
this is called Planting by the trench.   But there is another way
of planting *Manyoc*, much more expeditious and more eafie,
but the *Manyoc* is neither fo fair, nor fo much efteemed as the
other.   The way is only thus, to make a hole in the ground
with a ftick, and to thruft the *Manyoc* ftrait into it : care muft
be had in the planting of it, that the knots be not fet downwards, for if they fhould the *Manyoc* fticks would not grow.
The Indians never plant it otherwife ; but that it may ripen in
its feafon, they obferve a certain time of the Moon, and fee
that the ground be not too moift.

There are feveral kinds of thefe fhrubs differing one from
the other only in the colour of the bark of their wood and of
their root : Thofe which have the bark greyifh, or white, or
green, make a very good tafted bread, and grow up in a fhort
time ; but the roots they produce do not keep fo well, nor
thrive comparably to thofe of the red or violet *Manyoc*, which
is the moft common, the moft efteem'd, and the moft advantageous in houfe-keeping.

The juice of this root is as cold as Hemlock, and fo effectual
a poyfon, that the poor Indians of the greater Iflands being perfecuted with fire and fword by the Spaniards, to avoid a more
cruel death, made ufe of this poyfon to deftroy themfelves.
There is to this day to be feen in the Ifland of *Hifpaniola*, otherwife call'd S. *Domingo*, a place called the *Cave* of the Indians,
where there are the bones of above four hundred perfons, who
ended their lives there with this poyfon, to avoid the cruelties
of the Spaniards.   But let this juice, which is fo venemous to all
forts of living creatures, reft four and twenty hours after it is
taken from the root, and it lofes that malignant and dangerous quality.

PALMA-CHRISTI.

THere are in thefe Iflands an infinite number of the fhrubs
called *Palma-Chrifti* or *Ricinus* ; and they grow up fo
high, and fo big in fome places, that they would be taken for
a different kind from thofe commonly feen in *Europe*.   The
Negroes gather the feed, and extract an oyl from it, wherewith
they rub their hair to keep themfelves clear from vermine.
The qualities attributed to it by *Galen* and *Diofcorides*, confirm the ufe thefe Barbarians make of it : the leaf of this fhrub
is fovereign for the healing of fome kinds of Ulcers, as being
very attractive.

There grow in all thefe Iflands two kinds of fhrubs, or rather
great Reeds, fpongy within, growing of themfelves in fat
ground neer little rivulets, or in Valleys not annoyed by winds.
They are commonly called *Banana-trees*, or *Planes*, and *Fig-*

trees, or *Apple-trees of Paradiſe* : Theſe two kinds of ſhrubs have this common to both.

1 That they grow of equal height, to wit about twelve or fifteen foot above ground.

2 That their ſtalks, which are of a green colour, ſhining, ſpongious, and very full of water, ſhoot out of a great Onion, like a Pear, encompaſs'd with many little white roots, which faſten it to the ground.

3 That they have ſhooting forth at the foot of the ſtems certain Scyons, which bear fruit at the years end.

4 That when one ſtem is cut off for the getting of the fruit, the moſt forward next that ſucceeds in its place, and ſo the ſhrub is perpetuated, and multiplies ſo exceedingly, that in time it ſpreads over all the good ground neer it.

5 That the ſubſtance of both is very ſoft, and reducible into water, which though extreamly clear, yet hath the quality of dying Linen and white Stuffs into a dark browniſh colour.

6 That their Fruits lye at the top of the ſtem, like great cluſters or poſies.

And laſtly, that their leaves, which are about four foot or more in length, and a foot and a half in bredth, may ſerve for Napkins and Towels, and being dried make a ſoft kind of Couch or Bed to lye upon.

Theſe two ſhrubs have this further reſemblance, that which way ſoever their fruit be cut when it is come to maturity, the meat of them which is white as ſnow repreſents in the middle the form of a Crucifix, eſpecially when it is cut in thin ſlices. Hence the Spaniards are ſo ſuperſtitious as to think it a kind of mortal ſin to uſe a knife about it, and are ſcandaliz'd to ſee any thing employ'd about it but the teeth.

But there is this to be ſaid particularly of the *Banana-tree.*

1 That its fruit is in length about twelve or thirteen inches, a little bending towards the extremity, much about the bigneſs of a mans arm : whereas that of the Fig-tree is but half as big, and about ſix inches in length.

2 The *Banana-tree* hath not in its poſie or cluſter above 25 or 30 *Bananas* at the moſt, which do not lye over-cloſe one to another ; but the Fig-tree hath many times 120 Figs, which lye ſo cloſe together that they can hardly be gotten aſunder.

3 The meat of the *Bananas* is firm and ſolid, and may be dreſs'd either by roaſting it under the embers, or boiling it in a Pot with meat, or preſerv'd, and dry'd in an Oven, or in the Sun, and afterwards eaſily kept : But the Fig being of a ſoft ſubſtance hath not the ſame conveniences.

To get in theſe fruits, the trees, which it ſeems bear but once, are cut at the very foot, and the great cluſter is ſupported by a fork, that it may not be bruiſed in the falling : But they are ſeldom cut till ſome of the fruits of each cluſter be turn'd a little

tle yellowish; for that is a sign of their maturity, and then being carried into the house, those which were green ripen by
degrees, and so they have every day new fruit.

The cluster is commonly as much as a man can well carry;
nay sometimes it is laid on a Leaver, and carried upon their
shoulders between two, as that bunch of Grapes which the
Spies of the *Israelites* brought out of the Land of *Canaan.*
Some have thought this fruit so excellent and delicate, that
they have imagined it to be the same which God forbad our first
Parents to eat of in *Paradise:* accordingly they have named it
Adams Fig-tree, or the *Fruit-tree of Paradise:* the leaf of these
Reeds being of the largeness we have before described, may indeed be allow'd very fit to cover the nakedness of our first Parents; and as to the figure of the Crucifix which may be seen
within the fruit when it is cut, we leave it to find work for their
profound speculations who busie their thoughts in searching
out the secrets of Nature.

There are some who affirm that the figure of a Cross is also
marked in the seed of the Herb commonly called *Rue.* The
small *Gentiana,* or *Cruciata,* hath the leaves dispos'd in the
form of a Cross upon its stalk; and it is to be acknowledg'd
that Nature, as it were sporting her self, hath been pleas'd to
make several such representations in Plants and Flowers.
Hence it comes that some have the resemblance of Hair, others
of Eyes, others of Ears, others of a Nose, a Heart, a Tongue,
a Hand, and some other parts of the Body: There are in like
manner divers famous Plants which seem to represent several
other things, as Eagles, Bees, Serpents, Cats-clawes, Cocks-
combs, Bears-ears, Harts-horns, Darts, and the like: whence
many times those Plants derive their names from the said resemblance. But of these it is besides our design to give any
account.

CORAL-WOOD.

THere is also in several of the Islands a little shrub which
bears a seed as red as any Coral: it grows in bunches at
the extremity of its branches, which derive an extraordinary
lustre from it: But these little seeds have a small black spot at
one end, which disfigures them, and abates much of their
esteem with some; others on the contrary affirm that that
diversity of colours makes them more delightful to the
Eye. This may be called the *Coral-tree:* The seeds are used
for Bracelets.

JASMIN

JASMIN and CANDLE-WOOD

THe shrubs called by some *Jasmin*, and *Candle-wood*, may
be numbred among those that are confiderable in thefe
Iflands: The former bears a fmall white flower which perfumes all about it with its fweet fcent ; and thence it had the
name : The other cafts forth fo pleafant and fweet a fcent when
its wood is burnt dry, and does fo eafily take fire, and gives fo
clear a flame, by reafon of a certain Aromatick Gum lying
within it, that it is with reafon fought after by the Inhabitants
for their firing, and to ferve them for a Candle or Torch in the
night time.

CHAP. X.

Of the Plants, Herbs and Roots growing in the Caribbies.

HAving in the former Chapters reprefented the Trees and
Shrubs wherewith thefe Iflands are richly furnifhed ;
we come now to the Defcription of feveral rare
Plants, Herbs and Roots, whereby they are alfo abundantly
fupply'd.

PYMAN.

THe Plant called by the French and others *Pyman*, or *American Pepper*, is the fame which the natural Inhabitants
of the Country call *Axi*, or *Carive* ; it grows clofe like a little
Briar without any prickles: the ftem of it is covered with an
Afh-colour'd rind, and bears feveral little boughs loaden with
an infinite multitude of leaves, which are pretty long, full of
jags, and of a grafs-green colour : Of thefe there are three
kinds, differing only in the figure of the hufk or cod, or the
fruit they bear.   One bears only a little red button, fomewhat
long like a Clove, within which there are very fmall feeds,
much hotter then the Spices brought from the *Levant*, and in a
manner cauftick, which eafily communicates that picquant quality to all things wherein it is us'd.

The fecond kind hath a much larger and longer Cod, which
when ripe is of a perfect Vermilion colour, and being us'd in
Sauces, it makes them yellow, as Saffron would do.

The third hath yet a larger Cod then the precedent, which
is thick enough, red as any Coral, and not fmooth in all parts:

The

The feed, which is not fo biting, nor fo fpicy as thofe of the other two kinds, lies in the midft of it : Being ripe it is one of the moft delightful fruits that may be. The feed hath been brought over into *France* and other parts, and hath come to perfection ; but the fruit is not fo big as that of *America.* This cod and the feed within it is us'd inftead of pepper, becaufe it communicates a certain picquancy to things, like that fpice : But the operations of them differ much ; for after it hath bitten the tongue, and by its acrimony inflam'd the palate, inftead of fortifying and warming the ftomach, it weakens it, and caufes coldnefs in it ; or rather, according to the opinions of fome Phyficians, it over-heats it, and by its cauftick vertue weakens it, caufing coldnefs in it only by accident, inafmuch as it difperfes the radical moifture, which is the feat of heat. Whence it is obferv'd in the Iflands, that thofe who ordinarily ufe it in their meat are fubject to pains in the cheft, and apt to contract a yellow colour.

TOBACCO.

THe Plant called *Tobacco,* from the Ifland *Tabago,* where, as fome affirm, it was firft difcover'd by the Spaniards, had alfo the name *Nicotianum* from one *Nicot* a Phyfitian, who firft us'd it in *Europe,* and fent it from *Portugal* into *France :* It was alfo called *Queen-herb,* hence, that being brought from *America,* it was prefented to the Queen of *Spain* as a rare Plant, and of extraordinary vertues. The Spaniards give it further the title of *Holy-herb,* for the excellent effects they have experienc'd from it, as *Garcilaffo* in his *Royal Commentary of the Incas of Peru,* lib. 11. ch. 25. affirms. Laftly, the French call it *Petun,* though *de Lery* is much difpleas'd at the name, affirming, that the Plant they faw in *Brafil,* and which the *Topinambous* call *Petun,* differs very much from our *Tobacco.* The *Caribbians* in their natural Language call it *Touly.* Heretofore there were known in the Iflands but two kinds of *Tobacco-*Plants, commonly called by the Inhabitants *Green-Tobacco,* and *Tongu'd-Tobacco,* from the figure of its leaf ; but fince there have been brought from the Continent the feeds of *Virinus,* and the Tobacco of the *Amazons,* they are divided into four kinds : The two former are of a great produce, but the two others are more efteem'd by reafon of their fweet fcent.

All thefe kinds of Tobacco-Plants grow in the Iflands to the height of a man and higher, if their growth be not check'd by cutting off the tops of their ftems : They bear good ftore of leaves, which are green, long, downy on the lower fide, and feem in the handling as if they were oiled : Thofe which grow towards the ftock of the Plant are larger and longer, as deriving more nourifhment from the moifture of the root. At

the

the tops they fhoot forth little branches, which bear a flower like a fmall Bell, which is of a clear violet colour : And
when that flower is dry, there comes into its place a little
button, wherein is contained the feed, which is of a brownifh colour, and very fmall.

There are fometimes found under the leaves and branches of this Plant the nefts of the little Birds called *Colibris*,
which we fhall defcribe in its proper place.

INDICO.

THe material of which is made the Dying commodity
called *Indico* is got from a Plant which grows not a-
bove two foot and a half above the ground : It hath but a
fmall leaf, of a grafs-green colour, inclining to yellow when
it is ripe : The flower is reddifh : It grows from the feed,
which is fown by trenches in a ftreight line : It hath a very
bad fcent, quite contrary to that growing in *Madagafcar*,which
bears fmall flowers of a purple colour mixt with white, which
fmell well.

GINGER.

OF all the Spices of the *Levant* that have been planted in
America only *Ginger* hath thriv'd, and come to perfection. 'Tis the root of a Plant which grows not much above
ground, having green long leaves like thofe of Reeds and Sugar-canes : The root fpreads it felf, not in depth, but in
bredth, and lies neer the furface like a hand encompafs'd by
many fingers; whence the Inhabitants of the Iflands call it a
Paw. This Plant may be propagated by the feed, or, as is
moft commonly done, by certain fmall roots which grow like
fo many ftrings all about the old ftem and the greater roots,
as there do about Skirretts. It grows with eafe in all the I-
flands, efpecially at S. *Chriftophers*, many Inhabitants of which
Ifland have planted it, and traded in it with advantage, fince
Tobacco came to fo low a rate.

POTATOE.

THe *Potatoe* is a root much like the *Saligots* growing in
Gardens, which are called *Topinambous*, or *Jerufalem
Artichokes*, but of a much more excellent tafte, and more
wholfome.

Thofe *Topinambous* or Artichokes, which are now not only
very common in moft parts, but cheap, and flighted, as being a
tteatment for the poorer fort, were heretofore accounted delicacies : For in fome extraordinary Entertainments made at
Paris

Paris by the Princes to certain Embaſſadours, in the Year M. DC. XVI. they were ſerv'd up among the moſt exquiſite diſhes.

But the *Potatoe* is infinitely beyond it : It thrives beſt in a light ground, ſomewhat moiſt, and well ordered : It ſhoots forth abundance of ſoft leaves, of a very dark green, in figure like thoſe of *ſpinage :* They ſpring from certain fibres which creep along the ground, and in a ſhort time over-run the place where it is ſown.   And if the ground be well order'd, theſe fibres within a certain time frame divers roots by the means of certain whitiſh filaments which ſhoot forth below the knots, and eaſily faſten into the earth.   It bears a flower near the ſame colour with the root, and like a bell, within which lies the ſeed : But commonly to propagate this fruit they take only of theſe ſtrings or fibres, which lye ſcattered all over the ground, as we ſaid, and thruſt them into ground prepar'd for them, and at the end of two or three months they will have produc'd their root, which hath this further vertue, that being cut into ſmall pieces, and thruſt into the ground, it produceth its root and leaf as effectually as if the ſeed lay in each of its leaſt parts.

Theſe roots are of ſeveral colours, and in the ſame piece of ground there will be ſome white ones, which are the moſt ordinary, ſome of a violet colour, ſome red as beetroots, ſome yellow, and ſome marbled : They are all of an excellent taſte : For, provided they be not full of water, and grew in a ground moderately moiſt and dry, that is, participating of both, they taſte like Cheſt-nuts, and are a better nouriſhment then the *Caſſava*, which dries up the body ; for they are not ſo dry. Some, as particularly the Engliſh, uſe theſe roots inſtead of bread and *Caſſava*, and to that purpoſe bake them under the Embers, or upon the coals : For being ſo prepar'd they are of a better taſte, and are clear'd of that windy quality which is commonly obſerv'd to be in moſt roots.   But for the moſt part they are boyl'd, or ſtew'd in a great iron pot, into which there is a little water put to keep the bottom from burning ; then the pot-lid is ſet on as cloſe as may be, that they may ſtew by that ſmother'd heat.   This is the ordinary treatment of the Servants and Slaves of the Country, who eat them out of the pot with a ſauce made of *Pyman* and juice of Oranges.

If this root were not ſo common it would be more eſteem'd. The Spaniards think it a delicacy, and dreſs it with butter, ſugar, nutmeg, and cinamon : Others make a pottage of it, and putting into it ſome fat, pepper and ginger, account it an excellent diſh : But moſt of the Inhabitants of the Iſlands trouble not themſelves ſo much about the dreſſing of it. There are ſome will gather the tender extremities of the afore

I

ſaid

said strings, and having boil'd them eat them as a Sallet, like the tops of *Afparagus* or *Hops*.

ANANAS.

THe *Ananas* or *Pine-Apple* is accounted the moft delicious fruit, not only of thefe Iflands, but of all *America*. It is fo delightful to the eye, and of fo fweet a fcent, that Nature may be faid to have been extreamly prodigal of what was moft rare and precious in her Treafury to this Plant.

It grows on a ftalk about a foot high, encompaffed by about 15 or 16 leaves, as long as thofe of fome kinds of Thiftles, broad as the Palm of a mans hand, and in figure like thofe of *Aloes :* they are pointed at the extremity, as thofe of *Corn-Gladen*, fomewhat hollow in the midft, and having on both fides little prickles, which are very fharp.

The fruit which grows between thefe leaves, ftrait up from the ftalk, is fometimes about the bignefs of a *Melon :* its figure is much like that of a *Pine-Apple :* its rind, which is full of little compartiments like the fcales of fifh, of a pale-green colour, border'd with Carnation upon a yellow ground, hath on the out-fide feveral fmall flowers, which, according to the different Afpects of the Sun, feem to be of fo many different colours as may be feen in the Rain-bow; as the fruit ripens moft of thefe flowers fall. But that which gives it a far greater luftre, and acquir'd it the fupremacy among Fruit is, that it is crown'd with a great Pofie, confifting of flowers and feveral leaves, folid and jagged about, which are of a bright red colour, and extreamly add to the delightfulnefs of it.

The Meat or Pulp which is contained within the rind, is a little fibrous, but put into the mouth is turn'd all to juice: it hath fo tranfcendent a tafte, and fo particular to it felf, that thofe who have endeavour'd to make a full defcription of it, not able to confine themfelves to one comparifon, have borrow'd what they thought moft delicate in the *Peach*, the *Strawberry*, the *Mufcadine-grape*, and the *Pippin*, and having faid all they could, been forc'd to acknowledg that it hath a certain particular tafte which cannot eafily be exprefs'd.

The vertue, or fhoot by which this fruit may be perpetuated lyes not in its root, nor yet in a fmall red feed, which is many times found in its Pulp, but in that Garland wherewith it is cover'd; for as foon as it is put into the ground it takes root, fhoots forth leaves, and at the years end produces new fruit. It happens fometimes that thefe fruits are charg'd with three pofies or crowns, all which have the vertue of propagating their fpecies : but every ftalk bears fruit but once a year.

There are three or four kinds of them, which the Inhabitants diftinguifh by the colour, figure, or fcent, to wit, the

White-

White-Ananas, the *Pointed*, and that called the *Pippin*, or *Re-nette:* This laft is more efteem'd then the other two, inafmuch as being ripe it hath as to the tafte all the rare qualities before defcribed ; it hath alfo a fweeter fcent then the others, and does not fet the teeth fo much on edge.

The natural Indians of the Country, and the French who live in the Iflands make of this fruit an excellent drink, not much unlike *Malmfey*, when it hath been kept a certain time: there is alfo made of it a liquid Conferve, which is one of the nobleft and moft delicate of any brought out of the *Indies :* they alfo cut the rind into two pieces, and it is preferv'd dry with fome of the thioneft leaves, and then the pieces are neatly joyn'd together again, and they ice it over with Sugar, by which means the figure of the fruit and leaves is perfectly preferv'd ; and there may be feen in thofe happy Countries, notwithftanding the heats of the Torrid Zone, a pleafant reprefentation of the fad productions of Winter.

In Phyfick the Vertues of it are thefe: The juice does admirably recreate and exhilarate the Spirits, and comfort the Heart ; it alfo fortifies the Stomack, cureth Queafinefs, and caufeth Appetite: it gives prefent eafe to fuch as are troubled with the Stone, or ftoppage of Urine; nay it deftroys the force of Poyfon. If the fruit be not procurable, the root will do the fame effects. The water extracted from it by diftilling hath a quicker and more effectual operation; but in regard it is too corrofive, and offends the mouth, palat, and uretory veffels, it muft be very moderately ufed, and with the advice of an able Phyfician, who knows how to correct that Acrimony.

SUGAR-CANES.

THe Reed which by its delicious juice fupplies that fubftance whereof Sugar is made, hath leaves like thofe of other Reeds which grow in Marfhes and neer Ponds, but only they are a little longer and fharper; for if they be not taken with a certain care and fleight, they will cut a mans hands like a Rafour. It is call'd the *Sugar-Cane*, and grows up in height between five and fix foot, and two inches about: it is divided by feveral knots, which are commonly four or five inches diftant one from another; and the greater the diftance is between the knots, the more Sugar are the Canes apt to yield.

The leaves of it are long, green, and grow very thick, in the midft whereof rifes the Cane, which alfo at the top is loaden with feveral pointed leaves, and one kind of knot of them which contains the feed: it is as full as it can be of a white and juicy pith, out of which is drawn that liquor that makes the Sugar.

I 2

It

It thrives extreamly in a fat foil, fo it be light and fomewhat moift: it is planted in trenches made at equal diftances one from another, either with a Hoe, or a Plow, about half a foot deep: Having there laid the Canes, being ripe they cover them with earth, and a little while after out of every knot fhoots forth a root, and out of that a ftem which produces a new Cane. As foon as it appears above ground, it muft be carefully weeded all about, that the weeds choak it not: but as foon as it hath cover'd the ground it fecures it felf, and keeps its footing as well as any Copfe-wood might do, and it may laft fifty years without being renew'd, fo the main root be found and not injured by the worm; for if there be any jealoufie of that, the remedy is to take up the whole Plant as foon as may be, and to order it all anew.

Though the Canes be ripe at the end of nine or ten moneths, yet will they not be any way prejudic'd if continu'd in the ground two years, nay fometimes three, after which they decay: But the beft and fureft way is to cut them every year as neer the ground as may be, and below the laft knot or joynt.

Thofe who crofs the Fields when thefe Canes are come to maturity may refrefh themfelves with the juice of them, which is an excellent beverage, and hath the fame tafte with the Sugar: But if it be taken immoderately it may occafion fluxes and loofenefs, efpecially to fuch as are newly come into the Country; for thofe who by a long abode there are in a manner naturaliz'd, are not fo fubject to that inconvenience.

There grow alfo in fome of thefe Iflands thofe neat and precious Canes which are us'd in walking, naturally marbled, and enamell'd with feveral figures. The fides of great Ponds, and all Fenny and Marfhy places are alfo furnifh'd with a big fort of Reeds which grow up very high and very ftrait, whereof the Inhabitants commonly make the partitions of their Houfes, and ufe them inftead of Lats, for the covering of them. The Indians alfo make ufe of the tops of thefe Canes in the making of their Arrows.

CHAP. XI.

Of ſome other rare Productions of the Caribbies, *and
ſeveral ſorts of Pulſe, and Flowers growing in thoſe
Iſlands.*

Aving ſpoken of the Plants, Herbs, and Roots, conſiderable for their Leaves, Fruits, or Vertues, we now
come to treat of ſome other rare Productions of theſe
Iſlands, for the moſt part not known in *Europe.*

RAQVETTES.

That which the French call *Raquettes,* from the figure of
its leaves, which are like a *Racket,* is a great thorny buſh
creeping along the earth, and not able to raiſe it ſelf to any
height, in regard the ſtem, which is only a leaf grown big in
proceſs of time, grows not much more then half a foot above
ground; and though it be big enough, yet is it not to be ſeen
till the leaves, which are green, heavy, ill-ſhap'd, and about
an inch thick, and faſten'd one to another, encompaſſing it, be
firſt taken up: they are armed with prickles extreamly ſharp
and ſmall; and upon ſome of theſe long and prickly leaves
there grows a fruit about the bigneſs of a *Date-plumb,* which
hath alſo on the out-ſide ſeveral very ſmall prickles, which
prick their fingers who would gather them: being ripe it is red
within and without, of a Vermilion colour: the Hunts-men
of theſe Iſlands think it very delicate and refreſhing; but it
hath this property, that it colours a mans Urine as red as blood
as ſoon as he hath eaten it; inſomuch that ſuch as are ignorant
of this ſecret imagine they have broken a vein: Nay ſome
perceiving that alteration in themſelves have taken their Beds
out of an imagination that they were very ſick. Some report,
that in *Peru* there is a kind of Plumb which works the ſame effect: nay there are who affirm, that they have obſerv'd as much
after the eating of a Gelly of red Gooſe-berries.

Thoſe who have deſcribed *Tunal,* which is ſo much eſteem'd
for the precious Scarlet-dye lying in its leaves, make it like the
Plant we now deſcribe, ſave that they aſſign it no fruit. Some
others have ranked it among thoſe Thiſtles which bear Figs,
becauſe the fruit is of that figure, and when it is open, inſtead
of a ſtone, it hath only ſmall ſeeds like thoſe of the Fig.

There is alſo another kind of this Plant, whereof the fruit is
white, and of a ſweeter, and more ſavory taſte then the red
we ſpoke of before: nay there is yet another, which, no doubt,

is

is a kind of *Tunal*, on which there have been seen certain little worms in colour like a Ruby, which dye Linen or Woollen-Cloth, whereon they are crush'd, into a very fair and lively Scarlet-colour.

TORCH.

THe Plant called by the *Caribbians Akoulerou*, some of the *European* Inhabitants of these Islands call the *Torch*: it is a kind of great Thistle growing like a great bushy Briar, furnish'd of all sides with prickles, extreamly sharp and small: there shoot forth in the midst of it nine or ten stalks without either branches or leaves, growing up to the height of nine or ten foot, strait, and channelled like so many Torches: they have also very sharp prickles, like so many small Needles, which so secure them that they cannot be touch'd of any side: the rind, and what is within it, is soft and spongy enough. Every *Torch* bears at a certain season of the year, between the channels of the stalk, certain yellow or violet flowers, which are succeeded by a fruit like a great Fig, good to eat, and delicate enough. The Birds love it well, but they can only peck at it flying, because the prickles hinder them from lighting on any part of the Plant. The Indians get off the fruit with little forks or sticks cleft at one end.

LIENES.

THere are several kinds of Plants which creep along the ground, or are fasten'd to Trees; nay some which very much obstruct peoples passage through the Forests: The Inhabitants call them *Lienes*; some are like a great Cable, others bear flowers of several colours: nay some are loaden with great brownish husks a foot or better in length, four or five inches thick, and as hard as Oak-bark, wherein are contain'd those curious fruits called *Sea-Chestnuts*, which have the figure of a heart, and the pulp taken out, are made into Boxes to keep Sneezing-powder, or any other sweet powder. The fruit, called by the Inhabitants *Lienes-Apples*, grows on a kind of Willow, which is fasten'd to the greater sort of Trees like Ivy: it is about the bigness of a Tennis-ball, and cover'd with a hard shell, and a green out-side, containing within it a substance, which being ripe hath the figure and taste of Gooseberries.

SEMPER-VIVUM.

THere are in these Islands several kinds of Herbs that never dye or wither, whereof some grow on trunks of old
Trees,

Trees, as *Mistletoe* does on the *Oak*; others grow on the ground, and upon rocks. They have so much natural moisture, that being pluck'd, and hung with their roots upwards in the midst of rooms, where they are many times kept as rarities, and to recreate the eye, they lose nothing of their verdure.

SENSITIVE PLANTS.

THere is in the Island *Tabago* a kind of Herb, which besides its *perpetual growing* is also *sensible*, whence it is called the *Sensitive Plant*: it grows up about a foot and a half in height, encompass'd with a many leaves, in length a foot or better, in bredth three fingers, jagg'd almost like those of Fern, being at the extremities of a green colour checquer'd with litt'e brownish or red spots. In the season of fruits there grows out of the midst of this Plant a round flower, consisting of several leaves standing much after the same order as those of the Marigold; but they are of a bright violet colour, and being handled have a good scent; the nature of this Plant is such, that if one pluck off the leaves of it, or so much as touch them, the whole Plant withers, and all the other leaves fall to the ground, as if it had been trod under feet; and according to the number of the leaves that had been pluck'd off it will be a longer or shorter time ere it recover that loss.

There grows such another at *Madagascar*, which the Inhabitants call *Haest-vel*, that is, the *Living-herb:* but it is not the same kind as that which may be seen in the Kings Garden at *Paris*; for that hath a much lesser leaf, and it is neither spotted nor jagg'd and which is more, it bears no flowers: besides, its leaves being touch'd, close together by a certain kind of contraction; whereas that we describe sheds its leaves on the ground.

There is also another kind of living or sensitive Plant in some of the other Islands: it grows sometimes to the height of a shrub: it hath many little branches, which are at all times loaden with an infinite number of long and narrow leaves, which during the rains are enamell'd with small golden flowers, like so many stars. But what makes this Plant esteem'd one of the rarest and most admirable of any in the world, is, that as soon as one would fasten on it with his hand, it draws back its leaves, and wriggles them under its little branches, as if they were wither'd; and when the hand is remov'd, and the party gone away some distance from it, it spreads them abroad again.

Some call this Plant the *Chaste Herb*, because it cannot endure to be touch'd without expressing its resentment of the injury. Those who have pass'd by the *Isthmus* from *Nombre de Dios* to *Panama* relate, that there are whole Woods of a Tree called the *Sensitive-tree*, which being touch'd the branches and

leaves

leaves ſtart up, making a great noiſe, and cloſe together into the figure of a Globe.

Some years ſince there was to be ſeen in the Kings Garden at *Paris* a *Senſitive-ſhrub*, valued at a very great rate. But ſome body having advis'd the putting of it in the bottom of a Well to keep it from the cold, and the ſharpneſs of Winter, it there miſerably periſh'd, to the great regret of the Curious.

Of ſeveral ſorts of PEASE.

THeſe Iſlands are alſo fruitful in bearing all ſorts of Pulſe, ſuch as are ſeveral ſorts of *Peaſe* and *Beans* : The Savages call them by the general name of *Manconti*.

The *Peaſe* are in a manner of the ſame kinds as thoſe growing in *Europe*, thoſe only excepted, which are gather'd from a little ſhrub, which is about the height of *Broom*, and hath ſmall, green, and narrow leaves : it bears *Peaſe* in cods or huſks, which are faſtened to its branches : they are green and leſs then the ordinary ones, of an excellent taſte, and ſo eaſily boil'd, that they need but a walm or two : they are called in the Iſlands, The *Peaſe of Angola*, probably, becauſe the ſeed was brought from that Country.

There is another kind known by the name of Peaſe, which yet have the figure of Beans : they are ſmall enough ; and of this kind there are ſome white, ſome black, ſome red or brown, all very excellent, and are ripe in three moneths. Theſe in S. *Chriſtophers* are called *Engliſh Peaſe*.

BEANS.

OF *Beans* and *Faſels* there grow in the *Caribbies* ſeveral kinds, not to be ſeen in the Weſtern parts of *Europe*. The moſt common are white, to which the firſt Inhabitants gave an undecent name, by reaſon of their figure : their fruit may be eaten ſix weaks after they are planted : others are of ſeveral pretty colours, as thoſe which are called *Roman-Beans*, or *Lombardy-Beans*.

But the moſt conſiderable for their rarity are thoſe called the *Seven-years Beans*, becauſe the ſame ſtalk bears ſeven years one after another, and ſpreads it ſelf over Trees, Rocks, and whatever it can faſten on ; and what is to be yet further admir'd is, that at all times during the ſaid term of years it bears flowers, green fruit, and ripe fruit : So that he who ſees it,

——————— *may well admire*
Spring, Summer, Autumn in one bough conſpire.

The ſame thing is affirmed of a certain Tree in *Egypt*, called
Pharaohs

Pharaohs Fig-tree, on which there may be ſeen at all times fruit fully ripe, fruit ripening, and fruit newly knit.   Orange-trees have the ſame advantage.

Plants uſeful in Phyſick.

OF Plants uſeful in Phyſick there are many kinds in theſe Iſlands, whereof the vertues and temperament are not yet well known, and ſome others which are alſo to be had from other places : Such as are *Scolopendria,* and a kind of *Aloes,* and ſeveral ſorts of *Maiden-hair.*   There are alſo ſome, whereof trial hath been made, and they have been endued with great vertues, among which the moſt eſteem'd are the *Sweet-Ruſh,* the *Baliſier,* and the *Dart-Herb.*

SWEET-RUSH.

THe *Sweet-Ruſh* is like other Ruſhes which grow neer Ponds and Rivers, but it hath a round root about the bigneſs of a Small-nut, which caſts a ſweet ſcent like that of the *Flower-de-luce,* and being dried in the ſhade, and beaten to powder, hath a miraculous vertue to help Women in Labour, if they take but a ſmall doſe of it.

BALISIER.

THe *Baliſier* grows bigger and higher, according to the ſoil it meets with, but it thrives beſt in moiſt places : The leaves of it are ſo large that the *Caribbians,* in caſe of neceſſity, cover their little Huts therewith.   They are alſo apply'd to abate and mollifie the inflammations of wounds, and to make baths for ſuch as have had their Nerves cruſh'd, or have contracted any other weakneſs.   The flower of it, which grows like a Plume of Feathers, conſiſting of ſeveral yellow, or red cups, are ſucceeded by certain buttons, which are full of ſeeds as big as Peaſe, and ſo ſmooth and hard that Beads are made of them.

DART-HERB.

THe *Dart-Herb* is a ſad kind of Herb, for in the day time the leaves lye cloſe together, and in the night they are ſpread abroad : its leaves, which are of a bright-green, are about ſix or ſeven inches long and three broad : the root of it pounded, and applyed on the wound, takes away the venom of poyſoned Darts.

K

POT-

POT-HERBS.

MOst of the Pot-Herbs growing in several parts of *Europe* grow also in these Islands. 'Tis true, there are some, as Cabbages and Onions will not bear seed; yet is there no want of them. The Cabbages being ripe shoot forth many slips, which transplanted produce others, which come to be as fair and as large as if they grew from the seed. And for Onions, there are good store brought in the Ships, which produce abundance of Chibols, and those only are commonly used in Pottage, and with Pease.

MELONS.

THere is also abundance of ordinary *Melons*, the seed whereof is brought thither from these parts : but by reason of the heat of the Country they grow more easily ripe, the meat is firmer and of a better taste, and they have a sweeter scent : And what is a greater advantage, they are to be had at any time in the year.

WATER-MELONS.

THere grows in these Countries another kind of *Melons*, which are common in *Italy*, but must needs be incomparably better in *Egypt* and the *Levant*. There grow of them also in some parts of *France*, but they are naught : they are called *Water-Melons*, because they are full of a sugar'd water, intermingled with their meat, which ordinarily is of a Vermilion colour, and red as blood about the heart, wherein are contained their seed, which is also of the same colour, and sometimes black : their rind continues always green, and without any scent, so that it is rather by the stalk then the fruit that their ripeness is to be discover'd : they are sometimes bigger then a mans head, either round, or oval : they are eaten without Salt, and though a man feed liberally on them, yet do they not offend the stomack : but in those hot Countries they are very cooling, and cause appetite.

They plant also in these Islands *Mays*, otherwise called *Spanish-Wheat* or *Turkey-Wheat*, all sorts of *Millet*, *Cucumbers*, *Citrulls*, *Red-Parsnips*, and other Roots, all which are of an excellent taste.

LILLIES.

NOr is it to be doubted but that the flowers of these Countries are very beautiful, and admirable for their scent :
Among

Among others, there is a kind of *White-Lilly* that ſmells extreamly well; for the ſcent of it is like that of *Jeſſemine*, but
ſo communicative of it ſelf, that there needs but one flower to
perfume a whole Room.   The round top and the leaves are
like thoſe of the Lillies of *France*, but the flower hath its leaves
diſpers'd and divided into little Labels, as if they had been cut
with a pair of Sciſſers: there are alſo other Lillies which differ
in nothing from our Yellow and Orange-colour Lillies.

PASSION-FLOWER.

THere is another Plant in theſe Iſlands famous for the
beauty of its leaves, the ſweet ſcent of its flowers, and
the excellency of its fruit: The Spaniards call it *Grenadile*;
the Dutch, *Rhang-Appel*, and the French, *La Fleur de la Paſſion*,
that is, *The Paſſion-Flower*, becauſe it bears that rare flower
wherein may be ſeen, not without admiration, ſome of theInſtru-
ments of our Bleſſed Saviours Paſſion plainly repreſented. 'Tis
true, ſome curious Perſons, who have attentively conſidered
it do affirm, that they have obſerv'd therein a certain reſemblance of the Crown of Thornes, the Scourges, the Nails, the
Hammer, and the Pillar: but they add withall, that moſt of thoſe
things are therein repreſented or figured much after the ſame
manner as Virgins, Lyons, and Bears are ſeen among the Ce-
leſtial Bodies; ſo that to find all theſe repreſentations of the
Paſſion in thoſe flowers, they ſay with *Acoſta* in his Hiſtory,
Lib. 4. *Ch.* 27. that there is ſome piety requiſite to help on the
belief of ſome of them.

There are ſeveral ſorts of them, all which have this common,
that if they meet not with ſome Tree to faſten themſelves too,
they creep along the ground as Ivy doth; that their flowers are
diſplay'd after Sun-riſing, and cloſe again before it ſets; and
that they bear a delicate and very refreſhing fruit: but the
leaves, flowers, and fruits of ſome are ſo different, as to their
outward figure, that it is not to be wondred if the Authors
who treat of this Plant, imagining there had been but one
kind, agree not in their deſcriptions thereof.   The Inhabitants
of *Braſil* number ſeven kinds thereof; but in the *Caribbies* there
are but thoſe two known, which are repreſented among the
Sculps of this Chapter.

One hath very large leaves, which are divided into five leſſer leaves, whereof that in the midſt is round at the top, and
the four others pointed: its flower being fully blown is bigger then a Roſe; it is encloſ'd neer the ſtem in three little green
leaves, the body conſiſts of ſeveral other beautiful leaves,
whereof ſome are of a Sky-colour, chequer'd with little red
pricks, which have the figure of a Crown, and others are of
a purple colour: All this fair flower is encompaſs'd with an in-

K 2

finite

finite number of small waving filaments, which are as it were the beams of this little Sun among the flowers; they are enamell'd with White, Red, Blew, Carnation, and several other lively colours, which contribute an admirable grace thereto.

The other kind hath also its leaves divided into five parts as the former; but its flower, which is like a little bowl, bordered above with little white and red strings, is not so large: within it is adorned with white pointed leaves: there shoots as it were out of the heart of both these kinds of *Passion-Flowers* a small round Pillar, which hath on its chapter a button beset with three grains, somewhat like Cloves. From this Pillar there issue out also five white strings, which support little yellow knobs, like those which may be seen in the cavity of the Lillies; and these they say represent our Saviours five wounds.

These flowers, which are of a sweet scent, falling off, the button that is on the pillar grows so big, that it comes to be a fair yellow fruit, smooth, and about the bigness of an ordinary Apple. The rind of it is as thick as that of a Pomegranate, and it is full of a certain juice, very delicious to the taste, among which there is a great number of kernels, which are black, and extreamly hard. This fruit is prescrib'd as a sovereign refreshment to such as are in Fevers, and it hath been found by experience, that it hath a singular vertue to retrive lost Appetite, to comfort the vital Spirits, and to abate the heat of the Stomack. The Inhabitants of *Brasil* are very careful in the cultivation of this Plant, using it as a singular ornament for the covering of their Arbours, and other places in their Gardens; for its leaves and flowers make a very delightful shade, and they make of the fruit a cordial syrrup, which is highly esteem'd among them upon this account, that besides the properties assigned it in our description, it hath also this remarkable quality, that those who are once accustomed to use it shall never have an aversion against it. The rind of this fruit, and its flowers being preserv'd, work the same effects as the juice.

MUSK-HERB.

THere is also an Herb called the *Musk-Herb*: the stalk of it is of a considerable height, and it grows very thick and close together, as a little Briar, or Bush without prickles: its leaves are long enough, and rough; the flowers are yellow, very delightful to the eye, after the form of a Chalice, or little Bell, which afterwards becomes a button of a pretty bigness, and when it is ripe, is of a white Satin colour within, and of a Musk-colour without: the seed contained within this button is also of the same brownish colour; it hath the perfect scent

of

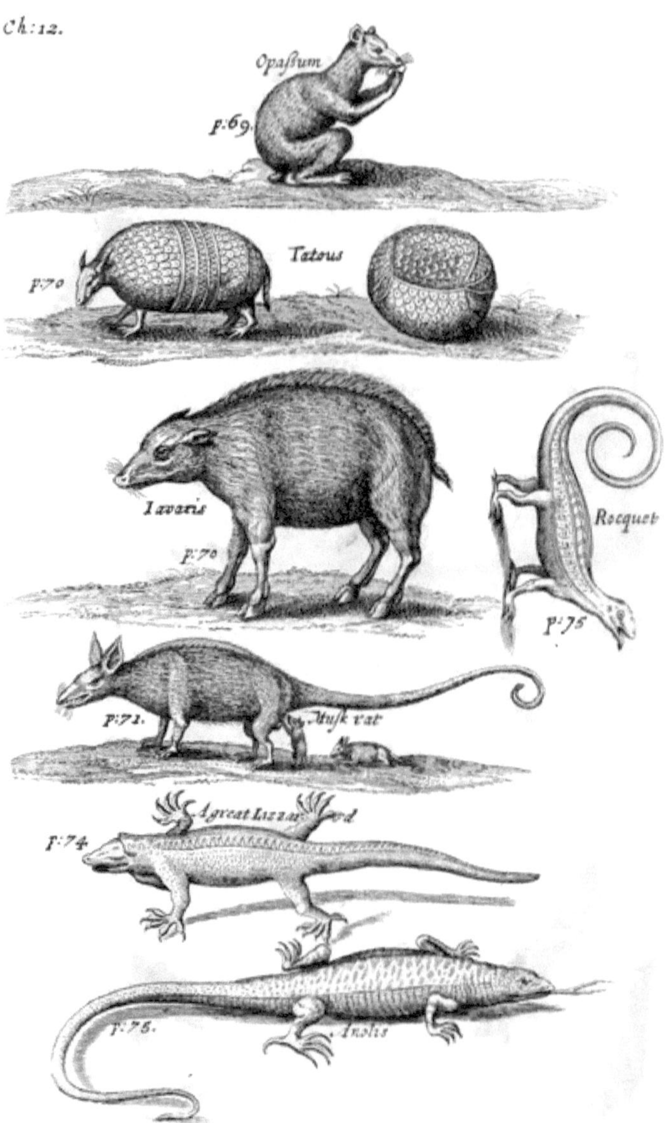
Opassum
F:69.
F:70
Tatous
Iavaris
F:70
Rocquet
P:75
P:71
Musk rat
A great Lizzard
F:74
F:75
Anolis

of Musk when it is newly gather'd.   And thence is it called
Musk-grain, and it keeps that scent a long time, provided it be
kept in a dry place, and in some vessel where it may take
no air.

In like manner, several other Herbs, several Shrubs, nay
most of those *Lienes,* or *Withies* which creep among the bushes,
and fasten for their support on the Trees growing in the *Carib-bies,* bear flowers as fair and delightful to the eye, as they are
sweet and acceptable to the nostril: insomuch that many
times as a man crosses through the Fields, he may come to
places where the Air is perfum'd all about.

CHAP. XII.

Of five kinds of four-footed Beasts found in these Islands.

BEfore the *Spaniards* and *Portuguez* had planted Colonies
in *America,* there were not in those parts any Horses,
Kine, Oxen, Sheep, Goats, Swine, or Dogs.   But for
the better convenience of their Navigations , and supply of
their Ships in case of necessity, they left some of these crea-tures in several parts of that new-found World, where they
have since multiply'd so exceedingly, that now they are more
common there then in any part of *Europe.*

Besides these Foreign kinds of Cattle, there were before in
these Islands certain sorts of four-footed beasts, such as are the
Opassum, the *Javaris,* the *Tatau,* the *Agouty,* and the *Musk Rat,*
whereof we shall here give the several descriptions.

O P A S S U M.

THe *Opassum* is the same creature which the *Brasilians* call
Carigueya, about the bigness of a Cat : it hath a sharp
Snout, the neather Jaw being shorter then the upper, as a Pigs,
the Ears long, broad, and strait, and the Tail long, Hairless
towards the extremity, and turning downwards : the Hair
on the Back is black intermix'd with grey, and under the Bel-ly, and about the Throat it is yellowish : it hath very sharp
Claws, and thence doth easily climb up Trees : he feeds on
Birds, and loves a Hen as well as the Fox does ; but for want
of prey he can make a shift to live on fruits.

What is particular in this Creature, is, that by a remarkable
difference it hath a purse or bag of its own skin, folded toge-ther under its Belly, in which it carries its young ones, which

it

it leaves upon the ground when it pleases, by opening that natural purse : when he would leave that place, he opens it again, and the young ones get in, and so he carries them with him where-ever he goes. The Female suckles them without setting them on the ground ; for her Teats lye within that purse, which on the inside hath a much softer skin then that which appears without. The Female commonly brings six young ones ; but the Male, who hath such another natural purse under his Belly, carries them in his turn to ease the Female, but cannot suckle them. These creatures are common in *Virginia*, and *New-Spain* : Nature having not thought fit to bestow on the Whale the convenience of such a bag, gave her the invention of hiding her young ones in her Throat, as *Philostratus* affirms. And the Weasil is so fond of her young ones, that out of a fear they might be taken from her, she also takes them into her mouth, and removes them from one place to another.

JAVARIS.

THere is also in some of these Islands, as at *Tabago*, a kind of wild Swine, which are to be seen in like manner in *Brasil*, and *Nicaragua* : they are in most things like the wild Boars in our Forests, but have very little fat : they have short Ears, almost no Tail, and their Navels are on their Backs : some of them are all black, others have certain white spots ; their grunting is also more hideous then that of tame Swine ; they are called *Javaris* : This Venison is of a taste good enough, but very hardly taken, in regard the Boar having a kind of vent, or hole on the Back, by which he refreshes his Lungs, is in a manner indefatigable ; and if he be forc'd to stop, and be pursued by the Dogs, he is arm'd with such sharp and cutting defensives, that he tears to pieces all those that shall set upon him.

TATOUS.

THe *Tatous*, or *Hedge-Hogs*, which also are to be seen in *Tabago*, are arm'd with a hard skaly coat, wherewith they cover and secure themselves as with armour : They have a Head and Snout like a Pig, and with the latter they turn up the ground: they have also in every Paw five very sharp Claws, which they use the more readily to thrust away the earth, and discover the roots wherewith they are fatten'd, in the night time. Some affirm, that their flesh is a very delicate meat, and that there is a small bone in their Tails which helps Deafness : It hath been confirm'd by experience, that it helps the Noise or Humming, and cures the pain of the Ear , being

thrust

thruft into it in a little **Cotton**; fome of thefe are as big as **Foxes**; but thofe which are in *Tabago* are much lefs.

When thefe creatures are purfu'd, and when they take their reft, which they commonly do in the day time, they clofe together like a bowl, and fo dextroufly get in their feet, head and ears under their hard fcales, that all parts of their body are by that natural armour fecur'd againft all the attempts of both Hunts-men and Dogs; and if they are neer fome precipice, they roll themfelves down without fear of receiving any hurt thereby. *Linfcot* relates, that in the *Eaft-Indies*, in the river of *Goa*, there was a Sea-monfter taken which was cover'd all over with fcales as hard as any Iron, and when it was touch'd it clos'd together, as it were into a ball.

AGOUTY.

THe *Agouty* is of a dark colour inclining to black, having a rough, light hair, and a little tail without any hair: it hath two teeth in the upper jaw, and as many in the neather: It holds its meat in the two fore-pawes, like a Squirrel: the cry of it is, as if it diftinctly pronounc'd the word *Coüye*. 'Tis hunted with Dogs, and its flefh, though tafting fomewhat rank, is by many preferr'd before that of Conies: When it is hunted it gets into hollow Trees, out of which it is forc'd by fmoak made, after it hath cry'd ftrangely: if it be taken young, it is eafily tamed, and when he is angred the hair on his back ftands up, and he ftrikes the ground with his hind-feet, as Conies do: He is much about the fame bignefs, but his ears are fhort and round, and his teeth as fharp as a Rafour.

MUSK-RAT.

THe *Musk-Rats* have commonly their abode in Holes, or Berries in the ground, like Conies, and they are much about their bignefs; but as to their figure it differs not from that of the great Rats which are to be feen elfewhere, fave that moft of them have the hair of their belly white, like Dormice, and that of the reft of their bodies black or tawny: there comes from them a fcent fweet as Musk, which caufes a certain dejection of fpirit, and makes fuch a ftrong perfume about their holes, that it is very eafie to find them out.

The Continent of *America* hath many kinds of four-footed Beafts, which are not to be found in any of the Iflands.

CHAP.

CHAP. XIII.

Of the Reptiles found in thefe Iflands.

WE come now to treat of the *Reptiles*, which, being naturally enemies to cold, muft needs exceedingly multiply in thefe hot Countries : Befides, the vaft Woods and the Rocks of thefe Iflands very much advance their production, in regard they afford them fecure retreats.

Several kinds of Serpents and Snakes.

THere are indeed very few venemous Beafts in the *Caribbies*, though there be many Serpents and Snakes of feveral colours and figures : There are fome nine or ten foot long, and as big as a mans arm or thigh : Nay there hath been heretofore kill'd one of thefe Snakes, which had in her belly a whole Hen, feathers and all, and above a dozen egges, the Hen having been furpriz'd as fhe was fitting : Another was found that had devour'd a Cat ; whence a guefs may be made at their bignefs.

But how prodigious foever they are, as to their bulk, yet are they not venemous in moft of thefe Countries : Nay fome Inhabitants having of them on the thatch of their houfes, which is commonly of Palm-leaves, or Sugar-Canes, drive them not thence, becaufe they force away and devour the rats. But we muft acknowledge withal, that there is an hoftility between them and the Poultry. It hath been obferv'd, that fome of them have been fo fubtle, as, having furpriz'd a Hen fitting, not to meddle with her during that time ; but affoon as the chickens are hatch'd, they devour them, and kill the Hen, if they be not able to fwallow her down whole.

There are others very fair and delightful to the eye ; for they are green all over, fave that under the belly they are of a very light grey : They are about an ell and a half in length, and fometimes two ; but, proportionably to that length, they are very fmall, as being at moft not above an inch about : They feed either on Frogs, which they find near fome brooks, or on Birds, which they furprize on the Trees, or in their nefts, when they meet with them. Accordingly, this kind of Snake is accounted noble in comparifon of the others ; for it fubfifts by its fifhing and hunting. Some of the Inhabitants, who have been us'd to fee all thefe kinds of Snakes, handle them without any fear, and carry them in their bofoms. Thofe who have travell'd into *Afia* and *Affrick* affirm, that they have there met with fomewhat of the like nature :

For

For they relate, that in *Great Tartary* there are mountains
where may be feen Serpents of a prodigious bulk, but not venemous at all, nay they are good meat: And that in the
Kingdom of *Syr* fome of thefe Creatures have been feen
playing with children, who fed them with bread. It is faid
alfo, that in the Provinces of the *Antes*, in the Kingdom of
Peru, there are dreadful Snakes between 25 and 30 foot in
length, which never hurt any body.

As to the Iflands of *Martinico* and S. *Aloufia* it is otherwife; for there fome are not dangerous at all, others are very
much fo: Thofe which are not, are bigger and longer then
the others; whence it comes, that thofe who know them
not are more afraid of them, then of fuch as fhould really
be feared: Yet do they not any harm; nay affoon as they
perceive any body, they make all the hafte they can away;
which hath occafion'd their being call'd the *fugitive snakes*.
They are alfo eafily diftinguifh'd from the others by the
black and white fpots on their backs.

Of the dangerous Snakes there are two kinds: Some are
grey on the back, and to the feeling like velvet; others are
all yellow or red, and dreadful to look upon by reafon of that
colour, though they be not more dangerous, nay haply lefs
then the former. Both kinds are great lovers of rats, as
well as thofe without venome; and when a Cott is much pe-
fter'd with rats, 'tis ftrange if there be not alfo Snakes a-
bout it. They are of different bignefs and length, and it is
conceiv'd the fhorteft are moft to be feared: Their heads are
flat and broad, their jaws extreamly wide, and arm'd with
eight teeth, and fometimes ten, whereof fome are forked like
a Crefcent, and fo fharp, that it is impoffible to imagine any
thing more: And thefe being all hollow, it is by that fmall
channel that they difperfe their poyfon, which lies in little
purfes on both fides of their throat, juft at the very roots of
their teeth: They never chew any thing they eat, but fwallow
it down whole after they have crufh'd and made it flat. Some
affirm, that if they did chew their food they would poyfon
themfelves, and that to prevent that they cover their teeth
with their gums when they take their nourifhment.

Thefe creatures are fo venemous in thofe two Iflands, that
when they have ftung any one, if there be not a prefent remedy immediately apply'd, the wound within two hours will
be incurable. All the commendation can be given them is
this, that they never fting any one if he do not touch either
them, or fomething on which they repofe themfelves.

L   LIZARDS.

LIZZARDS.

THere are also in these Islands several kinds of *Lizzards* :
The greatest and most considerable are those which some *Indians* call *Iguanas*, the *Brasilians*, *Senembi*, and our *Caribbians*, *Ouayamaca* : Being come to their full growth they are about five foot in length, measuring from the head to the extremity of the tail, which is as long as all the rest of the body ; and for their bigness they may be a foot about: their skins are of several colours according to the different soils they are bred in. Hence it is probably that the *Portuguez* have call'd them *Cameleons*, out of an imagination that they were a species of that creature. In some Islands the Females are of a light green, chequer'd with black and white spots, and the Males are grey : In others these last are black, and the Females of a light grey, intermixt with black and green : Nay in some places both Males and Females have all the little scales of their skin so glittering, and as it were studded, that seen at a distance one would think them cloth'd in rich cloth of gold or silver : They have on their backs prickles like combs, which they force up, and let down as they please, and appear less and less from the head to the end of the tail : They go on four feet, each whereof hath five claws which have very sharp nails : They run very fast, and are excellent at the climbing of Trees : But, whether it be that they love to look on men, or are of a stupid unapprehensive nature, when they are perceiv'd by the Huntsmen they patiently expect without stirring till they are shot : Nay they suffer to be put about their necks that gin with a running knot, which is fasten'd to the end of a pole that is often us'd to get them off the Trees where they rest themselves : when they are angry, a certain craw they have under their throat swells, and makes them seem the more formidable : Their jaws are very wide, their tongues thick, and they have some very sharp teeth : they will hardly let go what they have once fasten'd on with their teeth, but they are not venemous at all.

The Females lay egges about the bigness of those of Woodquists, but the shell is soft : they lay them deep enough under the sand on the Sea-side, and leave them to be hatch'd by the Sun, whence some Authors have rank'd them among the Amphibious creatures. The Savages taught the Europæans the way to take these Lizzards, and by their own examples encourag'd them to eat thereof: They are very hard to kill, insomuch that some having receiv'd three shots of a Gun, and thereby lost some part of their entrails, would not fall : And yet if a small stick be thrust into their noses, or a pin between their eyes, where there is a little hole into which the pin easily

enters,

enters, they presently dye : The *Caribbians* are very dextrous in the taking of them by a Gin with a running knot, which they cunningly get about their necks : or having overtaken them by running, they lay hold on them with one hand by the tail, which being very long gives them a good hold, and before they can turn back to bite them, they take them by the chine-piece of the neck, and then having turn'd their paws on their backs, they bind them, and so keep them alive above fifteen days without giving them any sustenance : Their flesh is white, and in some places over-laid with fat   Those who are accustomed to it think it very delicate, especially the lushious taste it naturally is of being taken away by good Spices, and some picquant sauce ; yet is it not safe to eat often thereof, because it over-dries the body, and abates somewhat of the good constitution thereof : the egges have no white, but are all yolk, which makes the Pottage they are used in as excellent as our Hens-egges might do.

Besides these greater sorts of Lizzards, there are in these Islands four others, which are much less ; and these are called, *Anolis*, *Roquets*, *Maboujats*, and *Gobe-mouches*, or *Fly-catchers*.

ANOLIS.

THe *Anolis* are very common in all the Plantations : they are about the bigness and length of the Lizzards seen in *France* ; but they have a longer head, the skin yellowish, and on their backs they have certain blew, green and grey streaks drawn from the top of the head to the end of the tail : their abode is in holes under ground, whence in the night time they make a very loud and importunate noise : In the day time they are in perpetual exercise, and they only wander about Cottages to get somewhat to subsist on.

ROQUETS.

THe *Roquets* are less then the *Anolis* : their skin is of the colour of a wither'd leaf, marked with little yellow or blackish points : they go on four feet, whereof the fore-feet are high enough : their eyes are very lively and sparkling : their heads are always lifted up, and they are so active that they perpetually leap up and down, like Birds when they would not make use of their wings : their tails are so turn'd up towards their backs that they make a circle and a half : They love to see men, and if they stay where they are they will ever and anon be staring on them : when they are a little pursu'd, they open their mouths, and put out their tongues like little Hounds.

L 2

MABOU-

MABOUJATS.

THe *Maboujats* are of several colours: those which have their abode in rotten Trees, and fenny places, as also in deep and narrow Valleys into which the Sun pierces not, are black and extreamly hideous, which no doubt occasion'd their being called by the same name the Savages give the Devil: their bigness commonly is little more then an inch, their length six or seven: the skins of them all are as if they were oyl'd.

GOBE-MOUCHES.

THose which the French call *Gobe-Mouches*, that is, in English *Fly-catchers*, from their most ordinary exercise; and the *Caribbians, Oulleouma*, are the least of all the Reptiles in these Islands: they are in figure like those the Latines call *Stelliones:* some of them seem to be cover'd with fine gold or silver Brocado; others with a mixture of green, gold, and several other delightful colours: they are so familiar that they come boldly into rooms, where they do no mischief, nay on the contrary, they clear them of Flies, and such Vermine. This employment they perform with such dexterity and nimbleness, that the sleights and designs of Hunts-men are nothing compar'd to those of this little Beast; for he sculks down, and stands as it were Sentinel on a plank, or some other thing that is higher then the floor, where he hopes the Fly will light; and perceiving his prey, he keeps his eye always fixt upon it, putting his head into as many different postures as the Fly shifts places; and standing upon his fore-feet, and gaping after it, he half opens his little wide mouth, as if he already devour'd and swallow'd it by hope: Nay though there be a noise made in the room, and some body come neer him, he is so attentive on his game that he quits not his post; and having at last found his advantage, he starts so directly on his prey, that he very seldom misses it. It is an innocent divertisement to consider with what earnestness and attention these little creatures shift for their livelihood.

Besides, they are so tame that they will come upon the Table while people are eating, and if they perceive a Fly, they will attempt the taking of it even upon their Trenchers who sit at Table, nay upon their hands or cloaths; and they are suffered to do so, because they are so smooth and cleanly, that their passing over the meat creates no aversion to those who are to eat of it: in the night time they bear a part in the Musick made by the *Anolis*, and other little Lizzards. And to propagate their species, they lay small Egges as big as Pease, which having cover'd with a little earth, they leave to be hatch'd by the Sun:

as

as soon as they are kill'd, which is very easie, by reason of their attention in pursuit of their game, they immediately lose all their lustre; the gold and azure, and all the sparkling beauty of their skin vanishes, and they become pale and earthy.

If any one of these Reptiles we have described might be accounted a kind of *Chamelion*, it should be this last named, because it easily assumes the colours of those things on which it makes its ordinary residence; for those which are seen about young Palm-trees are all green, as the leaves of that Tree are: those which frequent Orange-trees are yellow, as their fruit; nay there have been some, who having much us'd a Chamber where there was a Bed with Curtains of changeable Taffata, had afterwards an infinite number of young ones which had their bodies enamell'd with several colours suitably to the furniture of the place to which they had so often had access: some haply would have this effect attributed to the force of their little imagination; but we leave that speculation to the more addicted to such curious disquisitions.

LAND-PIKES.

THere are also in several of these Islands certain creatures which have the perfect figure, skin, and head of the Fish we call a *Pike*, and therefore may be termed the *Land-Pikes*: but, instead of Finns they have four feet, which are so weak that they can onely crawl along the ground, and wind their bodies as Snakes, or to keep to our former comparison, stir as Pikes, after they are taken out of the water. The largest are not above fifteen inches in length, and proportionably big: their skin is cover'd with little scales which shine extreamly, and are of a silver-grey colour: Some lovers of curiosities have young ones in their Closets, which they were perswaded to receive for *Salamanders*.

In the night time they make a hideous noise from under the rocks, and the bottoms of hollow places where they are lodg'd: It is more sharp and grating to the ear then that of Frogs and Toads; and they change their notes according to the variety of the places where they lurk: they are seldom seen but a little before night, and when any of them are met in the day time, their motion, which is such as we before described it, is apt to frighten the unwary beholder.

SCORPIONS *and other dangerous Reptiles.*

THere are also in these parts *Scorpions*, like those commonly seen in *France*, and other places: but they have not so dangerous a venom: they are yellow, grey, or dark-colour'd according to the different soils in which they are bred.
Some

Some who have broken up fenny places for Wells or receptacles for water, have often met with a moſt hideous kind of Lizzards: They are in length about ſix inches: the ſkin of their back is black, and beſet with ſmall grey ſcales, which by their extraordinary ſhining, a man would think were oyl'd: their bellies are alſo ſcaly, as well as their backs, but the ſkin which covers it is of a pale yellow: their heads are ſmall and picked: their mouths are wide enough, and furniſh'd with ſeveral teeth, which are extreamly ſharp: they have two little eyes, but not able to endure the light of the day, for as ſoon as they are taken out of the ground they immediately endeavour to make a hole in it with their pawes, which have each of them five hard and crooked clawes, wherewith they break the ground juſt as the Moles do, and ſo make their way whither they pleaſe: they are very deſtructive in Gardens, gnawing the roots of Trees and Plants: their biting is alſo as venemous as that of the moſt dangerous Serpent.

CHAP. XIV.

Of the Inſects commonly ſeen in the Caribbies.

NOt only the Heavens, and other vaſt, and more excellent parts of Nature declare the glory of their Almighty Maker; but even the leaſt and moſt deſpicable of his productions do alſo diſcover the work of his hands, and raiſe their minds who attentively conſider them to a grateful admiration of the greatneſs of his power, and an humble acknowledgment of his Sovereignty: Out of a perſwaſion therefore that there are ſome who delightfully ſearch into the ſecrets of Nature, and contemplate the wonders of God, who out of his inexhauſtible treaſures hath endued the moſt inconſiderable of his creatures with ſo many rich ornaments, occult qualities, and rare beauties, we ſhall beſtow this Chapter on the conſideration of certain Inſects commonly ſeen in theſe Iſlands, all which have ſome peculiar properties, as ſo many beams of glory to raiſe them from their natural lowneſs into ſome eſteem.

SNAILES.

AMong the Inſects which abundantly ſwarm in theſe hot Countries there is a kind of Snailes, called by the French *Soldats*, that is *Souldiers*, becauſe they have no ſhells proper and peculiar to themſelves, and make them not of their foam

or

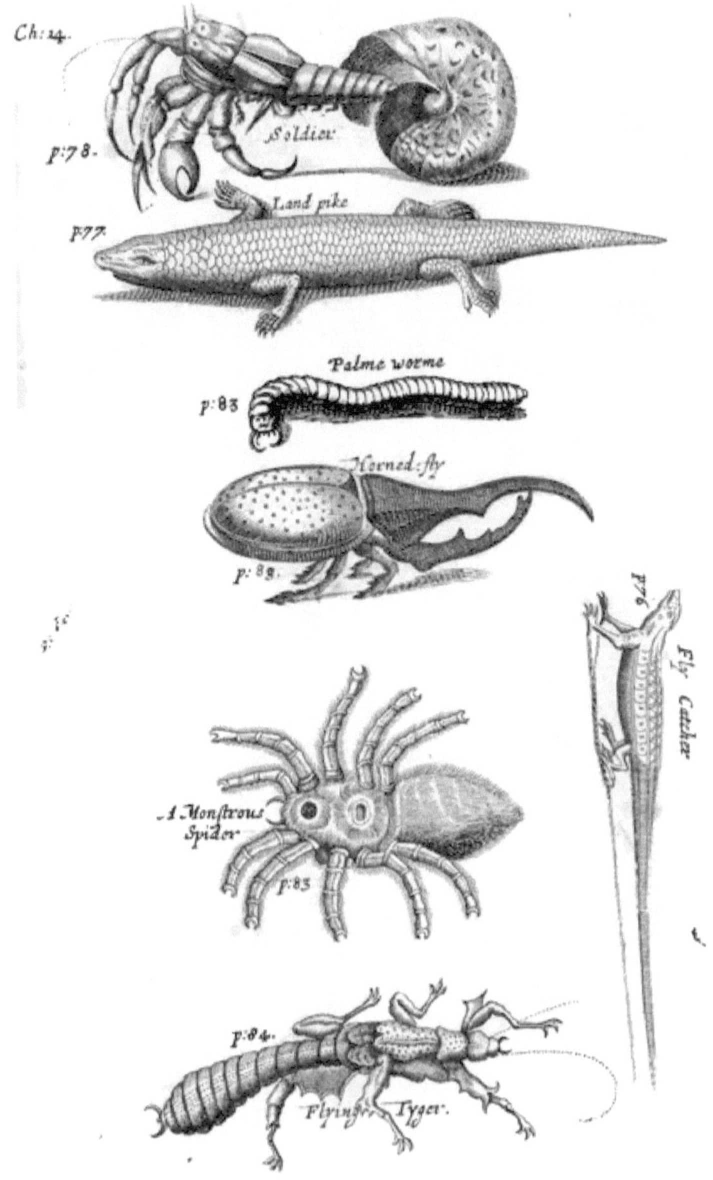

Ch: 14.
p:78.
Soldier.
Land pike
p:77.
Palme worme
p:83
Horned: fly
p:88.
Fly Catcher
p:76
A Monstrous
Spider
p:83
p:84.
Flyinge Tyger.

or ſlime, as the ordinary Snail does, but as ſoon as they are
produc'd out of ſome corrupted matter, or otherwiſe, they
have this inſtinct (to ſecure the weakneſs of their little bodies
againſt the injuries of the air, and the attempts of other Beaſts)
to ſeek out ſome empty habitation, and to take poſſeſſion of
ſuch a ſhell as they find moſt convenient for them, within
which they ſit and accommodate themſelves, as Souldiers,
who having no ſetled habitation take up their quarters in other
mens houſes, according to their neceſſities, and the then preſent poſture of their affairs.

They are commonly ſeen in the ſhells of Periwincles, or
great Sea-Snails, which they find on the ſhore, whither they are
caſt by the waves upon the death of the fiſh which had been
the firſt inhabitant thereof: but indeed theſe little Souldiers
are found in all ſorts of other ſhells caſt up by the Sea, nay
even the ſhells of the *Lieve-auts*, and ſome have took up their
quarters in the clawes of great dead Crabs. They have this
further induſtry, that as they grow bigger they ſhift ſhells according to the proportion of their bodies, and take a larger, into which they enter, quitting the former: ſo that they are of
ſeveral forms and figures, according to the diverſity of the
ſhells they poſſeſs themſelves of: It is probably of theſe *Souldi-*
ers that *Pliny* ſpeaks, under the name of a kind of ſmall Crab,
to which he attributes the ſame properties: their bodies are
very tender except their heads and clawes: they have inſtead
of a foot, and for a defenſive weapon ſome inſtrument that is
like the claw of a great Crab, wherewith they cloſe the entrance of their ſhells, and ſecure their whole body: it is all
jagged within, and it holds ſo faſt whatever it faſtens on, that
it takes away the piece with it. This Inſect marches faſter then
the common Snail, and fouls not with its foam or ſlimineſs the
place over which it hath paſs'd.

When this Souldier is taken he grows angry, and makes a
noiſe: to make him quit the habitation he hath taken up, there
needs only to ſet him neer the fire, and immediately he for-
ſakes his Quarters: if it be preſented to him to get into it
again, he goes in backwards: when there are many of them
met together with an intention at the ſame time to quit their
former lodgings, and to take up new ones, which they are all
much inclin'd to do, they enter into a great conteſtation, there
happens a ſerious engagement which is manag'd with the ſaid
claſping inſtrument, till at length the weaker is forc'd to ſub-
mit to the victorious, who preſently poſſeſſes himſelf of the
ſhell, which he afterwards peaceably enjoys as a precious
conqueſt.

Some of the Inhabitants eat of them, as the common Snails
are eaten in ſome parts among us: but they are more fit for
Phyſick then Food; for being got out of their ſhells there may
be

be extracted from them an oyl, which is excellent for the curing of cold Gouts, and is very succefsfully used to mollifie the hard and callous parts of the body.

There are befides, two other forts of fmall Snails which are very beautiful: One is flat, after the fafhion of a Scotchmans Bonnet, and of a dark colour: The other is fharp, and turned like the Vice of a Prefs, and hath fmall, red, yellow, or blew ftreaks or lines, for which they are much efteemed by the curious.

GLO-WORMES.

THere are in thefe Iflands feveral kinds of great Flies of divers figures and colours: but we muft affign the firft place to thofe which the *French* call *Mouches Lumincufes,* and we may Englifh *Glo-wormes:* Some Savages call them *Cucuyos,* and the *Caribbians* by a name not much differing from it, *Cojouyou.* This Fly is not recommendable for its beauty, or figure, as having nothing extraordinary as to either, but only for its *luminous* quality: they are of a dark colour, and about the bignefs of a Locuft: it hath two hard and ftrong wings, under which are two lefler wings very thin, which appear not but when it flies; and it is then alfo it may be obferv'd that under thofe lefler wings there is a brightnefs, like that of a Candle, which enlightens all about it: befides, the eyes of this Infect are fo luminous, that be it ever fo dark, it flies any where in the night, which is the time that this glittering light may be feen.

It makes no noife flying, and lives only on flowers which it gathers off the Trees. Being taken between ones fingers, it is fo fmooth and flippery, that by the little endeavours it makes to recover its liberty, it infenfibly gets away: Being kept in captivity it conceals all the light it hath under the wings, and communicates only that of its eyes, but even that very weakly in comparifon of the brightnefs it fheds being at liberty: it hath no fting, nor any claw for its defence: The *Indians* are glad to have of them in their houfes, for they ferve them inftead of Lamps: but indeed of their own accord, in the night time, they come into thofe rooms which are not kept too clofe.

There are in thefe Iflands certain *fhining Worms,* which alfo flie. All parts of *Italy,* and all the other parts of the *Levant,* are alfo full of them.

But how famous foever thefe little Stars of the Eaft may be, yet are they but fmall fparkles in comparifon of the great fire which thefe flying Torches of *America* caft forth: For they do not only guide the Traveller by fhewing him his way in the night, but with the affiftance of this light a man may eafily

write,

write, and read the ſmalleſt Print that may be. A *Spaniſh* Hiſtorian relates, that the Indians of *Hiſpaniola*, having theſe Flies faſten'd to their hands and feet, they ſerv'd them inſtead of Torches to go a hunting in the night time : it is affirmed alſo by others, that ſome other Indians extract that luminous liquor which theſe Flies have in their eyes and under their wings, and that they rub their faces and breaſts therewith in their nocturnal meetings, which makes them appear in the dark to the beholders, as if they were covered with flames, and like dreadful apparitions.

Theſe Flies are eaſily taken in the night time ; and that is done by turning a lighted ſtick in the air : For as ſoon as thoſe which at the cloſe of the evening are ready to come out of the woods perceive that fire, imagining it to be one of their companions, they immediately flye to the place where that light appears to them, and ſo they may be either ſtruck down with a Hat, or flying of themſelves againſt the lighted ſtick, they fall to the ground, not knowing where they are.

Nor will it be amiſs to inſert in this place what a learned and curious French Gentleman, one Monſ. *du Montel*, from whoſe generous liberality came ſeveral other remarks which enrich this Hiſtory, lately writ to a friend of his concerning theſe Flies.

    " Being in the Iſland of *Hiſpaniola*, (ſaith he) I have often at
" the beginning of the night walk'd about the little Huts we
" had ſet up for our abode there while our Ship was repairing,
" to conſider how that the Air was in ſome places enlightned by
" thoſe little wandring Stars : But the moſt pleaſant ſight of all
" was, when they came neer thoſe great Trees which bear a
" kind of Figs, and were not far from our Huts ; for ſometimes
" they flew about them, ſometimes they would be within the
" thick boughs, which for a time obſcur'd and eclips'd thoſe lit-
" tle Luminaries ; yet ſo as that their beams might ever and
" anon be ſeen to break through, though weakly, the inter-
" poſed leaves: thoſe pretty interruptions of light came to us
" ſometimes obliquely, ſometimes in a ſtraight line, and per-
" pendicularly : Afterwards thoſe glittering Flies extricating
" themſelves out of the obſcurity of thoſe Trees, and coming
" neerer us, we had our pleaſure heightned by ſeeing them on
" the adjacent Orange-trees, which they ſeem'd to ſet a fire,
" gilding thoſe beautiful fruits, enamelling their flowers, and
" giving ſuch a luſtre to their leaves, that their naturally de-
" lightful verdure was extreamly encreas'd by the pleaſant
" combination of ſo many little lights. I wiſh'd my ſelf at
" that time the Art of Painting or Drawing, that I might re-
" preſent a night enlightned, and as it were turn'd into day by
" ſo many fires, and ſo pleaſant and luminous a piece of Land-
" ſkip. Think it not much that I am ſo long about the ſtory of

M

" a

" a Fly, since *Du Bartas* sometime gave it a place among the
" Birds, and in the fifth Day of his first Week speaks very nobly
" of it in these terms :

New-Spain's Cucuyo *in his forehead brings*
Two burning Lamps, two underneath his wings ;
Whose shining rays serve oft in darkest night,
Th' Embroiderer's hand in royal works to light :
Th' ingenious Turner with a wakeful eye
To polish fair his purest Ivory :
Th' Usurer to count his glist'ring Treasures :
The learned Scribe to limne his golden measures.

" If five or six of these Flies were put into a vessel of fine Cry-
" stal, no doubt, the light of them would be answerable to the
" Poets description, and be a living and incomparable Torch.
" But it is to be noted, that these Flies shine not at all when
" once they are dead, their light being extinguish'd with their
" lives.

PHALANGES.

TO come to the other kinds of great Flies to be seen in
these Islands, and which some call *Phalanges,* besides the
Cucuyos there are some that be much bigger, and of a strange
figure : There are some have two snouts like that of an Elephant, one turning upwards, the other downwards : Some
others have three horns, one rising out of the back, and the
other two out of the head : The rest of their body, as also
their horns, is black, and shines like Jet. There are some have
one great horn about four inches in length, much after the fashion of a Wood-cocks bill, very smooth on the upper side,
and covered with a certain downiness on the lower, which
horn rising out of their back reaches in a direct line to the
head, on which there is another horn, like that of the horned
Beetle, which is as black as Ebony, and transparent as glass :
The whole body is of the colour of a wither'd leaf, smooth,
and flourished like Damask : their head and mouth are like
those of an Ape ; they have two large, yellow, and firm eyes,
a wide mouth and teeth like a little Saw. Hear what account
our curious Traveller gives of it.
" I have seen, saith he, one kind of these great Flies, which
" I thought extreamly beautiful : It was about three inches in
" length : the head of it was azure, not unlike that of a Grass-
" hopper, save that the two eyes were as green as an Emerald,
" and encompass'd by a small white streak : the upper side of
" the wings was of a bright violet colour, damask'd with se-
" veral compartiments of carnation, heightned by a small na-
"tural

" tural thread of silver : the compartiments were dispos'd with
" such an exact observance of Symmetry, that a man would
" think that the Compass and the Pencil had in the doing of it
" employ'd all the rules of Perspective , and the Shadows of
" Painting : The neather part of the body was of the same co-
" lour with the head, save that there were six black feet neatly
" bending towards the belly : When the wings, which were hard
" and solid, were spread abroad, there might be seen two other
" lesser wings which were thinner then any silk, and as red as
" Scarlet. This kind of Fly I saw in the Island of *S. Croix*, in
" the custody of an *English* Gentleman , and I immediately
" writ down this description of it. I thought at first it had
" been artificial, because of that lively Carnation colour, and
" the string of silver ; but having taken it into my hands, I
" acknowledg'd that Nature must certainly have been in an
" excellent good humor, and had a mind to divert her self,
" when she bestow'd such sumptuous robes on that little Queen
" among the Insects.

PALMER-WORM:

THere is a Worm, or Vermine in English called a *Palmer*,
in *French Millepied*, (thousand footed) from the almost
infinite multitude of its feet, which are as brittles under his body, and help him to creep along the ground with incredible
swiftness, especially when he finds himself pursu'd : This kind
of Insect in the *Caribbies* is about six inches long : The upper
part of his body is cover'd all over with swarthy scales, which
are hard and joynted one within another, like the Tiles of a
House : but what's dangerous in this creature, is, that he hath
a kind of claws both in his head and tail , wherewith he
twitches so home, and so poysons the place wounded, that for
the space of four and twenty hours, and sometimes longer, the
party hurt feels a very sharp pain.

SPIDERS.

THere are in several of the Islands certain great Spiders,
which some have ranked among the *Phalanges*, by reason
of their monstrous figure and bigness, which is so great, that
when their legs are spread abroad they take up a larger place
then the Palm of a mans hand : their whole body consists of
two parts, whereof one is flat, and the other of a round figure,
smaller at one end, like a Pigeons egge : They have all of
them a hole on their back, which is, as it were, their Navel :
their mouth cannot easily be discern'd, because it is in a manner
cover'd over with hair, which commonly is of a light grey, but
sometimes intermixt with red : it is armed with two sharp tushes

which are of a folid matter, and of a black colour, fo fmooth
and fhining, that fome curious perfons have them fet in gold for
Tooth-picks , and are highly efteemed by thofe who know
they are endued with a vertue to preferve from pain and all
corruption thofe parts that have been rubbed therewith.

When thefe Spiders are grown old they are covered all over
with a fwarthy Down, which is as foft and as clofe as Velvet:
their body is fupported by ten feet, which are a little hairy on
the fides, and have **below** certain fmall points like briftles,
which help them to faften more eafily on thofe places up which
they would climb: All thefe feet iffue out of the fore-part of
the Infect, having each of them four joynts, and at the ends
they are armed with a black and hard horn, which is divided
into two parts like a fork.

They every year fhift off their old fkin as the Serpents do,
as alfo the two tufhes which ferve them for teeth, and are their
defenfive arms; thofe who meet with thefe precious *exuviæ*
may therein obferve the perfect figure of their body, fuch as it
is reprefented among the Sculps of this Chapter.

Their eyes are very little; and lye fo deep in their heads that
they feem to be only two fmall points: they feed on Flies and
fuch vermine, and it hath been obferv'd, that in fome places their
Webs are fo ftrong, that the little Birds caught in them have
had much ado to get away: the fame thing is affirmed of the
Spiders which are found in the *Bermudez,* Iflands inhabited
by the Englifh: It is probable they are of the fame kind.

FLYING-TYGER.

THere is another Infect called by fome the *Flying-Tyger,*
becaufe its body is chequer'd with fpots of feveral colours, as the Tyger is: It is about the bignefs of the horned
Beetle: The head is fharp, and hath two great eyes as green
and fparkling as an Emerald: his mouth is arm'd with two hard
hooks extreamly fharp, with which he holds faft his prey,
while he gets out the fubftance of it: The whole body is cover'd with a hard and fwarthy cruftinefs, which ferves him for
armor: Under his wings, which are alfo of a folid matter,
there are four leffer wings which are as thin as any filk: It hath
fix legs, each whereof hath three joynts, and they are briftled
with certain little prickles: In the day time he is continually
catching other Infects; and in the night he fits on the Trees,
whence he makes a noife like that of the *Cigales.*

BEES, *and fome other Infects.*

THe *Bees* which are in the Iflands, differ not much from
thofe of the Southern part of *America,* but both kinds
are

American Swallow
p: 89.
Eagle
p: 93.
Flammant
p.88.
The Colibry
or
Humming bird.
p: 93
Craw-fowle
p: 87
Caat
p: 88.
Pintado
p: 89.

are leſs then thoſe of *Europe* : Some are grey, others of a dark colour, or blewiſh : theſe laſt make moſt wax , and afford the beſt hony : they all have their abode in the clefts of rocks, and hollow Trees : their wax is ſoft, and ſo black that no Artifice can whiten it : but in requital their hony is much whiter, ſweeter, and clearer then any we have in theſe Countries : They may be handled without any danger, for they have in a manner no ſtings.

There are alſo in theſe Iſlands *horned Beetles* or *Bull-flies,* and an infinite number of *Graſſ-hoppers,* and *Butter-flies,* the ſight whereof very much delights the eye. There are withall both on the ground, and in the air, ſeveral very troubleſome and dangerous Inſects, which extreamly annoy the Inhabitants : But of theſe, and ſome other inconveniences, we ſhall give an account in the two laſt Chapters of this firſt Book.

CHAP. XV.

Of the more conſiderable kinds of Birds which may be ſeen in the Caribbies.

ALL the works of God ſpeak the magnificence of the Worker, the diſpoſal of them declares his wiſdom, the Earth is full of his productions : but we muſt acknowledg that of all the Creatures, not endued with any thing above a ſenſitive life, the Birds do more loudly then any publiſh his goodneſs and Providence, and by the ſweet harmony of their ſinging, the activity of their flight, and by the lively colours and beauty of their feathers excite us to praiſe, and glorifie that Sovereign Majeſty which hath ſo advantageouſly adorn'd and embelliſh'd them with ſo many rare perfections. Having therefore in the precedent Chapters treated of the *Trees , Plants , Herbs , Four-footed Beaſts , Reptiles* and *Inſects* which the *Caribby* Iſlands do plentifully produce to furniſh the *Earth,* we ſhall in this Chapter deſcribe the rare *Birds* which inhabit the *Air* of theſe pleaſant Countries, and enrich the perpetual Verdure of ſo many precious Trees wherewith they are crowned.

FREGATES.

AS ſoon as any Ships come neer theſe Iſlands, ſeveral Birds which frequent the Sea come to them, as if they had been ſent to enquire whence they came : When the Sea-men perceive theſe Viſitants they are ſatisfi'd that it will not be long

ere

ere they shall see Land: Yet are they not to flatter themselves with that hope till they see them coming in great Companies; for there is one kind of them which many times flye above two hundred leagues from Land.

The *French* have bestow'd on them the name of *Fregates, Frigots,* because of the continuance and lightness of their flight. Their body is about the bigness of a wild Drake's; but their wings are very much larger, and they make their way through the air with such swiftness, that in a very short time they will be out of sight: There are several kinds as to their feathers; for some are all black, others all grey, save only the belly and wings, in which there are some white feathers: They are excellent good at fishing; and when they perceive a fish lying even with the water, they fail not, yet as it were only sporting themselves, to seise it, and immediately devour it: They have a strange dexterity in taking the *flying Fishes*; for as soon as they perceive that that delicate prey makes the water to rise and bubble a little, and is just upon the taking of its flight, to avoid the cruel pursuits of its Sea-enemies, they place themselves so directly on that side on which they should make their sally, that as soon as they are out of the water they receive them into their Beaks, or Claws: So these innocent and unfortunate fishes, to avoid the teeth of one enemy, many times fall into the claws of another who gives them no better quarter.

The Rocks which are in the Sea, and the little un-inhabited Islands are the places where these Birds make their abode and their nests: The meat of them is not much esteem'd; but their fat is carefully kept, it having been found by experience that it helpeth the Palsey, and all sorts of cold Gouts.

FAUVES.

THe Birds which the French call *Fauves,* that is, *Fallow,* by reason of the colour of their back, are white under the belly: they are about the bigness of the *Poule d'eau,* but for the most part so lean that they are valued only for their feathers: their feet are like those of Wild-Ducks, and their beaks sharp as those of Wood-cocks: they live on small fishes, as the *Frigots* do; but they are the most stupid of any Sea or Land-Fowl in the Islands; for, whether it be that they are soon weary of flying, or take the Ships for moving rocks, as soon as they perceive any one, especially if it be neer night, they immediately light in them, and suffer themselves to be taken without any trouble.

HERONS,

HERONS, *and several other Sea and River-Fowl.*

THere are seen neer these Islands, and sometimes at a great distance from them in the Sea, certain Birds perfectly white, whose beaks and feet are as red as Coral; they are somewhat bigger then Crows: they are conceiv'd to be a kind of Herons, because their tails consist of two long and precious feathers, by which they are distinguish'd from all other Birds frequenting the Sea.

Among the Birds frequenting Rivers and Ponds there are found in these Countries *Plovers*, *Duckers*, *Moore-hens*, or *Coots*, *Wild-Ducks*, and *Wild Geese*; as also a kind of *Ducks*, which having the whole body as white as snow, have their beaks and feet as black as may be; and a kind of *Herons* of an admirable whiteness, about the bigness of a Pigeon, but beaked like a Wood-cock: they live on fish, and delight in sandy places, and on rocks: They are much sought after for that precious Plume of fine Feathers, soft as any silk, which is had from them: but inasmuch as all these are common in other places, we may forbear the descriptions thereof.

CRAW-FOWL.

THere is in all these Islands a large Bird which lives only on fish: it is about the bigness of a great Duck, and the feathers are of an Ash-colour, and hideous to the eye: it hath a long and flat beak, a great head, small eyes deep set in his head, and a neck short enough, under which hangs a kind of craw or bag so big that it may contain a great pale of water: From which description we may call him the *Craw-Fowl*, as the *French* have properly termed him, *Grand-gosier:* These Birds are commonly found upon Trees on the Sea-side, where they lye in ambush to discover their prey; for as soon as they perceive a fish, as it were between wind and water, so as that they have them at advantages, they fall upon it, and seise it: they will swallow down great fishes whole: they are also so attentive on their fishing, that having their eye continually fixt on the Sea whence they expect their prey, they are easily shot, and become it themselves to others: they are a stupid and melancholy kind of Bird, suitably to their employment: they are so excellently well sighted, that they discover fish at a great distance in the Sea, and above a fathom under water; but they stay till they become up almost even with it before they offer at them: their flesh is not to be eaten.

COOT.

COOT.

THe Iſlands called the *Virgins* are of the *Caribbies* the beſt furniſhed with abundance of Sea and Land-Fowl: for beſides the forementioned, whereof they have good ſtore, there is a kind of *Coot*, or *Moor-hen*, admirable for the beauty of its feathers: they are no bigger then Pigeons, but have a much longer beak of a yellow colour, are higher ſet, and their legs and feet are of a bright red: the feathers of the back, wings and tail are of a ſhining carnation intermixt with green and black, which ſerves for a foil to ſet off the beauty of the other colours: Under the wings and on the belly their feathers are of a golden yellow: their neck and breaſts are adorned with a delightful mixture of all the colours they have about their bodies; and their head, which is very ſmall, and beſet with two little ſparkling eyes, is crowned with a tuft of ſeveral little feathers of ſeveral pleaſant colours.

FLAMMANS.

THe Ponds and fenny places which are not much frequented are the retreats of ſeveral great and beautiful Birds about the bigneſs of wild Geeſe, and of the ſame figure with thoſe which the Dutch call *Lepelaer*, from the form of their beak, which hath the reſemblance of a *ſpoon*: They have long necks, and their legs are of ſuch length, that their bodies are about three foot from the ground: But they differ as to colour, inaſmuch as when they are young their feathers are white, as they grow it becomes of a murrey colour, and when they are old of a bright carnation; from which colour the French took occaſion to call them *Flammans*: There are of theſe Birds ſeen neer *Montpelier* in *France*, which have the lower part of their body and under their wings of a carnation colour, the upper part black: there are in like manner in theſe Iſlands ſome that have a mixture of black and white feathers in their wings.

They are ſeldom ſeen but in great companies, and their hearing and ſmelling is ſo perfect, that they ſmell the Huntsmen and Fire-arms at a great diſtance: To avoid all ſurpriſes they pitch in open places, and in the midſt of Fens, whence they may at a great diſtance perceive their enemies; and there is always one of the party upon the guard while the reſt are ſearching in the waters for their livelihood; and as ſoon as he hears the leaſt noiſe, or perceives a man, he takes his flight, and gives a cry for a ſignal to the reſt to follow him: when the Hunts-men who frequent *Hiſpaniola* would kill ſome of theſe Birds, which are there very common, they take the wind of

them,

them, that the ſmell of the powder may not eaſily be carry'd
to them, then they cover themſelves with an Ox-hide, and
creep on their hands and feet till they come to a place whence
they may be ſure to kill. By this ſleight theſe Birds, who
are accuſtomed to ſee the wild Oxen that come out of the
Mountains to the watering-places below, become the prey of
the Huntſ-men. They are commonly fat, and a delicate
meat: Their ſkins are kept, which are cover'd with a ſoft
down, to be put to the ſame uſes as thoſe of Swans and
Vultures.

SWALLOW of America.

SOme years ſince there was brought to a curious Perſon
living at *Rochel* a Bird about the bigneſs of a Swallow, and
like it, ſaving that the two great feathers of the tail were a
little ſhorter, and the beak turn'd downwards like a Parrot's,
and the feet like a Duck's: It was black, ſave only that under the belly there was a little white like our Swallows; in
fine it was ſo like them, that it may well be called the *Swallow of America.* We have aſſign'd it a place among the Sea
and River-fowl, inaſmuch as its feet diſcover its ſubſiſtence by
the waters. And in regard it is ſo rare a Bird that no Author
that we know of hath ſpoken of it, we thought fit to give a
Sculp of it, the draught whereof was taken from the living
Bird.

LAND-FOWL.

BEſides all theſe Birds, which have their ſubſiſtence out of
the Sea, Rivers and Ponds, there are in theſe Iſlands a-
bundance of Partridges, Turtles, Ravens, and Wood-quiſts,
which make a ſtrange noiſe in the Woods: There are alſo
three ſorts of Hens; ſome, ordinary Hens, ſuch as are in theſe
parts; others, like Turkies; others, a kind of Pheaſants, which
are called *Pintadoes,* becauſe they are as it were painted with
colours, and have about them ſmall points like ſo many eyes
on a dark ground-work.

There are alſo *Black-birds, Feldivars, Thruſhes,* and *Horto-
lans,* in a manner like thoſe of the ſame name among us.

As to the other Birds which are peculiar to the Foreſts of
the *Caribbies,* there are ſo many kinds, and thoſe ſo richly a-
dorned, that it muſt be acknowledg'd, that if they are not
comparable to thoſe of *Europe,* as to their ſinging, they very
much excell them in the bravery of their feathers; as will appear by the deſcriptions we ſhall make of ſome of the more
conſiderable.

N

Arras.

ARRAS.

THe *Arras* are a kind of Birds extremely beautiful, about the bigness of a *Pheasant*, but as to the figure of the body they are like *Parrots*: They have all heads big enough, sprightly and stedfast eyes, crooked beaks, and a long tail consisting of very fine feathers of several colours, according to the difference of the Islands where they are bred. There are some have their heads, the upper part of the neck, and the back, of a bright sky-colour, the belly, the lower part of the neck, and the wings of a pale yellow, and the tail all red : Others have almost all the body of a flame-colour, save that they have in their wings some feathers which are yellow, azure, and red. There are yet others have all their parts diversify'd with a mixture of red, white, blew, green and black, that is, five lively colours, making a delightful enamell : They commonly flye in companies : A man would think them very daring and confident; for they are not startled at the discharging of guns, and if the first shot hath not hurt them, they will continue in the same place for a second : but this confidence is attributed rather to a natural stupidity then courage. They are easily tam'd, and may be taught to speak, but their tongues are too thick to do it so plainly as the other kinds of Parrots, to wit the *Canides*, and ordinary sort of Parrots, call'd by the French *Perriques*. They are such enemies to cold, that they are hardly brought over Sea alive.

CANIDES.

THe *Canides* are much about the same bigness with the precedent, but of a much more beautiful plumage, and therefore the more esteem'd. Monsieur *du Montell*, who hath made many Voyages into *America*, and visited all the Islands, and saw one of them in that of *Coraßao*, gives us this account of it. "It deserves to be numbred, *saith he,* among the most "beautiful Birds in the world. I took so particular notice of "it, having had of them in my hands many times, that I have "the Idæas of it still fresh in my memory. Under the belly, "wings, and neck, it was of a waving Aurora-colour, the back "and one half of the wings of a very bright sky-colour, the "tail and greater feathers of the wings were mixt with a "sparkling carnation, diversify'd with a sky-colour, as upon "the back a grass-green and a shining black, which very much "added to the gold and azure of the other plumage : But the "most beautiful part was the head, cover'd with a murrey "down, checquer'd with green, yellow, and a pale blew, which "reach'd down wavingly to the back : The eye-lids were
white,

" white, and the apple of the eye yellow and red as a Ruby ſet
" in Gold : it had upon the head a certain tuft or cap of fea-
" thers of a Vermilion red, ſparking like a lighted coal, which
" was encompaſs'd by ſeveral other leſſer feathers of a pearl
" colour.

" If it were recommendable for all theſe extraordinary or-
" naments, it was much more for its familiarity and innocency ;
" for though it had a crooked beak, and that the claws with
" which he held his meat and brought it to his beak were ſo
" ſharp as to take away whatever it faſtened on, yet was it ſo
" tame as to play with little Children and never hurt them ;
" and when one took him into his hand, he ſo contracted his
" claws, that the ſharpneſs of them could not be felt : He had
" this quality of a dog, that he would lick with his ſhort and
" thick tongue thoſe who made much of him and gave him
" ſomething he liked, put his head to their cheeks to kiſs and
" careſs them, and expreſſing his acknowledgments by a thou-
" ſand pretty inſinuations, he would ſuffer himſelf to be put
" into what poſture one would, and took a certain pleaſure in
" diverting thoſe he thought his friends : But as he was mild
" and tractable to thoſe who were kind to him, ſo was he as miſ-
" chievous and irreconcileable to ſuch as had injur'd him, and
" he could diſtinguiſh them from others, and make them feel the
" ſharpneſs of his beak and claws.

" He ſpoke the *Dutch*, *Spaniſh* and *Indian* Language, and in
" the laſt he ſung Airs as a natural *Indian* : He alſo imitated
" the cries of all ſorts of Poultry and other creatures about the
" houſe : he call'd all his friends by their names and ſirnames,
" flew to them as ſoon as he ſaw them, eſpecially when he was
" hungry : If they had been abſent, and that he had not ſeen
" them a long time, he expreſs'd his joy at their return by cer-
" tain merry notes : when he had ſported himſelf till they
" were weary of him, he went away, and perch'd himſelf on
" the top of the houſe, and there he talk'd, ſung, and play'd a
" thouſand tricks, laying his feathers in order, and dreſſing
" and cleaning himſelf with his beak : He was eaſily kept ; for
" not only the bread commonly uſed in that Iſland, but all the
" fruits and roots growing there, were his ordinary food ; and
" when he had more given him then he needed, he carefully
" laid up the remainder under the leaves wherewith the houſe
" was covered, and took it when he had need. In a word, I
" never ſaw a more loving or more amiable Bird : 'Twas a Pre-
" ſent for any Prince if he could have been brought over the
" Sea. This Bird had been brought from the *Caribby* Iſlands
" to Monſ. *Rodenborck* then Governour of the Fort and Dutch
" Colony, which is in the Iſland of *Coraſſao*.

PARROTS.

IN all these Islands almost there are *Parrots*, which the Indi-ans in their Language call *Koulehuec*, and they are seen in companies like Starelings: The Hunts-men rank them among the Wild-fowl, and think not their pains and powder ill spent to kill them; for they are as good and as fat as any Pullet, especially when they are young, and have corn and fruits to feed upon: their bigness and plumage differs according to the difference of the Islands, insomuch that the ancient Inhabi-tants know by their bulk and feathers what places they were bred in.

There is an admirable kind of them in one of the Islands called the *Virgins*: they are no bigger then that Bird which the Latines call *Upupa*, the English a *Whoope*, and almost of the same figure: But their feathers are of such a strange diversity of colours, as extreamly pleases the eye: they are apt to speak very distinctly, and imitate whatever they hear.

PARAQUITOES.

THe *Paraquitoes* are a small kind of Parrots, no bigger then *Black-birds*, nay some exceed not the bulk of a *Sparrow*: They are all green, save that under the belly and the extremities of the wings and tails they are a little yellow-ish: they are taught to speak and whistle, but retain somwhat of their wildness; for they will bite hard if they be angred: If they can get loose they will into the Woods, where they starve; for being taken young and kept in Cages where they have their meat made ready for them, they cannot pitch on those Trees which bear food fit for them.

TREMBLO.

IN some Islands, especially *Gardeloupe*, there is a little Bird called *Tremblo* from its perpetual trembling, or shaking of the wings, which it a little opens: it is about the bigness of a Quail, the feathers of a darker grey then the Lark.

SPARROW of America.

THe Islands of *Tabago* and *Barboudos*, being the more Sou-therly of all the *Caribbies*, are furnished with several sorts of beautiful Birds not to be found in the more Northerly: Among the rest there is one no bigger then a *Sparrow* is very remarkable for the beauty of its plumage; for his head, neck and back are of so bright and sparkling a red, that when a man hath

hath him faft in his hand, and fhews only his neck or back, he might be taken even at a fmall diftance for a lighted coal: Under the wings and belly he is of Sky-colour, and the feathers of the wings and tail are of a dark red, chequer'd with little white points di'pos'd at an equal diftance one from another, which have the figure of the apple of his eye: he hath alfo the beak and note of the Sparrow, and therefore we thought fit to call him the *Sparrow of America*.

EAGLE *of* Orinoca.

THere croffes over from the Continent a kind of large Bird, which may be ranked among the chiefeft of the Birds of Prey that are in the *Caribbies*: The firft Inhabitants of *Tabago* call'd him the *Eagle of Orinoca*, becaufe he is about the bignefs, and differs not much in figure from the Eagle, and that this Bird, who is but a Paffenger in that Ifland, is commonly feen neer the great River of *Orinoca*, in the Southerly part of *America*: All his feathers are of a iight grey marked with black fpots, fave that the extremities of his wings and tail are yellow: he hath a quick and piercing fight: his wings are very long, his flight fteady and fwift, confidering the weight of his body: he feeds on other Birds, on which he furioufly faftens his tallons, and having mafter'd them he tears them in pieces, and devours them: yet doth he fhew fo much generofity that he never fets upon the weaker fort, and fuch as are not able to defend themfelves; but he engages only againft the *Arras*, the *Parrots*, and all thofe which as himfelf are armed with crooked beaks, and fharp tallons: Nay it hath been obferv'd, that he falls not on his game while it is on the ground, or lodg'd in a Tree, but ftays till it hath taken its flight, that he may engage it in the open air with equal advantage.

MANSFENY.

THe *Manffeny* is alfo a kind of fmall Eagle, which, as the other, lives by prey, but hath not the courage of the forementioned; for his hoftility is only againft Wood-Quifts, Doves, Chickens, and other leffer Birds, which are not able to oppofe him.

There are moreover in thefe Iflands abundance of other Birds of different kinds, whereof moft have yet no names among the foreign Inhabitants of thofe parts.

COLIBRY.

WE will conclude this ftory of the *Caribbian* Fowl, with an account of the *Colibry*, or as it is otherwife commonly

monly called by English Writers the *Humming-Bird*, a Bird admirable for its beauty, bulk, sweet scent, and manner of life; for being the least of all Birds, he gloriously confirmes the saying of *Pliny*, that, *Natura nusquam magis quàm in minimis tota est:* Nature is ever greatest in its least productions. Some of these Birds are no bigger bodied then some of the greater sorts of Flies: Some are of so beautiful a plumage, the neck, wings and back represent the Rain-bow, which the Ancients call'd *Iris*, the Daughter of Admiration: There are others have such a bright red under their neck, that at a distance one would think it were a Carbuncle: The belly and under the wings are of a gilt-yellow, the thighs as green as an Emerald, the feet and beak as black as polish'd Ebony, and the two little eyes are two Diamonds set in an oval of the colour of burnish'd steel: The head is of a grass-green, which gives it such a lustre, that it looks as if it were gilt: The Male hath a little tuft, in which may be seen all the colours which enamel that little body, the miracle of the feather'd Commonwealth, and one of the rarest productions of Nature: He lets fall and raises up when he pleases that little crest of feathers wherewith the Author of Nature hath so richly crowned him, nay all his plumage is more beautiful and shining then that of the Female.

If this Bird be miraculous as to his bulk and plumage, he is no less as to the activity of his flight, which is such, that proportionably the greatest Birds make not their way through the air with so much force, and make not so loud a noise as this little *Colibry* does by the agitation of wings; for a man would think it a little whirle-wind rais'd of a sudden in the air, and blowing in his ears: And in regard he takes a pleasure to flye neer those who pass by, he sometimes by his sudden surprisal frightens those who hear him before they see him.

He lives only on the Dew which he sucks from the Flowers of Trees with his tongue, which is much longer then his beak, and hollow as a small reed, and about the bigness of a small needle: He is very seldom seen on the ground, nor yet standing on the Trees, but suspended in the air, neer the Tree whence he hath his nourishment: He is born up by a gentle agitation of his wings, and in the mean time he draws to him the dew which stays longest at the bottom of the flowers half-blown: 'Tis pleasant to look on him in that posture: For spreading abroad his little crest, a man would think he had on his head a crown of Rubies, and all sorts of precious stones; and the Sun adding somewhat to the natural lustre of his plumage makes him look as if he were a composition of precious stones animated, and flying in the air: In those places where there are most Cotton-trees is commonly the greatest store of *Colibris*.

Though

Though his plumage loſe much of its beauty when he is dead, yet is there ſo much left, that ſome Ladies have worn them for Pendants : Nay ſome have imagined they became them better then any other.

This miraculous Bird is not only extreamly delightful as to his colours, but there is one kind of it which having recreated the eye, ſatisfies alſo the noſtril by the ſweetneſs of his ſcent, which is like that of the fineſt Muſk and Amber.

He commonly makes his neſt under a ſmall branch of ſome Orange-tree, or Cotton-tree, and as it muſt be proportionable to the ſmallneſs of his bulk, he ſo covers it among the leaves, and ſo induſtriouſly ſecures it againſt the injuries of the weather, that it is in a manner imperceptible : he is ſuch an excellent Architect, that to prevent his being expos'd to the Eaſterly and Northerly Winds, which are the ordinary winds in thoſe parts, he places his neſt towards the South : It conſiſts on the out-ſide of little ſtrings taken from a Plant called *Pite*, and wherewith the Indians make their cordage : Theſe little ſtrings or filaments are as ſmall as a mans hair, but much ſtronger : He ties them and weaves them one into another ſo cloſely about the little forked branch which he hath choſen for the perpetuation of his ſpecies, that the neſt being thus among the leaves, and hanging under the branch, is, as we ſaid before, both out of ſight and out of danger : Having made it ſtrong and fortifi'd it on the out-ſide with theſe filaments, and by ſome little bits of bark and ſmall herbs interlaced one within another by a miraculous artifice, he furniſhes it within with the fineſt Cotton, and the Down of certain little feathers ſofter then any ſilk : The Female commonly lays but two egges which are oval, about the bigneſs of a Pea or ſmall Pearl.

To what is aboveſaid we ſhall add the account given of it by our noble Traveller (*du Montel*) in his familiar Relations to a friend of his : "There are, *ſaith he*, ſometimes found the "neſts of the *Colibris* under the branches of thoſe Plants of To-"bacco which are ſuffered to grow as high as they can for ſeed. "I remember a Negro of ours ſhew'd me one of them, which "was very neatly faſhioned, under one of thoſe branches : Nay "being in S. *Chriſtophers*, an *Engliſh-man* ſhew'd me one of them, "which was faſtened to one of the Reeds that ſuſtain'd the co-"vering of a Hut. I ſaw alſo one of theſe neſts, together with "the egges, which was faſtened to a branch that had been cut "off to adorn the Cloſet of a curious perſon, who had alſo the "Male and Female dried and preſerv'd entire ; and there it "was that I attentively conſidered both the Neſt and Bird ; and "having admired the operations of Divine Providence in that "little creature, how could I leſs then be aſtoniſh'd at the mira-"culous Architecture of the Neſt, which though built with "an unexpreſſible artifice, was nevertheleſs performed only "with his little beak ?   There

There are of thefe Birds feen in moft of the *Caribby* Iflands, but according to the diverfity of the Iflands they alfo differ as to bignefs and plumage : The moft beautiful and leaft as to bulk are in the Ifland of *Aruba*, which depends on the *Dutch* Colony at *Coraffao*.

It might haply be here expected we fhould fpeak of the finging of this Bird, and that having entertain'd the fight with its beauty, and the fmelling with its fcent, it fhould alfo fatisfie the ear with its harmonious mufick : Some affirm that there is a kind of them that fings at a certain feafon of the year : But it is probable that what is called the finging of the *Colibry*, is only a little noife like that of the *Cigale*, which is always the fame note. But though it fhould not fing at all, it is endued with fo many other extraordinary advantages of Nature, that it may be ranked among the moft beautiful, and moft excellent of Birds.

Thofe who have liv'd at *Brafil* do unanimoufly affirm, that there is in thofe parts a little Bird called *Gonambuch*, of a fhining white colour, whofe body is no bigger then that of a Hornet, and as to a clear and diftinct note is nothing inferiour to the Nightingale : It's poffible it may be a kind of *Colibry*, as indeed fome do make it; yet is it not comparable, either as to beauty of feathers or fcent, and other tranfcendent qualities, to that whofe defcription we have here made.

Thofe have come neerer the mark who have affirmed that this mafter-piece of Nature is a kind of thofe little Birds, which fome *Indians* call *Guaraciaba*, or *Guacariga*, that is to fay, *Sunbeam*, and *Guaracigaba*, that is, *Hair of the Sun* : The *Spaniards* call it *Tomineios*, forafmuch as having put one of them with his neft into a pair of Scales wherewith gold is weigh'd, it commonly weighs not above two of thofe little weights, which the fame *Spaniards* call *Tominos*, that is, four and twenty grains.

Some have been of opinion that fome of thefe excellent *Colibris* were at firft Flies, which were afterwards transform'd into Birds : Others have written that the *Caribbians* called thefe Birds *Renati*, or *New-born*, becaufe they fleep one half of the year, as the Dormice do, and that they awake in the Spring, recovering as it were a new life with that delightful feafon of the year : Nay there are fome affirm, that when the leaves fall they thruft their little beaks into the trunks of the Trees, and there remain immoveable, and as it were dead, for fix moneths, till the earth puts on a new livery of flowers : But thefe are frivolous ftories grounded on conjectures, which may be touch'd by the way, but not admitted to any competion with the true account we give of our *Colibry*.

We will conclude this Chapter with a thing worthy obfervation, which yet happens not in other parts, unlefs haply in

Guiny,

Guiny, as *Linſcot* reporteth: It is the wonderful inſtinct which God hath beſtow'd on all the ſmaller ſorts of Birds in *America*, to preſerve their ſpecies ; inaſmuch as there being in the Woods a kind of long Snakes green and ſmall, which crawling up the Trees might wriggling themſelves from branch to branch devour the egges of the Birds, which they are extream-ly greedy of : to prevent the coming of theſe to their neſts, all the leſſer Birds, which are not ſo well beaked as to make their party good againſt theſe enemies, make their neſts at the fork-ed end of certain ſmall filaments, which like Ivy growing on the ground crawl up the Trees, and being come to the top, and not able to get any higher, fall down again, and ſometimes reach two or three fathom below the branches. At the very extremity of theſe ligaments or filaments, by the French called *Lienes*, the Birds faſten their neſts with ſuch ſtrength and in-duſtry, that a man cannot ſufficiently admire either the materi-als or workmanſhip of thoſe little hanging edifices. The Par-rots and other ſtronger Birds make their neſts in hollow Trees, or upon the boughs, as thoſe in theſe parts do; for with the of-fenſive arms of their beaks and claws they are able to engage their profeſs'd enemies the Snakes.

CHAP. XVI.

Of the Sea and River-Fiſh of the Caribbies.

WE ſhall not promiſe ſo exact and full a Hiſtory of the Fiſh of theſe Iſlands as ſo ample a ſubject might re-quire : but having already given an account of the accommodations of theſe happy Countries, as to the Land, the order of our Deſign requires that we ſhould now ſpeak of the productions of the Sea which encompaſs them, and the Rivers that run through them. The buſineſs therefore of this Chap-ter ſhall be to give a ſhort deſcription of the moſt excellent Fiſhes wherewith they are plentifully furniſh'd, in order to the ſubſiſtance of men; that the conſideration thereof may work in us the deepeſt acknowledgments imaginable of that Provi-dence which hath diſplay'd its miracles in the deep waters, as well as on the dry land; and conſequently that it is juſt that the Heavens and the Earth ſhould praiſe him, the Sea and whatever moves therein.

FLYING-FISHES.

THere are some who think what is said of the *Flying-Fishes* a pure fiction, though confirmed by the relations of many famous Travellers: But what opinion soever they may have thereof who believe only what they have seen, it is a certain truth, that as soon as Ships have pass'd the *Canaries*, thence to the Islands of *America*, there are often seen rising out of the Sea great numbers of Fishes which flye about the height of a Pike above the water, and neer a hundred paces distance, but no more, in regard their wings are dried by the Sun: They are somewhat like Herrings, but have a rounder head, and they are broader on the back: their wings are like those of a Bat, which begin a little below the head, and reach almost to the tail: It happens many times that in their flight they strike against the sails of Ships, and fall even in the day time upon the Deck: Those who have dress'd and eaten of them think them very delicate: Their forsaking the Sea their proper Element, is occasion'd upon their being pursu'd by other greater Fishes which prey on them; and to avoid meeting with them they quit their proper Element, making a sally into the air, and changing their finnes into wings to eschew the danger; but they meet with enemies in the air as well as in the water; for there are certain Sea-fowls living only by prey, which have an open hostility against them, and take them as they flye, as was said in the precedent Chapter.

SEA-PARROTS.

THere are also in these parts certain Fishes scaled like a Carp, but as to colour are as green as a Parrot, whence they are by some called *Sea-Parrots*: They have beautiful and sparkling eyes, the balls clear as Chrystal, encompass'd by a circle argent, which is enclos'd within another as green as an Emerald, of which colour are the scales of their backs; for those under the belly are of a yellowish green: They have no teeth, but jaws above and below of a solid bone, which is very strong, of the same colour as their scales, and divided into little compartiments very beautiful to the eye: They live on Shell-Fish, and with those hard jaw-bones they crush, as between two mill-stones, Oysters, Muscles, and other Shell-fish, to get out the meat: They are an excellent kind of fish to eat, and so big, that some of them have weigh'd above twenty pounds.

DORADO.

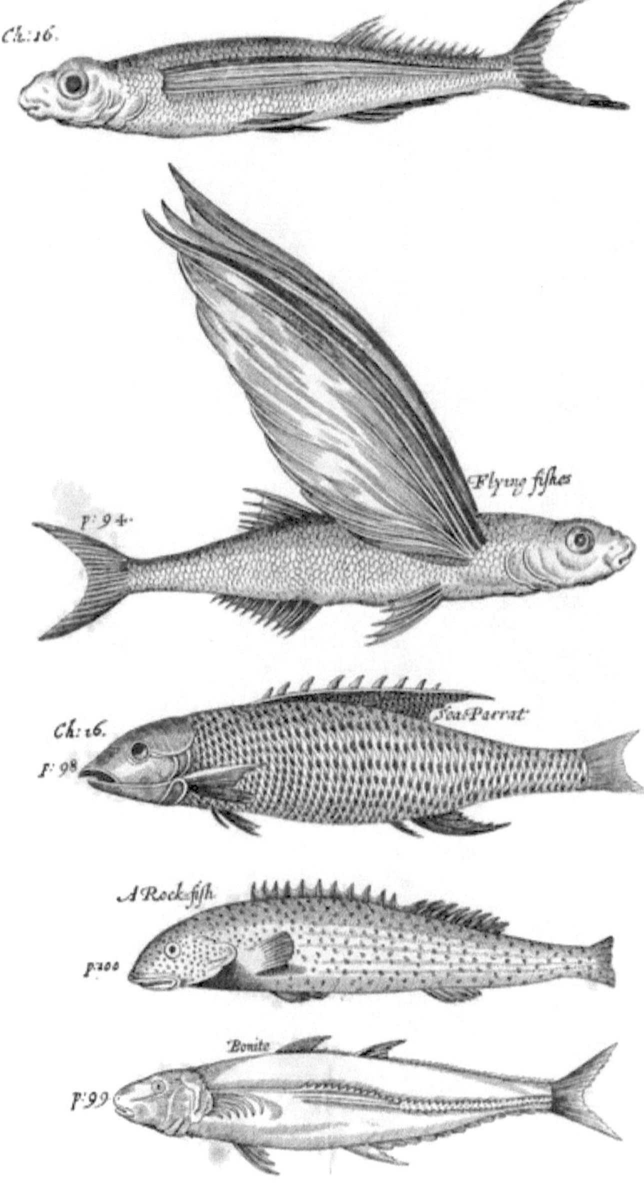

Ch: 16.
Flying fishes
P: 94.
Ch: 16.
F: 98
Sea Parrat
A Rockfish
p: 100
Bonite
F: 99

DORADO.

THe *Dorado*, by ſome called the *Sea-Bream*, by others the *Amber-Fiſh*, is alſo common in theſe parts : it is called *Dorado*, becauſe in the water the head of it ſeems to be of a green gilt, and the reſt of the body as yellow as gold, and azur'd, as a clear ſky : It takes a pleaſure in following the ſhips, but ſwims ſo ſwiftly that he muſt be very dextrous that ſhall take it either with the iron-hook, or long ſtaff with the caſting-net at the end of it, which are the inſtruments wherewith Sea-men are wont to take great fiſhes : Nor can a man imagine a fiſh better furniſh'd for ſwimming then this ; for he hath the fore-part of the head ſharp, the back briſtled with prickles reaching to the tail, which is forked, two fins of each ſide of the head, and as many under the belly, ſmall ſcales, and the whole body of a figure rather broad then big, all which give him a ſtrange command of the waters : ſome of them are about five foot in length : Many account the meat of this fiſh, though a little dry, as pleaſant to the taſte as that of a Trout or Salmon, ſo the dryneſs of it be corrected with a little good ſauce : When the *Portuguez* ſee theſe *Dorados* following their Ships, they ſtand on the Bow-ſprit with a line in their hand, at the end whereof there is only a piece of white linen faſten'd to the hook without any other bait.

BONITE.

THere is another Fiſh which commonly follows the Ships, called a *Bonite* : It is big, and hath much meat about it, and about two foot in length : The ſkin of it ſeems to be of a very dark green, and whitiſh under the belly : It hath ſcales only on both ſides, and there only two ranks of very little ones along a yellowiſh line, reaching from one ſide to the other, beginning at the head to the tail, which is forked : It is taken with great hooks caſt out on the ſides of the Ship ; which may be done without any hindrance to the Voyage : This Fiſh is as greedy as the Cod, and taken with any baits, even with the entrails of other fiſh : He is more common in the main Sea, then on the Coaſts, and very good meat eaten freſh ; but much more delicate having lain a little while in Pepper and Salt before it be dreſs'd : Some conceive this to be the ſame fiſh with another call'd by the French *Thon*, which is common on all the Coaſts of the *Mediterranean* Sea.

O 2   *NEEDLE-*

NEEDLE-FISH.

THere is a Fish without scales, four foot or thereabouts in length, called the *Needle-Fish:* The head of it is sharp, a foot or better in length, the eyes large and shining, and encompass'd with a red circle: The skin of his back is streaked with blew and green lines, and that under the belly is white intermixt with red: It hath eight fins which somwhat incline to yellow, and a very sharp tail, whence probably it came to be so called, as the figure of the head gave the Dutch occasion to name it *Tabac-pype*, that is, *Tobacco-pipe.*

The Coasts of these Islands are furnished also with *Carangues* and *Mullets*, which come sometimes into the fresh waters, and are taken in the Rivers; as also *Rock-Fishes*, which are red intermixt with several other colours: They are called *Rock-Fishes*, because they are taken neer the Rocks. There are also a kind of fish called *Negroes*, or *Sea-Devils*, which are large, and have a black scale, but their meat is white and excellent good; and an infinite number of Fish, which for the most part differ from those seen in *Europe*, and have yet no names among us.

Nor are the Rivers behind hand in supplying the Inhabitants of these Islands with abundance of excellent Fish: and if we may bring small things into competition with great, they are proportionably to their extent as plentiful thereof as the Sea it self. 'Tis true, there are not any *Pikes* or *Carpes*, nor some other fish which are common in these parts; but there is great store of others which are known only to the *Indians*, and whereof some are not much different as to figure from ours.

CHAP. XVII.

Of the Sea-Monsters found in these Islands.

THose who have writ the History of Fish have ranked among the Whales all such as are of extraordinary bigness, as they have comprehended under the name of Monsters all those that are of a hideous shape, or living by prey are the destructive Inhabitants of the Waters, as Lyons, Bears, Tygers, and other wild beasts are of the Earth: We shall treat in this Chapter of both, that is of all those which are of a prodigious bulk, or dreadful as to their ugly shapes, or to be feared by reason of the mischief done by them: So that we must for a time descend into the abysses of the Main, where there are *creeping things innumerable*, as the royal Prophet saith,

and

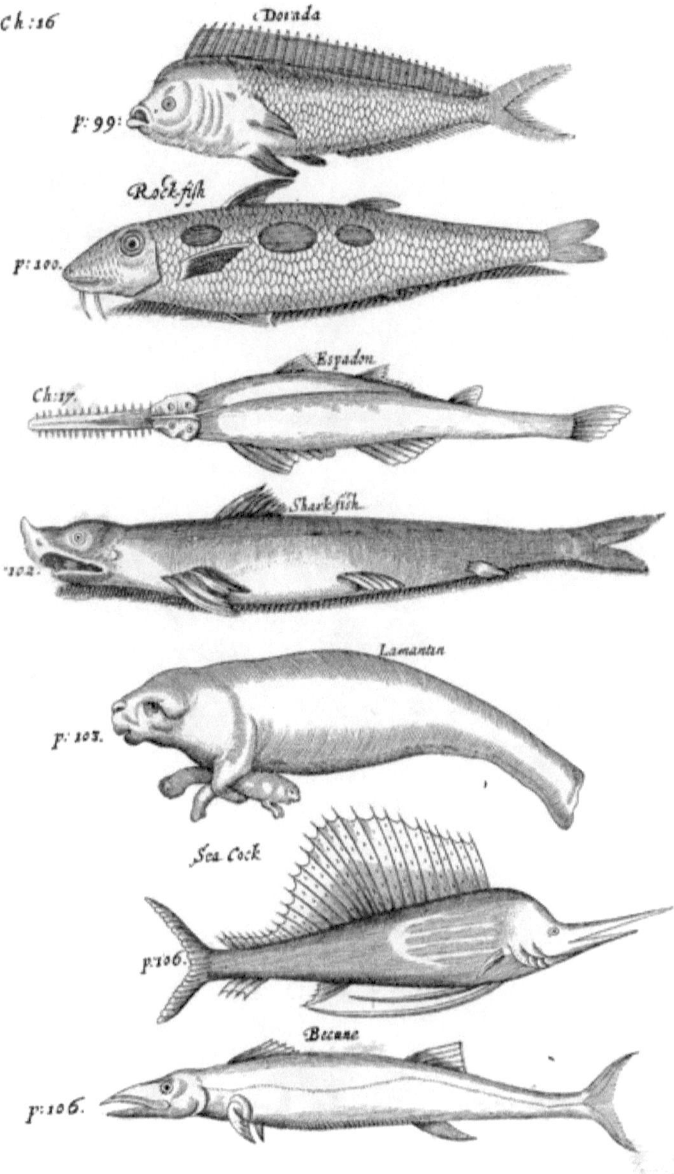

Ch:16
Dorada
P:99:
Rock-fish
P:100.
Espadon
Ch:17.
Shark-fish.
102.
Lamantin
P:103.
Sea Cock
p:106.
Becune
P:106.

and both ſmall and great Beaſts; and after we have contemplated the works of the Lord therein, riſe up again to celebrate his mercy towards the Children of Men.

ESPADON, *or* SWORD-FISH.

AMong the Sea-Monſters that which the *French* call *L'Eſpadon* (a word ſignifying a ſhort ſword) is one of the moſt remarkable : it hath at the end of the upper jaw a defenſive weapon, about the breadth of a great Courtelas, which hath hard and ſharp teeth on both ſides : Theſe defenſives in ſome of them are about five foot in length, and about ſix inches broad at the lower end, and palizadoed with twenty ſeven white and ſolid teeth in each rank, and the bulk of their bodies bears a porportion thereto · The head of this monſter is flat and hideous to behold, being of the figure of a heart : They have neer their eyes two vents at which they caſt out the water which they had ſwallowed : They have no ſcales, but a greyiſh ſkin on the back, and a white under the belly, which is rough like a file : They have ſeven fins, two of each ſide, two on the back, and that which ſerves them for a tail : Some call them *Saw-fiſhes*; ſome *Emperors*, becauſe there is an hoſtility between them and the Whale, which they many times wound to death.

MARSOUINS.

THe *Marſouins* are the *Sea-Hogs*, or *Porpoſes*, which go together in great companies, and ſporting themſelves leap up above the water, and following all of them as many as are together the ſame courſe : They many times of themſelves come neer enough to the ſhips, and ſuch as are dextrous do now and then take ſome of them · Their meat is of a dark colour; the fatteſt have not above an inch or two of fat : They have a ſharp ſnout, a very broad tail, greyiſh ſkin, and a hole upon the top of their heads, through which they breathe and caſt out water : They grunt almoſt like the Land-Swine : Their blood is hot, and their entrails like thoſe of a Pig, and they are much of the ſame taſte; but their meat is of hard digeſtion.

There is another kind of *Porpoſes* which have the ſnout round and hollow, and from the reſemblance there is between their heads and the frocks of Friers, ſome call them *Monks-heads*, and *Sea-Monks*.

REQUIEM.

REQUIEM.

THe *Requiem*, otherwise called the *Shark-Fish*, is a kind of *Sea-Dog* or *Sea-Wolf*, the moft devouring of all Fifhes, and the moft greedy of mans flefh : He is much to be feared by fuch as go a fwimming : He lives altogether by prey, and commonly follows the fhips to feed on the filth caft out of them into the fea.   Thefe Monfters feem to be of a yellowifh colour in the water : Some of them are of an unmeafurable length and bignefs, and fuch as are able to cut a man in two at one bite : Their fkin is rough, and there are made of it foft files to polifh wood : Their heads are flat, and the opening of their mouth is not juft before the fnout, but under it : Whence it comes, that to faften on their prey they are forc'd to turn their bellies almoft upwards : Their teeth are very fharp and very broad, being jagged all about like a Saw : Some of them have three or four ranks of thefe in each jaw-bone : Thefe teeth lye within the gums, but they make them fufficiently appear when there is occafion.

Thefe cruel *Sea-Dogs* are attended by two or three fmall fifhes, and fometimes more, which go before them with fuch fwiftnefs, and fo regular a motion, that they either advance or halt more or lefs according as they perceive the *Requiems* do : Some call them *Rambos*, and *Pilgrims*, and the French Mariners, the *Requiems Pilots*, inafmuch as thofe fmall fifhes feem to be their convoys : They are not much above a foot in length, and of a proportionable bignefs : But their fcales are beautified with fo many pretty and lively colours, that it might be faid, they were encompafs'd which chains of Pearl, Coral, Emerald, and other precious ftones : A man can hardly be weary of looking on them in the water.

It is in like manner affirmed, that the Whale where-ever fhe goes hath marching before her a little fifh like a *Sea-Gudgeon*, which from that fervice is called her *Guide* : The Whale follows him, fuffering her felf to be led and turn'd as eafily as the Rudder caufes the Ship to turn about ; and in requital of this fervice, whereas whatever elfe enters into the horrid Chaos of this Monfters throat is immediately loft and devour'd, this little fifh makes it his retiring, and his refting place ; and while he lyes there a fleep the Whale ftirs not, but as foon as he gets out fhe prefently follows him : and if it happen the faid fifh fhould be a little out of the way, fhe wanders up and down, ftriking many times againft the Rocks, as a Ship without a Rudder ; which thing *Plutarch* affirms that himfelf was an eyewitnefs of in the Ifland of *Anticyra*. There is fuch another friendfhip between the little Bird called the *Wren* and the *Crocodile* ; and that Shell-fifh called the *Naker* lives in the fame

man-

manner with the *Pinnothere*, and other Shell-fish not much unlike a Crab, as is affirmed by *Montagne*, lib. 2. ca. 12.

The meat of the *Requiem* is not good, and therefore not eaten, unlefs it be in cafe of great neceffity: yet is it conceiv'd by fome, that while they are young they may be tolerable meat. Some curious perfons do carefully fave the Brains found in the heads of the old ones, and being dried they keep it, and they fay it is very good for fuch as are troubled with the Stone or Gravel.

Some Nations call this Monfter *Tiburon* and *Tuberon*: But the *French* and *Portuguez* commonly call it *Requiem*, that is to fay, *Reft*, haply, becaufe he is wont to appear in fair weather, as the Tortoifes alfo do, or rather becaufe he foon puts to reft whatever he can take: His Liver being boiled yields a great quantity of oyl very good for Lamps, and the Skin of it is ufed by Joyners to polifh their work.

REMORA.

BEfides the Pilots before mentioned, the *Requiems* are many times accompany'd by another kind of little fifhes called by the Dutch *Sugger*, becaufe they ftick fo clofe to the bellies of the *Requiems* as if they would fuck them. The French account it a kind of *Remora*, which name they have becaufe they ftick to the Ship as if they would ftop their courfe: They are about two foot in length, and proportionably big: They have no fcales, but are covered with an Afh-colour'd fkin, which is as glutinous as thofe of Eeles. Their upper-jaw is a little fhorter then the lower; inftead of teeth they have little rifings, ftrong enough to break what they would fwallow: Their eyes are very fmall, of a yellow colour: They have fins and a certain plume as fome other Sea-fifhes have, but what's moft remarkable in them, is, that they have on their heads an oval piece made fomewhat like a crown: it is flat and ftreaked above with feveral lines which make it look briftly: It is by this part that thefe fifh ftick fo clofely to the Ships and *Requiems*, that fometimes they muft be kill'd ere they can be gotten off: They are eaten fometimes, but in cafe of neceffity, when other better fifh cannot be had.

LAMANTIN.

OF all the Sea-monfters that are good to eat, and kept for Provifion, as Salmon and Cod are in *Europe*, the moft efteemed in thefe Iflands is a certain fifh by the French called *Lamantin*, by the Spaniards *Namantin* and *Manaty*: It is a Monfter that in time grows to that bulk, that fome of them are eighteen foot in length, and feven in bignefs about the middle of
the

the body : His head hath ſome reſemblance to that of a Cow, whence ſome took occaſion to call him the *Sea-Cow :* He hath ſmall eyes, and a thick ſkin of a dark colour, wrinkled in ſome places and ſtuck with ſome ſmall hairs : Being dried it grows ſo hard that it may ſerve for a Buckler againſt the Arrows of the *Indians* ; nay ſome of the Savages uſe it to ward off the blows of their enemies when they go to fight : They have no fins, but inſtead thereof they have under their bellies two ſhort feet, each whereof hath four fingers very weak to ſupport the weight of ſo heavy a body ; nor hath he any other defenſive. This Fiſh lives on the graſs and herbage that grows about the Rocks, and on the ſhallow places that have not much above a fathom of Sea-water. The Females are diſburthen'd of their young ones much after the ſame manner as Cows are, and they have two teats wherewith they ſuckle them : They bring forth two at a time, which forſake not the old one till ſuch time as they have no longer need of milk, and can feed on the graſs as ſhe does.

Of all Fiſbes there is not any hath ſo much good meat as the *Lamantin* ; for many times there needs but two or three to load a great Canow ; and this meat is like that of a Land-creature, eating ſhort, of a Vermillon colour, not cloying or fulſom, and mixt with fat, which being melted never grows muſty : It is much more wholſom eaten two or three days after it hath been laid in ſalt then freſh : Theſe Fiſh are more commonly taken at the entrance of freſh-water Rivers then in the Sea. Some highly value certain ſmall ſtones found in the heads of theſe Monſters, as having the vertue reduc'd to powder to clear the Reins of Gravel, and diſſolve the Stone bred there : But the Remedy being violent, I ſhould not adviſe any to uſe it without the preſcription of an experienc'd Phyſitian.

WHALES and other Sea-Monſters.

SUch as Sail into theſe Iſlands do ſometimes in their Courſe meet with Whales which caſt up water by their Vent to a Pikes height, and commonly ſhew but a little of their back, which looks like a rock above the water.

The Ships are alſo many times attended for a good way by certain Monſters about the bigneſs of a Shallop, which ſeem to take a pleaſure in ſhewing themſelves : Some Sea-men call them *Souffleurs*, that is, *Blowers*, for that ever and anon theſe prodigious fiſhes put up ſome part of their head above water to take breath ; and then they blow, and cauſe a great agitation of the waters with their ſharp ſnouts : Some hold them to be a kind of *Porpoſes*.

SEA-

SEA-DEVILS.

ON the Coafts of thefe Iflands there is fometimes taken by the Fifhers a Monfter which is ranked among the kinds of *Sea-Devils*, by reafon of its hideous figure: It is about four foot long, and proportionably big: it hath on the back a great bunch full of prickles like thofe of a Hedg-Hog: The fkin of it is hard, uneven and rugged, like that of the Sea-dog, and of a black colour: The head of it is flat, and on the upper part hath many little rifings, among which may be feen two little very black eyes: The mouth which is extreamly wide, is arm'd with feveral very fharp teeth, two whereof are crooked and bent in like thofe of a wild Boar: it hath four fins, and a tail broad enough, which is forked at the extremity: But what got it the name of *Sea-Devil*, is, that above the eyes there are two little black horns, fharp enough, which turn towards his back like thofe of a Ram: Befides that this Monfter is as ugly as any thing can be imagin'd, the meat of it, which is foft and full of ftrings, is abfolute poyfon; for it caufes ftrange vomiting, and fuch fwoonings as would be follow'd by death if they be not foon prevented by the taking of a dofe of good *Mithridate*, or fome other Antidote. This dangerous creature is fought after only by the curious, who are glad to have any thing that comes from it to adorn their Clofets: And fo it comes to pafs that this Devil, who never brought men any profit while it lived, gives a little fatisfaction to their eyes after his death.

There is another kind of *Sea-Devil*, no lefs hideous then the precedent, though of another figure: The largeft of this kind are not much above a foot in length from the head to the tail: They are almoft as much in bredth; but when they pleafe they fwell themfelves up, fo as that they feem to be round as a bowl: Their wide mouths are arm'd with many little but very fharp teeth, and inftead of a tongue they have only a little bone which is extreamly hard: Their eyes are very fparkling, and fo fmall, and deep fet in the head, that the ball thereof can hardly be difcerned: They have between the eyes a little horn which turns up, and before it a pretty big ftring that hath at the end of it a little button: Befides their tail, which is like the broad end of an Oar, they have two plumes, one on the back which ftands as it were upright, and the other under the belly: They have alfo two fins, one of each fide over againft the midft of the belly, having at the extremities fomewhat like little paws, each whereof is divided into eight claws, which are armed with fharp nails: their fkin is rough, and prickly all over, like that of the *Requiem*, fave only under the belly: it is of a dark red colour and marked with black fpots: the meat of them is not to be eaten: They may be eafily flayed, and the

fkin

skin being fill'd with Cotton or dry'd leaves, finds a place among rarities; but it loses much of its lustre when the fish is dead.

BECUNE.

AMong the ravenous Monsters that are greedy of mans flesh, found on the Coasts of these Islands, the *Becune* is one of the most dreadful: It is in figure much like a *Pike*, but in length seven or eight foot, and proportionably big: He lives by prey, and furiously fastens like a Blood-Hound on the men he perceives in the water: He carries away whatever he once fastens on, and his teeth are so venemous, that the least touch of them becomes mortal if some sovereign remedy be not immediately apply'd to abate and divert the poyson.

SEA-WOOD-COCKS.

THere is another kind of *Becunes*, by some called *Sea-Wood-Cocks* from the figure of the beak, which is somewhat like a Wood-Cocks bill, saving that the upper part is much longer then the lower, and that this fish moves both jaws with like facility: Some of them are so big and long, that they are above four foot between the head and the tail, and twelve inches broad neer the head, measuring side-wife: The head is somewhat like that of a Swine, but enlightned by two large eyes which are extreamly shining: It hath two fins on the sides, and under the belly a great plume rising higher and higher by degrees, like a Cocks-comb, reaching from the head almost to the tail, which is divided into two parts: Besides the long and solid beak it hath, for which it is remarkable among all fishes, it hath two sorts of horns, hard, black, and about a foot and a half in length, which hang down under his throat, and are particular to this kind of fish; and these he can easily hide in a hollow place under his belly, which serves them for a sheath: It hath no scales, but is cover'd with a rough skin, which on the back is black, on the sides greyish, and under the belly white: It may be eaten without any danger, though the meat of it be not so delicate as that of several other fishes.

SEA-URCHIN.

THe Fish found on these Coasts, and called the *Sea-Urchin*, well deserves that name: It is round as a ball, and full of sharp prickles, for which it is feared: Some call it the *Armed Fish*. They who take of them, having dried them, send them as Presents to the Curious, who for rarity hang them up in their Closets.

CHAP.

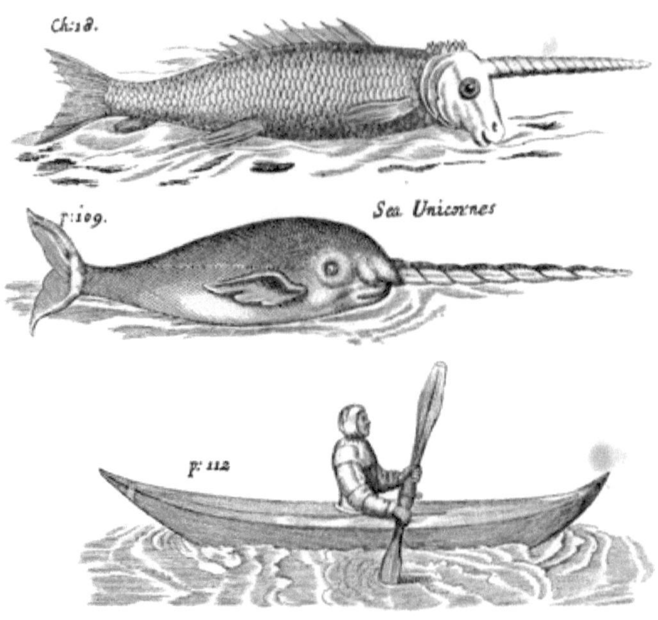

Ch: 18.
p: 109.
Sea Unicornes
p: 112

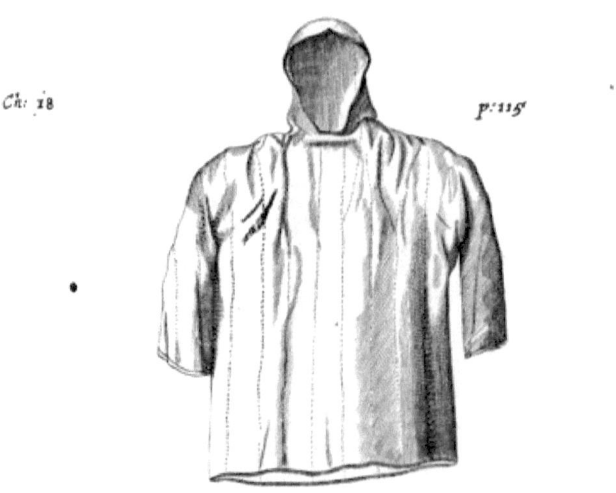

Ch: 18
p: 115

CHAP. XVIII.

A particular Description of the Sea-Unicorn *which was cast ashore at the Haven of the* Tortoise-Island, *in the Year* 1644. *and a pleasant Relation, by way of Digression, of several beautiful and rare Horns brought lately from* Davis-streight; *with an account of the Country, and the Dispositions of the Inhabitants.*

WE cannot better conclude the Account we had to give of the Sea-monsters, then with a description of so remarkable and miraculous a Fish, as may justly deserve a particular Chapter to treat of it: It is the *Sea-Unicorn*, which is sometimes seen in those parts. There was cast ashore, in the year 1644. a prodigious one, on the Coast of the *Tortoise-Island*, neer *Hispaniola*: Monsieur *du Montel*, having been an eye-witness thereof, gives us this curious description of it.

"This *Unicorn*, saith he, was pursuing a *Carangue*, or some
"other lesser fish, with such earnestness and impetuosity, that
"not considering that it needed a greater depth of water then
"the other, it stuck with half the body dry on a sand-bank,
"whence it could not recover the deeper waters ere it was de-
"stroy'd by the Inhabitants: It was about eighteen foot in
"length, being at the largest part of its body about the big-
"ness of a great Barrel: It had six great fins like the ends of
"Galley-oars, whereof two were placed neer the gills, and
"the other four on the sides of the belly at equal distances;
"they were of a Vermilion red colour: all the upper part of
"the body was cover'd with great scales about the bigness of a
"Crown-piece, which were of a blew colour intermixt with
"certain spangles of silver: neer the neck the scales were clo-
"ser, and of a dark colour, seeming as it were a collar: The
"scales under the belly were yellow; the tail forked, the
"head somewhat bigger then that of a horse, and neer the same
"figure: It was cover'd with a hard and dark colour'd skin;
"and as the Land-Unicorn hath one horn in his forehead, so
"this Sea-Unicorn had a very fair one issuing out of the fore-
"part of his head, about nine foot and a half in length: it was as
"strait as could be, and from the place whence it came out it
"grew smaller and smaller to the very point, which was so
"sharp, that being thrust hard it would enter into wood or
"stone, or some more solid substance: It was at the place where
"it came out of the head about sixteen inches about, and
"from thence to two thirds of the length it was like a screw,

"or

" or to fay better, made waving like a wreath'd pillar, fave
" that the channels grew fmaller and fmaller till they gently
" ended in a point, which was two inches beyond the fourth
" foot.   All that lower part had over it an afh-colour'd fkin,
" which was all over cover'd with a fmall foft hair, fhort as
" plufh, and of the colour of a wither'd leaf, but under that it
" was as white as Ivory.   As to the other part, which feemed
" naked, it was naturally polifh'd, of a fhining black, marked
" with certain fmall white and yellow ftroaks, and of fuch fo-
" lidity, that a fharp file could hardly get a little fmall powder
" from it.   It had no ears ftanding up, but two fpacious gills,
" as the other fifhes : The eyes were about the bignefs of a
" Hens egge; the Ball, which was of a fky-colour enamell'd
" with yellow, was encompafs'd with a certain vermilion, which
" had beyond it another as clear as Chryftal : The mouth was
" wide enough, and furnifhed with feveral teeth, whereof
" thofe before were extremely fharp, and thofe towards the
" throat in both jaws were broad, and a little knobbed : The
" tongue was of a length and thicknefs proportionable, and
" covered with a rough fkin of a vermilion colour. What was
" further remarkable, is, that this fifh had upon the head a kind
" of crown, rifing above the fkin about two inches, and made
" oval wife, the extremities whereof ended in a point. Above
" three hundred perfons of that Ifland did eat of the meat of
" it, and that plentifully, and thought it extremely delicate :
" It was interlarded with a white fat, and being boiled it came
" up in fleaks like frefh Cod, but it had a much more excellent
" tafte.

    " Thofe who had feen this rare fifh alive, and had with great
" Levers broken the back of it, affirmed, that he had made
" prodigious attempts to thruft them with his horn, which he
" turned with an inexpreffible dexterity and nimblenefs, and
" that if he had had as much water under him as would have
" born him up, he would have been too hard for them all.
" When the entrails were taken out, it was found that he liv'd
" by prey; for there were within him the fcales of feveral
" kinds of fifh.

    " What could be preferv'd of this miraculous Animal, efpe-
" cially the head, and the precious horn faften'd in it, hung up
" neer two years at the Guard-houfe of the Ifland, till Mon-
" fieur *Le Vaffeur*, the Governour of it, prefented one Monfieur
" *des Trancarts* (a Gentleman of *Xaintonge* who had given him
" a vifit) with the Horn.   Not long after, coming over in the
" fame Ship with the Gentleman who had that precious rarity
" put up in a long Cheft, our Ship was caft away neer the Ifland
" of *Fayala*, one of the *Affores*, and all the Goods were loft,
" but nothing fo much regretted as the lofs of that Cheft.
    There is in the Northern Seas another kind of Unicorns,
                                                        which

which are many times by the Ice carried to the Coaſt of *Iſe-land :* They are of ſo prodigious a length and bulk, that moſt Authors who have written of them rank them among Whales : They are not cover'd with ſcales as the formentioned deſcrib'd by us was, but with a hard black ſkin like the *Lamantin* : They have but two fins on both ſides, and a large plume upon the back, which being narrower in the midſt then at either end; makes as it were a double creſt riſing up for the more conveni-ent dividing of the waters : they have three vent-holes a little below their necks, at which they caſt up the ſuperfluous water they had ſwallow'd, as the Whales do : their heads are ſharp, and on the left ſide of the upper jaw there comes out a horn white all over as the tooth of a young Elephant, which horn is ſometimes fifteen or ſixteen foot in length : It is wreath'd in ſome places, and ſtreaked all over with ſmall lines of a pearl-colour, which are not only on the ſuperficies of it, but run through the ſubſtance : The horn is hollow to the third part, and all over as ſolid as the hardeſt bone.

Some will have this prominency to be rather a tooth then a horn, becauſe it riſes not out of the forehead, as that we have ſpoken of, nor yet from the upper part of the head, as thoſe of Bulls and Rams, but out of the upper jaw, in which it is ſet, as the teeth are in their proper places : Thoſe who are of this opinion ſay further, that it is not to be wondred theſe fiſhes ſhould have but one ſuch tooth, when the ſubſtance out of which others ſhould be produced is quite exhauſted in the making of that one, which is of ſuch a prodigious length and bigneſs as might ſuffice to make a hundred.

But whether this ſtrange defenſive wherewith theſe mon-ſtrous fiſh are armed be called Tooth or Horn, certain it is that they uſe it in their engagements with the Whales, and to break the Ice of the Northern Seas, wherewith they are often-times encompaſſed : Whence it came, that ſome times there have been ſeen of them ſuch as by reaſon of the violent ſer-vice they have been in, in diſingaging themſelves out of thoſe icy mountains, have not only had their horns blunted at the point, but alſo ſhattered and broken off : The figures of both this kind and that caſt aſhore in the *Tortoiſe* Iſland may be ſeen among the Sculps.

While we were ordering the foregoing ſtory for the ſatisfa-ction of the Publick, a Ship of *Fluſhing*, commanded by *Ni-cholas Tunes*, wherein M. *Lampſen*, one of the Deputies of that Province, in the Aſſembly of the States-General, and other conſiderable Merchants of the ſame Town were concern'd, co-ming in from *Davis-ſtreight*, brought thence among other rari-ties ſeveral excellent pieces of the Unicorns of the Northern Seas, of that kind we ſpoke of before; and in regard the Re-lation ſent us of that Voyage may very much clear up the matter

ter we treat of, we conceive the Reader will take it kindly to be entertain'd with it, assuring himself he hath it with the same sincerity as it was communicated to us.

The Captain of whom we have this Relation, leaving *Zealand* at the end of the Spring, 1656. with a design to discover some new Commerce in the Northern parts, arrived at the end of *June* following in *Davis-streight*, whence having entred into a River which begins at the sixty fourth degree, and ten minutes of the Line Northward, he sailed to the seventy second, under which the Country we intend to describe lyes.

As soon as the Inhabitants of the Country, who were then a fishing, perceived the Ship, they came towards it with their little Boats, which are so made as that they carry but one person: The first who attempted it occasion'd the joyning of so many others to them, that in a short time there was a squadron of seventy of those little vessels, which parted not from the foreign Ship till it had cast Anchor in the best Haven, where by their acclamations and all the signs of friendship and good will that could be expected from a Nation so far unacquainted with civility, they exprefs'd the extraordinary joy they conceived at its happy arrival : These little vessels are so admirable, whether we consider their materials, or the strange industry in the making of them, or the incomparable dexterity whereby they are conducted, that they may well be allow'd a place among the descriptions which this delightful digression shall furnish us with.

They consist of little thin pieces of wood, whereof most are cleft like Hoops: These pieces of wood are fasten'd one to another with strong cords made of the guts of fishes, which keep them together in a figure fit for the uses to which they are design'd : They are cover'd on the out-side with the skins of Sea-Dogs, which are so neatly sewn together, and so artificially done over with Rozin about the seams, that the water cannot make the least entrance into them.

These little Boats are commonly about fifteen or sixteen foot in length, and they may be in the midst where they are biggest about five foot circumference ; from that place they grow smaller and smaller, so that the ends or extremities of them are very sharp and plated as it were with a white bone, or a piece of the Unicorns horn before described : The upper-part is flat and even, and cover'd with leather as the rest, and the lower part is fashion'd like the belly of a great fish ; so that they are very swift upon the water : they have but one overture, or open place, which is just in the midst of the whole structure : It is rais'd a little about with a small ledge of Whale-bone, and it is made fit for the reception of one man, so as that being in it, his waste fills the hole. When the Savages who invented these kinds of Boats would make use of them,

either

either to go a fishing or to divert themselves on the water, they
thrust down their feet and thighs in at the hole, and then sitting
down they so fasten the short Coat they have about them to
the ledge which is about the hole, that they seem to be graf-
fed into the little vessel, and to be part of it.

Thus much of the figure and materials of these little vessels;
let us now consider the accoutrement of the men who have
the conduct of them: When they intend to go to Sea, they put
over their other cloths a certain short coat, which is kept only
for that purpose: This Sea-coat consists of several skins having
the hair taken off, which are well dress'd and set together, that
a man would think it to be all of a piece: It reaches from the
crown of the head to the Navel: it is rubb'd over with a
blackish gum, which is not dissolved in the water, and keeps
it from passing through; That *Capuchon* or part of it which
comes over the head, comes so close under the neck and upon
the forehead, that it leaves nothing but the face open: The
sleeves are ty'd at the wrist, and the lower part of the coat is
fasten'd to the ledge, about the hole of the vessel, with so
much care and industry, that the body thus covered is always
dry in the midst of the waves, which with all their tossing can
wet only the face and the hands.

Though they have neither Sail, nor Mast, nor Rudder, nor
Compass, nor Anchor, nor any thing of all those conveniences
which are requisite to make our Ships fit for the Sea; yet will
they undertake long voyages with these small vessels, upon
which they seem to be sewn: they have an experienc'd knowledg of the Stars, and need no other guide in the night time:
The Oars they use are broad at both ends like a Chirurgeons
palet, and that they may the more easily make their way
through the waves, and last the longer, they tip them with a
white bone which covers the edges of the wood; which ornament they fasten with pins of horn, which they use instead of
nails: The middle of these Oars is beautifi'd with a bone or
precious horn, as well the ends, and by that place they hold
them that they may not slip out of their hands: They handle
these double Oars with such dexterity and nimbleness, that
these small vessels will out-run Ships that have all the advantages of sails, wind, and tide: They are so confident in them,
and so vers'd in the guiding of them, that they shew a thousand
tricks in them, for the divertisement of the beholders: Nay
sometimes they will raise such waves, that the water will be all
foamy, as if there had been a great tempest; and then they seem
rather like Sea-monsters coursing one another then men: And
to make it appear they fear not dangers, and that they hold a
good correspondence with that Element which feeds them,
they shew several tricks, diving and rouling themselves in the
Sea three or four times together; so that they may be taken
for perfect *Amphibia.*   When

When they intend to take voyages longer then ordinary, or are afraid to be driven far into the Sea by some Tempest, they take with them in the hollow place of their vessel a bladder full of fair water to quench their thirst, and fish dry'd in the Sun or Frost to eat instead of fresh meat: But they are seldom reduc'd to the necessity of using those provisions; For they have certain Darts like little Lances, which are fasten'd to their Boats; these they so dextrously cast at the fish they meet with, that they are very seldom destitute of these refreshments: They need no fire to dress their meat, for on the Land, as well as at Sea, they are wont to eat it raw: They also carry along with them the teeth of certain great fishes, or pieces of sharp bones, which serve them for knives to dress and cut the fish they take: Besides, another advantage of these vessels is, that there can happen no mutiny in them, since one and the same person is Master, Mariner, Purser and Pilot of it, who may stop it when he pleases, or let go with the wind & water, when he would take the rest necessary to retrive his spent forces: In this case he fastens his Oar to certain straps of Hart-skin design'd for that purpose, which are fastened to the Boat, or else he ties it to a buckle which hangs before on his coat.

The Women have not the use of these little Boats; but that they may also sometimes divert themselves on the water, their husbands, who are very fond of them, bring them abroad in other vessels which are about the bigness of our Shallops or Long-boats, and such as may carry fifty persons: They are made of Poles ty'd together, and cover'd with Sea-Dogs skins, as the former: When it is calm they go with Oars, when there is any wind they fasten the Mast to certain Sails of Leather.

The Reader may see among the Sculps of this Chapter a Cut of one of these Boats, with the person that conducts it sitting therein, which may render the description we have given of it more intelligible and compleat.

As to the Country where these excellent Navigators are bred, the degrees under which we have placed it shew it to be of a very cold constitution: 'Tis true, in the moneths of *June* and *July*, which make the Summer of those parts, and are but one continu'd day, (as *December* and *January* make but one night) the air is warm, pleasant, and clear, but between those two seasons, the days growing alternately longer and shorter, are attended with thick Mists, Snow, or Icy-rains, which are extream cold and tedious.

That part of the Country which lyes neer the Sea, is dry, and full of rough and dreadful rocks; and when the Snow melts it is overflown in many places by certain impetuous torrents lying between them: But when a man hath travell'd one league of very bad way, he comes into pleasant fields, especially in the Summer time: There are also mountains cover'd

with

with little Trees, which extreamly recreate the eye, and feed abundance of Fowl and Wild-beaſts; and there are Valleys through which there run many clear and pleaſant Rivers of freſh water, which have ſtrength enough to make their way into the Sea.

The Captain who commanded the *Fluſhinger*, from whoſe late Voyage we have this Relation, being landed with ſome part of his men, and having made a diligent obſervation thereof, he found there, among other things worth his notice, a vein of a certain browniſh earth full of ſhining ſpangles, as it were of ſilver, wherewith he cauſed a barrel to be filled, that trial might be made thereof: But having been in the crucible, it was found fit only to be put on the covers of Boxes, and ſuch pieces of Joynery, to which it adds much beauty and luſtre: Yet is there ſome hope derived from this diſcovery, that upon further trial there may be Silver-Mines found in theſe parts.

Though this Country be very cold, yet are there in it many beautiful and large Birds of a black and white plumage, and ſome of divers other colours, which the Inhabitants flay that they may have their fleſh to eat, and their ſkins to cloath themſelves withall: There are alſo Harts, Elks, Bears, Foxes, Hares, Conies, and abundance of other four-footed beaſts, whoſe Furs are either black or of a dark grey, very thick, long, ſoft, and beſides the uſes may be made thereof as Furs, excellent for Hats.

Our Relation tells us that the Country is inhabited by two ſorts of Inhabitants, who live together in perfect friendſhip and good correſpondence: Some are of a very high ſtature, well-ſhap'd in their bodies, of a pretty clear complexion, and very ſwift in running: The others are much lower, of a dark Olive-colour'd complexion, and well proportioned as to their members, ſave that they have ſhort and big legs. The former ſpend their time in Hunting, whereto their activity naturally inclines them, while the latter employ themſelves in Fiſhing: Both kinds have their teeth very white and cloſe, black hair, lively eyes, and their faces ſuch as that there can no remarkable deformity be obſerv'd in them: They are all of them ſo vigorous, and of ſo healthy a conſtitution, that many of them being above a hundred years of age are very active and laborious.

In their ordinary converſation they ſeem to be of a cheerful humor, courageous and confident: They love thoſe ſtrangers who viſit them, becauſe they bring them Needles, Fiſhinghooks, Knives, Hedge-bills, Wedges, and all the other Implements of Iron they have need of, which they ſo highly eſteem that they will give their cloths, and what they account moſt precious for them: but they have ſuch an averſion from all novelty, as to feeding and clothing, that it were hard to induce

Q

them

them to admit of any change in either : nay though they are one of the pooreſt and moſt barbarous Nations under the Sun, yet do they think themſelves the moſt happy, and beſt provided for of any; and they are ſo well conceited of their manner of life, that the civilities of all other people are accounted by them unbeſeeming, ſavage, and extreamly ridiculous actions.

This high eſteem they have conceiv'd of their condition contributes not a little to that ſatisfaction and tranquility of mind which is legible even in their countenances : beſides that they are not diſturb'd by any vain deſigns which might interrupt their quiet : They know nothing of thoſe gnawing cares and pinching diſtractions wherewith the inordinate deſire of wealth torments the greateſt part of mankind. The conveniences of fair and ſumptuous buildings, the fame attending gallant actions, the delights of great entertainments, the knowledg of excellent things, and what we think moſt advances the pleaſure and enjoyments of life, having not yet found the way into theſe Countries, their thoughts accordingly are not troubled about the acquiſition thereof : but to get thoſe things which are preciſely neceſſary for their ſubſiſtence and clothing, with as little trouble as may be, is the end of all their conſultations and deſigns.

Their ordinary Exerciſes, nay indeed Employments, are Fiſhing and Hunting; and though they have no Fire-arms nor Nets, yet ingenious and inventive Neceſſity hath inſpir'd them with other ways whereby they effect their deſires. They eat whatſoever they feed on without any dreſſing, or any other ſauce then hunger : nay they laugh at thoſe who boil fiſh or fleſh, affirming that the fire takes away the natural taſte thereof, and what makes them acceptable to them.

Though they need no fire to dreſs their meat, yet they very much commend the uſe of it, and their Caves are not deſtitute of it in the winter time; both by its light to abate ſomwhat of the tedioufneſs of that long night which reigns in their Country, and by its heat the cold whereby they are beſieged of all ſides : But when they take their reſt, or are forc'd to go out of their Caves, they put on a certain Fur, which by the excellent diſpoſal of Divine Providence ſecures them againſt the injuries of the cold, though they lay in the midſt of the ſnow.

The mens cloths, are a Shirt, a pair of Breeches, a ſhort Coat, and a kind of Buſkins : The Shirt comes but a little below the Waſte : It hath a Capuchon, or Cap annexed to it, to come over the head and neck : It is made of the bladders of great fiſhes cut into long pieces of equal bredth, and very neatly ſewn together : It hath no opening at the breaſt as ours have; but that it may not rent when it is put on, the ends of the ſleeves, the head-piece, and the bottom of it are hemm'd

in

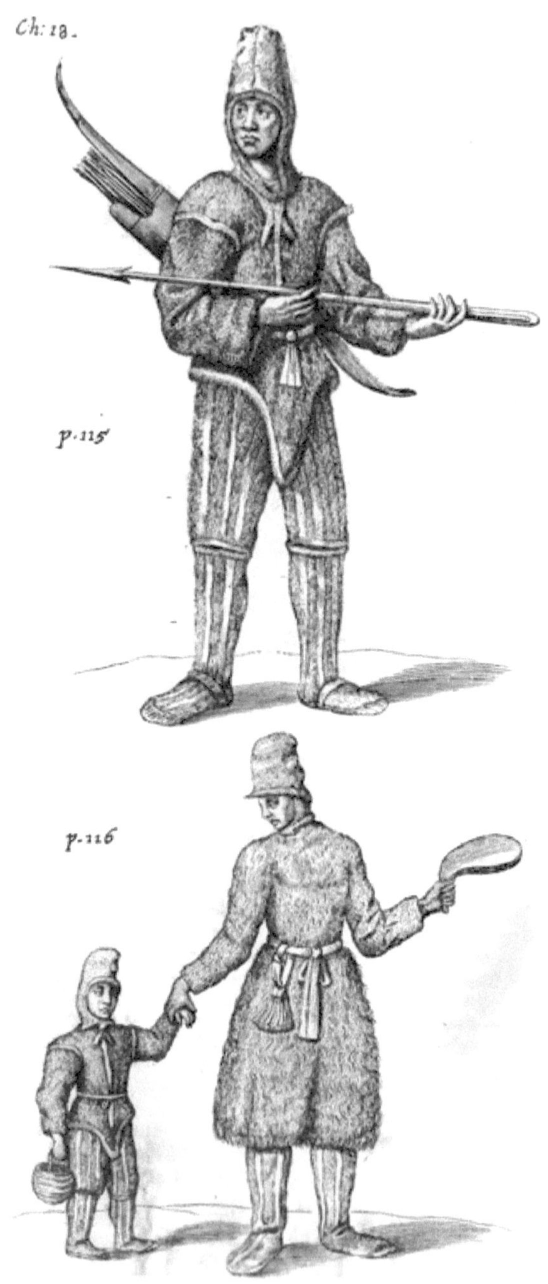
Ch: 18.
p. 115
p. 116

in with a very thin black ſkin; as it is repreſented among the
Braſs-cuts.

The reſt of their cloths, even their Buſkins, are of ſeveral
pieces cut proportionably one to another, as their Shirts are;
but they are of a ſtronger ſtuff, to wit, Harts-ſkins, or Sea-dogs-
ſkins very well dreſs'd with the hair on : The cloaths of the Savage whoſe pourtrait is to be ſeen among the Sculps, taken by
the Original, were of Leather of two ſeveral colours, the pieces
were cut of the ſame bredth, and put together ſo handſomly,
that a white piece was ſewn between two dark colour'd pieces,
which ſhew'd very prettily : The hair which was on the out-
ſide was as ſmooth and as ſoft as Velvet, and the ſeveral pieces
were ſo neatly joyn'd together, that a man would think by the
out-ſide that the Garment was all made of the ſame ſkin.   As
to the faſhion of the Coat, and the external ornaments of the
Savage, the Graver hath ſo naturally repreſented them in the
Sculp, that we need not trouble the Reader with any further
deſcription thereof.

The Savages inhabiting about the foreſaid Streight never go
abroad into the Country but they have at their back a Quiver
full of Arrows, and a Bow or a Lance in their hands : Their
Arrows are of ſeveral kinds, ſome are for the killing of Hares,
Foxes, great Birds, and all ſorts of ſmall Game; others for
Harts, Elks, Bears, and other greater Beaſts : The former are
not above two or three foot in length, and inſtead of iron at
the top they put a ſmall ſharp bone, which on one of the ſides
hath three or four little hooks, ſo that it cannot be taken out
of the place wounded without widening the wound : The latter, which are at leaſt four or five foot long, have alſo at the end
a ſharp bone jagged like the teeth of a Saw : They caſt theſe
latter with the hand; but to give them the greater force, and
make them do execution at a greater diſtance, they faſten to
their right arm a piece of wood a foot and a half long, which
on one ſide hath a deep channel into which they put the butt-
end of the Javelin, which being caſt thence goes off with a
greater violence.

They ſometimes alſo carry in their hands a kind of Lance, of
a tough and heavy wood, which is tipp'd at the ſmaller end
with a round bone, the point whereof had been ſharpened on
a ſtone, or they ſtrengthen it with the horns or teeth of the fiſh
before deſcribed : Theſe Lances are ſeven or eight foot in
length, and beautifi'd at the butt-end with two little wings of
wood, or Whale-bone, which make them a little more ſight-
ly then they would be otherwiſe.

Beſides the ſeveral ſorts of hooks wherewith they take the
ſmaller fiſhes frequenting their Coaſts, they have divers kinds
of Javelins, which with a wonderful dexterity they dart at
the great and monſtrous fiſhes they take in the Sea : And that

Q 2   thoſe

those they have hurt with these Darts may not sink to the bottom, and elude their expectation, there is fasten'd to the butt-end of them a thong of Harts-leather 25 or 30 fathom in length, and at the end of that thong or line of leather there is a bladder, which keeping above water shews where the fish is, and so they draw it to them, or gently drag it to land after it hath spent it self in strugling.

The young women differ not much in their cloaths from the men; but the more ancient are commonly clad with the skins of certain great Birds, whose feathers are white and black, and very ordinary in those parts. These women have the art to flay them so neatly, that the feathers stay in the skin: These cloaths reach but to half the leg: They are girt with a thong of leather, at which instead of keys there hang a great many little bones as sharp as any bodkins, and about that length: They wear neither Bracelets, nor Neck-laces, nor Pendants; nor mind any ornament, save that they make a gash in each cheek, and fill it with a certain black colour, which as they think adds very much to their beauty.

While the men are a hunting or fishing they stay at home, and employ themselves in making of Cloths, Tents, Baskets, and such things as are necessary about the house: They are extreamly fond of their little ones, and if they be forc'd to change their habitations, or to accompany their husbands in some journey, they either carry or lead them where-ever they go, and to recreate them by the way, and quiet them when they cry, they have little drums cover'd with fishes bladders, on which they can make as good Musick as any on the Taber: They also beat them to frighten away the Bears, and other wild Beasts which wander up and down neer the Caves where these Savages pass over the Winter with their families, and about the Tents where they are lodg'd in the Summer. Among the Sculps of this Chapter there is the pourtraiture of one of these women, to which we refer the Reader for further satisfaction.

Though these poor Barbarians cannot be imagin'd to study much Policy, yet have they among them petty Kings and Captains, who preside in all their Assemblies: They advance to these dignities those who have the handsomest bodies, are the best Hunts-men, and the most valiant: These wear the richest Skins and more precious Furs then their Subjects; and as a badge of their Supremacy they have a certain badge which is sown before on their Coats, and when they go abroad they are always attended by certain young men arm'd with Bows and Arrows, who punctually execute their commands.

They have not the invention of building houses; but in the Summer they live in the fields under Tents of Leather, which they carry along with them to be pitch'd where they think it

most

moſt convenient; and in Winter their abode is in Caves, which are naturally made in the Mountains, or they have taken the pains to make ſuch.

They neither Sow nor Reap any kind of Grain in order to their ſubſiſtence: Nor have they any Trees or Plants bearing fruits fit to eat, unleſs it be ſome Straw-berries, and a kind of Raſpices; but indeed their livelihood depends wholly on their Fiſhing and Hunting: Fair water is their ordinary drink, and their moſt delicate entertainment, as to drink, is the blood of Sea-dogs, and that of Deer, and other Land-creatures, which they either kill or take in Traps, at the ſetting of which they have an admirable induſtry.

The Winter being ſo long and hard in this Country, the Inhabitants muſt needs ſuffer great inconveniences during that ſeaſon, eſpecially that tedious night which keeps them in two whole moneths: But beſides that in caſe of neceſſity they endure hunger a long time, they have this foreſight that in the Summer they dry ſome part of their fiſhing and hunting, and lay it up with as much Fat and Suet as they can get together, in order to their ſubſiſtence during that comfortleſs time: Nay ſome affirm they are ſo ſucceſsful in their hunting by Moonlight, that they are ſeldom deſtitute of freſh meat, even during this long Eclipſe.

They deſire not to ſee any other Country beſides that they were born in, and if a tempeſt or other accident chance to caſt them upon ſome other, they perpetually ſigh after their own, and are never quiet in their minds till they have recover'd it: If they are deny'd or too long delay'd that favour, they will attempt it with the hazard of their lives, expoſing themſelves to the Sea in their little Veſſels without any other guide then the Stars, by which they regulate their courſe.

Their Language hath nothing common with any other in the World; there is a Vocabulary of it, but not to be publiſh'd till there be a further diſcovery made of theſe parts; what is ſaid here thereof being only by way of digreſſion.

Nor hath it been yet obſerved what Religion they have among them; but from their looking towards the Sun, and their pointing at him with a certain admiration, lifting up their hands on high, it is inferr'd that they account him a God.

The Ship from which we have this Relation, brought from *Davis-ſtreight* ſeveral conſiderable Commodities, whereof we ſhall here give a Liſt, to ſhew that the cold which reigns in that Country is not ſo inſupportable as to freeze up all manner of Commerce in thoſe parts.

1. Nine hundred Sea-dogs ſkins, moſt of them between ſeven and eight foot long, ſpotted and wav'd with black, red, yellow, tawny, and ſeveral other colours, which heightned

ned their price beyond thofe commonly feen in *Holland*.

2. Many rich Hides of Harts, Elks, Bears, as alfo the fkins of Foxes, Hares, and Conics, whereof moft were perfectly white.

3. A great number of precious Furs of divers kinds of four-footed Beafts particular to that Country, and not known yet by any name among us.

4. Several Packs of Whale-bone of extraordinary length.

5. Some compleat fuits of Cloths of the Inhabitants of the Country, whereof fome were of the fkins of Beafts, others of thofe of Birds, of the fafhion before reprefented.

6. Many of their Shirts made of Fifhes Bladders very neatly few'd; as alfo Caps, Gloves, and Bufkins, Quivers, Arrows, Bows, and other Arms ufed by them; as alfo fome of their Tents, Bags, Bafkets, and other little pieces of Houf-hold-ftuff.

7. A great number of thofe fmall Veffels made to carry only one man: A great Boat or Shallop forty five foot in length, which might conveniently carry fifty perfons.

8. But the moft rare and precious Commodity was a very confiderable quantity of the Teeth or Horns of the fifhes called Sea-Unicorns, which are thought to be the largeft, the faireft and the moft exactly proportion'd of any that have yet been feen.

Some of them were fent to *Paris*, and other parts of *Europe*, where they were well receiv'd: Nor is it unlikely but that they will be much more highly efteemed, when the admirable vertues they have in Phyfick are known: For though their beauty and rarity may procure them the beft places in the Clofets of the Curious; yet will they be more kindly received there, when fome others have found true what many famous Phyficians and Apothecaries of *Denmark* and *Germany*, who have made trial thereof upon feveral occafions, unanimoufly affirm of them, to wit, that they expell poyfon, and have all the properties commonly attributed to the Land-Unicorn's Horn.

CHAP. XIX.

Of certain Shell-Fiſh, rare Shells, and other remarkable productions of the Sea, found on the Coaſts of the Caribbies.

TO dive into the deep Secrets of the Waters to take a view of all the excellent Creatures ſporting themſelves therein, and obſerve the vertues and occult qualities wherewith they are endow'd, is a work might be expected from that Wiſdom which was communicated to *Solomon*, who treated of Trees, from the Cedar in *Libanon* to the Hyſſop growing on the Wall : For the watery Element is furniſhed with ſuch a miraculous plenty, that it abundantly produces not only Fiſhes of ſeveral kinds fit for the ſuſtenance of man, and thoſe of extraordinary bulk and monſtrous figures, as hath been ſhewn in the precedent Chapters, but alſo ſuch a multitude of precious Shells, and other Rarities, that we may well acknowledg that the Divine Wiſdom hath diſplay'd all theſe rich beauties of its inexhauſtible Treaſures, to ſhew its Omnipotency in the midſt of the Waves, and gently to win us into an admiration of his Goodneſs and adorable Providence, which humbles it ſelf to deſcend into the Abyſſes of the Sea to people them with ſome excellent Creatures not to be ſeen elſewhere, and an infinite number of others bearing the Characters and Idæas of the moſt conſiderable Bodies that either adorn the Heavens, flye in the Air, or embelliſh the Earth. Hence it comes, that there are found in the Waters, Stars, Cornets, Trumpets, Purcelains, Trees, Apples, Cheſt-nuts, and all the delightful curioſities which are ſo highly eſteemed among men. But to begin with the Shell-fiſh, there are in the Seas about, and in the Rivers of the *Caribbies* ſeveral kinds of them : The more particularly eſteemed are the *Homars*, the *Sea-Spiders*, and the *Crabs*.

HOMARS.

THe *Homars* are a kind of *Crevices*, of the ſame figure as thoſe of our Rivers ; but they are ſo big that there needs but one to make a good large diſh : Their meat is white, and of a good taſte, but a little hard of digeſtion : The Inhabitants of the Iſlands take them in the night time upon the ſands, or in the Shallows neer the low-water-mark ; and with the aſſiſtance of a Torch, or Moon-light, they catch them with a little iron fork.

SEA.

SEA-SPIDER.

THe *Sea-Spider* is by some conceiv'd to be a kind of *Crab*: It is cover'd with two very hard scales, whereof the uppermost is somewhat i rough, and the lowermost is more smooth, and jagged with sharp points: It hath many legs or claws, and a strong tail, sometimes about a foot in length: They are much sought after by some of the Savages to be employ'd about their Arrows: When this fish is dried in the Sun, the scale or shell of it becomes glistering, and in a manner transparent, though naturally it be of an Ash-colour.

CRABS.

THe ordinary *Crabs* of the *Caribbies* are of the same figure as those taken in these parts: There is a great difference among them as to bigness, but the rarest are those which live by prey: They are very common in most of the Islands, but above all in those called the *Virgins*: They lurk under the stumps and stocks of the Trees growing on the Sea-side, and as it were imitating a kind of Frogs, called the *Fishing-Frogs*, they discover from their lurking-holes the Oysters and Muscles, which they prey upon; and the sleight they use in the taking of them is worth our notice. Having found by experience that their Mordants or Claws are not strong enough to break the shells wherein those delicate fishes are contain'd; and having observed that several times of the day they open their shells to take the air, they diligently watch the time, and having furnish'd themselves with a little round pebble, they hold it ready in one of their claws, and coming to the Oyster or Muscle, let it fall so cunningly into the half-open'd shell, that not being able to close again, the fish becomes the prey of these subtle Crabs.

As to the *Shells* found in these Islands, in the Creeks and Nooks into which they are cast by the Sea there are abun- of them, and of several kinds: The most sought after and most considerable are these.

BURGAU.

THe *Burgau*, which is of the figure of a Snail, being uncas'd out of the outermost coat, presents to the eye a silver shell intermixt with spots of a bright black, a lively green, and so perfect and shining a grey, that no Enameller could come neer it with all the assistances of his art. As soon as the fish which had been lodg'd within this precious little Mansion hath been disseiz'd thereof, there is immediately seen a magnificent

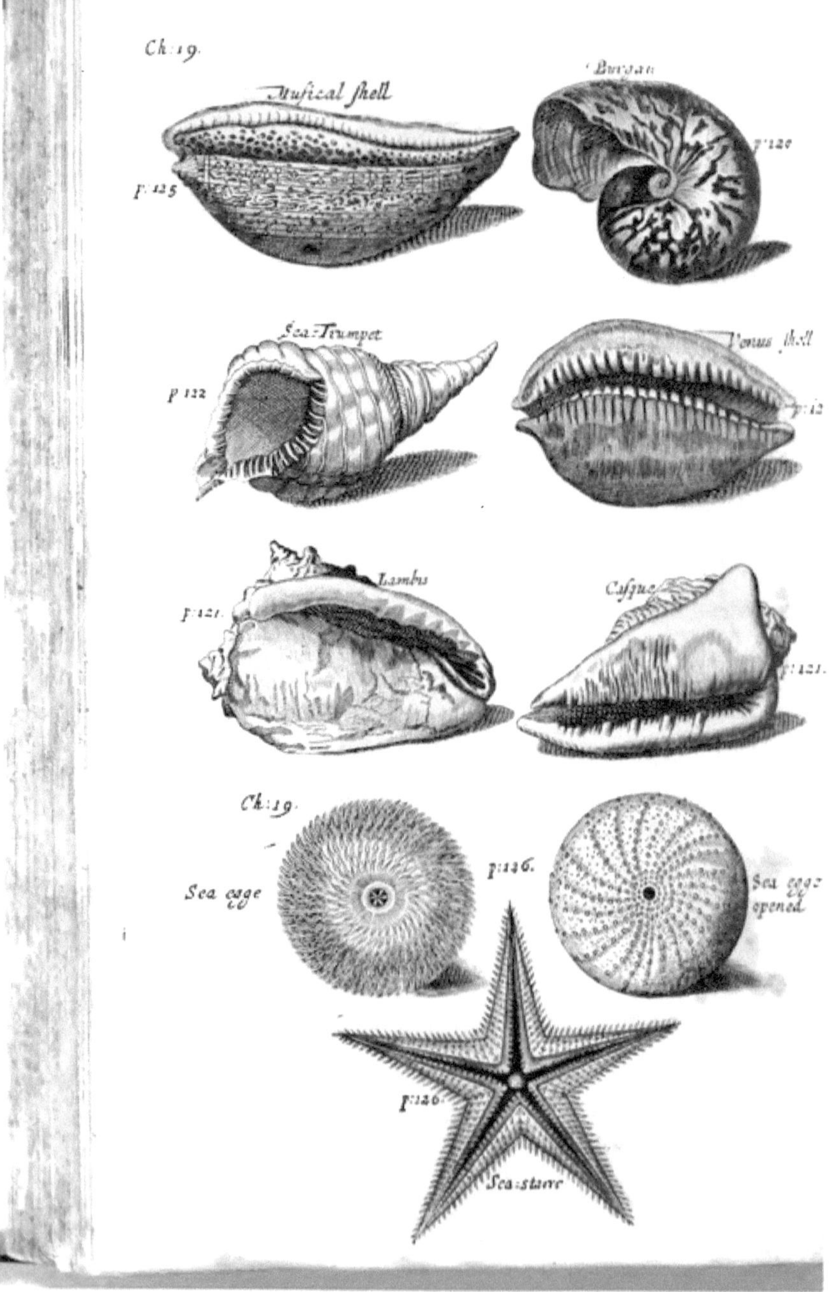

Ch: 19.
Musical shell
Bursa
p: 126
p: 125
Sea: Trumpet
Venus shell
p 122
p: 12
Lambis
Casque
p: 121.
p: 121.
Ch: 19.
Sea cage
p: 126.
Sea egg opened
p: 126.
Sea starr

ficent entry beſet with pearls', and afterwards ſeveral rich ap-
partements ſo clear, ſo neat, and enamell'd all over with ſo
bright a ſilver-colour, that there cannot in matter of ſhell any
thing be imagin'd more beautiful.

CASK.

THe *Cask*, or *Head-piece*, is of a different bigneſs proportionably to the heads of ſo many fiſhes as had worn it; and
it is ſo named from its figure: It is lin'd within and at the edges,
which are thick, flat and jagged, of a Satin carnation colour
extreamly bright and ſhining; and on the out-ſide it is faſhion'd
like a neat Country-building, having many little riſings which
are interlaced with a thouſand compartiments, on which there
may be ſeen a waving pannache or feather of divers rare
colours.

LAMBIS.

THe *Lambis* hath haply receiv'd that name becauſe the
fiſh which makes it move hath the figure of a great
Tongue, which licks that glutinous moiſture lying on the
rocks againſt which the waves of the Sea beat.   This is one of
the largeſt ſiz'd ſhells that are: One of the ſides is turned up,
as it were to make the greater diſcovery of the fair purple colour wherewith it is beautifi'd within: But it muſt be acknowledg'd, that the ſhape being none of the handſomeſt, and the
outer coat prickled with ſeveral rough and ſharp riſings, it
would hardly be receiv'd into the Cloſets of the Curious, if
Art taking off that outer coat did not diſcover **the beauty** and
ſmoothneſs of the divers-colour'd ſhell which **lay** within that
courſe ſhag: The fiſh which is lodg'd within the clefts of this
little moving rock is ſo big, that one of them will make a pretty round diſh: It may be ſerv'd up to the Tables of the daintieſt
Palats, ſo it be well dreſs'd with good ſtore of Pepper to correct its indigeſtion: The ſhells burnt to powder and mixt with
ſand make a cement which defies rain, and all other injuries of
the weather.   The *Lambis* yields a ſound like that of a Huntſ-
mans horn, and is heard at a great diſtance; whence ſome of
the Inhabitants of the Iſlands uſe them to bring their people together to meals.

VENUS-SHELLS.

THe *Venus-ſhells* may juſtly be numbred among the rareſt
productions of the Sea, whether we conſider the delightful ſmoothneſs wherewith they are glaz'd both within
and without, or the diverſity and livelineſs of their colours:
R   Their

Their jagged edges are turned inwards, and though all are not equally beautiful, yet are they all of the fame oval figure, gaping in the midft, and turning in a little: But they are very different as to bignefs and colour.

The ordinary ones are of a gilt-yellow, checquer'd with little white or red fpots, fo as that at a diftance a man would think them little Pearls, or grains of Coral: Of the reft, fome are blewifh, fome as it were befet with ftars, fome greyifh, fome like Chryftal, and fome colour'd like Agats, which are all delightful to the eye.

But the moft efteem'd by the Curious are on the out-fide of a colour between coral and carnation, and of a filver-colour, or of a bright fky-colour within, and a rich porphiry with fmall golden ftreaks: Thofe alfo are with reafon well efteem'd, which on the upper part are of a bright green like an Emerald, and within on the edges, and in the diftances of a pearl-colour: The fame account is made of thofe which on the back are black as Jet, and all elfewhere of a pale blew intermixt with little purple veins.

In fine, there are fome have fuch a delightful mixture of colours, as if the Rain-bow had communicated fome of its beauties to thefe little creatures: Nay there are abundance of them fo diverfifi'd with odd figures and characters, that it may be imagin'd Nature was in a very pleafant humor when fhe was deliver'd of thefe miracles.

But the mifchief of it is, that the Sea, which is poffefs'd of them as her moft precious jewels, never parts with them but againft her will: For if the Winds did not enrage her, and fhaking her bowels fearch into the bottom of her Treafures, and force them thence, fhe alone would enjoy thefe beauties, and never let us have any of them.

The Curious, to heighten their luftre, place them according to their value and efteem in feveral Cabinets, lin'd with green Plufh, or fome other rich ftuff: And after the example of the Flowrifts, who call their Tulips and Gilly-Flowers by the names of the *Cæfars*, and moft illuftrious Heroes, they in like manner give them the titles of Emperours and Princes.

SEA-CORNETS.

THere are alfo feen in the *Caribbies* two forts of thofe great Shells called *Sea-Cornets*, which are turned at the end like a fcrew: Some are white as Ivory, and not inferior to it in luftre: Others are within of a fhining pearl-colour, and without of feveral fair and lively colours, which are fometimes like fcales, fometimes waving, falling one upon another from the edge of the wide opening to the turn'd end, where they ceafe: If a little hole be made at the fmall end of thefe Cornets,

they

they become a kind of mufical Inftrument which makes a fharp
and piercing found, and forc'd through the windings of the
fhell, may be heard at as great diftance as the fmalleft kind of
Trumpet might be : But there is a great fecret in the found-
ing of it.

MOTHER *of* PEARL.

SHells do not only afford a pleafant divertifement which may
    excite men by a confideration of thofe fmall, but admira-
ble works of Nature, to blefs the Author thereof; but having
cloy'd the eye, they find fomewhat to fatisfie the tafte, and en-
creafe wealth : For *Oyfters*, and other fhell-fifh are welcome to
the greateft Tables; and the *Naker* or *Mother of Pearl* is big
with that Pearl which enriches the Crowns of Kings. 'Tis
true, there is feen only the feeds of thefe Pearls in the *Caribbies*, and that they are to be had in perfection only at S. *Margarets* Ifland, and the South-part of *America :* But though this
feed is not hardned into great Pearls in the *Caribbies*, yet are
not the fhells wherein it is found without their advantages;
for the meat within them is for food, and the two parts of the
filver fhell make fo many Spoons, which may creditably appear
upon the Table.

It is not eafie to determine whether the dew which falls in
the *Caribbies* be not fruitful enough to make the *Mother-Pearl*
produce its fruit in perfection; or whether after it hath receiv'd that feed from the Heavens they mifcarry, and have not
natural force enough to retain it : But not to enquire whence
the defect proceeds, it is moft certain they have as ftrong an inclination to avoid the reproach of fterility, as thofe fifh'd for on
the Coafts of S. *Margarets* : For he who will be at the curiofity
to obferve their fecret Loves from the rocks, at the foot whereof they moft delight to be, fhall find, that at the break of day
they ftart up feveral times to the furface of the water, as it were
to do homage to the Rifing-Sun; then of a fudden they open
themfelves upon that foft bed, expecting the firft beams of that
all-enlivening Star : If they be fo happy as to receive fome
drops of the dew he caufes to diftill from the Heavens at his
rifing, they immediately clofe their fhells, left any touch of
falt-water come in, and corrupt that celeftial fperm : And then
they cheerfully return to their deep cells.

A certain Author named *Fragofus* conceives, that the Pearls
ingender in the meat of the Oyfter, as the ftone does in fome
living creatures, of a thick and vifcous moifture which remains
of the aliment. Some learned Phyficians who are alfo of the
fame opinion, fortifie it with what is affirmed by *Jofephus Acofta*, a very creditable Writer, to wit, that the Slaves who fifh
for Pearls, dive fometimes twelve fathom deep in the Sea to

take the Oysters which are commonly fastened to the Rocks, that they get them thence by violence, and come up loaden with them: Whence they conclude, that it cannot be well maintained, that those Oysters which are fasten'd to the rocks suck in the dew, and that thence comes the generation of Pearls.

But not to enter into any contestation with these Gentlemen, nor yet absolutely to reject their opinion which hath its grounds, we may affirm, that the true account given by *Acosta* of the fishing for Pearls makes nothing against the opinion commonly receiv'd of their generation; for it is not impossible but that the Mother-Pearls which have conceived of the Dew, feeling themselves burthened with that precious fruit, have no great inclination to appear ever afterwards on the surface of the waters; and being satisfi'd with the treasure they are possess'd of, they from thenceforth fasten themselves to the rocks, whence they cannot be gotten off without violence.

Of several other sorts of Shells.

THose who living in populous Cities would counterfeit Deserts, Rocks and solitary Places, or in their Gardens raise little Hills, under which there should be Grotts encompass'd with all the most curious spoils of Sea and Land, might find in most of these Islands what may satisfie their humor: This only is to be feared, that abundance and diversity would puzzle their choice, and occasion a certain contempt of them. There are on the Coasts of these Islands an infinite multitude of several sorts of Shells, especially those of the *Sea-tops*, *Whelks*, *&c.* which have no names among us, whereof some are of a silver-colour, some full of stars, some sanguine, some green, some streaked with carnation, some checquer'd with several sorts of colours, which make them shine along the sands like so many precious stones: The Sun extreamly heightens their lustre and beauty; and when after an extraordinary tempest the Sea hath enrich'd the surface of those shores with these little sparkling gems, the eye is so dazzled at it, that a man cannot but acknowledg that Nature loves to make different demonstrations of her power, and shews what she can do, when she bestows so much beauty, and so many rich ornaments on these little inconsiderable Creatures.

The Savage Islanders sometimes gather these little play-games of the Sea, only for diversion sake, and having made holes in them put them on strings for Neck-laces and Bracelets: But most of the Southern part of *America* have a far greater esteem for them; for they drive a Trade with them, and they are in some places the current Money, and those who have most shells are accounted the richest. The Shells used for this purpose are of a

pretty

pretty bigneſs, ſolid, and of extraordinary luſtre; and to be current Money, they muſt be marked by certain Officers, who aſcertain the value thereof by certain little Characters engraved on them.

MUSICK-SHELL.

THere is a very conſiderable Shell, which Monſ. *du Montel* thinks may be found in ſome of the *Caribby-Iſlands*, though he never ſaw any of that kind but only at *Coraſſao:* It differs not much as to figure from the *Venus-ſhells:* It may be called the *Muſical-ſhell*, becauſe on the out-ſide of it there are blackiſh lines, full of notes, which have a kind of key for the ſinging of them, ſo that it might be ſaid there wants only the letter to that natural pricking: The forementioned Gentleman relates, that he ſaw ſome that had five Lines, a Key and Notes, which made good Muſick: Some perſon had added the Letter, which it ſeems Nature had forgotten, and caus'd it to be ſung, and the Muſick was not undelightful.

This might afford the ingenious many excellent reflections: They might ſay among other things, that if according to the opinion of *Pythagoras* the Heavens have their Harmony, the ſweetneſs whereof cannot be heard by reaſon of the noiſe made upon Earth; if the Air reſound with the melody of an infinite number of Birds who ſing their ſeveral parts there; and if Men have invented a kind of Muſick, after their way, which by the Ears recreates the Heart; it were but juſt that the Sea, which is not always toſs'd and troubled, ſhould have within its territories certain Muſicians to celebrate, by a Muſick particular to them, the praiſes of their Sovereign Maker. The Poets might adde, that theſe natural tablatures are the ſame which the *Syrens* had in their hands, when they had their melodious Conſorts; and that being perceiv'd by ſome eye which came to diſturbe their recreations, they let them fall into the water, where they have been carefully kept ever ſince: But leaving theſe imaginations to thoſe they belong to, let us purſue our deſign.

EYE-STONE.

THere is a little Stone found in theſe Iſlands, moſt commonly neer the Sea-ſide, and ſometimes at a good diſtance from the Sea, which from its vertues may be termed the *Eye-ſtone*; but in regard the more common opinion will have it to be a production of the waters, we ſhall treat of it in this place. Some of theſe Stones are about the bigneſs of the larger ſort of Braſs-farthings; but the leaſt are moſt eſteem'd: A man would think, looking on them in the Sun, that they were

of

of thofe Pearls called *Barroques* cut in two, they are fo cleer, tranfparent, and fmooth : Some of them have red or blewifh veins, which give them a very delightful luftre, according to the feveral afpects are caft on them : They have the figure of a Snail engrav'd on that fide which is even : Being put under the eye-lid, they roll about the ball of the eye, and it is affirmed, that they ftrengthen and cleer the fight, and force thence the motes, or trafh which might have fallen into it.

SEA-EGGES.

THere is found in the Ifland of S. *Martins* a production of the Sea, called *Sea-egges*, or *Sea-Apples*, full of fharp prickles rifing out of a dark-coloured fkin : But when the fifh which rouls them is dead, they lofe all thofe prickles, which become afterwards of no ufe ; and quitting that hard cruftinefs which had encompafs'd them, they difcover the whitenefs of their fhells, which are intermixt with fo many compartiments and little windings, that the needle of the moft ingenious Embroiderer would be much troubled to imitate them. Thefe Egges fhould rather be called *Sea-Urchins* or *Sea-Cheftnuts* ; for while they are living they have the figure and colour of a little Urchin, which formes it felf like a ball, and is arm'd ot all fides, the better to deal with his enemy : Or they are like thofe rough prickles which encompafs the Cheftnut while it is upon the Tree.

SEA-STAR.

TO confider narrowly all the rarities to be feen in the Sea, it might be faid, that of whatever is excellent in the Heavens there is a certain refemblance in the Sea, which is as it were the others looking-glafs. Hence it comes, that there are Stars to be feen in it, having five points or beams, fomewhat of a yellowifh colour. This *Star* is fomewhat better then a foot diametre, and an inch thick ; the fkin is hard enough, and full of little rifings, which adde much to its beauty. If thefe Sea-Stars may not enter into any competition with thofe of the Heavens, as to magnitude and light, they exceed them in this, that they are animate, and that their motion is not forc'd, and that they are not fix'd nor confin'd to the fame place: For the fifh, which hath taken up its abode in this ftarry manfion, moves which way it pleafes on the azure plains of the waters while the weather is calm, but as foon as it forefees any tempeft, out of a fear to be forc'd to the Land, which is not fit to entertain Stars, it cafts out two little anchors out of its body, whereby it is fo firmly faftened to the Rocks, that all the violent agitations

of

of the incens'd waves cannot force it thence. It is preſerv'd
alive by the means of the nouriſhment it takes by a little hole,
which is as it were its mouth, and lies juſt in the centre of
its body. Some curious perſons remove theſe Stars out of
their watery Element, and having dryed them in the Sun
make them the ornaments of their Cloſets.

SEA-TREES.

NOr can the ſandy ſhelfs or ſholes of thoſe Rocks, which
are covered with water, endure the reproach of barren-
neſs: For notwithſtanding the ſaltneſs whereby they are always encloſ'd, they make a ſhift to produce, among the graſs
which is upon them, certain Trees which are immediately
glaz'd with a ſalt-peter, which renders them extremely white.
Some conceive them to be a kind of Coral. There are taken
up of them of ſeveral figures, and ſo neatly made, that the eye
cannot be cloy'd with conſidering the odneſs of their ſhapes.

SEA-FANS.

THere are alſo certain *Pannaches*, or *Sea-Fans*, or Sea-
Feathers, which are, to ſpeak by way of reſemblance,
as it were the borders of that ſpacious liquid Garden which
never needs watering: They are woven very finely, and according to the quality of the Rocks whereon they are rooted,
they are of different colours: This only were to be wiſh'd,
that they had ſolidity enough to endure a tranſportation from
thoſe Iſlands into theſe parts.

CHAP. XX.

*Of Amber-greece ; its Origine ; and the marks of that
which is good, and without mixture.*

AMber-greece is found in greateſt abundance on the Coaſts
of *Florida*, beyond what is had of it in any other Country of *America*: Whence it comes, that the *Spaniards*
have built Forts there, to keep poſſeſſion of the Land, and
entertain with the Indians, who inhabit it, the Commerce of
that rich Commodity, which they carefully gather ſince they
have been acquainted with the value of it. There hath ſometimes been taken up of it, after extraordinary tempeſts, on the
Coaſts of *Tabago*, *Barboudos*, and ſome other of the *Caribbies*,
as we have received by very authentick Relations: Upon
which

which affurance, it will be no digreffion from the Natural Hiftory we treat of, if we perfume this Chapter with the fweet
fcent of this Aromatick Drug, which certainly is the rareft
and moft precious of all thofe productions which the Ocean
hath yet caft up out of its vaft and unexhaufted bofom to enrich that new world.

The *Maldives* call Amber-greece *Panahambar*, that is, *Amber of gold*, by reafon of its worth *:* The Inhabitants of *Fez*,
Morocco, and the *Æthiopians* call it by the fame name as they
do the Whale; whence it is probably conjectur'd, that they
thought it proceeded from the Whale.   Moft certain it is, that
neither *Hippocrates*, *Diofcorides*, nor *Galen*, ever heard any
thing of Amber-greece, no more then they had of the *Bezo-
ar-ftone*, *Guayacum*, *Saffafras*, *Saffaparilla*, *Rhubarb*, *Mechoa-
chan*, and many other Drugs : Amber-greece therefore is one
of thofe whereof the knowledge is wholly modern, and the
origine not well known.

Some have imagin'd that this Amber, not known among
the Ancients, is an excrement of the Whales : Others are of
opinion, that it comes from the Crocodiles, in regard their
flefh is perfum'd : Some others are perfwaded, that they are
pieces of Iflands and fragments of Rocks conceal'd in the
Sea, and carried away by the violence of the waves, forafー
much as there are fometimes found pieces of this Amber which
weigh a hundred pound, and of the length of fixty hands-
bredths, and that, as is affirmed by *Linfcot*, in the Year M. D.
L. V. there was a piece found neer *Cape Comorin*, which
weigh'd thirty hundred weight. There are alfo thofe who
conceive it to be a kind of Sea-foam, which gathers together and grows thick after a certain time by the agitation
of the Sea-water, and is hardned by the heat of the Sun.

But the moft probable conjecture is, that it is a kind of
Bitumen engendred at the bottom of the Sea; and when it
comes to be extremely agitated by fome extraordinary tempeft, it lets go this Bitumen, and forces it towards the fhores:
for indeed it is commonly found only after fome great tempeft.
Philoftratus in the life of *Apollonius* affirms, that the Panthers
which are neer the Mount *Caucafus* are very much delighted
with the fweet fcent of that place : But certain it is, that of
all creatures the Birds are very great lovers of this Amber-
greece, and that they will fcent it at a great diftance: Where-
fore as foon as the tempeft is laid it muft be fought after and
taken away, otherwife it will be devoured. Nor is it the
fweet fcent of it, but the ill, which caufes the Birds to flock to
it; for this precious and admirable perfume, when it is frefh
and foft, and newly come out of the Sea, fmells very ftrong,
and thofe creatures which run to it do but as they would do to
fome carrion; for the fcent of it is like that of rufty bacon,

and

and 'tis likely for that reaſon that it was ſo long ere 'twas known and uſed: The Ancients judg'd of its vertue by its ill ſcent, fit rather to injure the heart then refreſh it, and ſo they rejected it as unprofitable, nay hurtful. Beſides it is not ſo commonly, nor in ſo great quantities found towards the Coaſts of *Greece*, nor yet in *Europe*; and there were but very few Voyages heretofore made into the *Indies*.

The Foxes do alſo think it a good diſh, and eat much of it: In thoſe Countries where much of it is gather'd, theſe creatures wait at the Sea-ſide, and having diſcover'd any, they immediately devour it: But having kept it a while in their bellies, they caſt it up again before it be any way digeſted; yet does it loſe ſome of its vertue and ſweet ſcent: Whence it comes, that this kind of Amber-greece is leſs eſteem'd then the other, and us'd only in perfumes.

It will not be amiſs here to give the marks whereby the true Amber-greece is to be diſtinguiſh'd from the adulterate, ſince thoſe who have written of it, as *Garcias*, *Monard*, *Scaliger*, *Ferdinand Lopez*, *Cluſius*, and others, ſpeak very little thereof, and aſſign not the eſſential marks of it.

It is in the firſt place to be obſerv'd, that Amber-greece is generally diſtinguiſh'd into that which comes from the *Levant* Seas, and that which comes from the Weſtern Sea: That which is taken up on the Coaſts of the *Levant*, eſpecially on thoſe of *Barbary*, where there is much, and in great pieces had, is for the moſt part black, and cannot be dried ſo well as to be reduc'd to powder, as that of the Weſt, let what will be added to promote the pulverization of it: It is alſo more eaſily melted by the fire, hath not ſo ſweet a ſcent, and is of a lower value: There is little of the Amber brought into theſe parts, in regard it is not much eſteem'd, and not very uſeful either as to Phyſick, or Perfumes.

The Amber-greece of the Weſt, whereof the beſt is that found on our Coaſts, is commonly of an aſh-colour'd grey, looking as if aſhes were mixt with wax, yet ſo as that the aſhes appear diſtinctly, and are not perfectly mixt with the wax: The upper part of it having raked along the ſhore, and lain more open to the air, is commonly of a tawny colour, or at leaſt not ſo white as it is within, hard and ſolid like a cruſt, and ſometimes full of ſand and little ſhells: which happens hence, that being ſoft as Bitumen or Pitch, ſuch filth eaſily ſticks to it; and that abates ſomwhat of its price, but not of its goodneſs.

To know whether this Amber, which is of the beſt kind, be good, in the firſt place conſider the figure of it, which for the moſt part ſhould incline to roundneſs, inaſmuch as all things that are any way ſoft being toſs'd to and fro by the Sea are reduc'd to a certain roundneſs: It ſhould be alſo ſomewhat

S   ſmooth,

smooth, and of a dark colour between a dark-grey and tawny : If it be very dry it should be the lighter, proportionably to the bigness of the piece : Hereby it may be judg'd whether there be any mixture of Scamony, Bitumen, Wax, Pitch, or Rozin, all these adding much to its weight : By the same tryal it may be known whether there be any mixture of sand; as also whether it be not the black Amber-greece of the *Levant*.

If the Owners of it are unwilling to have the piece broken, take a needle heated, and thrust it into the piece, and if it enter easily, conclude there are no stones within it ; and if you smell at the liquor which will come forth by the heat of the needle whereby the Amber is melted, you will find it of a scent not unlike that of gumm'd wax, but at last will end in an odour sweet enough.

But the surest way is, having agreed about the price of the piece of Amber conditionally it be good, to break it ; so you will find whether there be any small pebbles in it.   The Amber, as we said before, must be of an ash-colour, having small specks, as our Water-nuts : When it is fresh it is of a darker colour then when it is very dry : but if it differ not much from that colour, and be not too black nor too white, it matters not ; above all it should appear of a mixt colour : Take also a little out of the middle of the piece, or from that part which you think worst, and put it on a knife heated in the fire, and it will presently melt like wax, and if the knife be very hot what was put upon it will be quite consum'd.

When you have thus melted it, observe whether it hath the scent we mentioned, which cannot be well known but only to such as have made tryal thereof, because it is particular thereto ; and by that means you will also discover whether there be any mixture in the Amber : You may also while it is melting put a little upon your hand, and spreading it you may see whether there be any mixture : It should stick so fast to your hand that it can hardly be got off : When it melts it becomes all of one colour, though before it seemed to be mixt, and inclines to that of some kind of Rozin : It should not dissolve in either water or oyl ; not but that there is a way to dissolve it in either of them, by the addition of a certain ingredient, which those who know it would not have discover'd : Nor should it be reduc'd to powder, unless being very dry it may be scraped or grated, and be mixt with some fine powder : It also sticks much to the Mortar, which therefore must be often made clean : The black will never be reduc'd to powder, neither this, nor any other way.

The difference between the black and the grey consists chiefly in the colour, which inclines to that of black pitch, and not mixt with whitish-grey seeds, but all over alike : The black is also softer and more weighty, and smells more like *Bitumen*.   There

Ch: 21.
Tortoise.
p:133
Crocadile.
p:133.
Sea Feather.
Sea Tree
p:127.
p:129.

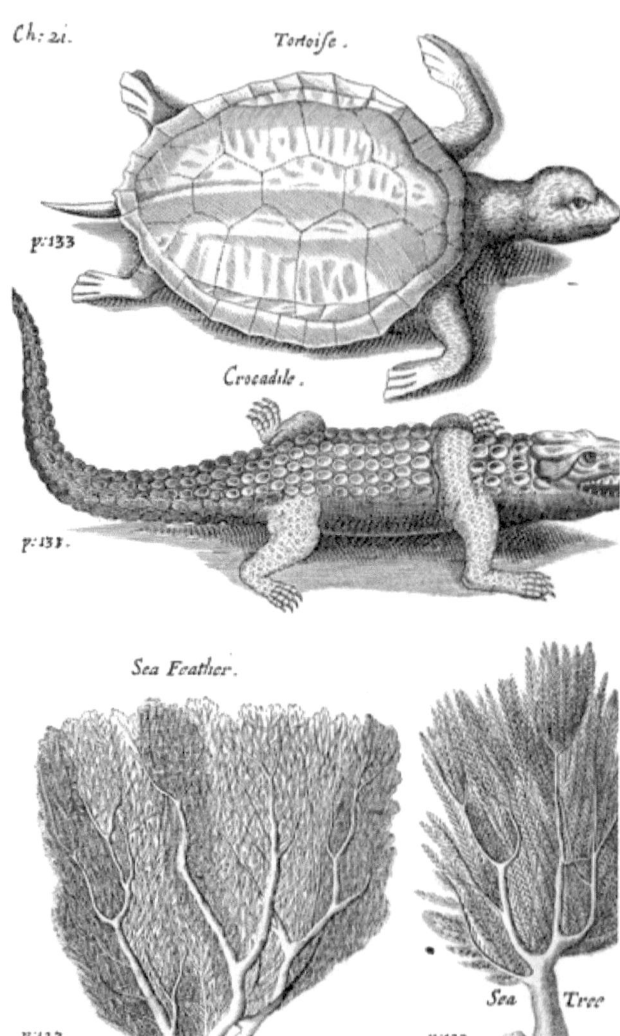

There is a third kind of Amber-greece, which is white, the rareſt, as *Ferdinand Lopez* affirms, but not the beſt as he accounts it. On the contrary, it is the moſt inconſiderable of any, and there being no account made of it, there is very little tranſported: But this is indeed ſome of the other kinds of Amber-greece, which having been devoured and digeſted by Birds that have very hot ſtomacks, turns white, as moſt of the excrements of Birds are: That which hath been devour'd by Fiſhes, as it happens many times, is not much alter'd either as to colour or ſubſtance: which proceeds hence, that their ſtomacks are not ſo hot as thoſe of the Birds, and perhaps finding the Amber-greece hotter then their ordinary ſuſtenance, and burthen'd therewith, they ſoon caſt it up again: But what had been eaten by the Fox is in a manner corrupted, and of little value, by reaſon of the heat of his ſtomack. This white Amber-greece is like ſalted or pickled Suet, eaſily melted, and ſmells like tallow; whence ſome conceive it is but ſome kind of ſuet ſo ordered.

Having given the marks of the right Amber-greece, we ſhall omit the adulterations of it, becauſe they are almoſt infinite: Nor ſhall we treat of its uſe in Phyſick, its excellent qualities, and eſpecially the ſweet ſcent it gives to liquid Conſerves, and all other things wherein it is uſed: Of theſe ſome other Books lately come forth, and experience may ſatisfie the curious Reader.

CHAP. XXI.

Of certain Creatures living partly on Land, partly in the Waters, commonly called Amphibia, *which may be found in the* Caribby-Iſlands.

WE ſhall begin with the *Crocodile*, by the Iſlanders called *Cayeman*: It is a very dangerous Monſter, which ſometimes grows to an extraordinary bulk and length: The Skeletons of ſeveral of them being frequently brought into theſe parts, we ſhall not be ſo large in our deſcription thereof, as otherwiſe we might.

This Creature keeps in or neer the Sea, and in the Rivers of the Iſlands that are not inhabited, and ſometimes on the Land among the Reeds, very hideous to look on: It is conceiv'd to live a long time, and that its body encreaſeth in all its dimenſions to the very laſt day: Whence it is not to be wondred, if there have been ſeen of them ſome which were eighteen foot in length, and as big about as a Hogſhead: It hath four feet

well

well arm'd with crooked claws : The skin, which is cover'd all over with scales, is so hard on the back, that a bullet from a Musket shot at him shall hardly make any impression on it : but if he be hurt under the belly, or in the eyes, he is soon gone : His lower jaw is immoveable, but hath so wide a mouth, and so well set with sharp teeth, that he makes nothing to divide a man in two.

He runs fast enough on land ; but the weight of his body causes him to make so deep a track in the sand, as a Coach-horse might do ; and having no *vertebræ* in the back-bone, no more then the *Hyæna's*, he goes streight forwards, not being able to turn his vast body, but with much difficulty ; so that the better to avoid his pursuit, a man need only turn several times a side.

Those which are bred in fresh water do so smell of Musk while they are alive, that the air is perfum'd a hundred paces about the place where they are : nay the water retains somwhat of the same smell. This observation of the sweet scent of the Crocodile may, by the way, discover the error of *Pliny,* who imagin'd that of all living creatures only the *Panther* had a sweet scent with it, as he somewhere affirms, though in another place he writes, that the entrails of the Crocodile smell very sweet, and that proceeds from the odoriferous flowers on which he feeds : Now this musky scent of the Crocodile of *America* is enclos'd in certain glandules in the Emunctories, which he hath under the thighs, and which being taken thence keep the said smell a long time : It may be imagin'd that God hath bestow'd this scent on them, that men and other creatures, which many times become the prey of these cruel Monsters, might by the scent discover the place where they lurk, and avoid them.

Those which have their abode in the Sea have no smell of musk, but both kinds are very dangerous, and to be dreaded by such as either go to wash themselves, or are forc'd to cross some river by swimming : This dreadful Monster hath a strange sleight to make his prey of Oxen and Cows : One of them will lye lurking at those places of the Ponds and Rivers where those creatures are wont to water, and finding one at his advantage, he half-shuts his eyes, and floats on the face of the water, as if it were a piece of rotten wood ; by which means getting neerer and neerer to the poor beast which is a drinking, and is not aware of him, he immediately fastens on him, taking him by the lips, and forcing him under water, he drowns him, and then feeds on him He taketh men also by the same sleight, as is affirmed by *Vincent le Blanc,* who hath a Relation of the servant of a Consul of *Alexandria,* who going to take one of these cruel beasts, thinking it had been a piece of wood, was drawn by it to the bottom, and never seen afterwards.

There

There are abundance of these monstrous Crocodiles in those Islands, which from them are called the Islands of *Cayeman*, and not frequented but only in the time of Tortoise-fishing : For having pick'd out the best meat out of the Tortoise, and a great deal cast away, the Crocodiles come in great numbers in the night time to feed on the entrails and carcases left on the sand : So that those who are watching for the Tortoises are oblig'd to carry about them great wooden Leavers to keep off those *Cayemans*, which they many times kill, having first broken their backs with those Leavers.

These creatures have a whitish fat, which was heretofore used by Physicians in fluxions proceeding from a cold cause; it being hot, and consisting of subtile parts : Upon the same account were such as had Fevers rubb'd therewith upon the approach of their fits, to cause sweating; Many other properties are attributed to the Crocodile by *Pliny*, in order to the curing of diseases : Some are very desirous to get certain little stones, like little bones, which are in his head, and having reduced them to powder, they use them to clear the Reins of Gravel : Some also affirm, that the sharpest teeth of this Animal, which are on the side of each jaw, cure the Tooth-ach, and preserve the teeth from corruption, being only rubbed every day therewith : There are in like manner in the heads of Dragons, and Toads, stones good against several diseases : So the cruel *Requiems*, by us before described, afford a remedy against the Stone and Gravel. Thus hath it pleas'd the wise Author of Nature, that we should have some advantages from those creatures which are otherwise most pernicious.

The *Chineses* have a way to take and tame these Crocodiles, as some Historians affirm: And when they have bred them a certain time, and made them fat enough, they kill them, and feed on them : But the *Europeans* who have tasted thereof, affirm, their flesh, though white and delicate, is not pleasant to the taste, as being too lushious, sweetish, and retaining much of the musk.

TORTOISES.

THere are taken in these Islands several sorts of *Tortoises*, for there are *Land-Tortoises*, *Sea-Tortoises*, and *Fresh-water-Tortoises*, which are of different figures : The *Caribbians* call them all by the name of *Catallou*; but when they speak of the Land-Tortoises, they adde the word *Nonum*, which in their Language signifies the Earth, or that of *Tona*, that is to say, of the River or Water.

The Sea-Tortoises are commonly divided by the Islanders into three kinds, that which the French call *Tortue Franche*, that called *Caouanne*, and the *Carets* : They are all of them almost moft of the fame figure; but the meat only of the firft kind is good to be eaten, unlefs it be in cafe of neceffity, and for want of other provifion; fo that of the two laft, only the fhell is of value.

The *Tortue-Franche*, and the *Caouannes* are commonly of fo vaft a bulk, that the upper fhell is about four foot and a half in length, and four in bredth: Which is not to be much admired, fince that in *Maurice-Ifland* there are fome which having four men on their backs, are neverthelefs able to go. *Ælian* relates, that the Inhabitants of *Taprobana* cover their houfes therewith: And if we may credit *Diodorus Siculus*, certain Nations of the *Eaft-Indies* convert them into Boats, in which they will crofs a great arm of the Sea that lies between them and the Continent.

Thefe Amphibious creatures feldom come to Land, but only to difpofe of their Egges, in order to propagation: To that end they make choice of a very light fand which they find on the Sea-fide, in fome place not much frequented, and to which they may have eafie accefs.

The Iflanders, who at a certain feafon of the year go to the *Cayeman-Iflands*, to make provifion of the meat of Tortoifes which come to land there in infinite numbers, affirm, that they make their recourfe thither from all parts within a hundred leagues and more to lay their egges, by reafon of the eafinefs of the accefs, the fhore being flat, and cover'd with a foft fand: The Tortoifes come to land about the latter end of *April*, and their landing continues till *September*, and then may they be taken in abundance; which is thus performed.

At the clofe of the evening fome men are fet afhore, who lying on the fands without making any noife, watch the Tortoifes when they come out of the Sea to lay their egges in the fand; and when they perceive that they are got a good way from the Sea-fide, and hear them making a deep hole in the fand with their claws, into which being a foot and a half deep, and fometimes more, they lay the egges, they come and furprize them at that employment, and turn them upfide-down; and being in that pofture they are not able to recover themfelves, but continue fo till the next day that they are brought thence in Shallops to the Ships: When they are thus turned upfide-down, they are obferv'd to fhed tears, and are heard to figh. 'Tis generally known that the Stag weeps when he is put to his extremities: And it is almoft incredible what cries and groans proceed from the Crocodiles about the *Nile*, and what tears they fhed when they find themfelves taken.

The Sea-men of thofe Ships which go to the *Cayeman-Iflands* to take in their loading of Tortoifes, may every night in lefs then three hours turn forty or fifty of them, the leaft whereof weighs a hundred and fifty pound, and the ordinary ones two

hundred

hundred pound ; nay ſome of them will have two great pails
full of egges in their bellies : Theſe egges are round , and
about the bigneſs of a Tennis-ball ; they have white and yolk
like Hens-egges, but the ſhell is not ſo hard, but ſoft, feeling as
if it were wet parchment. The *Fricaſſeys* and *Omeletts* made
of them are good enough, but a little drier then thoſe
made with Hens-egges. There is ſo much meat about one
Tortoiſe as may well maintain ſixty perſons a whole day :
When they are deſirous to eat of them, they cut off the ſhell
which is under the belly from that on the back, unto which it
is joyn'd by certain griſtles which are eaſily cut : What Tortoiſes are taken by the Sea-men in the night, finds them work
all day to cut into pieces and ſalt them. Moſt of the Ships
which come to theſe *Cayeman-Iſlands*, after they have taken in
their loading, that is, after ſix weeks or two moneths continuance there, return to the *Caribbies*, where they ſell that ſalted
Tortoiſe ; and it becomes the ſuſtenance of the ordinary ſort of
people, and the ſlaves.

But the Tortoiſes that have eſcaped, having laid their egges
at two or three ſeveral times, return to the place whence they
came, the egges which they have cover'd with ſand on the
Sea-ſide being about ſix weeks after hatch'd by the heat of the
Sun, and not by their looking on them, as *Pliny*, and ſome of
the Ancients imagined : as ſoon as the young Tortoiſes have
broken the ſhells wherein they were incloſ'd, they make their
way through the ſand, and get out of the grave which gave
them birth, and by an inſtinct of nature go ſtreight to the Sea
to the old ones.

The meat of this kind of Tortoiſe is as dainty as any Veal,
ſo it be freſh, and kept but one day : It is intermixt with fat,
which when it is dreſs'd is of a greeniſh yellow : It is of eaſie
digeſtion, and very wholſom, whence it comes, that thoſe ſick
perſons who cannot recover in the other Iſlands are carried to
that purpoſe to the *Cayemans* in the Ships that go for Tortoiſes ; and commonly having refreſh'd, and purg'd themſelves
with that diet, they return thence perfectly recover'd. The
fat of this kind of Tortoiſe yields an oyl, which while it is
freſh is good enough to fry withall , being ſtale it is employ'd
in Lamps.

CAOUANNE.

THe Tortoiſe called the *Caouanne* is of the ſame figure as
the precedent, ſave that the head of it is a little bigger : This ſtands upon the defenſive when people come neer
to turn it ; but the meat of it being black, full of ſtrings, and
of ill taſte, there is no account made of it, but only where
other is not to be had ; the oyl alſo got from it is good only for
Lamps.   *CARETS.*

CARETS.

THe third kind of Sea-Tortoise, called by the French *Ca-ret*, differs from the two others in bigness, as being much less, and that it lays not its egges in the sand, but in a kind of gravel which is mixt with small pebbles: The meat of this Tortoise is not pleasant, but the egges more delicate then those of the other two kinds: It would be as little regarded as the *Caouanne*, were it not sought after for its precious shell: It consists of fifteen greater and lesser leaves or pieces, ten where-of are flat and even, four a little bending, and that which covers the neck, made triangle-wise, hollow like a little buckler: All the shells of an ordinary *Caret* may weigh three or four pound; but there have been some taken whose shells have been so large and so thick, rhat all together have weigh'd about six or seven pounds.

Of the shell of this kind of Tortoise are made Combs, Cups, Boxes, Cases, Cabinets, and so many excellent things of great price: It also enriches Houshold-stuff, the borders of Looking-glasses and Pictures, and is used now in the covering of Pocket-books of Devotion. To get this precious shell, they put a little fire under the upper shell which consists of so many pieces; and as soon as they feel the heat they are easily taken off with the point of a knife.

Some affirm, that this kind of Tortoise is so vigorous, that its shell being taken away it will get another if it be immediately cast into the Sea. The most plentiful fishing for these Tortoises is at the *Peninsula* of *Jucatan*, and several little Islands within the Gulf of *Hondures*: So that honest *Pirard* was ill-inform'd, who in his Treatise of the Animals and Fruits of the *East-Indies*, Chap. 2. affirmes, that this kinde of Tortoise is to be found only in the *Maldivos* and the *Philippine-Islands*.

It is affirmed by some, that the oyl of this kind of Tortoise helpeth all kinds of Gouts proceeding from cold causes: It is also very successfully used to strengthen the Sinews, to take away the pain of the Reins, and cure all cold Fluxions and Distempers.

Having given so particular an account of the Tortoises, it will not be amiss to adde thereto the manner how they are fish'd for, and how all the great fishes of the *Caribbies* are taken.

How

How the Tortoiſes *and other great Fiſhes are taken* in the Caribbies.

THe Sea-Tortoiſes are not only taken upon the ſand, as we ſhew'd before, but alſo by means of an Inſtrument, which is a pole about the length of a half-pike, at the end whereof there is faſten'd a nail pointed at both ends, which is ſquare in the midſt, and about the bigneſs of a mans little finger: Some make notches on that ſide of it which ſtands out of the wood, that it may take faſter hold when it is entred into the ſhell of the Tortoiſe.

In the night time, the Moon ſhining and the Sea calm, the Maſter-fiſher being in a little boat with two others, one at the oar to turn it of any ſide as faſt as ever he can, that the boat may go much faſter and with leſs noiſe then if it were row'd; the other is in the midſt of the Canow or Boat, holding the line which is faſten'd to the nail, and in a readineſs to draw it it as ſoon as the inſtrument hath done execution on the Tortoiſe.

Being thus provided, they go where they think to find of them; and when the Maſter-fiſher, who ſtands up on the fore-part of the Canow, perceives one of them by the glittering of the Sea, which by getting up ever and anon to the face of the water it cauſeth to foam, he directs him who guides the little veſſel to make to the place where he would have him, and being gently got neer the Tortoiſe, he violently darts the inſtrument into its back: The nail piercing the ſhell, gets alſo a good way into the fleſh, and the wood keeps up above the water: As ſoon as the fiſh finds it ſelf hurt, it ſinks down to the bottom with the nail ſticking faſt in the ſhell: And the more it ſtrives and ſtruggles, the more it is entangled. At laſt having wearied it ſelf, and ſpent its forces in ſtriving by reaſon of its loſs of blood, it ſuffers it ſelf to be eaſily taken, and is either taken into the Canow, or drawn to the ſhore.

After the ſame manner they alſo take *Lamantins*, and ſeveral other great fiſhes; but inſtead of the nail there is put into the wooden inſtrument a great hook, or a ſmall dart of iron made like that of a ſharp lance: On one ſide of that piece of iron there is a hole, through which there paſſeth a line, which is alſo woond about the dart, ſo that when it is darted into the fiſh, the line eaſily is let looſe, that it may have the liberty to tumble up and down in the water, and when it hath ſpent its forces, and reduc'd to extremity, if it cannot be gotten into the Canow, it is eaſily drawn to the ſhore, where they divide it into quarters.

T

Land-Tortoifes, and Frefh-water-Tortoifes.

THe Land-Tortoifes are found in fome Iflands neer the frefh-water Rivers, which are leaft fubject to inundations, or in the ponds and fenny places that are fartheft from the Sea: They are cover'd all over with a hard and folid fhell, which is not to be rais'd by feveral pieces or leaves, as thofe of the Sea-Tortoifes, and it is fo thick in all parts, that it fecures the Animal living within it from any hurt, and will not be broken even though the wheels of a loaden Cart fhould go over it. But what is yet more ftrange, is, that the creature never finds this moving lodging too narrow for him; for it grows larger proportionably as the body of the poffeffor grows bigger: The upper covering is in fome of them about a foot and a half in length: it is of an oval figure, fomewhat hollow like a Buckler, and on the outfide hath feveral ftreaks, which as it were divide it into fo many compartiments, with a certain obfervance of Symmetry: All thefe intermixtures are laid on a black ground, which in feveral places is enamell'd with white and yellow.

This kind of Tortoife hath a very ugly head, like that of a Serpent: It hath no teeth, but only jaws, which are ftrong enough to break what it would fwallow down: It is fupported by four feet, fomewhat weak to fuftain the weight of its body; nor does it upon purfuit truft much to them: For if he be not neer fome river or pond into which he may caft himfelf, he places all refuge and fafety in the covering of his manfion, under which like a Hedg-hog he immediately draws in his head, feet and tail, upon the firft apprehenfion of any danger.

The Female lays egges about the bignefs of thofe of Pigeons, but a little longer: Having cover'd them with fand, fhe leaves them to be hatch'd by the Sun. Though there be fome who hold that the meat of thefe Land-Tortoifes is of hard digeftion, yet thofe who have eaten thereof rank it among the moft delicate difhes of *America*: The Phyficians of the Country advife thofe who are inclin'd to Dropfies to ufe it often for a preventive: They have alfo found by experience, that the blood of thefe Tortoifes dried and reduc'd to powder takes away the poyfon of Vipers and Scorpions, being apply'd to the wound: It is alfo certain, that the afhes of their fhells mixt with the white of an egge cures the chaps in Nurfing-womens nipples; and if the head be powder'd therewith, it prevents the falling of the Hair.

CHAP.

CHAP. XXII.

Containing the particular Deſcriptions of ſeveral ſorts of Crabs or Crab-fiſh, commonly found in the Caribbies.

There are found in all the *Caribby-Iſlands* certain Crabs or Crab-fiſh, which are a kind of amphibious *Crevices*, and very good meat, whereas thoſe of *Braſil* are unpleaſant, inaſmuch as they ſmell of the Juniper-root. Accordingly the Indian Inhabitants very highly eſteem theirs, and make them their ordinary entertainment : They are all of an oval figure, having the tail turning in under the belly : Their bodies, which are cover'd all over with a ſhell hard enough, is ſupported by ſeveral feet which are all full of little prickles, which facilitate their climbing up to thoſe places whither they would get up : The two fore-feet are very big, and of thoſe one is ſomewhat bigger then the other : The French call theſe two fore-feet or claws, *Mordants*, ſignificantly enough, foraſmuch as with theſe they twitch and ſecure whatſoever they have faſtened on : The fore-part which is ſomewhat broader, and ſtands up higher then the other, hath ſtanding a little out two eyes, which are ſolid, tranſparent, and of ſeveral colours : Their mouths are armed with two little white teeth diſpos'd on each ſide like a pair of ſharp pincers, wherewith they cut the leaves of Fruits, and the roots of Trees on which they feed.

TOURLOUROU.

There are three kinds of them, differing in bigneſs and colour, of which the leaſt are thoſe commonly called *Tourlourous :* They have a red ſhell marked with black-ſpots; they are pleaſant enough to the taſte, but in regard there is much picking work about them, and but little to be gotten from them, and that it is conceived they incline people to the bloody flux, they are uſed only in caſe of neceſſity.

WHITE-CRABS.

There are others all white, and have their abodes at the foot of Trees on the Sea-ſide, in certain holes which they make in the ground, into which they retreat, as the Conies do into their Clappers or Hutches : Theſe are the biggeſt of all the kinds, nay there have been thoſe taken which have had in one of their claws as much meat as an egge might con-

T 2

tain,

tain, and as delicate as that of the River-Crevices: They are seldom seen in the day time; but in the night they come in multitudes out of their holes to feed under the Trees; and it is then that they are taken with the help of a Lanthorn or Torches: They delight very much to be under the Arched-Indian-Fig-tree, and other Trees which are on the Sea-side, and in the most fenny places: If a man shall search into the ground, or in the sand to get them out of their lurking places, he shall always find half their bodies in water, as most of the other amphibious creatures are.

PAINTED-CRABS.

BUt those of the third kind, which as to bulk is between the two others before mentioned, are the most beautiful, the most to be admired, and the most esteem'd of all: They are indeed much of the same figure with the precedent; but according to the several Islands, and different soils wherein they are bred, they are painted with so many colours, and those so beautiful and lively, that there cannot be a greater divertisement then to see these creatures at mid-day creeping under the Trees where they seek for their sustenance: Of some of them the bodies are of a violet colour intermixt with white: others are of a bright yellow interlaced with several small greyish and purple lines, which begin at the mouth and are drawn down over the back: Nay there are some which upon a dark-colour'd ground are streaked with red, yellow and green, which makes the richest mixture of colours that can be imagin'd; looking on them at a little distance a man would think, that all those delightful colours wherewith they are naturally enamell'd, were not yet fully dry, such is their brightness, or that they were newly varnish'd over to give them the greater lustre.

These *Painted Crabs* are not like the white ones, which dare not appear in the day time; for these are to be seen morning and evening, and after the rains under the Trees, where they recreate themselves in great companies together: They will also suffer a man to come neer enough to them; but as soon as they perceive him make any attempt to take them (which is best done with a little wand, it being too dangerous to employ the hands) they make their retreat without turning their backs on those that pursue them, and as they go back they shew their teeth, and opening their defensives, which are those two Claws or Mordants they have in their feet, they therewith defend their whole body, and they ever and anon strike them one against another to frighten their enemies: And in that posture they get into their forts, which are commonly under the root, or in the cleft of some rotten Tree, or that of some rock.

These

Thefe Crabs have this natural inftinct, to go every year about *May*, in the feafon of the rains, to the Sea-fide to wafh themfelves, and difburthen themfelves of their egges, in order to the perpetuation of their fpecies: They come down from the Mountains in fuch multitudes, that the high-ways and woods are covered with them; and they have this ftrange direction given them, that they take their way towards that part of the Ifland where there are Creeks and defcents, whereby they may the more eafily come to the Sea.

The Inhabitants are at that time very much annoy'd by them, in regard they fill their Gardens, and with their little Mordants they cut the Peafe and young Plants of Tobacco: They obferve fuch an order in this defcent, that they look like an Army marching in rank and file: they never break their ranks, and whatever they meet with by the way, Houfes, Mountains, Rocks, or other obftacles, they attempt to get over them, that they may go on ftill in a ftrait line: Twice a day they make a halt, during the greateft heat, both to feed and reft themfelves a while: But they make greater journies in the night then in the day, till at laft they get to the Sea-fide.

When they are upon this expedition they are fat, and good to eat; the Males being full of meat, and the Females of egges: And indeed during that time, a man may have of them at his door: Nay fometimes they come into the houfe, if the palizadoes be not clofe enough, and that they meet with a place to get in at: The noife they make in the night time is greater then that of the Mice, and keeps people from fleeping: When they are come to the Sea-fide, having refted themfelves a little, and confider'd the Sea as the nurfe of their young ones, they approach fo neer it, that they wafh themfelves three or four times in the little waves which gently rife and fall on the fand: then having retired into the Woods or neighbouring Plains to recover their wearinefs, the Females return a fecond time to the Sea, and having wafh'd themfelves a little, they open their tails, which are commonly thruft up under the belly, and fhake out the egges faften'd thereto into the water: After which having once more wafh'd themfelves, they return in the fame order in which they came thither.

The ftrongeft of them foon recover the Mountains, every one making to the quarter from whence he came, and by the fame way through which he had pafs'd before: But then, that is, in their return, they are for the moft part fo weak and lean, that they are forc'd to make fome ftay in the next fields they come at to refrefh themfelves, and retrive their former vigour before they can get up to the tops of Mountains.

As to the Egges thus committed to the Sea, having been caft up by it on the fofter kind of fand, and warm'd fome time by the beams of the Sun, they are at laft hatch'd, and become little

tle Crabs, whereof there may be seen millions about the bigness of a large farthing, getting into the neighbouring bushes till such time as they are strong enough to get to the old ones in the Mountains.

Another considerable thing in these Crabs, is, that once a year, to wit, after their return from the Sea, they are under ground for the space of six weeks, so that there is not one of them to be seen: During this time they change their skin or shell, and become wholly new: They work out the earth so neatly at the entrance of their retreats, that there is no hole to be seen; which they do to prevent their taking of any air; for when they put off their old coat, their whole body is as it were naked, being only cover'd with a very thin pellicle, which grows thicker and harder by degrees, till it come to the solidity of the shell they had put off.

Monsieur *du Montel* relates, that he purposely caused some places to be digg'd where it was likely there were of them hidden: Having met with them, he found them wrapp'd in leaves of Trees, which no doubt was their sustenance, and serv'd them for a nest during that retirement; but they were so weak and unable to endure the air, that they seemed as it were half dead, though fat enough, and excellent meat, and as such highly esteemed by the Inhabitants: Close by them he found the shell they had put off, which seem'd to be as entire as if the animal had been still within it: And what was strange, though he look'd very narrowly, yet hardly could he find any hole, or cleft at which the body of it might get out of that prison: But having view'd it very exactly, he found a little disjunction neer the tail, at which the Crab had slipped out.

They are commonly dress'd as the Crevices in these parts are; but the more delicate will take the time and pains, after they are boiled, to pick out all that is good in the claws, and to extract a certain oily substance which is in the body, and by some called *Taumaly*, and to fry all together with the egges of the female, putting thereto a little of the Country Pepper, and some juice of Oranges; and this makes it one of the most dainty dishes in the *Caribbies*.

In these grounds where there are many of the Trees called *Manchenillos*, the Crabs which feed under them, or eat of the fruit, have a venemous quality, insomuch that those who eat thereof fall dangerously sick: But in other parts they are wholsom enough, and as the Crevices in *Europe* are numbred among the delicacies: Such as are careful of their health open them before they eat thereof, and if they be black within they think them dangerous, and use them not.

CHAP.

CHAP. XXIII.

Of Thunder, Earth-quakes, and the Tempests sometimes
happening in the Caribbies.

AS there is hardly any face so beautiful, but that it may
be subject to some defect, spot or mole; so these
Islands having all the excellencies and advantages before represented, have also some imperfections and defects
which take off much of their lustre, and abate of the enjoyments and pleasures they might otherwise afford : We shall
give a short account of the principal inconveniences happening
there, and the remedies which may be apply'd thereto.

THUNDER.

OF those *Thunder* may be named in the first place, which
though never heard on the Coasts of *Peru*, is in these
Islands so frequent, and in many places so dreadful, that by its
terrible claps it forces the most confident into terrour and astonishment.

EARTH-QUAKES.

EArth-quakes do also sometimes produce very sad effects, and
shake the very foundations of the Earth so violently,
that they make a man reel in those places where he might
think himself most safe: But through Gods goodness these
happen very seldom, and in some places the agitation is not
so great.

HURRICANE.

WHat is most to be feared is a general conspiracy of all
the Winds, which goes about the Compass in the
space of 24 hours, and sometimes in less.   This is that which is
called a *Hurricane*, and happens commonly in the moneths of
July, August, or *September :* at other times there is no fear of it.
Heretofore it happened but once in seven years, and sometimes
seldomer ; but within these few years it hath happened once
every two years, nay in one year there happened two of them :
Nay not long after Monsieur *Auber* was sent to command in
chief at *Gardeloupe*, there were three Hurricanes in one year.

This kind of Tempest is so violent, that it breaks and unroots
Trees, deprives those it takes not away of all verdure, makes
desolate whole Forests, removes Rocks from the tops of Mountains,

tains, and casts them into the Valleys, overthrows Houses, carries away the Plants it hath forc'd out of the Earth into the Sea, makes a general waste of all it meets with in the Fields; and in a word, leaves famine all over the Country, which groans a long time after that disaster, and will be a long time ere it recovers the ruines occasion'd thereby.

Nor does the Hurricane all this mischief only by Land, but it raises withall such a tempest on the Sea, that it seems to be mixt and confounded with the Air and the Sky: It breaks to pieces the Ships that happen to be on the Coasts at that time, casting some upon the shores, and swallowing others into the Abysses of the Deep: So that those which escape shipwrack at such a time, are extreamly oblig'd to acknowledg the great mercy of God towards them.

Those who observe the signs preceding this Tempest, have particularly noted these; That a little before it happens the Sea becomes of a sudden so calm and even, that there appears not the least wrinkle on her face; That the Birds by a natural instinct come down in multitudes from the Mountains, where they make their ordinary abode, to retire into the Plains and Valleys, where they keep on the ground to secure themselves against the injuries of the cruel weather which they foresee coming; And that the Rain which falls a little before is bitter and salt, as the Sea-water.

It is not many years since that there happen'd a memorable example of this Tempest upon several Ships lying in the Road of S. *Christophers* loaden with Tobacco, and ready to set sail; For they were all broken to pieces and cast away, and the Commodities wholly lost: Whereof there follow'd another strange and unexpected accident, which was, that most of the fish upon the Coast was poysoned by the Tobacco: The Sea seem'd in a manner cover'd with those poor creatures, which turn'd upside-down and languishing floated on the face of the water, and came to dye on the shore.

Nor are these disasters particular only to the New-World, but there have been seen in *France*, and other places such dreadful Tempests as might well be accounted Hurricanes. In the year M.D.XCIX. there rose neer *Bourdeaux* such a violent wind, that it broke and unrooted most of the great Trees which were able to resist, especially the Wall-nut-trees, whose boughs are commonly very large, and transported some of them above five hundred paces from the place where they grew: But the weaker Trees which gave way were spared: The Palace of *Poictiers* receiv'd much hurt; divers Steeples were batter'd, and that of *Cangres* neer *Saumur* quite blown down: Some persons on horse-back in the fields were carried above sixty paces out of their way: For the space of six or seven leagues, as far as it blew, there was nothing but ruine and confusion.

[To

[To this place may be reduced, among others, that Tempeſt which happen'd here in *England* at the removal out of this world of the late Uſurper *Oliver Crommel*; the miſchiefs whereof are yet freſh in mens minds; as alſo that in *February*, 1661.]

To give an example of a Hurricane that ſhew'd its malice here in *Europe*, particularly on the Sea, we ſhall adde the Copy of a Letter from a Merchant of *Rochel* to a Correſpondent of his at *Rouen*, dated *January* the 30th, M.DC.XLV.

"We have been in a very ſad condition theſe two days, by
"reaſon of the extraordinary Tempeſt which began Saturday
"night laſt, the 28th of this month, and continues yet: We ſee
"from our Walls between thirty and forty Ships caſt away, and
"forc'd to the ſhore, moſt Engliſh bottoms, and abundance of
"Merchandize loſt: One of theſe Ships of 200 Tun burthen
"was caſt neer a Wind-mill, which is twelve foot higher then
"any tide was ever ſeen; for the Tempeſt was not only in the
"Air, but it alſo forc'd the Sea much beyond its ordinary li-
"mits, inſomuch that the ſpoil it hath done by Land very
"much exceeds the loſs of the Ships. All the Salt on the low
"Marſhes was carried away; all the Wheat on the lower
"grounds and reduced marches overflown: And in the Iſle
"of *Ree* the Sea croſs'd it from one ſide to the other, ſpoil'd
"abundance of Vineyards, and drown'd much Cattel. In the
"memory of man the Sea never came up ſo high; nay it came
"to ſome places almoſt a league within the Land: So that
"thoſe who have been at S. *Chriſtophers* affirm, that the Hur-
"ricanes happening there are not more dreadful then this
"Tempeſt was here: The wind was North-weſt: The loſs
"both on Sea and Land is valued at five hundred thouſand
"Crowns: 'Tis conceiv'd there is as much Salt loſt as would
"have freighted two hundred Ships of three hundred Tun a
"piece. There are alſo loſt ſome Dutch Ships neer the Iſle of
"*Ree*, at *Bourdeaux*, and *Bayonne*, which were very richly
"laden. Whence it appears that theſe Tempeſts are as violent
"in *Europe* as thoſe ſo much feared in the *Caribbies*.

But in thoſe parts, ſome to ſecure themſelves from theſe Storms forſake their houſes, out of a fear to be over-whelm'd in their ruines, and make their abode in Caves and the clefts of Rocks, or lye flat on the ground in the open fields, till they be over: Others run to ſome houſe neer them, which they think ſo ſtrongly built, as that it may elude the ſhocks of that Tempeſt; for now there are in the *Caribbies* many ſtructures that in a manner defie the violence thereof: Nay there are ſome will get into the little Huts built by the Negroes, in imitation of thoſe of the *Caribbians*; for it hath been found by experience, that theſe Hutts, being round and having no place open but the door, and whereof the Raſters ſtand upon the ground, are

U

com-

commonly spared when the highest houses are remov'd from one place to another, if not quite overthrown by the impetuous agitation of the winds raising this Tempest.

CHAP. XXIV.

Of some other Inconveniences of the Country, and the remedies thereof.

BEsides the Thunder, Earth-quakes and Hurricanes, which shake the very foundations, and blast the beauty of the *Caribby-Islands*, there are some other Inconveniences which much annoy the Inhabitants, though not so much to be feared as the precedent. These we have reserv'd to be the subject of this last Chapter, wherein out of the desire we have to contribute all lyes in us to the well-being and satisfaction of those amiable Colonies, we shall propose the remedies which the experience of the ancient Inhabitants, and the judgment of several eminent Physicians have found most proper and effectual to secure them from those dangerous consequences.

MOUSTICOES, and MARINGOINS.

THere is then, in the first place, a sort of very small Flies, by some called *Mousticoes*, which are felt commonly before they are seen : But in that little weak body there is so sharp and venemous a sting, as causing an importunate itch that will not be satisfi'd till the skin be scratch'd off, the wound degenerates into a dangerous Ulcer if some remedy be not apply'd.

There is another kind somwhat bigger, and making a noise like that of the Flies, seen in these parts neer ponds and fenny places, by some of the Inhabitants of the *Caribbies* called *Maringoins :* They do the same effect with the former, being arm'd with a little sting which pierces through cloaths, nay through the Hammocks, or hanging-beds on which people rest themselves : But both kinds have this particular to them, that they never do any mischief, but they before-hand proclaim a war, and sound a charge with their little Trumpet, which many times does more frighten then their stinging hurts.

To avoid the annoyance of these two little Insects, the Inhabitants place their houses on a little eminency, give them air on all sides, and cut down all the Trees which may hinder the East-wind, which is the ordinary wind blowing in those Islands, and which drives away these wicked and importunate enemies :

Those

Thoſe alſo who have their lodgings and beds very cloſe are not ſo much troubled therewith.

But if notwithſtanding theſe precautions any be annoy'd thereby, they need only take Tobacco in the room, or make a fire that ſhall ſmoak much, and theſe diſturbers of mens reſt will be gone: And if they have ſtung any one, and he be deſirous to be rid of the itch which follows, let him only wet the place ſtung with Vinegar, or the juyce of the leſſer kind of Citron, and he ſhall have eaſe.

WASPES *and* SCORPIONS.

WAſpes alſo and *Scorpions* are common in moſt of theſe iſlands: Theſe Vermin are of the ſame figure and as dangerous as thoſe of the ſame kinds in moſt parts of *Europe*: The ſtingings of Waſpes are helped by the juice of Rue-leaves, and perfectly cured by a fomentation of the ſovereign remedy againſt all ſorts of poyſons, which is given out under the famous name of *Orvietan*; and that of Scorpions hath its remedy in the beaſt it ſelf, which muſt be cruſh'd upon the place affected, or for want thereof, recourſe muſt be had to the oyl called Scorpion-oyl, which ſhould be common in all thoſe parts where theſe Inſects are ſo.

MANCHENILLO.

IN moſt of theſe Iſlands there grow certain Trees called by ſome *Manchenillo-trees*, beautiful to the eye, bearing leaves like thoſe of Crab-trees, and a fruit called *Manchenillo*, like an *Appius-apple*; for it is ſtreaked with red, extreamly fair, and of a pleaſant ſcent, inſomuch that one can hardly forbear taſting it if he be not before-hand acquainted with its dangerous quality; for though it be ſweet in the mouth, yet is it ſo fatal that being eaten it ſends a man to ſleep, not for 24 hours, (as a certain ſeed of *Peru*, and an herb in the Eaſt, whereof *Linſcot* ſpeaks at large) but ſo as never to awake again; ſo that it is much worſe then thoſe Almonds of *Mexico*, which ſmell like muſk, but being eaten leave a taſte of rottenneſs behind them; as alſo then the fair Apples of *Sodom*, which being opened yield only ſoot and aſhes; for if a man have the miſchance to be deceiv'd in them, it is without any hazard of his life: But theſe venemous Apples may be compared to the *Indian-nut* which grows in *Java*: It is ſomwhat like a Gall, and at the firſt eating thereof it taſtes like a ſmall Nut; but afterwards it cauſeth mortal gripings, and is a moſt dangerous poyſon: There is alſo in *Africk* a Tree called *Coſcoma*, which bears deadly Apples: The Tree of the *Maldivas*, named *Ambon*, bears a fruit no leſs deceitful and pernicious: And neer *Tripoly* in *Syria* there are

certain large Apricocks, which are fair to the eye, and very
favoury to the palat; but the fubfequent qualities of them are
many times mortal, or at beft, caufe long and painful difeafes to
fuch as have eaten of them.

There grow *Manchenillo*-Trees on the Sea-fide and the
banks of Rivers, and if the fruit fall into the water, the
fifh eating thereof will certainly dye; nay though it continue long in the water, yet will it not rot, but is cover'd
with falt-peter, which gives it a folid cruftinefs, as if it were
petrify'd. In thofe Iflands where this Tree grows in abundance the Snakes are venemous, it being fuppofed by fome,
that they fometimes fuck the fruit of it: Nay the Crabs which
feed under thefe Trees contract a dangerous quality from
them, as we faid elfewhere; and many have been fick after
the eating thereof: Whence it comes, that when thefe fruits
fall to the ground, fuch as are careful of their health will forbear the eating of Crabs.

Yet do not the Snakes or Crabs wholly live on this fruit,
but feeding under the Tree they draw the infection thereof to
themfelves, efpecially if they fuck the venome of its fruit. It
may well be, that what is mortal to fome creatures is not fo to
all; and that thefe Infects often feeding on this poyfon, do by
cuftom and continuance turn it into their fuftenance, as is reported of *Mithridates:* And fo they may infect fuch as eat
thereof, receiving themfelves no hurt thereby.

Under the bark of the trunk and boughs of thefe Trees
there is contained a certain glutinous water, which is white as
milk, extremely malignant and dangerous : There being many of them along the high-ways, if one fhould careiefly break
one of their branches, that milk or rather poyfon comes forth,
and falls upon him : If it light on his fhirt, it makes an ugly
ftain as if it were burnt; if on the fkin, and the place be not
immediately wafh'd, it will be all bliftered : but if it fhould
chance that a drop of this cauftick and venemous water fhould
fall into the eye, it will caufe an infupportable inflammation,
and the party fhall lofe his fight for nine days, after which he
will have fome eafe.

The dew, or rain-water, having continu'd a while on the
leaves of thefe Trees, produces the fame effect, and if it fhould
light on the fkin, it would fcorch it like Aqua-fortis : So that
it is almoft as bad as the drops of rain falling under the Line,
which are fo contagious, as thofe who have felt them affirm,
that if they fall on the hands, face, or any uncover'd part of
the body, there immediately rife up bladders and blifters with
much pain; and if the party do not prefently fhift his cloths,
his body will be full of wheals all over; not to mention the
worms which are bred in the cloths.

Nay the very fhade of thefe Trees is prejudicial to men,
and

and if a man reſt himſelf under them, the whole body ſwells
after a ſtrange manner. *Pliny* and *Plutarch* mention a Tree of
Arcadia no leſs dangerous; and thoſe who have travell'd into
the *Eaſt-Indies* affirm, that there is an herb named *Sapony*, which
cauſes their death who lye upon it. But what heightens the ill
quality of the *Manchenillo*-Tree, is, that the meat dreſs'd with
a fire made of its wood derives a certain malignity from it,
which burns the mouth and throat.

Nor are the Savages of theſe Iſlands ignorant of the nature
of the *Manchenillo*; for the compoſition wherewith they are
wont to poyſon their arrows hath in it, among other ingredients, the milk of this Tree, and the dew falling from it, and
the juice of the fruit.

To cure, in a ſhort time, the ſwelling and bliſters riſing on
the body after ſleeping under the ſhade of theſe Trees, or
receiving the rain or dew falling from their branches, as alſo thoſe occaſion'd by the milk within the bark, recourſe
muſt be immediately made to a kind of Snails, whereof we
have ſpoken before, under the name of *Souldiers*, and let
the party take a certain cleer water which is contain'd within their ſhell, and apply it to the place affected : this remedy
immediately allays the venome of that ſcorching liquour,
and puts the party out of all danger : The oyl extracted
without fire from the ſame Snail operates the ſame effect.
But if any ſhall happen to eat of the fruit of theſe venemous
Trees, he muſt uſe the remedies preſcribed hereafter, to expell the venome of Serpents, and all other poyſons.

WOOD-LICE.

THere is alſo a kind of Ant, or worm, which hath a little black ſpot on the head, all the reſt of the body
being white : They are bred of rotten wood, and thence
ſome call them *Wood-lice :* Their bodies are ſofter then thoſe
of our ordinary Ants, and yet their tooth is ſo ſharp, that they
gnaw wood, and get into ſuch coffers as lye neer the ground :
And in leſs then two days, if they be not deſtroy'd, there will
get in ſuch abundance, that linen, cloaths, paper, and whatever is within them will be eaten and devoured; nay they
gnaw and eat the poſts which ſuſtain the ordinary hutts, inſomuch that if ſome courſe be not taken they will at laſt fall
down.

To prevent the breeding of theſe Inſects, and the miſchief
done by them, there are theſe cautions : At the building of
houſes not to leave any wood on the ground to rot, out of
which they may breed : To burn the ends of thoſe pieces of
wood that are planted in the ground : As ſoon as any of them
are perceiv'd, to caſt ſcalding water into the holes which they
have

have made : To hang up Chefts and Coffers in the air with cords, as they are fore'd to do in feveral parts of the *Eaft-Indies*, that they may not touch the ground : And laftly, to keep the rooms very clean, and leave nothing on the ground. It hath alfo been obferv'd, that the rubbing of their haunts with the oyl of that kind of *Palma-Chrifti* wherewith the Negroes rub their heads to avoid vermine, hath prevented their coming any more that way. The oyl of *Lamantin* hath the fame effect, and if it be poured on their rendezvouz, which is a kind of Ant-hill made up of their own ordure, and faften'd about the forks which fuftain the hutts, they immediately forfake it.

RAVETS.

ANother dangerous vermine are the *Ravets*, of which there are two kinds : The bigger are almoft like Locufts, and of the fame colour ; the others are not half as big : Both kinds have their walks in the night-time, get into Chefts if they be not very clofe, foul all things wherever they come, and do mifchief enough, yet not fo much, nor in fo fhort a time, as the Wood-lice. They are called *Ravets*, becaufe like Rats they gnaw whatever they come at : They are no doubt the fame which *de Lery* calls *Aravers*, according to the Language of the *Brafilians*. This vermine hath a particular malice to Books, and their covers. The Wood-lice are as good, if they can get at them ; but they are to be commended in this particular, that they have a refpect for the letters, and only nibble about the margents ; for whether they cannot away with the ink, or for fome other reafon, it muft be an extraordinary famine that fhall force them to feed on the impreffion, or writing : But they are very great lovers of linen above any thing, ard if they can get into a Cheft, they will defire but one night to make work enough for many Sempftreffes for a month.

As to the *Ravets*, though they be not fo quick at their work, yet they fpare nothing but filk and cotton-ftuffs ; nay they have no ftomach to filk or cotton even while it is raw ; infomuch that if the Chefts be hung up in the air, and the cords be done about with cotton, as foon as they find their little feet faften'd in it, they immediately endeavour to get away, and turn fomewhere elfe. Such as dwell in houfes of brick or ftone are not troubled with the Wood-lice, but with all their care they have much ado to avoid the mifchief done by the *Ravets* : Yet hath it been found by experience, that they cannot endure fweet fcents, and that they would not willingly get into Chefts made of Cedar, and thofe excellent fweet woods which are common in all thefe Iflands. At *Cairo*
they

they put the pedeſtalls of Cabinets in veſſels full of water, to prevent the creeping up of the Ants. This eaſie ſecret might produce the ſame effect in the *Caribbies* to keep off the Wood-lice and Ravets, nay alſo the Ants, which are there alſo extremely troubleſome.

CHEGOES.

BUt what is moſt to be feared in all theſe Iſlands is a certain kind of little worm, no bigger then a hand-worm, which breeds in the duſt, in the ſweepings caſt out into the dung-hill, and ſuch unclean places: Theſe are commonly called *Chegoes.* They get into peoples feet, and under the nails of their toes; but if they get any further, and are not taken away in time, they will get into all the other parts of the body. At firſt they only cauſe a little itching, but having once got through the ſkin, they cauſe an inflammation in the place affected, and though very little when they entred it, come in time to be as big as a pea, and produce abundance of nits, which may breed others; and ſo many times ulcers are bred in the places whence they are taken.

The Savages, as they relate who have liv'd among them, have a certain gum, wherewith having rubb'd their feet, eſpecially under the nails, they are not annoy'd with this vermine: But ſuch as know not that ſecret are advis'd to have their feet ſearch'd by thoſe who have the ſkill to diſcover and take out thoſe dangerous Inſects, as ſoon as they feel the leaſt itching; at which work the Indians are very expert and fortunate. Thoſe who take out theſe *Chegoes* muſt have a care that they break not the bag wherein they are encloſed; which if they do, ſome of their little egges will remain behind, which will infallibly breed others. It is conceived alſo, that the *Roucou,* which the *Caribbians* uſe to make themſelves more beautiful, more nimble, and more active to run, hath a ſecret vertue to keep off all theſe vermine.

It is alſo a good remedy often to ſprinkle ſalt-water about the room; not to go bare-foot; to wear ſtockings of Goats-leather; and to keep ones ſelf very clean : For commonly only ſuch as are careleſs of themſelves, and ſlovenly, are much troubled with them. Theſe little worms are the ſame with thoſe which the *Braſilians* call *Tons,* and ſome other Indians *Nigas.*

Thoſe who have Ulcers cauſed by theſe little worms, either for want of taking them out ſkilfully or in time, are among the French called *Malingres.* Theſe Ulcers come alſo many times after ſome little ſcratching, which at firſt ſeems to be little or nothing : But afterwards, the party may well wonder to ſee it as big as the palm of a mans hand; for the Ulcer muſt
have

have its courfe : Nay fome of them, though little, yet are very hard to be cured. Of thefe Ulcers there are two kinds ; one round, the other uneven : The round Ulcer is harder to cure then the other, for it is encompafs'd with dead flefh, which makes it the worfe ; for till that dead and loofe flefh be removed, the Ulcer cannot be cured : Therefore as often as the wound is drefs'd, that dead flefh muft be quite cut away, which caufes extraordinary pains.

Among the remedies for the healing of thefe Ulcers, there are ufed Verdi-greece, Aqua-fortis, the fpirit of Vitriol, and burnt Allom, which eat away the dead flefh : They ufe to the fame end the juice of the leffer Citron, which is extreamly fharp ; and when the wound is foul, it makes it clean, and look well : True it is, the pain which the party feels when the wound is rubbed therewith is fo great, that he would rather pitch on any of the other remedies ; but they do not heal fo foon : There is alfo an Unguent made of common honey, a little fharp Vinegar, and the powder of Verdi-greece, which cures Ulcers in a fhort time : And to prevent them, let not any one make flight of the leaft hurt or fcratch that happens in any part of the body whatfoever, efpecially the feet or legs, but to apply a plaifter thereto, to take away the heat which may be in the wound ; and in cafe there be no other remedy procurable, to put fome Tobacco-leaves to it, and to ufe the juice of Citron and Vinegar, to take away the itch which remains after the ftinging of the *Moufticoes* and the *Maringoins*, rather then to make ufe of the nails.

In the fixth Chapter of this Hiftory, we faid there were Serpents and Snakes in the Iflands of *Martinico* and St. *Aloufia*, which have a dangerous venom · We fhall here affign the Remedies which may be fuccefsfully ufed in order to the taking away thereof. In the firft place, be it obferv'd, that they are to be ufed both inwardly and outwardly : Inwardly to comfort the heart, and diffipate the venemous quality which might prevail over it, there are fuccefsfully ufed Treacle, Mithridate, the Confection of Alkermes, Egyptian-Balm, *Peru-Balm*, Rue, Scordium, Scorzonera, Vipers-grafs, Angelico, and Contrahierva : But above all, the party ftung muft take down in a little Burrage-water, Buglofs-water, or fome other liquor, the powder of the Liver and Heart of Vipers, the weight of a Crown-piece : In a word, he muft ufe all thofe things which fortifie the heart, and revive and refrefh the fpirits : Outwardly there are to be applyed all the Remedies which have the vertue to draw and difperfe all manner of venom : Such are Cupping-glaffes apply'd upon the fcarified wound, as alfo all hot and attractive Medicaments, fuch as are Galbanum, Ammoniacum, the fomentation of wine boil'd with the root of Dragon-wort, or the leaves of Mug-wort, Garlick, Onions, Pigeons dung, the

blood

blood of Land-Tortoiſes dry'd and reduc'd to powder, and the like.

It is alſo not only requiſite, but very ſafe, as ſoon as may be to bind up the member affected, a little above the place where the party was ſtung, and immediately to make an inciſion, nay indeed to take away the piece, or at leaſt, as ſoon as it is ſcari-fi'd to apply thereto the outermoſt feather of a Chicken or Pi-geons wing to take away the venom ; and that Chicken or Pi-geon being dead, to take another, till there be no venom left to be drawn.

It were alſo to be wiſh'd, that all the Inhabitants of the *Ca-ribbies* were furniſh'd with that excellent Antidote, approved in ſo many places in *France*, which is known under the famous name of *Orvietan*, and ſold at *Paris* at the *New-bridge* end, in the ſtreet called *Rue Dauphine*, at the ſign of the Sun: For that admirable ſecret, among many other rare qualities, hath the vertue to drive away the venom of all ſorts of Serpents, and to allay the force of the ſtrongeſt poyſons: Such as have been ſtung by venemous Serpents are to uſe it thus.

Take of it about the bigneſs of a Bean, diſſolv'd in wine ; and after ſcarification made on the place ſtung, and drawing blood by the Cupping-glaſs, apply thereto a little *Orvietan*, and let care be taken that the Patient be kept awake at leaſt for twelve hours after. This ſovereign remedy loſes nothing of its goodneſs, though it be kept many years, ſo it be put up in a place not too hot, where it may be dry'd up; and if it be, it may be reduc'd to its conſiſtence with *Mel roſatum* ; it may be alſo had in powder.

As to the diet to be obſerv'd during the uſe of this remedy ; the Patient muſt abſtain from all meats that enflame the blood, or cauſe melancholy: He muſt alſo forbear purging and bleed-ing, for fear of drawing the venom inward ; unleſs ſome of the nobler parts be in danger, in which caſe he may purge abundantly, and uſe baths, and things good to open the pores, and cauſe ſweating.

If a perſon be reduc'd to ſuch an extremity as that none of the forementioned Antidotes can be procured, let him make uſe of this which is very common and eaſily got: Let him who hath been bitten or ſtung by any venemous creature immedi-ately eat the rind of a raw Citron, for it hath the vertue to ſe-cure the heart from the venom: if it may be done, the place hurt muſt be bound as hard as can be endured, a little above the biting or ſtinging ; then it muſt be ſcarifi'd, and let there be often apply'd thereto a mans faſting ſpittle ; and if the beaſt which hath done the miſchief can be had, cut off the head of it, and pound it till it be reduc'd to a kind of Unguent, which muſt be apply'd hot to the wound: This is the ordinary reme-dy uſed by the natural Inhabitants of *Braſil* to free themſelves

X

from

from the violent poyſon of that dangerous and monſtrous Serpent, which in their Language they call *Boicininga*, and the Spaniards *Caſcavel*.

The laſt Letters we receiv'd from *Martinico* aſſure us, that ſome conſiderable families lately come from *Braſil* with their Negroes to live in that Iſland, acquainted the Inhabitants with ſeveral Herbs and Roots growing in the *Caribbies*, as well as *Braſil*, which are excellent to allay the venom of all kinds of Serpents and poyſon'd Arrows.

The forementioned remedies may alſo be uſed againſt the venom of the *Becune*, and all the other dangerous fiſhes. They may alſo be ſucceſsfully employ'd to prevent the pernicious effects of the juice of *Manyoc*, the *Manchenillo-tree*, and the ſtinging of Waſpes, Scorpions, and all other venemous Inſects.

SEA-FOAM.

THoſe who go a fiſhing, or to waſh themſelves in the Sea, do ſometimes meet with a certain foam which the wind blows to and fro like a little bladder, of a purple colour, of a different figure, and beautiful to the eye; but what part ſoever of the body it ſhall ſtick to, it immediately cauſes in it a very grievous pain, extreamly ſharp and burning: The readieſt remedy that can be apyly'd to alleviate that ſtinging pain, is, to anoint the place affected with the oyl of the *Acajou-nut*, mixt with a little good Aqua-vitæ; for one heat takes away the other.

RATS.

MIce and Rats were creatures heretofore unknown to the *Caribbians*; but now ſince the coming in of ſo many Ships to thoſe Iſlands, and the caſting away of divers of them in the very Roads, where they afterwards rot, they have got to land, and are ſo multiply'd, that in ſome places they do abundance of miſchief among the Potatoes, Peaſe, Beans, and particularly that kind of Wheat which is called Turkey-wheat: Nay did not the Snakes deſtroy them, and ſearch for them in their holes under ground, in the clefts of rocks, nay even in the coverings of houſes, which conſiſt of Palm-leaves, or Sugar-canes, it would no doubt be a very hard matter to ſecure Proviſions from them. Now indeed there are Cats in theſe Iſlands, which give them no quarter; nay, Dogs are taught to hunt them, and it is no ſmall diverſion to ſee how ſubtle they are to find them out, and expert in the hunting and killing of them.

Nor is this inconvenience particular to the *Caribbies*; nay it is much worſe in *Peru*; for *Garcilaſſo*, in his *Royal Commentary,*

tary, affirms, that thefe peftilent creatures being extreamly numerous in thofe parts commit very great fpoils, ranfacking the places through which they pafs, making the Fields defo-late, and gnawing the Fruits even to the ftalks, and roots of the Trees.

The Inhabitants of the Iflands have an invention which they call *Balan*, to keep the Rats from eating their *Caſſava*, and other Provifions. This *Balan* is a kind of round hurdle, or haply fquare, confifting of feveral ftakes, on which they place the *Caſſava* after it hath been dried in the Sun: It is faften'd at the top of the Hut, hanging down by a Witth or Cord; and that the Rats may not come down along the Cord, and fo get to the *Balan*, they put the Cord through a fmooth gourd which hangs loofe in the midft of it, fo that the Rats being come to that place, being not able to faften their feet in it, and fearing the motion of the Gourd, are afraid to venture any further: Were it not for this fecret, the Inhabitants would find it a hard tafk to keep their provifions.

Thus hath the wife Author of Nature been pleas'd, by an admirable equipollence of perfections and imperfections, that thofe Countries which have fome advantages above others fhould alfo be fubject to thofe inconveniences that are not to be found elfewhere. Thus hath the Divine Providence, whofe bufinefs it is liberally to fupply the exigencies of his Creatures, plac'd the prefervative neer the poyfon, the Remedy walking as it were hand in hand with the Difeafe, and fo laid open to Man the inexhauftible Treafures of Grace and Nature, to fecure him againft the injuries of Air, the outrages of the Seafons, the violence of Poyfons, and whatever the Earth produces that is moft dangerous, fince it became envenomed by the firft Tranfgreffion.

The End of the Firft Book.

THE
HISTORY
OF THE
Caribby-Iſlands.

THE SECOND BOOK.

Comprehending the MORAL Hiſtory of thoſe
Iſlands.

CHAPTER I.

*Of the Eſtabliſhment of thoſe Inhabitants who are Stran-
gers in the Iſlands of* S. Chriſtopher, Mevis, Gardeloupe, Martinico, *and ſome other Iſlands of the* Caribbies.

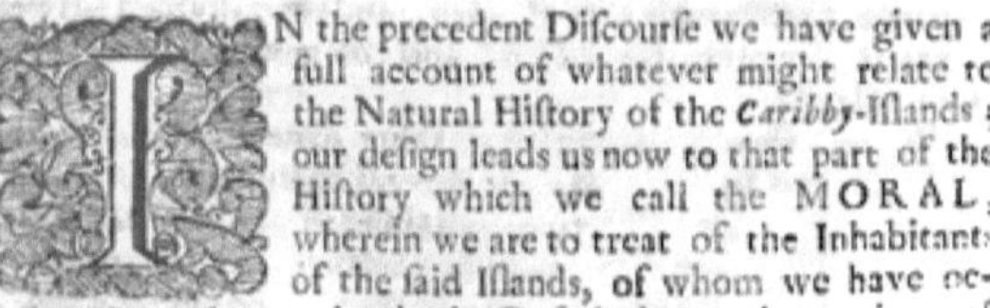

IN the precedent Diſcourſe we have given a
full account of whatever might relate to
the Natural Hiſtory of the *Caribby*-Iſlands ;
our deſign leads us now to that part of the
Hiſtory which we call the MORAL,
wherein we are to treat of the Inhabitants
of the ſaid Iſlands, of whom we have oc-
caſionally made mention in the Deſcription we have given of
thoſe places in the precedent Book.   In the firſt place we ſhall
ſpeak of thoſe Inhabitants thereof who are Strangers, or *Euro-*
peans,

peans, yet only fo far as the profecution of our Defign requires; which having difpatch'd, we fhall defcend to a more large and particular confideration of the *Indians*, the natural and originary Inhabitants of the Country ; a tafk which requires a more ample deduction, and a more exact and curious difquifition, upon this prefumption, that there hath yet been very little publifh'd upon that fubject.

The *Spaniards*, grounding their Title upon the Donation of Pope *Alexander* the fixth, and fome other apparent Reafons and Pretences, prefume that the right of Navigation into the late difcover'd part of the World, which is call'd *America*, and of eftablifhing and fetling Colonies there, whether it be in the Continent, or in any of the Iflands, properly belongs to them, exclufively to all others. But not to urge that the vanity of that arrogant prefumption is fufficiently difcover'd of it felf, and that it would prove a great digreffion from the defign of our Hiftory to engage our felves in a particular difquifition of that Controverfie, we need only fay, that *Bergeron*, a learned and curious Authour, hath fo exactly handled this Queftion, and fo cleerly fhewn the abfurdity of that chimerical pretence, in his Treatife of *Navigations*, that it would be loft labour for us to infift upon it, or to think of any thing new that can be produc'd upon that account. Accordingly all Chriftian Kings and Princes have always difputed thar pretended Right with the King of *Spain*, as unanimoufly concluding that he had unjuftly attributed the fame to himfelf : Nor have they engag'd againft him only by words and writings, but have effectually profecuted their own pretenfions, and from time to time fent Fleets into *America* to fetle Plantations there, and to take into their poffeffion feveral parts of that new World ; wherein the moft fuccefsful have been the *Englifh*, the *French*, and the *Dutch*.

But it is to be obferv'd, that of all the Colonies which thefe three European Nations have planted in *America*, thofe that fetled themfelves in the *Caribby-Iflands* are of greateft account, and the moft frequented by Merchants, as being the moft advantageous upon the fcore of Trade. The *Englifh* and *French*, as may have been noted in the firft Book of this Hiftory, are the moft confiderable in thofe parts, and have divided between them the greateft, the richeft, and the moft populous of all thofe Iflands.

We may further affirm it as a thing generally known, that thefe Nations have not in their feveral eftablifhments follow'd the inhumane and barbarous maximes of the *Spaniards*, nor after their example unmercifully exterminated the originary Inhabitants of the Country ; for if they found any of them in actual poffeffion of the Lands where they liv'd, they have for the moft part preferv'd them therein, and contracted alliances
with

with them. Yet muft it be acknowledg'd that the the *Caribbians* have had very great differences with the *Englifh*, and that the faid differences have continu'd a long time; but the ground of their quarrels proceeded from fome occafions of difcontent which the *Caribbians* receiv'd from fome particular perfons of that Nation, which reprefented in a Body hath difapprov'd their procedure, and upon all emergencies hath exprefs'd it felf fo far diffatisfi'd therewith, as to defire that they fhould be treated with the fame humanity, moderation, and Chriftian mildnefs, as thofe greater and flourifhing Colonies of *Virginia* and *New-England*, that are under the jurifdiction of the faid *Englifh*, have hitherto us'd towards the natural Inhabitants of that part of *America* which lies more Northerly, where they have eftablifh'd themfelves; for it is known that the *Englifh* hold fo facred and perfect a correfpondence with them, as hath opened a way for their inftruction in the Myfteries of Chriftian Religion, and the planting of a great number of fair Churches amongft thofe poor Barbarians.

But above all, this is moft certain, that when the *French* eftablifh'd themfelves in the Iflands of *Martinico, Gardeloupe,* and *Granada,* it was done with the confent of the moft confiderable perfons among the *Caribbians,* who thereupon difown'd thofe of their Country-men who would have obftructed the faid eftablifhment : Nay fuch was their earneftnefs therein, that they employ'd all their Forces and Councils to oppofe the defigns of the others, and to fecure the *French* in the peaceable poffeffion of what they had before granted them. This proceeding abfolutely clears the *French* of being guilty of the fame violences which are charg'd upon the *Spaniards,* and makes it appear, that the fetlement of the former in thofe Iflands was not like that of the latter in thofe places where they have the opportunities to eftablifh themfelves. And if it be objected to the *French,* that they have forc'd the natural Inhabitants out of S. *Chriftophers* and *Gardeloupe,* and that even at this prefent there is a War between the faid Nation and thofe of *Martinico;* it may be anfwer'd, that when the *French* peopled thefe Iflands, they propos'd to themfelves no other defign then the edification and inftruction of thofe poor Barbarians, and that if contrary to their firft intention they had been forc'd to ufe a fevere hand towards fome particular perfons, and to treat them as enemies, they were themfelves the occafion of their own misfortune, by being the firft Aggreffors, and guilty of previous violations of the facred Laws of Alliance, which they had contracted with them, and engaging themfelves in fanguinary counfels, fuch as would have fmother'd their Colonies ere they were fully fetled, had there not been a timely difcovery made thereof.

The *Englifh* and *French* Colonies had their beginning at the
fame

same time, which was in the year One thousand six hundred twenty and five : Monsieur *Desnambuc*, a French Gentleman, of the ancient House of *Vauderop*, and a Captain under the King of *France* in the Western Seas, and Sir *Thomas Warner*, an English Gentleman, joyntly took possession of the Island of S. *Christophers* on the same day, in the names of the Kings of *France* and Great *Britain*, their Masters, that they might have a place of safe retreat, and a good Haven for the reception of such Ships of both Nations as should be bound for *America*; that Island being furnish'd with all the advantages whereof we have given a full account in the Chapter particularly design'd by us for the description of it; upon which score it was visited by the *Spaniards*, who often put in there for refreshments, both as they were inward and outward bound in their long Voyages: Nay sometimes they left their sick there to be look'd to by the *Caribbians*, with whom they had made a peace upon those terms.

These two Gentlemen therefore considering with themselves, that if they were possess'd of that Country they might the better incommodate their common enemy in *America*, the *Spaniard*, and have withall a convenient and secure habitation, in order to the establishment of the Colonies they intended for those Islands, became Masters of it, and left men therein to keep it : But before they parted thence, having some grounds to fear that there might be some secret intelligence between the *Indians* and the *Spaniards*, or that in their absence they might execute the resolution, which by the perswasion of certain Sorcerers (a sort of people in great esteem among the *Indians*) they had undertaken, which was to put to death all the Strangers who were come into their Country, they in one night rid their hands of all the most factious of that Nation, and not long after forc'd all the rest, who had got together into several Bodies, and intended to stand upon their guard, to retire to some other places, and to leave that to their disposal.

Things being thus order'd, *Desnambuc* returns into *France*, and Sir *Thomas Warner* into *England*, where their conquest and all their proceedings thereupon were approved by the Kings their Masters; and having obtained a permission to carry over some recruits of men, they came back to the Island in the quality of Governours and Lieutenants, under the Kings of *France* and Great *Britany*.

But *Desnambuc* before he went over to cultivate and prosecute his conquest imagin'd to himself, that the most likely way to have a powerful support in *France*, such as should concern it self in the preservation of that Island, and so to secure and promote his designs, would be to get together a Company of persons of Authority, which should have the direction and signiory of the said Island, and what others might afterwards

be

be conquer'd and reduc'd under the jurifdiction of the King of
France; upon this provifion, that the faid Company fhould
have a care, and make it their earneft bufinefs to fupply the Colony with men for the keeping and cultivation of it; as alfo
with Ecclefiafticks to be maintain'd by allowances from the
faid Company; and laftly to build certain Forts there for the
fecurity of the Inhabitants, and to furnifh them with Canon,
Powder, and all forts of Ammunition; in a word, to maintain a fufficient Arfenal, wherein fhould be all things in readi-
nefs to oppofe the Enemy.

This Company, or Society, was eftablifh'd in the moneth of
October, in the year of our Lord, one thoufand fix hundred
twenty and fix, as well for the Government of S. *Chriftophers*,
as thofe other Iflands which are adjacent thereto, and was approv'd by the King of *France*. Since that time it hath been
further confirm'd, and favour'd with fome new Conceffions,
and very advantageous priviledges obtain'd from his moft Chriftian Majefty the eighth of *March*, one thoufand fix hundred
forty and two, for all the Iflands of *America* lying between the
tenth and thirtieth degree on this fide the Equator.

Defnambuc having thus order'd his affairs in *France*, returns
to S. *Chriftophers* with a recruit of three hundred men, which
the Gentlemen of the Company newly erected had raifed, in
order to the advancement of that Colony: He brought over
alfo along with him a confiderable number of gallant Volunteers, who look'd on it as no fmall honour to run fortunes with
fo famous an Adventurer, and to participate of his honourable
hazards, out of a confidence in procefs of time of reaping the
fruit of his Conquefts. They got all fafely to S. *Chriftophers*,
about the beginning of the year, M.DC.XXVII. and though
they had fuffered much during their Voyage, and were moft of
them either fick or much weakned, yet were they not difcou-
rag'd by thofe difficulties, but reflecting that the nobleft enterprifes are many times attended by great inconveniences, and
that Rofes cannot be gather'd without thorns, they immediately fell to work, and having in a fhort time learn'd of thofe
whom they found in the Ifle what they were to do in order to
their further eftablifhment, they behav'd themfelves anfwerably to the generous defigns of their Captain, who on his part
more and more encourag'd them by words and example.

How the Ifland was to be divided between the two Nations
had been defign'd before that Voyage; but the particular Articles of the Divifion were folemnly agreed to and concluded
on the 13th of *May*, in the faid year, M. DC. XXVII. For to
the end that every one might employ himfelf with fome affurance upon his own ftock, and that no differences might arife
between the *French* and the *Englifh*, M. *Warner* being return'd
from *England* fome time before the arrival of *Defnambuc*,

where he had also recommended his affairs to the direction of a
Company which undertook the advancement of his enterprifes,
they divided the whole Ifland between them, and fet thofe
Boundaries to their feveral divifions, which are remaining to
this day, but with this particular provifion that Fifhing and
Hunting fhould be equally free to the Inhabitants of both Nations, and that the Salt-ponds, the more precious kinds of Timber fit for Dying, or Joyners-work, Havens and Mines fhould
in like manner be common.

Nay it was further agreed upon by certain Articles concluded on both fides, that a good correfpondence fhould be
maintain'd between them, as alfo for the preventing of all jea-
loufies, and avoiding the occafions of difputes and conteftati-
ons, which might eafily arife between people of different humours: They further made a Defenfive League for the mutual relief of each other, if occafion fhould require, againft the
attempts of the common Enemy, or any other who fhould endeavour to difturb the peace and quiet which they hoped to enjoy together in thofe parts of the Country where they had
planted themfelves.

Thefe things thus fetled, the two Governours betray'd a
certain emulation in carrying on the eftablifhment of their Colonies; in the profecution whereof it is moft certain the *Englifh*
had very confiderable advantages above the *French* to compafs
their defigns: For befides that that Nation, which is as it were
nurs'd up in the bofom of the Sea, can better endure the hardfhip and inconveniences of long Voyages, and is better vers'd
in the making of new Plantations; the Company which was
eftablifh'd at *London* for the management of that of S. *Chriftophers*, made fuch generous provifions, that at its firft fetlement
it might be fupply'd with Men and Provifions, fuch as fhould be
neceffary for their fubfiftence, and took fo particular a care of
all things, that it was from time to time refrefh'd with new recruits, and whatever it might ftand in need of at the beginning, that it vifibly profper'd and advanc'd while the *French*,
which was unfurnifh'd with all thofe affiftances, feem'd to pine
and languifh, nay indeed would have quite fallen away if the
affection which it had for its chief Director, and the high
efteem it had conceiv'd of his valour had not kept it up.

While therefore the *French* Colony was reduc'd to thefe extremities, and in a manner fubfifted only by its courage, that
of the *Englifh* being in a good plight and condition, fpred it
felf into a new one, which planted it felf in the Ifland of *Mevis*, which is divided from S. *Chriftophers* only by a fmall arm of
the Sea, as we have faid elfewhere: But if the fmall number
whereto the *French* were reduc'd permitted them not to make
the like progreffes, their Governour *Defnambuc* had in the
mean time the opportunity to make feveral ufeful regulations
                                                            for

for the better fetlement of it : Of thefe we fhall not think it
befides our defign to infert here fome few of the principal Articles, to the end the memory of them may be precioufly preferv'd for the inftruction of pofterity.

In the firft place, taking it into his confideration, that by
peace and concord finall things come to be great, and that divifion diftracts and difperfes the greateft, he ordered that all
the Inhabitants of the Ifland who were fubject to his jurifdiction fhould maintain a perfect union among themfelves , and
that he prefs'd and recommended to them upon all occafions
as the Pillar of their little State, and the facred Channel through
which they were to expect the bleffings both of Heaven and
Earth abundantly to flow upon them : And whereas it is impoffible that in mutual converfation there fhould not happen many
things which might oftentimes offer fome violence to that ami-
cable correfpondence, if fome prefent provifion be not made
to the contrary, he defired that fuch differences might be with
the fooneft either decided or fmother'd , and all be reconcil'd with meeknefs, and that if poffible before the fetting of
the Sun.

Another command of his was, that his people fhould be faithful to their truft, and free, and fincere in all their affairs ; obliging and charitable towards their Neighbours, and as religious and punctual in the obfervance of the promifes they had
made, as if they had been put into writing, and feal'd and deliver'd before witneffes, or Publick Notaries.

And that their being continually employ'd about their Plantations might not caufe them to forget the bufinefs of War,
and out of a diftruft they would degenerate in point of courage, through a long and undifturbed quiet ; and that if occafion fhould require they might be able to handle their Arms,
and make ufe of them with dexterity, he appointed certain
days for the exercifing of them, that they might thereby be
minded of the Rules of Military Difcipline, and order'd, that
though all profefs'd the cultivation of the earth, yet that they
fhould have the generous looks and demeanors of Souldiers, and
that they fhould at all times have about them the Badges and
Liveries of that kind of Life, and fo never be feen out of their
Quarters without Fire-arms, or at leaft a Sword.

But if he requir'd them to be thus qualifi'd, to the end that
when occafion ferv'd they might make their enemies fenfible
of their valour and courage ; he on the other fide oblig'd them
to be mild and courteous one towards another, and that the
ftronger fhould not take their advantages of the weaker.
Thence it came that he made this commendable order, which is
ftill in force in all thofe Iflands ; to wit, that Mafters fhould
not take Servants for any longer term then three years, during
which time they fhould be oblig'd to treat them with all gentle-

nefs

nefs and moderation, and exact of them only fuch fervices as were rational and anfwerable to their ftrength.

Nay his care and tendernefs was very remarkable towards fuch as were newly brought into the Country: To the end therefore that at their arrival they might be fupply'd with all things requifite to fecure them againft the injuries of the air, and that their labour might not be hindred through want of convenient lodging, he defir'd, that as foon as the place which they had defign'd for their building was uncover'd, all the Neighbourhood fhould help them in the raifing of it up : This commendable Inftitution was fo well receiv'd, and fo carefully practifed, that all the Inhabitants generally acknowledg'd the equity of it, and took a certain pleafure in making a voluntary contribution of their pains and cares upon that occafion : Some went to cut down fuch Timber as might be neceffary ; others were to find Reeds and Palm-leaves for palizadoes and covering ; the ableft Architects planted the forkes, rais'd the couples, and faften'd the covering, and all feem'd to be kindly concern'd in the work, fo as that the narrow ftructure was in a few days become tenantable, yet without any charge to the owner, fave only to fee thofe charitable affiftants fupply'd with the ordinary drink of the Country, as long as they were at work upon his account.

In fine, he had a particular averfion againft thofe idle perfons who are bafely content to live by the fweat and labour of others, as the Drones do on the Hony which the laborious Bee had brought into the common Treafury. But to retrive in our days a little glimpfe of the Golden Age, fo much celebrated by the Ancients, he incited all the Inhabitants to be liberal, and apt to communicate to one another the goods which God had plentifully beftow'd on them, and to exprefs their charity and hofpitality towards all thofe who came to vifit them, that fo there might afterwards be no occafion to fetle Inns and Victualling-houfes among them, as being places which for the moft part ferv'd only for retreats to flothful, debauch'd, and diffolute perfons ; and the diforders and exceffes committed therein were fo great, as in time might haften the defolation and ruine of the whole Colony.

But while the *French* Governor was thus taken up with the ordering of his little Republick, and kept up the fpirits of his people with the expectation of fudden recruits, the Gentlemen of the Company not much differing in conftitution from many of that Nation who think of reaping as foon as they have difpos'd the feed into the ground, were for their parts in a continual expectation of fome Ships loaden with the richeft and moft precious Commodities of *America*, that fo they might be reimburs'd with intereft what they had laid out upon the firft embarquing, and till that return were come, they thought of

nothing

nothing lefs then running themfelves into new charges. The
Governor having ferioufly taken it into confideration, that all
the Letters he had fent to thofe Gentlemen upon that occafion
had not obtain'd any favourable anfwers from them, thought it
would be his beft courfe, ere the Colony were reduc'd to greater
extremities, to come over to them in perfon, and by a fecond
Voyage undertake the follicitation of that relief, upon which
the fafety of their firft advancements, and the fubfiftence of
the *French* in that Ifland wholly depended. This good defign,
which the zeal he had for the glory of his Nation had infpir'd
him withall, prov'd as fortunate as he could have wifh'd it :
For being come to *Paris*, he was fo prevalent in reprefenting
the importance and neceffity of that Recruit to the Gentlemen
of the Company, that they granted him three hundred men,
and Ships furnifh'd with all neceffary Provifions for their tranf-
portation to S. *Chriftophers*.

This Recruit fo impatiently expected by the Colony, happily arriv'd about the beginning of *Auguft*, M.DC.XXIX. and it
was receiv'd with fo great joy by them who had fo long ftood
in need of it, that now they thought nothing fhould obftruct
the execution of their defigns. But it feems the profperities of
this life are of a fhort continuance; they had hardly folac'd
themfelves two months in the enjoyments of that happinefs,
ere there comes upon them a powerful Fleet from *Spain*; *Dom
Frederick de Toledo*, who had the command of it, had receiv'd
exprefs order from his Catholick Majefty, that before he fell
down to the *Havanna*, *Carthagena*, and the other more eminent Ports of *America*, he fhould touch at S. *Chriftophers*, and
force thence all the *Englifh* and *French*, who had planted themfelves there fome years before.

The firft act of hoftility committed by this Naval force,
which confifted of four and twenty great Ships of burthen,
and fifteen Frigots, was the feifure of fome *Englifh* Ships then
lying at Anchor neer the Ifland of *Mevis*; which done, it came
and caft Anchor in the Road of S. *Chriftophers*, within Cannon-
fhot of the *Baffe-terre*, where Monf. *de Roffey* had the command
in chief. The Forts of both the Colonies were not yet in fuch
a condition as to ftand out a fiege, they were unfurnifh'd with
Provifions, and all the Ammunition, as to Powder and Shot, in
the whole Ifland could not amount to much; nay though both
the Nations fhould have joyn'd all their forces together, yet
could they not have oppos'd fo great an Army : But their courage in fome meafure fupply'd all thofe defects; for that the
Enemy fhould not brag of his having compafs'd his defigns
without fome oppofition, *Defnambuc* difpatch'd out of the
Cabes-terre, where he began to fortifie himfelf, all his moft experienc'd Souldiers, in order to the relief of the place which
was threatned by the Enemy, and the *Englifh* fent thither four
of their beft Companies.   Thefe

Thefe Forces being come to the appointed Rendezvouz, were joyntly employ'd with the Inhabitants of that Quarter to intrench themfelves along the Sea-coaft, to make a more vigorous refiftance againft the Enemy, and oppofe his landing; and no doubt they would have put him to fome trouble, had they been well commanded, and that firft earneftnefs had not receiv'd fome remiffion by the fright which fo feiz'd the heart of *de Roffey* that he would have fuffer'd them to land, and make their approaches without any refiftance, if a young Gentleman, Nephew to Monf. *Defnambuc*, and elder Brother to Monf. *Parquet* the prefent Governour of *Martinico*, had not got leave to pafs over the Works, and to engage the firft Company of the Enemy that appear'd upon the fands: He was feconded by fome Volunteers, who would needs participate of the glory of that action: but he went before them all, both as to courage and refolution;for he fo gallantly engag'd him who had the command of the party, that he kill'd him, and feveral others of the moft valiant about him, who had the confidence to make tryal of his valour: But being afterwards forfaken by thofe who had follow'd him in that encounter, he was over-power'd by number, knock'd down, and carry'd into one of the enemies Ships, where after all remedies apply'd in order to his recovery he dy'd, to the great regret of both fides, as bemoaning the misfortune of fuch a miracle of generofity and refolution.

During this encounter, which fhould have been maintain'd with more gallantry by thofe who were in actual poffeffion of the Ifland, the General of the *Spanifh* Fleet immediately gave order, that all the Ships fhould at the fame time fend out their Shallops full of Souldiers well arm'd, which got a fhore in very good order: This added not a little to the fright *de Roffey* was in before, inafmuch as being far from entertaining any thoughts of oppofition, out of a fear of being opprefs'd by that multitude, he thought it his only way to make an honourable retreat before his people were encompafs'd of all fides. This refolution tumultuoufly taken was grumbled at by thofe who wifh'd the Enemy had more dearly bought the defolation of their Colony; but fuch a general confternation was there in that fatal conjuncture, that it was carried, they fhould take their way towards the *Cabes-terre*, and that there it fhould be taken into futher confideration what were beft to be done in order to the common fafety.

The *Spaniard* perceiving that the *French* had quitted their Fort and their Works without making any great refiftance, imagin'd there might be fome defign in that retreat, and that it had been made purpofely to draw him into fome Ambufcado laid for him in the Woods. This fufpicion kept him from profecuting his victory, and fo occafion'd his ftay in the Quarter of the *Baffe-terre* till he had a better account brought him of

the

the ſtate of the whole Iſland, and himſelf had conſider'd what was moſt expedient for him to do, in order to a more ſudden and punctual execution of his Commiſſion.

While the Enemy continu'd in this ſuſpence, and conſider'd with himſelf how to compaſs his deſigns with leaſt danger, *Deſnambuc* extreamly ſurpriz'd at ſo ſudden a change, and ſo unexpected ſucceſs, endeavour'd to comfort his own people, and to encourage them to expreſs their conſtancy in the ſupporting of that miſcarriage. He thereupon took occaſion to remonſtrate to them, That the diſgrace was not paſt remedy; That it was not to be imagin'd the enemy would ſtay in the Iſland ſo long as to force all the Inhabitants out of it; That he had affairs of greater weight, which call'd him elſewhere; That he would not eaſily be drawn into the Foreſts, which it was abſolutely neceſſary he ſhould paſs through ere he could come into his Quarter; That they might put themſelves into ſuch a poſture of defence as ſhould not only give a check to his progreſs, but alſo force him to ſignalize his invaſion with his own blood; And laſtly, that there were in his way ſome places ſo fortifi'd by Nature, that a few men might force him to find his way back again.

This advice was very ſolid, and might have prevail'd ſomewhat with thoſe to whom it was given, but the terror wherewith their ſpirits were prepoſſeſs'd, and the conſternation was ſo general, that it was not weigh'd as it deſerv'd. The buſineſs therefore being taken into deliberation, it was concluded, that the Iſland ſhould be deſerted, and that the Colony ſhould tranſport it ſelf to ſome other place which might give leſs occaſion of jealouſie to the *Spaniard*, and lye more out of the ordinary courſe of his Fleets. *Deſnambuc* foreſeeing that what pretence ſoever might be made for the taking of that reſolution, it would ſtill be chargeable with ſomewhat of cowardice and baſeneſs, ſuch as ſhould blaſt the opinion conceiv'd of the gallantry of the *French*, and of a ſudden ſmother the great hopes which ſome had of the advancement of their Colony, could not be perſwaded to give his approbation thereto. However, though he were of a contrary ſentiment, that it might not be ſaid he forſook in ſo ſad a conjuncture thoſe whom he had brought thither through ſo many Seas and dangers, he comply'd with their humor, and embarqu'd himſelf with them in certain Ships which chanc'd to be in the Haven; and ſo to avoid a greater diſorder, doing his own inclinations a violence, he only aſſur'd them that he ſhould one day reproach them with the little eſteem they made of his remonſtrances.

The Quarters where the *Engliſh* had ſetled themſelves were alſo in a great diſorder; they had intelligence brought them, that the enemy was become maſter of all the *Baſſe-terre*; That he had demoliſh'd the Fortreſs of the *French*, after he had remov'd

mov'd the pieces that were in it ; That he had already burnt all their Huts, and made havock of all the Plantations of the Quarter. They were in perpetual expectation when he should come, and fall on them with all his forces, and in that apprehension some endeavour'd to make their escape by Sea, or shelter themselves in the Mountains, while others somewhat more courageous were consulting how to send Deputies to *Dom Frederic*, to entreat him to admit of some accommodation: But all the Answer they receiv'd, was an express command immediately to depart the Island, which if they did not, they should be treated with all the rigour which the Law of Arms permits to be used towards those who against all right possess themselves of what belongs not to them.

To facilitate the departure which *Dom Frederic* had so imperiously commanded, he gave order that those Ships which his Fleet had taken away from the *English* neer the Island of *Mevis* should be restor'd to them, and that they should embarque without any delay, and immediately set sail for *England*. But whereas it was impossible those Vessels should contain so great a number of people, he permitted the supernumerary to continue in the Island till they had a favourable opportunity for their transportation.

These things dispatch'd, *Dom Frederic* weigh'd Anchor, in order to the continuation of his Voyage, but as soon as the Fleet was out of sight, the *English* who had been left behind in the Island began to rally, and took a resolution courageously to carry on the setlement of their Colony.

While these things were in agitation at S. *Christophers*, the *French* who had left it at the beginning of the distraction had suffer'd so many inconveniences at Sea, partly through want of Provisions, and partly by reason of contrary Winds, that they were forc'd to put in at the Islands of S. *Martin* and *Montserrat*, after they had by the way touch'd at that of *Antego*. They wish'd themselves so happy, as that they might have setled in any of those places; but they look'd on them as dreadful Desarts in comparison of that out of which they had been so unhappily forc'd: The pleasant Idea of that was still before their eyes, it was the continual subject of their regret; and the delightful remembrance of that pleasant abode, to the recovery whereof they were by Divine Providence re-invited by ways unknown to them, rais'd in them a desire to be inform'd what condition the *Spaniard* had left it in, since they were then so neer it: To satisfie that commendable curiosity, they sent one of their Ships to S. *Christophers*, which returning gave them an account, that the Enemies Fleet was gone; and that the *English* who were left behind were courageously employ'd in rebuilding their Hutts, planting Provisions, and repairing their desolations.

This

This unexpected good News reviv'd their decay'd hopes, and heightned the courage of those who were most cast down, so that there needed not many arguments ro perswade them to a return into that delightful Country which was already posfess'd of their hearts and tenderest affections.

Being arrived there, every one resum'd his former place, with a resolution to make an absolute setlement; but the Famine, which press'd hard upon them, would no doubt have check'd the progress of all these promising designs, and they would have been crush'd by the extraordinary labours which they were at the same time oblig'd to undergo, as well in re-building their houses, as planting things necessary for their subsistence, if in those pressing extremities God had not directed thither for their relief some Ships belonging to the United Provinces, which, finding what a deplorable condition they were in, generously supply'd them with provisions, cloaths, and all things necessary; nay to put an absolute obligation upon them, they had no other security for their satisfaction then their bare words.

The *French*, having thus seasonably overcome the inconveniences which they had struggled with from the first beginning of their establishment, employ'd themselves so earnestly afterwards in their Plantations, that, through the blessing of God on their labours, the Earth furnish'd them with Provisions, and Tobacco in such abundance, that they honestly satisfy'd their charitable Creditors, and in a short time were better accommodated with all things then they had been before their defeat by the *Spaniards :* Yet were they still in want of Men to carry on their Enterprizes, and the Commerce which began to be establish'd among them.   To remedy that, *Desnambuc*, who found his constancy attended with so good success, thought it the surest and most likely expedient, to permit the principal Inhabitants of the Colony to return into *France* to make Levies there, and to bring over what numbers they should raise on their own charge.   This prudent advice being accordingly put in execution, the Island was in a few years supply'd with abundance of gallant persons, who brought it into reputation.

The *English* Colony made also a shift in a short time to make up all the breaches it had receiv'd by the invasion of the *Spaniards :* The Company at *London*, which had undertaken the direction of it, sending over continual supplies of Men and refreshments, the two Quarters whereof the *English* were possess'd in the Island of S. *Christophers* became too narrow to maintain so great a multitude, insomuch that besides the Island of *Mevis*, which they had peopled before their defeat by the *Spaniards*, they grew so powerful, as in less then four years to spread themselves into new Plantations in the Islands of the

Z

Barbouthos,

Barboutkos, Mountferrat, Antego, and the *Barbados,* which are grown very numerous there, and famous for the Trade of the rich Commodities they are furnish'd with, as may be seen by the particular descriptions we have given thereof in the precedent Book of this History.

What Colonies the *Dutch* have in the *Caribby*-Islands were establish'd some time after those of the *French* and *English,* and their establishments were not upon the account of the States, but upon that of some particular Companies of Merchants, who, the better to carry on the Trade which they have in all the Islands whereof the *English* and *French* are possess'd, were desirous to have some places of safe retreat for the refreshment of their Ships. The most ancient of those Colonies which have any dependence on the States-General of the United Provinces, is that in the Island of S. *Euftace:* It was establish'd much about the same time that Sir *Thomas Warner* setled that of *Mont-ferrat,* which was in the Year M. DC. XXXII. It is considerable upon this account, that it is a place naturally well fortify'd; as also for the number and quality of the Inhabitants, the abundance of good Tobacco which it still yields; and for several other remarkable advantages, whereof we have given an account in the fifth Chapter of the former Book.

Monsieur *Defnambuc* expres'd no less earneftness and generosity in the dilatation of his Colony then other Nations did in that of theirs; but having not been so seasonably reliev'd as was requisite at the beginning, and his designs having been many times check'd by several unhappy obstructions, he had this further displeasure, to see divers of the most considerable Islands possess'd by others before he was in a condition to put in for a share, and dilate his Conquest beyond the limits of S. *Christophers.* He had a long time before cast his eye on that of *Gardeloupe,* as being one of the noblest and greatest Islands of all the *Caribbies*; but while he was taking order for the transporting of men thither, he was prevented in his design by Monsieur *de l' Olive,* one of the principal Inhabitants of his own Colony, who making his advantage of a Voyage he had made into *France* about some private affairs of his own, as he pretended, joyn'd with Monsieur *du Pleffis,* and some Merchants of *Dieppe,* for the establishment of a Colony there by Commiffion from the Company which had the direction of the Islands of *America.*

These two Gentlemen being made joint Governours of the Island of *Gardeloupe,* and invested with equal authority, arriv'd there the 28ᵗʰ of *June,* M. DC. XXXV. with a Company of five hundred men, who presently after their arrival were press'd with a famine, and divers diseases, which took away a great number of them. It is conceiv'd that the former misfortune

fortune happen'd to them upon this occasion, that they had
planted themselves at their first landing in those parts of the
Island where the soil was most barren, and unfit for cultivation of any in it, and that they had upon too light grounds enter'd into a War with the *Caribbians,* the originary Inhabitants
of the place, who might have plentifully furnish'd them with
most of the provisions necessary for their subsistence at the beginning, till the earth and their own industry had supply'd
them better. Diseases were the consequences of that unwhol-
some nourishment which hunger forc'd them to make use of
for want of better: whereto this may be added, that the
ground being not reduc'd to culture, the air was the more easily corrupted.

Du Plessis reflecting on the misfortunes and inconveniences
which daily fell one in the neck of another upon that unsetled
Colony, and having just grounds to fear that other yet greater might happen to it, took it so much to heart, that he dyed
out of pure grief, in the seventh month after his arrival. The
loss of him was much regretted by all the *French,* who had
always express'd a great submission to his advice, and much
love and respect to his person. He was a man of singular prudence, of so affable and obliging a disposition, that he gain'd
the affections of all that treated with him.

After the departure of Monsieur *du Plessis, de l' Olive* became sole Governour. This latter was a Person of an humour
as active and stirring as that of his Collegue was gentle and
moderate; and he so much harkned to the violent counsels of
some restless spirits, who like so many pestilent Ear-wigs were
continually putting him upon new projects, that he soon after
engag'd himself in that fatal War against the *Caribbians,* which
had almost prov'd the destruction of that newly-planted Colony. True it is, that at first he press'd so hard upon them,
as to force them to leave him the absolute possession of *Gardeloupe;* but in regard that to compass the designs which he
had fram'd to himself from the time of his arrival he was ne-
cessitated to commit several cruelties, such as the very Barbarians themselves would not have exercis'd upon their greatest
enemies, it prov'd such a blast to his reputation, that the ap-
provers of his conduct were only some sanguinary persons and
Desperadoes.

The poor *Caribbians* which the Governour had forc'd out
of the Island of *Gardeloupe* retreated into that of *Dominico:*
Those of the same Nation who were possess'd of the latter
entertain'd them kindly, and to give them a greater assurance
how much they were sensible of their misfortune, they proffer'd to joyn with them to revenge by the way of Arms the
injury which had been done them; a proffer too obliging
to be refus'd. Their forces being thus united, they made

several incursions into *Gardeloupe*, and became such goads and thorns in the sides of the *French*, that they were forc'd to give over the culture of Tobacco, nay indeed the planting of those provisions which were necessary for their subsistence, to the end they might always be in Arms, to prevent the attempts and designs of those subtle enemies, whom they had by their own imprudence so much exasperated against them.

This cruel War, which lasted neer four years, reduc'd the Colony to great extremities, and brought it to so deplorable a condition, that it was out of repute in all places; and upon its being continually pester'd by the incursions and depredations of the irreconcileable *Caribbians*, it was concluded to be at no great distance from its utter destruction. The *French* being brought to this lowness, it pleas'd God that the Governour *de l' Olive* lost his sight, whereupon the Gentlemen of the Company sent over Monsieur *Auber* to be Governour of it, who remedied all the precedent disorders, appeas'd all troubles, and setled that Peace which afterwards brought in Trading and plenty of all things; as we shall shew more at large in the third Chapter of this Moral History.

As soon as M. *Desnambuc* had receiv'd intelligence that *Gardeloupe* was inhabited, he resolv'd with the first convenience to setle himself in some other of the best Islands which were yet at his choice; and to prevent a second supplantation, finding that he had about him a considerable number of resolute persons, and furnish'd with all provisions of War, and what was necessary for the belly, and all things requisite for the prosecution of such enterprizes, he went in person to take possession of the Island of *Martinico*, which having done, he left there for his Lieutenant Mr. *du Pont*, and for Commander in chief Mr. *de la Falice*. Not long after dying at S. *Christophers*, he left all his Estate, and Titles of what kind soever, which he had in *Martinico*, which he had peopled at his own charge, to M. *Parquet* his Nephew, who is the present Lord and Governour of it, as we have said elsewhere.

This Gentleman was a person of much gallantry, of easie access, familiar with all, and master of a happy kind of insinuation, such as gently forc'd the love and obedience of those who were under him. It is related of him, that the *English* having gone a little beyond the boundaries which by the mutual agreement concluded between both Nations had been set for the distinction of their several Quarters, he went to those of the *English*, attended by a small number of persons, and spoke with the *English* Governour, who expected him with a considerable number of Souldiers: But he behav'd himself with so much courage and resolution, and gave such good reasons, intermixt with menaces, for what he did, that the *English* Governour granted him what he desir'd. That accident

cident ſhews how careful he was to preſerve the Rights and
Priviledges of his Nation; and what he did then had this further conſequence, that the two Governours were ever afterwards very good friends.

CHAP. II.

Of the Eſtabliſhments of the French *in the Iſlands of*
S. Bartholomew, S. Martin, *and* Sante-Cruce.

AFter the death of Monſieur *Deſnambuc*, one Monſieur *du
Halde*, who was his Lieutenant in that Government, was
nominated to be Governour in Chief by the Gentlemen of the
Company : But not long after, the ſaid *du Halde* coming over
into *France*, Cardinal *Richelieu*, whoſe care extended to the
moſt remote places where the *French* had any thing to do, undertook the conſervation and advancement of that Colony in
America, out of an endeavour to render the name of *France*
as glorious in that part of the new World, as it was here. To
carry on that deſign he thought it requiſite that the Iſlands
ſhould be ſupply'd with a Governour accordingly : Having
therefore ſome while ſought for a perſon fit for that Employment, one eminent for his conduct, prudence, generoſity, and
the experience requiſite for ſo great a charge, he at laſt pitch'd
upon Monſieur *de Louvilliers Poincy* Knight, a Gentleman of a
very ancient Houſe.

The Cardinal preſented this excellent Perſon to King *Lewis*
the XIII. who approving the choice, inveſted him with the
Charge of Governour, and Lieutenant-General under his Majeſty in the Iſlands of *America :* Whereupon Letters Patents
were granted him in *September* M. DC. XXXVIII. That quality had not been given to any of thoſe who had preceded him
in the Government of thoſe Iſlands.

In the Year M. DC. XXXIX. the ſaid new Governour ſetting
ſail from *Diep* about the midſt of *January*, arriv'd about a
month after at the *Caribbies*, and was firſt receiv'd at *Martinico* by the Inhabitants in Arms. He afterwards went to *Gardeloupe* and S. *Chriſtophers* ; but his nobleſt reception was at the
latter : All the *French* Inhabitants being in Arms receiv'd him
in the quality of General with univerſal applauſe, and he was
conducted to the Church, attended by his Gentlemen and
Guards, where *Te Deum* was ſung.

Immediately upon his reception the Iſland began to put on
a new face, and within a ſhort time after things were viſibly
chang'd from better to better ; inſomuch that he not only anſwer'd

fwer'd but exceeded the expectations of his Majesty and the Cardinal. One of the first things he did, was to give order for the building of Churches in several Quarters of the Island: He took care that the Priests should be well lodg'd and maintain'd, that they might not be diverted from the employments of their Function: He made such provisions in the administration of justice, as rendred it expeditious, and without Fees, by means of a Council consisting of the most prudent and experienc'd among the Officers of the Island: His vigilance reform'd and prevented the disorders which easily creep in among persons shuffled together from divers places, and of different humours: His prudence in composing and setling matters of greatest difficulty was equally admir'd by those who were under his Government, and his Neighbours of other Nations. That greatness of mind, which successfully guided him to the accomplishment of all his designs, made him dreadful to all restless and dif-satisfy'd spirits: His affability, easiness of access, and his kind entertainment towards Strangers, brought Trading and plenty into the Island; and his goodness and liberality justly gain'd the hearts and affections of the *French:* In a word, his Generosity signaliz'd in many occurrences as well in *France,* during the noble Employments he had in his Majesties Armies, as in *America* since his Government there, in the preservation, dilatation, and reduction of so many considerable places, wrought such a terrour in the *Spaniard,* that he never since proffer'd to oppose his glorious Enterprizes.

Having setled S. *Christophers* in good order as to Trading, and all other Concerns, and made it the most flourishing Island of all the *Caribbies,* as we have represented it in the fourth Chapter of the precedent Book, he afterwards extended the *French* Colony into those of S. *Bartholomew,* S. *Martins,* and *Santa Cruce,* whereof we have given an account in their proper places, yet so as we still have many considerable circumstances to deliver concerning the Conquest of the Island of *Santa Cruce,* which we shall here take occasion to insert.

The Island of *Santa Cruce* hath been subject to many Masters in a short time, and for many years together the *English* and *Dutch* had some contestations about the propriety of it: At last they made a division of it between them; but in the Year M DC. XLIX. the *English* having observ'd that they much exceeded the *Dutch* in number, forc'd them to depart the Island. But they also continu'd not long Masters of it; for soon after the *Spaniards* who were Inhabitants of the Island of *Porto-Rico* made an incursion into it, burnt their houses, put to the sword all the *English* they found in Arms, and order'd the rest with their baggage and wives to be transported to the *Barbouthos.*

Having

Having thus laid the Ifland defolate, as they were fetting things in order for their returning aboard their Veffels, and to take their courfe back to *Porto-Rico*, there arrives thither a Ship from the Iflands of S. *Euftace* and S. *Martins*, wherein there were a confiderable number of men, who having receiv'd intelligence of the defeat of the *Englifh*, and imagining that the *Spaniards* were gone, would have reviv'd the pretenfions of the *Dutch* to that Ifland : but the *Spaniards* having the advantage, as being ten to one, the *Dutch* were forc'd to accept of fuch terms of accommodation as the others were pleas'd to give them. The crafty *Spaniards* had indeed promis'd them good quarter, but their defign was to tranfport them to *Porto-Rico* to their Governour, who, according to the *Spanifh* humour, would not have treated them over-chriftianly.

But as good fortune would have it, juft as the *Spaniards* were preparing for their return with the *Dutch* Prifoners, who had fo unfortunately fallen into their hands, two *French* Ships well mann'd, and furnifh'd with all forts of Provifions and Ammunition, arriv'd in the Ifland, fent thither by the *French* General *de Poincy*, to fend the *Spaniard* packing thence, and take poffeffion of it for the King of *France*. This relief came in very feafonably for the deliverance of the furpriz'd *Dutch*; for the *Spaniards*, perceiving the *French* landing cheerfully and in good order, and making a confiderable Body of gallant men, and ready to fight, immediately let go their Prifoners; and after a fhort capitulation, the *French* fent them an exprefs order to be gone aboard their Ships, with a menace that if they did not, they would fall upon them as Enemies, and that they were not to expect any Quarter. The *Spaniards* thought it their beft courfe rather to comply then ftand to the hazard of an engagement, though they much exceeded the *French* in number.

The *French* General taking it into his confideration, of what importance the Ifland in time might be, efpecially in order to the facilitation of other acquefts of greater concernment, thought it worthy his endeavours to fecure what he had fo fortunately poffefs'd himfelf of, and thereupon fent a prudent and experienc'd Governour to command there under him : The perfon he pitch'd on for that Employment was Monfieur *Auber*, Major of the Ifland of S. *Chriftophers*, who had exercis'd that Charge with great approbation for many years together; but now he was advanc'd to the quality of Governour of that Ifland : He died in the exercife of that Charge, to the great regret of all the Inhabitants, after he had fetled the Ifland in good order, recover'd its ruines, and laid the foundations of a Fort which he had defign'd himfelf for the fecurity of fuch Ships as fhould afterwards come into the Haven, and to defeat the hopes of the *Spaniards* to make any more incurfions there.

This

This reduction of the Island under the power of the *French*, as we have describ'd it, happen'd in the Year M. DC. L.

The *Dutch* had built a very fair Church upon a pleasant ascent of this Island, in the form of a Cross, which may still be standing, if the *Spaniards*, who should have a respect for that sacred Sign which was on the top of the Steeple, have not ruin'd it. The *French* are oblig'd for that House of Prayer to the devotion and zeal of a certain Company of Merchants belonging to *Flushing*, who first peopled the Island by a Commission from the States-General.

The present King of *France* being inform'd of all the glorious actions done in those parts by Monsieur *de Poincy*, and considering how necessary his continual residence in *America* was, granted him new Letters Patents, whereby he confirm'd him in the Charge of Governour and Lieutenant-General in those places; and the Queen, during her Regency, gave him a great commendation for his noble Enterprizes, and Fidelity to the Kings service.

In the Year M. DC. LI. the *French* Governour, with the Kings consent, treated with the Gentlemen of the Company we mentioned before, and having reimburs'd them all the charges they had been at in the establishment of that Colony, purchas'd to himself the Seigniory and Fee-simple of the Islands of S. *Christophers*, S. *Bartholomew*, S. *Martin*, *Santa-cruce*, and other adjacent Islands, and that in the name, and for the benefit of his Order of *Malta*; and it is one of the noblest, richest, and most honourable Seigniories of any that Order enjoys under the Sovereignty of his Majesty of *France*: And since that time the said King hath made an absolute bequest of all those Islands to the Order of *Malta*, reserving to himself the Sovereignty thereof, and the homage of a Crown of Gold, to be presented at every change of King, of the value of a thousand Crowns; as it appears by the Letters Patents dated in *March*, M. DC. LIII.

Monsieur *du Parquet*, Governour of *Martinico*, did the like for the Islands of *Martinico*, *Granada*, and *Saintaloufia*: Monsieur *d' Hewell*, Governour of *Gardeloupe*, did the same thing for the Islands of *Gardeloupe*, *Marigalanta*, *Defirado*, and the *Saints*. The two last mentioned are not yet inhabited; but he hath purchas'd the Seigniory of those places by way of advance, that others might not without breach of civility possess themselves thereof: For it is to be observ'd, that the Company which had the direction of the Islands of *America*, but is now dissolv'd, had obtain'd of the King all the Islands of the *Caribbies*, as well those then inhabited, as those in process of time to be so: So that these Gentlemen, who have treated with the Company, would needs have mentioned in their Grant, some Islands which are not yet inhabited, yet lye neer and very con-

venient

venient for them, inſomuch as when they ſhall have men e-
nough in their other Iſlands, they will be the more eaſily tranſ-
planted into thoſe, unleſs the *Engliſh* or *Dutch* chance to be before-hand with them : For it is a general Rule, That a Country deſtitute of Inhabitants belongs to him who firſt poſſeſſes
himſelf of it ; ſo that neither the King of *France*'s Grant, nor
yet that of the Company does any thing more then ſecure thoſe
Gentlemen againſt the pretentions of ſuch of their own Nation as might oppoſe their deſigns.

Thus of all the Iſlands which the *French* are poſſeſs'd of in
America the King of *France* reſerves to himſelf the Sovereignty, and M. M. *de Poincy, du Parquet,* and *d' Houel* have the
Seigniory thereof, without any acknowledgment of the Company, which hath abſolutely quitted all its pretentions to the
ſaid Gentlemen.

As for the *Engliſh* Governours of S. *Chriſtophers,* Sir *Thomas
Warner* dying, after he had glorioufly eſtabliſh'd his Country-
men in the *Caribbies,* and left the Iſland of S. *Chriſtophers* inhabited by twelve or thirteen thouſand *Engliſh,* Mr. *Rich,* who
was the principal Captain in the Iſland, was advanc'd to that
Charge ; and this latter alſo dying, Mr. *Everard* was advanc'd
to the Government, which he ſtill exerciſes with general approbation, as we had occaſion to ſhew when we treated of the
Iſland of S. *Chriſtophers.*

At the firſt coming of the forreign Nations into the Iſlands,
they were lodg'd much after the ſame manner as the natural
Inhabitants of the Country, in little cotts and hutts made of
the wood they had fell'd upon the place as they clear'd the
ground.　There are ſtill to be ſeen, in ſeveral of the newly-
planted Colonies, many of thoſe weak ſtructures, which are
ſuſtain'd only by four or ſix forks planted in the ground, and
inſtead of walls are encompaſs'd and palizado'd only with
reeds, and cover'd with Palm or Plantane-leaves, Sugar-canes,
or ſome ſuch material : But in all the other Iſlands, where
theſe Nations are better ſetled and accommodated, there are
many very fair houſes of Timber, Stone, and Brick, built after the ſame manner as thoſe in their own Countries, ſave that
for the moſt part they are but one or two Stories high at the
moſt, that they may the more eaſily reſiſt the winds, which
ſometimes blow in thoſe parts with extraordinary violence.
Of theſe Edifices we have ſpoken already in ſeveral places of
the precedent Book, when we gave a particular account of
the ſeveral Iſlands.

But we have this particularly to adde here, that the *Engliſh*
are the beſt accommodated for Lodgings of any of the Inhabitants of thoſe Iſlands, and have their houſes well furniſh'd,
which is to be attributed to their conſtant abode in their Colonies, where they endeavour to get all conveniences as much

as if they were the places of their birth: They are also most
of them married, whence it comes that they take greater pains
to supply themselves with all things requisite, then those are
apt to do who lead single lives, as most of the *French* do.

We had an intention to conclude this Chapter with the
course taken by M. *Auber* to make up a peace with the *Caribbians*, upon his taking possession of the Government of *Gardeloupe* ; but in regard the discourse is somewhat long, and may
conduce much to the discovery of the humours and dispositions of those *Indians*, of whom we are to treat more at large in
this second Book, we thought it better dispos'd into a Chapter
apart.

<hr>

CHAP. III.

Of the Establishment of the French *Colony in the Island
of* Gardeloupe, *consequently to the Peace concluded
with the* Caribbians *of* Dominico, *in the Year*
M. DC. XL.

THe first among the *French* who took possession of the
Island of *Gardeloupe*, landed there in the Year 1635.
by order from a Company of Merchants of the City of *Deep*,
which, under the Authority of the General Company of the
Islands of *America* constituted at *Paris*, sent thither two Gentlemen, *du Plessis* and *de l' Olive*, to command there upon their
account : But the former dying some few months after his
establishment, and the other becoming unfit for the government of a new-planted Colony, through the loss of his sight,
and his continual indispositions, as we have mentioned in the
precedent Chapters, the *French* Governour-General took order that the Inhabitants of that Island should be supply'd with
all things necessary : For it is probable they would have absolutely forsaken it, had not the said Governour sent over recruits of Auxiliaries to them, under the conduct of *Vernade*
and *Sabouilly*, to oppose the designs of the *Caribbians*, who
with much animosity disputed the possession of it with them :
So that if that Colony is not oblig'd for its establishment to
the General *de Poincy*, this at least must be acknowledg'd, that
its preservation and subsistence was the effect of his care. He
accordingly approv'd and confirm'd, in the Kings name, the
nomination which the Company of the Islands had made of
M. *Auber* to be Governour of that Island.

This new Governour took the Oath of Allegeance before
the General, the 20th of *October* M. DC. XL. but before he fell
down

down to S. *Chriſtophers*, the Ship which had brought him out
of *France* into *America* caſting Anchor neer *Dominico*, many
of the Savages, who had obſerv'd the Ship at a diſtance, and
concluded from the expreſſions of friendſhip which had been
made to them, that they had no enemies in that Veſſel, grew
ſo confident as to come into it.   It fortunately happen'd, that
thoſe who had come out upon the diſcovery were ſome of the
chiefeſt Captains of the Iſland : M. *Auber* reſolv'd to make all
the advantage he could of that opportunity, imagining it
might conduce very much to the making of an alliance with
that people, which had been exaſperated and incens'd againſt
the *French* by the violences and cruel uſage of *de l' Olive*, one
of his Predeceſſors in that Charge, as alſo by the ill conduct of
thoſe who commanded the Recruits which the General had
ſent over for the ſecurity of the Iſland : And having wi hal an
inkling that thoſe of that Nation are eaſily drawn in by kind-
neſſes and little Preſents, he omitted nothing which he conceiv'd might promote his deſign.

He thereupon acquainted them, that he was newly come
from *France*, and that he was ſent over to be Governour of
Gardeloupe ; that he had been much troubled to hear of the
differences which for ſome years had continued between them
and the *French* ; that he was come with an intention to make
a friendly compoſure thereof ; and that he would be their
Companion and good Neighbour, and live with them, as their
late old friend M. *du Pleſſis* had done.   Theſe proffers were
interrupted now and then with glaſſes of *Aqua-vitæ*, which he
order'd ever and anon to be preſented to them.

Theſe Savages finding ſo free and cordial a reception, after
they had diſcours'd a while among themſelves, in the Language
they ſpeak, concerning their military affairs, which is under-
ſtood only by the moſt ancient Conductors of their Enterprizes, reſolv'd to accept of the proffer which had been made
them, and to renew the ancient amity, by renouncing whatever might tend to the proſecution of that bloody War which
had ſo much incommodated both parties.   But before they
would promiſe any thing, they ask'd Monſieur *Auber*, whether
l' Olive, Sabouilly, and all thoſe who had follow'd their violent
courſes, ſhould be forc'd to depart the Iſland ? Whereto it being anſwer'd that they ſhould, they reply'd, that it muſt ne-
ceſſarily be ſo, and that otherwiſe they ſhould ſtill have an
animoſity againſt the *French*, ſaying, *l' Olive and Sabouilly are
not good for the Caribbians :* Thoſe were their words.   Whereupon M. *Auber* having aſſur'd them that their deſires ſhould be
ſatisfy'd, and that for his part he would be good to them, if
they on their parts would be good ; which they promis'd to
be.   Theſe things concluded, he gave them a very noble
treatment, beſtow'd ſome Preſents among them, and diſmiſs'd

them the moſt ſatisfy'd people in the world.

From the road of *Dominico* M. *Auber* went to *Gardeloupe,* where having diſpos'd his equipage he return'd to S. *Chriſto-phers,* to give the General an account of what had paſt, who was well ſatisfy'd with the choice which the Company had made of him for that Employment.

Being return'd to his Government, he was gallantly receiv'd by all the Inhabitants, who eſteem'd him for his experience in whatever might contribute to the advancement of newly-planted Colonies, as alſo out of a perſwaſion, that his prudence would remedy the diſorders paſt, and his generoſity oppoſe the preſent difficulties, and undertake all things requiſite for the quiet and welfare of the Iſland ; and his mildneſs and af-fability would gain him the affections of all there, as they had done at S. *chriſtophers,* where he had been accounted one of their beſt Captains.   His Commiſſion was read and publiſh'd two Sundays together, at the head of all the Companies of the Iſland.

The War which had been fomented between the Savages and the *French* by the ill counſel of ſome reſtleſs ſpirits, and the credulity of the precedent Governour who had harkned thereto, together with the differences, jealouſies and animoſi-ties which thoſe boutefeus had rais'd among the principal In-habitants of the Iſland, had rendred it the moſt deſolate of all the Colonies of *America :* Want of proviſions had reduc'd many to ſo great extremities, that life grew weariſom to them, and death was the object of their wiſhes : The continual fear they were in of being ſurpriz'd by the Savages, oblig'd them to be always in Arms, and to leave their Gardens and Plantations uncultivated ; and the inſupportable treatment they receiv'd from ſome Officers who abus'd their Authority, had brought them to the threſhold of inevitable deſtruction.

But aſſoon as M. *Auber* had aſſum'd the Government, by the unanimous acclamations of all the Inhabitants, and brought them the news of an aſſured peace, which he had concluded with the Savages their neighbours, and hop'd very ſuddenly to ſee confirm'd by all the aſſurances could be expected from a Nation ſo unciviliz'd as that of the *Caribbians,* the diſturbers of the publick tranquillity were diſpers'd, and the well-affe-cted found themſelves in ſafety under the prudent conduct of ſo worthy a Governour, who us'd all poſſible endeavours to bring the Iſland to a perfect ſetlement : Inſomuch that the Co-lony ſeem'd to have put on a new face ; Juſtice began to flou-riſh ; the unity and labours of the Inhabitants retriv'd the plenty, trading, and peace, which had been forc'd thence be-fore ; and the pious example of the Commander in chief had the expected influence over all the members of that Colony.

Though he had motion'd a Treaty of peace with the Sava-

ges,

ger, yet did he conceive it expedient, for fear of a furprize, that the Inhabitants fhould ftill keep their Guards: Accordingly he planted Sentinels in all thofe places where the *Caribbians* might moft eafily land without being difcover'd: He chang'd the Guards, and plac'd them in other more advantagious places; and he thought it prudence to keep under thofe who would have ruin'd the firft foundations he had laid of the firm peace and alliance with thofe reconciled enemies, charging the former by exprefs prohibitions to forbear all acts of hoftility, that they might not by their particular animofities obftruct the general agreement wherein all the Inhabitants were fo much concern'd.

The faid Governour taking further into his confideration, that the Iflands were to fubfift by Trading; that nothing puts a greater flurre upon them then the bad Commodities vented therein; and that Tobacco was the only Commodity at that time of any efteem at *Gardeloupe*; and that feveral perfons put off what was not merchantable, which procedure had caus'd the Ifland to be flighted by Forreigners, who upon that account had forborn fending any Ships thither; he appointed certain perfons who well underftood the management of Tobacco, and thefe carefully examin'd the making up of it, and had order to caft into the Sea what was decay'd, or wanted thofe qualities it ought to have to be allowable.

This good order taken, as well in order to military affairs as policy, brought the Ifland in a fhort time into a flourifhing condition; and the report of its amendment occafion'd the coming thither of many Merchants, and invited a great number of confiderable families to fetle themfelves there.

But to return to the Savages who had vifited M. *Aubert* in his Ship at his firft arrival, and had treated with him about a peace, upon the conditions before-mentioned; they were no fooner got home into their Country, where they were expected with much impatience, upon this fcore, that they had continu'd a great while in the Ship, but they celebrated all over the Ifland the noble entertainment they had receiv'd from the Governour newly come from *France.* The confiderable Prefents he had beftow'd on them was an authentick affurance of his goodnefs and liberality. To this they added, that their enemies, *t' Olive* and *Sabouilly*, being ordered to depart *Gardeloupe*, they had made a peace with that brave Companion, who had treated them fo kindly, that he was worthy of their alliance. That he might take no further occafion of diftruft, they urg'd the neceffity there was that they fhould forbear making thofe incurfions into *Gardeloupe* which they had been wont to make in the time of War: And that when certain news came that the new Governour was fully eftablifh'd in his Government, they would give him a vifit, carry him Prefents,

and

and folemnly confirm that peace which was likely to prove ſo advantagious for the future. The *Caribbians*, who had loſt many of their men in the former engagements againſt the *French*, and grew weary of dealing with ſuch expert enemies, were glad to hear what was propos'd to them by the principal Captains in their Country : So that they approv'd all that had paſs'd between them and the *French* Governour, and behav'd themſelves as they ſhould do in order to the confirmation of the peace.

About the ſpace of five months the Savages punctually obſerv'd the promiſe they had made to M. *Auber*, of not giving any further diſturbance to the *French :* Imagining that time ſufficient to let all the Inhabitants of *Gardeloupe* know what alliance had been contracted at the road of *Dominico*, they reſolv'd to ſend thither a ſolemn Deputation, to confirm the peace, and wiſh the Governour all proſperity. There was a great competition among the Savages who ſhould be honour'd with a Commiſſion of ſo great importance : They reſolv'd then, to ſatisfie the moſt eminent among them who were competitors for that Embaſſie, to pitch upon two of their moſt ancient and moſt renowned Captains, and to give each of them a conſiderable Convoy, conſiſting of the choice of their braveſt Officers and Souldiers : And that there might be no jealouſie among the Captains, they thought it fit they ſhould depart in two ſeveral *Piragas*, each of them with his retinue, and in ſuch order as that one ſhould precede the other by one day.

The chiefeſt of theſe Embaſſadours was call'd Captain *Amichon*, a perſon very conſiderable among them, and he was accompany'd by thirty of the moſt active and moſt expert of *Dominico*. M. *Auber* was wont to ſay, that he had never ſeen any Savages ſo well ſhap'd and active as they were. Theſe Savages therefore, relying on the promiſe he had made them in the Road, landed at *Gardeloupe*, where hearing by the Guards that M. *Auber* was in the Iſland, and in good health, they confidently landed, and deſired to ſee him, having in the mean time left ſome of the leſs conſiderable of their party to look to the *Piraga*. While ſome went to acquaint the Governour with the arrival of theſe Deputies of *Dominico*, Captain *Amichon*, who was to be the Speaker, diſpatch'd away two of his retinue loaden with the beſt fruits of their Country, which they had brought along with them for a Preſent.

The *French* Governour was extremely glad to hear of their arrival, and having immediately commanded all thoſe of his houſhold and the whole Quarter not to give them the leaſt occaſion to fear any ill treatment, he would needs go himſelf to meet them, with a countenance which ſufficiently

ently exprefs'd how welcome they were.   We fhall not trouble our felves to infert here the Speech and Complements
made by Captain *Amichon* at this firft interview : He was one
of thofe who had vifited M. *Auber* in his Ship, fo that he eafily knew him again.   He immediately gave him to underftand,
that he was come to confirm what they had refolv'd together
at the Road of *Dominico* concerning the peace ; and that all
the *Caribbians* of his Country were defirous of it.   The *French*
Governour in anfwer thereto, made them fenfible as well by
his Interpreter as his countenance, that for his part he would
inviolably obferve that union, provided they were not the
firft breakers of it.   Having afterwards brought them to his
houfe, and knowing that good cheer was the beft feal could
be put to that Treaty of peace, he call'd for fome Aqua-vitæ,
and order'd to be brought what was moft delicious in the
Ifland : At laft he crown'd the Entertainment with Prefents
of all the curiofities moft in efteem among the Savages.   And
that all the Deputies might participate of the good cheer and
liberality of the Governour, thofe who had been treated went
to relieve thofe who were left behind to look to the *Piraga*,
who alfo in their turn receiv'd the fame treatment and Prefents which the others had had.   Captain *Amichon* forgot
not, according to the cuftom they obferve towards their
friends, to take M. *Auber's* name, and to give him his own.

Having been thus civilly receiv'd and treated, they return'd
very joyfully to their *Piraga*, and fet fail towards their own
Ifland : They met at a certain rendezvouz, which they had
agreed upon before they had left *Dominico*, with the other
Piraga, which brought over the other Embaffadour, whofe
name was Captain *Baron*, with his retinue.   This fecond
Captain underftanding from the former what reception he
and his retinue had at *Gardeloupe*, got thither the next day.
This *Baron* had been a great friend of M. *du Pleffis*, who dy'd
Governour of *Gardeloupe*, but having equal authority with
M. *de l' Olive*, his Collegue, who after *du Pleffis* death impru-
dently engag'd the *French* into a War with the Savages.

This Captain then, who had often vifited M. *du Pleffis*, and
remembred the friendfhip he had born him, being fatisfy'd of
the generofity of the *French*, went afhore with his Company,
and was conducted to the Governour's, who treated him with
the fame ceremonies as he had done the former : But when he
came to hear that the Captain had been intimately acquainted
with M. *du Pleffis*, and that there had been a familiar correfpondence between them, he treated him with greater tefti-
monies of affection then he had done the others, and enter'd into a particular friendfhip with him, receiving his
name, and giving him his own.   Thus was the latter Deputation difmifs'd with greater fatisfaction then the former,
and

and promis'd to continue their visits for the future : But both
of them gave a large account at their *Carbetts*, of the civilities
and good entertainment of the new Governour.

Captain *Baron*, who had been so kindly receiv'd at his first
visit, staid not long ere he made a second : At the latter the
Governour shew'd him one of M. *du Plessis* Sons, to whom the
Captain made a thousand caresses, in remembrance of his Father, whom he call'd his Companion, and the Friend of his
Nation. True it is, that Gentleman had insinuated himself
into the affection of those *Barbarians*, who had a respect for
his merits and excellent endowments.

After this visit, and several others which the *Caribbians* daily made, M. *Auber* would be assur'd of them by Hostages, that
they would observe the alliance : To that purpose he apply'd
himself to Captain *Baron*, with whom he had contracted a
greater friendship then with the others, and whom he call'd his
Companion, as succeeding to the alliance there had sometime
been between him and M. *du Plessis*. M. *Auber* ask'd him one
day, whether he thought it not rational, that, to be assur'd of
those of his Nation, he should require some of their children
to be deliver'd up to him as Hostages ? The Captain, who was
of a judgment and understanding much beyond the ordinary
rate of Savages, immediately reply'd, that the mutual safety
was to be procur'd upon equal conditions ; and that if they
deliver'd up some of their children to the *French*, it was but
just the *French* should do the like with them.   He thereupon
presented to M. *Auber* some of his own children who had accompany'd him ; and the other accepting of the proffer, made
choice of one of them, a young lad, whose countenance and
demeanour was somewhat more pleasing and attractive, in a
word, one who was in several respects more amiable then any
of his brethren : The Father was content to part with his Son,
and the Son was content to stay with M. *Auber* ; an accident
that seldom happens among the Savages. His name was *Ima-
labouy*. From that day M. *Auber* treated him as his Son, and
alway call'd him so ; and the young Fellow call'd him Father. When he was put into cloaths, he made a shift to be-
have himself well enough ; nor did he find it any hard matter to enure himself to the *European* course of life. Captain
Baron desir'd to have as a counter-hostage one of Mistress *Auber*'s Sons, who had been first wife to M. *du Plessis*, and was
then married to M. *Auber :* But M. *Auber* having represented
to the Captain, that young *du Plessis* was of too soft a nature to endure the hardship of a *Caribbian* life, prevail'd
with him to accept by way of Hostage, instead of him, one
of his Servants, who willingly proffer'd to follow him. That
young man being of a strong constitution, continu'd some
moneths among the Savages, who treated him with much
                                                    kindness :

kindnefs ; but whether the change of air, or nourifhment caus'd fome alteration in him, he fell fick fome time after: Which Captain *Baron* hearing of, and fearing he might dye among them, he brought him back to M. *Auber*, and requir'd not any other perfon in his ftead, faying that he would have no other Hoftage then the word of his Companion.   True it is, he would have perfwaded his own Son to return along with him, but he could not prevail with him, the Youth telling him, that he thought himfelf in a better condition with M. *Auber* then with his Father.

Captain *Baron* having left at *Gardeloupe* fo precious an engagement, took occafion to make frequent vifits to M. *Auber*, and by that means to fee his Son: And finding himfelf extremely oblig'd to M. *Auber* for the many favours he receiv'd from him, efpecially for the tender affection he bore his Son, he bethought himfelf to find out fome occafions whereby he might exprefs his acknowledgments thereof : He refolv'd therefore to make a difcovery to him, that during the Wars between thofe of his Nation and the *French*, who were commanded by *l' Olive*, he had taken a young *French*-man Prifoner, and had given him his life only upon this fcore, that he had fometime been a Servant to M. *du Pleffis*, his old Companion : And that it was neer three years that he had him, and gave him more then ordinary liberty, though it had been in his power to put him to death, becaufe he was taken in Arms, and in the heat of the Engagement : But that he had not us'd extremity, remembring the ancient friendfhip between him and M. *du Pleffis*, in whofe attendance he had feen that *French*-man.   M. *Auber* compaffionating the young mans condition, entreated the Captain to deliver him up ; which he promis'd, and not many days after was as good as his word ; and he whofe good fortune it was to be thus retriv'd, ftaid a long time after at *Gardeloupe*.

The generous Captain, not thinking it enough to have thus oblig'd M. *Auber*, and parted with his Prifoner, told him of another Captain of *Dominico* who alfo had a *French*-man in his houfe, a Prifoner at War, and proffer'd to follicite that Captain to fet him at liberty.   He prevail'd, and fome days after brought over that other Prifoner, whofe name was *Jean Jardin*.   This being a fubtle young fellow had gain'd the affections not only of the Captain, whofe Prifoner he was, but alfo of all the *Caribbians*, who had as much kindnefs for him as if he had been of their own Nation : And he had fuch an excellent memory, that he had got their Language in perfection.

M. *Auber* defirous to make fome return of thefe good offices and expreffions of affection, befides the Prefents he daily made the Captain, would needs oblige his whole Nation:

It was when the Captain was engag'd for the War against the *Arouagues*, who inhabit *Trinity*-Island, and to that purpose had made extraordinary preparations. For this nobly-minded Savage coming to take leave of M. *Auber* before he went upon that expedition, he bestow'd on him, to be put into his party, one of his menial Servants, who was his Fowler, named *Des Scriffiers*, who had a long time wish'd himself present at the Engagements of those Savages; and he furnish'd him with good fire-arms, and all things requisite to make use thereof.

Captain *Baron* was much astonish'd at that favour, and having joyfully accepted of it, made extraordinary declarations thereof among those of his own Nation. This Volunteer very cheerfully follow'd the Captain, and was at the Engagement with the *Arouagues* of *Trinity*-Island, to which there came a powerful Army of Savages from all the *Caribby*-Islands. The *French*-man did as much upon that occasion as could be expected from a gallant Souldier; and being a good marksman, he hurt and wounded so many of the *Arouagues*, who were not accustomed to feel the effect of fire-arms, that at last they took the rout, and retreated into the mountains, leaving the spoil to the victorious *Caribbians*. From that time *Scriffiers* was ever look'd upon by those of that Nation as a great Captain; and they could not sufficiently admire the kindness of the *French* Governour, who voluntarily depriv'd himself of that young mans service, and lent him to them. All the particulars of this relation we have from very good hands, especially M. *Auber's*.

During all the time of M. *Auber's* government of *Gardeloupe*, the peace made with the *Caribbians* was inviolably observ'd on both sides, to the great advantage of both Nations : For the Savages by that agreement had the opportunity to treat with the *French* for wedges, hooks, knives, and several other instruments and commodities which they look upon as the most necessary : And the *French* receiv'd from them in exchange, Swine, Lizards, Sea-Turtles or Tortoises, and an infinite number of other fishes, and other refreshments, whereof they made a good advantage. So that the *Caribbians* were as it were the Pourvoyers of the *French*, who in the mean time labour'd in their Plantations without any disturbance.

CHAP.

CHAP. IV.

Of the Trading and Employments of the Forreign Inha-
bitants of the Country ; and firſt, of the culture and
ordering of Tobacco.

IN the *Caribbies* Money is not us'd in order to the carrying
on of ordinary Traffick, but this is perform'd by the ex-
changing of thoſe Commodities which are of the growth of
the Country for ſuch as are brought out of *Europe*, whether
they conſiſt in Cloaths, Linnen, Ammunition, or Proviſions,
and other neceſſaries requiſite for the better conveniences and
enjoyments of life. And this was the common courſe of all
Nations before the uſe of Money, and is to this day practis'd
in divers ſavage Countries, and particularly in *Colchida*, where
every one brings to the Market what he hath ſuperfluous, to
ſupply himſelf with what he wants.

The Store-houſes and Magazines of theſe Iſlands are commonly well furniſh'd with all ſorts of Commodities which are
brought out of *England*, *France*, *Holland*, and *Zealand*, nay as
plentifully as in any place in the world. The price of every Commodity is not left to the choice of the Merchants
who keep the Store-houſes, but ſet upon it by the Governours, with the advice of their Council. The Commodities
which the Inhabitants bring in exchange for thoſe before-
mentioned, are reducible to five ſpecies ; to wit, Tobacco,
Sugar, Ginger, Indico, and Cotton.

At the beginning all the forreign Inhabitants of the *Ca-*
ribbies apply'd themſelves wholly to the culture of Tobacco, whereby they made a ſhift to get a competent livelihood ;
but afterwards the abundance that was made bringing down
the price of it, they have in ſeveral places employ'd themſelves in the planting of Sugar-canes, Ginger, and Indico :
And it hath pleas'd God ſo to proſper their deſigns, that it
is almoſt a miracle to ſee with what improvement all theſe
Commodities grow in moſt of the Iſlands. And foraſmuch
as many who ſee them in *Europe* know not how they are order'd, it will be a great ſatisfaction to their curioſity, to
give a ſhort account of each of them ; whereto we ſhall
adde ſomewhat concerning Cotton.

True it is, that divers Authors have already treated of
them ; but in regard our Hiſtory would be defective, if nothing ſhould be ſaid concerning them, we are in the firſt
place to aſſure the Reader, that the whole diſcourſe we intend to make thereof is not a Copy or Extract out of any
other, but a true Original naturally taken with much care

and fidelity : So that if we fay the fame things as others have done before us, thofe who fhall perufe our work will not be much troubled to find here the confirmation of a truth which comes from fo remote a part of the world, and whereof they cannot have too great an affurance : And if they find any thing that feems to clafh with fome precedent relations, they are to look on it as a difcovery of the falfhood of thofe which are contrary thereto : Or at leaft ours will make it apparent, that in all places the Planters do not fo exactly follow the fame method in the ordering of thefe Commodities, but that fometimes fome alteration may be obferv'd therein. Befides, we have this further hope, that fome will find in the following defcriptions a certain exactnefs and cleernefs which they will think not unacceptable to them; nay they may haply meet with fomething therein that is new, and fuch as hath not been obferv'd by any other Authors : But if there be any who fhall think there is not any thing in this and the next Chapter which they know not already, that is, nothing which may either inftruct or divert them, they are defir'd not to blame our diligence, and imagine them written for others who may receive fome inftruction or divertifement thereby, and acknowledge themfelves oblig'd to us for our care.

For the getting of good and merchantable Tobacco, the firft thing to be done, is, in the proper feafon to prepare the beds in feveral places of the Gardens, fuch as have good fhelter from the winds; then they fow in them the feed which had been gather'd from the ftalks of the precedent year, which they fuffer to grow and ripen for that purpofe : They mix afhes with the feed when it is fown, that it may not fall too thick in fome places : When it begins to appear above ground, it is carefully cover'd with the leaves of the prickly Palms, or with branches of Orange, or Citron-trees, to fecure it from the exceffive heat of the Sun, the coolnefs of the night, and the fpoil which tame Fowl and Birds might make in it.

While the Plant is growing up to a condition that it may be tranfplanted, the place into which it is to be remov'd is prepared. If the Plantation be but newly eftablifh'd, it is requifite that it fhould have been cleer'd of wood fome confiderable time before, and that the branches fhould be burnt upon the ground, and over the beds : And if after all that there be any thing remaining, whatever is not burnt muft be convey'd quite away, that the place may be free. True it is, there's no need of digging the earth or turning it up, nor yet of delving, but only of cleering it of all weeds, fo as that there remain not any wood, nor bark, nor leaf, nor fo much as the leaft grafs. To do that, they make ufe of a kind of broad and fharp Hoes, which pare and take off the furface of the ground,

and

and if need be, carry along with them the roots of the weeds, whoſe after-growth they would prevent.

The ground being thus prepar'd, it is divided into ſeveral ridges or beds diſtant one from the other two or three foot. To do this, they make uſe of long cords, which at the diſtance of every two foot, or thereabouts, are marked with a little piece of cloth, which is ſew'd thereto; and then they place little ſticks at all the places anſwerable to thoſe marks; to the end, that when the time of tranſplanting the young Tobacco is come, which is immediately after it hath pleas'd God to ſend a good ſhower of rain, they ſhould have nothing elſe to do but to plant, and not loſe time in making thoſe diviſions of the Garden or Plantation.

The Tobacco-plant is ready for its removal out of the bed where it had been firſt ſown, when it hath four or five leaves ſtrong and thick enough, and about the bredth of a mans hand; for then, if it happen that the ground is ſoftned by a pleaſant ſhower of rain, all thoſe who are deſirous of having good Tobacco with the firſt ſeaſon matter not much the inconvenience of being wet, ſo they can but ſet a good quantity of it in the ground. At that time there is an emulation among the good huſbands, every one endeavouring to outvye the other in working: Some are employ'd in chuſing and taking off the Plants from the beds, and diſpoſing them into baſkets; others carry them to thoſe whoſe work it is to plant them exactly at the places which had been before marked by the cord, as we ſaid elſewhere.

Thoſe who are employ'd about the planting of them make a hole in the ground with a ſharp ſtick, into which they ſet the root of the Tobacco; then they thruſt the earth pretty hard about, yet ſo as that the upper part of the Plant be not cover'd: And thus they do all along every rank, and aſſoon as they have finiſh'd one they begin another. Having performed that exerciſe, at the next meeting of the Neighbours together their common diſcourſe is, to enquire one of another how many thouſands of Plants they have ſet in the ground, and thence calculate the hopes of the future harveſt.

The Plant being thus ſet in the ground, which is commonly done in ſeveral intervalls, in regard it ſeldom happens that there is ſo plentiful a fall of rain as that it might be done at once, or haply becauſe the ground is not all prepar'd at the ſame time, or that there are not Plants enough, is not thereupon neglected; on the contrary, this is but the beginning of the pains and care which the ordering of it requires; for the Planters muſt be very careful to viſit it often, and aſſoon as they have perceiv'd that it hath taken root, there muſt be a ſpecial care taken that the Caterpillars and other miſchievous Inſects, whereof there are abundance in thoſe Countries, do not gnaw it, and hinder its growth.   The

The next work is, at leaft once every month, to weed away whatever might endanger the fmothering of it, diligently to grub up and rake the earth all about it, and to carry away the weeds to the extremities of the Plantation ; for if they be left in the place where they are laid upon their being taken out of the ground, the leaft rain would make them take root afrefh, and they would require a fecond weeding. The moft troublefom herb of any, and that which caufes moft trouble to get out of the Plantations, is Purflane, which in thefe parts of the world grows not without the pains and induftry of Gardeners. This exercife is continu'd till fuch time as the Tobacco-plant hath cover'd all the adjacent ground, and that the fhade of it keeps down all other weeds.

But though all this be done, yet are not the Planters at reft, inafmuch as anfwerably to the growth of the Plant in height and bredth, fome muft be continually employ'd in cutting off the fuperfluous leaves, taking away thofe that are dry'd up, rotten or decay'd, cleering it of all thofe fhoots and fuckers which might hinder its coming to perfection, by diverting the fap from the larger leaves : In fine, when the ftalk is grown to a convenient height, it muft be check'd, by cutting off the top of every Plant, thofe only excepted which are referv'd for feed. After all this ordering, the Plant is to continue fome weeks in the ground ere it comes to maturity, during which there is a little ceffation of labour and attendance about it.

But if the laborious Planter be exempted from the great pains he had beftow'd about it, he fhall not want work ; for there muft be a place prepar'd, where it is to be difpos'd as foon as it is ripe. Care muft be taken, that the Grange or Store-houfe, where it ought to be dry'd to a certain medio-crity, be well cover'd and clofe of all fides ; that it be furnifh'd with good ftore of poles fit for it to be laid upon ; that provifion be made of a certain thin bark taken from a tree called *Mahot*, to faften every Plant to the poles ; and that the place defign'd for the making of it up into rolls or pricks fhould have all things requifite for that work.

While all thefe preparations are made, if the Tobacco-leaves lofe ever fo little of their firft verdure, and withal begin to bow down more then ordinary towards the ground, and if the fcent of them grows ftronger, it is a fign that the Plant is come to maturity : And then, taking a very fair day, after the dew is fallen off, it is to be cut about an inch a-bove ground, and left upon the place till the evening, turning it once or twice, that the Sun may take away fomewhat of its moifture : In the evening it is carry'd by armfuls into the houfe. It is faften'd by the lower end of the ftalk to the poles, fo that the leaves hang downwards : It is alfo requifite that they fhould not be laid too clofe one to the other, left they

be

be corrupted, or be not dry enough, for want of air.

This firſt cutting down of the Tobacco being over, they often viſit the Plants which are hung up a drying, while the reſt which had been left growing comes to ripeneſs; and when they find the leaves fit to be made up into rolls, that is, when they are neither too dry (for in that caſe they would not be able to endure the wheel), nor yet too moiſt (for then they would corrupt in a ſhort time), they are taken off the poles, they are laid in heaps at the end of the Grange, and every ſtalk is ſtript of its leaves, after this manner.

In the firſt place, they lay aſide all the longeſt and all the broadeſt leaves, and they take away the great ſtalk which runs through the midſt of them; the leſſer leaves are alſo laid by themſelves, to be diſpos'd within the roll, and the greater ſerve for coverings and ſhrowds for them. Theſe leaves thus diſpos'd are ranked on planks or tables, cloſe by him who is to make them up into rolls, which he makes bigger or ſmaller, as may be ſeen by thoſe brought over into theſe parts.

There is a certain art in making up the rolls, and thoſe who can do it with expedition and dexterity are highly eſteem'd, and get much more then thoſe who are employ'd about ordering the ground: They muſt have their hands and arms extremely ſupple and nimble, to make the wheel turn with ſuch ſpeed, and ſtill to obſerve the ſame proportion, that ſo the roll may be equally big in all parts.

There is a particular artifice, in the buſineſs of Tobacco, to diſpoſe and lay it after the winding ſo as that it may be the more eaſily put up on the ſticks, which are all to be of a certain bigneſs and length, to avoid deceit.

When the Tobacco is thus made up, it is convey'd to the Store-houſe, and cover'd with *Bananas* or ſome other leaves, that it may not be prejudic'd by taking wind, and be of a good fair colour. That which cuts ſomewhat unctuouſly, is blackiſh and ſhining, and hath a pleaſant and ſtrong ſcent, and burns eaſily in the Pipe, is accounted the beſt.

We told you, that the Tobacco-plant was cut almoſt even with the ground, and not pluck'd up by the roots; and it is purpoſely ſo cut, that it may ſhoot-forth new ſtalks: And indeed it produces a ſecond Plant, but ſuch as is neither ſo ſtrong nor ſo fair as the former; nor is the Tobacco made thereof ſo much eſteem'd, nor will keep ſo well: It is call'd by ſome Shoot-Tobacco, or Sucker-Tobacco, or Tobacco of the ſecond cutting or growth: Nay ſome will have three ſhoots from the ſame ſtalk; and that humour hath brought the Tobacco which comes from ſome Iſlands into diſ-eſteem.

Now ſince we have expreſs'd our ſelves ſo much at large concerning the manufacture of Tobacco, we ſhall not think

it

it improper to infert in this place what is practis'd by fome curious perfons, whereby it is made more excellent then that which commonly goes under the name of *Virinus-Tobacco*, keeps well, and hath a fcent which fortifies the brain.   After they have fet afide the Plants of the firft cutting, and while they are drying on the poles, they gather together all the caft leaves, the fmall fhoots, as alfo the filaments which are taken out of the midft of the leaves which have been already cleer'd; and after they have pounded them in a mortar, all is put into a bag, which is put into a prefs to force out the juice, which is afterwards boil'd over a foft fire till it be reduc'd to the confiftency of a Syrup : That done, there is put into that decoction a little *Copal*, which is an aromatick gum, the virtue whereof is to fortifie the brain.   This gum diftills from a tree of the fame name, which is common in the Continent of *America*, and in the Iflands about the gulf of *Hondures*.

After this drug is put into the compofition aforefaid, it muft be well ftirr'd, that its fweet fcent and other qualities may be communicated and diffus'd through the whole decoction : Then it muft be taken off the fire, and when it is cold it is fet in a veffel neer the perfon who makes up the roll of Tobacco, and as often as he takes a handful of the leaves to feed the roll, he muft wet his hand in that liquor, and wipe it with the leaves.   This fecret hath an admirable effect to make the Tobacco keep well, and derives to it a virtue which extremely heightens its price.

The Tobacco thus order'd is to be made up into a roll, at leaft as big as a mans thumb, and be afterwards divided into little rolls not weighing above ten pound at the moft, and then fent in little veffels or clofe bafkets made for that purpofe, to keep it the better.   Some Inhabitants of the Iflands having made tryal of this fecret, have put off theirs for right *Virinus-* Tobacco, and fold it at the fame rate.

Thofe who imagine that Tobacco grows without any trouble ; and that rolls of it are, as they fay, found growing on Trees in *America*, and that there is no more to be done but to fhake them down ; or haply are perfwaded that it requires no great trouble to bring them to perfection, will be undeceiv'd when they come to read this relation of the culture and preparation of Tobacco ; whereto we have only this to adde, that if they had themfelves feen the poor Servants and Slaves, who are employ'd about this painful work, expos'd the greateft part of the day to the fcorching heat of the Sun, and fpending one half of the night in reducing it to that pofture wherein it is tranfported into *Europe*, no doubt they would have a greater efteem for, and think much more precious that herb, which is procur'd with the fweat and labours of fo many miferable creatures.

We

We shall not need to insert here what Physitians write of the miraculous effects of Tobacco, but leave the more curious to consult their Books, wherein they give a strange account thereof: Only this we shall affirm, that the virtues of it must needs be very great, since it hath its courte all over the world, and that in a manner all Nations upon Earth, as well those that are civiliz'd as those that still continue in their Barbarism, have afforded it a kind reception, and have advis'd the taking of it : And though some Princes have prohibited the use of it in their Territories, out of a fear that the money of their Subjects, which is rare and precious, should be turn'd into smoak, and slip out of their hands for a thing which seems not to be so necessary to life ; yet is there not any but will allow it a place among the drugs and remedies of Physick.

The more delicate and curious among those Nations who are dispos'd into hot Countries, qualifie it with Sage, Rosemary, and certain Perfumes, which give it a very pleasant scent ; and having reduc'd it to powder, they take it in at the nostril.   Those Nations who inhabit cold Countries, forbid not Persons of Quality the use of it ; nay it is a perfection and certain gallantry in the Ladies of those Parts, gracefully to handle a Pipe, whereof the boal is of Coral or Amber, and the head of Silver or Gold, and to puff out the smoak of this herb without the least wrinkle or wry face, and to let it out of the mouth after several little intervalls, which raising so many little vapours of a brownish colour, seems a kind of foil to set off the cleerness of their complection.   The composition we have before described, which heightens the good scent of Tobacco, will no doubt be kindly receiv'd by those persons who place the smoking of a pipe of Tobacco among the pleasures and enjoyments of this life.

To conclude, it is not easie to affirm what quantities of Tobacco are sent away every year, only from the Island of S. *Christophers* ; and it is almost a miracle to see what numbers of Ships come over out of *England, France, Holland,* and especially *Zealand,* and yet none returns empty : nay the sole trading which the last named Province maintain'd with this and the neighbouring Islands, rais'd the greatest and wealthiest houses at *Middleborough* and *Flushing :* nay to this day the principal commerce of those two Cities, which are the most considerable of all *Zealand,* is from these Islands, which are to them what the Mines of *Peru* are to the Kingdom of *Spain.*

C c   CHAP.

CHAP. V.

*Of the manner how Sugar is made ; and of the prepara-
tion of Ginger, Indico, and Cotton.*

WHen the great plenty of Tobacco made at S. *Christophers* and the other Islands had brought down the
price of it so low, that it did not turn to accompt, it pleas'd
God to put it into the heart of the *French* General *de Poincy*,
to find out some other ways to facilitate the subsistence of the
Inhabitants, and carry on some Trade : He thereupon employ'd his Servants and Slaves about the culture of Sugar-
Canes, Ginger, and Indico ; and the design met with a success
beyond what was expected.

Though it may be granted, that the Plant of the Sugar-
Cane was known to the Ancients, yet is the invention of making the Sugar but of late years : The Ancients knew no
more of it then they did of *Sena, Cassia, Ambergreece, Musk,
Civet,* and *Benjamin :* They made no other use of this precious
Reed, then in order to drink and Physick.   And therefore
we may well oppose all these things, with much advantage,
as also our Clocks, the Sea-Compass, the Art of Navigation,
Prospective-glasses, Printing, Artillery, and several other excellent Inventions of the last Ages, against their right way of
dying Purple, their malleable Glass, the subtle Machines of
their *Archimedes,* and some such like.

Having in the precedent Book given a description of the
Sugar-Cane, our business here will only be to represent the
manner how Sugar is gotten out of it.

That work is performed by a Machine or Mill, which some
call an *Ingenio,* whereby the juice within the Canes is squeez'd
out.   These Mills are built of very solid and lasting wood,
and are more convenient in these Islands then those used to the
same purpose at *Madera* and *Brasil :* Nor is it to be fear'd in
the former, as many times in the latter, that the fire should
get to the boiling Coppers, and set all into a flame, to the destruction of those who are employ'd about the work ; for
the Coppers in these Islands are seen to boil, yet the fire
that causes it is made and kept in on the outside by furnaces,
which are so well cemented, that neither the flame nor the
smoak does any way hinder those who are at work, which
they may follow without any fear of danger or inconvenience.

The ordinary way of turning the Mills is by Horses or
Oxen ; but the *French* Governour hath one which is turn'd
by water, which falling on a wheel sets the whole Machine
going.

When

When the Sugar-Canes are ripe, they are cut fomewhat
neer the ground, above the firft knot which is without any
juice ; and having cut off the tops, and taken away certain
little, long, and very thin leaves, which encompafs them, they
are made up into bundles, and carry'd to the Mills to be there
prefs'd and fqueez'd between two rollers, turning one upon
the other

The juice which is fqueez'd out of them falls into a great
Ciftern, whence it is convey'd through long pipes or channels
into the veffels appointed for the boiling of it. In great Su-
gar-works there are at leaft fix Coppers, whereof three very
large ones are of copper, about the bredth and depth of thofe
us'd by Dyers, and are to clarifie the juice, which is to be
boil'd with a gentle fire, putting in ever and anon a fmall
quantity of a certain very ftrong Lye, made of water and afhes, commonly call'd *Temper*, which makes all the filth to boil
up, which as it appears is taken off with a great brafs fkimmer. When the juice is well purify'd in thefe three Coppers,
into which it had been convey'd alternately one after another,
it is ftrain'd through a cloth, and afterwards pour'd into three
other Coppers of fome other mettal, which are very thick,
broad enough, and about a foot and a half deep. In thefe
Coppers the Sugar receives its laft boiling ; for then there is a
more violent fire made, and it is continually ftirr'd, and when
it bubbles up fo as that it may be fear'd it fhould boil over the
Coppers, it is allay'd by the cafting in of a little fallet-oil ;
and as it begins to grow thick, it is pour'd into the laft of thofe
Coppers, from whence, as it inclines to a confiftency, it is difpos'd into veffels of wood or earth, and fo carry'd into the
Curing-houfe, where it is whiten'd with a kind of fat earth
mixt with water, which is fpred upon it ; then they open
the little hole in the bottom of every veffel or pot, that all
the filth or dregs that is about the Sugar may fall into another channel, which conveys it into a veffel prepar'd for
that purpofe.

The firft fkimmings which had been taken off the great
Coppers is laid afide only for Cattle, but the other ferves
well enough to make a certain drink for the Servants and
Slaves. The juice which is drawn from the Cane will continue good but one day, infomuch that if within that time it be
not boil'd, it grows fharp and turns to vinegar. There muft
alfo be a very great care taken, that the Refervatory into
which the fqueezed juice falls, and the pipes or channels
whereby it is thence convey'd into other places, be often
wafh'd ; for if they contract ever fo little fharpnefs, the juice
cannot be reduc'd to Sugar : The whole work would alfo
mifcarry, if any butter or oil chance to be caft into any of the
three greater Coppers, which are to be wafh'd with Lye ; or

in like manner, if ever fo little Lye fall into the three leffer ones, where the juice is form'd into a Syrup, and curdles by the violence of the fire, and the continual agitation and ftirring of it with a fkimmer.   But above all things there muft be a great care taken, that there fall not any juice of Citron into the Coppers; for that would abfolutely hinder the coagulation of the Sugar.

Many of the Inhabitants who are not able to get fo many Coppers, nor furnifh themfelves with thofe great Engines whereby the Canes are fqueez'd, have little Mills made like Preffes, which are wrought by two or three men, or driven about by one horfe; and with one or two Coppers they purifie the juice gotten out of them, reduce it to the confiftence of Syrup, and make good Sugar without any further trouble.

The greateft fecret in the bufinefs of making good Sugar confifts in the whitening of it: Thofe who have it are very loth to communicate it.   From what hath been faid, it may be eafily inferr'd what extraordinary advantages accrue to the Inhabitants of that Ifland by means of this fweet and precious Commodity, and what fatisfaction it brings to their Correfpondents in other parts of the world, who have it at fo eafie rates.

This plenty of Sugar hath put the Inhabitants upon the preferving of abundance of excellent fruits of the growth of the Ifland, as Oranges, Lemons, Citrons, and others, efpecially Ginger, whereof we fhall give an account anon, and the fruit call'd *Ananas*, and the flowers of Oranges and Citrons.

As concerning the preparation of Ginger, when the root is come to maturity it is taken out of the ground; then it is dry'd in places well air'd, and it is often ftirr'd to prevent corruption.   Some make no more ado then to expofe it to the Sun in order to the drying of it; but others think it requifite to caft lime on it, the more to facilitate the drawing away of the moifture.   This root, which is one of the moft confiderable among Spices, is tranfported all over the world; but it is moft fought after in cold Countries.

The *French* do fometimes take it out of the ground before it is fully ripe, and preferve it whole with fuch artifice, that it becomes red, and tranfparent as glafs.   The preferv'd Ginger which is brought over from *Brazil* and the *Levant* is commonly dry, full of filaments or little ftrings, and too biting to be eaten with any delight; but that which is prepar'd at S. *Chriftophers* hath no fibres or ftrings at all, and it is fo well order'd, that there remains nothing that is unpleafant to the tooth when it is eaten.

It hath a fingular property to fortifie the breaft, when it is weakned by a confluence of cold humours; as alfo to

clear

clear the voice, to ſweeten the breath, to cauſe a good colour in the face, to take away the crudities of the ſtomach,
to promote digeſtion, to ſharpen the appetite, and to con-
ſume that wateriſhneſs and phlegm which puts the body into a languiſhing condition; nay it is affirm'd by ſome, that
it preſerves and wonderfully fortifies the memory, by diſ-
perſing the cold humours, or the phlegm of the Brain. This
root may alſo be reduc'd into a paſte, of which there may be
made a Conſerve, or cordial Electuary that hath the ſame effects.

We come now to give a ſhort account of Indico. The
Plant being cut is bound up into little bundles or fagots, and
left to rot in ciſterns of ſtone or wood full of fair water, on
which there is caſt a certain quantity of oil, which according
to its nature covers all the ſurface of it: They lay ſtones upon
the fagots, that they may the better keep under the water;
and after three or four days that the water hath been boiling,
which it does by the meer virtue of the Plant, without any
aſſiſtance of fire, the leaf being rotted and diſſolv'd by that
natural heat which is in the ſtalk, they take great ſtakes and
ſtir the whole maſs that is within the ciſterns, ſo to get out all
the ſubſtance of it; and after it is ſetled again, they take out
of the ciſtern that part of the ſtalk which is not rotted: that
done, they ſeveral times ſtir what is left in the ciſtern, and after they have left it to ſetle, they let out the water at a cock;
and the lees or dregs which remains at the bottom of the ciſtern,
is put into molds, or left to dry in the Sun. Theſe dregs is that
which is ſo much eſteem'd by Dyers, and commonly known
by the name of Indico.

There are ſome make uſe of Preſſes, whereinto having put
little bundles of the rotted Plant, they by that means get out
all the juice of it: But in regard they are the leaves of the
Plant that the foreſaid Commodity is made of, thoſe who are
deſirous to have it of the higheſt price, think it enough to have
the dregs which remains after the corruption of thoſe leaves,
and is found, after ſo many ſtirrings, at the bottom of the ciſtern.

The *French* Inhabitants of the *Caribbies* were there a long
time ere they drove any trade in that Commodity, by reaſon
that the Plant whereof it is made, being of it ſelf of a very
ſtrong ſcent, exhales an inſupportable ſtink when it is rotted: But ſince Tobacco came to ſo low a rate, and that in
ſome places the ground would not bring forth that which
was good, as it had done ſome time before, they apply'd
themſelves to the culture of Indico, whereof they now make
a conſiderable advantage.

Laſtly, as concerning Cotton, the *French* make it not much
their buſineſs to gather it, though they have many of the trees
                                                          that

that bear it in the hedges of their Plantations: But all put together amounts but to little in comparison of what is said of a certain Quarter of the Province of *China*; for a certain Authour named *Trigant*, in the xvii. chap. of the fifth Book of his History, affirms, that there grows so much Cotton there as finds work enough for two hundred thousand Weavers.

The *English* who are the Inhabitants of the *Barbouthos* drive a great trade in this Commodity, as also those who liv'd formerly in the Island of *Santa-cruce*. There is no great trouble in the making of Cotton fit for the market; for all to be done, is to get out of the half-open'd button that matter which in a manner forces its way out it self: And whereas it is full of the seed of the tree that bears it, which are like little beans intangled within the Cotton, in the midst whereof they had their production, there are a sort of little Engines made with such artifice, that by the turning of a wheel, whereby they are put into motion, the Cotton falls on the one side, and the seed on the other: That done, the Cotton is thrust up as close as may be into bags, that so it may take up the less room.

Thus have we given a brief account of the principal Employments which keep up the Commerce of the Islands, and the Commodities wherein the Inhabitants do ordinarily trade.

CHAP. VI.

Of the more honourable Employments of the European *Inhabitants of the* Caribbies; *their Slaves; and their Government.*

THE *European* Colonies which have planted themselves in the *Caribbies*, do not consist only of a sort of Vagabonds and persons of mean condition, as some fondly imagine, but there are also among them many of Quality, and descended from noble Families: So that the Employments we mentioned in the precedent Chapter, are design'd only for the most inconsiderable of the Inhabitants, and such whose necessities have forc'd them to earn their bread with the labour of their hands, and the sweat of their brows: But the others, who are able to hire people to oversee their Servants and Slaves, and to see that they do their work, lead pleasant lives, and want not those enjoyments thereof which are to be had in other Countries. Their employments and divertisements, besides the frequent visits they make and receive with extraordinary expressions of civility, are Hunting, Fishing, and other commendable

mendable exercises; nay they endeavour to outvye one the other in their entertainments, wherein they are magnificent, there being a sufficient plenty of Beef, Mutton, Pork, wild and tame Fowl of all kinds, Fish, Pastry, and excellent Conserves, all in as great abundance as at the best Tables in the *European* parts of the world. And these mutual demonstrations of kindness are deriv'd from the Officers and those of the better rank to the meanest Inhabitants, who think it a great want of civility to dismiss any one from their houses, before they have presented them with somewhat to eat and drink.

Wine, Beer, Brandy, and *Aqua-vitæ*, and such drinks, are seldom wanting in these Islands; and if there should chance to be a scarcity of these, the Inhabitants have the art of making a delicious drink of that sweet liquor which is got out of the Sugar-canes, and that being kept for certain days becomes as strong as any Sack: Of the same liquor they also make an excellent kind of *Aqua-vitæ*, not much unlike that which is brought thither out of *France*; only this inconvenience it hath, that they who drink excessively of it are apt to fall dangerously sick. Moreover, they make several kinds of Beverage with the juice of *Oranges*, *Figs*, *Bananas*, and *Ananas*, which are all very delicious and pleasant to the taste, and may be ranked among Wines: They also make a sort of Beer of the *Cassava* and the roots of *Potatoes*, which is as pleasant, nourishing, and refreshing as that which is brought out of the Low-Countries.

As concerning those Employments which are equally honourable and necessary in order to the welfare of the Inhabitants of these Islands, it is to be observ'd, that all are taught the use of Arms, and the Heads of Families seldom walk abroad without their Swords. Every Quarter is dispos'd under the command of certain Captains and other Officers, who have the oversight thereof. They are all well-arm'd, and they often muster and are exercis'd even in the times of deepest peace; so that they are always in readiness, at the first beat of Drum, to march to the places where the Captains appoint their Rendezvouz. In the Island of S. *Christophers*, besides twelve Companies of Foot, there are also some Troops of Horse, as we said elsewhere.

And whereas all persons of Quality, whereof there is a considerable number in those Islands, have Servants and Slaves who are employ'd about the works before-mentioned, and that in most parts of *Europe* they do not make use of Slaves, there being only the *Spaniards* and the *Portugnez* who go and buy them up at the places of their birth, such as are *Angola*, *Cap-vert*, and *Guinny*, it will be but requisite that we here give a short account of them: But we shall in the first place speak of those who are hired Servants, and to continue such only for a certain time.

As

As for the *French* who are carried over out of *France* into *America*, to serve there, they commonly deliver obligatory acts to their Masters, which is done before publick Notaries; by which writings they oblige themselves to serve them during the space of three years, conditionally to receive from them so many pounds of Tobacco, according to the agreement they have made during that term. These *French* Servants, by reason of the three years service they are engag'd to, are commonly called the *Thirty-six-months-men*, according to the Language of the Islands. There are some so simple as to imagine, that if they be not oblig'd to their Masters in writing before their departure out of *France*, they are so much the less oblig'd when they are brought into the Islands; but they are extremely mistaken; for when they are brought before a Governour to complain that they were carried aboard against their wills, or to plead that they are not oblig'd by writing, they are condemn'd for the space of three years to serve either him who hath paid for their passage, or such other as it shall please the Master to appoint. If the Master hath promis'd his Servant no more then the ordinary recompence of the Islands, he is oblig'd to give him for his three years service but three hundred weight of Tobacco, which is no great matter to find himself in linnen and cloaths; for the Master is not engag'd to supply him with any thing but food: But he who before his departure out of *France* promises to give three hundred weight of Tobacco to him whom he receives into his service, is oblig'd exactly to pay it, nay though he had promis'd him a thousand: It is therefore the Servants best course to make his bargain sure before he comes out of his Country.

As concerning the Slaves, and such as are to be perpetual Servants, who are commonly employ'd in these Islands, they are originally *Africans*, and they are brought over thither from the Country about *Cap-vert*, the Kingdom of *Angola*, and other Sea-ports which are on the Coasts of that part of the world; where they are bought and sold after the same manner as Cattle in other places.

Of these, some are reduc'd to a necessity of selling themselves, and entring into a perpetual slavery, they and their children, to avoid starving; for in the years of sterility, which happen very frequently, especially when the Grass-hoppers, which like clouds spread themselves over the whole Country, have consum'd all the fruits of the earth, they are brought to such a remediless extremity, that they will submit to the most rigorous conditions in the world, provided they may be kept from starving. When they are reduc'd to those exigencies, the Father makes no difficulty to sell his children for bread; and the children forsake Father and Mother without any regret.   Another

Another fort of them are fold after they have been taken Prifoners in War by fome petty neighbouring Prince ; for it is the cuftom of the Princes of thofe Parts to make frequent incurfions into the Territories of their Neighbours, purpofely for the taking of Prifoners, whom they afterwards fell to the *Portuguez*, and other Nations with whom they drive that barbarous Trade : They receive in exchange for them Iron (which is as precious with them as Gold), Wine, *Aqua-vitæ*, Brandy, or fome poor Clothing : They make Slaves of the women as well as the men, and they are fold one with another, at a higher or lower rate, according to their youth, age, ftrength, or weaknefs, handfomnefs, or deformity of body. They who bring them over to the Iflands make a fecond fale of them, at fifteen or fixteen hundred weight of Tobacco every head, more or lefs, as the parties concern'd can agree.

If thefe poor Slaves chance to fall into the hands of a good Mafter, one who will not treat them with too much feverity, they prefer their prefent flavery before their former liberty, the lofs whereof they never afterwards regret : And if they are permitted to marry, they multiply extremely in thofe hot Countries.

They are all Negroes, and thofe who are of the brighteft black are accounted the faireft : Moft of them are flat-nos'd, and have thick lips, which goes among them for beauty ; nay there are fome affirm, that in their Country the Midwives do purpofely crufh down their nofes, that they may be flat, affoon as they come into the world : The hair of their heads is all frizled, fo that they can hardly make ufe of Combs; but to prevent the breeding of vermine, they rub their heads with the oil of that fhrub which is called *Palma-Chrifti* : They are very ftrong and hardy, but withal fo fearful and unwieldy in the handling of Arms, that they are eafily reduc'd under fubjection.

They are naturally fufceptible of all impreffions, and the firft that are deriv'd into them among the Chriftians, after they have renounc'd their Superftitions and Idolatry, they pertinacioufly adhere unto ; wherein they differ much from the *Indians* of *America*, who are as unconftant as Cameleons. Among the *French* Inhabitants of the *Caribbies* there are fome Negroes who punctually obferve abftinence all the time of Lent, and all the other Fafting-days appointed by the Church, without any remiffion of their ordinary and continual labour.

They are commonly proud and infolent ; and whereas the *Indians* are defirous to be gently treated, and are apt to dye out of pure grief, if they be put to more then ordinary hardfhip, thefe on the contrary are to be kept in awe by threats and blows ; for if a man grow too familiar with them, they are prefently apt to make their advantages of it, and to abufe

D d

that

that familiarity; but if they be chaftiz'd with moderation when they have done amifs, they become better, more fubmiffive, and more compliant, nay will commend and think the better of their Mafters: But on the other fide, if they be treated with exceffive feverity, they will run away, and get into the Mountains and Forefts, where they live like fo many Beafts; then they are call'd *Marons*, that is to fay, Savages: or haply they will grow fo defperate as to be their own Executioners. It is therefore requifite, that in the conduct of them there fhould be a mean obferv'd between extream feverity and too much indulgence, by thofe who would keep them in awe, and make the beft advantage of them.

They are paffionate Lovers one of another; and though they are born in different Countries, and fometimes, when at home, Enemies one to another, yet when occafion requires they mutually fupport and affift one another, as if they were all Brethren: And when their Mafters give them the liberty to recreate themfelves, they reciprocally vifit one the other, and pafs away whole nights in playing, dancing, and other paftimes and divertifments; nay, fometimes they have fome little Entertainments, every one fparing what he can to contribute to the common repaft.

They are great Lovers of Mufick, and much pleas'd with fuch Inftruments as make a certain delightful noife, and a kind of harmony, which they accompany with their voices. They had heretofore in the Ifland of *S. Chriftophers* a certain Rendezvouz in the midft of the Woods, where they met on Sundays and Holidays after Divine Service, to give fome relaxation to their wearied bodies: There they fometimes fpent the remainder of that day, and the night following, in dancing and pleafant difcourfes, without any prejudice to the ordinary labours impos'd upon them by their Mafters: nay, it was commonly obferv'd, that after they had fo diverted themfelves, they went through their work with greater courage and chearfulnefs, without expreffing any wearinefs, and did all things better than if they had refted all night long in their huts. But it being found, that the better to enjoy themfelves in thefe publick Meetings, they many times ftole the Poultry and Fruits of their Neighbours, and fometimes thofe of their Mafters, the *French* General thought fit to forbid thefe nocturnal affemblies: So that now if they are defirous to divert themfelves, they are enjoyn'd to do it within their own Neighbourhoods, with the permiffion of their Mafters, who are willing enough to allow them convenient liberty.

As to the Advantages accrewing from the labours of thefe Slaves, he who is Mafter of a dozen of them may be accounted a rich man: For befides that thefe are the People who cultivate the ground in order to its production of all neceffary

provifions

provisions for the subsistence of their Masters and themselves; being well order'd and carefully look'd after, they promote the making of several other Commodities, as Tobacco, Sugar, Ginger, Indico, and others, which bring in great profit. Add to this, that their service being perpetual, their number increases from time to time by the Children that are born of them, which have no other Inheritance than that of the slavery and subjection of their Parents.

All the Forreign Inhabitants who have planted themselves in those Islands are govern'd according to the Laws and Customs of their own Countries.

Among the *French* Inhabitants of S. *Christophers* Justice is administred by a Council consisting of the principal Officers who have the oversight of the Militia of the Island, of which Council the General is President: And though there are certain places appointed for that Administration, yet is the Council many times assembled as the General thinks fit, and occasion requires, under a kind of great Fig-tree, which is about the bigness of a large Elm, neer the Court of Guard of the *Basse-terre*, not far from the Haven.

In this Council, abating all the Formalities which have been invented to make Suits immortal, all differences that happen between the Inhabitants are amicably compos'd, and decided most commonly at the first sitting, without any charge to the Parties, save only that he which is found guilty of the wrong is to make satisfaction according to the Custom, whereof part goes to the relief of the Poor, and maintenance of the Church, and the rest for the satisfaction of the party concern'd. This Council doth also pass sentence of death, without appeal to any other Power.

The Governours of the other Islands do also administer Justice every one in his Government: So that no man should be guilty of so great a weakness as to imagine that people live in those Countries without any order or rule, as many do: Nay, it is rather to be look'd on as a kind of Miracle, that (the Inhabitants of those Countries being a confluence of people from so many several Countries, and consequently of different humors and constitutions) disorders should not creep in, and that all are kept in awe and subjection to the Laws established.

Thus much of the Forreign Inhabitants of the *Caribbies*; we come now to treat of the Natural and Originary.

CHAP. VII.

Of the Origine of the Caribbians, *the natural Inhabitants of the Country.*

THe Method we had propos'd to our felves for the profecution of this Hiftory requires that henceforth we treat of the *Indians*, the natural Inhabitants of the *Caribbies*.   And here we conceive it not to be our bufinefs to bring upon the Stage that great and difficult Queftion, to wit, How the race of Men came to fpread it felf into *America*, and whence they came into that new World? There are fome eminent Perfons have treated of this matter with fo much fufficiency, exactnefs, and folidity, that it were a tedious and fuperfluous Work at the prefent to trouble the Reader with any thing concerning it. Befides, the Hiftory of the Originals of our Savage Inhabitants of the *Caribbies* requires not that we fhould defcend fo low to find them.

The ancient and natural Inhabitants of the *Caribbies* are thofe who have been called by fome Authors *Cannibals*, *Anthropophagi*, or *Eaters of Men* ; but moft others who have written of them, commonly call them *Caribbians* or *Caribes* : But their primitive and originary Name, and that which is pronounc'd with moft gravity is, as the *French* Writers would have it, that of *Caraibes* Nay, if we may credit thefe laft mentioned Authors, not only the *Caribbians* themfelves of the Iflands do fo pronounce their name, but alfo thofe of their Nation who live in the Continent of *America*, both the Septentrional and Meridional : So that that being the moft common appellation of them among the *French* Inhabitants of the Iflands, we fhall alfo have occafion to ufe it fometimes in the fequel of this Hiftory, in regard the prefent Work is render'd out of that Language.

Some are of opinion, that this word *Caraibes* (or *Caribbians*) is not natural to the favage Inhabitants of the *Caribbies* , but that it was impos'd upon them by the *Spaniards*, as they had given the fame denomination to many Savages of the Meridional Continent, who are known thereby ; as alfo that of *Calibis*, or *Calibites*, to their allies the Inhabitants of the fame Continent.

Thofe who maintain this opinion affirm, that the *Spaniards* might well give to thofe People that name of *Caraibes*, in regard they over-ran all the Quarters of the Southerly part of *America* ; and that having made the firft Maps thereof, they fet down thofe Nations under that Name, which hath ftuck to them ever fince.   To prove this they alledge, that they are never call'd *Caraibes* or *Caribbians* among themfelves, but only when they are drunk , and that having their heads full of Wine they

leap

leap up and down and rejoyce, ſaying in their corrupt Language, *Moy bonne Caraïbe, I am an honeſt Caribbian:* That otherwiſe they only make uſe of that word when they are amongſt Strangers, and that in their trading and their communication with them, to make a certain diſcovery of themſelves, as being ſenſible that the ſaid name is known to them: But that when they are among themſelves, not only they, but alſo thoſe of their Nation Inhabiting the Continent, and the *Calibites,* call themſelves by the name of *Calinago,* which is the name of the Men, and *Calliponan,* which is that of the Women. And they further affirm, that they are called *Oubao-bonou,* that is, *Inhabitants of the Iſlands,* or *Iſlanders;* as the call thoſe of the Continent *Batoüe-bonon,* that is, *Inhabitants of the Firm Land.*

But all this preſuppos'd as probable, there is but little likelihood that the word *Caribbians* ſhould have been impos'd upon them by the *Spaniards,* and that our Iſlands ſhould not have had it before they were known by them. The firſt reaſon we give of this aſſertion is, that before either the *Spaniards* or *Portuguez* had found a paſſage into *Brazil,* there were in thoſe Parts certain men more ſubtle and ingenious then the reſt, whom the *Braſilians* call'd *Caraïbes,* or *Caribbians,* as *Johannes de Lery* hath obſerv'd in his Hiſtory. Secondly, it is a thing out of all controverſie that there are certain Savages who bear the name of *Caribbians* in ſome Quarters of the Southerly part of *America,* where the *Spaniards* never had any Commerce: For not only thoſe of the ſame Nation with our Iſlanders, who inhabit along thoſe Coaſts of the Meridional *America,* and are neer Neighbours to the *Dutch* Colonies of *Cayenna* and *Berbica,* but thoſe alſo who live far within that Meridional Continent, beyond the ſources of the moſt remarkable Rivers, call themſelves *Caribbi-ans.* Moreover, we ſhall find in the ſequel of this Chapter, that there is in the Septentrional Continent a powerful Nation conſiſting for the moſt part of certain Families, who at this preſent take a great pride in being called *Caribbians,* and ſtand upon it, that they had receiv'd that name long before *America* was diſcover'd. Add to this, that though it were granted that the *Spaniards* would have impos'd that name on all thoſe Nations, how can it be prov'd that they were as willing to accept of it from People unknown and Enemies to them? Now it is certain, that not only all thoſe people do call themſelves *Caribbi-ans,* but alſo that they withal think it a glory, and derive an advantage from that name, as Monſieur *du Montel* hath heard it from their own mouths: How then is it to be imagin'd that they ſhould triumph in a name which they had receiv'd from their Enemies? Nay if it be urg'd further, as we ſhall ſee anon, that the Anceſtors of our Savage Inhabitants of the Iſlands receiv'd from the *Apalachites* the name of *Caribbians,* inſtead of that of *Coſachites,* under which they went before; it may be replyed,

That

That they took it from such as were their friends and confederates, and that as an Elogy of honour. In fine, we also affirm, that it is not only in their drunkenness and debauches, that our *Indian* Inhabitants of the Islands call themselves *Caribbians*, but they do it also when they are sober and in cold blood; And as to their calling themselves *Calinago*, it is possible they may have many different names, whence it does not ever the more follow, that they had received any of them from the *Europæans*. For the denomination of *Oubao-bonon*; the signification of the word sufficiently shews, that it is not particular to them, and that it may be generally applyed to any Inhabitants of Islands. And whereas they make use of the name of *Caribbians* rather than of any other, when they speak to strangers, it is because they are apprehensive enough that that name is best known to them: but it is not to be concluded thence, that they received it from the *Spaniards*, nay it might be more probably affirmed that the *Spaniards* themselves having learnt it of them, should afterwards have communicated it to other *Europæans*. But as to our design, it matters not much whether opinion be embrac'd, and every one may follow which sentiment liketh him best; only we have taken the liberty to propose what we conceived most probable.

As to the originals of the insulary *Caribbians*, those who have hitherto given any account of them, have had so little light to guide themselves by in that obscure piece of Antiquity, that they may be said to have grop'd all their way: some imagine that they are descended from the *Jews*, grounding their conjecture, among other things, on this, that the *Caribbians* are obliged to marry those Kinswomen of theirs that are next of kin to them, and that some among them eat no swines flesh nor Tortoises: But this is to fetch a thing too far off, and to ground an imagination on too weak conjectures. There are others who would have them to come over from the Haven of *Caribana*, and pretend that they were transported thence: But this opinion is grounded only on the clinching of the words *Caribana* and *Caribbians*, without any other confirmation.

There are yet others who affirm, and that upon a simple conjecture, that these Savages are the originary Inhabitants of the greater Islands, and that it is not long since they came into those now called the *Caribbies*, where they took refuge as the remainders of the horrid Massacres committed by the *Spaniards*, when they possess'd themselves of St. *Domingo, Cuba, Jamaica*, and *Porto-Rico*: But this is confuted by the certainty of History, which assures us, that at the first beginning of the discovery of *America*, the *Caribbies* were possessed and inhabited by the *Caribbians*; that at first they were surprized and ill-entreated by the *Spaniards*; but that afterwards these

last

laſt being beaten off with diſadvantage, and meeting with many inconveniences in the proſecution of that war, made a kind of agreement with ſome among them, as we ſhall ſee more particularly hereafter in the Chapter of their Wars. Add to this, that the *Indians* of *Coraſſao*, who, without all diſpute, are ſome of thoſe perſons who eſcaped the Maſſacres, and who have among them ſome yet living, who lived in the Port called at the preſent, the Port of the *Kow-Iſland*, or as the *French* call *Le port de l' Iſle à vache*, in the Iſland of *Hiſpaniola*, when the firſt *Spaniards* landed there, have not a word of the *Caribbian* Language in theirs, nor any thing of Carriage; whence it may be dedue'd, that there never was any communication or correſpondence between them and the *Caribbians*. Beſides, thoſe of the greater Iſlands who might have fled to avoid the tyranny of the *Spaniards*, would have had greater encouragement to retreat into the Territories which were below them, and whereto the regular winds lay more fit to carry them, than to direct their courſe againſt the wind, and ſo retarding their flight, expoſe themſelves to a thouſand hazards by Sea, and engage themſelves in a voyage twenty times as long: For it is almoſt a miracle, that ſuch Veſſels as theirs are can advance a league in a day againſt the wind; nay it many times happens that very great veſſels are in their aſcent fore'd back more in three hours than they had advanc'd in ſix daies: For we have it from very skilful Pilots, that they have been three months geting up from the *Cul-de-Sac* of St. *Domingo* to St. *Chriſtophers*; whereas to fall down from St. *Chriſtophers* to St. *Domingo*, there needs commonly not above four or five days at moſt.

As concerning the opinion the *Caribbians* themſelves have of their origine, we find, that, being as ignorant of all Monuments of Antiquity, as free from all curioſity of enquiring after things to come, they believe for the moſt part, that they are deſcended from the *Calibites* or *Calibis*, their Allyes and great friends, the Inhabitants of the Meridional part of *America*, & the neighbouring people of the *Arouagoes* or *Alouagues*, in that Country or Province which is commonly called *Gujana*, or the *Savage-Coaſt*. And thoſe who adhere to this opinion, ground their perſwaſion on the conformity of Language, Religion and Manners, obſervable between the *Caribbian* Inhabitants of the Iſlands, and the *Calibites*; though it may as well be preſum'd that the ſaid reſemblance might partly proceed from the allyance and particular friendſhip there was between them; partly from the Neighbourhood of the *Caribbians* of the Meridional Continent and thoſe *Calibites*; and partly from ſome other cauſes, whereof we ſhall give an account hereafter.

But theſe poor Savages of the Iſlands agree not among
them-

themſelves in the particular relation they make of their Extra-
ction, and the occaſion that brought them into thoſe Iſlands;
nor can they give any account of the time of their coming thither. We ſhall here ſet down what thoſe of S. *Vincent* and
ſome others have related to Monſieur *du Montel* concerning
themſelves, which we have taken out of his curious Collections.

All the *Caribbians* were heretofore ſubject to the *Arouagues*,
and obey'd their Prince; but ſome among them not able to endure that yoke, broke out into a Rebellion: And that they
might the better live undiſturb'd, and at a diſtance from their
Enemies, they retreated to the *Caribby*-Iſlands, which were
not at that time inhabited; and their firſt landing was in the
Iſland of *Tabago*, which is one of the neereſt to the Continent:
Afterwards the other *Calibites* ſhook of the Domination of the
Arouagues; but finding themſelves ſtrong enough, or not having the ſame inclination with the former, they continu'd in
their Country; and what they had at the time of their revolt
they have kept ever ſince, and live free in the Country, but
Enemies to the *Arouagues*, having a Captain-General of their
own Nation, by whom they are commanded. They have alſo
continu'd to this preſent Friends and Confederates to the *Caribbians.*

Upon this Relation it is that ſome ground the explication
they make of the word *Caribbians*, as if it ſignified *Rebells*;
whether it was impos'd upon them by the *Arouagues*, or that
thoſe people aſſum'd it of themſelves by way of triumph, as
deriving a certain glory from their noble Inſurrection, and the
generous Rebellion which eſtabliſh'd them in peace and liberty: But there needs no more to ſhew that the word *Caribbian*
does not ſignifie *Rebel*, as among others a certain Journal of a
Dutch-man, than that there are many Colonies in ſeveral parts
of the Continent of *America*, both the Septentrional and Meridional, which no body pretends or can pretend were ever under the power of the *Arouagues*, which yet are known by the
name of *Caribbians*. And as to the being among them any that
have rebell'd againſt other Sovereigns, only this may be inferr'd
thence, **That** being ſince reconcil'd to them, and living to
this day in the midſt of them, under the ſaid name of *Caribbians*, as we ſhall ſee more particularly anon, there is no likelihood that it ſhould ſignifie *Rebels*, ſince it were a blaſting of
their Reputation, and a mark of Infamy to them.

But thoſe who have convers'd a long time together among
the Savages of *Dominico* relate, that the *Caribbian* Inhabitants
of that Iſland are of opinion, that their Anceſtors came out of
the Continent, from among the *Calibites*, to make a War
againſt a Nation of the *Arouagues*, which inhabited the Iſlands,
which Nation they utterly deſtroy'd, excepting only the Women, whom they took to themſelves, and by that means re-
peopled

peopled the Iſlands : Whence it comes that the Wives of the *Caribbian* Inhabitants of the Iſlands have a language different from that of the Men in many things, and in ſome conſonant to that of the *Arouagues* of the Continent. He who was the Commander in chief in that Enterpriſe beſtow'd the conquer'd Iſlands on his Confidents; and he to whoſe lot the Iſland of *Dominico* fell was called *Ouboutou-timani*, that is to ſay, King, and cauſed himſelf to be carried on the ſhoulders of thoſe whom the Iſlanders call *Labouyou*, that is, Servants.

There is ſo little certainty and ſo much variety in all theſe Relations, and others of the like nature, which theſe poor ignorant people make upon this occaſion, that the moſt prudent ſort of people conceive there cannot any judgment be grounded thereon : And indeed theſe Savages themſelves ſpeak not thereof but at adventure, and as people tell ſtories of what they had ſeen in their dreams; ſo careleſs have they been in preſerving the tradition of their Origine; and they palpably contradict and confute one the other by the difference of their Relations : However, we ſhall find at the end of this Chapter what ſeems moſt probable to have given occaſion to moſt to believe that they are deſcended from the *Calibites*.

In all the ſeveral ſentiments whereof we have given an account, either out of the Writings or Diſcourſes of divers others, there is this that's commendable, That thoſe who advance them, proceed conſequently to the diſcoveries they had made, and that they do all that lies in their power to unravel and diſengage ancient and unknown Truths. But if the Relation we are about to give of the Origine of the *Caribbian* Inhabitants of the Iſlands, be the moſt ample, the moſt particular, the moſt full of Curioſities, and the beſt circumſtanc'd of any that hath hitherto appear'd, it is but juſt we ſhould think it accordingly the trueſt and moſt certain; yet with this caution, that we ſtill leave the judicious Reader at liberty to follow that ſentiment which ſhall ſeem moſt rational to him. And whereas we ought to render every one the commendation he juſtly deſerves, we are to acquaint the Publick, that it is oblig'd for theſe Particularities and Diſcoveries to the obliging Communication we have receiv'd thereof from one Maſter *Brigſtock* an *Engliſh* Gentleman, one of the moſt curious and inquiſitive Perſons in the World, who, among his other great and ſingular accompliſhments, hath attained the perfection of the *Virginian* and *Floridian* Languages, as having in his noble Travels ſeen all the Iſlands, and a great part of the Septentrional *America* : By that means it was that he came exactly to underſtand, upon the very place whereof we ſhall make mention, and from ſuch intelligent Perſons as could give him an account thereof with ſome certainty, the enſuing Hiſtory of the Origine of our Savages, the truth whereof he will make good whenever occaſion ſhall require.   E e   The

The *Caribbians* were originary Inhabitants of the Septentrional part of *America*, of that Country which is now called *Florida*: They came to Inhabit the Islands after they had departed from amidst the *Apalachites*, among whom they lived a long time; and they left there some of their people, who to this day go under the name of *Caribbians*: But their first origine is from the *Cofachites*, who only chang'd their denomination, and were called *Caribbians* in the Country of the *Apalachites*, as we shall see anon.

The *Apalachites* are a powerful and generous Nation, which continues to this present planted in the same Country of *Florida*: They are the Inhabitants of a gallant and spacious Country called *Apalacha*, from which they have received their name, and which begins at the altitude of thirty three degrees and twenty five minutes, North of the Equinoctial Line, and reaches to the thirty seventh degree. This people have a communication with the Sea of the great Gulf of *Mexico* or *New Spain*, by the means of a River, which taking its source out of the *Apalachæan* Mountains, at the foot whereof they inhabit, after it hath wandred through many rich Campagnes, disembogues itself at last into the Sea neer the Islands of *Tacobago*: The *Spaniards* have called this River *Riu del Spirito Santo*; but the *Apalachites* call it still by its ancient name of *Hitanachi*, which in their Language signifies fair and pleasant. On the East-side they are divided from all other Nations by high and far-spreading Mountains, whose tops are cover'd with snow most part of the year, and which separate them from *Virginia*: on the other sides they adjoin to several inconsiderable Nations, which are all their friends and confederates.

These *Apalachites* make it their boast, that they had propagated certain Colonies a great way into *Mexico*: And they show to this day a great Road by land, by which they affirm that their Forces march'd into those parts. The Inhabitants of the Country, upon their arrival gave them the name of *Tlatuici*, which signifies *Mountaineers* or *High-Landers*, for they were more hardy and more generous than they. They planted themselves in a quarter like that from which they came, scituate at the foot of the Mountains, in a fertile soil, where they built a City, as neer as they could like that which they had left behind them, whereof they are possess'd to this day. They are so united there by inter-marriages and other bonds of peace, that they make up but one people with them; nor indeed could they well be discern'd one from the other, if they had not retain'd several words of their originary language, which is the only observable difference between them.

After the *Apalachites* had planted this Colony, the *Cofachites*, who liv'd more towards the north of *America*, in a fenny and

some-

ſomewhat barren Country, and who had continu’d till then
in good correſpondence with them, knowing that they were
then far from their beſt and moſt valiant men, took an advantageous opportunity to fall upon their Neighbours the *Apalachites*, and to force them out of their habitations, or at leaſt
to participate with them of the land where they had ſetled
themſelves, after they ſhould become Maſters thereof. This
deſign having been carried on very cunningly among the chiefeſt of the *Cofachites*, they afterwards publiſh’d it in all their
Villages, and got it approv’d by all the heads of Families, who
inſtead of minding the buſineſs of Husbandry and ſetting things
in order for the ſowing of Corn at the beginning of the Spring,
as they were wont to do other years, prepar’d their Bows, Arrows, and Clubs; and having ſet their habitations on fire, and
furniſh’d themſelves with ſome little proviſions out of what was
left of the precedent Winter, they took the field, with their
wives and children, and all the little baggage they had, with a
reſolution either to conquer or dye, ſince they had cut off all
hopes of returning to a place which they had deſtroy’d and
deſpoil’d of all manner of conveniences.

In this equipage they in a ſhort time got to the frontiers of
their Neighbours: The *Apalachites* who thought of nothing
leſs than having an enemy ſo neer them, were then very buſie
about the planting of their *Mais*, and the roots from which they
derive their ordinary ſuſtenance: Thoſe who liv’d about the
greatLake at the foot of the Mountains, which they call in their
Language *Theomi*, having perceiv’d this powerful Army ready
to fall on them, immediately made their retreat into the neighbouring Mountains, and left their villages and cattel to the diſpoſal of the enemy; thence they took their march through
the woods, to carry intelligence of this erruption to the Cities
which are in the vallies among the firſt mountains, where re-
ſided the *Paracouſſis*, who is the King of the Country, with all
the conſiderable forces thereof. Upon this ſo unexpected
news, the ſaid Prince, while he was making his preparations to
go againſt the Enemy, poſted thoſe who were moſt in a readineſs for the expedition in the Avenues of the mountains, and
placed Ambuſcadoes in ſeveral parts of the great Foreſts,
which lye between the great Lake and the Mountains, and
through which there was a neceſſity of paſſing to get into that
pleaſant and ſpacious valley, which is above ſixty leagues in
length, and about ten in bredth; where are the habitations
of the chiefeſt Inhabitants of the Country, and the moſt conſiderable Cities in the Kingdom.

While the *Cofachites* were buſie about the plundering and
pillaging the houſes they had found neer the great Lake, the
Apalachites had the opportunity to prepare themſelves for the
reception of them: But the former, inſtead of taking the or-

dinary Roads and ways which led to the flat Country, which, as we said, lie between the Mountains, having left their Wives and Children neer the great Lake, under the guard of some Forces they had drawn off from the main Body, and being guided by some of the *Apalachites*, whom they had surprized fishing in the great Lake, cross'd through the woods, and made their way over mountains and precipices, over and through which the Camels could hardly have pass'd, and by that means got into the heart and centre of the Country, and found themselves of a sudden in a Province, called that of the *Amanites*: They without any resistance surpriz'd the chiefest places of it, wherein they found to guard them only Women, Children, and some old men, such as were not able to follow their King, who with his people lay expecting the Enemy at the ordinary descents which led into the Country.

The *Cofachites* perceiving that their design had prov'd so successful, and that there was a great likelihood that in a short time they should become Masters of the whole Country, since they had met with so good fortune immediately upon their first appearance, prosecuted their conquests further, and having Cities for their retreat, where they had left good strong Garrisons, they marched towards the King of *Apalacha*, with a resolution either to fight him, or at least oblige him to allow them the quiet possession of some part of the Country. The *Apalachite* was extreamly surpriz'd, when he understood that the Enemy, whom he had all this while expected on the Frontiers, and at the known avenues of the Country, had already possess'd himself of a Province that lay in the centre of his Dominions, and that he had left Garrisons in the Cities and most considerable places thereof: However, being a magnanimous and gallant Prince, he would try whether the chance of Arms would prove as favourable to him, as he thought his cause good and just; he thereupon came down with his people out of the Mountains, where he had encamped himself; and having encourag'd those that were about him to do their utmost, he confidently set upon the van-guard of the *Cofachites*, which was come out to observe his motion: having on both sides spent all their arrows, they came to a close fight, and having taken their Clubs, there was a great slaughter in both Armies, till that night having separated them, the *Cofachites* observ'd that they had lost a great number of theirs in the engagement, and found that they had to do with a people that behav'd themselves more valiantly than they had imagined to themselves they would have done; and consequently that their best course would be to enter into a friendly treaty with them, rather than venture another hazard of their Forces in a strange Country.

Upon this they resolv'd, that the next morning they would
send

send Embassadours to the King of the *Apalachites*, with certain Overtures of Peace, and in cafe of a refufal (diffembling the lofs they had receiv'd in the former Engagement) to declare open War, and to challenge him to be immediately ready to receive their Charge, which fhould be much more violent then what they had met withal the day before; and that then all their Forces were come together.

The *Paracouffis* of the *Apalachites* having given audience to thefe Embaffadours, defir'd that days time to confider of the Propofitions which had been made to him; and thereupon having requir'd of them the Articles and Conditions under which they would Treat with him, in cafe he might be inclin'd to Peace, they told him, That they had left their own Country with a refolution to plant themfelves either by friendfhip or by force in that good and fat Country whereof he was poffefs'd; and that if he would condefcend to the former of thofe means, they defired to become one People with the *Apalachites*, to dwell in their Country, and to cultivate it, and fo to fupply the empty places of thofe who not long before had gone from among them to plant a new Colony in fome remote parts of the World.

The *Apalachite* affembled his Council upon thefe confiderations, and having acquainted them therewith, he reprefented, That the Army of the *Cofachites* hindred the coming in of the Affiftances which they might receive from the other Provinces that had not been ready to come in to them at the beginning of the War; That by the fame means the paffage of Provifions was abfolutely obftructed; That the Enemy was Mafter of the Field, and that without any refiftance he had got into one of the beft Provinces of the whole Country, where he had alfo poffefs'd himfelf of places of Importance; and, That though in the precedent Engagement he had taken particular notice of the incomparable fidelity and gallantry of his People, in fetting upon and fighting againft the Enemies, over whom they had very confiderable Advantages, yet had that good Succefs been bought with the lofs of his moft valiant Captains, and the beft of his Souldiers, and confequently it concern'd them to bethink themfelves of fome means to preferve the reft of the Kingdom, by fparing what was then left of the choiceft Men : And fince the Enemies were the firft Propofers of the Conditions of Peace, it would be the fafeft way to hearken thereto, if it might be done without any derogation from their Glory, and the great Reputation they had acquir'd before; inafmuch as there was wafte grounds enough in feveral places, and that the Country, by reafon of the tranfplantation of fome part of their Inhabitants, was fpacious and fertile enough to fuftain them all.

All the chief Commanders of the *Apalachites* having heard
what

what had been propos'd by their King, and concluding it was
not fear that oblig'd him to hearken to an Accommodation
with the *Cofachites*,since that the day before he had ventur'd his
Person among the most forward ; but that it proceeded purely
from the desire he had that they might not be rashly expos'd to
further danger, and his care of preserving his People, which
was already at the mercy of the Enemy,who had possess'd himself of one of the richest Provinces ; and having also understood by some Spies who were come into the Kings Army by
some secret ways,and made their escape out of the Cities where
the *Cofachites* had their Garisons, that they treated with great
mildness and respect the women and old men whom they had
found there ; having, I say, taken all these things into consideration, they unanimously subscribed to the sentiments of their
Prince, and made answer, That there was a necessity of condes-
cending to an Accommodation, and making some Agreement
upon the most advantageous Conditions they could, according
to the present posture of their Affairs : And after they had
confirm'd this resolution by their *Ha Ha*, which is the sign of the
applause and ratification wherewith they are wont to conclude
their Deliberations, they signified the same to the Embassadors
of the *Cofachites*, who expected it with impatience.

This news being carried over to the Camp of the *Cofachites*,
was receiv'd with great joy, as being consonant to the end they
had propos'd to themselves when they first undertook the War
and left their Country : They thereupon immediately deputed
some of the chiefest among them to agree with the *Apalachites*
about the absolute conclusion of that Peace,and to sign the Articles of the Treaty.   These Deputies being come to the place
where the Prince of the *Apalachites* expected them, attended
by the most considerable Persons about his Court, sitting on a
Seat somwhat higher then any of the rest, and cover'd with a
rich Fur, were very kindly receiv'd ; and having taken their
Seats, the King drank to them of a certain Beverage call'd
Cassina, out of a Bowl of which he first tasted himself : All that
were present at the Council drank afterwards in order ; which
done,they fell upon the business of the Treaty, which was concluded upon these Conditions ;

That the *Cofachites* should inhabit promiscuously in the
Cities and Towns of the *Apalachites* ; That in all respects they
should be esteem'd and accounted as the natural Inhabitants of
the Country ; That they should absolutely enjoy the same
Priviledges ; That they should be subject to the King, as the
others were ; That they should embrace the Religion, and observe the Customs of the Country : Or if they would rather,
the *Apalachites* would resign up to them the rich and great
Province of *Amana*, to be enjoy'd only by them, according to
the limits which should be agreed upon:Provided nevertheless,
                                                      That

That they should acknowledge the King of the *Apalachites* for their Sovereign, and that from thence forward they should render him reasonable homage.

This Agreement being thus reciprocally concluded, was attended with mutual acclamations: Not long after, the Deputies of the *Cofachites* having given an account of their negotiation to their Commander in chief and his Councel, and represented to them the choice which had been left them either of living promiscuously among the *Apalachites*, or being sole possessors of the Province into which they were entered; they unanimously accepted of the latter, and so became absolute Masters of that Province of *Amana*, whereof the King of the *Apalachites* put them himself into quiet possession: The Women, Children, and Old men, who had been left behind, when all such as were able to bear arms had follow'd their Prince, were transported into some of the other Provinces, where the King appointed a setled habitation for them, and all the gallant men of that Province who had ventur'd their lives against the Enemy, and for the preservation of their Country.

All things being thus setled, both parties laid down their arms, and the *Cofachites* went to fetch their Wives, Children, Cattel, Baggage, and the Souldiers they had left neer the great Lake of *Theomi*; and being safely return'd, they dispos'd themselves into the Cities appointed them, congratulating their good fortune in the conquest of so noble a Country, answerably to their expectation at the first undertaking of the War.

From that time the *Apalachites* gave the name of *Caribbians*, or as the *French* would have it, *Caraibes*, to those new comers, who of a sudden and contrary to their expectation, forc'd themselves upon them, to repair the breach which had been made by the transplantation of some of their people into another Country of *America*: so that this word *Caraibes* signifies, in their language, a sort of *people added*, or *suddenly and unexpectedly coming in, strangers*, or *stout and valiant men*; as if they would express, that a generous people, whom they expected not, were come upon them, and had been added to them: and this denomination continu'd to these new comers instead of that of *Cofachites*, which hath been kept up only in some weak and wretched Families which liv'd more towards the north of *Florida*, and after the departure of the true *Cofachites*, possess'd themselves of their habitations, and would also have pass'd under the name of those who had preceded them in the possession of that Country: Whereas on the other side, these true *Cofachites* were known by the name of *Caribbians* in the Province of *Amana*; and therefore henceforward we shall speak of them, and the Colonies which they have since sent abroad, only under that name.

These

These two Nations being thus united by the determination of their differences, and the period they put to a cruel war which might have ruin'd them both, liv'd afterwards in good correspondence for many years. But in process of time, the *Caribbians* finding themselves multiply'd in the Country which they had conquer'd by their arms, would not embrace the Religion of the *Apalachites*, who ador'd the Sun, as shall be shewn hereafter, nor be present at their Ceremonies in the Temple they had in the Province of *Bemarin*, where the Court was; nor in fine render the King the homages that were due to him for the Province they were possess'd of, according to their promise, and the Articles of the Treaty.

This breach of promise on the part of the *Caribbians*, and that unjustifiable act, prov'd the occasion of many bloudy Wars which happen'd afterwards between the two Nations: the *Caribbians* were surrounded of all sides by their adversaries, who kept them in so, that they could not any way enlarge their quarters; and on the other side the *Apalachites* had in the bowels of their Country a cruel and irreconcileable enemy, who kept them perpetually in alarms, and oblig'd them to be always in arms: during which, both the one and the other, sometimes victorious, sometimes beaten, as the uncertain chance of war was pleas'd to carry it, liv'd a very sad life; insomuch that, many times, either for want of cultivating the ground, or by reason of the waste committed in the fields of one another, a little before the Harvest, they were reduc'd to such an extreme Famine, as destroy'd more people than the Sword.

Above an age was spent in these contests, during which the *Caribbians*, who had for their Commander in chief and King of their Nation, one of their most valiant Captains, whom they called *Ragazim*, added to their former acquests another Province, which lay next to them on the South side, and is called *Matica*, which reaching through the Mountains by an interva' that receives a torrent descending from the same Mountains, afterwards extends towards the West, as far as the River, which taking its source at the great Lake, after it hath made several Islands, and flown through divers Provinces, falls at last into the Ocean: This is the famous River which the *French* have called the River of *May*; but the *Apalachites* name it *Bafainim*, which signifies in their language, *the delicious River*, or *abounding* in fish. The *Caribbians* having thus dilated their territories, and forc'd their Enemies to retreat, made for some years a truce with the *Apalachites*, who being wearied out with the Wars, and discourag'd by the loss of a considerable Province, willingly hearkned to that cessation of arms, and all acts of hostility.

But these *Apalachites* being exasperated to see their Country grown lefs by one of the beft Provinces belonging to it, taking the advantage of the opportunity of that Truce, fecretly confulted feveral times among themfelves how they might carry on their defigns more fuccefsfully againft the *Caribbians* then they had done before ; and having found by fad experience, that they had not advanc'd their affairs much by aflaulting their Enemies openly, and by fetled Engagements, they refolv'd to fupplant them by fubtlety, and to that end to think of all ways imaginable to make a divifion among them, and infenfibly to engage them in a Civil War within their own Country. This advice being receiv'd and generally approv'd of all their Priefts, who are in very great efteem among them, and have Voices in their moft important Aflemblies, immediately furnifh'd them with expedients, and fuggefted to them the means, which were to this effect.

They had obferv'd that thofe people who came in fo flily and furpriz'd them in their own Country, were without Religion, and made no acknowledgment of any Divinity, whereto they conceiv'd themfelves oblig'd to render any publick Service, and that they ftood in fear only of a certain evil Spirit which they called *Mabouya*, becaufe he fometimes tormented them ; yet fo as that in the mean time they did not do him any homage : Thence it came that for fome years after their arrival, during which they had liv'd in good correfpondence with them, they endeavour'd to induce them by their example to acknowledge the Sun to be the fovereign Governour of the World, and to adore him as God. Thefe Exhortations and Inftructions had a great influence over the Spirits of the chiefeft among the *Caribbians*, and had made ftrong impreflions in them ; fo that having receiv'd the firft Principles of that Religion while the time of their mutual correfpondence continu'd , many left the Province of *Amana* wherein they had their habitations, and went into that of *Bemarin*, the principal Province of the *Apalachites*, whence they afcended into the Mountain of *Olaimi*, upon which the *Apalachites* made their folemn Offerings ; and upon their invitation the *Caribbians* had participated of thofe Cermonies and that Service : Thefe Priefts, whom the *Apalachites* call *Jaouas*, which is as much as to fay, *Men of God*, knew that the feeds of Religion are not fo eafily fmother'd in the hearts of men ; and that, though the long Wars they had had with the *Caribbians* had hinder'd the exercife thereof, yet would it be no hard matter for them to blow up, as we may fay, thofe fparks in them which lay hid under the afhes.

The Truce and Ceflation of all acts of Hoftility, which had been concluded between the two Nations, prefented the *Apalachites* with a favourable opportunity to profecute their defign ; whereupon the Priefts of the Sun advis'd, with the Kings Confent, that there fhould be a publication made among the

F f

Caribbians,

Caribbians, that at the beginning of the Month of *March*, which they call *Naarim* in their language, they would render a solemn Service in honour of the Sun, on the high Mountain; and that the said Service should be attended with Divertisements, Feasting, and Presents, which they should liberally give to such as were present thereat. This Ceremony was no new thing among the *Apalachites*, so that the *Caribbians* could not suspect any circumvention, nor fear any surprise; for it was a very ancient custom among them to make extraordinary Prayers to the Sun at the beginning of the Month of *Naarim*, which is precisely the time that they have done sowing their *Mais*. That which they desire in this Service is, That the Sun would be pleas'd to cause that which they had recommended to his care, to spring, grow, and come to maturity. They have also the same solemnity in the Month of *May*, at which time they have got in their first Harvest, to render him thanks for the fruits they conceive that they have receiv'd from his hands. Besides, the *Caribbians* knew well enough, that during these Festivals the *Apalachites* hung up their Bows and Arrows; that it was accounted a hainous crime among them to go arm'd into their Temple, and to raise the least dispute there; and that during those days of Solemnity, the greatest Enemies were commonly reconcil'd, and laid aside all enmity. In fine, they made not the least doubt but that the Publick Faith, and the promise solemnly made, would be inviolably observ'd.

Upon this assurance they dispose themselves to pass over into the Province of *Bemarin* at the time appointed; and that they might be thought to contribute somwhat on their part to the publick Solemnity, they dress themselves with all the bravery and magnificence they could; and though that even then they were wont to go very lightly clad, and expose their bodies almost naked, yet the more to accommodate themselves to the humours of their Neighbours, whom they were going to visit, they caused all the Furs, spotted Skins, and Stuffs that they had, to be made into Cloaths: They forgot not also to cause their faces, their hands, and all those places of their bodies which lay expos'd to be seen, to be painted with a bright red; and they crown themselves with their richest Garland, interwoven with the different plumage of several rare Birds of the Country. The Women for their parts, desirous to participate of this Solemnity, leave nothing undone that might contribute any thing to the adorning of themselves; the Chains of Shells of several colours, the Pendants, and the high Coifs enrich'd with the precious and glittering Stones which the Torrents bring down along with them out of the high Mountains, made them appear with extraordinary lustre. In this equipage the *Caribbians*, partly out of curiosity, partly out of the vanity to shew themselves, and some out of certain motives of Religon,

undertake

undertake that Pilgrimage: And that they might not raise any jealousie in those who had so kindly invited them, they leave their Bows, Arrows, and Clubs at the last Village within their Jurisdiction, and enter into the Province of *Bemarin* only with a walking stick, singing and dancing, as they are all of a merry and divertive disposition.

On the other side, the *Apalachites* expected them with great devotion, and answerably to the Orders they had to that purpose receiv'd from their King, whose name was *Teltlabin*, and whose race commands at present among that people; they kindly entertain'd all those who came to the Sacrifice; nay, from the first entrance of the *Caribbians* into their Province, they treated them at all places as cordially as if they had been their Brethren, and that there had never been any difference between them: They feasted them all along the way, and conducted them up to the Royal City, which to this day they call *Melilot*, that is, the *City of Councel*, inasmuch as it is the habitation of the King and his Court: The chiefest of the *Caribbians* were magnificently entertain'd at the Palace-Royal, and those of the common sort were receiv'd and treated by the Inhabitants of the City, who spar'd no cost to heighten the satisfaction of their Guests.

The day dedicated to the sacrifice of the Sun being come, the King of the *Apalachites* with his Court, which was very much encreased by the arrival of the *Caribbians*, and a great number of the Inhabitants of the other Provinces, who were come up to the Feast, went up very betimes in the morning to the top of the Mountain of *Olaimi*, which is not a full league distant from the City: This Prince, according to the custome of the Country, was carried in a chair, on the shoulders of four tall men, attended by four others of the same height, who were to relieve the former when they were weary: There marched before him several persons playing on Flutes and other musical Instruments; with this pomp he came to the place appointed for the Assembly; and when the Ceremony was over, he made a great distribution of Cloaths and Furs, more than he had been accustomed to do upon such occasions before: But above all, his liberality was remarkable towards the most considerable persons among the *Caribbians*; and in imitation of the Prince, the wealthiest of his people made presents in like manner to those of that Nation who had vouchsafed their solemn Sacrifice with their presence; so that most of the *Caribbians* return'd home well satisfy'd, and in better Liveries than they had brought thence with them: After they were come down from the Mountain, they were again treated and entertain'd with the greatest expressions of good will, in all the houses of the *Apalachites*, through whose habitations they were to return into their quarters: In fine, to encourage them

F f 2   to

to a second visit, there were solemn protestations made to them from the King and his Officers, that they should be at all other times receiv'd with the like demonstrations of affection, if they were desirous to accompany them four times in the year to the celebration of the same Ceremonies.

The *Caribbians* being return'd into their Province could not make sufficient acknowledgments of the kind entertainment they had receiv'd: Those who had stay'd at home being ravish'd to see the rich presents which their Country-men had brought home, immediately resolv'd to undertake the same pilgrimage at the next ensuing Feast: And the day on which it was to be drawing neer, there was so great a contestation among them who should go, that if their *Cacick*, or chief Captain, had not taken some course therein, the Province would have been destitute of Inhabitants: The *Apalachites* on the other side continu'd their entertainments and liberalities; and there was a certain emulation among them who should be most kind to the *Caribbians*: Their Priests, who knew what would be the issue of all this imposture, recommended nothing so much to them, as the continuation of those good Offices, which they said were very acceptable to the Sun.

Three years slipp'd away in these visits; at the end whereof the *Apalachites*, who had exhausted themselves in liberalities towards their Neighbours, perceiving they had gain'd extreamly upon their affections, and that the greatest part of them were grown so zealous for the service of the Sun, that nothing would be able to force out of their apprehensions the deep sentiments they had conceiv'd of his Divinity; resolv'd, upon the instigation of their Priests, for whose advice the King and all the people had great respects and submissions, to take occasion from the expiration of the Truce to renew the war against the *Caribbians*, and to forbid them access to their Ceremonies, if they would not, as they did, make a publick profession of believing the Sun to be God, and perform the promise they had sometime made of acknowledging the King of the *Apalachites* for their Sovereign, and do homage to him for the Province of *Amana*, upon which account they had been admitted to be the Inhabitants thereof.

The *Caribbians* were divided about these proposals: For all those who were inclin'd to the adoration of the Sun, were of opinion, that satisfaction should be given to the *Apalachites*, affirming, that, though they were not oblig'd thereto by their promise, yet would there be an engagement to do it, though it were only to prevent their being depriv'd of the free exercise of their Religion, and debar'd their presence at the sacrifices made to the Sun, which they could not abandon without much regret: The *Cacick* or chief Commander, and a great number of the most considerable among the *Caribbians* alledged

on

on the contrary, that they would not blaft their reputation, and
the glory of all their precedent Victories, by fo fhameful a
peace, which, under pretence of Religion, would make them
fubject to the *Apalachites*; That they were free-born, and that,
as fuch, they had left the place of their birth, and tranfplanted
themfelves into a better Country than their own, by force of
Arms; That their greateft concernment was to endeavour the
continuance of that precious liberty, and to cement it with
their own blood, if occafion requir'd; That they were the
fame men who had fometime forc'd the *Apalachites* to refign
up to them the moft confiderable of their Provinces, fuch a one
as was the centre, and as it were the eye of their Country;
That they had not remitted any thing of that generofity, and
that that valour was fo far from being extinguifh'd, that on the
contrary they had enlarg'd their jurifdiction by the acqueft of
a noble and fpacious Country, which gave them paffage beyond
the Mountains, whereby they were furrounded before; That
having thus remov'd out of the way whatever might obftruct
their defigns, it would be thought an infupportable cowardice
in them, only under pretence of Religion, and out of pure
curiofity of being prefent at Sacrifices, to quit the poffeffion
of what they had reduc'd under their power with fo much
trouble and bloodfhed: In fine, that if any were defirous to
adore the Sun, they needed not to go out of their own Territories to do it, fince he fhined as favourably in their Provinces
as thofe of the *Apalachites*, and look'd on them every day as gra-
cioufly as on any other part of the world; and if there were
any neceffity of confecrating a Mountain to him, or a Grot,
they might find among thofe which feparated their Country
from the great Lake, fome that were as high and as fit for
thofe myfteries as that of *Olaimi*.

Thofe who maintained the fervice of the Sun, and were
againft engaging in a new war, which muft be the fequel of
refufing conditions which were as advantageous to them as to
the *Apalachites*, made anfwer; that fince they had for fome
years enjoy'd the fweetnefs of peace, and experienc'd upon fo
many occafions the kind entertainments and generofity of
their Neighbours, it would be the greateft imprudence in the
world to run themfelves into new troubles, which they might
avoid upon fuch eafie terms, and that without any lofs of the
reputation they had acquir'd; That the acknowledgments
which the *Apalachites* requir'd for the Province they were poffeffed of, might be fuch, and of fo little importance, that it
would not be any diminution of their Honour, or prejudice to
their Authority; That as to what concern'd the Service and
Sacrifices of the Sun, they were not furnifh'd with fuch Priefts
as were inftructed in that Science, and acquainted with the
Ceremonies thereof; That it was much to be fear'd that if they
fhould

should undertake to imitate the *Jaoüas* of the *Apalachites*, they would, by the miscarriages likely to be committed therein, draw upon themselves the indignation of the Divinity which they would serve, instead of gaining its favour; That they had found upon enquiry, that there was not any Mountain in the whole Country so kindly look'd upon by the Sun, and so pleasant as that of *Olaimi* : Nor was there any other that had a Temple naturally made in the Rock, after so miraculous a manner, which was such, that all the art and industry of man could never bring to that perfection, and that it could be no other than the work of the beams of that Divinity which was there ador'd; That though it were suppos'd they might find out a Mountain and a Cave that came somewhat neer the other, which yet they thought impossible, it was questionable whether those Birds who were the Sun's Messengers would make their habitation there; And that the Fountain consecrated in honour of him, which wrought admirable effects, and unheard of cures, would be found there; And consequently, that they should expose themselves to the derision of the *Apalachites*, who would still have occasion to make their brags of an infinite number of prerogatives peculiar to their ancient Temple and Service, which the new one they pretended to build would never have. From all which considerations the Religious party concluded, that their best course was to make a firm peace, that so they might have the convenience of participating of the same Ceremonies for the future, which they had frequented during the Truce.

But those who were resolv'd on the contrary side were so obstinate, that all those remonstrances prevail'd nothing upon them, nor could in the least divert them from the resolution they had taken never to acknowledge the *Apalachites* for their Sovereigns, nor lose their liberty under pretence of Religion and way of Worship, which their fore-fathers had been ignorant of : So that, in fine, this contrariety of sentiments made an absolute rupture among the *Caribbians*, so as to divide them into two factions, as the Priests of the *Apalachites* had foreseen; whereupon being divided also in their Councels, they could not return an unanimous answer to the propositions of peace or war which had been made to them by the *Apalachites* : But either party growing stronger and stronger daily, that which voted for an allyance with the *Apalachites*, and stood for the adoration of the Sun, became so powerful as to be in a condition to oblige the other either to embrace their opinion, or quit the Province.

It would be too tedious a Relation to set down here all the mischiefs and miseries which that Civil War brought among the *Caribbians*, who mutually destroy'd one the other, till at last, after many fights, the *Apalachites* joyning with that party which

which carried on their Interest, the other was forced to quit
the Provinces of *Amana* and *Matica*, and to find out a more
setled habitation elsewhere.

The victorious *Caribbians* having, by the assistance of the
Apalachites, rid themselves of those who were the disturbers of
their Peace, fortified their Frontiers, and placed up and down
on the avenues the most valiant and most generous of their
Forces, to deprive the Banish'd of all hope of ever returning :
That done, they contracted a most strict Alliance with the *Apalachites*, submitting themselves to their Laws, embracing their
Religion, and so making themselves one people with them ;
and that incorporation continues to this day ; yet not so, but
that those *Caribbians* do still retain their ancient name, as we
have already observ'd in the beginning of this Chapter ; as also
many words which are common between them and the Inhabitants of the *Caribbies* : Of this kind are, among an infinite
number of others, the terms of *Cakonnes*, to express the little
curiosities which are preserv'd for their rarity ; that of *Bouttou*,
to signifie a Club of a weighty kind of wood ; that of *Taumali*,
to express a certain picquancy or delightfulness of taste ; that
of *Banaré*, to signifie a familiar Friend ; that of *Etoutou*, to denote an Enemy : They also call a Bow, *Allouba* ; Arrows, *Al-
louani* ; a great Pond, *Taonaba* ; the evil Spirit, *Mabouya* ; and
the Soul of a Man, *Akamboué* ; which are the proper terms
which the *Caribbian* Inhabitants of the Islands make use of at
the present to signifie the same things.

As concerning the *Caribbians* forc'd out of their Country by
those of their own Nation, and driven out of the limits of
their ancient Habitation, and all the places they had Conquer'd ;
having straggled up and down a while neer the River which
derives its source from the great Lake, and endeavour'd to no
purpose to enter into some Accommodation with the Inhabitants of either side of it, they at last resolv'd to make their way
through their Country, either by fair means or foul, and so to
get into some place where they might perpetuate themselves,
and make a secure establishment of what was left of them :
With this resolution they made a shift to get to the Sea-side,
where having met with a people which took compassion on
their misery, they winter'd among them, and pass'd over that
disconsolate Season in much want : And while they spent their
time in continual regrets, for their loss of a Country so pleasant
and fertile as that which they had liv'd in, and considered that
they should never enjoy themselves in that whereto their misfortune had cast them as Exiles, there arrived where they were,
at the beginning of the Spring, two little Vessels, which came
from the Islands called the *Lucayos*, and had been driven by the
Winds into the Road neer which our *Caribbians* had pass'd over
the Winter : **There** were in those two Vessels, which they call
Canows

Canows or *Piragos*, about thirteen or fourteen persons, Inhabitants of *Cigateo*, one of the *Lucayan* Islands, who being got ashore, related to the natural Inhabitants of the Country how they had been forc'd thither by a Tempest; and among other things, they told wonders of the Islands where they liv'd, adding, that there were yet divers others beyond them, towards the Æquator, which lay defart, and were not inhabited, and those such as were accounted better then the others whereof they had given them an account: That for their parts, all they desired of the Inhabitants of the Country was only some Provisions, and a little fresh Water, to enable them to get home to their own Country, from which they conceiv'd themselves to be distant not above four or five days Sailing.

The *Caribbians*, who were studying where to find out some new habitation, and extreamly troubled that they had no setled place, where they might no longer be expos'd to the inconveniences of a wandring kind of life, having heard so much of these Islands, and that they were not far from the *Lucayas*, resolv'd to make their advantage of the opportunity of those Guides, whom they had met with by so extraordinary a good fortune, to follow them, when they should depart thence, and after their arrival at home, to plant themselves in some of those defart Islands whereof they had given so advantagious an account.

They doubted not but that the execution of this enterprize would put a period to all their miseries: But there was yet a great obstacle lay in their way, which at first they knew not how to overcome, to wit, the want of Vessels to crossthe Sea, and bring them to the places whereof they desir'd to possess themselves: The first Proposals were to fell down Trees, and to make them hollow with fire, as other Nations did, nay that among whom they then were: But that expedient requir'd a long time to compass it, while in the interim, those whom they hoped to have for their Conductors would be gone: Whereupon they thought it the surest way to find out Vessels ready made: To that end they resolv'd in the night time to seize on all those which the Nations of the neighbouring Creeks, and and such as liv'd neer the Rivers which fall thereabouts into the Sea, had ready in their Ports, and in condition fit for the Sea. The day being come for the departure of the *Lucayans*, who were to be their Guides, our *Caribbians* who had furnish'd themselves before-hand with all necessary provisions, met together the most secretly they could, along the River-sides and neer the Ports, and having possess'd themselves of all the *Canows* or Vessels they met with, joyn'd with the *Lucayans*, with whom, without taking any leave of their Hosts, they set Sail for the *Lucayas*.

The Wind having prov'd favourable to these Fugitives, they
got

got in a few days to *Cigateo*, where they were very civilly entertain'd by the Inhabitants, who, having fupply'd them with all neceffary refrefhments, conducted them to the moft remote of their Iflands, and thence gave them a Convoy to bring them to the next of the defart Iflands whereof they had given them a relation, which they call'd *Ajay*, but it is now call'd *Santa Cruz*: In their paffage they fail'd by the Ifland of *Boriquen*, now call'd *Porto-Rico*, which was inhabited by a very powerful Nation.

It was then in the faid Ifland of *Ayay* that our *Caribbians* laid the firft foundations of their Colony, and where enjoying an undifturbed Peace, which made them forget all precedent misfortunes, they multipli'd fo, that within a few years they were forc'd to fpread themfelves into all the other Iflands now known by the name of the *Caribbbies*: And fome Ages after, having poffefs'd themfelves of all the inhabitable Iflands, they tranfported themfelves into the Continent of the Meridional part of *America*, where they have at this day many great and numerous Colonies, wherein they are fo well fetled, that though the *Taos*, the *Sappayos*, the *Paragotis*, the *Arouacas* or *Arouagues*, who are their Neighbours in the Ifland of *Trinity*, and the Provinces of *Orinoca*, have often attempted to force them out of their habitations, and engag'd againft them with all their Forces, yet do they ftill continue in them in a flourifhing condition, and entertain fo good a correfpondence and fo perfect a friendfhip with our *Caribbians*, the Inhabitants of the Iflands, that thefe latter march out once or twice a year to their relief, joyning all together with the *Calibites*, their Friends and Confederates, againft the *Arouagues*, and other Nations, their common Enemies.

There is yet another Story concerning the origine of the Infulary *Caribbians*, which is, That they are defcended from their Confederates the *Calibites*; and we are apt to believe fomwhat of it may be true, as being the only account which moft of them can give of themfelves: For thefe *Caribbians* being lefs powerful then the *Calibites*, when they firft came among them into the Continent, and having afterwards enter'd into Alliance with them by Marriages and common concernments, they made up together but one people, and fo there enfu'd a mutual communication of Language and particular Cuftoms: And thence it comes that a great part of the *Caribbians*, having forgot their firft origine, would have it believ'd that they are defcended from the *Calibites*: And it is to be prefum'd, that it being out of all memory of man, when their Predeceffors came from the Northern parts into thefe Iflands, they have not any knowledg of their Native Country, which having caft them out of her bofom, and treated them as Rebels, was not fo far regretted by thofe poor Fugitives, as that they fhould be over-careful

G g

to

to preferve the memory of it. On the contrary, it is credible, that the fooner to forget the miferies they had fuffer'd, they effac'd the fad ideas therof as much as they could, and were glad of any other Origine : It may be alfo, that when the *Caribbians* firft enter'd the Iflands, upon their coming from the North, they were not fo deftitute of Inhabitants, but that there were here and there fome Families which might have pafs'd over thither from the Iflands of *Hifpaniola* or *Porto-Rico*, which they deftroy'd, referving only the Women, whom they might make ufe of for the propagation of their Colony: And of this there is yet a greater probability, in that thefe *Caribbians* being banifh'd from among the *Apalachites*, and by War forc'd to leave the Country to the victorious Party, many of their Wives ftaid behind among the *Apalachites*, and the reft of their own Nation who had joyn'd with them : And thence poffibly may proceed the difference there is between the Language of the Men and that of the Women amongft the *Caribbians*.

But to give a more particular account of thofe Colonies of the *Caribbians* which are in the Meridional Continent of *America*, in the firft place, the Relations of thofe who have entred into the famous River of *Orenoca*, diftant from the Line, Northward, eight degrees and fifty minutes, affirm, that at a great diftance within the Country, there live certain *Caribbians* who might eafily have pafs'd over thither from the Ifland of *Tabago*, which, of all the *Caribbies*, is the neereft to that Continent.

The *Dutch* Relations acquaint us, that, advancing yet further towards the Æquator, there lies, at feven degrees from that Line, the great and famous River of *Effequeba*, neer which are planted firft the *Aroüagues*, and next to them the *Caribbians*, who are continually in war with them, and have their habitations above the falls of that River, which defcend with great violence from the Mountains ; and thence thefe *Caribbians* reach to the fource of the fame River, and are very numerous, and poffefs'd of a vaft territory.

The fame Travellers relate, that within fix degrees of the Line lies the River *Sarname*, or *Suriname*, into which falls another River named *Ikouteca*, all along which there are many Villages inhabited by *Caribbians*.

There is befides a numerous people of the fame Nation, Inhabitants of a Country which reaches a great way into the Continent, the coafts whereof extend to the fifth and fixth degree North of the Æquator, fcituate along a fair and great River named *Marouyne*, about eighteen Leagues diftant from that of *Sarname*, which from its fource croffes up and down above two hundred leagues of Country, in which there are many Villages inhabited by *Caribbians* ; who, obferving the fame cuftome with the Iflanders, make choice of the moft valiant

among

among them for their *Cacicks*, or Commanders in chief, and are somewhat of a higher stature than those Inhabitants of the *Caribbies*, yet not differing much from them, save only that some of them cover their privy parts with a piece of cloth, but rather for ornament, than out of any consideration of shame or modesty: Those therefore who have travell'd into those Countries affirm, that, from the mouth of the River *Marouyne*, which lies at five degrees and forty five minutes of the Line to the North, to the source of it, there are twenty days sail, and that all along it the *Caribbians* have their Villages like those of our Islanders.

We observe further out of the Voyages of some *Dutch*, that the Inhabitants of that Continent, through which the River of *Cayenna* makes its passage into the Ocean, are naturally *Caribbians*.

In fine, it is not impossible but that these *Caribbians* might cross those Countries as far as *Brasil*; for those who have made voyages thither, affirm, that among the Provinces, which lie along the coasts of the South-Sea, there are some people, commonly known by the name of *Caribbians*; and that being of a more hardy and daring constitution, as also more apprehensive and subtle than the other *Indians*, Inhabitants of *Brasil*, they are so highly esteemed among them, that they conceive them to be endu'd with a more excellent kind of knowledge than the others; whence it comes that they have a great submission for their Counsels, and desire them to preside at all their Festivals and rejoicings, which they seldom celebrate without the presence of some one of these *Caribbians*, who upon that account take their progress up and down the Villages, where they are receiv'd with acclamations, entertainments and great kindness, as *John de Lery* hath observ'd.

Were it necessary to produce any further confirmation to prove that these *Caribbians*, scattered into so many places of the Continent of the Meridional part of *America*, are of the same Nation with the *Islanders*, we might alledge what is unanimously affirm'd by the two *Dutch* Colonies planted in those coasts, to wit, those of *Cayenna* and *Berbica*, both neighbours to the *Caribbians* of the Continent, to shew the conformity and resemblance there is in many things, as constitution, manners, customs, &c. between them and the *Indian* Inhabitants of the *Caribbies*, of whom we shall give an account hereafter: But it is time we conclude this chapter, which is already grown to a great length; yet could it not be divided, by reason of the uniformity and connexion of the matter.

Yet have we a word further to add, in answer to a question, which the curiosity of some person might haply take occasion to start, which is, How long it may be since the *Caribbians* came out of *Florida* into these Islands? We must acknowledge

G g 2

there

there can no certain account be given of it, inafmuch as thefe
Nations have commonly no other Annals than their own memories: But in regard thofe people ordinarily live two hundred years, it is not to be thought ftrange that the occurrences
happening among them, fhould be tranfmitted to pofterity to
three or four Generations.   And to confirm this, we may aver
that there are many men and women among them who can
give an exact account of the firft arrival of the *Spaniards* in
America, as if it had happened but yefterday: So that the remembrance of the departure of the *Caribbians* out of *Florida*,
and the wars they have had there, being yet frefh among the
Apalachites, thofe who have heard them difcourfe, conjecture
that it may be about five hundred years fince thofe things came
to pafs. But if it be further queftion'd, why they did not endeavour to make their way back again into *Florida*, to be reveng'd of the *Apalachites*, and thofe of their own Nation, who
had forc'd them thence, efpecially after they had multiply'd
and recruited themfelves fo powerfully in the Iflands? it may
be anfwered, That the difficulty of Navigation, which is very
eafie from the *Caribbies* to *Florida*, but very dangerous from
Florida to the *Caribbies*, the winds being commonly contrary,
chill'd the earneftnefs they might have to make any fuch attempt.   In the next place it is to be noted, that the air of the
Iflands being warmer, and the foil as good, and in all appearance more fuitable to their conftitution than that of *Florida*,
they apprehended, that thofe who had forc'd them thence,
had, contrary to their intentions, procur'd them a greater happinefs than they could have defir'd, and, thinking to make
them miferable, had made them fortunate in their exile.

CHAP. VIII.

By way of Digreffion giving an account of the Apalachites, *the Nature of their Country*, *their Manners*, *and
their ancient and modern Religion.*

SInce we have had occafion to fpeak fo much concerning the
Apalachites, and that above one half of the ancient *Caribbians*, after the expulfion of thofe among them who would not
adore the Sun, have to this prefent made up one people and
one Common-wealth with thofe *Apalachites*, it will be confo-
nant to our defign, efpecially fince the fubject thereof is rare
and little known, if we give fome account of the nature of
their Country, and the moft remarkable things that are in it;
as alfo of the manners of the Inhabitants, the Religion they

have

have had heretofore, and that which they profefs at this day, as we have the particulars thereof from the *Englifh*, who have traded among them, and have not long fince laid the foundations of a Colony in the midft of the nobleft, and beft known of their Provinces.

The Territories of the *Apalachites* confift of fix Provinces, whereof three are comprehended within that noble and fpacious Vale which is encompafs'd by the Mountains of the *Apalates*, at the foot whereof thefe people inhabit: The moft confiderable of thofe Provinces, and which lies towards the Eaft, wherein the King keeps his Court, is called *Bemarin*: That which is in the midft, and as it were in the centre of the three, is called *Amani* or *Amana*: And the third of thofe which are within that Vale, is known by the name of *Matica*. True it is, that this laft, which begins in the Vale, reaches a great way into the Mountains, nay goes yet much beyond, even to the South-fide of the great Lake, which they call *Theomi*: The other Provinces are *Schama* and *Meraco*, which are in the *Apalatean* Mountains; and *Achalaques*, which is partly in the Mountains, and partly in the Plain, and comprehends all the Marfhes and Fenny places, confining on the great Lake *Theomi*, on the North-fide.

The Country under the King of the *Apalachites* being thus divided into fix Provinces, there are in it fome Mountains of a vaft extent and prodigious height, which are for the moft part inhabited by a people living only upon what they get by hunting, there being great ftore of wild beafts in thofe Wildernefles: Befides which, there are alfo certain Vales, which are peopled by a Nation that is lefs barbarous, fuch as addicts it felf to the cultivation of the earth, and is fuftain'd by the fruits it produces: And laftly, there are abundance of Marfhes and Fenny places, and a great Lake, whereof the Inhabitants are very numerous, maintaining themfelves by fifhing, and what the little good ground they have furnifhes them withall.

The three Provinces which are within the Vale, which, as we faid in the precedent Chapter, is fixty leagues in length, and about ten more in bredth, lie as it were in a Champion Country, fave only, that in fome places there are certain rifings and eminences, on which the Towns and Villages are commonly built; many little Rivers, which defcend from the Mountains, and abound in Fifh, crofs it up and down in feveral places: That part of it which is not reduc'd to culture is well furnifh'd with fair trees of an exceffive height: For inftance, there are *Cedars, Cyprefs, Pines, Oaks, Panamas*, which the *French* call *Saxafras*, and an infinite variety of others which have no proper names among us.

As concerning the Fruit-trees of this Country, befides Cheftnut

nut and Walnut-Trees, which grow naturally there, the *English* who have planted themselves in those parts, as we shall relate more at large towards the end of this Chapter, have planted Orange-trees, sweet and sharp Citrons, Lemons, several sorts of Apples and Pears, and divers Stones, as of Plumbs, Cherries, and Apricocks, which have thriv'd and multiplied so, that in some places of this Country there are more *European* fruits then in any other part of *America*.

There is also good store of those lesser sort of Trees which bear leaves or flowers of sweet scent, such as Laurel, Jessemine, Roses, Rosemary, and all those others that are so ornamental in the Garden: Nor is there any want of Pinks, Carnations, Tulips, Violets, Lillies, and all the other Flowers which adorn Knots and Borders.

Pot-herbs also, and all sorts of Pulse and Roots, thrive very well there: Citruls, Cucumbers, and Melons are common all Summer long, and as well tasted as those which grow in any part of the *Caribbies*.

Strawberries and Raspberries grow in the Woods without any culture: They have also Small-nuts, Gooseberries, and an infinite variety of other small Fruits, which in their degree contribute to the delight and refreshment of the Inhabitants.

The Wheat, Barly, Rie, and Oats which some sow'd there at several Seasons, and in different Soils, hath grown only to the blade; but in requital, there grows every where such abundance of small Millet, Lentils, Chick-pease, Fetches, and Mais, or Turkish Wheat, which are sown and harvested twice a year, that the Inhabitants of the Plain Country have enough to supply those who live towards the Mountains, who bring them in exchange several sorts of Furs. The Lands that are sown with Turkish Wheat are enclos'd with Quick-set Hedges, planted on both sides with Fruit-trees, most whereof are cover'd with wild Vines, which grow at the foot of the Trees.

As to the Volatiles of this Country, there are Turkeys, Pintadoes, Parrots, Woodquists, Turtles, Birds of prey, Eagles, Geese, Ducks, Herons, white Sparrows, *Tonatzuli*, a kind of bird that sings as sweetly as the Nightingal, and is of an excellent plumage; and abundance of other Birds commonly seen neer Rivers and in the Forests, quite different from those that are seen in other parts of the World.

The *Apalachites* have no knowledge at all of Sea-fish, as being at too great a distance from the Coasts; but they take abundance in the Rivers and Lakes, which are extreamly nourishing, of an excellent taste, and much about the bigness and in figure somwhat like our Pikes, Carps, Perches, and Barbels: They also take Castors and Bevers neer the great Rivers, Lakes, and Pools; they eat the flesh of them, and make Furs of the Skins, for Winter-caps and other uses.

There

There is no venemous creature nor any wild beast in the lower part of the Country; for the Inhabitants of the Mountains, who are expert Huntsmen, drive them into the Forests, where they find them continual work and sport: So that the flocks of sheep, and herds of cattel and swine graze up and down the skirts of the Mountains without any body to look after them. But within the woods, and in the desarts, which are not much frequented by men, there are divers Monstrous and dangerous Reptiles, as also Bears, Tygers, Lions, Wolves, and some other kinds of cruel Beasts, which live by prey, and are particular to those Countries.

The men in these Countries are for the most part of high stature, of an Olive-colour, and well proportion'd, their hair black and long: Both men and women are very neat and curious in keeping their hair clean and handsomely order'd: The women tie up theirs about the crown of the head after the form of a Garland; and the men dispose theirs behind the ears: But upon days of publick rejoicing, all have their hair loose, dishevel'd, and dangling over their shoulders; a fashion becomes them well. The Inhabitants of those Provinces that lie towards and among the Mountains, cut off all the hair on the left side of the head, that so they may the more easily draw their Bows, and they order that which grows on the other side, so as to make a crest standing over the right ear: Most of them wear neither Caps nor any thing instead of Shoes, but they cover the body with the skins of Bears or Tygers, neatly sown together, and cut after the fashion of close coats, which reach down to their knees, and the sleeves are so short that they come not over the elbow

The Inhabitants of the other Provinces which are seated in the Vales and Plains, went heretofore naked from the Navel upwards, in the Summer-time, and in Winter, they wore garments of Furrs; but now both men and women are clad all the year long: In the hottest seasons, they have light cloaths, made of cotton, wooll, or a certain herb, of which they make a thred as strong as that of Flax: The women have the art of spinning all these materials, and weaving them into several kinds of stuffs, which are lasting, and delightful to the eie. But in the winter, which many times is hard enough, they are all clad in several kinds of skins, which they have the skill to dress well enough: They leave the hair on some, and so make use of them as Furs: They have also the art of tanning Ox-hides, and other skins, and making Shoes and Boots of them.

The men wear Caps made of Otter-skins, which are perfectly black and glittering, pointed before, and set out behind with some rich feathers, which hanging down over their shoulders make them look very gracefully: but the women have no
other

other ornament about the head, but what is deriv'd from the several dresses of their hair: They make holes in their ears, and wear pendants of Chrystal, or made of a certain smooth stone they have, which is of as bright a green as that of an Emrald: Of the same materials they also make great Necklaces, which they wear when they would appear in state: They make great account of Corral, Chrystal, and yellow Amber, which are brought to them by Strangers; and they are only the Wives of the principal Officers that have Bracelets and Necklaces made of them: Though there be some *Spanish* and *English* Families among them, yet have they not alter'd any thing either as to their Cloaths or course of Life.

The ordinary sort of people wear only a close coat without sleeves, over a thin garment of Goat-skins, which serves them for shirts: The Coat which comes down to the calf of the leg, is ty'd about the wast with a leathern girdle, which is set out with some little embroidery: But the Officers and Heads of Families wear over that a kind of short Cloak, which covers only the back and the arms, though behind it falls down to the ground: This Cloak is fasten'd with strong leathern points, which make it fast under the neck, and lye close to the shoulders: The womens garments are of the same fashion with those of the men, save that those of the former come down to the ankles, and the Cloak hath two open places on the sides, through which they put forth their arms.

To keep themselves clear of Vermine, they often wash their bodies with the juice of a certain root, which is of as sweet a scent as the *Flower-de-luce* of *Florence*, and hath this further vertue, that it makes the nerves more supple, and fortifies and causes a smoothness all over the body, and communicates an extraordinary delightful scent thereto.

The Cities of the three Provinces that are in the spacious Plain, which is at the foot of the Mountains, are encompassed on the outside by a large and deep Moat, which on the inside, instead of wals, is all planted with great posts pointed at the top, thrust a good depth into the ground; or sometimes with quick-set hedges intermixt with very sharp thorns; they are commonly about five or six foot in bredth: The Gates are small and narrow, and are made fast with little pieces of wood, which lie cross between small ramperts of earth that are on both sides, and which command the avenues: There are commonly but two Gates to every City; to enter in at them, a man must pass over a bridge so narrow, that two men cannot well march on a front upon it: The Bridge is built upon piles, which sustain certain planks, which they draw up in the night when they fear the least trouble.

It is seldom seen that there is above one City in every Province; nay there are some that have not above eight hundred
houses

houfes in them : The Metropolis of the Country, which is called *Melilot*, hath above two thoufand ; they are all built of
pieces of wood planted into the ground and joined one to another : The covering is for the moft part of the leaves of reeds,
grafs, or rufhes : Thofe of the Captains are done over with a
certain Maftick, which keeps off the rain, and preferves the
thatch from decaying in many years: The floors of all the
houfes is of the fame material, whereto they add a certain golden fand which they get out of the neighbouring Mountains,
and which gives fuch a luftre as if they were fown with little
fpangles of Gold.

The Rooms of the ordinary fort of people are hung only
with a kind of Mat , made of Plantane-leaves and rufhes,
which they have the art of dying into feveral colours ;
thofe of perfons confiderable among them, are hung with precious Furs, or Deer-skins painted with divers figures, or with
a kind of Tapiftry made of Birds-feathers, which they fo in-
duftrioufly intermingle, that it feems to be embroidered: Their
Beds are about a foot and a half from the ground, and are cover'd with skins that are drefs'd, and as foft as can be wifh'd :
Thefe skins are commonly painted with Flowers, Fruits, and a
hundred fuch inventions, and their colours are fo well fet on
and fo lively, that at a diftance one would take them for rich
Tapiftry: The wealthier fort in the winter time have their beds
covered with the skins of Martins, Beavers, or white Foxes,
which are fo well drefs'd, and perfum'd with fuch artifice, that
they never admit any thing of ordure : The Officers and all
the moft confiderable Inhabitants lie on Mattreffes fill'd with a
certain down that grows on a little plant, and is as foft as filk ;
but the common people take their reft on dry'd fern, which hath
the property of taking away the wearinefs of the body, and
retriving the forces exhaufted by hunting, gardening, and all
the other painful exercifes confequent to their courfe of
life.

The Veffels they ufe in their houfes are either of wood or
earth, enamel'd with divers colours, and very delightfully
painted : They fharpen upon ftones the teeth of feveral wild
beafts, and therewith arm their Arrows and Lances : Before
ftrangers came among them and traded in their Country, they
knew not there was fuch a thing as Iron ; but they made ufe
of extraordinary hard and fharp ftones inftead of wedges, and
certain fmooth and cutting bones, inftead of knives.

They all live very amicably together under the conduct of a
King, who keeps his Court at *Melilot*, the Metropolis of the
Kingdome : In every City there is a Governour, and other
fubordinate Officers, who are appointed by him, and chang'd
at his pleafure, as he thinks moft convenient : The Villages
alfo have Captains and heads of Families, by whom they are

H h   governed.

governed. All immoveable goods are common among these people, and excepting only their houses, and the little gardens belonging to them, they have no propriety in any thing: they carry on the business of Agriculture in common, and they share the fruits of the earth among themselves: At sowing-time the Governors and their Officers oversee the work; and at that time all those who are of age to do any thing abroad, go out betimes in the morning to their work, and continue there till the evening, at which time they return to their Towns and Villages to take their rest: While they are at work, it is the business of their Chiefs to provide them somewhat extraordinary in meat and drink: They dispose their Harvest into the publick Granaries, which are in the midst of their Towns and Villages; and at every full Moon, and at every new Moon, those who are entrusted with the distribution thereof, supply every Family, according to the number of persons whereof it consists, with as much as will suffice.

They are a temperate people, and hate all kind of voluptuousness, and whatever tends to effeminacy: And though Vines grow naturally in their Country, yet do they not make any wine but what is requisite for the divine service: Fair water is their ordinary drink, but at great entertainments, they make use of a pleasant kind of Beer, which is made of *Turkey* wheat: They also have the art of making an excellent kind of Hydromel, or Mead, which they keep in great earthen vessels: The great abundance of honey which they find among the Rocks, and in the clefts of hollow trees, supplies them with that whereof they make that delicious drink, which is such as may well pass for Sack, especially after it hath been kept a long time.

Those of the same Family live so lovingly together, that there are among them some houses where an old man hath his children, and his children's children, to the third, nay sometimes to the fourth generation, all living under the same roof, to the number of a hundred persons, and sometimes more. Most of the other Nations of the Septentrional part of *America* who inhabit along the Sea-coast, are so slothful, that in the winter time they are in great want, because they had not sown any thing when the time served, or had consumed the fruits of the precedent harvest in extraordinary entertainments and debauches: But the *Apalachites* hate nothing so much as idleness, and they are so addicted to pains-taking, that the fruits of the earth, being answerable to their labour, and being distributed with prudence and moderation, maintain them plentifully, nay so that they can, in case of necessity, assist their Neighbours the Inhabitants of the Mountains: Both men and women are perpetually employ'd, after seed-time and harvest, in spinning of Cotton, Wooll, and a certain Herb, which is soft

and

and strong, for the making of cloth, and several ordinary sorts of stuffs, wherewith they cover themselves : Some among them employ themselves in making of earthen ware; others in making Tapistry of the plumage of Birds; others, in making of Baskets, Panniers, and other little pieces of houshold-stuff, which they do with a strange industry.

They are of a very loving and obliging disposition : And whereas their distance from the Sea exempts them from being subject to receive any displeasure from Strangers, they are in like manner ignorant what entertainments to make them, when they chance to visit them, and are never weary of expressing all manner of friendship towards them : They are docible and susceptible of all sorts of good disciplines ; but they have this discommendable in them, that they are very obstinate in their opinions, easily angred, and much addicted to revenge, when they are convinc'd that they have been injur'd : They are extreamly apt to give credit to their dreams, and they have some old dotards among them, who openly make it their business to interpret them, and foretell what things shall happen after them.

They have had a long continuance of peace; however they think it prudence to stand always upon their guard, and they have always Sentinels at the avenues of their Cities, to prevent the incursions of a certain savage and extreamly cruel people, which hath no setled habitation, but wander up and down the Provinces with an incredible swiftness, making havock where-ever they come, especially where they find no resistance.

The Arms of the *Apalachites* are, the Bow, the Club, the Sling, and a kind of great Javelin, which they dart out of their hands, when they have spent all their Arrows : And whereas those that inhabit towards the woods and in the Mountains, live only by hunting, continual exercise makes them so expert in shooting with the Bow, that the King, who alwaies hath a Company of them about his person, hath no greater diversion than to see them shoot at a mark for some prize, which he gives him who in fewest shots came to the place assign'd, or hath shot down a Crown set up upon the top of a Tree.

They are passionate lovers of Musick, and all instruments that make any kind of harmony, insomuch that there's very few among them but can play on the Flute, and a kind of Hawboy, which being of several bigness, make a passably good harmony, and render a sound that is very melodious : They are mightily given to dancing, capering, and making a thousand postures, whereby they are of opinion they disburthen themselves of all their bad humours, and that they acquire a great activity and suppleness of body, and a wonderful swiftness in running. They heretofore celebrated solemn dances at the end of every

H h 2   harvest,

harveft, and after they had made their Offerings to the Sun upon the Mountain of *Olaimi* ; but now they have no fet and appointed time for thefe divertifements.

Their voice is naturally good, mild, flexible, and pleafant ; whence it comes that many among them make it their endeavour to imitate the finging and chirping of Birds ; wherein they are for the moft part fo fortunate, that like fo many *Orpheus*'s they entice out of the woods to follow them, thofe Birds which think they hear only thofe of their own fpecies: They do alfo by finging alleviate the hard labour they are addicted unto, and yet what they do, feems to be done rather out of divertifement, and to avoid idlenefs, than out of any confideration of advantage that they make thereof.

Their Language is very fmooth, and very plentiful in comparifons : That fpoken by the Captains and all perfons of quality, is more elegant and fuller of flourifhes than that of the common fort of people : Their expreffions are very precife, and their periods fhort enough : While they are yet children, they learn feveral fongs, made by the *Jaouas* in honour and commendation of the Sun ; they are alfo acquainted with feveral other little pieces of Poetry, wherein they have comprehended the moft memorable exploits of their Kings, out of a defign to perpetuate the memory thereof among them, and the more eafily tranfmit it to their pofterity.

All the Provinces which acknowledge the King of *Apalacha* for their Sovereign, underftand the language commonly fpoken in his Court ; yet does not this hinder but that each of them hath a particular dialect of its own, whence it comes that the language of fome, is in fome things different from that of others of the Inhabitants : The Provinces of *Amana* and *Matica*, in which there are to this day many *Caribbian* Families, have retained to this prefent many words of the ancient idiome of thefe people, which confirms what we have laid down for a certain affertion, to wit, that being known by the fame name, and having many expreffions common to them with the Inhabitants of the *Caribby*-Iflands, thofe Families have alfo the fame origine with them, as we have reprefented in the precedent chapter.

They heretofore adored the Sun, and had their Priefts, whom they called *Jaouas*, who were very fuperftitious in rendring to him the fervice which they had invented in honour of him : their perfwafion was, that the raies of the Sun gave life to all things ; that they dried up the earth ; and that once the Sun having continued four and twenty hours under an eclipfe, the earth had been overflown ; and that the great Lake which they call *Theomi*, was rais'd as high as the tops of the higheft Mountains that encompafs it ; but that the Sun having recovered the eclipfe, had, by his prefence, forc'd the waters to

return

return into their abyſſes; that only the Mountain dedicated to his honour, and wherein his Temple was, was preſerv'd from that deluge; and that their Predeceſſors, and all the beaſts which are at preſent in the woods and upon the earth, having retir'd to the ſaid Mountain, were preſerv'd for the repopulation and recruit of the whole earth : So that they conceive themſelves to be the moſt ancient people of the world; And they affirm, that from that time they have ac-knowledg'd the Sun for their God.

They were of opinion, that the Sun had built himſelf the Temple which is in the Mountain of *Olaimi*, the aſcent where-of is diſtant from the City of *Melilot* ſomewhat leſs than a league; and that the *Tonatzuli* (which are certain little birds about the bigneſs of a Quail, and whoſe bellies and wings are of a bright yellow, the back of a sky-colour, and the head of a plumage, partly red, and partly white) are the meſſen-gers and children of the Sun, which alwaies celebrate his praiſes.

The ſervice they rendred the Sun conſiſted in ſaluting him at his riſing, and ſinging hymns in honour of him : They ob-ſerved the ſame Ceremonies alſo in the evening, entreating him to return, and to bring the day along with him : And be-ſides this daily ſervice which every one performed at the door of his houſe, they had alſo another publick and ſolemn ſervice, which conſiſted in ſacrifices and offerings, and was perform'd by the *Jaonas*, four times in the year, to wit, at the two ſeed-times, and after the two harveſts, upon the Mountain of *Olaimi*, with great pomp, and a general concourſe of all the Inhabitants of the ſix Provinces.

This Mountain of *Olaimi* is ſeated, as we ſaid before, in the Province of *Bemarin*, about a league diſtant from the Royal City of *Melilot*; but there is about another league of aſcent and winding from the foot of it, ere a man can get to the top of it : It is certainly one of the moſt pleaſant and moſt mira-culous Mountains in the world : Its figure is perfectly round, and the natural deſcent extream ſteepy; but to facilitate the acceſs thereof to ſuch as are to go up, they have cut a good broad way all about it, and there are here and there ſeveral reſting places gain'd out of the Rock, like ſo many neeches : All the circumference of it, from the foot to within two hundred paces of the top, is naturally planted with goodly trees of *Saxafras*, *Cedar*, and *Cypreſs*, and ſeveral others from which there iſſue *Roſins*, and *Aromatick gums*, of a very delightful ſcent : On the top of it there is a ſpacious plain, ſmooth and eaven all over, and ſomewhat better than a league in compaſs; it is covered with a delightful green livery of a ſhort and ſmall graſs, which is intermixt with Thyme, Marjoram, and other ſweet ſmelling herbs : And it was upon the top of this Moun-

tain,

tain, and upon this pleasant verdure that the people stood, while the Priests of the Sun performed the divine service.

The place which serv'd them for a Temple, is a large and spacious Grott, or Cave, which is naturally cut in the Rock, on the East-side of the Mountain: It hath a vast and large mouth, as the entrance of a magnificent Temple: As soon as the Sun is risen, he darts his rays on that entrance, which hath before it a fair and spacious square place, which a man would say were made by art in the Rock: And there it is that the *Jaouas*, the Priests of the Sun, stay expecting his rising to begin their ordinary Ceremonies on Festival days. This Cave within is oval, two hundred foot in length, and proportionably broad: The Vault, which is naturally cut in the Rock, rises up circularly from the ground to about a hundred foot high: There is just in the midst of it a great hole, or Lanthorn, which enlightens it from the top of the Mountain: This Lanthorn is encompass'd with great stones, laid close together to prevent peoples falling in: The Vault on the inside is perfectly white, and the surface cover'd with a certain *Salt-peter*, which a man might take for white Coral diversy'd into several different figures; the whole compass of it is of the same lustre: The floor of it is also extreamly eaven and smooth, as if it were all of one piece of marble. In fine, the greatest ornament of this Temple consists in its perfect whiteness: At the bottom of it there is a great Basin or Cistern, just over against the entrance, which is full of a very clear water, which perpetually distilling out of the Rock, is receiv'd into that place. Just in the middle of this Temple, directly under the Lanthorn which enlightens it, there is a great Altar all of one stone, of a round figure, three foot in height from the floor, and sustain'd by a short pillar, which Altar and the Pedestal seem to have been cut out of the place where it stands, that being in all probability a piece of a Rock which jutted out upon the floor of that miraculous Cave.

The Sacrifices which the *Jaouas* offered to the Sun, consisted not in the effusion of mans blood, or that of some certain beasts; for they were of a perswasion, that the Sun, giving life to all things, would not be pleas'd with a service that should deprive those creatures of the life which he had bestow'd on them; but the Sacrifice consisted only in Songs, which they had compos'd in honour of him, as also in the perfumes of certain aromatical drugs, which they appointed to be burnt on his Altar, and in the offerings of garments, which the rich presented by the hands of the Priests, to be afterwards distributed among the poorer sort of people.

All this Ceremony, which was performed four times a year, lasted from Sun-rising till noon, at which time the Assembly was dismiss'd: The Priests went up to the Mountain on the

Eve of every Festival, to prepare themselves for that solemn Action; and the people, which came thither from all the Provinces, were there present some time before Sun-rising. The way which led up to the Mountain was enlightned by great Fires, which were kept in all that Night, for the convenience of those who went thither to adore. All the people remain'd without upon the Mountain, and none but the Priests durst come neer the Grot, which serv'd them for a Temple. Those who brought any Garments to be distributed to the poor, presented them to the Priests who stood at the entrance, and they hung them on the Poles which were on both sides of the Portal, where they remained till after the Service, and then they were distributed among the poor, as were also the other presents which the rich offered, and which were in like manner kept till the same time: Those also who brought Perfumes to burn on the Altar, deliver'd their presents to the Priests.

As soon as the Sun began to appear, the Priests who stood before the Temple began their Songs and Hymns, adoring him several times on their knees; then they went one after another to cast the Incense and Perfume which they had in their hands upon the Fire, which they had before kindled on the Altar, as also upon a great Stone which stood before the entrance of the Grot: This Ceremony being ended, the chiefest of the Priests powr'd some Honey into a hollow Stone, made somwhat like those Stones wherein the Holy-water stands in some places, which Stone stood also before this Temple; and into another, which was of the same figure and the same matter, he put some corns of *Turkey*-wheat a little bruis'd, and destitute of their outward Shell, as also some other small grains, which the Birds consecrated to the Sun, called the *Tonatzuli*, do greedily feed upon: These Birds, whereof there are great numbers in the Woods which lie round about this Mountain, were so accustomed to find these Treatments which were prepar'd for them in that place, that they fail'd not to come there in great companies as soon as the Assembly was retir'd.

While the Priests continu'd burning the perfume, and celebrating the praises of the Sun, the People who were upon the Mountain having made several bowings at the rising of the Sun, entertain'd themselves afterwards in some kinds of recreation, dances, and songs, which they sung in honour of him; and afterwards sitting down on the grass, every one fell to what he had brought along with him for his *Viaticum*.

Thus they continu'd there till noon; but when it came neer that time, the Priests, quitting the gate of the Temple, went into the body of it, and disposing themselves about the Altar, which stood in the midst, they began to sing afresh: Then as soon as the Sun began to cast his golden beams on the border of the opening or Lanthorn, under which the Altar was erected

éted, they put Incense and other perfumes upon the fire which they had kindled the night before, and very carefully kept in upon that Altar : Having ended their Songs, and consum'd all their Perfumes, they all retir'd to the entrance of the Temple, before the Gate, excepting only six, who remain'd neer the Altar ; and while those who stood at the entrance lift up their Voices more then ordinary, the others who remain'd at the Altar let go out of their hands, at the same time, every one six of the *Tonatzuli*, which they had brought thither, and kept in Cages for that purpose : These Birds having flown about the Temple, and finding the entrance possessed by the Priests, who were at the Gate with Boughs in their hands, and frighted them with their Voices, took their flight out at the open place in the midst of the Temple ; and after they had flown about a while, the Assembly which was upon the Mountain entertain'd them with loud cries of rejoycing, as accounting them to have put a period to the Ceremony, and looking on them as the Children and Messengers of the Sun, they immediately got into the Woods.

As soon as these Birds were gone the people march'd down in order from the Mountain, and passing neer the Temple, the Priests, who were still in their Office, caus'd them to enter into it ; and after they had washed their hands and their faces in the Fountain, they order'd them to go out at the same entrance, which was divided by a small partition, purposely made there to prevent confusion and disorder : Then at their coming out they took another way, which led them into the Road that conducted to the Mountain, and was the same by which they had ascended ; and so every one made towards his own home.

The poor, whereof the Priests had a Catalogue, staid till all the rest were gone, and receiv'd from their hands the Garments, and all the other Presents which the rich had made to the Sun, to be distributed among them ; which done, all left the Mountain, and there was an end of the Ceremony.

But now, since the greatest and most considerable part of the people who are Inhabitants of the Provinces of *Bemarin* and *Matica*, and particularly the King and City of *Melilot*, have embraced the Christian Religion, this Mountain and its Temple are not much frequented, unless it be out of curiosity : Nor does the King permit his Subjects of the other Provinces, who have not receiv'd Baptism, to go up thither to perform their Sacrifices and all their ancient Superstitions.

They believ'd the immortality of the Soul ; but they had so disguis'd this Truth with Fables, that it was in a manner smother'd thereby. They embalm'd the bodies of their deceased Relations with several sorts of Gums and Aromatical Drugs, which had the virtue of preserving them from corruption ;

tion; and after they had kept them ſometimes above a year in their houſes, they buried them in their Gardens, or in the neighbouring Foreſts, with great lamentations and ceremonies. They ſhew to this day at the foot of the pleaſant Mountain of *Olaimi*, the Sepulchres of ſeveral of their Kings, which are cut in the Rock; there is planted before every one of them a fair Cedar, for the better obſervation of the place, and more exact continuance of their memories.

To make a greater expreſſion of their mourning, and to ſhew how much they bewail'd the death of their Friends and Kinred, they cut off ſome part of their hair; but when any King died they ſhav'd the whole head, and ſuffer'd not their hair to grow again, till they had bewail'd him for the ſpace of fifteen months.

The Knowledge which the *Apalachites* have of God, they have attain'd to by ſeveral degrees: For, to go to the bottom of the buſineſs, it is about an Age ſince that the firſt Seeds of Chriſtian Religion were ſown in that part of *Florida*, by a *French* Colony conſiſting of ſeveral Perſons of Quality, which was brought thither and eſtabliſh'd there by one Captain *Ribauld*, in the time of *Charles* the Ninth King of *France :* The firſt thing he did was to build a Fort, which he named *Carolina*, in honour of His Chriſtian Majeſty : He impos'd alſo on the Capes, Ports, and Rivers of that Country, the names they are at the preſent known by; ſo that along the Coaſt a man finds a place called the *Port Royal*, the *French Cape*, the Rivers of *Seine, Loyre, Charante, Garonne, Daufins, May, Somme,* and ſeveral other places, which have abſolute *French* names, and conſequently are a manifeſt argument that the ſaid Nation have heretofore had ſome command there.

But what is more worthy obſervation, and conduces more to our purpoſe, is, that at this firſt Expedition for *Florida*, there went along with the Adventurers two Learned and Religious Perſons, who immediately upon their arrival in the Country made it their buſineſs, by all ſorts of good offices, to inſinuate themſelves into the affections of the Inhabitants, and to learn their Language, that ſo they might give them ſome knowledge of God, and the ſacred myſteries of his Goſpel. The Memorials which Captain *Ribauld* left behind him as to that particular, ſhew how that the King *Saturiova*, who govern'd the Quarter where the *French* had eſtabliſh'd themſelves, and who had for Vaſſals to him ſeveral little Kings and Princes who were his Neighbours, receiv'd thoſe Preachers very kindly, and recommended it to all his Subjects, that they ſhould have a ſingular eſteem for them; ſo that the affection thoſe poor people bore them, and the fidelity and zeal the others expreſs'd for the advancement of their Converſion, rais'd even then very great hopes that the work of the Lord would proſper in their

I i

hands,

hands, and that that little portion of his Vineyard being carefully dreſs'd, would in time bring forth many good and precious fruits, to the praiſe of his grace.

Theſe happy beginnings and firſt-fruits of the Goſpel of our Saviour *Jeſus*, were afterwards augmented and advanc'd by the cares of Monſieur the Admiral *de Coligny*, who gave a Commiſſion to one *de Laudoniere*, to carry over thither a conſiderable ſupply of Soldiers and all ſorts of Tradeſmen, which arriv'd in the year One thouſand five hundred ſixty and four : But theſe laſt Adventurers had hardly taken the air in the Country after their arrival thither, ere the *Spaniard*, who imagines that all *America* belongs to him, and who hath ever been jealous of the *French* Nation, made his advantage of the diſorders which were then in that Country, to traverſe the generous deſigns of the Directors of that hopeful Colony, and ſmother it as 'twere in the Cradle : To that purpoſe he ſent thither *Peter Melandez* with ſix great ſhips full of men and ammunition, who fell upon it on the nineteenth of *September*, MDLXV.

Monſieur *de Laudoniere* and Captain *Ribauld*, who had not long before brought the Colony a ſmall recruit of men, conſidering that it would be madneſs to think to oppoſe ſuch a powerful force, reſolv'd, with the advice of moſt of the Officers, to capitulate and deliver up the place to the ſtronger party, upon ſuch honourable conditions as people beſieg'd are wont to demand. *Peter Melandez* granted them moſt of the Articles they had propos'd ; but aſſoon as he was got into the Fort, and had ſecur'd the Guards, he broke the promiſe he had made them, and violating the Law of Nations, he cruelly maſſacred not only the Soldiery, but alſo all the women and children, whom he found within the place, and who could not make their eſcape by flight.

Captain *Ribauld* fell in the Maſſacre ; but *de Laudoniere* made a ſhift to eſcape, through the Fenns, to the ſhips newly come from *France*, which by good fortune were ſtill in the Road : Some others of the Inhabitants, who, upon the firſt arrival of the *Spaniards*, had foreſeen the danger likely to fall upon them, got in time into the woods, and in the night time came to the Village of their good friend *Saturiova*, who, hating the *Spaniard*, gave them protection, and ſupply'd them with proviſions for a competent ſubſiſtance, till the year MDLXVII. when Captain *de Gorgues*, coming to *Florida* with three ſtout ſhips full of reſolute men and all ſorts of Ammunition, ſeverely puniſhed the cruelty of the *Spaniards*, and being aſſiſted by *Saturiova*, and all his Neighbours and Allies, he reveng'd the publick injuries of the *French*, putting to the ſword all the *Spaniards* he met with, not only in the Fort of *Carolina*, which they had repair'd and fortified after their uſurpation

pation of it, but alſo thoſe he found in two other Forts which they had built along the Coaſt, which he burnt and demoliſh'd, as may be ſeen in the xii. Chapter of the fourth Book of the Deſcription of the *Weſt-Indies*, writ by *John de Laet*.

The Memorials which Captain *de Gorgues* cauſed to be printed, giving an account of his Expedition into *Florida*, tell us of a certain *French-man* named *Peter du Bre*, who having made his eſcape to King *Saturiova*, to avoid the cruelty of the *Spaniards*, related to him, that there eſcaped of that Maſſacre but ten men, of which number he was one; that they all met with a ſafe retreat in the territories of the ſaid Prince, who liv'd not far from their deſolated Colony; that three of the eſcaped perſons dy'd there ſome months after that defeat; that of the ſeven remaining, there were ſix were ſo charm'd with the advantageous relation which the ſubjects of *Saturiova* made to them daily of the Treaſures of King *Mayra*, of the powerfulneſs of another whoſe name was *Ollaca*, who commanded forty Princes, and of the generoſity and prudent conduct of the King of *Apalacha*, who govern'd many fair and large Provinces ſeated at the foot of the Mountains, and reaching into ſeveral delightful Vales which they encompaſs'd; that they importun'd *Saturiova*, who had entertain'd them ſo kindly, that he would be pleas'd to allow them guides, to conduct them to the Frontiers of the Kingdom of the laſt named, of whom they had heard ſo many miracles, and had particularly this recommendation, that he was a lover of Strangers, and that his Subjects were the moſt civilly govern'd of all the Septentrional part of *America*; that *Saturiova*, willing to add that favour to all thoſe they had receiv'd from him before, gave them a good convoy, conſiſting of the moſt valiant of his ſubjects, to conduct them with all ſafety to all his Allies, and to the Dominions of the King of *Apalacha*, if they were deſirous to viſit him.

The relation of the ſucceſs of this Progreſs, which theſe few *French-men* undertook to ſatisfie their curioſity, and to make the beſt uſe they could of this interval of their misfortune, aſſures us, that after they had viſited *Athorus*, the Son of *Saturiova*, and moſt of his Allies, who had their Villages all along a delightful River which in their Language they call *Seloy*, to avoid meeting any of the ſubjects of *Timagoa*, who was then engag'd in a War againſt *Saturiova*, there was a neceſſity they ſhould croſs Rivers upon boughs of trees faſten'd together, climb up Mountains, and make their way through Fens and thick Foreſts, where they met with ſeveral cruel beaſts; that before they came within the Dominions of the King of *Apalacha*, they were many times ſet upon by Troops of Savages, who ſcout up and down among thoſe vaſt deſarts; that two of their Guides were kill'd in thoſe encounters, and moſt of the reſt

dange-

dangeroufly wounded ; that the fubjects of King *Timagoa*, having obferv'd their march, had follow'd them for feveral days, and not being able to overtake them, they laid ambufhes for them, thinking to have met with them in their return ; that after they had run through abundance of dangers, and many times endur'd much hunger and thirft, they got at laft to the Province of *Matica*, which is under the jurifdiction of the King of *Apalacha* ; that the Governor of the City of *Akoveka*, which is the Metroprolis of that Country, caus'd them to be brought to the King, who was then gone to vifit the Province of *Amana* ; that that Prince entertain'd them with fo much kindnefs, and exprefs'd fo much friendfhip towards them, that they refolv'd to fend back their Guides into their Country, and to fetle themfelves amongft the *Apalachites*, fince they found them anfwerable to the account they had received of them.

The remembrance of the dangers they had run through ere they could get into the Province of *Matica* ; the lively apprehenfion they had of the difficulties which were unavoidable in their return ; the little hope there was that the *French* would ever undertake the re-eftablifhment of their Colony ; the pleafantnefs and fertility of the Country into which divine Providence had brought them ; and the good natures of the Inhabitants, befides feveral other confiderations, prevail'd with them to refolve on that fetlement. But the Guides whom *Saturiova* had given them, obftructed their refolution fo much, and fo earneftly remonftrated to them, that they durft not prefent themfelves before their Lord without them, that to compofe the difference, and prevent the reproach they were afraid of at their return into their own Country, they prevail'd fo far, that two of thofe Travellers fhould come back along with them to *Saturiova*, to teftifie their care and fidelity in the execution of the Commiffion he had given them.

The fame Relation adds further, that thofe four *French-men* who voluntarily ftay'd among the *Apalachites*, being well inftructed in the ways of God, left them fome knowledge of his Sovereign Majefty : And the *Englifh*, who have fome years fince found the way into thofe Provinces, write, that the Inhabitants of the Province of *Bemarin* do ftill talk of thofe ftrangers, and it is from them that they have learnt feveral words of the *French* Language, fuch as are among others thofe that fignifie God, Heaven, Earth, Friend, the Sun, the Moon, Paradife, Hell, Yea, No. Befides which there are many other words common among thofe people, and are us'd by them to exprefs the fame thing which they fignifie in *French*.

After the death of all thefe *French-men*, who were very much lamented by all the *Apalachites*, excepting only the Priefts of the Sun, who bore them an irreconcileable hatred, becaufe they turned the People from Idolatry, and inclined
them

them to the knowledge of the true God who created the Sun, whom they adored as God, the Provinces which are seated in the Vales of the *Apalachæan* Mountains, and had been enlightned but by a very weak ray of cœlestial light, would easily have returned to the darkness of their ancient superstition, if God, by a remarkable disposal of his Providence, had not sent to them some *English* Families, which at their arrival thither blew up that little spark, which lay hid under the embers, into a weak flame.

These Families came out of *Virginia* in the year M DC XXI. with an intention to go to *New-England*, to avoid the frequent incursions and massacres committed there by the Savages; but the wind proving contrary to their design, they were cast on the Coasts of *Florida*, whence they pass'd into the Province of *Matica*, and thence into those of *Amana* and *Bemarin*, and in the last they setled themselves, and have drawn thither a considerable number of Ecclesiasticks and persons of quality, who have there laid the foundations of a small Colony. Most of those who are retir'd into those places so remote from all commerce in the world, undertook that generous design, in the midst of the great revolutions which happen'd in *England* during the late troubles, and the main business they propos'd to themselves at that time, was only to make their advantage of so seasonable a retreat, that they might the more seriously, and with less distraction, mind the attainment of their own salvation, and dilate the limits of Christianity among those poor people, if God gave them the means.

We understand also by the last papers that have been sent us from *America*, that, God blessing the endeavours of the first Inhabitants of this small Colony, they have within these twelve or thirteen years baptiz'd most of the Officers and the most considerable Heads of Families in the Provinces of *Bemarin* and *Amana*; That at the present, they have a Bishop and many learned and zealous Ecclesiasticks among them, who carry on the work of the Lord; and the more to advance it, they have built Colledges in all those places where there are Churches, that the Children of the *Apalachites* may be instructed in the mysteries of Christian Religion and true piety.

The same Papers add further, that though the King of *Apalacha* hath received Baptism, and seems to have much affection for these Strangers, who have procur'd him that happiness; yet hath he of late entertain'd some jealousie of them, out of an apprehension, as it was represented to him by some of his Councel, that if he suffer'd them to grow more numerous, they might in time become Masters of the Country : He thereupon in the first place dispers'd them into several Cities, that they might not be able to make any considerable body, or foment any factions; and afterwards, there was an order pass'd, that

all

all thofe who have at the prefent any fetlement in the bofom of his Country, might peaceably continue in their habitations, and participate of the fame priviledges with the Natives, provided they held no correfpondence with any abroad, to the prejudice of the publick tranquillity; but that henceforward no other ftrangers fhall be permitted to make any further eftablifhments there.

Thofe who are acquainted with the Nature of the Country, affirm, that the King of the *Apalachites* hath no juft caufe to fear that either the *Englifh* or any other ftrangers fhould be guilty of any defign againft him, as to the maftering of his Country: For, befides the neceffity there is of having a very powerful Army, ere any fuch enterprife can be undertaken, and that the *Englifh* who are eftablifh'd there, are no more amongft that great Nation, than a handful of fand on the Sea-fide; this Country being fo remote from all the reft of the world, and deftitute of Gold, Silver, precious Stones, and in a manner all rich Commodities, whereby Commerce is kept up and continu'd; it is moft certain, that it will never be much fought after or envy'd by any *Europæan* Nations, which fend out Colonies only to thofe places, where there is hope of making fome confiderable advantage by way of Trade. Whereto may be added this further confideration, that, though thefe Provinces were poffefs'd of as great Treafures and Rarities, as they are deftitute thereof; yet lying at a great diftance from Sea-Ports, and having no navigable Rivers falling into it, by means whereof there might in time be fome correfpondence between them and other parts, there is no likelihood that there fhould be many perfons either in *England* or any where elfe, who would be perfwaded to crofs over fo many Seas, to go and end their days in a Country which is deftitute of all thofe conveniences, and cannot receive thofe refrefhments which are brought out of *Europe*, and contribute much to the comfortable fubfiftance of all the other Colonies of *America*; and in a word, a Country, which can give its Inhabitants nothing but clothing and nourifhment.

Some time after the *Englifh* had eftablifh'd themfelves in this Country, as we have reprefented before, the *Spaniards* (who as it were keep the keys of one part of *Florida*, by means of the Forts they have built near the moft eminent Havens, and along the moft confiderable Rivers) brought in there a company of religious men of the Order of the *Minimes*, whom Pope *Urban* the eighth had fent into the Septentrional *America*, in the quality of *Apoftolical Miffionaries*, and endow'd with moft ample priviledges, for their better encouragement in the carrying on of that work: They arriv'd in thofe Provinces in the year, One thoufand fix hundred forty and three; and fince that time they have taken their progrefs through moft of

the

the Villages that lie about the great Lake, and upon the descent of the Mountains which look towards the Country of the *Cofachites*: It is reported, that they have baptized with great pomp the *Paracoussis* of the Province of *Achalaca*, and a great number of his Subjects.

When these religious men return from their Missions, they live in a solitary, yet delightful place, which lies upon the descent of a high Mountain, not above a quarter of a league distant from the great Lake, and about as much from the greatest Village of the Province of *Achalaca*. Before a man comes to their habitation, he must cross through several fair Gardens, in the midst whereof there is a pleasant walk, planted with trees on both sides, which reaches to the skirt of the Mountain: And though they have seated themselves on an eminent place, yet they have many springs, which, falling down from the upper part of the Mountains, are receiv'd into great Cisterns and great Ponds, where they have abundance of good Fish: The Lord of the Country visits them often, and hath a great respect for them; for the most part, he hath some one of them about his person, who serves him as a Chaplain.

In the year One thousand six hundred fifty and three, in which Mr. *Brigstock*, that most inquisitive *English* Gentleman, from whom we have receiv'd all the account we have given of the *Apalachites*, arriv'd in that Province of *Achalaca*, the foremention'd Religious men entertain'd him very kindly, and did him all the good offices lay in their power: From them it was, that, during his aboad in the Country, he learnt all the particulars we are now going to describe, and which he hath liberally communicated to us.

They show'd him an admirable Flower, which grows abundantly in the Mountains of those parts: The figure of this Flower is much like that of a Bell, and there are as many colours observable in it as in the Rain-bow; the under leaves, which being fully blown, are much larger than those of our greatest Roses, are charged with a great many other leaves, which appear still less and less to the lower part or bottom of the Bell: Out of the midst of them there rises a little button, like a heart, which is of a very delicious taste: The Plant hath a little bushiness at the top, much like Sage: The leaves and the flower smell like a Violet: It is also a kind of sensitive Plant, for it cannot be touch'd, either in its leaves or flower, but it immediately withers.

These Religious men carryed the said *English* Gentleman to a Village of the *Indians*, who inhabit in the Mountains, where there is a miraculous Grott or Cave, wherein the waters have fashion'd all the most delightful rarities, that a man can desire from a divertisment of that kind: They shew'd him particularly

larly one place in the said Grott, where the waters falling upon a bare stone, and distilling drop after drop, of a different
bigness, make so exact a musick, that there is no harmony can
well be preferr'd before it.

There is found in the Mountains, on the East-side of the Province of *Achalaca*, some Rock-Christal, and certain red and
bright stones, which have such a lustre as that they might pass
for right Rubies: 'Tis possible there may be some Copper-
mines in those parts; but they are not yet discovered, only
what confirms this opinion is, that they find a kind of golden
sand there, which is wash'd down by the torrents, and hath a
wonderful lustre: Mr. *Brigstock* having given of it to some
Goldsmiths to make a test thereof, it was in a manner quite consum'd by the fire, and the little that remained in the Crucible
might well pass for very fine Copper.

These same Religious men shew'd the said Gentleman, as
they pass'd through the woods, several sorts of trees which
yielded Gums of excellent scent, as also many other Rarities,
a particular account whereof would require a considerable Volume: But above all, they show'd him the tree, whereof the
Floridians make that excellent drink which they call *Casina*,
the description whereof may be seen in the History of *de Laet*.
It is absolutely conformable to the Relation of Mr. *Brigstock*,

Before the Inhabitants of *Achalacha* were converted to Christianity, they took several Wives; but now their Marriages
are regulated, and they content themselves only with one:
They interr'd their Lords as the *Apalachites* do, in the Caves
that are at the foot of the Mountains: then they made up the
entrance thereof with a stone-wall: they hung before the
Cave the most considerable Vessels which those Princes had
made use of at their Tables: And all the Captains fasten'd
all about the place, their Bows, Arrows, and Clubs, and mourn-
ed for several days at the Sepulchre: They worshipped the
Sun, and held the immortality of the Soul as well as their
Neighbours: They believ'd also that such as had liv'd well,
and serv'd the Sun as they ought, and made many presents to
the poor, in honour of him, were hapyy, and that after death
they were chang'd into Stars: But on the contrary, that those
who had led a wicked life, were carried into the precipices of
the high Mountains, whereby they were surrounded, and there
endur'd extream want and misery, amongst the Lions, Tygers,
and other beasts of prey, which hunt after their sustenance
therein.

The Inhabitants of this Country are all long-liv'd, insomuch
that there are many among them, both men and women, who
are neer two hundred years of age.

This curious digression we receiv'd from the forementioned
English Gentleman, Mr. *Brigstock*, and we have inserted it
here

here, out of a preſumption that it will not be undelightful to
thoſe, who ſhall make it their divertiſement to read this Hiſtory; at leaſt while we are yet in expectation that that excellent
perſon will give us a perfect accompt of the ſtate of the *Apalachites*, and ſome others of the Neighbouring Nations, as he
puts us in hope that he will.

CHAP. IX.

Of the Bodies of the Caribbians, *and their Ornaments.*

WE are now to re-aſſume our former diſcourſe, and return from *Florida* to the *Caribby-Iſlands*, to conſider
there, with all the exactneſs imaginable, what concerns thoſe
Inhabitants thereof on whom we intend to beſtow the remaining part of this Hiſtory, and particularly what relates to their
Bodies, Minds, Diſpoſitions, Manners, Religion, Cuſtoms, and
other remarkable occurrences concerning the ſavage *Caribbians* or *Cannibals*, of whoſe origine we have already given ſo
large an account.

And whereas ſome of the *Caribbians* who inhabit in the ſame
Iſlands wherein the *French* and other *Europæan* Nations have
planted *Colonies*, or at leaſt come often among them, accommodate themſelves in many things to their manner of life, and
that they may be the more kindly received by them, they quit
many of their old Cuſtoms; thoſe who are deſirous to be acquainted with the ancient manners of the *Caribbians*, are not to
learn them of the *Caribbians* who live in *Martinico*, or thoſe
who converſe moſt with the *Europæans*; but from thoſe of St.
Vincent, who of all others have held leaſt correſpondence with
any Forreigners: It is accordingly from them that we have receiv'd what we ſhall hereafter relate concerning the *Caribbians*: But before we enter into the relation, we ſhall make ſome
general obſervations, to prevent the aſtoniſhment which the
Reader might conceive at the difference there is between the
account we give of them, and what he may receive from others,
either by word of mouth or writing.

In the firſt place, it is to be acknowledged a thing almoſt impoſſible, that the Relations of Countries and Cuſtoms at ſo
great a diſtance from us, ſhould agree in all things, eſpecially
ſince we find that thoſe of neighbouring Countries are for the
moſt part differing among themſelves.

Secondly, it is to be obſerved, that ſince the *Caribbians* became familiar, and have converſed with forreign Nations, they
have remitted much of their ancient Cuſtoms, and quited many
K k   things

things which they practis'd before with an inviolable strictness: So that there may be seen in them now a remarkable change from what they were heretofore: That the case stands thus with them now, is to be attributed partly to the conversation of the *Europæans*, who in some things have oblig'd them to abate somewhat of their original simplicity; and in others have made them worse than they were, as to our own shame we cannot but acknowledge: Hence it comes that Monsieur *du Montel* tells us in his Relations, that two ancient *Caribbians*, considering that degeneration of their Country-men, took occasion to entertain him with a discourse to this purpose: "Our "people are become in a manner like yours, since they came "to be acquainted with you; and we find it some difficulty to "know our selves, so different are we grown from what we "have been heretofore: It is to this alteration that our peo-"ple attribute the more frequent happening of *Hurricanes* than "they were observ'd to be in the days of old; and conclude "thence, that *Maboya* (that is to say, the evil spirit) hath reduc'd "us under the power of the *French, English, Spaniards* and others, "who have driven us out of the best part of our Country.

Thirdly, it is possible they may have different Customs, according to the diversity of the Islands, though they all make up but one people; as may be observed in the diversity of the Customs of one and the same Kingdom, according to the several Quarters and Provinces of it: Whence it may have proceeded, for example, that those that have conversed most at *Dominico* will give an account of the Opinions, Customs, and Ceremonies of the *Caribbians*, much different from what shall be related thereof by those persons who shall have frequented other places; and yet the Relations of either side shall be true.

Fourthly, as in the Continent of *America*, the *Caribbians*, who inhabit a good way within the Country, and consequently seldom see any forreigners, retain much more of their ancient Customs, and their old course of life, than those who living neer the *Dutch* Colonies of *Cayenna* and *Berbica*, drive on an ordinary trade with the Christians; so among our *Caribbians*, the Inhabitants of the Islands, those who converse least with the *Europæans*, such as are those of St. *Vincent*'s, are more strict observers of their ancient course of life, than are, for example, those of *Martinico* or *Dominico*, who are oftner seen among them.

Fifthly, thence it proceeds that those persons who have seen them only in these last mentioned places, or have heard of them only from such as have been acquainted with them only in those places, will haply find many things in the prosecution of our History, which may clash with the Relations they had received of them from others; which if they do, they are not to wonder

der therear, ſince moſt of our Obſervations relate to the *Ca-*
ribbians of *St. Vincents.*

Laſtly, we deſire our Readers to take this further adver-
tiſement, that it is our deſign to give a deſcription of the ancient Manners and Cuſtoms of theſe *Caribbians,* to the end that
no body may think it ſtrange, if their preſent demeanour be
not in all things anſwerable thereto : Theſe advertiſements being thus premis'd, we proceed to give the Reader ſatisfaction
conſequently to the title of this Chapter.

Moſt of thoſe people whom we call *Barbarians* and *Savages,*
have ſome thing hideous and deformed or defective, either in
their Countenances or ſome other part of the body, as Hiſtorians affirm of the *Maldiveſes,* the Inhabitants about the
Magellane ſtreights, and ſeveral others which we need not name
here.

But the *Caribbians* are a handſome well-ſhap'd people, well
proportion'd in all parts of their bodies, gracefull enough, of
a ſmiling countenance, middle ſtature, having broad ſhoulders,
and large buttocks, and they are moſt of them in good plight,
and ſtronger than the *French*: Their mouths are not over large,
and their teeth are perfectly white and cloſe : True it is their
complexion is naturally of an Olive-colour, and that colour
ſpreads even into the whites of their Eyes, which are black,
ſomewhat little like thoſe of the *Chineſes* and *Tartars,* but very
piercing: Their foreheads and noſes are flat, not naturally,
but by artifice : For their mothers cruſh them down at their
birth, as alſo continually during the time they ſuckle them,
imagining it a kind of beauty and perfection; for were it
not for that, their noſes would be well ſhap'd, and they would
have high foreheads as well as we : They have large and thick
feet, becauſe they go barefoot, but they are withall ſo hard,
that they defie Woods and Rocks.

Among thoſe of the Country a man cannot meet with any
wanting either one or both eyes, lame, crook-back'd, or bald,
or having any other deformity naturally; as is in like manner
affirmed of the *Braſilians,* the *Floridians,* and moſt Nations of *De Lery c.8.*
America; whereas thoſe who have walked through *Grand* *Voyage de*
Cairo relate, That in the Streets they have met with many one- *Breves.*
eyed, and many ſtark blind people; thoſe infirmities being ſo
frequent and ſo popular in that Country, that of ten perſons
five or ſix are ſubject thereto: But if any among the *Caribbi-*
ans are thus deformed, or have loſt, or are maimed in any limb,
it hapned in ſome Engagement againſt their Enemies; and ſo
thoſe ſcars or deformities being ſo many demonſtrations of their
Valour, they glory in them; ſo far are they from being in any
danger of miſchief, or being caſt into a furnace by their Country-men, as thoſe poor Children were among the people of
Guyana, and among the *Lacedemonians* in the time of *Lycurgus,*

K k 2

who

who came out of their Mothers wombs imperfect and deformed.
Nay, there are some handsom Maids and Women amongst the
Savage *Caribbians,* witness *Madamoiselle de Rosselan,* wife to the
Governour of *Saintaloufia.*

Trigaut.Hist.   All the *Caribbians* are black-hair'd, as the *Chinefes* are , who
Chin.l.1.c.8. for that reason are sometimes call'd the *Black-hair'd* People:
The hair of the *Caribbians* is not curl'd or frizzled, as that of
the *Moors,* but streight and long, as those of the *Maldivefes:*
And the Women attribute the highest perfection of Beauty to
this black colour, as to what concerns the hair. It is reported
Garcilaffo, also, That the *Indian* Women of *Peru* are so enamour'd of
l. 8. c. 13. black hair, that to make their own of that colour by artifice,
when Nature does it not, they are willing to endure incredible
pains and torments: On the contrary, in *Spain* many Ladies,
to make their hair seem to be of a golden yellow colour, perfume it with *Sulphur,* steep it in *Aqua-fortis,* and expofe it to
the Sun in the heat of the day, nay in the very Dog-days: And
in *Italy* the same colour is much affected.

The *Caribbians* are very careful in combing themselves, and
they think it commendable so to do: They anoint their hair
with Oil, and have certain Receipts to advance the growth
thereof: The Women commonly comb their Husbands and
their Children : Both Men and Women tie up their hair towards the hinder part of the head, winding it about so as that
it stands up like a horn on the Crown; on both sides they leave
locks hanging down like so many Muftachioes, according to
natural liberty. The Women part their hair so as that it falls
down on both sides of their heads; but the men part theirs the
quite contrary way, so as that one half falls down behind, the
other before, which obliges them to cut off the fore-part of it,
otherwise it would fall down over their eyes: This they did
heretofore with certain sharp Herbs, before they had the use
of Scissers; not to mention, that they were also accuftomed to
cut off their hair when they were in mourning; whereas on the
contrary, in *Madagafcar* the Men never cut off their hair, but
the Women shave it clear off; a custom contrary to that of
those people among whom S. *Paul* liv'd.

The *Caribbians* seem not to have any Beards at all, but as
soon as they grow they pluck them off by the roots, as the *Bra-*
Carpin in *filians,* the *Cumanefes,* and certain Nations subject to the Em-
Bergeron. pire of the *Tartars* do, who have always an iron inftrument in
their hands, wherewith they pluck out the hair of their Beards
as soon as they come out: But the *Caribbians* are seldom seen
to put themselves to that trouble, insomuch that it is conceiv'd
they have a secret to prevent the growth of hair when it is once
gotten off; an invention which would have been of great convenience to the ancient *Romans*: For it is affirm'd, that they
would not suffer their Beards to grow till after the time of the
Emperour

Emperour *Adrian*, who first suffer'd his to grow; before that time it was thought among them so honourable a thing to wear no beard, that there was a prohibition made that Slaves should not shave theirs: The same prohibition extended also to all persons charg'd with any Crime, as it were to set a mark of infamy on them, till such time as they were clear'd, as *Aulus Gellius* affirms; which proceeding was contrary to what is pra-ctis'd in the *Grand Seignior's* Territories, who causes the Beard to be shaven, as a mark of ignominy: In the year One thousand six hundred fifty two, that hapned to the *French* Consul at *Alexandria*, being charg'd with having done some unhandsom things in his Employment; his Beard had such a natural graceful curl, and was of so fair a flaxen colour, that some Turks would have given him a considerable sum of money for it, and kept it for a Rarity; but he chose rather to bring it along with him into *France*.

   The *Caribbians* wonder very much to see our *Europeans* suffer their Beards to grow so long, and think it a great deformity to wear any, as they account it a perfection in themselves to have none; but they are not the only Savages who are fantastick in matter of gracefulness and beauty: All barbarous Nations, nay some that are civiliz'd, are wedded to their particular sentiments, as to that point: For instance, among the *Maldiveses* it is accounted an accomplishment of Beauty to have the body all over hairy, which among us would be thought more becoming a Bear then a Man: Among the *Mexicans*, to have a little narrow forehead, and that full of hair: Among the *Japoneses*, not to have any hair at all; whence it comes, that they are ever employ'd in the plucking of it off, leaving only a little tuft on the crown of the head: Among the *Tartarian* Women it is thought a piece of Beauty to be flat-nos'd, but to heighten the attractions of their noses, they rub them with a very black unguent: Among the Inhabitants of *Guinny* they make the same account of great nails and flat noses; and thence it comes that assoon as the children are come into the world, they crush down their noses with their thumbs, as do also the *Brasilians*: Among those of the Province of *Cusco* in *Peru*, and some oriental Inhabitants of the *Indies*, as also among the *Calecutians*, and the *Malabars*, it is thought very graceful to have extraordinary large ears, hanging down over their shoulders; insomuch that some among them use divers artifices to make them such: Among the *Æthiopians*, great lips and a skin black as Jet, are thought beautiful: The Negroes of *Mosambico* are extreamly pleas'd to have their teeth very sharp, so that some use Files to make them such: Among the *Maldiveses* they are no less desirous to have them red, and to that end, they are continually chewing of *Petel*: Among the *Japoneses* and the *Cumaneses*, they are industrious to have

them

them black, and they purpofely make them fuch : And among the latter, it is accounted beauty to have a long face, lean cheeks, and exceffively big legs: And hence it is that they fqueeze the heads of their children between two cufhions as foon as they are born, and that after the example of the Inhabitants about the River of *Effequebe*, they bind the legs very hard a little below the knee, and a little above the ankle, that fo the calf may fwell : Among fome *Peruvians*, to have the face cut and chequer'd, as it were with Lancets, and to have flat and broad heads, huge foreheads, and the head very narrow from the forehead to the nape of the neck, is accounted beautiful : And to reduce it to this comely fhape, they kept their childrens heads prefs'd between two thin boards, from the time of their birth till they were four or five year old. To be fhort, among fome oriental Nations, and fome *Africans*, it is accounted a great perfection in the Women, to have their breafts hanging down over their fhoulders; and among the *Chinefes*, it is the principal part of beauty to have the foot extreamly little and thin; and the better to have it fo, while they are yet children they bind their feet fo hard, that they are in a manner lam'd, and it is with much ado that they are able to ftand : It were a hard matter to make a defcription of beauty, according to the different opinions of all thefe nations: But to return to the *Caribbians*.

They go ftark-naked, both men and women, as many other Nations do : And if any one among them fhould endeavour to hide the privy parts, all the reft would laugh at it : Though the Chriftians have converfed very much among them, yet have all the perfwafions that have hitherto been ufed to induce them to cover themfelves been to no purpofe : And whereas fometimes, when they come to vifit the Chriftians, or to treat with them, they have comply'd fo far with them, as to cover themfelves, by putting on a fhirt, drawers, a hat, and fuch cloaths as had been given them, yet affoon as they were return'd to their own habitations, they ftrip themfelves, and put up all in their Clofets, till fome fuch other occafion fhould oblige them to put them on again : To requite this compliance of the *Caribbians*, fome among the *French*, having occafion to go among them, made no difficulty to ftrip themfelves after their example : This defiance of cloaths reigns in all places under the Torrid Zone, as every one knows.

Vin. Le Blanc. par. 3. c. 16.

Dutch Relations.

When the *Brafilians* are reproach'd with their nakednefs, they reply, that we came naked into the world, and that it were a mad thing for us to hide the bodies beftowed on us by nature. The Inhabitants of the Kingdom of *Benin* in *Africa*, are to be commended, that they cover themfelves when they are to be married, and would do it fooner if their King would permit it: The women of the *Lucayan* Iflands ought alfo to

par-

participate of that commendation, for they were wont to cover themselves when they came to be marriageable, and solemnized that action with great rejoicing : But now that custome is abrogated, for that poor Nation hath been utterly destroy'd by the *Spaniards*, or carryed away and made slaves to work in the Mines, and there are not in any of the Islands known under that name, any of the natural Inhabitants, but only some few *English* who were transported thither out of the Island of *Bermudez*. But come we to the Ornaments of our Savages.

They change their natural colour by dying their bodies with some composition which makes them red all over: For living neer Rivers and Springs, the first thing they do every morning is to go and wash themselves all over: And this was the practice of the ancient *Germans*, as *Tacitus* affirms. Assoon as the *Caribbians* have wash'd themselves, they return to their houses, and drie themselves by a little fire ; being dry'd, the Wife, or some one of the houshold takes a gourd full of a certain red composition which they call *Roucou*, from the name of the tree which produces it, and whereof we have given an account in its proper place in the precedent Book : With this colour mixt with oil, they rub the whole body and the face ; the better to apply this paint, they make use of a spunge instead of a Pencil ; and to appear more gallant, they many times make black circles about the eyes, with the juice of *Junipa* Apples.

Lib. de mor. German.

This red painting serves them both for Ornament and for a Covering ; for besides the Beauty they imagine to themselves therein, they affirm that it makes them more supple and active ; which may be the more likely to be true, for that the ancient Wrestlers were wont to rub themselves with oil for the same end : They affirm further, That by rubbing themselves thus with *Roucou*, they secure themselves against the coldness of the night and rains, the stinging of the *Mesquitos* and the *Maringoins*, and the heat of the Sun, which otherwise would cause risings and ulcers in the skin: This Unction hardens their skins, and withal gives it an extraordinary lustre and smoothness, as all know who have seen and felt them.

Most Savages do thus paint and trick up themselves after a strange manner ; but they do not all use the same colours, nor observe the same fashion : For there are some who paint their Bodies all red, as our Inhabitants of the *Caribbies* do ; as for instance, those of the *Cape de Lopes Gonsalvez* ; but others make use of other colours, as Black, White, Chestnut, Gingioline, Blew, Yellow, and the like. Some use only one particular colour ; others paint themselves with several colours, and represent divers figures on their bodies: Some others, without applying any colour, rub themselves all over with the oil of Palmtrees :

This is affirmed by divers Historians.

trees :

trees: Some anoint themfelves with the oil of Balm, and then caft on it a fmall powder, which feems as if it were the filings of Gold.   In fine, there are fome who anoint their bodies with a glewy oil, and blow on that the downe or fmalleft Feathers of divers Birds; or haply they cover themfelves with a kind of gummy pafte, which is of a very fweet fcent, and faften thereon the moft delightful Flowers growing in their Country. There is fufficient choice of all thefe modes; and it were a pleafant fight to fee a company of thefe Morris-dancers dancing together.   We might add thereto, to make the divertifement the more compleat, thofe *Turkish Pilgrims* who commonly go in long Garments made of thoufands of pieces of all forts of colours.

But this is to be noted, That the painting of the body is a very ancient kind of Ornament; and among other Monuments *Lib.22.c.1.* of this piece of Antiquity, *Pliny* and *Herodian* affirm, that cer-*In the life of* tain people of *Great Brittany*, not ufing any kind of cloathing, *Severus.* painted their bodies with divers colours, and reprefented thereon the figures of certain living Creatures, whence they were called *Picti*, that is, Painted people.   But among all the Savages who at this day paint themfelves, the *Caribbians* have this advantage, that they adorn themfelves with a colour which the Ancients honour'd moft of any; for it is reported, that the *Goths* made ufe of Vermilion to make their faces red; and the *Lib.33.c.7.* ancient *Romans*, as *Pliny* affirms, painted their bodies with *Minium* upon the day of their Triumph; and he particularly tells us that *Camillus* did fo: and he further adds, that upon Feftival days they fo painted the face of the Statue of their *Jupiter*; and that heretofore the *Æthiopians* made fo great account of this Vermilion colour, that their principal Lords apply'd it all over their bodies, and that their Gods wore it in their Images.

Our *Caribbians* do for the moft part content themfelves with this ordinary drefs of red painting, which ferves them inftead of Shirts, Cloths, Cloaks and Coats: But on folemn days and times of publick rejoicing, they add to the red divers other colours, fpreading them fantaftically over the face and the whole body.

But this kind of painting is not the only ornament in ufe among them; they adorn the crown of the head with a little Hat made of birds feathers, of different colours, or with a Plume of *Herons* feathers, or thofe of fome other Bird: They alfo fometimes wear a crown of feathers, which covers their heads, fo that there may be feen among them a great many crowned heads, though there be no Kings: And yet they may be better look'd upon as Kings with their feather Crowns, than the Lord of the Gulf of *Antongil* be taken for a Sovereign Prince, when he hath for his Scepter and the badge of his
Royal

Royal dignity, but a great Gardiner's Pruning-hook, which he always carries about him.

The women among the *Maldeveſes*, make about a dozen holes in each ear, at which they faſten little gilt nails, and ſometimes Pearls and Precious Stones: The Ladies of *Madagaſcar* and *Braſil* make a hole as big as that a man may thruſt his thumb through it in the lower part of the ear, at which they hang pendants of wood and bone: And the *Peruvians*, under the reign of their Kings the *Incas*, were accuſtomed to make in their ears a hole of an incredible bigneſs, at which they faſtened chains of a quarter of an Ell in length, with Pendants of Gold at the bottom, of an extraordinary bigneſs: But our *Caribbians* are content with a ſmall hole, according to the *Europæan* mode, in the ſofteſt part of the ear, through which they put the bones of certain Fiſhes very ſmooth, pieces of that kind of *Tortoiſe* ſhells which they call *Carets*; and ſince the Chriſtians came among them, Buckles of Gold, Silver, Latten, at which they hang very fair Pendants: They know how to diſtinguiſh between thoſe that are right and the counterfeit, but they are moſt taken with ſuch as are made of Chryſtal, Amber, Coral, or ſome other rich material, provided the buckle, and all the other workmanſhip be of Gold: Some have endeavoured to put upon them ſuch as were only Copper gilt, and would have perſwaded them they were Gold; but they refuſed them, ſaying that they intended to deceive them, and that it was but *Kettle-gold*: and to make a tryal thereof, they were wont to put them into their mouths: So great is their experience in theſe things beyond thoſe of *Madagaſcar*, who when the *Hollanders* coming thither in the year MDCXLV. offered them a Silver-ſpoon, put it between their teeth, and finding it was hard refus'd it, deſiring one of Tin: Whence it may eaſily be imagined what account they made of Tin, ſince they gave a young maid in exchange for a Spoon of that mettal. *Herodotus* affirms that heretofore among the *Æthiopians*, Copper was in better eſteem than Gold, the uſe whereof was ſo vile, that they bound Malefactors with chains of Gold.

The *Caribbians* do ſometimes alſo make holes through their lips, and put through them a kind of little Bodkin, which is made of the bone of ſome beaſt or fiſh: Nay they bore through the ſpace between the Noſtrils, that they may hang there ſome Ring, a grain of Chryſtal, or ſome ſuch toy: The necks and arms of our *Caribbians* have alſo their reſpective ornaments; for they have their Neck-laces and Bracelets of Amber, Coral, or ſome other glittering material: The men wear Bracelets on the brawny part of the arm, neer the ſhoulder; but the women wear theirs about the wriſts: They adorn alſo their legs with Chains of *Raſſada*, inſtead of Garters: Thoſe among them who have no acquaintance with the *Europæans*, commonly wear about their necks Whistles made of the bones of their enemies, and great chains made of the teeth of *Agoutys*, Tygers, wild Cats, or little shells bor'd through and fasten'd together with a thread of fine Cotton of a red or violet colour: And when they would make the greatest show they can, they add to all this a kind of Caps, certain Bracelets, which they fasten under their armpits, Scarfs, and Girdles of Feathers very industriously dispos'd together by a delightful intermixture, which they suffer to hang down over their shoulders, or from the navel to the middle of the thigh.

But the most considerable of all their Ornaments, are certain large Medals of fine Copper extreamly well polished, without any graving on them, which are made after the figure of a crescent, and enchac'd in some kind of solid and precious wood; these in their own language they call *Caracolis*: They are of different largeness, for there are some so small that they hang them at their ears like Pendants, and others about the bigness of the palm of a mans hand, which they have hanging about their necks, beating on their breasts: They have a great esteem for these *Caracolis*, aswell by reason the material whereof they are made, which never contracts any rust, glisters like Gold, as that it is the rarest and most precious booty they get in the incursions they make every year into the Country of the *Arouagues* their Enemies; and that it is the livery or badge, whereby the Captains and their Children are distinguish'd from the ordinary sort of people: Accordingly those who have any of these jewels make so great account of them, that when they die, they have no other inheritance to leave their Children and intimate Friends: Nay there are some among them who have of these *Caracolis* which had been their Grandfathers, wherewith they do not adorn themselves but on extraordinary occasions.

The women paint the whole body, and adorn themselves much after the same manner as the men do, excepting only those differences we have mentioned before, and that they wear no Crowns on their heads: There is this also particularly observable in them, that they wear a kind of buskins, which fall no lower than the ankle: This kind of ornament is very neatly wrought, and edg'd above and below with a certain intertexture of rushes and cotton, which lying streight on the calf of the leg makes it seem more full.

CHAP.

CHAP. X.

Certain Remarks upon the Caribbian *Language.*

IT is our intention at the end of this Hiſtory, for the ſatisfaction of the more curious Reader, to add a large Vocabulary of the *Caribbian* Language ; and therefore, in this Chapter, we ſhall only make ſome principal remarks upon it, ſuch as may in ſome meaſure diſcover the grace, the ſmoothneſs, and the proprieties thereof.

1. The *Caribbians* have an ancient and natural Language, ſuch as is wholly peculiar to them, as every Nation hath that which is proper to it.

2. But beſides that ancient Language, they have fram'd another baſtard-ſpeech, which is intermixt with ſeveral words taken out of forreign Languages, by the commerce they have had with the *Europæans :* But above all they have borrowed many words of the *Spaniards,* for they were the firſt Chriſtians that came among them.

3. Among themſelves, they alwaies make uſe of their ancient and natural Language.

4. But when they have occaſion to converſe or negotiate with the Chriſtians, they always make uſe of their corrupt Language.

5. Beſides that, they have alſo a very pleaſant intermixture of words and expreſſions when they would undertake to ſpeak in ſome forreign Language : As for example, when they uſe this expreſſion to the *French,* ſaying, *Compere Governeur,* that is, Goſſip Governour, uſing the word *Compere* generally towards all thoſe who are their Friends or Allies: In like manner they would ſay, without any more ceremony, *Compere Roy,* that is, Goſſip, or Friend King, if there were any occaſion to do it: It is alſo one of their ordinary complements to the *French* , when they ſay with ſmiling countenance, *Ah ſi toy bon pour Caraibe, moy bon pour France, If thou art good for the* Caribbian, *I am good for* France : And when they would commend, and expreſs how much they are ſatisfy'd with thoſe of the ſame Nation, they ſay, *Mouche bon France pour Caraibe,* France *is very good for the* Caribbian; they ſay alſo, *Maboya mouche fache contre Caraibe,* Maboya *doth much againſt the* Caribbian, *when it thunders, or in a Hurricane ;* and, *Moy mouche Lunes, I have lived many Moons,* to ſignifie that they are very ancient : They have alſo theſe words often in their mouths, when they find that the *French* would abuſe their ſimplicity, *Compere, toy trompe Caraibe, Friend thou deceiveſt the* Caribbian:

And they are often heard to say when they are in a good humour, *Moy bonne Caraibe, I am an honest* Caribbian.

6. Yet is it to be observ'd, that though the *Caribbians* of all the Islands do generally understand one another, yet is there in several of them some dialect different from that of the others.

7. There is no great use made of the letter *P.* in their Language; but that only excepted, there is no want of letters, as there is in the Language of *Japan*, *Braseel* and *Canada*, which want the letters *F. L. R.* Or in that of *Peru*, wherein *B. D. F. G. J.* consonant and *X* are wanting, as Historians affirm.

8. The Language of the *Caribbians* is extreamly smooth, and for the most part pronounced with the lips, some few words with the teeth, and in a manner nothing at all from the throat. For though the words we shall set down hereafter, seem to be rough, as they are written, yet when they pronounce them, they make elisions of certain letters, and give such an air thereto as renders their discourse very delightful to the ear: Whence it came, that *Monsieur du Montel* hath given this testimony of them: " I took great pleasure, said he, in hearkning " unto them when I was among them, and I could not suffici- " ently admire the grace, the fluency, and the sweetness of their " pronunciation, which they commonly accompany with a lit- " tle smiling, such as takes very much with those who converse " with them.

9. The *Caribbians* who are Inhabitants of the Islands have a sweeter pronunciation than those of the Continent: but otherwise they differ only in a dialect.

10. By the same word, according as it is diversly pronounced they signifie several things : For example, the word *Anban* signifies, 1. *Yes*, 2. *I know not*, 3. *Thine*, or *take it*, according to the pronunciation that is given it.

11. The *Europæans* cannot pronounce the *Caribbian* Language with the grace and fluency natural thereto, unless they have learnt it very young.

12. They hear one another very patiently, and never interrupt one the other in their discourse: But they are wont to give a little hem at the end of every three or four periods, to express the satisfaction they have to hear what is spoken.

13. What advantage soever the *Europæans* may imagine they have over the *Caribbians*, either as to the natural faculties of the mind, or the easiness of pronunciation of their own Languages, in order to the more easie attainment of theirs, yet hath it been found by experience, that the *Caribbians* do sooner learn ours than we do theirs.

14. Some among the *French* have observ'd, that the *Caribbians* have a kind of aversion for the *English* tongue, nay so far, that some affirm they cannot endure to hear it spoken

where

where they are, becaufe they look on them as their Enemies. And whereas there are in their corrupt Language many words taken out of the *Spanifh*, a people whom they alfo account their Enemies, it proceeds hence, that they learn'd them during the time they held a fair correfpondence with that Nation, and before they began to treat them as they afterwards did.

15. They are very fhie in communicating their Language, out of a fear the fecrets of their Wars might be difcovered; nay, thofe among them who have embrac'd the Chriftian Religion, would not be perfwaded to reveal the grounds of their Language, out of a belief it might prejudice their Nation.

16. We fhall here fet down fome of the moft particular proprieties of their Language : In the firft place, the men have many expreffions proper only to themfelves, which the women underftand well enough, but never pronounce : And the women have alfo their words and phrafes, which if the men fhould ufe they would be laugh'd at; whence it comes, that in this Difcourfe one would think the women fpoke a Language different from that of the men, as will be feen in our Vocabulary, by the difference of expreffions which the men and women make ufe of to fignifie the fame thing : The Savages of *Dominico* affirm, that it proceeds hence, that when the *Caribbians* came to inhabit thefe Iflands, they were poffefs'd by a Nation of the *Arouagues*, whom they abfolutely deftroy'd, fave only the Women, whom they married for the re-peopling of the Country ; fo that thofe Women having retain'd their own Language, taught it their Daughters, and brought them to fpeak as they did; which being practis'd to the prefent by the Mothers towards their Daughters, their Language came to be different from that of the Men in many things : But the male Children, though they underftand the fpeech of their Mothers and Sifters, do neverthelefs imitate their Fathers and Brethren, and accuftom themfelves to their Language when they are five or fix years old. To confirm what we have faid concerning the caufe of this difference of Language, it is alledg'd, That there is fome conformity between the Language of the *Arouagues* who live in the Continent, and that of the *Caribbian* Women : But it is to be obferv'd, That the *Caribbians* of the Continent, as well Men as Women, fpeak the fame Language, as having not corrupted it by inter-marriages with ftrange Women.

17. The old men have alfo fome terms particular to themfelves, and certain affected expreffions, not at all us'd by the younger fort of people.

18. The *Caribbians* have alfo a certain Language which they make ufe of only among themfelves, when they entertain any warlike Refolutions ; it is a very hard kind of fuftian-language: The Women and Maids know nothing of that myfterious Language,

guage, nor yet the young Men, till they have given some assurances of their generosity, and the zeal they have for the common Quarrel of their Nation against their Enemies: This is to prevent the discovery of their designs before the appointed time.

19. For the variation of their Cases, Persons, Moods, and Genders, they have no distinct particles as we have, but they lengthen their words by certain syllables or letters at the beginning or end of the word, and sometimes by the change of the letters: Thus they say in the Imperative, *Bayoubaka, Go*; but in the Indicative, *Nayoubakayem*, I go: In like manner, *Babinaka*, dance; *Nabinakayem*, I dance; much like the formation of the Hebrew Verbs.

20. Indefinite and absolute Nouns are not much in use among them, especially the names of the parts of the body; but they are always in a manner restrain'd to a first, second, or third person.

21. The first person is commonly express'd by the Letter N; at the beginning of a word, as *Nichic, my Head*; the second by a B, as *Bichic, thy Head*; and the third by an L, as *Lichic, his Head*.

22. The neuter and absolute Gender is express'd by a T, as *Tichic, the Head*; but this is not much in use.

23. They have different names in speaking to persons when they are present, and others when they speak of them; thus they say *Baba*, Father, speaking to him, and *Toumaan*, speaking of him; *Bibi*, Mother, speaking to her, and *Ichanum*, speaking of her; which, with the difference there is between the Language of the Men and the Women, the young and the old, their ordinary Discourse, and that us'd by them when they are engag'd in Military Deliberations, must needs cause a great multiplication of words in their Language.

24. Their proper Names are many times deriv'd from certain Accidents, as we shall see more particularly in the Chapter of the Birth and Education of their Children.

25. They never name any one when the party is present; or at least, out of respect, they do but half name him.

26. They never pronounce the whole Name of either Man or Woman; but they do those of Children; so that they will say, the Father or Mother of such a one; or else they say half the Name; as for instance, *Mala*, insteed of saying *Malakaali*, and *Hiba* for *Hibalomon*.

27. The Uncles and Aunts, as many as are of the collateral Line, are called Fathers and Mothers by their Nephews; so that the Uncle is called *Baba*, that is to say, *Father*: But when they would expresly signifie the true and proper Father, they many times add another word, saying, *Baba tinnaca*.

28. Consequently to the precedent appellation, all the He-
Cousins

Cousins are also called Brothers, and all the She-Cousins, Sisters.

29. But between He-Cousin and She-Cousin, the former calls the latter *Tonëilleri*, that is to say properly, *My Female*, or my betrothed; for naturally among them the She-Cousins become Wives to the He-Cousins.

30. The Months they call *Lunes*, that is, *Moons*; and the Years *Poussinieres*, that is, the *Seven Stars*.

31. We shall now give a taste of the naturalness and elegance of their Language, setting down the signification of their words, without expressing the words themselves, so to avoid the setting of them down twice, as reserving that for our Vocabulary.

32. To signifie that a thing is *lost* or *broken*, they commonly say it is *dead*.

33. They call a *Capuchin* Friar, Father *Aioupa*; and the word *Aioupa* signifies in their Language a *Covering* or a *Penthouse*; as if they said, It is a man by whom one may be cover'd, by reason of his great *Capouche*: By the same name they also ironically call an Ape or Monkey, by reason of his long Beard.

34. A Christian, *a Man of the Sea*; because the Christians came to them in Ships.

35. A Lieutenant, *the track of a Captain*, or *that which appears after him*.

36. My Son in Law, *he who makes me little Children*.

37. My younger Brother, *my half*.

38. My Wife, *my heart*.

39. A Boy, *A little Male*.

40. A Girl, *A little Female*.

41. The Spaniards and English, *Deformed Enemies*, *Etouton noubi*; because they are cloath'd, in opposition to their Enemies who are naked, whom they call simply *Etouton*, that is to say, *Enemies*.

42. A Fool, *Him who sees nothing*, or *who hath no light*.

43. The Eye-lid, *The Covering of the Eye*.

44. The Eye-brows, *The Hair of the Eye*.

45. The Ball of the Eye, *The Kernel of the Eye*.

46. The Lips, *The Borders of the Mouth*.

47. The Chin, *The prop of the Teeth*.

48. The Neck, *The prop of the Head*.

49. The Arm and a Wing are express'd by the same word.

50. The Pulse, *The Soul of the Hand*: The *Germans* make such another composition, when they call the Glove the *Shooe of the Hand*.

51. The Fingers, *The little ones*, or *Children of the Hand*.

52. The Thumb, *The Father of the Fingers*; or *that which is opposite to them*: Of that kind is the *ἀντίχειρ* of the *Greeks*.

53. A Joint, *A thing added*; they call also by that name, a piece set on a Garment.

54. The

54. The Bladder, *The Urine Vessel.*
55. The Ham, *That which draws the Leg.*
56. The Sole of the Foot, *The inside of the Foot.*
57. The Toes, *The little ones, or children of the Foot.*
58. The number Ten, *All the Fingers of both hands.*
59. Twenty, *The Fingers of the Hands, and Toes of the Feet.*
60. A Pocket-pistol, *A little Arquebusse.*
61. A Candlestick, *That which holds somthing.*
62. Thorns, *The hair of the Tree, or the eyes of the Tree.*
63. The Rainbow, *Gods Plume of Feathers.*
64. The noise of Thunder, *Trerguetenni.*

65. This Language hath also in its abundance and its naturalness some imperfections which are particular thereto; yet are they such as that some of them do not so much deserve blame as commendation.

66. The *Caribbians* in their natural Language have very few words of injury or abuse; and what they say that is most offensive in their Railleries is, *Thou art not good,* or *thou hast as much wit as a Tortoise.*

67. They have not so much as the names of several Vices; but the Christians have sufficiently supplied them therewith. Some have admir'd that in the Language of *Canada* there is no word answerable to *Sin*; but they might have observ'd withal, that there is not any whereby to express *Virtue.*

68. They have no words to express *Winter, Ice, Hail, Snow,* for they know not what they are.

69. They are not able to express what does not fall under the Senses, save that they have certain names for some both good and evil Spirits; but that excepted, they have no word to signifie Spiritual things, as *Understanding, Memory, Will*; as for the *Soul,* they express it by the word *Heart.*

70. Nor have they the names of Virtues, Sciences, Arts, Trades, nor those of most of our Arms and Tools, save only what they have learn'd since their Commerce with the Christians.

71. They can name but four Colours, whereto they make all the rest to relate; to wit, White, Black, Yellow, and Red.

72. They cannot express any number above Twenty; & their expression of that is pleasant, being oblig'd, as we said elswhere, to shew all the Fingers of their Hands, and Toes of their Feet.

73. When they would signifie a great Number, which goes beyond their Arithmetick, they have no other way then to shew the hair of their Heads, or the sand of the Sea; or they repeat several times the word *Mouche,* which signifies *Much*; as when they say in their Gibberish, *Moy mouche mouche Lunes,* to shew that they are very ancient.

74. In fine, They have neither Comparatives nor Superlatives; but for want thereof, when they would compare things together, and prefer one before all the rest, they express their

The   *sentiment*

ſentiment by a demonſtration which is natural and pleaſant
enough : Thus, when they would repreſent what they think
of the *Europæan* Nations which they are acquainted withall,
they ſay of the *Spaniards* and the *Engliſh*, that they are not
good at all ; of the *Dutch*, that they have as much goodneſs as
a mans hand, or as far as the elbow ; and of the *French*, that
they are as both the arms, which they ſtretch out to ſhew the
greatneſs thereof: This laſt Nation they have a greater affection for than for any other, eſpecially thoſe of it who have
gone along with them to their wars ; for they give thoſe part
of their booty : And as often as they return from their wars,
though the *French* had not gone along with them, yet do they
ſend them part of the ſpoil.

CHAP. XI.

Of the Diſpoſitions of the Caribbians, *and their* Manners.

THE *Caribbians* are naturally of a penſive and melancholy temperament, fiſhing, ſloth, and the temperature of
the air contributing much to the continuance of that humour :
but having found by experience, that that uncomfortable conſtitution was prejudicial to their health, and that the mind
ore-preſs'd dries up the bones, they for the moſt part do ſo
great violence to their natural inclination, that they appear
chearful, pleaſant, and divertive in their converſation, eſpecially when they have got a little wine in their heads : Nay they
have brought themſelves to ſuch a paſs, that, as the *Braſilians*, De Lery c.12.
they can hardly endure the company of ſuch as are melancho-
ly : and thoſe who have converſed much with them have alwaies found them very facetious, and loth to let ſlip any occaſion of laughing, without making their advantage of it : nay
ſometimes they have burſt out into laughter, at what the moſt
inclin'd thereto among us would hardly have ſmil'd.

Their diſcourſes among themſelves are commonly concerning their hunting, their fiſhing, their gardening, or ſome other
innocent ſubjects ; and when they are in ſtrange company, they
are never troubled if any body laugh in their preſence, ſo far
are they from thinking it done as any affront to them : And
yet, they are ſo far from the ſimplicity of a certain Nation of
New-France, who acknowledge themſelves to be *Savages*, not
knowing what that denomination ſignifies, that they think
themſelves highly injur'd when any one gives them that name :

M m

for

for they underſtand what the word means, and ſay that term belongs only to the wild beaſts, the Inhabitants of the woods: Nor do they take it well to be called *Cannibals*, though they eat the fleſh of their Enemies, which they ſay they do to ſatisfie their indignation aud revenge, and not out of any delicacy they find in it more than in any thing elſe whereby they are ſuſtain'd: But they are extreamly pleas'd when any one calls them *Caribbians*, becauſe it is a name they pride themſelves much in, as being a certain acknowledgment of their generoſity and courage: For **they are not only** the *Apalachites*, from amongſt whom they came, who by that word ſignifie a *Warlike and valiant man*, endu'd with force and a particular dexterity in military affairs; but even the *Arouagues* themſelves their irreconcileable Enemies, having often experienc'd their valour, underſtand thereby the ſame thing, though by the ſame word they would alſo denote a *Cruel perſon*, by reaſon of the miſeries the *Caribbians* have occaſioned them. But howere it be, this is certain, that our Savages of the *Caribbies* are ſo much pleaſed with that name, that ſpeaking to the *French* they have this perpetually in their mouths, *Toy Francois, moy Caraibe*, *Thou art a* French-man, *I am a* Caribbian.

In all other things they are of a good and tractable diſpoſition; and they are ſo great Enemies to ſeverity, that if the *Europæan* or other Nations who have any of them ſlaves (as among others the *Engliſh* have ſome, cunningly trapan'd and carryed away by them from the places of their birth) treat them with any rigour, they many times die out of pure grief: But by fair means they will do any thing, contrary to the *Negroes*, who muſt be roughly dealt with, otherwiſe they grow inſolent, ſlothful, and perfidious.

They commonly reproach the *Europæans* with their avarice, and their immoderate induſtry in getting of wealth together for themſelves and their Children, ſince the earth is able to find ſufficient ſuſtenance for all men, if ſo be they wil take ever ſo little pains to cultivate it: as for themſelves, they ſay they are not perplex'd with caring for thoſe things whereby their lives are preſerv'd; and indeed it muſt be acknowledged, that they are incomparably fatter, and have their health better than thoſe that fare deliciouſly: Moſt certain it is, that they live without ambition, without vexation, without diſquiet, having no deſire of acquiring honours or wealth, ſlighting Gold and Silver, as the ancient *Lacedemonians*, and the *Peruvians*, and contenting themſelves with what Nature had made them, and what the earth ſupplies them withall for their ſuſtenance: And when they go a hunting, or a fiſhing, or root up trees for ground to make a little Garden, or to build houſes, which are innocent employments, and ſuitable to the nature of man, they do all without eagerneſs, and as it were by way of divertiſement and recreation.   But

But it raises a particular astonishment in them, when they see how much we esteem Gold, considering we are so well furnish'd with Glass and Chrystal, which in their judgment are more beautiful, and consequently ought to be more highly prized: To this purpose, *Benzoni* a *Milanese* Historian, relates a strange story of the New-world, how that the *Indians* detesting the insatiable avarice of the *Spaniards,* who subdu'd them, took a piece of Gold in their hands, and said, "Be-
"hold the God of the Christians; for this they come from *Ca-*
"*steel* into our Country; for this they have made us slaves, ba-
"nish'd us out of our habitations, and committed horrid things
"against us; for this they are engag'd in wars amongst them-
"selves; for this they kill one the other;for this they are alwaies
"in disquiet, they quarrel, rob, curse and blaspheme : In fine,
"there is no villany, no mischief but they will commit for this.

In like manner, our *Caribbians,* when they see the Christians sad and perplext at any thing, are wont to give them this gentle reprehension : "*Compere* (a word they have learnt of the *French,*and commonly use to express their affection, as the women do also call our *Europæans Commeres,* as a mark of their friendship; both words signifying in *English* Gossip, or familiar friend) "how miserable art thou, thus to expose thy person to
"such tedious and dangerous Voyages, and to suffer thy self to
"be orepress'd with cares and fears ! The inordinate desire of
"acquiring wealth puts thee to all this trouble, and all these
"inconveniences; and yet thou art in no less disquiet for the
"Goods thou hast already gotten, than for those thou art desi-
"rous to get : Thou art in continual fear lest some body should
"rob thee either in thy own Country or upon the Seas, or that
"thy Commodities should be lost by shipwrack, and devour'd
"by the waters : Thus thou growest old in a short time, thy
"hair turns gray, thy forehead is wrinkled, a thousand incon-
"veniences attend thy body, a thousand afflictions surround
"thy heart, and thou makest all the haste thou canst to the
"grave : Why art thou not content with what thy own Coun-
"try produces ? Why dost not thou contemn riches as we do ?
And to this purpose, the great Traveller *Vincent le Blanc* hath *Part.3.c.16.*
a remarkable discourse of some *Brasilians*: "That wealth which
"you Christians pursue with so much earnestness, do they any
"way promote your advancement in the grace of God ? Do
"they prevent your dying ? Do you carry them along with
"you to the grave ? To the same purpose was their discourse
to *J. de Lery,* as he relates in his History.   *Ch.* 13.

The *Caribbians* have this further reproach to make to the *Europæans,* to wit, that of their usurpation of their Country, and they stick not to do it as a manifest injustice : "Thou
"hast driven me, *says this poor people,* out of St. *Christophers,*
"*Aleuis, Montserrat, St. Martins, Antego, Gardeloupe, Barbou-*

M m 2   "thos,

" *thos*, *St. Euftace's, &c.* neither of which places belonged to
" thee, and whereto thou couldeft not make any lawful pre-
" tence: And thou threatneft me every day to take away that
" little which is left me: What fhall become of the poor mife-
" rable *Caribbian*? Muft he go and live in the Sea with the
" fifhes? Thy Country muft needs be a wretched one, fince
" thou leaveft it to come and take away mine: Or thou muft
" needs be full of malice, thus to perfecute me out of a frolick.
This complaint may well exempt them from the opprobrious
denomination of Savages.

Lycurgus would not permit his Citizens to travel, out of a
fear they might learn the manners of forreign Countries: But
our Savages ftand in need of much travel to unbarbarize themfelves, if we may ufe fuch an expreffion: And yet they are not
only free from that infatiable covetoufnefs, which makes the
Chriftians undertake fo great and fo dangerous voyages, but
alfo from the curiofity of feeing any other Country in the
world, as being enamoured of their own more than any other.
And thence it comes, that, imagining we fhould not be more
curious than they are, nor lefs lovers of our Countries, they
are aftonifh'd at our Voyages; wherein they have the honour
to be like *Socrates*, of whom *Plato* gives this teftimony, that
he had no more defign to leave *Athens*, with any intention to
travel, than the lame and the blind; and that he defired not
to fee other Cities, nor to live under other Laws; being, as to
this particular, as far as our *Caribbians*, from the opinion of
the *Perfians*, among whom it is come into a Proverb, that
he who hath not travell'd the world may be compared to a
Bear.

But we are to note further, that our *Caribbians* of the Iflands
have not only an averfion from travelling into any other parts
of the world, but they would not alfo willingly fuffer any of
theirs to be carried away into a ftrange Country, without an
abfolute promife within a fhort time to bring them back again:
But if it happens through fome misfortune that any one of
them dies by the way, there is no thinking of any return among
them, for there is no hope of reconciliation.

But if they have no curiofity for things at a great diftance
from them, they have much for thofe that are neerer hand, infomuch that if a man open a cheft in their prefence, he muft
fhew them all that is in it, otherwife they will think themfelves
dif-obliged: And if they like any thing of what they fee
therein, though it be of ever fo little value, they will give the
moft precious thing they have for it, that fo they may fatisfie
their inclination.

As concerning Traffick, true it is, that having treated about
fomething, they will fall off from what they have promifed:
But the fecret to make them ftand to their bargain, is to roll
them,

them, that a Merchant ought to be as good as his word: For when they are preſs'd upon in point of honour, and reproached with inconſtancy as if they were children, they are aſhamed of their lightneſs.

Theft is accounted a great crime amongſt them; wherein it muſt be acknowledged they ſhew themſelves more rational than *Lycurgus*, who allowed that vice in the *Lacedæmonian* children, as a very commendable employment, provided they did their buſineſs cleaverly, and Hocus-pocus-like: But the *Caribbians* have ſo natural and ſo great an averſion for that ſin, that there is no ſuch thing found among them, which is very rare among *Savages*: For moſt of them are Theeves; and thence it is that ſome of their Iſlands have their name thence.

Pluta. in his Life.

Iſlands of Robbers.

But for the *Caribbians*, as they are are not of their own nature any way inclined to thieving, ſo they live without any diſtruſt one of another: So that their Houſes and Plantations are left without any body to look to them, though they have neither doors nor incloſures, after the ſame manner as ſome Hiſtorians relate of the *Tartars*: But if the leaſt thing in the world be taken from them, ſuch as may be a little knife, wherewith they do ſtrange things in Joyner's work, they ſo highly prize what is uſeful to them, that ſuch a loſs is enough to ſet them a weeping, and grieving for the ſpace of eight days after it, nay will engage them in combinations with their friends to get reparations, and to be reveng'd on the perſon whom they ſuſpect guilty of the theft: Accordingly in thoſe Iſlands where they have their habitations neer thoſe of the Chriſtians, they have often revenged themſelves of thoſe who had, as they ſaid, taken away any of their little houſhould-ſtuff: And in thoſe places when they find ſomething wanting in their houſes, they preſently ſay, *Some Chriſtian hath been here*: And among the grievances and complaints which they make to the Governours of the *French* Nation, this comes alwaies in the front, *Compere Governour, thy Mariners* (ſo they call all the forreign Inhabitants) *have taken away a knife out of my Cot,* or ſome other piece of houſhold-ſtuff of that kind. The Inhabitants of *Guinny* would not make any ſuch complaints: For if they chance to loſe ſomething, they are of a perſwaſion that ſome of their deceaſed Relations, having occaſion for it in the other world, came and took it away.

Carpin s Travels into Tartary.

The *Caribbians* are a people as it were aſſociated in one common intereſt, and they are of all people the moſt loving one to another; being in that particular far from the humour of thoſe *Aſiaticks* of *Java*, who ſpeak not to their own Brothers without a dagger in their hands, ſo diſtruſtful are they one of another: From this affection which our Savages mutually bear one another, does it proceed that there are few quarrels and animoſities among them.

But

But if they are once injur'd, either by a Stranger or one of their own Countrymen, they never forgive, but contrive all the waies they can to be revenged: Thus when any of those Imposters, whom they call *Bogez*, makes them believe that one of those whom they account Sorcerers is author of the mischief that hath happened to them, they endeavour all they can to kill him, saying, *Taraliatana, he hath bewitched me; Nebanebouibatina, I will be revenged of him*: And this furious passion and desire to be revenged, is that which makes them so brutish, as we said before, as to eat the very flesh of their Enemies, whereof we shall give the particulars in their proper place: This implacable animosity is the vice generally reigning among them; and it exercises the same Tyranny, without any exception, over all the Savages of *America*: The revenge of the Inhabitants of *Canada* is sometimes very pleasant; for they eat their own lice, because they have bitten them: If the *Brasilians* hurt themselves against a stone, to be revenged they bite it as hard as they can; It is observed also that they bite the Arrows which light upon them in fighting.

De Lery c. 11. & 14.

Without any obligation to *Lycurgus*, or his Laws, the *Caribbians*, by a secret law of nature, bear a great respect to ancient people, and hear them speak with much attention, expressing by their gesture, and a little tone of the voice, how much they are pleas'd with their discourses: And in all things the younger sort comply with the sentiments of the ancient, and submit to their wills: It is reported they do the same in *Brasil* and *China*.

Linscot & Semedo.

The Young men among the *Caribbians* have no conversation either with the Maids or married Women: And it hath been observed, that the men are less amorous in this Country than the women, as they are in several other places under the Torrid Zone: Both the men and women among the *Caribbians* are naturally chast, a quality very rare among Savages: And when those of other Nations look over-earnestly upon them, and laugh at their nakedness, they are wont to say to them, *Friends, you are to look on us only between both the eyes*; a vertue worthy admiration in a people that go naked, and are as barbarous as these.

It is related of Captain *Baron*, that in one of the incursions made by him and his party into the Island of *Montserrat*, then possest by the *English*, he made great waste in the Plantations that lay neerest to the Sea, so that he carried a great booty, and that among the Prisoners there being a young Gentlewoman, Wife to one of the Officers of the Island, he caused her to be brought to one of his houses in *Dominico*: this Gentlewoman being big with child when she was carried away, was very carefully attended during the time of her lying in, by
the

the Savage women of the ſame Iſland : And though ſhe liv'd
there a good while after among them, neither Captain *Baſon*
nor any other ever touched her ; a great example of reſerved-
neſs in ſuch people.

Yet muſt it be acknowledged, that ſome of them have ſince
degenerated from that chaſtity, and many other vertues of
their Anceſtors : But we muſt withall make this acknowledgment, that the *Europæans* by their pernicious examples, and the
unchriſtian-like treatment they have us'd towards them, baſe-
ly deceiving them, perfidiouſly upon all occaſions breaking
their promiſes with them, unmercifully rifling and burning
their houſes and villages, and raviſhing and debauching their
Wives and Daughters, have taught them (to the perpetual infamy of the Chriſtian name) diſſimulation, lying, treachery,
perfidiouſneſs, luxury, and ſeveral other vices, which were unknown in thoſe parts, before they had any Commerce with
them.

But as to other concerns, theſe Savages are remarkable for
their civility and courteſie, beyond what can be imagined in
Savages : Not but that there are ſome *Caribbians* very brutiſh
and unreaſonable; but for the greater part of them their
judgment and docility is obſervable upon many occaſions, and
thoſe who have converſed long with them, have found ſeveral
experiences of their fair dealing, gratitude, friendſhip and generoſity : But of this we ſhall ſpeak more particularly in the
Chapter where we ſhall treat of their *Reception of ſuch Stran-*
gers as come to viſit them.

They are alſo great lovers of cleanlineſs (a thing extraordinary among Savages) and have ſuch an averſion for all naſtineſs, that if one ſhould eaſe himſelf in their Gardens
where their *Caſſava* and *Potatoes* are planted, they will preſently forſake them, and not make uſe of any thing growing
therein : Of this their neatneſs in this and other things, we ſhall
have occaſion to ſay more in the Chapter *Of their Habitations,*
and their Repaſts.

CHAP. XII.

Of the natural ſimplicity of the Caribbians.

Aᴅmiration being the Daughter of Ignorance, we are not
to think it ſtrange that the *Caribbians*, who have ſo little
knowledge of thoſe excellent things which ſtudy and experience have made familiar amongſt civiliz'd Nations, ſhould be
ſo

so much aftonifh'd when they meet with any thing whereof the caufe is unknown to them, and that they fhould be brought up in fo great fimplicity, that it might be taken in moft of thefe poor people for a brutifh ftupidity.

This fimplicity is remarkable, among other things, in the extraordinary fear they conceive at the fight of Firearms, which they look on with a ftrange admiration ; but their aftonifhment is greateft at Fire-locks, much beyond what they have for great Guns and Muskets, becaufe they fee Fire put to them ; but for Fire-locks, they are not able to conceive how it is poffible they fhould take Fire ; and fo they believe it is the evil Spirit *Maboya* who does that Office : But this fear and aftonifhment is common to them with divers other Savages, who have not found any thing fo ftrange in their encounters with the *Europæans*, as thofe Arms which fpit Fire, and at fo great a diftance wound and kill thofe whom they meet with : This was it, together with the Prodigy of feeing Men fighting on Horfeback, which principally made the *Peruvians* think the *Spaniards* to be Gods, and occafioned their fubmiffion to them with lefs refiftance. It is reported alfo that the *Arabians*, who make Incurfions along the River *Jordan*, and fhould be more accuftomed to War, are not free from this fear and aftonifhment.

Among the feveral difcoveries of the fimplicity of our *Caribbians*, we fhall here fet down two very confiderable ones. When there happens an Eclipfe of the Moon, they believe that *Maboya* eats her, and they dance all night, making a noife with Gourds, wherein there are many fmall Pebbles : And when they fmell any thing of ill fcent, they are wont to fay, *Maboya cayeu eu*, that is, *The Devil is here* ; *Caima Loary*, *Let us be gone becaufe of him*, or *for fear of him* : Nay they attribute the name of *Maboya*, or Devil, to certain Plants of ill fcent, fuch as may be Mufhrooms, and to whatever is apt to put them into any fright.

Some years fince, the greateft part of the *Caribbians* were perfwaded that Gun-powder was the Seed of fome Herb ; nay, there were thofe who defir'd fome of it to fow in their Gardens ; nay, fome were fo obftinate, that, though diffwaded from it, they put it into the ground, out of a perfwafion that it would bring forth fomwhat, as well as other Seeds : Yet was not this Imagination fo grofs as thofe of certain Brutes of *Guinny*, who, the firft time they faw *Europæans*, thought the Commodities they brought them, fuch as Linnen, Cloathes, Knives, and Fire-arms, grew on the Earth fo prepar'd, as the Fruits did on Trees, and that there was no more to be done than to gather them : That certainly is not fo pardonable a piece of fimplicity as that of the *Caribbians* : And we may further alledg, to excufe that fimplicity, or at leaft to render it the more fupportable, the ftupidity of thofe Inhabitants of *America*,

ca,

ca, who, upon the firſt Diſcovery of the *New-World*, imagin'd that the Horſe and the Rider made up one Creature, like the imaginary Centaurs of the Poets: And that of thoſe others, who after they were ſubdu'd, coming to deſire peace and pardon of the Men, and to bring them Gold and Proviſions, went and made the ſame Preſents to the Horſes, with a Speech much like that which they had made to the Men, interpreting the neighing of thoſe Creatures for a Language of compoſition and truce : And to conclude theſe inſtances, we ſhall add only the childiſh ſottiſhneſs of thoſe ſame *Indians* of *America*, who roundly believ'd, that the Letters which the *Spaniards* ſent one to another were certain Meſſengers and Spies, ſpeaking, and ſeeing, and diſcovering the moſt ſecret actions; and upon this perſwaſion, fearing one day the eye and tongue of one of theſe Letters, they hid it under a ſtone, that they might freely eat ſome Melons of their Maſters.   In fine, there will be no cauſe to think it ſo ſtrange that the *Caribbians* ſhould take Gun-powder, a thing abſolutely unknown to them, for ſome ſeed that might be ſown, when there were ſome people living in *France*, whoſe habitations being at a great diſtance from the places where Salt was made, thought out of a like imagination that it was gather'd in Gardens.   It hapned alſo, not many years ſince, that a Woman, an Inhabitant of *Martinico*, having ſent ſeveral pounds of *Caret*-ſhells and Tobacco to a She-Merchant of S. *Malo's*, when this latter had put off the Commodity, ſhe gave an account thereof to her Correſpondent at *Martinico*, and advis'd to plant *Carets* in her Garden rather then Tobacco, for that the former was much dearer in *France*, and that there was no danger of its rotting in the Ship, as there was of Tobacco. But let us conſider what there is yet to be ſaid concerning the natural ſimplicity of our Savages of the *Caribbies*.

It is a pleaſant thing to conſider that theſe poor people ſhould be ſo ſimple, as that though they have many places fit for the making of Salt, yet dare they not make uſe of it, as accounting Salt extreamly prejudicial to health, and the preſervation of life; thence it proceeds that they never either eat of it, or ſeaſon their meat therewith ; and when at any time they ſee our people make uſe of it, they ſay to them, out of a compaſſion worthy compaſſion, *Compere, thou haſteneſt thy own death :* But inſtead of Salt, they ſeaſon all their meſſes with *Pyman*, or American Pepper.

Nor is there any Swines-fleſh eaten among them, which they call *Coincoin*, and *Bouirokou* ; nor yet Tortoiſe, (or as ſome call them Turtles) which they call *Catallou*, though there be abundance of thoſe Creatures in their Country : Of this their abſtinence they give the ſimpleſt reaſons imaginable : For as to the Swine, they are afraid to taſte of it, leſt they ſhould have ſmall eyes like thoſe of that Beaſt ; now in their judgment it is the

N n

greateſt

[marginal notes:]
Montagne's Eſſays, l. 1. c. 8.
De Lery, c. 16 Garcilaſſo, l. 9. c. 29.
Caret is a kind of Tortoiſe-ſhell.

greateſt of all deformities to have ſmall eyes, and yet there are few among them but have them ſuch. As for the Tortoiſe, the reaſon of their abſtinence from that is no leſs ridiculous; they will not feed on that, ſay they, out of a fear leſt if they did, they ſhould participate of the lazineſs and ſtupidity of that Creature.

Moſt of thoſe people who are known by the name of Savages are alſo full of ſtrange and fantaſtical imaginations concerning the matter and manner of eating: For example, the *Canadians* abſtain from Muſcles, only out of a pure fancy; but they are ſuch Beaſts that they cannot give any reaſon for that abſtinence: They will not caſt the Beavers bones to the Dogs, leſt the ſoul of that Beaſt ſhould go and tell the other Beavers, and ſo oblige them to leave the Country: It is reported alſo, That they do not eat the marrow of the back-bone of any Creature, for fear of having any pain in the back. The *Braſilians* eat no hens egges, out of an opinion they are poiſon: They abſtain alſo from the fleſh of Ducks, and that of every Creature that goes ſlowly, as alſo from Fiſhes that do not ſwim ſwiftly, for fear of participating of the ſlowneſs of thoſe Creatures. The *Maldiveſes* forbear the meat of Tortoiſes, as the *Caribbians* do; but it is becauſe of the conformity there is, in their judgment, between them and Man. The *Calecutians*, and ſome others who live more towards the Eaſt, never taſte of the fleſh of wild Oxen, Cows, and Bulls, out of a perſwaſion that mens Souls, when they depart out of their Bodies, go and animate thoſe of the ſaid Beaſts. In fine, certain *Peruvians* of the Province of *Paſſu* abſtain from all kinds of fleſh whatſoever; and if they are intreated to taſte thereof, their anſwer is, *That they are not Dogs.* All theſe Inſtances are brought upon the Stage, to ſhew that the averſion of the *Caribbians* to eat Salt, Swines-fleſh, and Tortoiſes, ſhould not cauſe them to be accounted the moſt ſelf-will'd and moſt extravagant of all the Savages.

Beſides the diſcoveries we have already made of their ſottiſhneſs and ſimplicity, there is this yet to be added, That they are ſo ſtupid, that they cannot count a number exceeding that of the Fingers of their Hands and the Toes of their Feet, which they ſhew to expreſs the ſaid number, what exceeds it ſurpaſſing with them all Arithmetick; ſo that they would be very unfit for Bankiers; an humour contrary to that of the *Chineſes*, who are ſuch excellent Accomptants, that in a moment they caſt up ſuch Sums as it would trouble us much to do, and that with greater certainty.

But the *Caribbians* have the priviledge not to be the only Nation in the World which may be reproach'd with this ignorance; for it is as great among the people of *Madagaſcar* and *Guinny*, to cite no more; nay, ſome ancient Hiſtorians affirm,

That

That there were fome people who could not count above five, and others who could not exceed four.

The Inhabitants of *Guinny* having counted to Ten, were wont to fet a mark, and then begin again. Certain Savages of the Septentrional part of *America*, to exprefs a great number, which it was impoffible for them to name, make ufe of an eafie kind of demonftration, taking their hair or fome fand in their hands; a fort of comparifons which are frequent in holy Scripture. The Inhabitants of the *Caribby*-Iflands have alfo their invention to fupply the defect of Arithmetick; for when they are to go to the Wars, and are to be ready at their general Rendezvouz on a certain day, they take each of them one after another an equal number of Peafe, in their folemn Affembly; as for inftance, thrice or four times Ten, and fome certain number under Ten, if need be, according as they are refolv'd to advance their Enterprife; they put up thefe Peafe in a little Gourd, and every morning they take out one, and caft it away, till there are none left, and then the appointed time for their departure is come, and the next day they are to be upon their march: Another way they have is this, every one of them makes fo many knots on a little Cord, and every day they unty one, and when they are come to the laft they make ready for the Rendezvouz: Somtimes alfo they take little pieces of Wood, upon which they make fo many notches as they intend to fpend days in their preparation; every day they cut off one of the notches, and when they come to the laft, they take their march towards the place appointed.

The Captains, the *Boyez*, and the moft ancient among them, have more underftanding than the common fort, and by long experience, join'd to what they had receiv'd by tradition from their Anceftors, they have acquir'd a grofs knowledge of divers Stars; whence it comes that they count the Months by Moons, and the Years by the Seven Stars, taking particular notice of that Conftellation: Thus fome *Peruvians* regulated their Years by their Harvefts: Thofe Inhabitants of *Canada* who live in the Mountains obferve the number of the Nights and Winters; and the *Soriquefes* count by Suns. But though the more judicions among the *Caribbians* difcern the Months, and the Years, and obferve the different Seafons, yet have they not any Monuments of Antiquity, and cannot tell how long it is fince the firft of their Nation left the Continent, and fetled themfelves in the Iflands; but all the account they are able to give of it is, That neither themfelves, nor their Fathers, nor their Grandfathers could remember any thing of it; nor can they tell what age they are of, nor give any precife account of the time when the *Spaniards* came into their Country, nor of feveral other things of that nature; for they take no notice of ought of this kind, and make no account of knowing what is done in the World.   N n 2   CHAP.

CHAP. XIII.

Of that which may be called Religion *among the* Caribbians.

THere is no **Nation** so savage, no People so barbarous, but they have some opinion and perswasion of a Divinity, said *Cicero*; nay, Nature her self seems to have been so indulgent to Mankind, as to make some impression of a Divinity in the minds of Men; for what Nation, what kind of Men are there, but have, without any previous learning it from others, a natural sentiment of the Divinity? We may with just reason admire these noble Illuminations proceeding out of the mouth of a man groping in the darkness of Paganism: But things are come to that pass now, that it will be a hard matter to make good the famous words of that incomparable Orator and Prince of Roman Eloquence: For the poor Savages of the ancient People of the *Antes* in *Peru*, and of the two Provinces of the *Chirrhuanes* or *Cheriganes*, those of most of the Countries of *New-France*, *New-Mexico*, *New-Holland*, *Brasil*, *New-Netherlands*, *Terra del Fuego*, the *Arouagues*, the Inhabitants about the River *Cayenna*, the *Islands of Robbers*, and some others, if we may credit Historians, have not any kind of Religion, **and** do not adore any Sovereign Power.

Those also who have convers'd among the Originary Inhabitants of the *Caribby*-Islands, are forc'd to acknowledge, That they have, by the violence of their brutish passions, smother'd all the apprehensions Nature had bestow'd on them of a Divinity; that they have rejected all the Directions and Instructions which might guide them to the knowledge thereof; and consequently, that by the just judgment of God they are surrounded by so dreadful a night, that there is not to be seen among them either Invocation, or Ceremonies, or Sacrifices, or, in fine, any Exercise or Assembly whatsoever in order to Devotion: nay, they are so far from having any of these things, that they have not so much as a name to express the Divinity, so far are they from serving it; so that when any one would speak to them concerning God, he must use these circumlocutions; *He who hath created the World, who hath made all things, who gives life and sustenance to all living Creatures,* or somthing of that kind: They are accordingly so blinded and brutish, that they do not make any acknowledgment of the Lord of Nature, in that admirable work of the Universe; wherein he hath been pleas'd to represent himself in a thousand immortal colours, and make his adorable Omnipotency as it were visible to the

eye:

eye : Thence comes it that they are deaf to the voices of an infinite number of creatures which continually preach unto them the preſence of their Creator : And ſo they daily uſe the benefits of their Sovereign Maſter, without ever reflecting that he is the Author thereof, and making any acknowledgment of his goodneſs, who hath ſo liberally ſupplyed them therewith.

They ſay that the Earth is the indulgent Mother, who furniſhes them with all things neceſſary to life : But their terreſtrial minds are not raiſed to any apprehenſion of that Almighty and all-merciful Father who fram'd the Earth, and by the continual influence of his Divinity impregnates it with the vertue of producing all things for the nouriſhment of man : If any one ſpeak to them concerning that Divine Eſſence, and diſcourſe with them of the myſteries of Faith, they will hearken to all that is ſaid with much patience : But when the diſcourſe is at an end, they anſwer as it were in jeſt, *Friend thou art very eloquent, thou art very ſubtle, I would I could talk as well thou doſt:* Nay ſometimes they ſay as the *Braſilians* do, that if they ſhould ſuffer themſelves to be perſwaded by ſuch diſcourſes, their Neighbours would laugh at them.

A certain *Caribbian* being at work on a Sunday, Monſieur *du Montel* relates how that he ſaid to him, "Friend, he who hath "made Heaven and Earth will be angry with thee for working "on this day ; for he hath appointed this day for his ſervice : "And I, *reply'd very bluntly the Savage*, am already very angry "with him ; for thou ſayeſt he is the Maſter of the world and "of the ſeaſons : He it is therefore who hath forborn to ſend "rain in due time, and by reaſon of the great drought hath "cauſed my *Manioc* and my *Potatoes* to rot in the ground : "ſince he hath treated me ſo ill, I will work on every Sunday, "though 'twere purpoſely to vex him. See here a pregnant example of the brutality of this wretched people. This diſcourſe is much like that of thoſe ſenceleſs people among the *Topinambous*, who, when it was told them that God was the Author of the Thunder, argued, that it followed he was not good, ſince he took ſuch pleaſure in frighting them after that manner. But to return to the *Caribbians*.

Thoſe of the ſame Nation who live in the Meridional Continent of *America*, have no more Religion than the Inhabitants of the *Caribbies* : Some among them have a certain reſpect for the Sun and the Moon, and imagine that they are animated ; yet do they not adore them, nor offer, nor ſacrifice any thing to them : It is probable they have retain'd that veneration for thoſe two great Luminaries from the remembrance of the *Apalachites*, among whom their Predeceſſors had ſometimes ſojourned. Our Iſlanders have not preſerved any thing of that Tradition ; but we ſhall here ſet down all that may be called

Religion

Religion among them, and what bears a grofs reprefentation thereof.

They have a natural fentiment of fome Divinity, or fome fu-perior and obliging power, which hath its refidence in the Hea-vens; They fay, "That the faid power is content quietly to
"enjoy the delights of its own felicity, without being offended
"at the ill actions of men, and that it is endued with fo great
"goodnefs, that it does not take any revenge even of its Ene-
"mies: whence it comes that they render it neither honour nor adoration, and that they interpret thofe Treafures of cle-mency, whereof it is fo liberal towards them, and that long-fuffering whereby it bears with them, either to weaknefs or the indifference it hath for the conduct of mankind.

Their perfwafion therefore is, that there are two kinds of fpi-its, fome good, others evil: The good fpirits are their Gods; and they call them in general *Akamboue*, which is the word ufed by the men; and *Opoyem*, which is that of the Women: True t is, the word *Akamboue* fignifies fimply a *Spirit*, and thence t comes that it is alfo called the fpirit of man; but this appel-ation they never attribute to the evil fpirits: Thefe good fpi-its, which are their Gods, are more particularly exprefs'd by he men under the word *Icheiri*, and by the women under hat of *Chemiin*, which we cannot render otherwife than by that of *God*, and *Chemiignum*, the *Gods*: And every one fpeaking particularly of his God, fays *Icheirikou*, which is the word of the men, and *Nechemerakou*, which is that of the women: But both men and women call the evil fpirit, which is their De-vil, *Mapoya*, or *Maboya*, as all the *French* pronounce it; but the *Caribbians* in that word pronounce the B according to the *Ger-man* pronunciation.

They believe that there is a great number of thefe good Spirits, or Gods, and every one imagines that there is one of them particularly defign'd for his conduct: They fay there-fore, that thefe Gods have their abode in Heaven, but they know not what they do there, and of themfelves they never propofe to themfelves the making of any acknowledgment of them as Creators of the world, and the things contained there-in: But only when it is faid to them, that the God we adore is he who hath made Heaven and Earth, and that it is he who caufeth the Earth to bring forth things for our nourifhment; they anfwer; *True, thy God hath made the Heaven and the Earth of* France *(or fome other Country, which they name) and caufes thy Wheat to grow there: But our Gods have made our Country, and caufe our Manioc to grow.*

It is affirmed by fome, that they call their falfe Gods *des Rio-ches*; but that word is not of their Language, but is derived from the *Spanifh*: The *French* affirm the fame thing after the *Spaniards*; and if the *Caribbians* make ufe of it, they do it not

among

among themſelves but only among Strangers: So that from what hath been ſaid it is apparent, that though theſe Barbarians have a natural ſentiment of ſome Divinity, or ſome ſuperior Power, yet it is intermixt with ſo many extravagances, and involv'd in ſo great darkneſs, that it cannot be ſaid thoſe poor people have any knowledge of God: For the Divinities they acknowledge, and to whom they render a certain homage, are ſo many Devils, by whom they are ſeduc'd and kept in the chains of a damnable ſlavery, though they make a certain diſtinction between them and the evil Spirits.

They have neither Temples nor Altars particularly dedicated to theſe pretended Divinities which they acknowledge, and ſo they do not ſacrifice to them any thing that hath had life; but they only make them offerings of *Caſſava*, and of the firſt of their Fruits; and when they think they have been healed by them of ſome diſeaſe, they make a kind of wine or a feaſt in honour of them, and by way of acknowledgment, and as it were to expreſs their gratitude, they offer them ſome *Caſſava*, and *Ouicou*; all theſe offerings are called by them *Anaeri*. Their Houſes being made after on oval figure, and the roof reaching to the ground, they ſet at one end of the Hut their Offerings in Veſſels according to the nature of the thing, upon one or more *Matoutous*, or little Tables made of Bull-ruſhes and the leaves of the tree called the *Latanier*: Every one may make his Offerings to his God in his own Houſe, or Cot; but when it is done in order to invocation, there muſt be one of the *Boyez* preſent: All theſe Offerings are not accompany'd with any adoration, or Prayers, and they conſiſt only in the bare preſentation of thoſe gifts.

They alſo invocate their falſe Gods when they deſire their preſence; but that is to be done by the interpoſition of the *Boyez*, that is to ſay, their *Prieſts*, or to ſay better, their *Magicians*; and this they do eſpecially upon four occaſions.

1. To demand revenge on ſome body who hath done them any miſchief, and to bring ſome puniſhment upon him.

2. To be healed of ſome diſeaſe wherewith they are troubled, and to know what will be the iſſue thereof: And when they are recovered, they make *Wines*, as they are called in the Iſlands, that is, *Aſſemblies of rejoycing and congratulation*, and debauches in honour of them, as it were by way of acknowledgment of their favour: And their Magicians do alſo perform the office of Phyſitians among them, by an aſſociation of Magick and Medicine, never doing any cure, or applying any remedies but what are accompany'd by ſome act of ſuperſtition.

3. They conſult them alſo to know the event of their wars.

4. Laſtly,

4. Laſtly, they invocate thoſe ſpirits by the means of their *Boyez*, to obtain of them that they would drive away *Maboya*, or the evil Spirit : But they never invocate *Maboya* himſelf, as ſome have imagined.

Every *Boyé* hath his particular God, or rather his familiar Devil, which he invocates by the ſinging of certain words, accompanied with the ſmoke of Tobacco, which they cauſe to be burnt before that Devil, as a perfume which is very delightful to him, and the ſcent whereof is able to make him appear.

When the *Boyez* invocate their familiar Devil, it is alwaies done in the night-time, and great care muſt be taken that there be no light neer, nor any fire in the place where they exerciſe their abominations; for theſe ſpirits of darkneſs perfectly abhor all light : And when ſeveral *Boyez* invocate their Gods at the ſame time, as they ſpeak, thoſe Gods, or rather Devils, rail one at another, and quarrel, attributing to one another the cauſes of every ones evil, and they ſeem to fight.

Theſe Demons ſhelter themſelves ſometimes in the bones of dead men taken out of their graves and wrapt in Cotton, and thereby give Oracles, ſaying it is the ſoul of the deceaſed perſon : They make uſe of them to bewitch their Enemies, and to that end the Sorcerers wrap up thoſe bones together with ſomething that belongs to their Enemy. Theſe Devils do alſo ſometimes enter into the bodies of Women, and ſpeak by them: When the *Boyé* or Magician hath by his Charms obliged his familar Spirit to appear, he bids him appear under different ſhapes, and thoſe who are about the place where he exerciſes his damnable ſuperſtitions, ſay, that he clearly anſwers the queſtions made to him, that he foretels the event of a war or diſeaſe, and after the *Boyé* is retired, that the Devil ſtirs the Veſſels, and makes a noiſe with his jaws, as if he were eating and drinking the preſents prepared for him : but the next day they find he hath not meddled with any thing : Theſe profane offerings which have been defiled by theſe unhappy Spirits, are accounted ſo holy by the Magicians and the poor people whom they have abuſed, that only the moſt ancient and moſt conſiderable perſons among them, have the liberty to taſte of them; nay they durſt not do that, unleſs they have that cleanneſs of body which they ſay is requiſite in all thoſe that are to be admited thereto.

Aſſoon as theſe poor Savages are troubled with any ſickneſs or pain, they believe that they are ſent upon them by the Gods of ſome of their Enemies; and then they make their applications to the *Boyé*, who conſulting his Dæmon, tells them it is the God of ſuch a one, or ſuch a one, who hath cauſ'd thoſe miſchiefs to them : And this raiſes in thoſe who conſult, enmity and a deſire to be revenged of thoſe whoſe Gods have treated them in that manner.   Be-

Beſides the *Boyez* or Magicians who are highly reſpected and honoured among them, they have alſo Sorcerers, at leaſt they think them ſuch, who, as they ſay, ſend charms upon them, and dangerous and fatal enchantments; and thoſe whom they account ſuch, they kill, if ever they light on them: 'Tis many times a plauſible pretence to be rid of their Enemies.

The *Caribbians* are ſubject to ſome other miſchiefs, which they ſay proceed from *Maboya*, and they often complain that he beats them: True it is, that ſome perſons of worth, who have converſed a certain time among this poor people, are perſwaded that they are neither moleſted, nor effectually beaten by the Devil; and that all the complaints and dreadful relations they make as to that, are grounded only on this, that being of a very melancholick conſtitution, and having for the moſt part their ſpleens ſwell'd and inflam'd, they are many times ſubject to terrible dreams, wherein they imagine the Devil appears to them, and beats them: whereupon they ſtart up frighted out of their wits, and when they are fully awake, they ſay that *Maboya* hath beaten them; and having the imagination thus hurt, they are perſwaded that they feel the pain.

But it is manifeſt by the teſtimonies of ſeveral other perſons of quality and exquiſite knowledge, who have ſojourned a long time in the Iſland of St. *Vincent*, which is inhabited only by the *Caribbians*, and ſuch as have alſo ſeen thoſe of the ſame Nation who live in the Continent of the Meridional part of *America*, that the Devils do effectually beat them, and that they often ſhew on their bodies the viſible marks of the blows they had received: We are aſſured further by the Relations of divers of the *French* Inhabitants of *Martinico*, that going into the Quarter of theſe Savages, who live in the ſame Iſland, they have many times found them making horrid complaints that *Maboya* had immediately before their coming thither treated them ill, and ſaying that he was *Mouche fache contre Caraibes, mightily incens'd againſt the Caribbians*; ſo that they accounted the *French* happy, that their *Maboya* did not beat them.

Monſieur *du Montel*, who hath often been preſent at their aſſemblies, and converſed very familiarly and a long time together with thoſe of that Nation who inhabit in the Iſland of St. *Vincents*, as alſo with thoſe of the Meridional Continent, gives this teſtimony upon this ſad occaſion: "Notwithſtanding the ig-
"norance and irreligion wherein our *Caribbians* live, they know
"by experience, and fear more than death the evil Spirit,
"whom they call *Maboya*; for that dreadful Enemy doth ma-
"ny times appear to them under moſt hideous ſhapes: And
"what is particularly obſervable, that unmerciful and bloudy
"executioner, who is an inſatiable murtherer from the begin-
"ing of the world, cruelly wounds and torments thoſe miſe-
O o
rable

" rable people, when they are not fo forward as he would
" have them to engage themfelves in wars ; fo that when they
" are reproached with that over-eager paffion which hurries
" them to the fhedding of mans blood, their anfwer is, that
" they are forced thereto againft their wills by the *Ma-*
" *boya.*

But thefe are not the only people whom that implacable Enemy of Mankind treats as his flaves : There are feveral other barbarous Nations who can alwaies fhow on their bodies the bloudy marks of his cruelties : For it is reported, that the *Brafilians* fhake and fweat with horrour at the remembrance of his apparitions, and many times out of the pure apprehenfion they have of the cruel treatment they are wont to receive from him : Thence it proceeds that fome of thofe Nations flatter that old Dragon, and by adorations, offerings, and facrifices, endeavour to abate his rage and appeafe his fury ; as among others, not to mention the people of the Eaftern part of the World, fome of the Inhabitants of *Florida* and *Canada :* For that is the only reafon they can give for the fervice they do him : Nay it is affirmed that the Nation of the *Jews* was heretofore inclin'd to make offerings to that Devil, to be delivered out of his temptations and fnares : And one of their own Authors cites this Proverb as ufed among them ; *Make a prefent to Samael, on the day of expiation.*

But how great foever the apprehenfions which the *Caribbians* have of their *Maboya* may be, and how ill foever they may be treated by him, yet do they not honour him with any offerings, prayers, adorations, or facrifices : All the remedy they ufe againft his cruel vexations, is, the beft they can, to make little Images of wood, or fome other folid matter, in imitation of the fhape under which that wicked fpirit hath appeared to them : Thefe Images they hang about their necks, and fay they find eafe thereby, and that *Maboya* does not torment them fo much when they have thofe about them : Sometimes alfo in imitation of the *Caribbians* of the Continent, they make ufe of the mediation of the *Boyez* to appeafe him, and they thereupon confult their Gods, as, upon the like occafions thofe of the Continent have recourfe to their Sorcerers, who are highly efteemed among them.

For though the *Caribbians* of thofe parts are all generally fubtle enough, yet have they among them a fort of crafty companions, who to gain greater authority and reputation among the reft, make them believe that they hold a fecret correfpondence with the evil Spirits whom they call *Maboya,* as our Iflanders do, whereby they are tormented, and that they learn of them things abfolutely unknown to others : Thefe Impoftors are looked upon among this poor people that have no knowledge of God, as Oracles, and they confult them in
all

all things, and superstitiously give credit to their Answers.
This occasions irreconcileable Enmities among them, and many times Murthers; for when any one dies, his Friends and Relations are wont to consult the Sorcerer how he came to his death; if the Sorcerer answers, that such or such a one was the cause of it, they will never rest till they have dispatch'd him whom the *Piais* (so they call the Sorcerer in their Language) hath nam'd to them. The *Caribbians* of the Islands do also in this follow the custom of their Country-men of the Continent, as we have represented before.

But this is most certain, and a thing which all the Savages daily acknowledg themselves by experience, That the wicked one hath no power to do them any hurt in the company of any *Christians*; hence it comes, that in those Islands where the *Christians* live jointly with the *Caribbians*, those wretched people being persecuted by the Adversary, make all the haste they can to the next houses of the *Christians*, where they find a certain refuge against the violent assaults of that furious Oppressor.

It is also a manifest truth, confirm'd by daily experience all over *America*, That the holy Sacrament of Baptism being conferr'd on these Savages, the Divel never beats nor torments them afterwards as long as they live.

A man would think, that this seriously consider'd, these people should earnestly desire to embrace the Christian Religion, that so they might be deliver'd out of the jaws of that roaring Lion. True it is, that while they feel the cruel pricks in the Flesh, they wish themselves Christians, and promise to become such; but as soon as the pain is over, they laugh at Christian Religion and its Baptism. The same brutish stupidity is found *De Lery, c. 16* among the people of *Brasil.*

CHAP. XIV.

A Continuation of that which may be called **Religion** *among the* Caribbians : *Of some of their* **Traditions**; *and of the Sentiment they have of the Immortality of the Soul.*

WE have seen in the precedent Chapter how the Spirits of darkness take occasion in the night-time, by hideous apparitions and dreadful representations, to frighten the miserable *Caribbians*; and how to continue them in their Er-

O o 2

rors,

rors, and a fervile fear of their pretended power, they punifh them if they be not fo forward as they would have them to comply with their wicked fuggeftions; and how they charm their Senfes by Illufions and ftrange Imaginations, pretending to the Authority of revealing to them things to come, healing them of their Difeafes, revenging them of their Enemies, and delivering them out of all the dangers whereto they fhall be expos'd: All this well confider'd, is it to be admir'd that thefe Barbarians, who knew not, nor in the leaft reflected on the honour which God had done them, in making a difcovery of himfelf to them in the many delightful Creatures he hath fet before their eyes, to conduct them to the light of their inftructions, fhould be deliver'd up to a reprobate fenfe, and that at this prefent they fhould be deftitute of all underftanding to perceive the true way of Life, and without hope, and without God in the World?

We have alfo reprefented, That what indeavours foever they might ufe to fmother all the fentiments of Divine Juftice and its Jurifdiction in their Confciences, yet hath there ftill remain'd in them fome fpark of that Knowledge, which awakens them, and raifes in them from time to time divers fears and apprehenfions of that Vengeance which their Crimes might bring upon them: But inftead of lifting up their eyes to heaven, to implore the affiftance thereof, and by confidence and amendment of life to appeafe the Sovereign Majefty of the true God, whom they had offended, they defcend to the abyffes of Hell, to invocate the Devil by the facrilegious Superftitions of their Magicians, who after they have render'd them thofe fatal offices, involve them, by thofe infamous Contracts, in the deplorable flavery of thofe cruel Tyrants.

Thefe poor Barbarians are fo tranfported and befotted by thofe furious paffions, that to obtain fome favour from thofe enemies to all goodnefs, and to appeafe thofe Tygers, they render them feveral fmall Services; for they not only confecrate to them the firft of their fruits, but they alfo devote to them the moft fumptuous Tables of their Feafts; they cover them with the moft delicate of their Meats, and the moft delicious of their Drinks; they confult them in their affairs of greateft importance, and are govern'd by their wicked counfels; they expect, in their Sicknefs, the Sentence of their Life or Death from thofe deteftable Oracles, which they receive by the means of thofe Puppets of Cotton, wherein they wrap up the worm-eaten Bones of fome wretched Carcafs taken out of the Grave; and to free themfelves from the weight of their blows, and divert their rage, they burn in honour of them the leaves of Tobacco; and fomtimes they paint their ugly fhapes in the moft confiderable place of their Veffels which they call *Piragas*, or they wear hanging about their necks a little Image

representing

repreſenting ſome one of thoſe curſed Spirits, in the moſt hideous poſture in which they had ſometime appear'd unto them, as we have hinted in the precedent Chapter.

It is alſo conceiv'd, That it is out of the ſame deſign of inſinuating themſelves into the favour of thoſe Monſters, that many times they macerate their Bodies by many bloody inciſions and ſuperſtitious abſtinences, and that they have ſo great a veneration for the Magicians, who are the infamous Miniſters of theſe infernal Furies, and the Executioners of their enraged Paſſions: Yet have not theſe abus'd wretches any Laws determining the preciſe time of all theſe damnable Ceremonies; but the ſame wicked Spirit which inclines them thereto, finds them occaſions enough to exerciſe them, either by the ill treatment they receive from him, or their own curioſity to know the event of ſome military Enterpriſe, or the ſucceſs of ſome Diſeaſe, or laſtly to find out the means of revenging themſelves of their Enemies.

But ſince thoſe who have liv'd many years in the midſt of that Nation unanimouſly affirm, That in their greateſt diſtreſſes they never ſaw them invocate any of thoſe Spirits, we are perſwaded, that all thoſe little Services, which fear forces from them rather then reverence or love, ought not to be accounted a true Worſhip, or acts of Religion; and that we ſhall give thoſe fooleries their right denomination, if we call them Superſtitions, Enchantments, Sorceries, and ſhameful productions of that Art which is as black as are thoſe Spirits of darkneſs whom their *Boyez* conſult: And we may conclude alſo, that the meat and drink which they preſent to thoſe counterfeit Divinities, cannot be properly called Sacrifices, but expreſs Compacts between the Divels and the Magicians, obliging them to appear when they call for them.

So that it is not to be thought ſtrange, that in all theſe weak ſentiments which moſt of the *Caribbians* have of whatever hath any appearance of Religion, they ſhould among themſelves laugh at the Ceremonies of the Chriſtians, and think the worſe of thoſe of their Nation who expreſs any inclination to be Baptiſed: The ſureſt way therefore for thoſe whoſe hearts God ſhould open to believe the holy Goſpel, would be to leave their Country and Friends, and to go into ſome of thoſe Iſlands which are inhabited only by Chriſtians: For though they are not ſo ſuperſtitious as the people of the Kingdom of *Calecut*, who think it a horror only to touch a perſon of a contrary perſwaſion to theirs, as if they were thereby defil'd; nor yet ſo rigorous as they are in the Kingdom of *Pegu*, where when a man embraces the Chriſtian Religion, the wife celebrates his Funeral as if he were dead, and erects a Tomb, at which having made her Lamentations, ſhe is at liberty to marry again, as if ſhe were effectually a Widow; yet he among the *Caribbians* who ſhould

embrace

embrace Christianity, would expose himself to thousands of reproaches and affronts, if he continu'd his aboad among them.

When they see the Assemblies and Service of the Christians, they are wont to say, is is pretty and divertive, but it is not the fashion of their Country; not expressing in their presence either hatred or aversion to the Ceremonies, as did the poor Savages who liv'd in the Island of *Hispaniola*, and the neighbouring Islands, who would not be present at the Service of the *Spaniards*, much less embrace their Religion, because, as they said, they could not be perswaded that persons so wicked and so cruel, whose unmerciful barbarism they had so much experienc'd, could have any good belief.

Some Priests and Religious men, who had been heretofore in that Country, having been over-forward in the baptizing of some before they had instructed them in that Mystery, have been the cause that that Sacrament is not in such reputation among the *Caribbians* as otherwise it might have been: And whereas their Godfathers and Godmothers gave them new Cloathes, and made them some other little Presents on the day of their Baptism, and treated them very sumptuously, within eight days after they had received that Sacrament they desired to receive it again, that they might have other Presents and good cheer.

Not many years since, some of those Gentlemen took into their charge a young *Caribbian*, their *Catechumen*, born in *Dominico*, whose name was *Ya Marabouy*, a Son of that Captain whom the *French* call the *Baron*, and the Indians *Orachora Caramiana*, out of a design to shew him one of the greatest and most magnificent Cities in the World, which was *Paris*; they brought him over-Sea, and after they had shewn him all the Rarities of that great City, he was baptiz'd there with great solemnity, in the presence of many Persons of Honour, and named *Lewis*: Having sojourn'd a while in those Parts, he was sent back into his own Country, loaden indeed with Presents, but as much a Christian as when he came out of it, because he had not been fully instructed in the Mysteries of Christian Religion: As soon as he had set foot in his own Island he laugh'd at all he had seen, as if it had been but a May-game, and saying the Christians were an extravagant sort of people, he return'd into the Company of the other Savages, put off his Cloathes, and painted his Body over with *Roucon*, as he had done before.

To shew the inconstancy and lightness of the *Caribbians* in the Christian Religion, when they have once embrac'd it, there is a Story, how that while M. *Auber* was Governour of *Gardeloupe* he was often visited by a Savage of *Dominico*, who had liv'd a long time at *Sevil* in *Spain*, where he had been baptiz'd; but being return'd into his Island, though he made as many Signs of the Cross as one would desire, and wore a great pair

of

of Beads about his Neck, yet he liv'd like a Savage, went naked among his own people, and retain'd nothing of what he
had seen and been taught at *Sevil*, save that he put on an old
Spanish Habit, the more to ingratiate himself when he came to
visit the Governour.

They have a very ancient Tradition among them, which
shews that their Ancestors had some knowledg of a Superior
Power which took a care of their Persons, and whose favourable assistance they were sensible of; but this Light their brutish Children have suffer'd to be extinguish'd, and through their
ignorance never reflected on it: They say then, That their
Ancestors were poor Savages, living like Beasts in the midst of
the Woods, without Houses or places where they might retreat, living on the Herbs and Fruits which the Earth produc'd
of it self without manuring; whilst they were in this miserable condition, an old man among them, extreamly weary of
that brutish kind of life, wept most bitterly, and, orewhelm'd
with despair, deplor'd his wretched condition; whereupon a
Man all in white appear'd to him descending from Heaven, and
coming neer, he comforted the disconsolate old man, telling
him, That he was come to assist him and his Countrymen, and
to shew them the way to lead a more pleasant life for the future; That if any one of them had sooner made his complaints
to Heaven, they had been sooner relieved; That on the Sea-
shore there was abundance of sharp Stones, wherewith they
might fell down Trees to make Houses for themselves; And,
That the Palm and Plantine Trees bore Leaves fit to cover the
Roofs of them, and to secure them against the injuries of the
Weather; That to assure them of the particular care he had
of them, and the great affection he bore their *species*, beyond
those of other Creatures, he had brought them an excellent
Root, wherewith they might make Bread, and that no Beast
should dare to touch it when it was once planted; and that he
would have them thence-forward make that their ordinary sustenance: The *Caribbians* add further, That thereupon the
charitable unknown person broke a stick he had in his hand into three or four pieces, and that giving to the old man, he commanded him to put them into the ground, assuring him that
when he should come a while after to dig there, he should find
a great Root; and that any part of what grew above-ground,
should have the virtue of producing the same Plant: he afterwards taught him how it was to be used, telling him the Root
was to be scraped with a rough and spotted Stone, which was
to be had at the Sea-side; that the juice issuing by means of
that scraping, was to be laid aside as a most dangerous poison;
and then with the help of fire a kind of savory Bread might be
made of it, on which they might live pleasantly enough. The
old man did what had been enjoin'd him, and at the end of nine
Moons

Moons (as they say) being extreamly defirous to know the fuccefs of the Revelation, he went to fee the pieces he had planted in the ground, and he found that each of them had produced many fair and great roots, which he difpofed of as he had
been commanded : Thofe of *Dominico* who tell this ftory, fay
further, that if the old man had vifited the pieces at the end of
three days, inftead of nine months, he would have found the
roots grown to the fame bignefs, and that they had been produc'd in that time : But in regard he went not to look what
became of them, till after the expiration of fo long a time, the
Manioc continues to this prefent all that time in the ground,
before it be fit to make *Caffava* of.

This is all we could get from the *Caribbian* Tradition, and
we conceiv'd it might well be fet here at length, fince it is the
only one that is related among this ignorant people, who trouble themfelves not to know the Name and Quality of that kind
and heavenly Benefactor who hath obliged them fo much, nor
to render him any acknowledgment or honour : The Pagans
were much more grateful in honouring *Ceres,* from whom they
faid they received Corn, and the invention of making bread :
And the *Peruvians,* though they knew not the great *Pachaca-*
mac, that is, him whom they held to be the foul of the Univerfe,
and the Sovereign Author of their lives and all they had, yet
did they adore him in their hearts with much refpect and veneration, and rendring him externally by their geftures and
words great expreffions of their fubmiffion and humility, as
to the unknown God.

The *Caribbians* believe they have every one of them fo many fouls as they feel beatings of Arteries in their bodies, befides that of the heart : Now of all thefe fouls the principal,
as they fay, is in the heart, and after death it goes to Heaven
with its *Icheiri,* or its *Chemiin,* that is, with its God, who carries
it thither to live there in the company of the other Gods : And
they imagine that it lives the fame kind of life as man lives
here below : Thence it comes that to this day they kill flaves
on the Tomb of the dead, if they can meet with any that had
been in the fervice of the deceafed, to go and wait upon him
in the other world : For it is to be obferved, that they do not
think the Soul to be fo far immaterial as to be invifible ; but
they affirm it to be fubtile, and of thin fubftance as a purified
body ; and they have but the fame word to fignifie heart and
foul.

As for the other fouls, which are not in the heart, they
believe fome go after death and live on the Sea-fide, and that
they caufe Veffels to turn : They call them *Oumekou* ; the
others, as they conceive, go and live in the Woods and Forefts,
and they call them *Maboyas.*

Though moft of this poor people believe the immortality
of

of the soul, as we have represented it, yet they speak so confusedly, and with so much uncertainty of the state of the soul
separated from the body, that we should sooner have done to
say they were absolutely ignorant thereof, than set down their
extravagant Relations. Some affirm, that the most valiant of
their Nation are carried after their death into certain *Fortunate Islands,* where they have all things at their wish, and that
the *Arouagues* are there their slaves; that they swim unwearied
in great Rivers; that they live deliciously, and spend the time
in dancing, playing, and feasting, in a land which produces in
abundance all sorts of excellent fruits without any cultivation: On the contrary they hold, that those who were cowardly
& afraid to go to the wars against their Enemies, do after death
serve the *Arouagues,* who inhabite barren and desart Countries
beyond the Mountains: But others who are more brutish never trouble themselves about their condition after death, nor
ever think or speak of it: And if any question be put to them
concerning it, they know not what answer to make.

Yet they have all had heretofore a certain belief of the immortality of the Soul, but after a very gross manner, as may be
deduc'd from the Ceremonies of their Interrments, and the
prayers they make to the dead, that they would return to
life, as we shall represent more at large in the last Chapter of
this History; as also from this, that the most polite among them
are at present of that perswasion, that after death they shall
go to Heaven, to which place they say their Ancestors are gone
before them; but they never enquire after the way they are
to take to attain that happy abode. Accordingly, when their
Boyez, who also act the part of Physitians, despair of curing
their diseases, and that the Devils have foretold by their mouths
that there is no further hopes of life, they give them this comfort, that their Gods will conduct them to Heaven, where they
shall live at ease without any fear of sickness.

The belief of the *Calecutians* as to this Article is worse than
that of our *Caribbians,* and their transmigration is an extravagant kind of immortality: For they believe that their souls
at the departure out of their bodies are lodg'd in those of wild
Oxen, or some other beast. The *Brasilians* are in this point
more rational; for they conceive that the souls of the wicked
go after death to the Devil, who beats and torments them, but
that the souls of the just are entertain'd with dancing and good
cheer in delightful plains beyond the Mountains: And it is
pleasant to think that most of the Savages of *America* place the
sovereign felicity of the other life in dancing.

The Resurrection of the body is by the *Caribbians* accounted a pure foolery; their Theology is too obscure to receive so
great an illumination: We may therefore well wonder at a small
glimpse of this sacred truth in the poor *Virginians,* since it is

*Pirard's
Travels part
1. c. 27.*

De Lery, c. 16

*Garcilasso,
l. 2. c. 7. De
Lact, l. 5. c. 7.*

a point wherein the ancient Pagans saw as little as our *Caribbi-ans* : There is also a small spark of it among the *Indians* of *Pe-ru*, as most Authors affirm.

But though the *Caribbians* have so little knowledge and fear of God, as we have represented, yet are they extreamly afraid of his voice, that is Thunder ; that dreadful voice which makes such a stir in the clouds, which is attended by such flames of fire, which shakes the foundations of the Mountains, and makes the *Neroes* and *Caligulaes* of this world to tremble : Our Sava-ges therefore assoon as they perceive the approaches of the Tempest, which commonly comes along with that voice, make all the haste they can to their little houses, and sit down on low stools about the fire, covering their faces and resting their heads on their hands and knees; and in that posture they fall a weeping, and say in their Gibberish, *Maboya mouche faobe contre Caraibe*, that is. *Maboya is very angry with them* : and they say the same when there happens a Hurricane : They give not over that la-menting exercise, till the Hurricane is quite over; and they are extreamly astonish'd, that the Christians should express so so little affliction and fear upon those occasions. Thus the Grand *Tartars* are mightily afraid of Thunder, and when they hear it, they drive all strangers out of their houses, and wrap themselves up in Garments of coarse cloth, which they put not off till the noise be over : And divers other barbarous Na-tions are no less frighted than the *Caribbians* upon the like occa-sions : Nay it is reported that the *Peruvians*, the *Cumaneses*, the *Chineses*, and the *Moluckeses* imitate them in lamentations and frights, when there happens an Eclipse.

Yet is it true, that since the *Caribbians* have conversed fami-liarly with the Christians, some of them are grown so resolute as not to be afraid of the Thunder : for some have been seen to laugh when it thundred most, and others counterfeited the noise, pronouncing a word which is not easily written, and whereof the sound comes somewhat neer these letters, *Trtrque-tenmi* : But it is very certain withall, that they do their natu-ral inclination a great violence when they pretend that they are not afraid of the Thunder, and it is pure vanity which eggs them on to personate that confidence, to perswade those who see them, that upon those emergencies their generosity is as great as that of the Christians : For some of the *French* In-habitants of *Martinico* who have surpriz'd them in their Quar-ters when it thundred and lightned, affirm that they found the most resolute among them shivering with fear in their poor Huts.

Now this trouble and these disturbances which they discover at the hearing of that cœlestial voice, are they not a visible effect of the sentiment they have of an infinite and sovereign Power, imprinted by Nature on the minds of all men, and a pregnant
proof,

proof, that though these wretches endeavour all they can to
smother the stings of their Consciences, yet can they not do
it so fully but that they prick and torment them, though against
their wills? And is not this enough to make good the saying
of *Cicero*, at the begining of the precedent Chapter? For
though all men do not in words acknowledge that Divinity,
yet are they convinc'd in themselves, by a secret but irresista-
ble hand, which writes this first of all Truths in their hearts
with the point of a Diamond: So that to conclude, we shall
say with that great man, whose words will put an excellent period to this discourse, as they have begun it, That it is innate,   *De Nat. De-*
and as it were graven in the minds of men, that there is a   *or. lib. 2.*
Divinity.

CHAP. XV.

Of the Habitations and House-keeping of the Caribbians.

HIstorians relate, that heretofore some of the ancient Inha-   *Garcil. Com.*
bitants of *Peru* liv'd scattered up and down the Moun-   *Royal, l. 2.*
tains and Plains, like savage beasts, having neither Villages nor   *c. 12. & l. 6.*
Houses; That others made their retreat into Caves, and de-   *c. 11.*
sart and solitary places; and others took up their quarters in
ditches and hollow trees: But the *Caribbians* at the present
are in a condition much different from this savage and brutish
kind of life: True it is we shall find it no great task to give a
description of their Habitations, for they are at no great trouble about the architecture of them; for they require only a
tree and a hedge-bill to build themselves a lodging.

Their Habitations are somewhat neer one to another, and
dispos'd at certain distances, after the manner of a Village;
and for the most part they plant themselves upon some little
ascent, that so they may have better air, and secure themselves
against those pestilent Flies which we have elsewhere called
Mesquitos and *Maringoins*, which are extreamly troublesome,
and whereof the stinging is dangerous in those parts where
there is but little wind stirring: The same reason it is that obliges the *Floridians*, beyond the Bay of *Carlos* and *Tortugues*, to
lodge themselves for the most part at the entrance of the Sea,
in Huts built on Piles or Pillars: The Inhabitants of the *Caribbies* are also desirous to be somewhat neer Springs, Brooks,
and Rivers, because of their washing of themselves every morning before they put the red paint on their bodies.

Among us, and several other Nations of this part of the
world, the Architects break their brains in studying to make

such strong and sumptuous Edifices, as if they would have
their duration to be equal with that of the world : The *Chineses*, at the late coming of the Christians among them, expressed a certain astonishment thereat, and charged us with Vanity : For their parts they measure the continuance of their
Houses by that of their short lives : But our Savages of the *Caribbies* are willing to abate much of that term, and order their
structures so as that they are oblig'd to build often in their
lives : Their little Huts are made in an oval form, of pieces of
wood planted in the ground, over which they put a Roof of
Plantane-leaves or Sugar-canes, or some herbs which they can
so dispose and intermix one among another, that under that
covering which reaches to the ground, they are secured against
rain and all injuries of the weather : And this Roof, as weak as
it seems to be, makes a shift to last three or four years, without
being much the worse, unless there happens to be a Hurricane:
Pliny affirms, that some Northerly people made use of Reeds
for the covering of their houses; and they are used to this
day in the Low-Countries, *France,* and other parts : The *Cari-
bians* do also make use of small Reeds fasten'd across for the *Pa-
lisadoes*, which are instead of walls to their Habitations; under
every covering they have as many partitions made as they
would have Rooms : A simple piece of Mat does among them
the office of our doors, bolts, and locks : There's nothing
above their heads but the roof it self, and under their feet only the bare earth; but they are so careful in keeping of it clean,
that they sweep it as often as they see the least filth upon it :
This they observe in their private houses; for commonly their
Carbet, or publick house, where they meet upon some rejoicing
account, is not kept over-clean, insomuch that many times the
place is full of *Chegoes*.

Besides the little room where they take their rest, and entertain their friends, every considerable family hath two other
little rooms : One serves for a Kitchin, and the other for a
kind of Store-house, where they put up their Bows, their Arrows, and their *Boutous*, which are Clubs of a heavy and smooth
wood, which they use in their wars instead of swords, when
they have spent all their Arrows : There they also put up
their Baskets, their supernumerary beds, with all the toys and
ornaments they make use of at publick meetings and upon
days of Triumph : All that trumpery they call by the name
of *Caconnes*.

As to furniture, our Savages have only a kind of hanging
beds, which they call *Amais*, which are as it were great Co-
verlets made of Cotton, very neatly woven, and folded together at both ends, that they may join the two corners of the
bredth : Then they fasten the *Amais* by the two folded ends,
to the principal pillars of their Edifice : Those who have no

Cotton-

Trigaut's
History of
China, c. 4.

L. 16. c. 38.

Cotton-beds, make use of another kind of Bed, which is called *Cabane*; and this is made of several small sticks laid across, on which they put a good quantity of *Banana*-leaves; this *Cabane* is hung up and suftain'd by the four corners with great cords of *Mahot*: They have also little Stools or Chairs made all of a piece, of a red or yellow Wood, and as smooth as Marble: There are also some among them who have little Tables, which have four wooden Pillars, and those cover'd with the leaves of that kind of Palm which is called the *Latanier*.

Their Vessels, as well of the Kitchin as others, are all of Earth, as those of the *Maldiveses*; or of certain Fruits like our Gourds, but which have a thicker and harder rind, cut after divers figures, and made smooth and painted as well as they are able to do it: of these they make such Vessels as serve instead of Platters, Porringers, Basins, Trenchers, Drinking-cups, and Dishes: All these Vessels made of Fruits, they call *Coïs* or *Couis*; and it is the same name which the *Brasilians* give theirs made of the same materials: Their earthen Vessels they make use of as we do of our Kettles and Cauldrons; among others they have one kind which they call *Canary*; of these *Canarys* there are some very large, others little; the little ones serve only for the making of sawces or haut-gousts, which they call *Taumalis*; but the great ones are employ'd about the making of that kind of Drink which they call *Ouicou*: The *Caribbians* of *Martinico* do often bring some of these little *Canarys* to the Quarter of the *French*, who give them in exchange certain *Caconnes*, that is, some toys or other, wherewith they are pleas'd: Those little Vessels are the more esteem'd, because they are not so easily broken as our earthen Pots: These Vessels which we have described, as wretched as they are, are preserv'd by them with as much curiosity and care as can be imagined.

The *Caribbians* have also, at a pretty distance from their houses, a place for the easing of their natural necessities, to which when they have need they resort, carrying along with them a sharp stick, wherewith they make a hole in the ground, into which having put their Ordure, they afterwards cover it with earth; so that there is never any thing of that kind seen among them: We take the more particular notice of this Custom of theirs, because it is consonant to what was done by the Army of *Israel* as long as they were in the Field: To the same ^{*Deut. c.13.*} may also be referred the Custom of the *Turks*, who in that case *Busbequius* make a pit with a piece of Iron to cover their Excrements, *in his Em-* which keeps their Camp very clean when they are in the Field. *bassies,* l. 3. An ancient Author affirms, that in the *East-Indies* a certain *Ctesias.* Bird named *Justa* does somwhat of this kind, burying its own Ordure so as that it may not be seen; but this smells too much of the Fable to be credited. The *Tartars*, as some affirm, will *Carpin's* not so much as make water within the inclosures of their Habi- *Travels into* tations, as accounting it a sin.   But *Tartary.*

But to return to our Savages: There are to be seen within the inclosures of their houses a great number of Poultry and Turkeys, which they breed not so much for their own Tables, as to make Presents to their Friends the Christians who come to visit them, or to be exchang'd for Hedg-bills, Wedges, Hoes, and other Instruments of Iron which they stand in need of.

They have also about their habitations good store of Orange-Trees, Citron-Trees, Guavas, Fig-Trees, Bananas, and other Fruit-Trees; many of those little Trees which bear the *Pyman*, and the Shrubs and Simples whereof they have any acquaintance, to be us'd when they have any need of them; and with these their little Gardens are bordered; but within they are full of Manioc, Potatoes, and several sorts of Pulse, as Pease of divers kinds, Beans, Mais, small Millet, and some others: They have also Melons of all sorts, excellent Citruls, and a kind of Cabbge called the *Caribbian*-Cabbge, which are of a very delicious taste: But they bestow their greatest pains about the culture of the *Ananas*, which they prefer before all other Fruits.

But though they have no Villages, nor movable Houses, such as may be remov'd from one place to another, as is reported of the *Bedowins* a poor people of *Ægypt*, certain Moors inhabitants on the South-side of *Tunis* in *Africa*, and certain Nations of *Great-Tartary*; yet do they often change their Habitations, as the humour takes them; for as soon as they take the least disgust to their Habitations, they immediately transplant themselves to some other place; and this is done of a sudden, and without desiring any permission of the *Cacick*, as the ancient *Peruvians* were oblig'd to do of their King upon such occasions.

Among the occasions of this change of habitation among the *Cariblians* of the Islands, one is a perswasion that they shall have their health better in some other place; the same cause occasions many times a removal of house-keeping among the *Brasilians*: Somtimes it is caus'd by some nastiness done in their Habitations, for which they conceive a certain horrour; and somtimes the death of one of the house, which causing in them an apprehension of going the same way, obliges them to take up their Quarters in some other place, as if death could not as easily meet with them there; but this foolish apprehension is much more prevalent with the *Caribbians* of the Continent, who upon such occasions will be sure to burn their habitations, and march to some other place: This pleasant Superstition is observable also among the *Indians* of the Island of *Corassao*, though those poor people have receiv'd Baptism; for Mont. *du Montel* relates, That being in the great Village of those *Indians* named the *Ascension*, and having observed in two or three places some houses without any Inhabitants, though they were not

deficient

deficient in ought, and others quite ruined, he asked how those houses came to be so; whereto the *Caciok*, or Captain, made answer, That it was because some persons had dy'd in those places. The ancient *Peruvians* put themselves to the trouble of such a removal, if their habitations receiv'd any prejudice by Thunder; for then they conceiv'd such an abomination thereat, that they made up the doors thereof with stones and dirt, that no body might ever enter there any more.

It is reported, That heretofore the men of the Province of *Quito* in *Peru* thought it no shame to employ themselves in all things relating to house-keeping, while their Wives went abroad walking at their pleasures: And the ancient *Ægyptians* did the like, if we may credit *Herodotus*. And we are to acknowledg, *Lib.* 2. that the employment of dressing Meat in the Kitchen was accounted honourable in ancient *Greece*; for honest *Homer* in *Lib.* 9. his Iliad represents *Achilles* making a *Hash*, and spitting the Meat, and all his Courtiers busie in the Kitchen for the entertainment of the Embassadors of *Agamemnon*: And as to Fish, it hath always had this priviledge, that Persons of Quality have thought it no disparagement to have a finger in the ordering of it.

But among the *Caribbians* the men think all these employments below and unbefitting them; they for the most part spend the time abroad, but their Wives keep at home, and do all that is requisite about the house: True it is, the men fell down Timber for the building of their Houses, and when they are built it is their business to keep them in repair; but the women take care for all things necessary for the subsistence of the Family: The men go a hunting and a fishing, as we shall declare more at large elsewhere; But the women fetch home the Venison from the place where it was kill'd, and the Fish from the Water-side: It is the womens work, in fine, to get in *Manioc*, to prepare the *Cassava*, and the *Oüicou*, which is their ordinary Drink, to dress all the Meat, to set the Gardens, and to keep the house clean, and all the houshold-stuff in good order; not not to mention the pains they take in painting their Husbands with *Roucou*, and spinning Cotton for the use of the Family: so that they are continually employ'd, and their work is never at an end, while their Husbands divert themselves abroad; and so they are rather to be accounted Slaves then Companions.

In the Islands of S. *Vincent* and *Dominico* there are some *Caribbians* who have many *Negroes* to their Slaves, as the *Spaniards* and some other Nations have; some of them they got from the *English* Plantations, and some from *Spanish* Ships heretofore cast away on their Coasts; and they call them *Tamons*, that is, *Slaves*: They are so well ordered, that they serve them in all things about which they are employ'd with as much obedience, readiness, and respect, as if they were the most civiliz'd people in the World.   Now

Now that we are treating of the Houses and Housekeeping of the *Caribbians*, some might take occasion to ask, Whether, as we have the use of Lamps, Candles, and Torches, they do not also make use of some light, and some artifice in the night-time, to supply the want of the days light? True it is, they have learnt of the Christians to make use of the Oil of Fishes, and to put Cotton into Lamps, to light them in the night-time; but most of them have no other light in the night than a kind of wood very apt to take fire, which they have ready in the house for that purpose, whence we call it *Candle-wood*; it is full of an unctuous Gum, which makes it burn like a Candle, and being once lighted, it gives a sweet scent : In like manner the Inhabitants of *Madagascar*, instead of Candles and Torches, in the night time make use of certain Gums which easily take fire, and they put them into earthen Creusets, where they make a delightful and sweet smelling Fire: And if the Fire chance to go out among the *Caribbians*, they have the secret of supplying that want by rubbing two pieces of *Mabot* one against the other, and by that collision they take fire, and in a short time burn into a clear flame : Thus the *Brasilians*, insteed of a Steel and Stone, the use whereof they have not, make use of two several kinds of Wood, whereof one is almost as tender as if it were half rotten, and the other, on the contrary, very hard; and by that friction and agitation the fire takes in the former : The same thing is affirm'd of some sorts of Canes, which may be seen in the Cabinets of the Curious.

De Lery, c. 19.

Those who have sail'd to the mouth of the River of the *Amazones* relate, that they there saw some *Indians* strike fire with two sticks, but after a manner different from that of our *Caribbians*; for in that part of the World they have also two pieces of Wood, one soft, which they make flat and even like a Busk, and the other very hard, like a stick sharpened at the end, which they thrust into the soft, which they keep close to the ground under their feet; and they turn the other with both hands so swiftly, that at last the fire takes in that below, and sets it of a flame: And whereas it many times happens one person may be weary of that exercise, another immediately takes the stick in hand, and turns it with the same swiftness, till they have got fire. Some may imagine, that these ways of lighting fire are modern; but there are some marks thereof in Antiquity, as may be seen in *Theophrastus*.

History of Plants, L. 7. c. 10.

CHAP.

CHAP. XVI.

Of the ordinary Repaſts of the Caribbians.

MOſt of thoſe people who have the denomination of *Sa-vages* and *Barbarians* are gluttonous and beaſtly in their Repaſts: The *Braſilians* eat and drink exceſſively, naſtily, and at all hours, nay they riſe many times in the night to that em-ployment: The *Canadians* are ſuch gluttons, that they eat till they are ready to burſt; nay they are ſo ravenous, that they will not loſe ſo much as the ſkimmings of the Pot: They are ne-ver ſeen either to waſh their hands, or the meat they eat: They have no other napkins than the hair of their own heads, or that of their dogs, or the firſt thing they meet with: The *Grand-Tartars* do the like: They never waſh their Diſhes or Kettles, but with the pottage made in them, and are ſo naſty that what they do is not be related: The other *Tartars* come not much ſhort of them in naſtineſs and gluttony, uſing their hands in-ſtead of ſpoons to take up their pottage, and eating the fleſh of dead horſes, without any other dreſſing than ſetting of it an hour or two between their ſaddles and horſes-backs. In like manner (to make an end of theſe ſlovenly inſtances) the Inha-bitants of *Guinny*, thoſe of the *Cape* of *Good Hope*, and certain other Savages eat raw and ſtinking fleſh, together with the hair and feathers, guts and garbage, like ſo many dogs: But we are to give our *Caribbians* this commendation, that they are temperate and cleanly in their ordinary Repaſts, as well as thoſe of the Continent, though ſome among them deſerve not this elogy, as there is no rule ſo general but may have ſome ex-ception. Monſieur *du Montel*, a worthy and faithful witneſs, gives this teſtimony of ſobriety and cleanlineſs to thoſe whom he had ſeen at St. *Vincents* and elſewhere: But as we ſaid be-fore, they are not all ſuch; for thoſe who have ſeen them at *Dominico* give them not the ſame Character.

This people eat many times together in a publick houſe, as we ſhall ſee more particularly hereafter, either upon the ac-count of divertiſement and to be more than ordinarily merry, or to diſcourſe concerning their wars and common affairs, as the *Lacedæmonians* were heretofore wont to do: The women, according to the cuſtome of ſome other barbarous Countries, eat not till their huſbands have done, and they have no ſet time for their Repaſts: Their ſtomacks are their Clocks and Re-membrancers: They ſo patiently endure hunger, that after they are returned from fiſhing they will have the patience to broil their fiſh over a ſoft fire on a wooden frame made like a

De Lery, c. 9.

Relation of New-France.

Rubriques & Carpin.

Busbequius, Des Hayes, & Bergeron

Vin.leBlanc. & Garci-laſſo.

Q q

Grid-

Gridiron, about two foot high, under which they kindle so small a fire, that sometimes it requires a whole day to make ready their fish as they would have it : Some of the *French* affirm, that have eaten some of their dressing , they have lik'd it very well : It is observable generally in all their meat, that they dress all with a very gentle fire.

They commonly eat sitting on low stools, and every one hath his little table by himself, which they call *Matoutou*, as *Tacitus* affirms, that it was practised among the ancient *Germans*, and as it is reported at this day to be done in *Japan :* Sometimes also they eat their meat on the ground, kneeling round one by another : For Table-cloths, they have no linnen, as we have, nor skins, as the *Canadians*; nor Mats as the *Maldiveses*, nor Carpets as the *Turks* and some other Nations, but fair and large *Banana*-leaves newly gathered, which are very fit for Table-cloths, being so large as we have represented elsewhere: the same serve also for Napkins, and they wipe their hands therewith : They are alwaies very careful to wash their hands before meals: And when they are about the dressing of any meat, they never touch any thing that is to be eaten, ere they make their hands clean : In fine, in all their ordinary Repasts, their sobriety and cleanliness is so observable as can hardly be imagined among Savages.

We have said elsewhere that their ordinary bread is a thin Cake which they call *Cassava*, made of the *Manioc*-root : Other Writers have set down the manner how it is made; yet that our History may not be thought imperfect, we shall here give a description of the composition thereof : The root, though it be sometimes about the bigness of a mans thigh, is easily got out of the ground : Assoon as it is taken out it is scraped with a knife to take off a little hard skin which covers it, and then it is scraped or filed with with a Rasp or flat File of Iron or Copper, of a good bigness; and they press the meal which comes from it in a linnen bag, or in a long kind of pokes, which they call in the Islands, *Snakes*, neatly woven of Rushes or *Latanier* leaves by the *Caribbians*, that the juice may be squeezed out of it : The Savages before they knew the use of those Rasps, made use instead thereof, of certain hard and sharp stones which are to be found on the sea-shore : They are somewhat like our Pumice-stones : When the moisture of the *Manioc* is got out, the meal is sifted through a coarse cloth, and without mixing it with any liquor, it is put upon an Iron Plate, or Plank, and sometimes on a broad stone, under which there is fire; when it is baked on one side, they turn it on the other; and when it is fully baked, it is exposed to the Sun to make it harder, that it may keep the better : It is commonly made no thicker than a mans little finger, and sometimes thinner, according to the fancy of the Inhabitants : It will keep many
months,

months; but it eats best after a day or two making; there are some who would rather eat of it than of our ordinary bread: And the greatest miracle is, that of a root so dangerous of it self people should by artifice get so excellent nourishment: Thus the *Moors* drying a kind of poisonous Apricocks which grow in their Country, in the Sun, and afterwards boiling them over a fire, make a certain drink thereof, which is pleasant and may be drunk without any danger.

But the *Caſſava* which the *Caribbians* make is very delicate; for they have so much patience to go through with any thing they undertake, that they do better than the *French*, who are so hasty, that they would make an end of any thing assoon as they have begun it: But the *Caribbians* go leasurely to work, and never consider the time spent, so the business be done to their minds.

And whereas some *Europæans* who have used *Caſſava*, complain that it is no good nourishment, that it injures the stomack, corrupts the blood, changes the colour, weakens the nerves, and dries the body; it is to be considered, that as custom is a second nature, so that many things, though bad in themselves, do not prejudice health when one is accustomed thereto; so on the contrary, those which are good and innocent, nay the best of their own nature, if a man be not accustomed thereto, are many times prejudicial and hurtful: To confirm this truth, it is to be attributed to want of custom, what is related by some Historians of certain *Braſilians*, who being shut up with the *Dutch* in St. *Margarets* Fort, could not brook the bread and other provisions distributed to them as Soldiers, and on which it was necessary they should subsist, and complained that they made them sick, and were the occasions of their death: To this purpose there is a remarkable passage in the Travels of Monsieur *des Hayes* into the *Levant*; to wit that the said person entertaining some *Tartars* at his Table, who knew not what bread was, caused them to eat some; for within two hours after, they thought they should have dyed when the bread they had eaten began to swell, and to cause them great pains.

There is another kind of bread among the *Caribbians* made of the *Spaniſh* wheat which they call *Mais:* The *Engliſh* Inhabitants of the *Barmouthos* use no other: There are some also who instead of bread eat the root called Potatoe, whereof we have given a description elsewhere.

As concerning the other provisions used by the *Caribbians*, their most ordinary dishes, and which are used also by the *Caribbians* of the Continent, are Lizards, Fish of all sorts, Tortoises only excepted; and Pulse, as Pease, Beans, &c. but their ordinary food (contrary to the Inhabitants of *Madagaſcar*, who have a horrour for that kind of sustenance) is Crabs, got very

Q q 2   clean

clean out of their shells, and fryed with their own fat, juice of Citron, and Pyman, which they are great lovers of, and which they put abundantly into all their sawces: And yet when they entertain the *French*, or other *Europæans*, they are not so prodigal thereof, and then they accomodate themselves to their palates, out of a compliance and discretion, which argues them to be somewhat better than Savages. They call the inner part of the Crab *Taumaly*; and of that it is they make their ordinary Ragoust with water, the fine flower of *Manioc*, and good store of *Pyman*. In the last course they bring in fruits as we do; and ordinarily they content themselves with Figs, Bananas, or Ananas: If they eat flesh or any thing that is salted, it is only out of compliance with strangers, to avoid being troublesome to those who entertain them, and so they accommodate themselves to their humours who come to visit them; for then they order most of their meat to please them: And to this must be referred what we have said concerning their not eating of salt, Swines-flesh, Tortoises, and *Lamantin*.

True it is, there are among this people certain men extreamly slothful and melancholy, who lead a wretched kind of life: For they live only upon *Burgaus*, *Shell-fish*, *Crabbes*, *Soldiers* and such like Insects: They never eat any Pottage, nor Flesh, unless it be that of certain birds which they broil on the coals with their Feathers about them, and their Guts within them; and all the Sawce they use consists of the water of *Manioc* (which being boiled loses its venemous quality) fine flower of the same *Manioc*, and good store of *Pyman*.

Sometimes they have a detestable kind of seasoning for their meats, and that is the fat of the *Arouagues* their irreconcileable Enemies: But this hath no place in their ordinary Repasts, as being used only on solemn days of debauches and rejoicing.

As to their drink, as they do in several parts of *America*, the same grains of *Mais* which serve to make bread, are used for the composition of a Drink which is accounted as good as Wine; and as among us the Wheat which makes Bread will also make Beer; so in these Islands, of the Roots of *Potatoes* and *Manioc*, which serve to make Bread, there are made two several sorts of Drinks, which are ordinary in the Country: The former and most common, which is made of *Potatoes* boiled with water, is called *Maby*: It is excellent good to refresh and quench thirst, and it hath also an appetitive vertue, which causes an evacuation of the sandiness, and all the viscosities of the lower parts: Whence it comes, that those who make use of that Drink, never complain of the Stone or Gravel: The other Drink is called *Ouicou* (from a name coming neer the *Caouin* of the *Brasilians*) and is made of the *Cassava* it self, boiled in like manner with water: It is strained through a coarse cloth, which the Savages call *Hibichet*: This Drink is more excellent

cellent than the *Maby*, and differs not much from Beer, either as to colour or ſtrength. The *Indians* make it very pleaſant, but of ſuch ſtrength withall, that much drunk it intoxicates, as Wine does: They make it of *Caſſava* well and throughly baked on the plank, then chew'd by the Women, and put into Veſſels full of Water: or, after it hath been infus'd, and boiled for about the ſpace of two days by its own vertue, without any fire, as new Wine does, the infuſion is ſtrain'd through the coarſe or hair-cloth; and the juice which is gotten from it by that ſtraining, being kept two daies more, is ready for drinking: To make this compoſition boil the better they put into the Veſſel two or three Roots of Potatoes, ſcraped very ſmall. It muſt indeed be acknowledged that this cuſtom which the Savages obſerve in chewing the *Caſſava* before it be put into the Veſſel, is enough to turn the ſtomachs of ſome; but it is moſt certain withall, that the Drink made after that manner is incomparably better than that which is made otherwiſe.

The *Ouicou* is alſo made after another manner, without the Roots of Potatoes, which is this; after the *Caſſava* is taken off the Plank, it is laid ſomewhere about the houſe and covered with the leaves of *Manioc*, and ſome heavy ſtones laid thereon, to ſet it into a heat; and this is done for the ſpace of three or four days: That done, it is broken into ſeveral pieces which are ſpread on *Banana*-leaves, and then they are lightly ſprinkled with water, and ſo left: When the *Caſſava* hath remained ſo for the ſpace of one night, it becomes all red: and then it is good to make *Ouicou*, and will make its water boil without the Roots of *Potatoes*.

Beſides theſe two ſorts of Drinks which are the moſt ordinary in the *Caribbies*, there are alſo made in divers places ſeveral ſorts of delicious Wines: The *Negroes*, who are ſlaves in theſe Iſlands, make inciſions in the prickly Palms, out of which there diſtils a certain liquor like White-wine, which they gather in ſeveral little Gourds faſten'd to the overtures of thoſe trees, whereof each will yield two pints every day, and ſometimes more: The moſt ancient Authors aſſure us, that among the *Eaſt-Indians*, the Wine of Palms was very much in uſe, as indeed it is at this day: It is alſo uſed in ſome parts of *Africk*, as at *Monomotapa*.

Moreover there is in the *Caribbies* another kind of Drink made of *Bananas*, which is alſo in other parts, and by ſome called *Couſcou*: But in regard this ſort of Wine, though very pleaſant and ſtrong, cauſes great ventoſities, it is not much uſed.

To conclude, there is made in theſe Iſlands an excellent kind of Wine of thoſe precious Reeds out of which the Sugar is gotten: And this is the moſt eſteemed Drink of any made in the *Caribbies*: It is called by ſome *Cane-wine*, and there is a

par-

particular secret in the making of it : There is more made at
S. *Christophers* then any where else, by reason of the abundance
of Canes planted there : The juice of these Canes is got out by
a Mill made purposely for that use ; afterwards it is purified by
fire in great Caldrons : It may be kept a long time in its perfection, and it hath a sweetness, and withal a certain picquancy,
which might make it pass for Sack.   Of the same Canes there
is also made a certain *Aquavitæ* called *Cane-Aquavitæ*, which
keeps better then the Wine of those same Reeds.

There is not any thing in the substance of these ordinary Repasts of our *Caribbians*, which seem to savour of the Savage,
unless it be haply the Lizards ; But why may not they be as
good Meat as the Frogs and Snails eaten in some parts of
France? And who knows not that in *Spain* they eat abundance
of young Asses? Nay, compare the sustenance of our *Caribbians* with that of the *Canadians*, who, besides the skimmings of
the Pot, which we said they eat, do commonly drink filthy
and nasty grease, and prefer the flesh of Bears before any other ;
with that of the Inhabitants of the Island of *Good-fortune*,
one of the *Canaries*, who eat abundance of Suet ; with that
of the *Tartars*, the *Persians*, the *Chineses*, the *Huancas*, a Nation
of *Peru*, of the Negroes of *Angola*, who commonly live on the
flesh of Horses, Cammels, Mules, Wolves, Foxes, Asses,
Dogs, and drink the Blood of those Creatures ; with that of
the *East-Indians*, who think the Flesh of Bats and Mice as delicious as that of Partridges ; with that of the *Brasilians*, who
feed on Toads, Rats, and Worms ; or, lastly, with that of the
Tapuyes, and some other *Barbarians*, who eat hair minc'd very
small, and mix'd with wild honey, and season all their Meat
with the ashes of the burnt Bodies of their deceas'd Relations,
and mix them with the meal they bake, which causes horrour
only to represent, much more to do : Let there be, I say, a
comparison made between all these infamous Ragouts, and those
of the *Caribbian* Nation, and it will be found, that in their ordinary Commons there is nothing barbarous : Yet are we not
to dissemble what some of the *French* relate, to wit, That they
have seen the *Caribbians* eating the Lice and *Chegoes* they had
taken ; as it is reported of the *Mexicans* and *Cumaneses* : but
they do not make their Ordinary out of them, and it is particular only to some among them ; besides that they do it not
out of any delicacy they find in those Vermine, but only to
be revenged of them.

Moreover, the horrour which the *Caribbians* conceiv'd heretofore at the eating of Swines-flesh, Tortoises, and Lamantin,
for the pleasant reasons before alledged, was so great, that if
any of the *Europæans* had got them to eat any of them by sur-
prize, and they came afterwards to know it, they would be
reveng'd of them one time or other ; witness what happened to

a perſon of ſome note among the *French* : This perſon receiving
a Viſit from the *Cacick* or Captain of the Savages of the Iſland
where he liv'd, entertain'd him in jeſt with *Lamantin*, diſguis'd
in the faſhion of a Haſh; the *Cacick* miſtruſting what indeed
afterwards happened to him, intreated the Gentleman not to
deceive him; and upon the aſſurance given him thereof, he
made no difficulty to eat: after Dinner the Gentleman diſcover'd the abuſe to the *Cacick* and his Company, that he might
have the pleaſure of their Diſcourſes thereupon, and ſee what
faces they would make after ſuch a Treatment; but they had
at that time ſo much power over themſelves as to ſmother their
indignation, and the *Cacick* only ſaid to him ſmiling, *Well Friend
we ſhall not dye of it* : Some time after the Gentleman went to
return him his Viſit; he receiv'd him with great civility, and
made him extraordinary cheer; but he had given his people
order to put into all the Sauces ſome fat of the *Arouagues*,
whereof the principal *Indians* are always well provided : After
this infamous Repaſte was ended, the *Cacick*, glad in his heart,
ask'd the Gentleman and his Company how they lik'd his
Treatment; whereupon they commending it very much, and
giving him thanks for it, he acquainted them with the trick he
had put upon them; moſt of them were ſo troubled at the
thought of it, and had ſuch an inclination to caſt up all they
had eaten, that they grew very ſick; but the *Indian* laughing
at the ſpectacle, told them that he was then reveng'd.

Thoſe who have lately been among the *Caribbians* of *Dominico* and *Martinico* affirm, That now moſt of them make no
difficulty to eat *Lamantin*, Tortoiſes, and Swines-fleſh, nay, all
other Meats in uſe among the *Europæans*; and that they laugh
at the ſimplicity which oblig'd them to abſtain from them, for
fear of participating of the nature and qualities of thoſe Animals.

They have alſo remitted much of that ſeverity which they
uſed towards their Wives; for now they are ſeldom ſeen to
fetch home the Fiſh their Husbands had taken: And when they
have been a fiſhing, the Husband and Wife eat together: The
Women go alſo oftener to the *Carbet*, to participate of the
Feaſt and the publick rejoycing there made, then they did before their Husbands became ſo familiarly acquainted with
Strangers.

CHAP.

CHAP. XVII.

Of the Employments and Divertifements of the
Caribbians.

Plut. *in his
Life.*
Des Hayes
*Travels to
the* Levant.
Garc. *Com.
Royal,* li. 5.
c. 11. *&* l. 6.
c. 35.

A Lexander the Great accouuted Labour to be a thing truly
Royal ; and there are to be feen at this day in the Se-
raglio at *Adrianople,* the Tools which *Amurath* made ufe of to
make the Arrows he fent to fome of his principal Officers : The
Peruvians are much to be commended as to this particular ; for
the Kings of *Peru* had made Laws, and appointed particular
Judges for the regulation of Idle perfons and Vagabonds, infomuch that it was ordered, That Children of five years of age
fhould be employ'd in fome Work fuitable to their age ; nay,
they fpared not the blind, the lame, and the dumb, but employ'd them in divers things, wherein they might do fomthing
with their hands : But there are fome people fo lazy, that they

Herod. *l.* 5.

De Laets
Hift of Ame-
rica.

think Idlenefs a thing very commendable; and the Hiftorians
who have written of the *Weft-Indies* tell us of certain ftupid
and brutifh *Indians* of *New-Spain* and *Brafil,* who pafs away the
whole day fnoring in their Cots, while their Wives go abroad
to get in certain Roots for their fuftenance.

But our *Caribbians* are not like thefe laft ; for they are found
taking pains and their pleafure in feveral forts of exercifes :
The chiefeft, and thofe which are moft ordinary among them
are Hunting and Fifhing, wherein they beftow the greateft part
of their time, but efpecially in Fifhing : They are feldom feen
to go out of their Houfes without their Bows and Arrows; and
they are wonderfully expert in the ufe of them, being accuftomed to that exercife from their Infancy, as the *Turks* alfo are ;
whence it comes, that in time they come to be fo excellent at
the Bow, that within a hundred paces they will hardly ever fail
ftriking a half-Crown piece; nay, as they are making their Retreat they can do execution on their Enemies, as the *Parthians*
were fomtimes wont to do : How much therefore are we the

*Judg.*20.16.
more to wonder at thofe *left-handed* Benjamites, *who could
fling ftones at an hairs-breadth, and not mifs ?*

When the *Caribbians* go abroad a hunting or a fifhing, they
do not take their Wives along with them, as fome *Brafilians* do,
who caufe theirs to walk before them, fo great is their jealoufie;
but when they have taken any thing, they leave it upon the
place, and the Women were heretofore oblig'd to go and bring
it home, as we have already hinted : It is reported that the *Canadians* do the fame.

Among the *Caribbians* of the Iflands there is no diftinction of
quality

quality as to Hunting; but the exercife of it is as free to the meaneſt as to the greateſt among them : The cafe is the fame among all the other *Indians* of the *Weſt-Indies*.

As in their private Repaſts they never ufe no kind of Fleſh, if they have not Strangers to entertain, fo ordinarily their hunting is only for Lizards; and if they engage themfelves in any other kind of hunting, it is upon fome extraordinary occafions, when they would treat fome of their Friends among the *Europæans*, or when they intend to vifit them, and would get fomthing of them in exchange for what they had taken.

They are extreamly expert in fiſhing with the Hook, and in taking of Fiſh with the Dart; and a man cannot fufficiently admire their patience in that Exercife; for they would be content to continue half a day in the fame place, without betraying any wearinefs: And when, after they have waited a long time for the Fiſh, they come at length to perceive fome great one to their mind, and within their reach, they caſt the Dart at it, as the *Braſilians* do; which having faſtned, they immediately leap into the water after the Dart, to feize their prey : But befides the Hook and Dart wherewith they take Fiſh, they are alfo very excellent in diving neer the Rocks, and forcing them out of the holes where they ſhelter themfelves; as being in that particular equally expert with the *Floridians*, who, not De Lery, *c.* expecting that the Fiſh ſhould come and ſhew themfelves, 12. go and find them out in the bottom of the water, and there Acoſta, *l.*3. kill them with their Clubs; fo that they are feen coming up *c.*15. again with the Fiſh in one hand, and the Club in the other. 'Tis Fr. Pirard, a common thing among the Savages to be excellent Swimmers part 1.*c.*2. and Divers; and it is particularly affirm'd of the *Braſilians*,the *Maldiveſes*, fome *Peruvians*, and the Inhabitants of the Iſlands of *Robbers*, that they may pafs for a kind of amphibious Creatures.

But if the other inventions for fiſhing ſhould fail our *Caribbians*, they have their recourfe to a certain wood, which they bruife after they have cut it into little pieces; which done,they caſt it into Ponds, or thofe places where the Sea is quiet and calm; and this is as it were a Sovereign Mummy, wherewith they take as much Fiſh as they pleafe ; but they are fo prudent as not to make ufe of this laſt expedient but only in cafe of neceſſity, for fear of making too great a waſte among the Fiſh.

After Hunting and Fiſhing, they apply themfelves to feveral kinds of Works, as to make Beds of Cotton, very neatly woven, which they call *Amacs:* The Women fpin the Cotton on the knee, and commonly they make ufe of neither Diſtaff nor Spindle; but fome of them in the Iſland of *Martinico* have learn'd the ufe thereof of the *French* : They have alfo the perfect Art of twiſting it; but in fome Iſlands the Men weave the Beds : Befides this, they make Baskets of Bull-ruſhes, and Grafs,

R r

of

of divers colours; wooden chairs all of one piece; little Tables, which they call *Matoutou,* weav'd of the leaves of the *Latanier*-tree; the straining-cloths called *Hibichets*; the *Catolis,* which are a kind of great baskets to carry things on the back; several forts of Vessels fit for eating and drinking, which are polish'd, painted, and adorn'd with abundance of pretty figures delightful to the eye: They make also some other little ornaments, as Girdles, Hats, and Crowns of feathers, wherewith they set out themselves on solemn days: And the women make for themselves a kind of Buskins, or half-stockings of Cotton. But above all they take abundance of pains in ordering and polishing their Arms, that is, their Bows, their Arrows, and their *Boutous* or Clubs, which are of a hard and smooth wood, and neatly wrought about the handles with wood and bones of divers colours.

They take no less pains about their *Piragas,* or Vessels wherein they go to Sea, and whatever belongs to Peace or War. These Vessels are made of one great Tree, which they make hollow, smooth, and polish with an unimaginable dexterity: The greater sort of *Piragas* are many times rais'd higher all about, especially towards the poop, with some planks: Sometimes they paint in them their *Maboya*; sometimes they represent Savages, or some other fantastick figures. These Shallops are so large as many times to carry fifty men with all their Arms. Before they had any acquaintance with the *Christians,* who furnish'd them with all sorts of Wedges, and other Carpenters and Joyners tools, they were put to a great deal of trouble to make their Vessels; for they were oblig'd, as the *Virginians,* and some other Savages were, to set fire at the foot of the Trees, and to compass them about a little above the

De Lery,
c.13.

foot with wet moss, to keep the fire from ascending; and so they undermin'd the Tree by little and little: Afterwards to pierce the wood they us'd certain hard stones sharpened at one end, wherewith they cut and made their *Piragas* hollow, but with so great trouble and expence of time, that they acknowledge how much they are oblig'd to the *Europeans,* who have taught them easier ways to do it, by the iron-instruments wherewith they have supply'd them. Thence it came that the

Comment.
Royal,l.1.
c.11.

Peruvians thought it so great a happiness to have the tools which were brought them by the *Europeans,* that the use of Scissers being introduc'd into *Peru* by the means of the *Spaniards,* an *Indian* of Quality admiring the invention, said to one of them, That though the *Spaniards* did not furnish them with any thing but Rasors, Scissers, Combs and Looking-glasses, it sufficiently oblig'd them liberally to bestow on them all the gold and silver they had.

The *Caribbians* employ themselves also in making earthen Pots of all sorts, which they bake in furnaces, as our Potters
do:

do: And of the same material they also make those Plates or Planks on which they bake the *Cassava.*

The dexterity they express in these little Exercises, is a sufficient discovery that they would easily learn other Trades, if they were taught them. They delight very much in handling the tools of Carpenters and Joyners; and though they have not been taught how they are to be us'd, yet are they able to do many things since the *Europeans* have supply'd them therewith: So that it is to be presum'd, that if they had good Masters, they would do well at those Trades.

They are great Lovers of divertisements and recreation; and thence it comes they seek after whatever may keep them in a good humour, and divert melancholy: To that purpose they take a pleasure in keeping and teaching a great number of Parrots and Paraquitos.

To divert themselves they also make several Musical Instruments, if they may be so called, on which they make a kind of harmony: Among others they have certain Tabours or Drums made of hollow Trees, over which they put a skin only at one end: To this may be added a kind of Organ which they make of Gourds, upon which they place a cord made of the string of a reed which they call *Pite*; and this cord being touch'd makes a sound which they think delightful. The concerts of divers other Savages are no better then theirs, and no less immusical to their ears who understand Musick. In the morning, as soon as they are up, they commonly play on the Flute or Pipe; of which Instrument they have several sorts, as well polish'd and as handsom as ours, and some of those made of the bones of their Enemies: And many among them can play with as much grace as can well be imagin'd for Savages. While they are playing on the Flute, the Wives are busie in making ready their breakfast.

Sometimes also they pass away the time in singing certain Airs, the burthens whereof are pleasant enough; and in that Exercise they sometimes spend half a day together, sitting on their low stools, and looking on their fish while it is broiling. They also put pease or small pebble-stones, as the *Virginians* do, into gourds, through the midst whereof they put a stick which serves for a handle, and then shaking them they make a noise: This is the invention the women have to quiet their children. Most of the *Caribbian* Songs consist of bitter railleries against their Enemies; some they have also on Birds, and Fishes, and Women, commonly intermixt with some bawdery; and many of them have neither rhime nor reason.

Many times also the *Caribbians* of the Islands joyn Dancing to their Musick; but that Dancing is regulated according to their Musick. There are some Barbarians excessively addicted to that Exercise, as for instance the *Brasilians*; who, as *de Lery*

    affirms,

affirms, spend day and night in dancing : And we have said elfewhere, that there are many Savages who make their imaginary felicity of the other life to confist in dancing.

But the *Caribbians* use Dancing particularly at their solemn
Entertainments in their *Carbet*, or publick house. These Entertainments are ordered after this manner : Some days before
the meeting the Captain gives notice to every house, that all
may appear at the *Carbet* at the day appointed : In the mean
time the Women make a kind of strong drink of bak'd *Caffava*, and better prepar'd then that which they ordinarily drink;
and as they adde to the dose of the Ingredients, so is the
drink the stronger, and more apt to intoxicate : The men go
a fishing, or catching of Lizards; for as to other meat they
seldom prepare any for their own Tables, unless they have
Strangers to entertain : On the day appointed both men and
women paint their bodies with divers colours and figures, and
adorn themselves with their Crowns of Feathers, their richest
Chains, Pendants, Bracelets, and other Ornaments: Those
among them who would appear most gallant rub their bodies
with a certain Gum, and blow the Down of diverse Birds upon
it. In fine, they all put on their best faces, and endeavour to
make the greatest shew they can at this solemnity, priding it in
their Plumes, and all their other gallantry : The women bring
thither the Drink and Messes they have prepared, and are extreamly careful that nothing be wanting, which may contribute to the solemn entertainment : Our *Caribbians* spend all
that day and the best part of the night in eating and drinking,
dancing, discoursing and laughing : And in this Debauch they
drink much more than ordinary, that is, they make a shift to
get drunk; and the women will not be much behind them,
especially when they can get any Wine, or *Aqua-vitæ* to promote the work : So that what we have said of their ordinary
sobriety holds not at these Meetings; no more than it does at
their going to their Wars, and at their return thence : and yet
take them at the worst, their excesses come much short of those
of the *Brasilians*, who in their Debauches drink three or four
days without ceasing, and in their drunkenness engage themselves in all kind of Vices.

Their drunkenness and their debauches are frequent, as
hapning upon these several occasions: 1. When there is any Councel held concerning their Wars : 2. When they return from
their Expeditions, whether they have prov'd successful or not:
3. Upon the birth of their first Male Children : 4. When they
cut their Childrens hair : 5. When they are at age to go to the
Wars : 6. When they cut down trees, in order to the making
of a Garden and building of a House : 7. When they launch a
new Vessel : And lastly when they are recovered of some dif-
ease : They call these assemblies *Ouicou*, and since they have
conversed with the *French*, *Vin*, that is, *Wine*.　　　　　But

But on the contrary they have also their Fasts, wherein they betray the ridiculousness of their humour : For, 1. they fast when they enter into adolescency : 2. When they are made Captains : 3. At the death of their Fathers or Mothers : 4. At the death of the Husband or Wife : 5. When they have killed one of their Enemies the *Arouagues* ; this last occasion of fasting they glory very much in.

CHAP. XVIII.

Of the Entertainment which the Caribbians *make those who come to visit them.*

HEre it is that our *Caribbians* triumph over all other Savages in point of civility : For they receive strangers, who come to their Islands to visit them, with all manner of kindness and testimonies of affection.

They have sentinels all along the Sea-side in most of those Islands whereof they are solely possessed : These sentinels are placed on the Mountains, or such eminent places whence they may see a good way into the Sea; and they are so dispos'd, that they overlook those places where there is good anchorage for Ships, and an easie descent for men to land : Assoon as ever these perceive a Ship or Shallop coming towards them, they give notice thereof to such of their people as are next to them : Whereupon of a sudden there come out together several Canows or Vessels, in each whereof there are not above three men at most, who are sent out to discover what they are, and call to them at a distance to declare themselves; for they trust not the Flagg, as having been often deceived thereby : and they know by their voices whether they be *French, Spaniards, English* or *Dutch.* Some affirm, that the *Brasilians* and the *Peruvians* are so exact in their smelling, that they will discern a *French-man* from a *Spaniard* by the scent.

When the *Caribbians* are not well-assured who they are who come towards them, and perceive that they intend them some mischief, they put themselves into a posture of defence, possess themselves of the narrowest avenues of their Country, place ambushes in the Woods, and without being perceiv'd keep an eye on their Enemies, retreating through obscure waies till they have found their advantage, and joined all their Forces together ; and then they let flie a shower of Arrows on their Enemies : That done, they surround them, close with them, and cut them all off with their Clubs. In some Islands they make

up

up a body of fifteen hundred men and more, as may be guess'd by their appearance; for their number cannot be certainly known, inasmuch as they themselves not knowing how to reckon, cannot tell what numbers they are: But if they are pressed by their Enemies, they get into the Woods, or climb up Rocks that are inaccessible to all others; or if they are neer the Sea, they leap in and dive, and rise up again at a hundred, nay sometimes two hundred paces from the place where they had been seen: And afterwards they rally together, at certain Rendezvouses known to themselves, and charge afresh when it is least expected, and when they were thought to be absolutely routed.

But when they find those coming to them to be friends who come only to visit them, after they have cry'd to them that they are welcome, some cast themselves into the water and swim to them, enter into their Vessel, and when they come neer land proffer to carry them ashore on their backs, as an assurance of their affection: In the mean time the Captain himself, or his Lieutenant, expects them on the shore, and receives them in the name of the whole Island: Thence they are conducted by a considerable number of them to the *Carbet*, which is as it were the Town-House, where the Inhabitants of the Island, every one according to the age and sex of the New-comers, bid them welcome: The old Man complements and makes much of the old Man; the young Man and Maid do the like towards those of their age; and a man may read in their countenances how much they are satisfied with the visit.

But the first discourse they make to the Stranger is to ask him his name, and then to tell him theirs: And for an expression of great affection and inviolable friendship, they call themselves by the names of those whom they entertain: But to crown the Ceremony, they will have the person whom they receive in like manner to assume their name: Thus they make an exchange of names; and they have such excellent memories, that ten years after such a meeting they will remember the names of their friends, and relate some circumstance of what had passed at the former interview: And if they were presented with any thing, they will be sure to call it to mind; and if the thing be still in being, they will shew it to him who had bestowed it on them.

After all these complements which are passed at the first meeting, the next is to present their Guests with those pensile Beds which they call *Amais*, very clean and white, whereof they have store against such occasions: They desire them to rest themselves thereon, and then they bring in Fruits; and while some are busie preparing some treatment, others entertain them with discourse, observing still the conformity of age and sex.

This

This kind of entertainment may well be accounted more
rational than that of the *Caribbians* of the Southerly part of the
Continent, who receive their Guests after a very odd fashion, not
much unlike what is practised by the *Canadians :* For the *Cacick* of those *Caribbians* conducts him who comes to see them to
the Publick-house, without speaking at all to him : then he is
presented with a stool and some Tobacco, and so they leave him
for a time, without speaking a word to him, till he hath rested
himself and taken his Tobacco : Then the *Cacick* comes and
asks him, whether he be come ? The other answering yes, he
sits down by him and falls into discourse : Afterwards those of
the common sort come asking him after the same manner, whether he be come ? And having thereupon brought him something to eat, they also fall into discourse with him : True it is
indeed, that our Insulary *Caribbians*, in the reception of their
Guests, towards those of their own Nation, who are strangers
in their Islands, practise the same thing as the *Caribbians* of the
Continent : But when they entertain *French* and other *Europæans* who would be loth to keep silence so long, they speak to
them, and fall immediately into discourse, as we said before, ac-
commodating themselves to their humour, and, to comply
with them, crossing the rules of their own Ceremonies.

But the Banquet they intend them was prepared before hand,
let us now see how it is ordered, and how they demean themselves therein : They give every one his little Table, and his   Trigaut,
Messes apart, as the *Chineses* do: Some bring in broil'd Lizards;   *l. 1. c. 7.*
others, fry'd Crabs; some, Pulse; and others, Fruits, and so of
the rest : During the Repast, they discourse with them, and
wait on them with the greatest care imaginable : They think it
the greatest kindness can be done them to eat and drink hearti-
ly; and all their business is to fill the Cups, and see that every
Table be furnished : When a man drinks he must take all off,
otherwise they are disobliged; and if one cannot eat all the
Caſſava that is given him, he must put up the rest and carry it
along with him, otherwise they will take it unkindly : Thus Busbequius,
the *Turks* when they are at a friends Table, are wont to fill *lib.* 4.
their Handkerchers, and sometimes the sleeves of their Garments
with fragments of meat and bread, which they carry away with
them. And among the *Grand-Tartars*, when a Guest cannot eat all Rubriques
that is presented to him, he must give the remainders to his *in his Tra-*
Servant to lay up for him, or carry it away himself in his bag *vels into*
or pouch, wherein he puts up also the bones, if he hath not pick- Tartary.
ed them clean enough, that he may afterwards do it at his lea-
sure : But among the *Chineses*, when the Guest goes home, the
Servants of the person who invited him, carries along with him
the dishes that were left.

After the Repast, the *Caribbians* conduct you to their private Houses, and into their Gardens, shew you their Arms,
their

their curiofities and their trinkets, and prefent you with Fruits, or fome little pieces of their own workmanfhip.

If any one be defirous to continue a while among them, they take it for a great favour, and are extreamly glad of it, and find the fame treatment as at firft : But if they are willing to be gone from them, they are troubled, and ask whether you diflike your entertainment, that you fhould be gone fo foon. With that fad countenance they all re-conduct you to the Sea-fide, nay will carry you into your Shallops, if you will fuffer it : And at that final parting they again prefent you with fruits, which they force you to accept, faying to thofe who would re-fufe them, *Friend, if thou haft no need of it thy felf, thou mayft give it to thy Marriners*; fo they call all the Servants and Dome-fticks of thofe to whom they fpeak. The *Brafilians* and the *Cana-dians*, as fome affirm, do alfo make prefents upon the like occa-fions : And *Tacitus* relates, that the ancient *Germans* made pre-fents to the Strangers who came to vifit them; but they reci-procally demanded fomething of them : In this point the *Ca-ribbians* fhew themfelves more generous, for they give, and re-quire nothing back in lieu of it.

But it would be an incivility to go and vifit thefe good peo-ple and to receive their kindneffes, and not to prefent them with fomething : Whence it comes that the Strangers, who go to fee them, never go without fome grains of Chryftal, Fifhing-hooks, Needles, Pins, or little Knives, or fome fuch toies : And af-foon as they have done eating, they fet on the little Table, on which they have eaten, fome of thofe things : Thofe who have prepared the Banquet think themfelves requited a hundred-fold, and make extraordinary acknowledgments thereof.

We have hitherto reprefented what treatment the *Caribbi-ans* have heretofore made to fome of their friends, *French* and *Dutch*, who took occafion to vifit them : But they ufe other Ceremonies at the reception of Strangers of their own Nation, or their Confederates, who chance to come into their Iflands : There is in every *Carbet* a Savage, who hath a Com-miffion to receive Paffengers, and is called *Niouakaiti* : If they are of the common fort, he prefents them with Seats, and what is fit for them to eat, efpecially a *Caffava*-cake folded double, which fignifies that they may eat as much as they can, and leave the reft behind them.

If thofe who come to fee them, or pafs by occafionally are confiderable to them upon any other account, as being fome way related to them, or Captains, they comb their hair both at their coming and their going away, they hang up Beds, and invite them to reft themfelves, faying, *En Bouckra*, behold thy Bed They alfo prefent them with *Matoutous*, which are little Tables made of Rufhes, or the leaves of Palms or *Lataniers*, as we said elsewhere, on which they set the meat and the *Cassa-va* not folded, but as they come off the Plank : The women set them at their feet, and the men standing about, shew that which was brought, saying, *En Terebaili, behold thy meat* : Afterwards the women bring in Gourds full of *Ouicou*, and make them drink : Then having set them on the ground before them, the Husband who stands behind the women, says, *En batoni, behold thy drink* : And the other makes answer to these two complements, *Tao*, that is to say, *very well*, or *I thank you*. The *Cassava* unfolded signifies, eat thy fill and carry away the rest ; which they fail not to do : When they have dined well without being interrupted by any one, they all come to salute them one after another, saying to him, *Halea-tibou*, that is, *be welcome* : But the women are not much concerned in this Ceremony. As for the Visitants when they would depart, they go and take leave of every one in particular ; which they express by the word *Huichan* in their language.

CHAP. XIX.

Of what may be accounted Polity amongst the
Caribbians.

THere are in every Island of the *Caribbies*, inhabited by the *Caribbians*, several sorts of Captains : 1. The Captain of the *Carbet*, or of a Village, whom they name *Tiouboutouli hauthe* : This is when a man hath a numerous Family and retires with it at a certain distance from others, and builds Houses or Huts for to lodge it in, and a *Carbet*, where all of the Family meet to be merry, or to treat of the affairs which concern it in common ; thence it is that he is named a Captain of a Family, or of Houses.

2. A Captain of a *Piraga*, that is, either he to whom the Vessel belongs, or he who hath the command of it when they go to the Wars ; and these are named *Tiouboutouli Canaoa*.

3. Amongst those who have every one the command of a Vessel in particular, they have also an Admiral or General at Sea, who commands the whole Fleet : Him they call *Nhalenè*. In fine, they have the grand Captain, or Commander in chief, whom they call *Ouboutou*, and in the plural number, *Ouboutou-num* : This is the same whom the *Spaniards* call *Cacique* (and we in this History call *Cacick*) as some other *Indians*, and sometimes also our Savages do in imitation of them : He is during his life, from his first election to that charge, the General of
S f   their

their Armies, and he is always highly respected among them: He appoints the meetings of the *Carbet*, either for merry-making or deliberations in order to a War : And he alwaies goes abroad attended by all of his own house, and some others who do him the honour to wait on him : Those who have the greatest retinue are the most highly honoured : If any one gives him not the respect due to him upon the account of his charge, it is in his power to strike him : Of these there are but two at the most in an Island, as at *Dominico* : They are also commonly the Admirals when a Fleet goes out : Or haply that charge is bestowed on some young man, who is desirous to signalize himself upon that occasion.

This charge is obtain'd by election : and commonly he who is advanced thereto must have killed divers of the *Arouagues*, or at least one of the most considerable persons among them. The Sons do not succeed their Fathers in that charge, if they be not worthy thereof. When the chief Captain speaks all others are silent : and when he enters into the *Carbet*, every one makes him way ; he hath also the first and best part of the entertainment : The Lieutenant to this Captain is called in their Language *Onbouton maliarici*, that is to say properly, the *Track of the Captain*, or *that which appears after him*.

None of these Chiefs hath any command over the whole Nation nor any superiority over the other Captains : But when the *Caribbians* go to the Wars, among all the Captains they make choice of one to be General of the Army, who makes the first assault : and when the expedition is over, he hath no authority but only in his own Island: True it is, that if he hath behav'd himself gallantly in his enterprises, he is ever after highly respected in all the Islands : But heretofore, before the commerce between the *Caribbians* and forreign Nations had alter'd the greatest part of their ancient Politie, there were many conditions requisite to obtain that degree of honour.

It was in the first place requisite that he whom they advanc'd to that dignity, had been several times in the Wars, and that to the knowledge of the whole Island whereof he was to be chosen Captain, he had behaved himself couragiously and gallantly : Next to this it was necessary, that he should be so active and swift in running, as to surpass all competitors in that exercise : Thirdly, he who stood for the Generalship of an Island, should excell all others in swimming and diving : A fourth condition was, that he should carry a burthen of such weight as his fellow-pretenders should not be able to stand under : Lastly, he was obliged to give great demonstrations of his constancy : for they cruelly cut and mangled his shoulders and breasts with the tooth of an *Agonty* ; nay his best friends made deep incisions in divers parts of his body : And the wretched person who expected that charge was to endure all this, with-

out

out betraying the least sign of resentment and pain; nay, on the contrary, it was requisite that he receiv'd all with a smiling countenance, as if he were the most satisfied man in the World: We shall not wonder so much that these Barbarians should endure such Torments, in order to the acquisition of some Dignity, when it shall be considered, that the *Turks* do not shew themselves somtimes less cruel towards themselves, upon the account of pure gallantry, and as it were by way of divertisement; witness what is related by *Busbequius* in the fourth Book of his *Embassies*, which were too tedious to set down in this place.

To return to the *Caribbians* of the Islands: This ancient ceremony, which they observed in the election of their chief Governours, will no doubt be thought strange and savage; but there is somthing of the same kind observable in other Nations: For in the Kingdom of *Chili* they chuse for the Sovereign Captain him who is able longest to bear a great Tree upon his shoulders: In the Country of *Wiapoco*, towards the great River of the *Amazons*, to be advanc'd to the dignity of Captain, he must endure, without the least stirring of the Body, nine extraordinary strokes with a Holly-wand from every Captain, and that three several times; but that is not all; he must also be put into a Bed of Cotton, over a Fire of green Leaves, the thick Smoke whereof ascending upwards, must needs be very troublesom to the wretch who is so mad as to expose himself thereto; and he is oblig'd to continue there till he be in a manner half dead; this speaks a strange desire to be Captain : Nay, heretofore among the *Persians*, those who were desirous to be admitted into the Fraternity of the Sun, were requir'd to give proofs of their Constancy in fourscore several sorts of Torments: The *Brasilians*, without any other ceremony, make choice of him for their General who hath taken and kill'd most Enemies: And now also in some of the *Caribbies* the *Caribbians* themselves laugh at their ancient Ceremonies at the election of their Captain; for having observ'd that their Neighbours think that kind of proceeding ridiculous, they now make choice of him for their Chief, who having behav'd himself valiantly in the Wars against their Enemies, hath acquir'd the reputation of a brave and gallant person.

As soon as the *Cacick* is receiv'd into his Charge, he is highly respected by all, insomuch that no man speaks if he do not ask or command him to do it; and if any one cannot forbear speaking as he ought, all the rest immediately cry out, *Cala la bocca*, which they have learn'd from the *Spaniard*; But it suffices not to be silent in the presence of their Chief, but they are also very attentive to his Discourse, look upon him when he speaks; and to shew that they approve of what he says, they are wont to smile, and that smile is accompanied by a certain *Hun-*
Hun.   S f 2   These

These expressions of respect are such as are not to be accounted savage, as being us'd generally all over the World; but the *Maldiveses* have a particular way of honouring a person; for as they think it a kind of disrespect to pass behind any one, so to express a great submission they take their passage just before him, and making a low obeisance, say as they go by, *May it not displease you*: The *Incas*, a people of the Kingdom of *Peru*, to express the respect they bear their God, enter into his Temple backwards, and go out of it after the same manner; quite contrary to what we do in our ordinary Visits and Civilities : The *Turks* account the left hand the more honourable among Military persons : The Inhabitants of *Java* think the covering of the Head is the greatest act of submission : The *Japonneses* think it a great incivility to receive those who would honour them standing; they take off their Shooes when they would express how much they honour any person: In the Kingdom of *Gago* in *Africk* all the Subjects speak to the King kneeling, having in their hands a Vessel full of Sand, which they cast on their Heads : The Negroes of the Country of *Angola* cover themselves with Earth when they meet with their Prince, as it were to signifie, that in his presence they are but dust and ashes : The *Maronites* of Mount *Libanus* meeting their Patriarch, cast themselves at his feet and kiss them; but he immediately raising them up, presents them with his hand, which they taking in both theirs, and having kiss'd it, lay on their heads : But they who live about the Streight of *Sunda* have a very strange Custom, which is, that to honour their Superiors they take them by the left foot, and gently rub the Leg from the Anckle-bone to the Knee; and that done, they in like manner rub the Face, and the fore-part of the Head; an action which I doubt would be far from being thought respectful in these Parts.

From what hath been said it may be deduc'd, That this Worlds Honour, whatever it may be, Virtue excepted, consists only in Opinion and Custom, which differ, and somtimes clash, according to the diversity of Mens humours.

But to return to the Captain of our *Caribbians*; It is his business to take the Resolutions of War, to make all Preparations in order thereto, and to go upon any Expedition in the head of his Forces : He also appoints the Assemblies of his Island, and takes care for the reparations of the *Carbet*, which is the House where all Resolutions that concern the Publick are taken: In fine, he it is who in the name of the whole Island, as occasion serves, gives Answers, and appoints the days of divertisement, as we mentioned before.

The administration of Justice among the *Caribbians* is not exercis'd by the Captain, nor by any Magistrate; but, as it is among the *Tapinambous*, he who thinks himself injur'd gets

such

ſuch ſatisfaction of his adverſary as he thinks fit, according as his paſſion dictates to him, or his ſtrength permits him: The Publick does not concern it ſelf at all in the puniſhment of Criminals; and if any one among them ſuffers an injury or affront, without endeavouring to revenge himſelf, he is ſlighted by all the reſt, and accounted a Coward, and a Perſon of no eſteem: But, as we ſaid before, there happen few quarrels or fallings out among them.

A Brother revenges his Brother and Siſter, a Husband his Wife, a Father his Children; ſo that when any one is kill'd, they think it juſtly done, becauſe it is done upon the account of revenge and retaliation: To prevent that, if a Savage of one Iſland hath kill'd another Savage, out of a fear of being kill'd by way of revenge by the Relations of the deceaſed, he gets into another Iſland and ſetles himſelf there. Thoſe whom they think Sorcerers do not exerciſe that profeſſion long among them, though for the moſt part they are rather imagin'd to be ſuch, than that they are really ſo.

If the *Caribbians* ſuſpect any one to have ſtollen ſomthing from them, they endeavour to lay hold on him, and to cut him over the Shoulders with a Knife or the Tooth of an *Agouty*, as a mark of his crime and their revenge: Theſe *Agoutys* Teeth among the *Caribbians* ſupply the want of our Raſors, and indeed they are in a manner as ſharp: Thus the ancient *Peruvians* and the *Canarians*, before they had the uſe of our Iron Inſtruments, made uſe of a certain kind of Flint inſtead of Sciſſers, Lancets, and Raſors.

The Husband ſuffers not his Wife to break her conjugal Faith towards him without puniſhment; but he himſelf acts the part of both Judge and Executioner, as we ſhall declare more particularly in the Chapter of their *Marriages.* They know not what it is to puniſh publickly, or to obſerve any form in the execution of Juſtice; nay, they have no word in their Language to ſignifie *Juſtice* or *Judgment.*

CHAP. XX.

Of the Wars of the Caribbians.

IT is commonly at their publick Feaſts and Entertainments that the *Caribbians* take their Reſolutions of engaging upon any War; which humour is not particular to their Nation; for the *Braſilians* and the *Canadians* do the like: And that it may not be thought this is found only among Savages, *Herodo-* Lib. 1.

tus

Lib. 15.

ius and *Strabo* affirm, That heretofore the *Persians* consulted concerning their most important affairs at their great Feasts, and when they had their heads well stor'd with Wine. And not only the *Persians*, but also several *Grecian* Nations held their Councels of War at Table, if we may believe *Plutarch.*

Symp. l. 5.
qu. 2.
Trigaut,
l. 1, c. 7.

The same thing is at this day practis'd among the *Chineses*, as some Historians affirm.

But to return to the Councels of War of our *Caribbians*: When they begin to have their brains warm'd with their drink, an old Woman comes into the Assembly with a sad countenance and deportment, and with tears in her eyes demands audience; which being easily granted her, by reason of the respect and reverence they bear to her age, with a doleful voice, interrupted by sighs, she represents the injuries which the whole Nation hath receiv'd from the *Arouagues*, their ancient and inveterate Enemies: And having reckon'd up the greatest cruelties which they have heretofore exercis'd against the *Caribbians*, and the gallant men they have kill'd or taken in the Battels that were fought between them, she comes to particularize in those who were lately made Prisoners, massacred, and eaten, in some later Engagements: And at last she concludes, that it were a shameful and an insupportable disparagement to their Nation, if they should not revenge themselves, and generously imitate their Predecessors, those brave *Caribbians*, who minded nothing so much as to gain satisfaction for the injuries they had receiv'd; and who after they had shaken off the yoke, which the Tyrants would have impos'd on them for the taking away of their ancient Liberty, have carried their victorious Arms into the Territories of their Enemies, whom they have pursu'd with darts and fire, and forc'd to make their retreats into their highest Mountains, the clefts of Rocks, and the dreadful recesses of their thickest Forests; and this with so great success, that at present they dare not appear at their own Sea-coasts, and can find no habitation so remote where they think themselves secure from the assaults of the *Caribbians*; fear and astonishment having been their constant attendants after such signal Victories: That they are therefore couragiously to prosecute their advantages, and not to rest till that pestilent Enemy be utterly destroy'd.

As soon as the old Woman hath made an end of her discourse, the Captain makes a Speech to the same purpose, to make a greater impression in the minds of the Audience; which ended, the whole Assembly unanimously applauds the Proposition, and make all demonstrations imaginable of the justice of their Cause. From that time, being encourag'd by the words they had heard, they breathe nothing but blood and wounds. The Captain, concluding by the applause of the whole Assembly, and by their gestures and countenances, that

they

they are resolv'd for the War, though they do not say so much,
immediately orders it, and appoints the time for the Enterprize by some of their ways of numbring, as we have hinted
in the Chapter of their *Natural Simplicity*. In this place we
are to make this particular Remark, That they take these
bloody resolutions when they are well-loaden with drink, and
after the Divel hath tormented them to egge them on thereto,
as we have said elsewhere.

The next day after the Assembly, nothing is seen or heard
in all parts of the Island but preparations for the War: Some
polish their Bows; others order their Clubs; others prepare,
sharpen, and poison their Arrows; and others are employ'd to
make ready the *Piragas:* The Women, for their parts, are
busie about disposing and getting together the necessary provisions for the Army: So that on the day appointed they all
meet at the Sea-side with all things in a readiness to embarque.

They all furnish themselves with good Bows, and every one
with a good sheaf of Arrows, which are made of a small smooth
Reed, with a little piece of iron or some sharp bone at the
point: The Arrows us'd by the *Brasilians* are made after the
same manner; but the *Caribbians* adde to theirs, to make
them more dreadful, a mortal poison made of the juice of the
Manchenillo-trees, and other poisons; so that the least scratch
made by them becomes a mortal wound. It hath hitherto
been a thing impossible to get out of them the Receipt of that
composition. They have also every one of them that wooden
sword which they call *Boutou*, or to say better, that massy
Club which they use instead of a sword, and wherewith they
do miracles in point of fencing. These are all their Arms;
for they have no Targets or Bucklers, as the *Tapinambous,* but De Lery,
their bodies are naked. c.14.

Next the care they take about their Arms, they also provide themselves sufficiently with belly-timber, and take along
with them in their little vessels good quantities of *Cassava,*
broil'd Fish, Fruits, and particularly *Bananas,* which keep a
long time, and the meal of *Manioc.* The *Icaqueses* in their
Wars never trouble themselves about any such thing; and
what they do in this particular is so peculiar to them, that it
deserves to be mentioned: for they are content with so little
for their sustenance, and delight so much in living upon certain
Plumbs which grow abundantly in their Parts, and from which
they have their name, that when they go to the Wars they
are never seen to carry any provisions for the belly along with
them.

Our Savages of the *Caribbies,* as well as those of *Brasil,* take De Lery,
along with them to the Wars a certain number of Women, to c.14.
dress their meat, and look to the *Piragas* when they are got
ashore. Their Arms and Provisions are well fasten'd to these

Piragas ; so that if the Vessel comes to overturn, which happens often, they set it right again without losing any thing of what was in it : And upon those occasions, being so good Swimmers as we have represented them, they are not troubled for their own persons, so far that they have sometimes laugh'd at the Christians, who, being neer them upon those occasions, endeavour'd to relieve them.   Thus the *Tapinambous* laugh'd at some *French* men upon the like accident, as *De Lery* relates. The sails of the *Caribbians* are made of Cotton, or a kind of Mat of Palm-leaves : They have an excellent faculty of rowing with certain little Oars, which they move very fast.   They take along with them also some *Canows*, which are their least kind of Vessels, to attend their *Piragas*.

Their custom is to go from Island to Island to refresh themselves, and to that end they have Gardens even in those which are desert, and not inhabited : They also touch at the Islands of their own Nation, to joyn their Forces, and take in as they go along all those that are in a condition to accompany them ; and so their Army increases, and with that equipage they get with little noise to the Frontiers.

When they sail along the Coasts, and night comes upon them, they bring their Vessels ashore, and in half an hours time they make up their lodging-place under some Tree with *Balisier* and *Latanier*-leaves, which they fasten together on poles or reeds, sustain'd by forks planted in the ground, which serve for a foundation to this little structure, and to hang their beds on : These lodgings thus made in haste they call *Aioupa*.

The *Lacedæmonian* Law-giver had forbidden, among other things, that War should be always wag'd against the same Enemies, for fear they might thereby grow more experienc'd in Military Affairs : But the *Caribbians* follow not those Maximes, nor fear any such inconvenience ; for they always make War against the same Nation : Their ancient and irreconcileable Enemies are the *Arouacas*, *Arouaques* or *Arouagues*, which is the name commonly given them in the Islands, though the *Caribbians* call them *Alouagues*, who live in that part of the Meridional *America* which is known in the Maps under the name of the Province of *Guyana* or *Guayana*, not far from the Rivers which fall down out of that Province into the Sea. The cause of this immortal enmity between our Insulary *Caribbians* and those people hath been already hinted in the Chapter of the Origine of the *Caribbians*, to wit, that those *Arouagues* have cruelly persecuted the *Caribbians* of the Continent, their Neighbours, the Relations of our Islanders, and of the same Nation with them ; and that they have continually warr'd against them to exterminate them, or at least, to drive them out of their habitations.   These *Arouagues* then are the people whom our Islanders go and find out in their own Country,

try,

De Lery,
c.13.

Chap.12.

Plut. *in the*
Life *of* Ly-
curgus.

try, commonly once or twice a year, to be reveng'd of them as much as they can. And it is to be obferv'd on the other fide, that the *Arouagues* never make any attempts on the *Caribbians* of the Iflands, in the Iflands where they live, but only ftand on the defenfive; whereas they are fure to have our Savages among them oftner then they wifh, coafting along, as they are wont to do, all the other Iflands wherein they have Gardens or Colonies, though the furthermoft of the *Caribby-*Iflands, which is *Santa-Cruce*, is diftant from the Country of the *Arouagues* about three hundred Leagues.

It was *Alexanders* generofity made him ufe this expreffion, that a Victory was not to be ftollen: but *Philip* of an humour different from his Son, thought there was no fhame in a Conqueft, howere it were obtain'd : Our *Caribbians*, with moft of the old Inhabitants of *America*, are of the fame opinion : For they carry on all their wars by furprize, and think it no difhonour to make their advantage of the night : Contrary to the *Icaquefes*, who would think their reputation blafted, if coming to the Territories of their Enemies, they did not fend them notice of their arrival, and challenge them to come and receive them armed.   The *Arraucanes*, next neighbour to the *Chili*, a warlike people, and whom the *Spaniard* hath not been yet able to overcome, nay was fometimes worfted by them, do much more : For when they are to engage againft an Enemy, they have the War proclaim'd by Heraulds, and fend this meffage to them ; *We fhall meet thee within fo many Moons, be ready.* And fo the *Yncas*, the Kings of *Peru*, never undertook any war, till they had firft advertis'd their Enemies thereof, and declar'd it two or three times : Whence it may be inferred by the way, that *L'Efcarbot* is miftaken in his Hiftory of *New-France*, where he affirms, that all the *Weft-Indians* generally wage their wars by furprize.

The *Caribbians* have this imagination, that the War they fhould begin openly would not profper : So that having landed in the Country of the *Arouagues*, if they are difeovered before they give the firft fhock, or that a dog, as one would fay, did bark at them, thinking it ominous, they immediately return to their Veffels, and fo to their Iflands, leaving the defign to be profecuted fome other time.

But if they are not difeovered, they fall upon their Enemies even in their Houfes : If they cannot eafily come at them, or find them well fortified in fome Houfes that have good Palifadoes, whence they play upon them with their Arrows with fome advantage, they are wont to force them out by fhooting fire to the Houfes with their Arrows, at the points whereof they faften lighted Cotton : And thefe arrows being fhot on the roofs, which confift of Grafs or Palm-leaves, they prefently fet them on fire : Thus the *Arouagues* are forced out of their

T t   holes,

Q. Curt. Juftin. l. 9.

Garcilaf. l. 5. c. 12.

Lib. 3. c.25.

holes, and to fight in the open field, or run away: When our Savages have thus gotten them into the field, they presently shoot away all their arrows, which being spent they take their *Boutous*, and do strange things therewith; they are in perpetual motion all the time they are fighting, that the Enemy may have the less time to observe them: Fire-arms, especially great Guns, which make so great noise, and do such execution, especially when they are loaden with Nails, Chains, and other pieces of old Iron, have abated much of their courage when they have had to do with *Europæans*, and makes them afraid to come neer their Ships and Forts: But though they do not take *Opium*, to make them less sensible of danger, before they go to fight, as the *Turks* and the *East-Indians* of *Cananor* do; nor yet feed on Tygers and Lions to make themselves more couragious, as the people of the Kingdom of *Narsinga* towards *Malabar*; yet when they fight equally armed with the *Arouagues*, and have begun the Battel, especially if they are animated with some good success, they are as bold as Lions, and will either overcome or die. Thus did the warlike Savages of the Country of *Carthagena*, when they were assaulted by the *Spaniards*; for they fell in among them with such fury, both men and women, that a young maid laid several *Spaniards* upon the place ere she was killed her self. They say also that the *Mexicans* and *Canadians* will rather be cut to pieces than taken in fight.

If the *Caribbians* can take any one of their Enemies alive, they bind him and bring him away captive into their Islands; but if any one of theirs fall dead or wounded in the field, it would be an eternal and insupportable reproach to them to leave him in the power of the Enemy: That consideration makes them break furiously into the midst of the greatest dangers, and resolutely make their way through whatever opposes them, to retrive the bodies of their Comrades; and having gotten them by force from amongst the Enemies, they carry them to their Vessels.

When the fight is over, our Savages make their retreat to the Sea-side, or into some neighbouring Island; and if they have received some considerable loss by the death of some of their Chief Commanders, or their most valiant Soldiers, they fill the air with dreadful howling and crying before they get into their Vessels; and intermixing their tears with the blood of the deceased, they mournfully dispose them into their *Piragas*, and accompany them with their regrets and sighs to some of their own Territories.

But when they have had the Victory, they spend not the time in cutting off the heads of their slain Enemies, in carrying them in triumph, and in taking the skins of those poor bodies, to make Standards in their Triumphs, as the *Canadians* do, and as heretofore was the custom of the *Scythians*, as *Herodotus* affirms,

firms; nay, as was that of the ancient *Gauls*, if we believe *Livy.* Lib. 10.
The *Caribbians* think it enough to expreſs their joy by outcries
over the bodies of the *Arouagues*, and afterwards all along their
Coaſts, as it were to inſult over that hateful Country before
they leave it : But after they have ſung in that ſtrange Country ſome of their triumphal ſongs, they make what haſte they
can to their Veſſels, to carry away the reſt into the boſom of
their native ſoil; and the poor *Arouagues* they have taken, they
carry away chain'd, to be dealt with as ſhall be ſeen in the
next Chapter.

The end they propoſe to themſelves in theſe Expeditions, is
not to become Maſters of a new Country, or to load themſelves with the ſpoils of their Enemies; but only the glory of
ſubduing and triumphing over them, and the pleaſure of ſa-
tiating their Revenge for the injuries they have received from
them.

Next the *Arouagues*, the greateſt Enemies the *Caribbians* have
are the *Engliſh* : this enmity took its riſe hence, that the *Engliſh*, having under the Flags of other Nations got divers of
the *Caribbians* aboard their Ships, where they had at firſt
charmed them with kindneſs, and little preſents, eſpecially
Aqua-vitæ, which they extreamly love; when they ſaw their
Veſſel full of theſe poor people, who never dreamed of any
ſuch treachery, weighed anchor, and carried the *Caribbians*,
men, women, and children into their Plantations, where they
are ſtill kept as ſlaves: It is reported that they did the like
in ſeveral of the Iſlands, wherein they followed the example of
the *Spaniards* : Whence it comes that they ſtill bear a grudge
to the *Engliſh*, and can hardly endure to hear their Language
ſpoken: Nay, their diſſatisfaction is ſo great, that if a *French-
man*, as ſome of that Nation affirm, chance to make uſe of ſome
Engliſh expreſſions in his diſcourſe, he runs the hazard of their
enmity : Accordingly, in their turns, by the law of retaliation,
they have often made incurſions into the Iſlands of *Montſerrat*,
Antego, and others which are in the hands of the *Engliſh*; and
after they had ſet ſome houſes on fire, and taken ſome Goods,
they carried away men, women, and children, whom they
brought to *Dominico* and St. *Vincents*; but it was never heard
that they did eat any of them, it ſeems they reſerve that cruelty for the *Arouagues* : Nay before the *Caribbians* had any war
with the Inhabitants or *Martinico*, when the Parents or Friends
of the *Engliſh* who had been carried away Priſoners of War
by thoſe *Caribbians*, employed the mediation of the *French*,
they were eaſily enlarged and put into the hands of the *French*,
who gave the *Caribbians* in exchange for them, ſome of thoſe
trifles which they highly value, or haply an Iron wedge, or
ſome ſuch neceſſary tool : Nay, upon the preſenting them with
ſome of thoſe things they have delivered up ſome of the *Arou-*

agues appointed to be eaten. They have at this prefent in the Ifland of St. *Vincents* fome young Boys and Girls of the *Englifh* Nation, who being carried away very young, have clearly forgot their Parents, and would hardly return with them, fo well are they pleafed with the humour of the *Caribbians*, who for their part treat them as mildly as if they were of their own Nation; they are now known only by the fairnefs and flaxennefs of their Hair, whereas the *Caribbians* are generally black-hair'd.

As for the *Spaniards*, at the firft difcovery of *America*, the *Caribbians* who were then poffefs'd of all the *Caribby*-Iflands, were cruelly treated by them; they perfecuted them with fire and fword, and purfu'd them even into the woods, as wild beafts, that they might carry them away Captives to work in the Mines: Which kind of procedure forc'd this people, which is valiant and generous, to oppofe the violence, and to lay ambufhes for their Enemies, nay to affault them in their Ships which lay in their Roads, which they borded without any fear of fire-Arms, making their way through Swords and Pikes: In which attempts they were many times fo fortunate, that they became Mafters of divers Ships richly loaden, difpatching all that oppos'd them, carrying away all the booty, and then feting the Ships on fire: True it is, they pardoned the *Negro-flaves* they met with, and having brought them afhore put them to work in their Habitations; thence came the *Negroes* which which they have at prefent in St. *Vincents* and fome other Iflands.

The *Spaniards* being fenfible of thefe loffes, and perceiving they had a ftubborn Enemy to deal with, and that when they had ruin'd that Nation, they fhould not advantage themfelves; and confidering further, that the Iflands they were poffeffed of lay convenient for their Ships in their long Voyages, to take in refrefhments of water, wood, and provifions if need were, and to leave fuch as were fick in their Fleet, they refolved to treat the *Caribbians* more kindly; and thereupon having fet fome of them at liberty whom they had Captives, and fent them back into their Country with prefents, they made ufe of them to treat concerning a peace with that People, the conditions whereof being accepted by fome of the Iflands, they fet afhore therein fome fwine which they had brought out of *Europe*; and afterwards they left there behind them the fick they had in their Ships, and took them in again recovered at their return. But the *Caribbians* of St. *Vincents*, and thofe who lived at *Dominico* would not confent to that agreement, but ftill perfift in the averfion they had for the *Spaniards*, and the defire they have to be revenged of them.

As to what concerns their defenfive wars, they have learnt by their acquaintance with the Chriftians, and the differences they

they have had with them upon several occasions, to keep their
ranks, and to encamp in advantagious places, and to make some
kinds of fortifications in imitation of the others: The *French*
found it so by experience, some years since, at the taking of
Granada: They imagined that the *Caribbians* would not have
made any resistance; but they found them in a defensive posture, to prevent their landing, and contest their possession of
that place; for besides the mischief they did them by an extraordinary shower of Arrows, and the Barricadoes they placed in the avenues, they couragiously opposed their landing,
and laid several ambushes for them; and when they saw that
the *French*, notwithstanding their resistance, were resolv'd to
come, and forced them to make their retreat into the woods,
they rallied on an eminent place which they had fortified: and
whereas it was somewhat steepy on all sides save only one,
which had a spacious avenue, they had cut down certain trees,
of the boals whereof they had made long Rollers, which being
lightly fasten'd at the top of the Mountain, might be rolled
down the descent, with a more than ordinary force and violence against the *French*, if they had attempted any assault:
Out of this Fort they also made several sallies upon the Enemy,
who was building one where they might safely expect the supply which was to be sent them from *Martinico*; there they
kept them in as it were besieged for certain days, during which
they had made hollow places in the earth to secure themselves
from the Muskets; and thence shewing only their heads, they
shot their Arrows at those who had the confidence to come
without the Trenches; nay, in the night time they made a shift
to get a pot full of burning coals, on which they had cast a handful of *Pyman*-seed, into the Hut which the *French* had set up
at their first arrival in the Island, purposely to stifle them, if
they could, by the dangerous fume, and the stupifying vapour
of the *Pyman*: But their stratagem was discovered; and some
time after the expected supply being come to the *French*, the
Caribbians treated with them, and left them the absolute possession of the Island; but the differences they have since had
with the *French* Inhabitants of *Martinico* have occasioned another War which lasts still.

CHAP.

CHAP. XXI.

Of the Treatment which the Caribbians *make their Prisoners of War.*

WE are now going to dip our Pen in Blood, and to draw a Picture which muft raife horrour in the beholder; in this there muft appear nothing but Inhumanity, Barbarifm, and Rage; We fhall find rational Creatures cruelly devouring thofe of the fame *fpecies* with them, and filling themfelves with their Flefh and Blood, after they had caft off Humane Nature, and put on that of the moft bloody and furious Beafts: A thing which the Pagans themfelves, in the midft of their darknefs, heretofore thought fo full of execration, that they imagin'd the Sun withdrew himfelf, becaufe he would not fhew his light at fuch Repafts.

When the *Cannibals*, or *Anthropophagi*, that is, *Eaters of Men* (for here it is that we are properly to call them by that Name, which is common to them with that of the *Caribbians*); when I fay they bring home Prifoner of War from among the *Arouagues*, he belongs of right to him who either feiz'd on him in the Fight, or took him running away; fo that being come into his Ifland, he keeps him in his houfe; and that he may not get away in the night, he ties him in an *Amac*, which he hangs up almoft at the roof of his dwelling; and after he has kept him fafting four or five days, he produces him upon fome day of folemn debauch, to ferve for a publick Victim to the immortal hatred of his Country-men towards that Nation.

If there be any of their Enemies dead upon the place, they there eat them ere they leave it: They defign for flavery only the young Maids and Women taken in the War: They do not eat the Children of their She-prifoners, much lefs the Children they have by them themfelves: They have heretofore tafted of all the Nations that frequented them, and affirm, That the *French* are the moft delicate, and the *Spaniards* of hardeft digeftion; but now they do not feed on any Chriftians at all.

They abftain alfo from feveral cruelties which they were wont to ufe before they kill'd their Enemies; for whereas at prefent they think it enough to difpatch them at a blow or two with the Club, and afterwards cut them into pieces, and having broyl'd them, to devour them; they heretofore put them to feveral torments, before they gave them the mortal blow: We fhall not think it befides our purpofe to fet down in this place fome of the inhumanities which they exercis'd upon thefe fad occafions, as they themfelves have given an account thereof to

thofe

those have had the curiosity to inform themselves from their own mouths.

The Prisoner of War who had been so unfortunate as to fall into their hands, and was not ignorant that he was design'd to receive the most cruel treatment which rage could suggest, arm'd himself with constancy, and, to express how generous a people the *Arouagues* were, march'd very chearfully to the place of execution, not being either bound or drag'd thereto, and presented himself with a smiling and steady countenance in the midst of the Assembly, which he knew desir'd nothing so much as his death.

As soon as he perceiv'd those people who express'd so great joy at the approach of him, who was to be the mess of their abominable Entertainment, not expecting their discourses and their bitter abuses, he prevented them in these termes; "I know "well enough upon what account you have brought me to this "place; I doubt not but you are desirous to fill your selves with "my blood, and that you are impatient to exercise your teeth "upon my body; but you have not so much reason to triumph "to see me in this condition, nor I much to be troubled there- "at: My Country-men have put your Predecessors to greater "miseries than you are now able to invent against me; and I "have done my part with them in mangling, massacring, and "devouring your people, your friends, and your fathers; be- "sides that I have Relations who will not fail to revenge my "quarrel with advantage upon you and upon your Children, "for the most inhumane treatment you intend against me: "What torments soever the most ingenious cruelty can dictate "to you for the taking away of my life, is nothing in compa- "rison of those which my generous Nation prepares for you "in exchange: therefore delay not the utmost of your cruelty "any longer, and assure your selves I both slight and laugh at "it. Somwhat of this nature is that brave and bloody Bra- vado which may be read of a *Brasilian* Prisoner, ready to be devour'd by his Enemies; "Come on boldly, *said he to them*, "and feast your selves upon me; for at the same time you "will feed on your Fathers and Grandfathers, who serv'd for "nourishment to my Body: These Muscles, this Flesh, and "these Veins are yours, blind Fools as you are; you do not "observe, that the substance of the Members of your Ance- "stors are yet to be seen in them; taste them well, and you "will find the taste of your own Flesh. But let us return to our *Arouagues*.

Montagn's, Essays, l. 1. c. 30.

His soul was not only in his lips, but shew'd it self also in the effects which follow'd that Bravado; for after the Company had a while endur'd his menaces and arrogant defiances with- out touching him, one among them came and burnt his sides with a flaming brand; another cut good deep pieces out of him,

and

and would have made them bigger, had it not been for the bones, in several parts of the body : Then they cast into his smarting wounds that sharp kind of Spice which the *Caribbians* call *Pyman :* Others diverted themselves in shooting Arrows at the poor Patient ; and every one took a pleasure in tormenting him ; but he suffer'd with the same countenance, and expressed not the least sentiment of pain : After they had made sport thus a long time with the poor wretch, at last growing weary of insulting, and out-brav'd by his constancy , which seem'd still the same, one of them came and at one blow dispatch'd him with his Club.   This is the Treatment which the *Caribbians* made heretofore to their Prisoners of War ; but now they think it enough to put them to a speedy death, as we have already represented.

As soon as this unfortunate person is thus laid dead upon the place, the young men take the body, and having wash'd it cut it in pieces, and then boyl some part , and broil some upon wooden Frames, made for that purpose, like Gridirons *:* When this detestable Dish is ready , and season'd according to their palates, they divide it into so many parts as there are persons present, and joyfully devour it, thinking that the World cannot afford any other repast equally delicious : The Women lick the very sticks on which the fat of the *Arouague* dropp'd ; which proceeds not so much from the deliciousness they find in that kind of sustenance, and that fat, as from the excessive pleasure they conceive in being reveng'd in that manner of their chiefest Enemies.

But as they would be extreamly troubled that the enraged hatred they bear the *Arouagues* should ever end, so do they make it their main endeavour to foment and heighten it: thence it comes, that while this poor Carcass is a dressing, they carefully gather and save all the fat that comes from it ; not to put into Medicines, as Chirurgeons sometimes do ; or to make wildfire of it, to set their Enemies houses on fire, as the *Tartars* do ; but they gather together that fat to be afterwards distributed among the chiefest of them, who carefully keep it in little Gourds, to pour some few drops thereof into their Sauces at their solemn Entertainments, so to perpetuate, as much as lies in their power, the motive of their Revenge.

I must needs acknowledge, the Sun would have more reason to withdraw himself from these Barbarians, than to be present at such detestable Solemnities ; but it would be requisite that he withdrew himself at the same time from most of the Countries of *America*, nay from some parts of *Africk* and *Asia*, where the like and worse cruelties are daily exercis'd *:* For instance, the *Tapinambous* make in a manner the same treatment to their prisoners, as the *Caribbians* do to theirs ; but they add thereto divers expressions of barbarism, which are not to be seen in the
Cnribbiei :

Caribbies : They rub the bodies of their Children with the De *Lery,c.*
blood of thoſe miſerable Victims, to animate them to future ¹5.
Cruelties : He who had been the Executioner of the Captive *l b.*8.
caus'd himſelf to be mangled and ſlaſh'd, and cut in ſeveral
parts of the body, as a Trophey of Valour, and a mark of
Glory: And what is yet ſuperlatively ſtrange, is, That thoſe
Barbarians beſtowing their Daughters for Wives on thoſe Enemies, as ſoon as they fall into their hands, when they come to
cut them in pieces, the Wife her ſelf eats firſt, if it be poſſible,
of the fleſh of her Husband ; and if it happen that ſhe hath
any Children by him, they are ſerv'd in the like manner, kill'd,
roſted, and eaten ; ſomtimes as ſoon as they come into the
World. The like Barbariſm hath ſomtimes been obſerv'd in Garcilaſ. *l.*
ſeveral Provinces of *Peru*.   ɪ.c. ɪ2.

Divers other barbarous Nations do alſo exceed the *Caribbians*
in their inhumanity ; but above all, the Inhabitants of the
Country of *Antis* are more cruel then Tygers: If it happens *Ibid.*
that by right of War or otherwiſe, they make a Priſoner, and
that they know him to be a perſon of ſmall account, they immediately quarter him, and beſtow the Members on their
Friends or Servants, that they may eat them if they pleaſe,
or ſell them in the Shambles; but if he be a perſon of quality,
the chiefeſt among them meet together, with their Wives and
Children, to be preſent at his death: Then theſe unmerciful
people having ſtrip'd him, faſten him ſtark naked to a poſt,
and cut and ſlaſh him all over the body with a ſort of Knives
and Raſours made of a certain Stone, ſuch as may be Flint: In
this cruel Execution they do not preſently diſmember him, but
they only take the fleſh from the parts which have moſt, as the
calf of the Leg, the Thighs, the Buttoeks, and the Arms; that
done, they all pell-mell, Men, Women, and Children, dye
themſelves with the blood of that wretched perſon; and not
ſtaying for the roſting or boyling of the Fleſh they had taken
away, they devour it like ſo many Cormorants, or rather
ſwallow it down without any chewing: Thus the wretch ſees
himſelf eaten alive, and buried in the bellies of his Enemies:
The Women adding yet ſomwhat to the cruelty of the Men,
though exceſſively barbarous and inhumane, rub the ends of
their Breaſts with the blood of the Patient, that ſo their Children may ſuck it in with their Milk. And if theſe inhumane
Executioners have obſerv'd, that amidſt all the torments they
put the miſerable deceas'd perſon to, he expreſs'd the leaſt ſence
of pain, either in his countenance or other parts of his body;
or that he ſo much as groan'd or ſigh'd, then they break his
bones, after they have eaten the fleſh about them, and caſt
them into ſome naſty place, or into a River, with an extream
contempt.

Thus alſo do ſeveral other Nations cruelly inſult over the

wretched remainders of their murthered Enemies, and exercise
their inhumane revenge and barbarous animosity on that which
hath no feeling thereof: Thus some Inhabitants of *Florida*, to
satiate their brutality, hang up in their houses, and carry about
them, the skins and hair of their Enemies; the *Virginians* wear
about their necks a dry'd hand; some Savages of *New-Spain*
hang about some part of their bodies, after the manner of a
Medal, a piece of their flesh whom they had massacred: The
Lords of the Island by the *French* call'd *Belle-Isle* neer *China*,
wear a Crown made up of Deaths-heads, hideously dispos'd,
and interlac'd with silk strings: The *Chineses* make drinking-
cups of the *Spaniards* skuls whom they have kill'd, as heretofore
the *Scythians* were wont to do with their Enemies, as *Herodotus* affirms: The *Canadians* and the *Mexicans* dance on their
Festival days, wearing about them the skins of those whom they
had fley'd and eaten: The *Huancas*, an ancient Nation of *Peru*,
made Drums of such skins, affirming, that when they were beaten they had a secret virtue to make those who fought against
them to run away.

From all this Discourse it may be deduced, to what degree of
rage and fury Hatred and the desire of Revenge may ascend:
And in these Examples there are many circumstances more
bloody, and some more detestable discoveries of cruelty and
barbarism, then there are in the treatment which our *Cannibals*
make to their Prisoners of War, the *Arouagues*.

But to make this treatment appear the less horrid, it were
easie to bring on the Stage divers Nations, who besides that furious animosity, and that unquenchable thirst of Revenge, do
further discover a barbarous and insatiable gluttony, and an absolutely brutish passion of feeding on Mans flesh.

And in the first place, whereas our *Cannibals* ordinarily feed
only upon the *Arouagues*, their irreconcileable Enemies, sparing
the Prisoners they take of any other Nation, some *Floridians*,
who live neer the Streight of *Bahama*, cruelly devour all the
Strangers they can get into their hands, what Nation soever they
be of; so that if any people land in their Country, and that
they chance to be the stronger party, they must infallibly expect
to be their next days Commons: They think Mans flesh
extreamly delicate, from what part soever of the Body it be taken; but they affirm, that the sole of the foot is the most delicious bit of any; thence it comes, that the said part is ordinarily serv'd up to their *Carlin*, who is their Lord, whereas anci-
ently the *Tartars* cut off the breasts of young Maids, and reser-
ved them for their chief Commanders, whose ordinary food
they were. To these *Barbarians* we may add those of the Province of *Hascala*, and of the Region of the City of *Darien* in
New-Spain, who did eat not only the flesh of their Enemies,
but also that of their own Country-men: And Historians affirm,

*De Laet. hist.
of America.*

*Somedo hist.
of China, P.
1. c. 2.*

Lib. 4.

*Garcil. l. 6.
c. 10.*

*Bergeron's
Treatise of
the Tartars.*

*Garcil de
Latt, &
Linscot.*

firm, that the *Yncas*, Kings of *Peru*, subdued divers Provinces, the Inhabitants whereof thought no Law so rigorous and insupportable, among all those which the said victorious Princes imposed on them, as those which prohibited the eating of mans flesh, so much were they addicted to that execrable diet; for not staying till he whom they had mortally wounded, had given up the ghost, they drunk off the blood which issued out of his wound; and they did the like when they cut him up into quarters, greedily sucking it, lest a drop should be lost: They had publick Shambles for the selling of mans flesh, whereof they took pieces and minc'd them very small, and of the entrails they made puddings and saucages : And particularly the *Cheriganes*, or *Chirrhuanes*, a people inhabiting the Mountains, had so strange and so insatiable an appetite to mans flesh, that they gluttonously eat it raw, not sparing their neerest Relations when they dyed : The same thing is at this day affirmed of the *Tapuyes*, a certain other oriental Nation; and *Herodotus* assures us of such a thing in his time; nay it is averred, that the people of *Java* are so barbarous and so great lovers of that abominable nourishment, that, to satisfie their damnable appetite, they deprive their Parents of their lives, and toss the pieces of their flesh one to another like balls, to see who shall have most of them : The *Amures*, a people of *Brasil*, are yet more inhumane and detestable; so that we need not feign *Saturnes* devouring their own children; for if we may credit Historians, these Barbarians eat in effect their own Children, member after member, and sometimes opening the wombs of great belly'd women, they take out the fruit thereof, which they immediately devour, longing so strangely after the flesh of their own species, that they go a hunting of men, as they do beasts, and having taken them they tear them in pieces, and devour them after a cruel and unmerciful manner.

By these examples it is sufficiently apparent, that our *Cannibals* are not so much *Cannibals*, that is, Eaters of men, though they have the name particularly attributed to them, as many other savage Nations; and it were an easie matter to find yet elsewhere certain discoveries of Barbarism answerable to that of our *Caribbian Cannibals*, nay such as far exceeds theirs : But we have done enough, let us draw the Curtains on these horrours, and leaving the *Cannibals* of all other Nations, return to those of the *Caribbies*, to divert our eyes, wearied with beholding so many inhumanities and bloudy Tragedies, by a prospect of their Marriages.

CHAP. XXII.

Of the Marriages of the Caribbians.

THere are in *America* some Savages so savage and so brutish, that they know not what Marriage is, but go indifferently together like beasts. This, among others, is affirm'd of the ancient *Peruvians*, and the Inhabitants of the Islands of *Robbers:* But the *Caribbians*, with all their barbarism, subject themselves to the Laws of this strict Alliance.

They have no set time of the Year appointed for their Marriages, as the *Persians*, who ordinarily marry in the Spring; nor yet are they oblig'd to do it at any certain age, as several other Savages, whereof some marry commonly at [a] nine years; others at [b] twelve; some at [c] four and twenty; and others only at [d] forty : Nor is it the custom among the *Caribbians*, as in a manner among all other Nations, that the young Men should ordinarily make choice of the Maids according to their own minds and inclinations; nor on the other side, do the young Maids make choice of their Husbands, as those of the Province of *Nicaragua* do, at their publick Feasts and Assemblies; and as it was done heretofore in *Candia*, as Historians affirm.

But when our Savages are desirous to marry, they have a priviledge to take all their Cousin-germans, and have no more to say, then that they take them to their Wives; for they are naturally reserv'd for them, and they may carry them to their houses without any other ceremony, and then they are accounted their lawful Wives. They may all take as many Wives as they please; especially, the Captains pride it much in having a great number of them : They build a particular Hut for every Wife : They continue what time they please with her whom they fancy most, yet so as that the others conceive no jealousie thereat. She whom they most honour with their company, waits on them with the greatest care and submission imaginable; she prepares *Cassava* for them, paints them, and goes along with them in all their Expeditions.

Their Husbands love them all very well; but this love is like a fire of straw, since that many times they forsake them with as much ease as they take them; yet are they seldom seen to leave their first Wives, especially if they have had children by them.

If there chance to be among the She-prisoners of War any that they like, they make them their Wives; but though the children born of them are free, yet are the Mothers, for their parts, still accounted Slaves. All the Wives speak with whom they please; but the Husband dares not discourse with the Relations

lations

lations of his Wife, but upon extraordinary occasions.

When it happens that any one among them hath no Coufin-germans, or that having ftaid too long ere they took them to Wives, their friends have difpos'd of them to others, they may now marry fuch as are not of any kin to them : but it is requi-fite that they demand them of their Fathers and Mothers, and as foon as the Father or Mother hath granted their requeft, they are their Wives, and they carry them to their own habi-tations.

Before they had alter'd fome part of their ancient Cuftoms, by reafon of the converfe they have had with the Chriftians, they took none for their lawful Wives but their Coufins, who were theirs by natural right, as we faid before, or fuch young Maids as their Fathers and Mothers willingly proffer'd them at their return from the Wars. This ancient Cuftom of theirs hath many particular circumftances worthy our remark ; and therefore we fhall give an account of it at large, as we have it from the moft ancient of that Nation who have related it, to fhew the great changes which have crept into their Manners and Cuftoms, fince they became acquainted with forreign Na-tions.

When the *Caribbians* return'd with fuccefs from their Wars, and that there was a folemn reception made for them in their Iflands, and a great entertainment at their *Carbet*, after that Solemnity, which is ftill in ufe among them, the Captain gave an account of the fuccefs of their Expedition, and commended the generofity and gallantry of thofe who had behav'd them-felves valiantly : But his main defign was to recommend the valour of the young men, the better to animate them to make future expreflions of the fame courage upon the like occafions. It was ordinarily at the end of that difcourfe that Fathers of families, who had Daughters marriageable, took occafion to prefent them for Wives to thofe among the young men whofe performances they had heard fo much celebrated, and whofe courage and undauntednefs in fighting had been fo highly com-mended : There was an emulation among them who fhould get fuch for their Sons-in-law : And he who had kill'd moft Ene-mies, had much ado that day to fcape with one Wife, fo many would there be proffer'd to him : But Cowards and perfons of no worth met with no courtfhip to that purpofe ; fo that, to be married among them, there was a neceflity of being cou-ragious ; for a Wife in that Nation then was the reward of ge-nerofity. Thus among the *Braflians*, the young men were not admitted to marry till they had kill'd fome Enemy : And in a   Vin.le Bian.
City of *Grand-Tartary*, called *Palimbrota*, thofe of higheft qua-   p.1. c. 30.
lity could have no Wives till they had brought proof that they
had kill'd three Enemies of their Prince. It is reported alfo,   Alex. ab A-
that heretofore in *Carmania*, if any one were defirous to marry,   lexandro, l.
it 1. c. 24.

it was requisite that he brought the King the head of an Enemy. The same Custom in a manner was observ'd among a certain people neer the *Caspian* Sea. And who knows not that King *Saul* demanded of *David* the lives of an hundred *Philistines*, for the dower of his Daughter, before he gave her him in Marriage?

But happy did that Father think himself among our *Caribbians*, who could first approach and seize about the body of some one of those valorous Sons-in-Law whom the Captain had commended ; for there was nothing to be expected for that time by him that came next ; and the marriage was concluded as soon as the other had said to the Young-man, *I bestow my Daughter on thee for thy Wife* ; the like expression from a Mother was as effectual : And the Young-man durst not refuse the Daughter when she was thus presented to him ; but it was requisite, that whether she were handsome or unhandsome, he took her to Wife. Thus the *Caribbians* married not after previous courtships and Love-suits.

And if the young *Caribbians*, after they were married, continued the same gallantry in ensuing Wars, they had accordingly other Wives bestowed on them at their return : this Poligamy is still in use among them, and it is indeed common among other Barbarians. The *Chileses*, Inhabitants of the Island of *Mocha*, make no more ado, but as often as they are desirous to have a new Wife, they buy one for an Ox, a Sheep, or some other Commodity : And there are some places where the number of Wives belonging to the same Husband is prodigious, as in the Kingdom of *Bennin*, the King whereof hath sometimes seven hundred Wives and Concubines ; and where the ordinary subjects, as well as those of *Mexico*, have each of them about a hundred, or a hundred and fifty Wives. On the other side there are some places where every Wife in like manner is permitted to have many husbands, as among the *Pelhuares*, a Nation of *Brasil*, in the Kingdom of *Calecut* ; and heretofore in some of the *Canaries*.

The Young-men among the *Caribbians* do not to this day converse with either Maids or Women till they are married ; wherein certainly they are at a great distance from the humour of the *Peguans*, who are so passionately amorous, that to make it appear, that the violence of the secret fire which consumes them, extinguishes in them the sentiment of all other ardors, they sear their own arms in the presence of their Mistresses with a flaming Torch, or suffer to die and be spent upon their flesh, a piece of linnen cloth all of a flame, and dipped in Oil : And to shew that being wounded to death by Love, all other wounds must needs be slight, they cut and slash their bodies with Ponyards. The *Turks* do somewhat of the same kind, as *Villamont* affirms ; for upon the like occasions they

De Laets
History.

*The Dutch
Relations.*

De Laet, Pirard, p. 1.
c. 27.
*Conquest of
the Canarys
by Berencourt.*
Vin.leBlanc.
p. 1. c. 3.

Lib 3.

they give themselves several cuts and great wounds with their
knives, in divers parts of their bodies.

The number of Wives among the *Caribbians* is not limited,
as it is among the *Maldiveses*, where a man may have but three
at the same time: But as that number was heretofore proportioned to their courage and valour, (for as often as they returned from the wars with the commendation of gallant men, they
might pretend to & hope for a new Wife)so at the present, they
have as many as they desire and can obtain; so that among
them, as well as among the *Topinambous*, he who hath most Wives
is accounted most valiant, and the most considerable person in
the whole Island. And whereas in the Island of *Hispaniola* all
the wives lay in the same Room with their Husbands, the *Carib-*
bians as we said before, to prevent all differences and jealou-
sies, keep their wives, as the *Turks* and *Tartars* do theirs, in distinct Habitations; nay, sometimes they dispose them into several Islands: Or haply another reason of their ordering such
a distance between the several aboads of their wives, is that
they may the more conveniently apply themselves to the culture of their Gardens, which lie scattered up and down in divers places: and it is upon the same account that some affirm
the *Caribbians* of the Continent do the like, their wives having
this commendation, that they are not troubled with jealousie.
Our Savages of the Islands, if they have no more wives than
one, are very careful not to be far from them; and if they have
many, they visit them by turns one after another: But in this
they observe the same Custom with the *Floridians*, that they
meddle not with those who are with child.

It is somewhat to be wondred at, that *Lycurgus* and *Solon*
those Lights of *Greece*, should shew themselves so blind and
withal so dishoneft, as to open a gap for Adultry to get in among
their Citizens; for there is hardly any Nation so Barbarous
and Savage, but hath of it self light enough to read this Law
drawn by the hand of nature; that Adultry is a crime, and
that a certain horrour ought to be had for it; nay there is not
any but expresses a certain detestation of it, and severely pu-
nishes it. The punishment of Adultery is pleasant enough
among the Inhabitants of *Guiana*; for the Wife, if she hath a
mind to continue still with her Husband, pays him by way of
satisfaction, some ounces of Gold. But there is no jesting with
those of *Bengala*, and the *Mexicans*, who cut off their wives noses and ears in that case: Divers other barbarous Nations punish this crime with death; nay, the *Peguans* are so severe upon
these occasions, and have so great a horrour for this breach of
conjugal love, that both men and women who are found guilty thereof are buried alive.

Nor are the *Caribbians* the most indulgent, and the least jealous of their honour in this case; heretofore they knew not
how

how to punish this Crime, because it reigned not among them before their commerce with the Christians: but now if the Husband surprises his Wife prostituting her self to some other, or have otherwise any certain knowledge of it, he does himself justice, and seldom pardons her, but dispatches her, sometimes with his Club, sometimes by ripping up the upper part downwards with a Rasor or the tooth of an *Agouty*, which is neer as sharp.

This execution being done, the Husband goes to his Father-in-law, and tells him in cold blood, *I have killed thy Daughter because she proved unfaithful to me* : The Father thinks the action so just, that he is so far from being angry with him, that he commends him, and conceives himself oblig'd : *Thou hast done well*, replies he, *she deserved no less* : And if he hath any more Daughters to dispose of, he immediately proffers him one of them, and promises to bestow her on him at the first opportunity.

The Father marries not his own Daughter, as some have affirmed; they abhor that crime, and if there have been any incestuous Fathers among them, they were forc'd to absent themselves; for had they been taken by the rest, they would have burnt them alive, or torn them into a thousand pieces.

CHAP. XXIII.

Of the birth and education of Children among the Caribbians.

THere is hardly any Custom among these poor *Indians* so brutish, as that which they use at the birth of their children; their wives are delivered with little pain, and if they feel any difficulty, their recourse is to the root of a certain Rush, out of which they get the juice, and having drunk it, they are immediately delivered : Sometimes the very day of their delivery, they go and wash themselves and the child at the next River or Spring, and fall about their ordinary business : The *Peruvian*, the *Japonnesses*, and the *Brasilian* women do the like ; and it was ordinary among the *Indians* of *Hispaniola*, and the ancient *Lacedemonians* to wash their children in cold water, immediately after their birth, to harden their skins. The *Maldiveses* wash theirs so for several daies together ; and it is affirmed by some, that the *Cimbri* were heretofore wont to put those little newly-born creatures into snow, to accustom them to cold and hardship, and to strengthen their members.

Garcil. Lincot. & De Laet.

Pirard.

They

They make no feaft at the birth of their Children, fave only at that of the firft-born, and they obferve no fet time for
that, but every man according to his humour : But when they
affemble their friends to rejoice with them upon the birth of
their firft-born, they fpare nothing that may contribute to the
entertainment and merry-making of the invited ; whereas
heretofore the *Thracians* accompanied with their tears the cries   Herod. *l.* 5.
of thofe who came into the world, reflecting on the miferies
they were to fuffer in this life.

But behold the brutality of our Savages in their enjoyments,
for the augmentation of their Family ! Affoon as the Wife is
delivered the Husband goes to bed, to bemoan himfelf there,
and act the part of the woman in that condition ; a cuftome,
which, though favage and ridiculous, is yet ufed, as fome affirm among the Peafants of a certain Province of *France*, where
they have this particular phrafe for it, *faire la couvade* : But
what is moft troublefome to the poor *Caribbian*, who hath put
himfelf into bed inftead of his newly-delivered Wife, is, that
they oblige him to a certain diet for ten or twelve days together, allowing him every day only a little piece of *Caffava*,
and a little water, wherein there had been boiled a little of that
root-bread ; afterwards his allowance is a little encreafed, yet
ftill continued in that fame diet ; but he breaks the *Caffava*
which is prefented to him only in the middle, for the fpace of
about forty days, leaving the extremities entire, which he hangs
up in his Hut, to ferve at the entertainment he afterwards
intends to make for all his friends ; nay after all this, he ab-
ftains, fometimes for the fpace of ten months, or a whole year,
from feveral kinds of meat, as Lamantin, Tortoifes, Swines-flefh,
hens, Fifh, and delicious things, being fo pitifully fimple as to fear
that thofe things might prejudice the child : but this great abftinence they obferve only at the birth of their firft-born ;
for at thofe of the reft, their fafts are much lefs rigorous, and
fhorter, not lafting ordinarily above four or five days.

Among the *Japonnefes* and the *Brafilians*, the Husbands are   De Laet, &
alfo fubject to the fame extravagance of perfonating the wo-   Maffæus.
men delivered ; but they are not fuch fools as to faft in their
beds ; on the contrary, they are delicioufly and plentifully
treated with all things : Some affirm, that heretofore the fame
thing was obfervable among the *Tibarians*, a people not far   Alex. *ab* A-
from *Cappadocia*, and fome others : But the natural Inhabitants   lexandro.
of *Madagafcar* imitate this faft of the *Caribbians*, when they   Fran. Cau-
would have their children circumcis'd.   che.

Some of our *Caribbians* are yet guilty of another extravagance, worft of all for the poor Father who hath a child born ;
for at the expiration of his faft, his fhoulders are fcarified
and open'd with the Tooth of an *Agouty* ; and it is requifite
that the befotted wretch fhould not only fuffer himfelf to be

so ordered, but he must also endure it without expressing the least sentiment of pain : Their perswasion is that the more apparent the Fathers patience shall be in these tryals, the more recommendable shall be the valour of his Son; but this noble blood must not be suffered to fall to the ground, since the effusion thereof contributes so much to future courage; it is therefore carefully sav'd to rub the childs face withall, out of an imagination he will be the more generous : This is also done in some parts towards the Daughters; for though they are not to be in their military engagements, as the *Amazons* heretofore were, yet do they go to the Wars with their Husbands, to provide Victuals for them, and look to their Vessels while they are engaged with the Enemy.

Assoon as the Children are born, the Mothers make their foreheads flat, and press them so that there is a descent backwards, for besides that that form of the forehead is accounted one of the principal pieces of beauty among them, they affirm, that it facilitates their shooting up to the top of a tree standing at the foot of it, wherein they are extreamly expert as being brought up to it from their child-hood.

They do not swathe their children at all, but leave them at liberty to turn themselves which way they will in their little *Amacs*, or Beds of Cotton, or upon little Couches of *Banana*-leaves laid on the ground in some corner of their Huts; and yet their limbs are not any way distorted, but the whole body is perfectly well-shap'd. Those who have liv'd among the *Maldiveses* and the *Topinambous*, affirm the same thing of the children of those people, though they never bind them up in any thing, no more then the *Caribbians* are. The *Lacedæmonians* heretofore did the like.

They do not impose Names on their children as soon as they are born, but after twelve or fifteen days, and then they call a Man and a Woman, who stand as it were for Godfather and Godmother, and make holes in the child's ears, the under-lip, and the space between the nostrils, and put a thred through, that there may be places to hang Pendants : But if they conceive the children too weak to endure the boring of those parts, they defer that ceremony till they are grown stronger.

Most of the Names the *Caribbians* give their children, are deriv'd from their Ancestors, or from divers Trees which grow in their Islands, or else from some accident that happen'd to the Father while his Wife was with child, or during the time of his own lying in : Thus ones Daughter, in the Island of *Dominico*, was called *Ouliem-banna*, that is to say, *The leaf of the wild Vine*, which is a Tree whereof we have given a description in its proper place. Another of the same Island, having been at S. *Christophers* whilst his Wife was with child, and having there seen the *French* General, nam'd the child he

had

had at his return, *General,* upon remembrance of the kind entertainment he had receiv'd at the General's.

Something of this kind is also observ'd among other Nations : For instance, the *Canadians* borrow Names from Fishes and Rivers : The *Virginians* and *Brasilians* take theirs from the first thing they think of, as from Bows, Arrows, living Creatures, Trees, Plants : The Grand Seignors of *Turkey* are wont to give to the Eunuchs who keep their Wives, the Names of the fairest Flowers; to the end that those Women calling them by the same Names, there should proceed nothing out of their mouths but what were decent and delightful : The *Romans,* as may be seen in *Plutarch,* sometimes took their Names from Fishes, sometimes from their Country-divertisements, sometimes from the marks and imperfections of their bodies, and sometimes from their most Heroick Actions, in imitation of the *Greeks :* Nay the Holy Scriptures furnish us with abundance of examples of Names taken from divers accidents, as among others those of *Benoni, Pharez, Icabod,* and the like.

The Names which the *Caribbians* impose on their male children some time after their birth, are not to be continu'd while they live; for they change their Names when they come to the age requisite to be receiv'd into the number of Souldiers : and when they have behav'd themselves valiantly in the Wars, and have kill'd one of the chief Commanders of the *Arouagues,* they assume his Name, as a mark of Honour : Which Custom relates somewhat to what was practis'd among the *Romans* after their Victories, when they assum'd to themselves the Names of the Nations whom they had subdu'd; as may be instanc'd in *Scipio Africanus,* and divers others whom we need not cite.   These victorious *Caribbians* have also, in their *Wines* or publick rejoycing days, some particular person chosen to give them a new Name, to whom they say, after they have taken a sufficient dose of drink, *Teticlée y atec,* that is, *I would be named, name me*; whose desire the other presently satisfies : and in requital he receives some Present, such as may be a knife, or a grain of Chrystal, or some other trifle much esteem'd among them.

The *Caribbian* Women suckle their own children, and are very good Nurses and indulgent Mothers, having all the care imaginable to bring them up; nay when their neighbours are gone to the wars they look to their Children. All the *Peruvian* and the *Canadian* women, and most of the *West-Indians* are also their own Nurses : And in the *East-Indies,* in the Kingdom of *Transiana* and the *Maldivos,* the women, of what quality soever they be of, are obliged to suckle their own Children : And *Tacitus* affirms, that all Mothers nurs'd their own Children among the ancient *Germans :* Nay it is reported that heretofore

Lescarbot.

Garcil. &
Lescarbot.

Le Blanc &
Pirard.

De Mor. Ger-
man.

X x 2   fore

Bergeron
in his Trea-
tife of Navi-
gations.

Effays, l. 2.
c. 3.

fore the Queens of *Peru* took the pains to bring up their own children : And we have the examples of fome Queens of *France*, who have not thought thofe maternal endeavours below them ; a Cuftom much contrary to that of thofe *Canarian* Women, who commonly caus'd their Children to be fuckled by Goats : The fame thing was alfo done by fome Country-women of *Guyenne*, in *Montaigne*'s time.

The Mothers of our little *Caribbians* do not only give the breaft to their Children, but affoon as they are grown a little ftrong, they chew the *Potatoes*, *Bananas* and other fruits, to feed them withall : And though they fuffer the little ones to tumble up and down ftark naked upon the ground, and that many times they eat and lick duft, and other filth which they are apt to put into their mouths, yet do they thrive extreamly, and for the moft part become fo ftrong, that at fix months they are able to go alone.

At two years of age their hair is cut, and then there is a Feaft made for the whole Family ; fome Parents defer till that time the piercing or boring of their ears, lips, and the fpace between the noftrils ; yet is not this much in ufe, but only when the weaknefs of the child will not permit it to be done fooner. When they are a little more advanc'd in years, the Boys eat with their Fathers, and the Girls with their Mothers : Fathers-in-Law, and all Relations which are in the collateral line with their true Fathers, they call by the general name of Fathers.

Though the Children of the *Caribbians* are not inftructed to do any reverence to their Parents, nor to exprefs the refpect and honour they owe them by any geftures of the body ; yet have they a natural affection for them, and if any injury be done them, they immediately efpoufe their quarrel, and endeavour all the ways they can to be revenged : For inftance, a *French-man* of *Gardeloupe* having cut the cords of the *Amac* wherein an old *Caribbian* lay, by which means falling down he bruifed himfelf and put his fhoulder out of joint, the old man's Son-in-Law immediately got together fome young men, who making an incurfion into the Ifland of *Marigalanta*, maflacred the *French* who were then beginning to plant themfelves there.

But the main bufinefs which the *Caribbians* mind in the education of their Children, is to teach them the ufe of the Bow : And to bring them the better on, affoon as they are able to go the Parents put their Breakfaft on the branch of a tree, whence they muft ftrike it down with their Arrows before they eat ; if they cannot there is no compaffion : As the Children grow up, their portion of meat is hung up higher : Sometimes alfo they cut off a *Banana*-tree, and plant it in the ground as a But, to teach their Children to fhoot at the Fruit : by this means

in

in proceſs of time they come to be expert in that exerciſe. Ancient Hiſtories tell us of other people, who not differing much from this Cuſtom of the *Caribbians*, obliged their Children to fling down their meat from the place where they ſet it.

They commonly deſign all their Sons to bear Arms, and to revenge them of their Enemies, in imitation of their Predeceſſors: But before they are ranked among thoſe who may go to the wars, they are to be declared Souldiers in the preſence of all their kindred and friends, who are invited to be preſent at ſo ſolemn a Ceremony: The manner of it is thus; The Father, who had before got all his Friends together, cauſes his Son to ſit on a low ſtool, which is placed in the midſt of the Hut, or in the *Carbet*; and after he hath repreſented to him the whole duty of a generous *Caribbian* Soldier, and made him promiſe that he will never do any thing which may derogate from the glory of his Predeceſſors, and that he will to the utmoſt of his power revenge the ancient quarrel of his Nation, he takes by the feet a certain Bird of prey, which they call *Atansfennis* in their language, and which had been prepared long before for that purpoſe, and with that he diſcharges ſeveral blows on his Son, till ſuch time as the bird is killed, and the head of it cruſhed to pieces: After this rough treatment, which puts the young man as it were into a maze, he ſcarifies his whole body with the tooth of an *Agouty*, and to cure the wounds he hath made, he puts the dead bird into an infuſion of *Pyman-ſeeds*, and he rubs all the wounded parts therewith, which cauſes an extraordinary pain to the poor Patient; but it is requiſite he ſhould ſuffer all this with a cheerful countenance, without the leaſt diſcovery of pain: Then they make him eat the heart of the bird; and to cloſe the Ceremony, he is laid into a kind of *Amac*, where he is to continue ſtretched out to his full length, till his ſtrength be in a manner ſpent, by reaſon of much faſting: That done, he is acknowledged by all to be a Souldier; he is admitted into the Aſſemblies of the *Carbet*, and may go along with the reſt in all their military Expeditions which they undertake againſt their Enemies.

Beſides the exerciſes of war, which are common to all the young *Caribbians* who would live in any eſteem among the Bravos of their Nation, their Fathers do many times deſign them to be *Boyez*, that is Magicians, and Phyſitians: To that end they ſend them to ſome one of the beſt skill'd in that damnable profeſſion, that is, one who hath the reputation of invocating the evil Spirits, inſtructing people how to be revenged of their enemies by ſorceries, and in curing divers diſeaſes whereto thoſe of that Nation are ſubject: But it is requiſite that the young man who is preſented to the *Boyez* to be inſtructed in his Art, ſhould be conſecrated thereto from his
child-

childhood by abstinence from several kinds of meat, by rigorous Fasts, and that to begin his apprenticeship, there is blood drawn from all parts of his body with the tooth of an *Agouty*, after the same manner as those are to be treated who are received Souldiers.

The *Caribbians* do also teach their Children to fish, swim, make Baskets, Clubs, Bows, Arrows, Girdles, Beds of Cotton and *Pyragas*: But to have any care of cultivating their minds, and instructing them in any thing of civility, or vertue, is more than could be expected from those poor Savages, who have no other light than their own blinded understanding, nor follow any other rule in all the actions of their lives, than the sad disorder of vicious and corrupt nature.

CHAP. XXIV.

Of the ordinary Age of the Caribbians, *their Diseases;
the Remedies used by them in order to the Recovery
of their Health ; their Death, and Funeral Solemnities.*

THe *Caribbians* being naturally of a very good temperament, and endeavouring all they can to avoid trouble and disquiet, and consequently to spend their lives with the greatest enjoyment of mind ; it is no wonder, considering withall their ordinary temperance and sobriety, that they should be free from an infinite number of inconveniences and indispositions whereto other Nations are subject, and that they should come to their graves later than most other people : The good air they live in does also in some measure contribute to their health and long life.

If therefore they do not die of violent deaths, they all of them live to a very great age; nay they are so vigorous in the extremities of age, that at fourscore and ten they commonly get children: There are many among them who being above a hundred years of age, have not so much as a grey hair : *De Lery* an Author worthy credit, affirms, that he seldom saw any grey hairs in the heads of the *Tapinambous* of the same age : Other Historians affirm, that the wives of those Savages bear Children till they are fourscore years of age: And some *French* took notice of a Savage in the Country of *Canada*, who had a better sight than any of them, and the hair of the head absolutely black, though he were above a hundred years of age.

The *Caribbians* live ordinarily a hundred and fifty years,
and

Ch. 8.

De Laets
Hist.of America.

Lescarbot.

and ſometimes longer : For though they cannot number their
years, yet is the number thereof deduced from the account
they give of certain accidents : And among others, there were
not long ſince living among them ſome perſons who remembred
the firſt arrival of the *Spaniards* in *America* : Whence it is to
be concluded, that they muſt be a hundred and ſixty years of
age at the leaſt : And indeed theſe are ſuch a people as may
paſs for the ſhadow of a body, and have nothing but the heart
living, being continually bed-rid, immoveable, and reduced to
pure skeletons ; yet are they ſtill obſerved to be in health :
And it is ſufficiently apparent, that their tongues are living as
well as their hearts, and that their Reaſon is not expir'd ; for
they do not only ſpeak with much eaſe, but alſo their memory
and judgment are not chargeable with any defect.

Nor is it much to be admired that the *Caribbians* ſhould live
ſo long, ſince both ancient and modern Hiſtories furniſh us with
examples enough to confirm this truth ; and among others the
Dutch who have traded to the *Moluccoes*, affirm, that in that
Country the Inhabitants live ordinarily a hundred and thirty
years : *Vincent le Blanc* affirms, that in *Sumatra Java*, and the
neighbouring Iſlands, they live to a hundred and forty, as they
do alſo among the *Canadians* ; and that in the Kingdom of
Caſuby they hold out to a hundred and fifty : *Pirard* and ſome
others aſſure us, that the *Braſilians* live no leſs, nay that ſometimes they exceed a hundred and ſixty : And in *Florida*, and
Jucatan, ſome have gone beyond that age : Nay it is reported
that the *French*, at the time of *Laudoniere*'s voyage into *Florida*, in the year MDLXIV. ſaw there an old man, who ſaid
he was three hundred years of age, and Father of five Generations : And if we may credit *Maffæus*, an Inhabitant of *Bengala*, in the year 1557. made it his boaſt, that he was three hundred thirty five years of age. So that all this conſider'd, it is no
incredible thing that our *Caribbians* ſhould live ſo long.

Aſclepiades, as *Plutarch* relates, was of opinion, that generally the Inhabitants of cold Countries liv'd longer than thoſe
of hot, giving this reaſon, that the cold keeps in the natural heat, and cloſes the pores to that end, whereas that
heat is eaſily diſperſed in thoſe Climates where the pores are
kept open by the heat of the Sun : But experience, in the *Caribbians* and ſo many other Nations of the Torrid Zone who
ordinarily live ſo long, while our *Europæans* commonly dye
young, deſtroies that argument.

When it happens that our *Caribbians*, as ſometimes it muſt,
are troubled with any indiſpoſition, they have the knowledge
of abundance of Herbs, Fruits, Roots, Oils, and Gums, by the
aſſiſtance whereof they recover their health in a ſhort time,
if the diſeaſe be not incurable : They have alſo an infallible
ſecret to cure the ſtinging of Snakes, provided they have not

touch'd

Dutch
tions. l
c. 24.
Leſcar

*Part
& p.* 1

Berge
Leſca.
De La

Plac. Phil.
l. 5. *c.* 30.

touch'd a vein; for then there is no remedy: This is the juice of a certain Herb which they apply to the wound, and in four and twenty hours they are infallibly cured.

The bad nourishment of Crabs, and other insects on which they commonly feed, is the cause that they are most of them subject to a troublesome disease, which in their language they call *Pyans*, as the *French* call it a kind of small Pox: When those who are fallen into this disease, eat of the *Fram-Tortoise*, or of *Lamantin*, or of *Caret*, which is another kind of Tortoise, they are immediately full of little risings, inasmuch as these meats force the disease out; they have also many times great Impostumes, Cornes, and Carbuncles, in divers parts of the body: To cure those, which proceed for the most part from the bad nourishment they use, they have the bark of a tree called *Chipiou*, bitter as soot, which they steep in water, and having scrap'd into that infusion the inner part of a great shell called *Lambys*, they drink up that potion: They also sometimes pound the bark newly taken from certain trees of *Miby*, or other *Withyes* which creep along the ground, or fasten on trees, and drink the juice gotten from it: but they do not willingly make use of this remedy but when the trees are most full of sap.

Besides these Medicines wherewith they purge the ill humours within, they also apply outwardly certain unguents, and liniments, which have a particular vertue of taking away the blisters and marks which commonly remain on their bodies who have been troubled with the *Pyans*: They make up these Remedies with the ashes of burnt Reeds, mixt with the water which they get out of the leaves at the top of the *Balisier*-tree: They also use to the same end the juice of the *Junipa* fruit, and they apply on the botches the husks of the same fruit, which hath the vertue of drawing away the matter of the wounds, and to close up the Ulcers: They have not the use of Phlebotomy, but they use scarifications upon the place affected, by scratching or opening it with the Tooth of an *Agouty*, and causing it to bleed a little. And to take off somewhat of the astonishment, which might be conceived at what we have represented elswhere concerning the incisions which these Barbarians make on themselves upon divers occasions, whereby it might be imagin'd their bodies should be as it were mangled and covered with scars, it is to be noted, that they have also certain secrets, and infallible remedies to cure themselves presently, and to close the wounds so that a man cannot easily observe the least scar about their bodies.

They also make use of artificial Baths, and provoke sweat by a kind of stove, wherein they inclose the Patient, who receives his absolute cure by that remedy: The *Sorriquefes* do also sweat their sick, but sometimes they moisten them with
their

their breath: And for the cure of wounds, they and the *Floridians* suck out the blood, as was practis'd by the ancient Physitians, when any one had been bitten by a venemous beast, causing him who was to do that office to be prepar'd for that purpose: It is reported also that our *Caribbians*, when they have been stung by some dangerous Serpent, cause the wound to be sucked by their Wives, after they have taken a drink which hath the vertue of abating the force of the venome: The *Topinambous* do also suck the affected parts, though there be no wound; which is also sometimes done in *Florida*: And the *Turks* when they are troubled with any defluxion and pain, either in the head, or any other part of the body, burn the part affected.

Some Barbarian Nations have much stranger remedies in their Diseases, as may be seen in Histories: It is reported that the *Indians* of *Mechoacam* and *Tabasco* in *New-Spain*, to cure themselves of Fevers, cast themselves stark-naked into the River, thinking thereby to drown the disease: Some thing of the same kind hath also been seen among the *Caribbians*; for Monsieur *du Montel* met there one day an old man washing his head in a very cold spring, and having asked him the reason of it, the man replyed, that it was to cure himself, for he was much troubled with cold; and yet contrary to all rules of our Medicine, this strange remedy prov'd fortunate to the old man; for the same Gentleman met him the next day very well and lusty, and quite cur'd of his indisposition; and the Savage failed not to brag of it, and laugh at the *French*-man for pitying him the day before.

The *Caribbians* are very shye in communicating their secrets in Medicine, especially the women, who are very skilful in all those cures; nay they are so careful in keeping to themselves the sovereign Remedies they have against the wounds made by poisoned Arrows, that no rewards could yet prevail with them to discover them to the Christians: But they are very willing to come and visit them, and to dress them when they stand in need of their assistance: For a person of quality among the *French* having been dangerously bitten by a Serpent, was happily recovered by their means: Which kindness of theirs makes them differ much from those brutish people of *Guinny* and *Sumatra*, who have no compassion on their own sick, but leave them to shift for themselves like so many poor beasts: But the ancient people of the Province of *Babylon* concern'd themselves so particularly in all Diseases, that the sick were there disposed into a publick place, and every one was to teach them that remedy which he had try'd upon himself: Those who have made Voyages to *Cambaya* affirm, that there is an Hospital there for the entertainment of birds that are troubled with any indisposition.

Y y

When

Margin notes:
Lescarbot & De Laet.
De Lery, c. 20.
Linscot, c. 1.
Villamont's Travels, l. 3.
Dutch Relations, & V. le Blanc. P. 1. c. 24.

When the ordinary Remedies which our *Caribbians* are wont to make use of when occasion requires, have not the success they had promised to themselves, their recourse is to their *Boyez*, that is their Magicians, who also pretend to the profession of Physick, and having sent for them, they ask their advice concerning the event of their sickness : These unhappy instruments of Satan have by their enchantments gain'd so great reputation among these poor besotted people, that they are looked upon as the Judges of life and death, and so dreaded by reason of their sorceries, and the revenge they take on those who slight them, that all think themselves obliged to express a complyance with their advice.

As concerning the Ceremonies observed by them upon these occasions, we have already given some account thereof in the Chapter of their *Religion* : It is requisite above all things, that the House or Hut into which the *Boyé* is to enter, should be very neatly prepared for his reception ; that the little Table, which they call *Matoutou*, should be furnished with *Anakri* or *Maboya*, that is, an offering of *Cassava* and *Onicou*, for the evil Spirit, as also with the first-fruits of their Gardens, if it be the season of fruits : It is further requisite, that at one end of the Hut, there should be as many low stools or seats as there are to be persons present at that detestable action.

After these preparations, the *Boyé*, who never does this work but in the night time, having carefully put out all the fire in and about the House, enters into it, and having found out his place by the weak light of a piece of Tobacco set on fire, which he hath in his hand, he first pronounces some barbarous words, then he strikes the ground several times with his left foot, and having put the end of Tobacco which he had in his hand into his mouth, he blows upwards five or six times the smoke which comes out of it, then rubbing the end of Tobacco between his hands he scatters it in the air : Thereupon the Devil, whom he hath invocated by these apish Ceremonies, shaking very violently the roof of the house, or making some other dreadful noise presently appears, and answers distinctly to all the questions put to him by the *Boyé*.

If the Devil assures him, that his disease for whom he is consulted, is not mortal, the *Boyé*, and the Apparition which accompanies him, come neer the sick person to assure him that he shall soon recover his former health ; and to confirm him in that hope, they gently touch those parts of his body, where he feels most pain, and having press'd them a little, they pretend that there come out of them Thorns, pieces of Bones, splinters of Wood and Stone, which were, as these damnable Physitians affirm, the cause of his sickness : Sometimes also they moisten the part affected with their breath, and having suck'd it several times, they perswade the Patient that by that

means

means they have got out all the venome which lay in his body, and cauſed him to languiſh : In fine, to put a period to this
abominable Myſtery, they rub the ſick perſon all over with
the juice of the *Junipa*-fruit, which dies his body of a very
dark brown, which is as it were the mark and ſeal of his cure.

He who is perſwaded that he hath recovered his health by this
damnable means, is wont by way of acknowledgment to
make a great feaſt, at which the *Boyé* hath the chiefeſt place
among thoſe who are invited : He is by no means to forget the
Anakri for the Devil, who fails not to be there : But if the
Boyé finds by the communication he hath had with his familiar, that the ſickneſs is to death, he comes and comforts the
ſick perſon, telling him that his God, or to ſay better his familiar Devil, having compaſſion upon him, will take him into
his company, and carry him along with him to be delivered
out of all his infirmities.

Certain people of old finding themſelves unable to endure
the trouble and inconveniences of decrepit age, were wont
to diſpatch their wearied ſouls out of their infirm bodies with a
glaſs of Hemlock : And ſome others, as *Pliny* affirms, being
weary of their lives, caſt themſelves into the Sea : But in other
Countries the Children thought it too long to ſtay till their
Parents were come to ſo great age, and ſo became their Executioners, and this they were authorized to do by a publick
Law. And even at this day the Sun ſhines upon ſome Provinces
of *Florida*, where there are people ſo curſed, as upon a certain
motive of Religion and Piety, to put their Parents to death
when they are old, as perſons uſeleſs in this world, and chargeable to them.

But how old ſoever they may be among the *Caribbians*, the
Children are never troubled to ſee their Fathers and Mothers
in that condition : True it is, that ſome *Caribbians* heretofore
have haſtened the death of their Parents, and have killed their
Fathers and Mothers out of a perſwaſion that they did a good
work, and rendred them a charitable office, by delivering them
out of many inconveniences and troubles which attend old age.
An old Captain among them, whom the *French* called *Le Pilote*,
made it his boaſt that he had done that deteſtable ſervice to
many of his Anceſtors : But it is to be obſerved that the *Caribbians* did not practiſe that inhumanity, but only towards thoſe
who deſired to be delivered in that manner out of the miſeries
of this life ; and ſo it was a certain compliance with their ear-
neſt entreaties who were weary of their lives : Moreover that
piece of barbariſm was never univerſally received among them,
and the more prudent ſort do at the preſent deteſt it, and maintain their Fathers and Mothers to the laſt gaſp, with all the
care, and all the expreſſions of love, honour, and reſpect that
can be expected from a Nation which hath no other light for

Ælian, *l.* 3.
c. 38.

Lib. 4. *c.* 12.

Æl. *l.* 4. *c.* 1.

Y y 2

its

its direction, than that of a corrupt Nature : They patiently bear with their imperfections, and the frowardness of their old age, are never weary of miniſtring unto them, and as much as they can, keep neer them, to divert them, as the *French* have obſerv'd in ſome of their Iſlands ; which demeanour of theirs is the more commendable, in that it is done amongſt Barbarians: So that if any among them do not honour their Fathers and Mothers, they have degenerated from the vertue of their Anceſtors.

But when after all their care and pains they chance to loſe any one of their Friends or Relations, they make great cries and lamentations upon his death : Wherein they differ much *Herod. l. 5.* from the ancient *Thracians*, and the Inhabitants of the *Fortu-* *& Philoſt in* *nate Iſlands*, who buried their dead with rejoicing, dancing, *the Life of* and ſinging, as perſons delivered out of the miſeries of humane *Apollonius,* life After the *Caribbians* have wept over their dead, they *l. 5. c. 1.* waſh them, paint the bodies with a red colour, rub their heads with Oil, comb their hair, thruſt up the legs to the thighs, and the elbows between the legs, and bend down the face upon the hands, ſo that the whole body ſomewhat reſembles the poſture of the child in the mothers womb ; and then they wrap it up in a new bed, till all things be ready to diſpoſe it into the ground.

There have been ſome Nations who caſt the bodies of the *Drake's Voy-* dead into Rivers, as ſome *Æthiopians* did : Others caſt them *ages, part 2.* to Birds and Dogs, as the *Parthians*, the *Hircanians*, and ſuch others, who were ſomewhat of the ſame humour with *Dioge-* *nes* the Cynick : Some others covered them with heaps of ſtones. It is reported of ſome Inhabitants of *Africk*, that they diſpoſed their dead in earthen Veſſels ; and that others put them into glaſs : *Heraclitus*, who maintained that fire was the principle of all things, would have the bodies of the dead burnt, that they might return to their firſt origine : And this Cuſtom, obſerved for ſeveral ages among the *Romans*, is at *Xenoph. Cy-* this day practiſed among divers oriental Nations : But *Cyrus* *ropæd. l. 8.* at his death affirmed, that there was nothing happier than to be diſpoſed into the boſom of the earth, the common Mother of *Plin. l. 7. c.* all mankind : The firſt *Romans* were of the ſame opinion, for *54.* they interr'd their dead : And of the ſeveral ways of diſpoſing of the dead, interring is that which is in uſe among the *Carib-* *bians* : They do not make their Graves according to our faſhion, but like thoſe of the *Turks*, *Braſilians*, and *Canadians*, that is about four or five foot deep, and round like a Tun : and at the bottom of it, they ſet a little ſtool, on which the Relations and Friends of the deceaſed place the body ſitting, leaving it in the ſame poſture as they put it in immediately after the death of the party.

They commonly make the grave within the houſe of the
deceaſed,

deceaſed ; or if they bury him elſewhere, they always make a
covering over the place where the body is to be laid, and after
they have let it down into the grave, and wrap'd it in an *Amac,*
they make a great fire about it, and all the more ancient both
men and women kneel down : The men place themſelves behind the women, and ever and anon they ſtroke them with their
hands over their arms, to incite them to lament and weep :
Then ſinging and weeping they all ſay with a pitiful and la-
menting voice : "Alas, why didſt thou dye ? Thou hadſt ſo
"much good *Manioc,* good *Potatoes,* good *Bananas,* good *Ana-*
"*nas* : Thou wert belov'd in thy Family, and they had ſo
"great care of thy perſon : Why therefore wouldſt thou dye ?
"Why wouldſt thou dye ? If the party were a man, they add,
"Thou wert ſo valiant and ſo generous ; thou haſt overthrown
"ſo many Enemies ; thou haſt behav'd thy ſelf gallantly in ſo
"many ſights ; thou haſt made us eat ſo many *Arouagues* ;
"Alas ! who ſhall now defend us againſt the *Arouagues* ? Why
"therefore wouldſt thou dye ? And they repeat theſe expoſtulations ſeveral times over.

   The *Topinambous* make in a manner the ſame lamentations
over the graves of their dead : "He is dead, *ſay they,* that brave De Lery, *c.* 5.
"Huntſman ; that excellent Fiſherman ; that valiant Warriour ;
"that gallant eater of Priſoners ; that great Deſtroyer of *Por-*
"*tuguez* and *Margajats* ; that generous Defender of our Coun-
"try, he is departed this world : And they often repeat the
ſame expreſſions : The Inhabitants of *Guinny* do alſo ask their Dutch Rela-
deceaſed what obliged them to dye, and they rub their Faces *tions, l.* 1.
with a wiſp of ſtraw, to try if that will awake them : And
Busbequius, in the Relation of his Embaſſies into *Turkey* relates,
that paſſing through a Town of *Servia,* named *Tagodena,* he
heard the women and young maids lamenting over a deceaſed
perſon, and ſaying to him in their Funeral ſongs, as if he had
been able to hear them : "What have we deſerved, and where-
"in have we been deficient in doing thee ſervice, and com-
"forting thee ? What cauſe of diſcontent have we ever given
"thee that ſhould oblige thee to leave us ? Which ſomewhat
relates to the complaints of our *Caribbians.*

   The howlings and expoſtulations of the *Topinambous* and the
Virginians upon the like occaſions laſt ordinarily a month : The
people of *Ægypt* continu'd their lamentations ſeventy dayes :
And ſome *Floridians* employ old women to bewail the decea-
ſed for the ſpace of ſix months : But *Lycurgus* limited mourn- Plut. *in his*
ing for the dead to eleven days ; and that is much about the *Life.*
time that our *Caribbians* took to do the ſame office, before they
put the dead body into the ground : For during the ſpace of
ten dayes or thereabouts, twice every day the Relations, and
the moſt intimate friends came to viſit the deceaſed party at
his grave ; and they always brought him ſomewhat to eat and
drink,

drink, saying to him every time: "Alas! why wouldst thou
"dye? why wilt thou not return to life again? say not at
"leaft that we refufed thee wherewithall to live upon; for we
"have brought thee fomewhat to eat and drink: And after
they have made this pleafant exhortation to him, as if he fhould
have heard them, they left the meat and drink they had brought
with them at the brink of the grave till the next vifit, at which
time they put it on his head, fince he thought it much to ftretch
forth his hand to take it.

Acofta, De
Lery, P. Ju-
nius, Fran.
Cauche, Th.
Nicholas in
Bergeron,
Carpin, &
Trigaut.

The *Peruvians*, the *Braſilians*, the *Canadians*, the Inhabitants
of *Madagaſcar*, the *Canarians*, the *Tartars*, the *Chineſes*, do alfo bring certain difhes of meat to the graves of their neereft
Relations. And not to go to Countries at fo great a diftance, is
there not fomething of this kind done among us? for during
certain dayes they ferve the Effigies of our Kings and Princes
newly dead, and they are prefented with meat and drink, as
if they were living, nay fo far as to tafte the meats and drinks
before them.

The *Caribbians* of fome Iflands do ftill fet meat at the graves
of the deceafed, but they leave them not fo long as they did
heretofore, ere they covered them with earth: For after the
Funeral lamentation is ended, and that the women have wept
as much as they can, fome friend of the deceafed laies a plank
over his head, and the reft put the earth together with their
hands till they have filled the grave; that done, they burn
all that belonged to the deceafed.

Acofta's Hiſt.
of China, De
Laet, Garcil.
Pirard, Lin-
fcot, &c.

They alfo fometimes kill Slaves to attend the Ghofts of the
deceafed, and to wait on them in the other world: But thefe
poor wretches get out of the way when their Mafters dye, into fome other Ifland. We may juftly conceive a horrour at the
relation of thefe inhumane and barbarous Funerals, which are
drench'd with the blood of Slaves, and divers other perfons,
and among others women, who have their throats cut, are
burnt and buried alive, to go and accompany their Husbands
into the other world, whereof frequent examples may be found
in divers Nations: But our *Caribbians* think it enough upon
thefe occafions to put to death only the Slaves of the deceafed,
if they can catch them.

Virgil, Ari-
an, Tacitus.

Lib. 7. c. 12.
Carpin.
De Lery,
Dutch Rela-
tions, De La-
et, & Junius.

It was forbidden the *Lacedæmonians* to bury any thing with
the deceafed perfon; but the contrary hath been and is ftill
practifed in divers Nations: For not to mention the many precious things which were confumed with the Bodies that were
burnt among the ancient *Romans*, *Macedonians*, *Germans* and
other people, we read in the Hiftory of *Jofephus*, that King
Solomon put up great wealth with the body of *David* his Father: Thus the *Tartars* put into the grave with the dead perfon all his Gold and Silver: And the *Braſilians*, *Virginians*, *Canadians* and feveral other Savages inter with the bodies, the
cloths and whatever elfe belonged to the deceafed.   The

The same thing was also practised among the *Caribbians* in their Funerals, before they conversed with the *Christians*: For at the last visit they made to the deceased, they brought along with them all the things he had used or worn about him in his life time, to wit, his Bow and arrows, the *Boutou*, or Club, the Crowns of Feathers, Pendants, Chains, Rings, Bracelets, Baskets, Vessels, and other things, and buried all with him, or burnt them over the grave: But now they are grown better Husbands; for the Relations of the deceased reserve all those things for their own use, or else they bestow them as presents on those who come to the Interment, who keep them in remembrance of the deceased.

After the body is covered with earth, the nearest Relations cut off their hair, and fast very rigorously, out of a perswasion that by that means they shall live longer and more happily: Others forsake the houses and the place where they have buried any of their kinred, and go and live elsewhere: When the body is neer rotted, they make another assembly, and after they have visited, and sighing trampled on the Sepulchre, they have a merry meeting, at which they drown all their grief in *Ouicou*. Thus the Ceremony is concluded, and the poor Carcass is no further tormented.

FINIS.

A CARIBBIAN VOCABULARY.

ADVERTISEMENT.

We said elsewhere, that the Men and Women among the Caribbians use several words to express the same thing, so that the Men have a term peculiar to themselves, and the Women another to them. Those words therefore of this Vocabulary, *after which the letter* M. *is set, are such as are properly used by the Men: And those which have a* W *after them, are the proper terms of the Women. The accent denotes the syllable to be pronounced long. Note also that* ch *is every where to be pronounced like* sh *in the* Caribbian *words.*

I. *The* PARTS *of* MAN'S Bodie.

MY Body, Nókobòu.
Fat, Takellé.
My skin, Nora. *This signifies generally whatsoever serves for a covering.*
My bones, Nabo. *This signifies also a gristle, and the tender sprig of a Plant.*
The Caribbians *make no distinction between the Veins and the Nerves, and they express both by the word* Nillagra, *which signifies* my Nerves *or* my Veins; *as* Lillagra, *his Nerves or his Veins. By the same name they also call the roots of trees.*
My blood, Nitta. *M.* Nimoinalou. *W. The hair of my head or Body,* Nilibouri.

My head, Nicheucke.
My Eyes, Nakou.
The ball of my eye, Nakoueuke, *that is properly, the kernel of my Eye.*
My eye-lid, Nakou-ora, *that is, the skin of my eye.*
My Eye-brow, Nichicouchi, *properly a piece of my Eye.*
The hair of the Eyelids, Nakou-iou, *properly the hair of the Eye.*
My forehead, Nérébé.
My face, Nichibou.
My Nose, Nichiri.
My mouth, Niouma.
My lip, Nioumarou.
My tooth, Nati.
My cheek-teeth, Nackeuke.
My jaws, Nari-aregrick, *properly, that which is next to my teeth,*

Z z   *My*

My *ear*, Narikae.
My *Temples*, Nouboyoubou.
My *cheeks*, Nitigné.
My *chin*, Nariona.
My *breaſt*, Nouri.
My *boſome*, Narokou.
My *ſhoulder*, Néché.
My *arm*, Narreuna; *it ſigni-
fies alſo a wing.*
My *elbow*, Neugueumeuke.
My *hands*, Noucabo.
My *fingers*, Noucabo-raün; *as
if you ſaid the little ones or
Children of my hand.*
My *thumb*, Noucabo-iteignum,
*that is properly, what is oppo-
ſite to the fingers.*
The *pulſe*, Noucabo-anichi, *that
is properly, the ſoul of the
hand.*
My *nail*, Noubara.
My *ſtomack*, Nanichirokou.
My *heart*, Nioüanni, M. Na-
nichi, W. *this word ſignifies
alſo my ſoul.*
My *lungs*, Noara.
My *Liver*, Noubana.
My *Entrails*, Noulakae, *that
ſignifies alſo the belly.*
My *Reins*, Nanaganè.
My *ſide*, Nauba.
The *Spleen*, Couëmata.
The *Bladder*, Ichicolou-akae.
My *Navil*, Narioma.
The *natural parts of the Man*,
Yaloukouli, M. Neheuera,
W.
The *natural parts of the Woman*,
Touloukou.
My *back-parts*, Narioma-ro-
kou.
My *buttock*, Niatta.
My *Thigh*, Nebouik.
My *knee*, Nagagirik.
My *Ham*, Nichaoua-chaoua.
My *Leg*, Nourna.
My *ſhin*, Nourna-aboulougou.
My *joint*, Napataragoune, *that

is a thing added; which word
they apply alſo to a piece ſet
on a garment.*
My *ankle*, Noumourgouti.
My *foot*, Nougouti.
My *heel*, Nogouti-ona.
My *toes*, Nougouti-raim, *that
is properly, the little ones of
the foot.*
The *ſole of my foot*, Nougouti-
rokou, *that is properly, the in-
ſide of the foot.*
Whereas they very ſeldome
expreſs themſelves by the indefinite names, eſpecially when they
ſpeak of the parts of the body,
but reſtrain them to one of the
three perſons, we have here ſet
them down under the firſt : Whoever therefore would put them
under any of the other two,
needs only change the firſt letter
of every word, as may be ſeen in
the chapter of their Language.

II. KINDRED
and
ALLYANCE.

MY *Kinſman*, Nioumou-
likou, M. Niroucke, W.
My *marriage*, Youëlleteli.
My *Husband*, Niraiti.
My *Father, ſpeaking to him*,
Baba, M. *and* W.
My *Father, ſpeaking of him*,
Youmaan, M. Noukouchili,
W.
My *Grandfather*, Itamoulou,
M. Nargouti, W.
My *Unkle by the Fathers ſide,
they call him Father*, Baba.
*And to ſignifie the true and
proper Father , when they
would expreſly diſtinguiſh
him, they ſometimes make
this*

this addition, Baba tin-
naka.

The Uncle by the Mother side,
Yao, M. Akatobou, W.

My Son, Imakou, Imoulou,
Yamoinri, M. Niraheu, W.

My Grand-child, Hibali, *when
there is but one: But when
there are more*, Nibagnem.

My Elder-Brother, Hanhin, M.
Niboukayem, W.

My younger-Brother, Ouanoüe
and Ibiri, M. *that is properly,
my half:* Namouleem, W.

My Brother-in-law, *and my
Cousin-german by the Mother-
side*, Ibamouy, M. Nikeliri,
W.

*The Cousin not married to the
Cousin-German*, Yapataga-
num.

My Nephew, Yanantigané.

My Son-in-law, Hibali mou-
kou, *that is properly, he who
makes little ones.*

My Wife, Yenenery, M. *the women say*, Liani, *his Wife.*

*My Mother, speaking to her, both
men and women say*, Bibi;
*which word is also an excla-
mation.*

A mother, speaking of her, Ichanum, M. Noukouchourou,
W.

*My mother-in-law by a second
marriage*, Noukouchorou-
teni.

*My mother-in-law, whose daugh-
ter I have married*, Imenou-
ti.

My Grand-mother, Innouti, M.
Naguette, W.

*My Aunt by the mothers-side is
called mother*, Bibi.

The Aunt by the Fathers-side,
Naheupouli.

My Daughter, Niananti, M. Niraheu, W.

My Sister, Nitou.

The elder sister, Bibi-Ouanou-
an.

The younger sister, Tamoule-
louan.

*Step-daughter, Daughter-in-law
and Neece*, Nibaché.

My she-Cousin-german, Youelle-
ri, M. *that is to say, my female, or she who is promised
me; because naturally, they are
to be wives to their Cousins.
The women say*, Youellou.

*The Children of two Brothers
are called brothers and sisters;
the children of Sisters the
like.*

III. CONDITIONS

and

QUALITIES.

A *man, or a male*, Ouekelli,
M. *in the plural number*,
Ouekliem. Eyeri, W. *in the
plural*, Eyerium.

A Woman, or a Female, Ouelle,
M. *in the plural number*, Ouliem: Inarou, W. *in the
plural*, Innouyum.

A Child, Niankeili.

A Boy, Mouléke.

A Girl, Niankeirou.

A little boy, Ouekelli-raeu, *properly a little male.*

A little girl, Ouelle-raeu, *properly, a little female.*

An old man, Ouaiali.

A Father of a Family, Tiouboutouli authe.

A Widdow and Widdower,
Moincha.

A Comrade, Banaré.

A Friend, Ibaouanale, M. Ni-
tignon, W.

An Enemy, Etoutou, M. Akani, W.

An Enemy who goes clad in opposition to those who go naked, Etoutou noubi.

Savage, Maron: *The* Caribbians *attribute that name only to animals and wild fruits.*

An Inhabitant, Bonon.

An Islander, or Inhabitant of the Islands, Oubao-bonon.

An Inhabitant of the Continent, Baloüe-bonon.

A man come thither by Sea, Balanaglé: *Thus they call the* Christians, *because they come to their Country by Sea.*

An Admiral, or General of a naval Army, Nhaléné.

A Captain of a Vessel, Tiouboutouli Canaoua.

A Commander in chief, or General, Ouboutou; *in the plural numb.* Ouboutounum.

A Lieutenant, Tiouboutoumaliarici, *that is properly, the track of the Captain, or that which appears after him.*

A Souldier or Warriour, Netoukouiti.

A Sentinel, or Spie, Arikouti, Nabara.

My Prisoner of war, Niouitouli, Niouemakali.

He who hath the charge of entertaining Guests, Niouakaiti.

My hired servant, such as the Christians *have*, Nabouyou.

A servant who is an absolute Slave, Tamon.

A Huntsman, Ekerouti.

Fat, Tibouleli.

Lean, Touleeli.

Great, Mouchipeeli.

Big, Ouboutonti.

Little, Nianti, racu.

Pretty little one, Pikenine, *in the bastard Language.*

High, Inouti.

Low, Onabouti.

Deep, Ouliliti, Anianliti.

Broad, Taboubéreti.

Long, Mouchinagouti.

Round, Chiririti.

Square, Patagouti.

Fair, Bouitouti.

Deformed, Nianti ichibou.

Soft, Nioulouti.

Hard, Téleti.

Dry, Ouärrou, Ouärrouti.

Moist, Kouchakouali.

Heat and cold are express'd in the ix. Section.

White, Alouti.

Black, Ouliti.

Yellow, Houëreti.

Red, Ponati.

They have no names but only for those four colours, and they refer all the rest to them.

A Thief, Youalouti.

An incestuous person, Kakouyoukouatiti.

An Adulterer, Oulimateti.

A Fornicator, Huereti.

Quarrelsome, Oulibimekoali, Koauaiti.

A treacherous person, Niroubouteiti.

Evil, Oulibati, Nianouanti.

Good, Iroponti.

Wise, Kanichicoti.

Cunning, Manigat.

A fool, Leuleuti ao, *or* Talouali ao; *that is properly, he who hath no light.*

Valiant, Ballinumpti.

Cowardly, Abaouati.

Joyful, Aouerekoua, Liouani.

Sad, Imouemeti.

Drunk, Nitimainti.

Rich, Katakobaiti.

Poor, Matakobaiti.

Piequant, Chouchouti.

Dead, Neketali.

IV. ACTIONS
and
PASSIONS.

HE puts his trust in him, Moingatteti loné.
Stay for me, Jacaba, Noubara.
Hope, expect, Alliré.
Hope in him, Emenichiraba.
Hope, Emenrchira.
My hope, Nemenichiraeu.
My fear, Ninonnoubouli.
My joy, Naoueregon, M. Niouanni, W.
My sadness, Nitikaboué.
He is born, Emeïgnouali.
Tou are welcome, Halea tibou.
I am hungry, Lamanatina.
I am thirsty, Nacrabatina.
Give me to eat, or give me some bread, Yerebali um boman, M. Nouboute um boman, W.
Give me some drink, Natoni boman
Eat, in the Imperative, Baika.
To eat, in the Infinitive, which is seldome used, Aika.
I eat, Naikiem.
Drink thou, Kouraba.
I drink, Natiem, Natakayem.
I am warm with drinking, or have drunk plentifully, Nacharoüatina.
Come hither, Hac-yeté.
Go thy wayes, Bayouboukaa.
Speak, Ariangaba.
I speak, Nanangayem.
Hold thy peace, Maniba.
Sit down, Niourouba.
Lie down on the ground, Raoignaba.
Rise up, Aganekaba.
Stand up, Raramaba.
Look, Arikaba.
Hear, Akambabaë.
Blow, Irimichaba.
Tast it, Aochabaë.
Touch it, Kourouabaë.

Go, Bayoubaka.
I go, Nayoubakayem.
Walk, Babachiaka.
Run, Hehemba.
Dance, Babenaka.
I dance, Nabinakayem.
Leap, Choubakouaba.
I am going, or about to leap, Choubakoua niabou.
Laugh, Béérraka.
I laugh or am glad, Naouërekoyem.
Weep, Ayakouaba.
Sleep, Baronka.
Awake, Akakotouäba.
Watch, Aromankaba.
Labour or pains-taking, Youategmali, M. Noumaniklé, W.
Rest, Nemervoni.
A Fight, Tibouikenoumali.
War, Nainchoa, M. Nihuctoukouli, W.
Peace, Niuëmboulouli.
He is defeated, Niouellemainti.
He is overcome, Enepali.
Breathe, Aouraba banichi, *that is properly, refresh thy heart*.
Blow, Phoubaë.
Spit, Chouëba.
Cough, Hymba.
Wipe thy nose, Nainraba.
To ease ones self, Homoura.
Wash thy self, Chibaba.
Moisten, Touba boubara.
Go to wash thy self, Akao bouka
I swim, Napouloukayem.
I swim well, Capouloukatiti.
He was drown'd, Chalalaali.
He was choak'd, Niarakouali.
Open, Talaba.
Shut it, Taba.
Seek, Aloukaba.
Find, Ibikouabaë.
Fly, Hamamba.
Thou fallest, Batikeroyen.
Loose it, Aboulekouabaë.
Sell it, Kebeciketabaë.
Buy, Amouliakaba.
He trades, Haouanemeti.

Go a hunting, Ekrekabouca.

That which I have taken in hunting, Nekeren.

He shoots well with the Bow, Kachienratiti, Boukatiti.

He shoots well with a gun, Katouratiti.

Go a fishing, Tikabouka authe, *I fish,* Natiakayem.

What I have got a fishing, Natiakani.

He is come into the Port, Abourricaali.

I sing in the Church, Nallalakayem.

I sing a song, Naromankayem.

He is in love with her, or makes much of her, Ichoatoati tao.

Kiss me, Chouba nioumolougou.

I would be named, name me, Yetikleé yatek.

He loves him, Kinchinti loné, Tibouinati.

He hates him, Yerekati loné.

A quarrel, Liouelébouli.

Drunkenness, Liuetimali.

Strike, beat, Baikoaba.

A whip or wand, Abaichaglé.

Beat him, Apparabaë.

Scratch, Kiomba.

Kill him, Chiouibae.

He is well, Atouattienly.

He is sick, Nanegaeti, Nanneteiti.

Sickness, Aneck.

He hath bewitched me, Nataliatina.

I will be revenged, Nibane bouibatina.

Revenge, Nayouïbanabouli.

He hath bitten him, Kerrelialo.

He is wounded, Niboukabouali.

He is yet living, Noulôukeili, M. Kakekeili, W.

Life, Lakakechoni.

He is dead, Aouéeli, Nikotamainali, M. Hilaali, W.

Bury him, or it; which is not said only of a man, but generally of whatsoever is put into the ground, as of a Plant, Bonambaë.

Buriall, Tonamouli.

V. Things relating to HOUSE-KEEPING and TRADE.

A Village, Authe.

A Publick-House, Karbet.

An ordinary house, Toubana, M. Touhonoko, W.

A Penthouse, Covering, or Hut suddenly erected, Aïoupa.

A Garden, Maina.

My Garden, Imaïnali, M. Nichali, W.

A Trench for the planting of Manioc, Tomonack.

The Roof, Toubana ora, *properly, the covering of the House or Hut.*

A Wall or Pallisado, Kourara.

Floor of boards they have not any.

A Plank, Iboutou.

A door, Béna.

A Window, Toullepen, *properly a Hole.*

A Bed, Amac *and* Akat, M. Nekera, W.

A Table, Matoutou.

A Seat, Halaheu.

A Cage, Tonoulou-banna.

A Vessel, Takae, *which is generally applyed to all Vessels.*

A Vessel made of a Gourd, Couï.

Half the Couï, which serves for a dish, Tauba; *this word signifies properly, a side.*

A Drinking-cup, Ritta.

A

A Glass, Flagon, bottle, Boutel-
la, *from the* Spanish.
*The wooden frame which serves
for a Gridiron, and is by o-
ther Savages called* Boucan,
Youla.
An Iron Pot or Kettle, Touraë.
An Earthen Pot, Taumali akaë,
and Canary.
*A Candlestick, or any thing
that holds a thing,* Taketaklé.
A Candle, Lamp, Torch, Touli,
*which is a Sandal-wood
which yields a Gum.*
A pair of snuffers, Tachackou-
taglé.
A Hook, Keouë.
A needle, Akoucha.
A pin, Alopholer.
A Coffer, Arka.
A basket, Alaouata, Catoli.
*The hair-cloth to sift the meal
of the* Manioc, *and to strain
the* Ouïcou, Mouchache.
Flesh that may be eaten, Te-
keric.
Roast-meat, Aribelet, Ache-
routi.
Sauce, Taomali, *or* Taumali.
A dish of hash'd meat, Natara.
A Feast, Natoni, Laupali, Ele-
toak.
Poison, Tiboukoulou, M. Ti-
baukoura, W.
Merchandise, Eberitina.
A Merchant, Baouanemoukou.
*A Piraga, or great vessel of the
Savages,* Canaoüa.
*A little vessel of the Savages,
which we call Canow,* Cou-
liala.
A Ship, Kanabire ; *this pro-
bably is derived from the
French word* Navire.
A Cord, Ibitarrou.
A Cable, Kaboya ; *'tis a word
no doubt fram'd by them since
their acquaintance with*

*strangers ; as are also some
of the ensuing.*
An Anchor, Tichibani, *and*
Ankouroute.
A Knife, Couchique.
Scissers, Chirachi.
Much, Mouche, *a word of the
corrupt Language.*
Ten, Chonnoucabo raim, *that
is, all the fingers of both
hands.*
Twenty, Chonnougouci raim,
*that is, all the fingers of both
hands, and all the toes of
both feet ; they cannot num-
ber any farther.*
Behold thy bed, Bouekra.
Behold thy meat, En yerebaili.
Behold thy drink, En batoni.
Gramercy, or well, Tao.
Yes, Anhan.
Nay, Ouä.
To morrow, Alouka.
Good morrow, Mabouë.
Farewel, Huican.

VI. ORNAMENTS and ARMES.

*T*Oyes *and trifles in gene-
rall,* Cacones.
A Crown, Tiamataboni.
A Ring, Toukabouri.
A Chain or Necklace, Eneka.
My Chain, Yenekali.
A Bracelet, Nournari.
Pendants for the ears, Narikae-
la.
A Girdle, Jeconti, Niranvary.
Spanish Leather, Tichepoulou.
A Comb brought out of Europe,
Baïna.
A Comb of Reeds, Boulera.
A Handkercher, Naïnraglé.
A Looking-glass, Chibouchi.

A

A Sword, Echoubara.

An Arquebuss or Musket, Rakabouchou.

A Pistol, Rakabouchou racu, *properly, a little Musket.*

Great Guns, Kaloon.

A Pike, Halberd, Ranicha.

The point of it, Lichibau, M. Laboulougou, W.

The middle, Lirana.

The end, Tiona.

A bow, Oullaba, M. Chimala, W. *these two words signifie also a tree.*

The string of the bow, Ibitarrou.

Arrows, Alouani, Bouleouä, Hippé.

The Club which the Savages use instead of a sword, Bouttou.

VII. *LIVING CREATURES.*

A *Dog*, Anly.

A Bitch, Ouelle anly, *properly the female of the dog.*

A swine, Bouirokou, *sometimes they also call that creature*, Concoin.

An Ape or Monkey, Alouata.

A Tortoise, or Turtle, Catallou, *and in the corrupt Language*, Tortillé.

The great Lizard, Ouayamaka; *the same which other Indians call* Iganas.

The little Lizard, or Catch-flye, Oulleouma.

A mouse, Karattoni.

A Cat, Mechou.

The Soldier, a kind of Snail so called, Makeré.

A Pismire, Hagué.

A Spider, Koulaélé.

A Serpent, Héhué.

A Snake, Couloubera, *from the Spanish.*

A Scorpion, Akourou.

A Fish, Authe; *and in the corrupt Language*, Pisket.

The shell of a Fish; they name the fish, and then add ora, *as much as to say, the shell or covering of the fish: Thus* Ouataboui-ora , *is that which we have elsewhere called a* Lambis.

A Mesquito, a kind of flye, Aëtera.

Another kind of small flyes commonly called Maringoins, *and known under that name*, Malu Kalabala: *It seems their feet are white.*

A Flye, Hueré-hueré.

The glittering flye, Cogouyou, *not differing much from the* Cocuyos *of the other Indians.*

A bird, Tonoulou.

A Turkey-cock, Ouekelli-pikaka.

A Turkey-hen, Ouelle-pikaka.

An ordinary hen, Kayou.

A Duck, Kanarou.

A Goose, Iriria.

A Parrat, Koulehuec.

A Pigeon, Ouakoukoua.

A Turtle, Oulleou.

A Partridge, Ouallami.

A Feather, Toubanna, *this signifies also a leaf.*

A wing or arm, Tarreuna.

A beak, or mouth, Tiouma.

A foot or claw, Tougouti.

VIII. *TREES* and *PLANTS.*

A *Tree*, Huéhué.

A Plant, Ninanteli.

A Flower, Illehué.

Fruit, or seed, Tun.

A leaf, Toubanna, *this signifies also a feather.*

A branch, Touribouri.

A Thorn, a Cyon, Huëhuëyou, *properly, the hair of the tree,* or Huëhuëakou, *as if one would say the cies of the tree.*

A Forrest, Arabou.

Figs, Bakoukou. *Orenges, and Lemons, or Citrons they call as we do, because these fruits were brought thither out of* Europe.

The Cassia-tree, Malimali.

Cotton, Manoulou.

The Cotton-tree, Manoulou-akecha.

The wild-Vine, Ouliem.

Raquette, *a fruit so named by the French,* Batta.

A great kind of Thistle, Akoulerou.

Tobacco, Youli.

A Melon, Battia.

Pease or Beans, Manconti.

A Cane, or Reed in general, Maboulou; Tikasket.

The Sugar-cane, Kaniche.

The juice of the Canes, or the wine thereof, Kanichira.

Sugar, Choucre, *a corrupt word.*

An herb, Kalao.

A root that may be eaten, Torolé.

IX. THINGS ELEMENTARY and INANIMATE.

The Heavens, Oubekou.

A white cloud, Alürou.

A black cloud, Ouällion.

Misty weather, Kemerei.

A Star, Ouäloukouma.

The Sun, Huyeyou, M. Kachi, W.

The Moon, Nonum, M. *which word signifies also the earth,* Kati, W.

A day, Lihuycouli.

Light, Lalloukoné.

Lightsome, Laguenani.

Night, Ariabou.

Darkness, Bourreli.

It is day, Haloukaali.

It is night, Boureokaali.

The air, Naouaraglé.

The wind, Bebeité, *it sometimes also signifies the air.*

Fire, Ouattou.

Ashes, Ballissi.

Rain, Konoboui.

Hail, Ice, Snow, are things they are not acquainted withall: *Winter is also unknown to them.*

Summer, Liromouli.

Cold, Lamoyenli.

Heat, Loubacha.

Fair weather, Ieromonmééli. *They call it also by the name of Summer.*

It is fair weather, Hueoumeti.

It is foul weather, Yehumeti.

Thunder, Oualou ouyoulou.

The noise of Thunder, Trtrguetenni.

A tempest, Youallou, Bointara, Ourogan, *which is the most common name.*

The Rain-bow, Alamoulou, *or* Youlouca, *as if they would say God's plume of feathers.*

A Mountain, Ouëbo.

A Valley, Taralironne.

An ascent, Tagreguin.

A plain, Liromonobou.

Water, a River, Tona.

A Pond, Taonaba.

A Spring or Fountain, **Tabou**likani.

A Well, Chickati.

A Brook, Tipouliri.

The Sea, Balanna, M. Balaoua, W.

The earth, Nonum, M. *that sig-nifies also the Moon*, Mona, W.

Excrement, Itika.

Sand, Saccao.

A way, Ema.

A Stone, Tebou.

A Rock, Emetali.

A Island, Oubao.

The Continent, Baloüe.

Wood, Huëhuë, *it signifies also a tree.*

Iron, Crabou.

Gold and silver, Boulâta.

Brass, Tialapirou.

Latten, Kaouanam.

A hole, Toullepen, *it signifies also a window.*

A Haven, Beya, *not much diffe-ring from the word* Bay.

X. Things relating to RELIGION.

THe Soul is expressed by the same word which sig-nifies the heart: *See before in the Section of the Parts of Man's Body.*

A Spirit, Akambouë, M. O-poyem, W. *These names are ge-neral: thence it comes that they are sometimes applyed to the Spirit of Man. But they are particularly attributed to good Spirits, at least those whom the* Caribbians *account such, and allow the place of Gods.*

A Good Spirit, which they hold to be a Divinity, and where-of every one of them hath one peculiar to himself for his God, is also called Icheiri, *which is the term of the men, and* Che-mun, *which is that of the wo-men, and whereof the plural is* Chemignum: *So that those words are answerable to God and Gods.*

My good Spirit, or my God, Icheirikou, M. Nechemera-kou, W.

The evil Spirit, or Devil, both men and women call him Maboya, *as all the French pro-nounce the word: but the Ca-ribbians pronounce it as if it were written with a* p, Mapoya.

They also attribute the name of Maboya *to certain Mush-rooms, and some other Plants of ill scent.*

The Devil, or evil Spirit is here, let us get away from him, Maboya kayeu eu, kaima Loa-ri *They are wont to say so when they smell any ill scent.*

The Offerings they make to the false Gods or Devils, Ana-kri.

Invocations, Prayers, Cere-monies, Adorations, are things they have no knowledge at all of.

FINIS.

A TABLE

Of the

CHAPTERS

Of the first Book of this History.

CHAP.

A Table of the Chapters of the second Book of this History.

CHAP.

CHAP.

FINIS.